# The Morrow Anthology of
# Great Western Short Stories

◙

# The

# Morrow Anthology of

# Great Western

# Short Stories

◙

### Edited with an Introduction and Headnotes by
### Jon Tuska and Vicki Piekarski

William Morrow and Company, Inc.

New York

Published by The Reader's Digest Association Inc., 1999, by permission of
William Morrow & Company, Inc. All Rights Reserved

It is the policy of William Morrow and Company, Inc., and its imprints and affiliates,
recognizing the importance of preserving what has been written, to print the books we
publish on acid-free paper, and we exert our best efforts to that end.

Library of Congress Cataloging-in-Publication Data

The Morrow anthology of great Western short stories / edited with an introduction and
headnotes by Jon Tuska and Vicki Piekarski.—1st ed.
   p.  cm.
  ISBN 0-688-14783-6
  1. West (U.S.)—Social life and customs—Fiction.  2. Short stories. American—West
(U.S.)  3. Western stories.  I. Tuska, Jon.  II. Pierkarski, Vicki.
PS648.W4M69  1997
813'.08740805—dc21                                  96-51442
                                                                 CIP

Printed in the United States of America

First Edition

1  2  3  4  5  6  7  8  9  10

BOOK DESIGN BY LEAH S. CARLSON

# Acknowledgments

"Monty Price's Nightingale" by Zane Grey first appeared in *Success Magazine* (April 1924). Copyright © 1924 by Street & Smith Publications, Inc. Copyright © renewed 1952 by Zane Grey, Inc. Reprinted by arrangement with Golden West Literary Agency. All rights reserved.

"On with the Dance" by B. M. Bower first appeared in *Short Stories* (January 10, 1934). Copyright © 1934 by Doubleday, Doran, and Company, Inc. Copyright © renewed 1962 by Dele Newman Doke. Reprinted by arrangement with Golden West Literary Agency. All rights reserved.

"The One-Way Trail" by Max Brand™ first appeared under the byline George Owen Baxter in *Western Story Magazine* (February 4, 1922). Copyright © 1922 by Street & Smith Publications, Inc. Copyright © renewed 1950 by Dorothy Faust. Acknowledgment is made to Condé Nast Publications, Inc., for their cooperation. Copyright © 1997 by Jane Faust Easton and Adriana Faust Bianchi for restored material. The name Max Brand is trademarked by the United States Patent and Trademark Office and cannot be used for any purpose without express written permission. Published by arrangement with Golden West Literary Agency. All rights reserved.

"Breaking the Blue Roan" by Honoré Willsie Morrow first appeared in *Everybody's Magazine* (December 1921). Copyright © 1922 by Ridgway Publications, Inc. Reprinted by arrangement with Golden West Literary Agency. All rights reserved.

"Shadows of Granite Ridge: At Kunman's Bend" by Vingie E. Roe first appeared in *Western Story Magazine* (October 20, 1923). Copyright © 1923 by Street & Smith Publications, Inc. Copyright © renewed 1951 by Condé Nast Publications, Inc. Reprinted by arrangement with Condé Nast Publications, Inc., in cooperation with Golden West Literary Agency. All rights reserved.

"The Bells of San Juan" by Alan LeMay first appeared in *Adventure* (November 15, 1927). Copyright © 1927 by the Butterick Publishing Company. Copyright © renewed 1955 by Alan LeMay. Reprinted by arrangement with Golden West Literary Agency. All rights reserved.

"Ghost Town Trail" by Cherry Wilson first appeared in *Western Story Magazine* (October 25, 1930). Copyright © 1930 by Street & Smith Publications, Inc.

# Contents

✪

| | |
|---|---|
| Introduction | xi |
| "Monty Price's Nightingale" by Zane Grey | 1 |
| "On with the Dance" by B. M. Bower | 11 |
| "The One-Way Trail" by Max Brand™ | 35 |
| "Breaking the Blue Roan" by Honoré Willsie Morrow | 95 |
| "Shadows of Granite Ridge: At Kunman's Bend" by Vingie E. Roe | 116 |
| "The Bells of San Juan" by Alan LeMay | 128 |
| "Ghost Town Trail" by Cherry Wilson | 143 |
| "Wagon Wheel Exile" by Cliff Farrell | 229 |
| "The Quickest Draw" by T. T. Flynn | 256 |
| "Valhalla" by Conrad Richter | 298 |
| "A Storm Comes to Crazy Horse" by Tom W. Blackburn | 315 |
| "Three-Way Double Cross" by C. K. Shaw | 323 |
| "Spawn of Yuma" by Peter Dawson | 338 |
| "Marked Man" by Eli Colter | 373 |
| "Night Guns Calling" by Steve Frazee | 398 |
| "Brother Shotgun" by Jeanne Williams | 420 |
| "Bonaparte McPhail" by Robert Easton | 435 |
| "The Girl Who Busted Broncos" by S. Omar Barker | 448 |
| "Mule Tracks" by Dwight Bennett Newton | 461 |
| "Ride the Red Trail" by Wayne D. Overholser | 480 |
| "The Ghost of Jean Lafitte" by Les Savage, Jr. | 491 |
| "Night Marshal" by Verne Athanas | 551 |
| "Journey of No Return" by T. V. Olsen | 565 |
| "Virginia City Winter" by Dorothy M. Johnson | 578 |
| "Deep in This Land" by Ernest Haycox | 591 |
| "The Business of Dying" by Richard S. Wheeler | 609 |
| "Moving On" by Jane Candia Coleman | 618 |
| "Guipago's Vow" by Cynthia Haseloff | 634 |

# Introduction

⌖

*Over whose campfires' ashened embers*
*The steadfast Northern Star remembers*
*That boldly they rode and lived and died,*
*Westerners all in hardy pride!*
**—S. Omar Barker**

*YES I had the right to life,*
*to laughter, to the use of my own voice.*
*These are inalienable rights—of the spirit*
*—yet they are never handed to us.*
*They must be worked for.*
*They must be earned.*
*What we begin with at birth*
*is simply the right to try.*
**—Jane Candia Coleman**

**I**t is unfortunate that in this century when writers came to tell stories of the Western frontier, they were met with myriad restrictions as to what was acceptable in the genre by editors and publishers. This, in contrast to the source of its origins, which was concerned with following one's own path or vision. There is perhaps no better illustration of the limitations placed on the Western story than that Western fiction in its traditional form—the heroic adventure story—is generally perceived to be a genre written by men, for men, about men. Notwithstanding this male-centered focus, women read Western fiction. Many stories about women have been written and enjoyed by readers, and a surprising number of women have had Western stories successfully published. Unfortunately, in all too many cases their accomplishments have gone unrecognized by literary historians, scholars, and anthologizers who put together collections of Western stories.

Part of the reason that women's Western fiction has been overlooked is due to where their stories originally appeared—pulp magazines. Pulp magazines provided a format by which writers could practice and perfect their craft. Conrad Richter, who wrote briefly for the pulps, credited this experience with teaching him how to plot out a story. For the author who could produce quickly and steadily, the reward, regardless of sex, was a regular income. Additional income, prior to the advent of paperback reprints in the 1940s, could be generated through hardcover book sales. Oddly enough, quite often for women the only available book market for their longer Western fiction was with British publishers, and many never published outside the magazine market. But even publication in book form did not secure women writers a place in literary history as it often did their male counterparts.

A more important factor that has contributed to the obscurity of female writers of Western fiction is that their identities were often concealed through sexually ambiguous pseudonyms, most commonly the use of initials. Whether this practice was begun by editors to fool the reading audience, which they believed to be composed largely of misogynistic males, or by female authors to garner an unbiased reading from an editor and thus gain entrance into a male-dominated field, or for some other reason, may never be known for certain. Nonetheless, the fact remains that even through the 1980s, almost any woman, with but a few exceptions, attempting to publish a traditional Western novel or story automatically affixed a sexually blurred identity to her work. Yet, clearly, for the majority of women writers, what had begun as a perceived necessity became a restrictive tradition.

In spite of the lack of encouragement or support from the publishing establishment, the critics, and, over the long term, the literary historians, women have persisted and, in many cases, prevailed. Women writers have made contributions to traditional Western fiction in that they have helped to refine, reshape, and redefine the Western story in its traditional form to embrace wider frontiers. Women, along with their male counterparts, have long recognized that the West is, as was once said, "the territory of the imagination." For this reason, among others, ten of the twenty-eight stories in this collection were written by female authors, many of whom are being collected here for the very first time.

It is our conviction that, whether written by men or by women, the Western story constitutes the single most important literary movement in the history of the United States and that it comprises the only unique body of literature that this country has contributed to the wealth of world culture. The Western story is unique to this country because of where it is set: in the American West. There was no place in all history quite like it before, and there is no place quite like it now.

The Western story at base is a story of renewal, and that is what has made it so very different from any other form of literary enterprise. It is refreshing, even revitalizing, in these days of a medically overeducated culture obsessed with health and terrified of old age and dying to behold once again generations of Americans to which such obsessions and terrors meant nothing. It is spiritually encouraging in these days of political correctness, timidity, and herd notions such as one-settlement culture that wants everyone to believe in a lockstep approach to life to contemplate those generations when individual, cultural, and ethnic differences were abundant, when not one culture but many coexisted even if warfare between them was unceasing. We have benefited from that time. There is no one idea and no one cause that can possibly ever win endorsement from everybody. We still live now with that reality of the frontier as part of our social existence.

Above all, the greatest lesson the pioneers learned from the Indians is with us still: that it is each man's and each woman's *inalienable* right to find his own path in life, to follow his own vision, to achieve his own destiny—even should one fail in the process. There is no principle so singularly revolutionary as this one in the entire intellectual history of the Occident and the Orient before the American frontier experience, and it grew from the very soil of this land and the peoples who came to live on it. It is this principle which has always been the very cornerstone of the Western story. Perhaps for this reason critics have been wont to dismiss it as subversive and inconsequential because this principle reduces their voices to only a few among many. Surely it is why the Western story has been consistently banned by totalitarian governments. Such a principle undermines the very foundations of totalitarianism and collectivism because it cannot be accommodated by the political correctness of those who would seek to exert power over others and replace all options with a single, all-encompassing, monolithic pattern for living.

There is no other kind of American literary endeavor that has so repeatedly posed the eternal questions—How do I wish to live? In what do I believe? What do I want from life? What have I to give to life?—as has the Western story. There is no other kind of literary enterprise since Greek drama that has so invariably posed ethical and moral questions about life as a fundamental of its narrative structure, that has taken a stand and said: this is wrong; this is right. Individual authors, as individual filmmakers, may present us with notions with which we do not agree, but in so doing they have made us think again about things that the herd has always been only too anxious to view as settled and outside the realm of questioning.

The West of the Western story is a region where generations of people from every continent on earth and for ages immeasurable have sought a second chance for a better life. The people forged by the clash of cultures in the American West produced a kind of human being very different from any the world had ever known before. How else could it be for a nation emerging from so many nations? And so stories set in the American West have never lost that sense of hope. It wasn't the graves at Shiloh, the white crosses at Verdun, the vacant beaches at Normandy, or the lines on the faces of their great men and women that made the Americans a great people. It was something more intangible than that. It was their great willingness of the heart.

What alone brings you back to a piece of music, a song, a painting, a poem, or a story is the mood that it creates in you when you experience it. The mood you experience in reading a Western story is that a better life *is* possible if we have the grit to endure the ordeal of attaining it; that it requires courage to hope, the very greatest courage any human being can ever have. And it is hope that distinguishes the Western story from every other kind of fiction. Only when courage and hope are gone will the Western story cease to be relevant to all of us.

# Monty Price's Nightingale

## Zane Grey

☒

*Born Pearl Zane Gray in Zanesville, Ohio, Zane Grey took his first trip to Arizona in 1907 and, following his return, wrote* The Heritage of the Desert *(Harper, 1910). The profound effect that the desert had had on him was so vibrantly captured, it still comes alive for the reader. Motion-picture rights brought in a fortune and, with 109 films based on his work, Grey set a record yet to be equaled by anyone. His masterpieces include, surely,* Riders of the Purple Sage *(Harper, 1912) and its sequel,* The Rainbow Trail *(Harper, 1915),* The Light of Western Stars *(Harper, 1914),* Wildfire *(Harper, 1917),* The Man of the Forest *(Harper, 1920), and* Wild Horse Mesa *(Harper, 1928). Some of his finest novels have only recently been published as he wrote them, including* Last of the Duanes *(Five Star Westerns, 1996),* Rangers of the Lone Star *(Five Star Westerns, 1997), and* Women of the Frontier *(Five Star Westerns, 1998). Zane Grey was not a realistic writer, but rather one who charted the interiors of the soul through encounters with the wilderness. He provided characters no more realistic than one finds in Balzac, Dickens, or Thomas Mann, but nonetheless they have a vital story to tell. More than stories, Grey fashioned psychodramas about the odyssey of the human soul. "Monty Price's Nightingale" was first published in Street & Smith's* Success Magazine *(April 1924) and wasn't collected in book form until* The Wolf Tracker and Other Stories *(Walter J. Black, 1976).*

**A**round camp fires they cursed him in hearty cowboy fashion and laid upon him the bane of their ill will. They said that Monty Price had no friend—that no foreman or rancher ever trusted him—that he never spent a dollar—that he would not keep a job—that there must be something crooked about a fellow who bunked and worked alone, who quit every few months to ride away, no one knew where, and who returned to the ranges, haggard and thin and shaky, hunting for another place.

He had been drunk somewhere, and the wonder of it was that no one in the Tonto forest ranges had ever seen him drink a drop. Red Lake and Gallatin and Bellville knew him, but no more of him than the ranges. He went farther afield, they said, and hinted darker things than a fling at faro or a fondness for red liquor.

But there was no rancher, no cowboy from one end of the vast range country to another, who did not admit Monty Price's preeminence in those peculiar attributes of his calling. He was a magnificent rider; he had an iron and cruel hand with a horse, yet he never killed or crippled his mount; he possessed the Indian's instinct for direction; he never failed on the trail of lost stock; he could ride an outlaw and brand a wild steer and shoe a vicious mustang as bragging cowboys swore they could; and supreme test of all he would endure, without complaint, long toilsome hours in the piercing wind and freezing sleet and blistering sun.

"I'll tell you what," said old Abe Somers. "I've ranched from the Little Big Horn to the Pecos, an' I've seen a sight of cowpunchers in my day. But Monty Price's got 'em all skinned. It shore is too bad he's unreliable . . . packin' off the way he does, jest when he's the boy most needed. Some mystery about Monty."

The extra duty, the hard task, the problem with stock or tools or harness—these always fell to Monty. His most famous trick was to offer to take a comrade's night shift. So it often happened that while the cowboys lolled round their camp fire, Monty Price, after a hard day's riding, would stand out the night guard, in rain and snow. But he always made a bargain. He sold his service. And the boys were wont to say that he put his services high.

Still they would never have grumbled at that if Monty had ever spent a dollar. He saved his money. He never bought any fancy boots or spurs or bridles or scarfs or chaps; and his cheap jeans and saddles were the jest of his companions. Nevertheless, in spite of Monty's shortcomings, he rode in the Tonto on and off for five years before he made an enemy.

There was a cowboy named Bart Muncie who had risen to be a foreman and who eventually went to ranching on a small scale. He acquired a range up in the forest country where grassy valleys and parks lay between the wooden hills, and here in a wild spot among the pines he built a cabin for his wife and baby.

It came about that Monty went to work for Muncie and rode for him for six months. Then, in a dry season, with Muncie short of help and with long drives to make, Monty quit in his inexplicable way and left the rancher in dire need. Muncie lost a good deal of stock that fall, and he always blamed Monty for it. Some weeks later it chanced that Muncie was in Bellville the very day Monte returned from his latest mysterious absence. And the two met in a crowded store.

Monty appeared vastly different from the lean-jawed, keen-eyed, hard-riding cowboy of a month back. He was haggard and thin and shaky and spiritless and somber.

"See here, Monty Price," said Muncie with stinging scorn, "I reckon you'll spare me a minute of your precious time."

"I reckon so," replied Monty.

Muncie used up more than the allotted minute in calling Monty every bad name known to the range.

"An' the worst of all you are is that you're a liar!" concluded the rancher passionately. "I relied on you an' you failed me. You lost me a herd of stock. Put me back a year! An' for what? God only knows what! We ain't got you figgered here ... not that way. But after this trick you turned me, we all know you're not square. An' I go on record callin' you as you deserve. You're no good. You've got a streak of yellow. An' you sneak off now an' then to indulge it. An' most of all you're a liar! Now, if it ain't all so ... flash your gun!"

But Monty Price did not draw.

The scorn and abuse of the cowboys might never have been, for all the effect it had on Monty. He did not see or feel it. He found employment with a rancher named Wentworth and went at his work in the old, inimitable manner, that was at once the admiration and despair of his fellows. He rolled out of his blankets in the gray dawn, and he was the last to roll in at night.

In a week all traces of his weakened condition had vanished, and he grew strong and dark and hard, once more like iron. And then again he was up to his old tricks, more intense than ever, eager and gruff at bargaining his time, obsessed by the one idea—to make money.

To Monty the long, hot, dusty, blasting days of summer were as moments. Time flew for him. The odd jobs, the rough trails, the rides without water or food, the long stands in the cold rain, the electric storms when the lightning played around and cracked in his horse's mane, and the uneasy herd bawled and milled—all these things that were the everlasting torment of his comrades were as nothing to Monty Price.

And when the first pay day came and Monty tucked away a little roll of greenbacks inside his vest and kept adding to it as one by one his comrades paid him for some bargained service—then in Monty Price's heart began the low and insistent and sweetly alluring call of the thing that had ruined him. Thereafter, sleeping or waking, he lived in a dream with that music in his heart, and the hours were fleeting.

On the mountain trails, in the noonday heat of the dusty ranges, in the dark, sultry nights with their thunderous atmosphere, he was always listening to that song of his nightingale. To his comrades he seemed a silent, morose, greedy cowboy, a demon for work, with no desire for friendship, no thought of home or kin, no love of a woman or a horse or anything, except money. To Monty himself, his whole inner life grew rosier and mellower and richer as day by day his nightingale sang sweeter and louder.

And that song was a song of secret revel—far away—where he gave up to this wind of flame that burned within him—where a passionate and irresistible strain in his blood found its outlet—where wanton red lips whispered, and wanton eyes, wine dark and seductive, lured him, and wanton arms twined around him.

The rains failed to come that summer. The gramma grass bleached on the open ranges and turned yellow up in the parks. But there was plenty of grass and water to last out the fall. It was fire the ranchers feared. And it came.

One morning above the low, gray-stoned and black-fringed mountain range rose clouds of thick, creamy smoke. There was fire on the other side of the mountain. But unless the wind changed and drew fire in over the pass, there was no danger on that score. The wind was right; it seldom changed at that season, though sometimes it blew a gale. Still the ranchers grew more anxious. The smoke clouds rolled up and spread and hid the top of the mountain and then lifted slow, majestic columns of white and yellow toward the sky.

On the day that Wentworth, along with other alarmed ranchers, sent men up to fight the fire in the pass, Monty Price quit his job and rode away. He did not tell anybody. He just took his little pack and his horse, and in the confusion of the hour he rode away. For days he had felt that his call might come at any moment, and finally it had come. It did not occur to him that he was quitting Wentworth at a most critical time. It would not have made any difference to him if it had occurred to him.

He rode away with bells in his heart. He felt like a boy at the prospect of a wonderful adventure. He felt like a man who had toiled and slaved, whose ambition had been supreme, and who had reached the pinnacle where his longing would be gratified.

His road led to the right, away from the higher ground and the timber. To his left the other road wound down the ridge to the valley below and stretched on through straggling pines and clumps of cedar toward the slopes and the forests. Monty had ridden that road a thousand times. For it led to Muncie's range. And as Monty's keen eye swept on over the parks and the thin wedges of pine to the black mass of timber beyond, he saw something that made him draw up with a start. Clearly defined against the blue-black swelling slope was a white-and-yellow cloud of smoke. It was moving. At thirty miles' distance, that it could be seen to move at all was proof of the great speed with which it was traveling.

"She's caught!" he ejaculated. "Way down on this side. An' she'll burn over. Nothin' can save the range!" He watched, and those keen, practiced eyes made out the changing, swelling columns of smoke, the widening path, the creeping dim red. "Reckon that'll surprise Wentworth's outfit," soliloquized Monty thoughtfully. "It doesn't surprise me none. An' Muncie, too. His cabin's up there in the valley."

It struck Monty suddenly that the wind blew hard in his face. It was sweeping down the valley toward him. It was bringing that fire. Swiftly on the wind!

"One of them sudden changes of wind!" he said. "Veered right around! An' Muncie's range will go. An' his cabin!"

Straightway Monty grew darkly thoughtful. He had remembered seeing Muncie with Wentworth's men on the way to the pass. In fact, Muncie was the leader of this firefighting brigade.

"Sure he's fetched down his wife an' the baby," he muttered. "I didn't see them. But sure he must have."

Monty's sharp gaze sought the road for tracks. No fresh track showed! Muncie must have taken his family over the short-cut trail. Certainly he must have! Monty remembered Muncie's wife and child. The woman had hated him. But little Del with her dancing golden curls and her blue eyes—she had always had a ready smile for him.

It came to Monty then suddenly, strangely, that little Del would have loved him if he had let her. Where was she now? Safe at Wentworth's, without a doubt. But then she might not be. Muncie had certainly no fears of fire in the direction of home, not with the wind in the north and no prospect of change. It was quite possible—it was probable that the rancher had left his family at home that morning.

Monty experienced a singular shock. It had occurred to him to ride down to Muncie's cabin and see if the woman and child had been left. And whether or not he found them there the matter of getting back was a long chance. That wind was strong—that fire was sweeping down. How murky, red, sinister the slow-moving cloud!

"I ain't got a lot of time to decide," he said. His face turned pale and beads of sweat came out upon his brow.

That sweet little golden-haired Del, with her blue eyes and her wistful smile! Monty saw her as if she had been there. Then like lightning flashed back the thought that he was on his way to his revel. And the fires of hell burst in his veins. And more deadly sweet than any siren music rang the song of his nightingale in his heart. Neither honor nor manliness had ever stood before him and his fatal passion.

He was in a swift, golden dream, with the thick fragrance of wine, and the dark, mocking, luring eyes on him. All this that was more than life to him—to give it up—to risk it—to put it off for an hour! He felt the wrenching pang of something deeply hidden in his soul, beating its way up, torturing him. But it was strange and mighty. In that terrible moment it decided for him; and the smile of a child was stronger than the unquenchable and blasting fire of his heart.

Monty untied his saddle pack and threw it aside; and then with tight-shut jaw he rode down the steep descent to the level valley. His horse was big and strong and fast. He was fresh, too, and in superb condition.

Once down on the hard-packed road he broke into a run, and it took an iron arm to hold him from extending himself. Monty calculated on saving the horse for the run back. He had no doubt that would be a race with fire. And he had been in forest fires more than once. . . .

Muncie's cabin was a structure of logs and clapboards, standing in a little clearing, with the great pines towering all around. Monty saw the child, little Del, playing in the yard with a dog. He called. The child heard and, being frightened, ran into the cabin. The dog came barking toward Monty. He was a big, savage animal, a trained watch dog. But he recognized Monty.

Hurrying forward, Monty went to the open door and called Mrs. Muncie. There was no response. He called again. And while he stood there waiting, listening, above the roar of the wind he heard a low, dull, thundering sound, like a waterfall in a flooded river. It sent the blood rushing back to his heart, leaving him cold. He had not a single instant to lose.

"Missus Muncie," he called louder. "Come out! Bring the child! It's Monty Price. There's forest fire! Hurry!"

He stepped into the cabin. There was no one in the big room—or the kitchen. He grew hurried now. The child was hiding. Finally he found her in the clothespress, and he pulled her out. She was frightened. She did not recognize him.

"Del, is your mother home?" he asked.

The child shook her head.

With that Monty picked her up along with a heavy shawl he saw and, hurrying out, he ran down to the corral. Muncie's horses were badly frightened now. Monty set little Del down, threw the shawl into a watering trough, and then he let down the bars of the gate.

The horses pounded out in a cloud of dust. Monty's horse was frightened, too, and almost broke away. There was now a growing roar on the wind. It seemed right upon him. Yet he could not see any fire or smoke. The dog came to him, whining and sniffing.

With swift hands Monty soaked the shawl thoroughly in the water and then, wrapping it round little Del and holding her tightly, he mounted. The horse plunged and broke and plunged again—then leaped out straight and fast down the road. And Monty's ears seemed pierced and filled by a terrible, thundering roar.

He had to race with fire. He had to beat the wind of flame to the open parks. Ten miles of dry forest, like powder! Though he had never seen it, he knew fire backed by heavy wind could rage through dry pine faster than a horse could run. Yet something in Monty Price welcomed this race. He goaded the horse. Then he looked back.

Through the aisles of the forest he saw a strange, streaky, murky something, moving, alive, shifting up and down, never an instant the same. It must have been the wind, the heat before the fire. He seemed to see through it, but there was nothing beyond, only opaque, dim, mustering clouds.

Ahead of him, down the road, low under the spreading trees, floated swiftly some kind of a medium, like a transparent veil. It was neither smoke nor air. It carried pinpoints of light, sparks, that resembled atoms of dust floating in sunlight. It was a wave of heat propelled before the storm of fire. Monty did not feel pain, but he seemed to be drying up, parching. All was so strange and unreal—the swift flight between the pines, now growing ghostly in the dimming light—the sense of rushing, overpowering force—and yet absolute silence. But that light burden against his breast—the child—was not unreal.

He must have been insane, he thought, not to be overcome in spirit. But he was not. He felt loss of something, some kind of sensation he ought to have had. But he rode that race keener and better than any race he had ever before ridden. He had but to keep his saddle—to dodge the snags of the trees—to guide the maddened horse. No horse ever in the world had run so magnificent a race.

He was outracing wind and fire. But he was running in terror. For miles he held that long, swift, tremendous stride without a break. He was running to his death whether he distanced the fire or not. For nothing could stop him now except a bursting heart. Already he was blind, Monty thought.

And then, it appeared to Monty, although his steed kept fleeting on faster and faster, that the wind of flame was gaining. The air was too thick to breathe. It seemed ponderous—not from above but from behind. It had irresistible weight. It pushed Monty and his horse onward in their flight—straws on the crest of a cyclone.

Ahead there was light through the forest. He made out a white, open space of grass. A park! And the horse, like a demon, hurtled onward, with his smoothness of action gone, beginning to break.

A wave of wind, blasting in its heat, like a blanket of fire, rolled over Monty. He saw the lashing tongues of flame above him in the pines. The storm had caught him. It forged ahead. He was riding under a canopy of fire. Burning pine cones, like torches, dropped all around him, upon him.

A terrible blank sense of weight, of agony, of suffocation—of the air turning to fire! He was drooping, withering, when he flashed from the pines out into the open park. The horse broke and plunged and went down, reeking, white, in convulsions, killed on his feet. There was fire in his mane. Monty fell with him and lay in the grass, the child in his arms.

Fire in the grass—fire at his legs roused him. He got up. The park was burning over. It was enveloped in a pall of smoke. But he could see. Drawing back a fold of the wet shawl, he looked at the child. She appeared unharmed. Then he set off running away from the edge of the forest. It was a big park, miles wide. Near the middle there was bare ground. He recognized the place, got his bearings, and made for the point where a deep ravine headed out of the park.

Beyond the bare circle there was more fire, burning sage and grass. His feet were blistered through his boots, and then it seemed he walked on red-hot coals. His clothes caught fire, and he beat it out with bare hands.

Then he stumbled into the rocky ravine. Smoke and blaze above him—the rocks hot—the air suffocating—it was all unendurable. But he kept on. He knew that his strength failed as the conditions bettered. He plunged down, always saving the child when he fell. His sight grew red. Then it grew dark. All was black, or else night had come. He was losing all pain, all sense, when he stumbled into water. That saved him. He stayed there. A long time passed till it was light again. His eyes had a thick film over them. Sometimes he could not see at all.

But when he could, he kept on walking, on and on. He knew when he got out of the ravine. He knew where he ought to be. But the smoky gloom obscured everything. He traveled the way he thought he ought to go and went on and on, endlessly. He did not suffer any more. The weight of the child bore him down. He rested, went on, rested again, went on again, till all sense, except a dim sight, failed him. Through that, as in a dream, he saw moving figures, men looming up in the gray fog, hurrying to him.

�✪

Far south of the Tonto range, under the purple shadows of the Peloncillos, there lived a big-hearted rancher with whom Monty Price found a home. He did little odd jobs about the ranch that by courtesy might have been called work. He would never ride a horse again. Monty's legs were warped, his feet hobbled. He did not have free use of his hands. And seldom or never in the presence of anyone did he remove his sombrero. For there was not a hair on his head. His face was dark, almost black, with terrible scars.

A burned-out, hobble-footed wreck of a cowboy! But, strangely, there were those at the ranch who learned to love him. They knew his story.

# On with the Dance

## B. M. Bower

☉

*Any list of women writers of Western fiction must include B. M. Bower, one of the first women to write traditional Western stories, and to this day her work probably generates more attention by scholars than any other female writer of the Western story. A contemporary of Owen Wister's, Bertha Muzzy Bower was born in Cleveland, Minnesota, and moved to Montana when she was sixteen. She celebrated romantic cowboys in her own inimitable and unsophisticated style, de-emphasizing violence and gun play—at least until late in her career. She often flavored her stories with a lighthearted humor, and her best works are those that stress a strong sense of family and camaraderie. It was the success of her inter-linked Flying U stories—originally appearing in pulp magazines and eventually in hardcover books as fifteen novels and short story collections featuring Chip Bennett and/or members of the Happy Family—along with the longevity of her career, spanning forty years, that secured her current position in the literary history of the Western story. Bower's novels have often been hard to come by, being out of print for decades, but recently they have begun to be successfully reissued. Foremost among these reprints are* Chip of the Flying U *(Dillingham, 1906), reissued by the University of Nebraska Press in 1994; in Chivers's Gunsmoke hardcover Western series,* The Whoop-Up Trail *(Little, Brown, 1933), re-printed in 1994; and* The Flying U Strikes *(Little, Brown, 1934), reprinted in 1996. "On with the Dance," a story Bower herself favored, first appeared in* Short Stories *(January 10, 1934).*

The tall young fellow in fringed leather chaps and big-roweled silver spurs stood still as carven granite beside the kitchen table. A holstered six-shooter hung snug at his right hip in odd contrast to the checked gingham apron tied behind around his neck. Above the pink cheeks his browned face was tilted, staring fixedly at a point considerably lower than the slant of his gun belt at his right side. He was wondering what would happen if he should kiss the cute dimple in the girl's elbow. But she looked up at him and he instantly began wiping four saucers, expertly shifting the top one to the bottom of the stack as he wiped.

"My goodness! Look out or you'll break Ma's new saucers!" she cried with a breathless giggle, excited by the close presence of the best-looking cowboy in that country.

"I ain't broke any so far," the wiper said equably. "You better look out yourself. If them soapsuds foam any higher, you're liable to drown that dimple."

"My goodness! What dimple, for pity sake?"

"In your elbow." His tone was deceptively casual. "Soapy dimples don't taste good."

Hattie blushed furiously and pulled the dishpan six inches toward the end of the table, trying to look indignant. But the cowboy noticed that she did not remove herself any farther from him but rather tempted him with the elbow under discussion.

So he dropped a knife. When he stooped to pick it up, he paused midway and kissed the dimple daringly.

"For . . . ever*more*!" cried Hattie, highly affronted.

The cowboy noticed that her outcry was carefully kept within the compass of the kitchen. Scarcely more than a murmur of protest, and that not half meant. So he kissed her on the mouth, the dishtowel with the knife in it swathing her shoulders as his arm slid around.

"You stop! I'll tell Ma. . . ." At least what she said had the sound of some such words. His lips were warm, tingly—interfering lips that brushed mere words aside. Then a panicky breath. "She's *coming*!"

It was Josie, the homely one, coming out of the sitting room with the coal bucket. She did not look at either of them as she walked through the kitchen and opened the door to the shed. The cold swooshed in like a white cloud that vanished when the heat ate it. The cowboy wiped a teacup and wondered if that other girl had caught onto anything.

When she came back, he remembered his manners and took long steps to meet her. He took the heavy bucket of lump coal from her hand, smiling down into her face when she looked up to protest. No one had ever thought to tell him that he had a most disturbing kind of smile. The homely girl's heart beat a swifter tempo, but no one suspected it, she looked so unimpressed.

"Thank you, Mister Farrow," she said when he had filled the sitting-room heater.

"Say, I'm lonesome enough in this man's country without everybody mistering me," he objected plaintively. "Folks have always called me Lynn . . . to my face," he hinted, giving her another look unconsciously devastating. "Make her behave, Missus Baldwin, can't yuh?"

"We're neighbors, Lynn. There ain't anybody got any reason to hold you off with a mister to your name that I know of." Mrs. Baldwin looked at him indulgently over her glasses. "You've been hunting them stray horses over this way steady for a month now. If we ain't all friends by this time, we never will be, I guess." With that gentle jab she went back to slip-stitching—whatever that was—on the sock she was knitting.

"Them stray horses just about saved my life," Lynn grinned shamelessly. "I expect I'll be hunting 'em over this way about all winter, if I don't get run off."

"Did you finish the dishes, Lynn?" Josie asked. And because she was the homely one Lynn hurried back to the task that had suddenly become exceedingly pleasant.

The door failed to close behind him, having a habit of swinging back against the wall unless deliberately latched. Lynn lacked the nerve to go back and pull it shut, so the dishwashing proceeded with decorum.

They presently talked of dancing. Lynn wished there was a dance somewhere within riding distance. They'd all go. He'd hitch the hay team to the sleigh, throw in a few forkfuls of hay, and take the bunch of them—Pa, Ma, Josie, and Hattie whose red mouth set his pulse jumping.

"Well, there won't be a dance now till Washington's Birthday, maybe not then," sighed Hattie, moving her bare elbows distractingly so that the dimples showed deepest. "The school board won't let the schoolhouse be used except on legal holidays."

"Why not give one here?" Lynn rashly suggested, lifting a handful of knives and forks from the pan of hot water.

"Pa won't have dances here," Hattie sighed, dripping foam from her pink hand. "It keeps him up all night looking after the teams and saddle horses. He just hates the fussing. I . . . why don't you give one, Lynn?"

"*Me?*" Lynn dropped another knife, without intention this time. And he did not kiss her elbow when he stooped to get it. "I never did give a dance. I wouldn't know the first thing about it. Besides. . . ."

"Besides what? There's that great empty house over at the Rolling M, and nobody in it but you. The Jamesons used to have dances all the time over there before they sold out. That big long sitting room was just *made* for dances. If you take out the stove in the middle, there's room for two sets. By putting the music up on the table right by the door, another set can dance in the kitchen without bothering the refreshment end. And it's an awfully good floor. The Jamesons had lots of money when they built the house. They lost it afterwards before they sold the stock to your outfit. Of course we can have a dance. I don't know why I didn't think of it before. We'll have lots of dances this winter, Lynn."

That was how it started. Lynn didn't want to tackle it and said so. But Hattie went on planning and persuading while the dishwater cooled, and the foamy white suds went to nothing. For a girl who had just thought of it she seemed to have a terribly clear idea of every small detail. Lynn wished it had been the homely one who had thought of a dance at the ranch where he was wintering alone. He could have thought of reasons why he couldn't go through with the scheme. With Hattie standing so close, the elbow he had kissed kept touching his gun belt, and he couldn't think of anything except that dimple and how her mouth felt against his lips.

But he tried. "If it was to storm," he said, "there's all of them cattle I've got to shovel hay to, and horses to feed. The Rolling M never put me on any dance committee when they sent me over here to winter the Jameson stock. I'm s'posed to feed up that hay before spring, so as not to waste it, and at the same time bring the stock through in good shape to trail 'em home next spring."

"Well," Hattie inquired archly, "and what has that got to do with having a dance?"

Lynn did not know, not in a sense that could be put into words. "I'd sure hate to make a fizzle of it," he hedged uncomfortably. "If I started a thing like that, I'd have to go through with it. I'm kinda stubborn that way."

Hattie found an errand into the sitting room. When she came out, the door closed after her so that it stayed closed. Lynn might have thought that indicated experience, but he didn't. He had something else to worry about.

So, the door being closed, Hattie managed to convince him that a dance was the simplest thing in the world to manage. She and Josie would make lots of doughnuts and sandwiches and bring over plenty of coffee and cream. All Lynn had to do was ride around and tell everybody, and get old Bill Saunders to come and play. He would, for a collection. They'd just pass the hat before supper. It wouldn't cost Lynn a cent. All he need do was have the house ready and the heating stove moved out of the front room. They'd even bring over some corn meal to make the floor slick. There wouldn't, Hattie eagerly assured him, be any trouble at all and he needn't worry a minute.

But female prophets are nearly always inspired by their own desires rather than by any prescient knowledge of the future. Lynn did worry. Riding back across the frozen brown prairie, he surprised three gray wolves feeding off a dead colt at sundown, and he shot two of them, throwing dust around the third with the last two bullets in his gun. But even the thought of the double bounty and the thick winter pelts that made such fancy rugs could not warm his thoughts from foreboding.

Nor did the fight afterwards with Seal, his brown horse, nor the victory of making Seal carry those two wolves to the Jameson place where he could skin them by lantern light. All the way home, sandwiched between the dead wolves, all through chore time when the lantern went here and there, drawing dancing bars of light across the bare brown sod—all the while he was eating supper, and afterwards while he skinned the wolves down in the blacksmith shop, he kept thinking what a fool he was to make promises to a girl.

Just because she had a cute dimple in her elbow, and because her lips were for the fellow who dared, here he was now with three deep wrinkles between his fine straight eyebrows and hot flushes of stage fright surging over his body. He even started talking to himself, a lapse he had always said was the earmark of a sheepherder going batty. But he did it, right out loud in the solitude of that big, deserted house of the Jamesons'. While he was pulling off his boots, he gave a snort. "Me give a dance to folks I don't hardly know by sight! Letting 'em lay their babies on my bed . . .! Them old sage hens cacklin' around in here where I've got it fixed up bully for the winter. Snoopin' around, criticizing my things . . . oh good *Godfrey!*" And he slammed a boot down on the floor and added fiercely: "Darn a girl, anyway! Getting around a fellow with dimples and kisses . . . oh, Godfrey!" Only, you must understand, he had much more forcible epithets that he applied to himself that night and afterwards.

But a promise is a promise. Lynn got up an hour earlier next morning and hauled a load of hay out to the feed ground. While the wise team walked slowly in an acre-wide circle, the lines winding around the front standard of the rack, he scattered the hay neatly in little piles. The bawling herd of weaned calves and poor cows trailed after in a long queue, thinking each forkful as it fell into the cold wind must be better than the last but at last settling down to their breakfast when Lynn drove the empty wagon back to the corral.

Once the team was unharnessed and left comfortably in their stalls, he was a free man until four o'clock, when he would have to haul another ton or two out and scatter it as before. A simple life— a contented life, even though it was lonesome at times. If it wasn't for that darned dance Saturday night.

He saddled Seal then, buttoned himself into his gray wolfskin coat, buckled on his spurs and his gun and rode over to see old Bill Saunders about the music. Old Bill was a case. When he fiddled, he chewed tobacco and stomped both feet, keeping time of a sort, and called off in a high singsong whine that carried far off above the shuffle of feet, the swish of skirts, and the squeal of his fiddle. He had bleak blue eyes, a red beard, and a fiery disposition.

Old Bill said all right, he'd be there with bells on. So Lynn loped on over to Squaw Creek and invited everybody along the creek, and they all said they'd come. In the teeth of a raw wind he loped home again and hauled two loads of hay because it looked as if it might take a notion to snow. And after supper he rode over to tell Hattie that Bill Saunders would come, all right, and so would all the folks from Squaw Creek. There were no kisses to reward him, but curiously enough Lynn did not think much about that. His thoughts were chiefly given to the ordeal he would have to face on Saturday night.

Next day he again hurried through his work, because Hattie had told him he must ride over Wolf Butte way and invite everyone who lived within twenty miles at least. She wanted this first dance of his to be something they'd all remember. Well, she had her wish, so far as that goes—though perhaps this is running ahead of the story.

That evening he stopped by to see Hattie, although he knew he shouldn't because it was getting past feeding time, and he knew those darned Rolling M critters would be standing around the feed ground, bawling their heads off. It was a sorry stop he made, because Hattie had a wonderful idea of lights all along the porch, and on the gate-posts, and wherever a light would hang. She was sorry she hadn't thought of it before, but still, it wouldn't be so very much trouble, would it Lynn, to ride around and tell everybody to bring their lan-terns—all the lanterns they could rustle? Lynn said sure, it wouldn't be any trouble at all. Which Hattie apparently believed, because she added archly that all a cowboy ever did was ride around anyway.

Well, he managed to get the cattle fed, though a pale moon watched him throw off the last of the load, and half the herd had given him up in disgust and gone off to the sheds to bed. That night he ached, and he had nightmare dreams of the terrible condition of the house. He thought he was waltzing with Hattie, and she kept stubbing her toe over those darned pack saddles he had brought in to mend when he got around to it. And he thought all the other women stood around and talked about the dirt.

So next day he started an uproar which he called hoeing out. It lasted until late afternoon, and he went off with wet feet to shovel hay to the cattle—wet feet caused by sloshing buckets of water on the floors and scrubbing it vigorously around with a broom, and then sweeping it out through the nearest doorway where it immediately froze and gave an icy approach to each door. He found that out when he walked hurriedly onto the porch after feeding time and nearly broke his neck. But the floors were clean, thank the Lord. No old hen was going to turn up her nose at *his* housekeeping.

That night it was the lanterns that haunted him. So he rode back to Squaw Creek next day between feedings and notified everyone to bring lanterns. And the day after that he did the same by Wolf Butte folks. But he didn't see any sense in it, and on his way back by way of the Baldwin ranch he remarked with sudden sarcasm to his brown horse Seal: "Not a *bit* of trouble to give a dance! No trouble . . . *hell!*"

He looked in the mood to say that to Hattie, though he was a nice-mannered young man and probably would have controlled himself. But Hattie wasn't home. Josie was frying doughnuts. She had two large milk pans full as they would hold, and she told Lynn to help himself. Lynn helped himself to five, one after the other. The last one he pulled off the fork Josie held out to him and burned his fingers. That tickled them both, and they laughed and laughed. It was the first time Lynn had so much as smiled since Hattie thought of giving a dance. He told Josie about the lanterns, and Josie couldn't see any sense in it either. He thought on the way home that he had kinda misread Josie's brand, thinking her homely and all. Maybe she wasn't any cigar ad, but she sure had brains in her head.

It seemed a shame he couldn't get a decent night's sleep any more, but five hot doughnuts—not to mention the dozen which Josie had laughingly distributed through his coat pockets—and no man could reasonably expect any better than he got. He went to bed (excuse me) belching greasy flavors of those doughnuts. He tossed, and he rolled until his blankets were all up around his neck, and his dreams were horrible. He awoke to Saturday morning and a gloomy conviction that trouble was headed his way. Naturally, he laid it to the doughnuts and tried to dismiss his melancholy and drove off to feed the cattle.

He was just throwing off the last few forkfuls of hay and thinking he'd lie around all day and rest up for the dance, when here came old Bill Saunders galloping across the field, his heels drumming his horse's ribs—the way an Indian rides as a rule.

"Good Godfrey, what now!" Lynn muttered into his collar and swung the team toward the corral to meet his visitor.

Bill Saunders wasted no words but told his bad news around a fresh chew of tobacco. One eye was closed completely; the other looked like polished turquoise. He held up a bandaged left hand.

"Hustled right over t'tell yuh I cain't play for yore dance," was his way of announcing it. "Had me a run-in with a blank blank blankety blank sheepherder. Licked 'im to a frazzle, but the damn' hydrophoby skunk got m'two string fingers in his mouth an' chawed 'em up like a dog chaws a chicken bone. Come 'ere and I'll show yuh."

Lynn stopped the team, and old Bill rode close to the rack and untied the bloody bandage with his yellowed teeth. Lynn looked and sucked in his breath. "Yep, he sure chawed you," he agreed dully.

"Well, blankety blank blank, I shore as hell cropped an ear for 'im," old Bill boasted while he rewound the stiffened bandage. "I'd 'a' sent 'im off with a bunch of dewlaps, but he broke away on me." And he added a string of words that sizzled the air.

Leaning over the edge of the rack, Lynn retied the bandage and said how sorry he was. "Anybody else in the country able to saw off a few tunes?" he asked worriedly.

Old Bill pondered, shaking his head. Then he spat into the trodden grass and squinted his good eye. "Feller visitin' Mullens'," he said cryptically. "Professional vi'linist, they tell me. You might git him. I don' know."

Lynn was doubtful. "These professionals . . . they're the jaspers that plays classical music," he objected. "Hell, I want somebody that can *fiddle*."

Old Bill thought the jasper over at Mullens' might be able to foller a mouth harp anyway. "Most generally these blank blank professionals are tol'able fair on waltzes. Purty slow an' weepy, but Lynn, yuh might prod 'im up with a pitchfork now an' then an' keep 'im ramblin'. Be better'n nothin', mebbe."

Old Bill would come over and do the callin' off and, if necessary, he'd stomp time and kinda keep the professional leanin' ag'in' the collar. He was a kind-hearted old ruffian, was old Bill Saunders, even if he did chew the ears half off sheepherders in the heat of an argument.

So Lynn saddled Seal and headed for Mullens' in a long lope. The men were out hauling hay. Mrs. Mullen held the door open just wide enough to let her face out and denied at first that she had a guest of any sort. But when Lynn told her about old Bill and smiled at her in the devastating way he had—though he didn't know he had it—Mrs. Mullen blushed and let him into the warm kitchen. Fat does many things to a woman but has never been known to make her absolutely impervious to smiles such as Lynn Farrow's.

Mrs. Mullen went upstairs to confer with the professional violinist, who was still in bed. She was gone a long time. Lynn could hear her voice raised in argument, sharpened with expostulation, lowered in pleading. Finally she returned to say that her old school mate, H. LaVerne Churchill, thought he was coming down with grippe. He certainly could play a violin, she said. He could play "Over the Waves" to bring tears from a rock, and you just wanted to go on waltzing till you dropped. But he was awful sensitive and shy. It was just like pulling teeth to get LaVerne out among strangers. She didn't know—if Lynn could promise him there wouldn't be any big crowd but just a few neighbors. . . .

With that hint to guide him, Lynn unbuttoned his fur coat and went upstairs behind Mrs. Mullen's toiling bulk and added all his persuasion to hers. Eventually H. LaVerne Churchill yielded to the flattery of their coaxing. He even consented to get up and dress himself and come downstairs to a belated breakfast. While he was waiting for his hotcakes, he condescended to play "Over the Waves"—Mrs. Mullen watching Lynn's face to see how he liked it.

Privately, Lynn thought the time was rotten. But he was no judge of professionals, and he left with both H. LaVerne Churchill and Mrs. Mullen promising that he would be there and bring his violin. In spite of that Lynn rode back around by old Bill Saunders's place and told him to bring his fiddle along and to come early because he might have to kinda egg the "vi'linist" into speeding up his tunes. He played, said Lynn, kinda long-drawn-out like a wolf howling before a storm. Sounded good, but nothing you could dance to.

He was still suffering from the effect of all those doughnuts, but there was no time to pet himself along. He was not afraid that H. LaVerne would fail to show up, because he had shown a rare diplomacy in adding a ten-dollar gold piece to his persuasions and had hinted that there would be another after the dance. Not that Lynn was overstocked with gold pieces. He was just a nice young man determined to finish whatever he started, which in this case was the dance for Hattie.

That day he fed the cattle so early he had to drive out into the three-hundred-and-twenty-acre field and toll the cattle in with the first load, they were so surprised that he should have hay for them at that hour. But he knew the Baldwins would be over early with the refreshments, and he wanted to be all shaved and in his good clothes before they came and have the plank benches laid around the wall in the front room. It was going to be pretty cold that night. He ought to keep the old cookstove red hot to kinda take the chill off the other rooms. There'd be plenty to do, especially after the crowd began to roll in along about seven, a little before, some of them.

He was just trying for the seventeenth time to slick the wave out of his hair and make his cowlick lie down when the Baldwins drove into the yard. Lynn hurried out bareheaded into the wind and helped the women down from the wagon and carried in the bundles of food. It took four trips. Then he went to show Baldwin the snuggest stalls for his team. He was just leaving the stable after that was done when there came the Mullens' covered buggy. Mrs. Mullen leaned out and beckoned him. Lynn hurried over.

"I'm awful sorry, Mister Farrow. I made Jim hitch up and come right over. LaVerne isn't coming at all. Right after supper he said he felt worse and was goin' to bed and see if he couldn't break up his cold. But I don't believe that's it, Mister Farrow. He just can't bear to set up and face a crowd of strangers. He's just lost his nerve, is what ails him. I do wish you'd've been there, Mister Farrow . . . I'm most sure you could've coaxed him into comin'."

"Yeah, well, I'll fork my horse and get right over there," Lynn promised. "Maybe I can git him to change his mind."

He left Mullen to put his team wherever he pleased, and Mrs.

Mullen to waddle up the slippery path alone to the house. He had changed from buttoned shoes to boots, had buckled on his gun and his big fur coat and his spurs, and was surging out into the raw dusk before Mrs. Mullen arrived puffing at the porch. A group of horsemen were arriving, collars pulled up around their shaven jaws. But he recognized old Bill Saunders's pacing pinto and hurried over to meet him.

"You'll have to ride herd on the bunch till I git back, Bill," he announced without preface. "I'm liable to be a little late with the music. That buttermilk-eyed buzzard of a vi'linist broke down on me. Backed out at the last minute and wouldn't come."

"Wouldn't, ay? Why, the blank blank blankety blank . . . !"

Lynn left him warming the atmosphere with his opinion of professional violinists who broke their engagements, saddled his horse, and rode forth into the teeth of a cold north wind.

H. LaVerne Churchill was in bed with the lamp on a box beside his pillow. He was reading "East Lynne" and his lip was trembling over the saddest part of all, where she came back hidden behind dark glasses to be governess—or was it nurse?—to her own darling—anyway, it was sad and H. LaVerne's pale blue eyes were moist and his lip was trembling. It trembled worse when Lynn burst into the room and yanked him out of bed.

Lynn was not a bad man, but he acted bad. He thought that was the way to handle pasty-faced runts like H. LaVerne Churchill, and perhaps he was right. He jerked out his gun and fired one shot. It left a burnt hole almost in the exact center of the braided rag rug. H. LaVerne Churchill's feet were near its edge. It was not a big rug, either.

"Git into your pants," Lynn ordered with a deadly calm. "You're due at that dance right now, so don't waste any time."

H. LaVerne dressed himself in less time than you would believe possible. Almost as quickly, in fact, as Lynn saddled the horse he found in the stable. He did not think a professional violinist would be likely to know much about horseback riding, and he was right. But this one rode that night.

They arrived just in time to start the music before the milling crowd began to lose its temper. Hattie was sulking a little because

Lynn had gone off without telling her where he was going, and there were not enough lanterns to make the porch look pretty. Josie gave him a smile, beckoned him to her, and led him into the pantry where she had a cup of hot coffee, a sandwich, and two kinds of cake all nicely spread out on a fringed napkin.

"Old Bill Saunders told me about the violinist," she said. "I just knew you had to go off without your supper. You stand there and eat that, and I'll keep watch."

Lynn hesitated, heard the twanging of the violin and the plunk of a guitar being tuned, and relaxed. Old Bill was getting things started all right. While he bit into a beef-tongue sandwich, he heard Bill's high rasping voice. *"Git yer partners fer a square dance!"* Josie looked over her shoulder and smiled at him, and Lynn smiled back.

"Let's dance this," he suggested, chewing fast so that he might swallow the last mouthful and be ready to make merry with the crowd.

"Oh, but this is Hattie's dance," Josie reminded him loyally. "She'll expect the first one with you. You're the host, you know. You have to see that everyone else is having a good time before you think about enjoying yourself."

"Yeah, that's right. I'm starting in with you." Lynn gave her a look.

"Well, you needn't worry about me," said Josie with a toss of her head (though her heart must have been beating furiously). "You better get out there and see if everybody has found partners. And you want to keep an eye on those Wolf Butte cowboys. If they brought bottles with them as they generally do, they'll pick a fight. They just love to break up dances. I can't see why Hattie wanted you to invite them, anyway. She knows they're rowdies."

"All right, I'll ride herd a while," Lynn promised, drinking the last of his coffee. "But you save a dance for me, Josie. A waltz. Will you do that?"

"Maybe . . . after you've danced with Hattie." She pushed him out of the pantry, her cheeks red as if she had painted them so, which of course she had not. Only the bold hussies used paint on their faces in those simple times.

Lynn went off to keep cases on the crowd. Already three sets had formed. Hattie stood in the first set. She couldn't have waited more than half a minute for Lynn, and he chalked that up against her as he slipped along the wall toward the front door. Through the window he had seen vague figures out there on the unused porch, and he thought he'd just see what they were hanging around out there for.

Half a dozen Wolf Butte men stood just beyond the light from the window. A round, ribbed bottle was making the rounds—a little early but they'd had a long, cold ride. Lynn paused in the doorway sizing up the situation and trying to see who they were before he went among them. But at that moment a loud voice behind him rose in raucous dispute above the first notes of the music. Lynn whirled about, closing the door behind him.

A tall, ungainly fellow with a red bandanna draped around his neck was trying to push a man out of the quadrille set nearest the door. One of these mouthy gazabos, Lynn tagged him. Claimed that was his place, he had it first, and he and his partner had just sat down a minute to wait till the music started.

"You ain't supposed to dance setting down," Lynn told him reasonably. "Stand up if you want to dance, brother. Folks ain't going to read your mind." He looked across at old Bill Saunders standing on a box beside the table where the musicians had their chairs. Old Bill turned and ejected his tobacco cud delicately into the corner. H. LaVerne drew his bow cannily across the strings of the violin cuddled beneath his weak chin.

*"S'lute yer pardners . . . ! Corners the same! Gran' right 'n' left . . . an' don't . . . go . . . lame!"*

The half-grown boy with the guitar was half a beat behind and didn't remember just when the chord should change, but the violin twanged right merrily along. The beat and shuffle, the swish of starched petticoats, the high nasal singsong of old Bill Saunders's calling the changes, all proclaimed that the dance was on. But near the door rose a dissonant note.

"'S my dance an' I'm a goin' to dance it!"

"You sed down, brother."

"I will like hell! I come here to dance and no this and that. . . ."

So Lynn got him by the ear and led him outside where a laugh greeted them and the little knot of men parted to let them through.

"Paste 'im one, Bob! Don't let him run any whizzer on yuh!"

Thus encouraged, Bob swung half around and did his pasting. The blow landed on Lynn's cheek, scraping off skin.

"You would, huh? Come on down to the blacksmith shop and lemme show yuh something." And Lynn rushed Wolf Butte down there at a trot.

The group followed, one man snatching a lantern off the gatepost as they went through. And after that Lynn was terribly busy for half an hour or more, fighting Wolf Butte men who rashly attempted to take Bob's part. It seemed to him that they all piled in at once, though actually four of the bunch were trying to pacify Bob and pull the other two off Lynn. They were practically sober and not aching to fight, as they would be later. Had Bob been a Squaw Creek man they would have laughed him out of it. But Wolf Butte boys had to stick together and do their fighting amongst themselves.

Down in the blacksmith shop with the door closed and the one lantern dimly lighting the scene, Lynn set himself grimly to the task. He polished Bob off, saw him let himself out to do something for his nose which was bleeding on his store clothes. He exchanged blows and hard words with two of Bob's friends, smashed their bottle which happened to be nearly empty, and saw them go off somewhere after another. He then brushed himself off, slicked his hair down with his hands, took off his coat, and sorrowfully inspected an alarming rip in the right armhole, put it back on, and returned to the house. Maybe Josie could pin it up or something.

How long he had been away he did not know, not over half an hour, he was sure. But in that short time a sinister change had come over the crowd. He went in through the kitchen, looking for Josie. What he saw was a hushed, whispering group of women. The men were standing in uneasy groups near the doors and, beside the table where the musicians had sat perched upon kitchen chairs, the young guitar player was pushing his instrument into a green denim bag as Lynn approached.

Lynn stared, astonished. Two women came out of the bedroom putting on their wraps, whispering together. Even at two o'clock in the morning one would not expect such definite evidence that the dance was over. Then Mrs. Mullen saw him and came waddling toward him like a flustered duck. Tears were dripping from her eyes.

"Oh, Mister Farrow! What shall we do?" she cried distractedly. "They've got LaVerne! They came and took him right off the table! Right in the middle of a two-step!"

Lynn led her to one side and got the story. She had known LaVerne was having some kinda trouble with his wife. That's why he hated to get out among people. But she never dreamed it was two wives he was hiding from. Poor LaVerne was so sensitive and so kinda innocent, she didn't much believe he realized how serious it was to marry two women. . . .

"Who got him? The sheriff?" Lynn's eyes were beginning to blaze.

"No, a deputy. A new one. He had a warrant, and he wouldn't wait but walked right up and served it on LaVerne, right in the middle of the dance. He made him put down his fiddle and go, and he wouldn't listen to nobody!"

"I see," said Lynn, and left her standing there. He went to old Bill Saunders. "Bill," he said with a snap in his voice, "see if you can't dig up somebody that can play a mouth harp for this kid to chord by. And you call off some good old square dances. Keep 'em hoeing 'er down for a while, till I get back."

Old Bill pried the corner off a plug, eyeing Lynn curiously. "What yuh figure on doin', Lynn?"

"Who, me? I'm going to scare up a fiddler. I know where I can get one. You tell 'em, I'll be back in an hour or so, and the dance'll go right on. Tell 'em that."

In his extra room where he had moved his personal belongings Lynn was buckling on his gun when Hattie appeared. Her eyes were full of tears, and her mouth was trembling. "They've spoiled my lovely dance!" she wailed. "Lynn, can't you *do* something?"

"I can sure try," Lynn told her, reaching for his coat. "Don't you worry a minute. You go on back and dance."

But it was Josie's face he remembered, her eyes questioning him over Hattie's shoulder. He did not speak to Josie at all, but he thought of her all the while he was saddling Seal. Without a word between them he felt sure that Josie understood and would ride hard on the crowd till he got back. There sure was a lot of *sabe* in that girl, even if she wasn't what you could rightly call pretty.

With the moon dodging in and out of gray clouds that carried snow in their folds, Lynn rode away from the corral and down the creek. When he swung into the beaten cow trail through the willows, he lifted Seal into a lope with his spurs. The road to the county seat led up along the ridge, and on it somewhere H. LaVerne Churchill was riding with the deputy sheriff to the town that was nearly forty miles off. They had, Lynn judged, more than half an hour start on him, and he could not hope to overtake them with Seal already leg weary from the errands he had run that day. But the main road swung back and crossed this creek about four miles farther down, and Lynn was taking a chance on meeting them somewhere along there.

The moon served for a while and then went under to stay. The quiet snowflakes came sifting down, and the night turned a whitish gray, with a silver spot in the clouds where the moon was swimming deep. Lynn knew to a hair what Seal could stand and kept him just safely under his limit until he reached the main road where it crossed the creek. There he dismounted and made sure, by the skim of unbroken ice, that no one had passed that way within the last hour. So then he turned back along the road and took it easy, letting his horse walk up the gentle slope of the prairie.

Topping the rise, he saw the two horsemen riding toward him through the white blur. They were coming along at a lope, so he touched Seal up with his spurs and galloped to meet them. Ten jumps away he pulled his gun and rode at them, setting Seal up in the trail before their horses.

"Hold on," he gave crisp command. "I've got you covered. Get your hands up, both of you."

H. LaVerne's arms shot straight up alongside his hat crown. The officer's lifted more slowly, but they went up. "If it's money you want," he called gruffly, "you've stuck up the wrong parties. I'm an officer of the law. I ain't any gold mine."

"You can keep your dough, if you've got any," Lynn said impatiently. "I want that prisoner of yourn. I hired him to play the fiddle at my dance, and by Godfrey, he's going to play it. You turn right around, H. LaVerne, and amble back to my kitchen table. They're spellin' you with mouth harps, and they're liable to git sore mouths and quit. So mosey right along."

The deputy made a choking sound. "This man is my prisoner," he blustered. "I've got him under arrest for bigamy and breakin' jail. He's wanted for forgery besides."

"He's wanted a damn' sight worse to play for my dance," Lynn bluntly stated. "You'd oughta waited till morning, anyhow. It ain't good manners to go and break up a dance on folks that've rode miles just to git a few hours of pleasure."

"What the hell's that to me? I come after this escaped prisoner, and I got him. I'm takin' him back to jail where he belongs."

"Not just yet, you ain't. This little squirt may be all you say. I wouldn't put it past him. But he's got to finish up the job he's been paid for." Lynn's voice eased down to a persuasive note. "I'm willing to be reasonable. You come on back with me and dance till morning. They'll be handing out some damn' good grub in a little bit now. I'll see to it you're treated like a king. Then in the morning, when the folks have danced all they want to, you can take H. LaVerne and hang him for all of me. How's that strike yuh?"

"It strikes me you're headed straight for the pen," snarled the deputy. "Interfering with an officer in the performance of his duty . . . I'll get you five years for it! Holding me up like this . . . !"

Lynn rode ominously closer. "Keep your hands up! If that's the way you feel about it, I'll make a damn' good job of it and, if I have to feed you a bullet or two, that'll be fine and dandy."

Even the murk of the thickening snow could not hide the sinister warning of the six-gun in his hand. With his knees he edged Seal closer alongside, leaned and lifted the gun from the deputy's holster.

"You'll do time for this," snarled the officer.

"Shut up, before I crown you with this gun. LaVerne, you take his bridle reins and lead out where I tell yuh. I ain't taking any chances with this jasper. He's liable to be wearing a shoulder holster or some such thing. Over to the left," he directed. "Now keep straight ahead till I tell yuh to stop. There's a claim shack over here a little ways. You'll see it."

Whatever H. LaVerne Churchill thought about the affair, he said never a word but was scrupulously careful to obey Lynn's slightest command. They arrived at the claim shack, a black, lonesome spot in the snowy void.

"Git down, LaVerne. You too, officer. All right. Now, LaVerne, search him thorough. Don't be afraid, 'cause he knows damn' well I'll shoot if either one of you makes a mismove. Another gun, huh? I thought so. Well, hold it on him till I get off. If you have to shoot him, that'll be all right with me. I've got no use for a man as mean and ornery as he is."

"Here's a knife," quavered H. LaVerne. "What'll I do with it?"

"Hand it over here. Now, I'll take the gun. Slip it in my coat pocket. Shaking the way you are, you ain't safe with a gun nohow. Furthermore, you're a prisoner. Don't forget that."

"Y-you're just pilin' up trouble for yourself," the deputy warned Lynn. But his tone was not convincing and, when he was told to get into the shack and stay there, he went and did his swearing through the doorway. Lynn holstered his gun, picked up the reins of the deputy's horse, and mounted Seal. He reined in close to the shack.

"You had your chance, and you've got no kick coming," he yelled above the steady flow of language from within. "If you'd been a gentleman about it, things would 'a' turned out more comfortable for yuh." He listened a moment for a reply, but nothing he heard seemed especially pertinent. The deputy was busy describing Lynn Farrow's character and ultimate fate. Lynn waited for a pause. "Go ahead, cuss and keep warm," he yelled. "Soon as the dance is over, I'll bring back your prisoner and you can have him. He ain't going to break away from me, if that's what's worrying yuh. So try and keep your shirt on till daybreak anyway." He wheeled his horse and waved H. LaVerne forward. "Here, pull up alongside. And don't try anything brave or there's liable to be a flock of brand new widows wearing black on your account."

"I . . . I won't," H. LaVerne promised in trembling sincerity, probably remembering the bullet hole in Mrs. Mullen's braided rug.

"And shake up that old pelter, can't you? That dance of mine'll be a complete fizzle if we don't look out."

H. LaVerne obediently kicked his horse in the ribs and went bouncing painfully through the night. Lynn drove him relentlessly along the shortcut trail, up to the stable, held him there by the sole power of his relentless purpose until the horses were stabled, then on to the house at a trot. H. LaVerne arrived at his post on the kitchen table with cold perspiration on his face and a hunted look in his eyes, but he caught Lynn's look and reached for his violin as a drowning man reaches for a life raft. Being a professional, he could fiddle, even though his fingers did shake.

Women always had felt sorry for H. LaVerne Churchill and wanted to bring a sparkle into his eyes. Now it was Josie, bringing him coffee and sandwiches and telling him there was no use starting in just now, because they were going to serve refreshments the minute old Bill called promenade home. Which Bill, catching sight of that cup and high-piled plate, did with his next breath.

"And here's your reward, Lynn," said Josie at his elbow just as he was shucking his fur coat and thinking no one appreciated his efforts anyway. "I won't ask how you performed the miracle, but you certainly have saved Hattie's dance. Folks were just beginning to growl about the music, so I hurried up the refreshments to keep them in a good humor and give you a little more time. I suppose you'll want to eat with Hattie. She's over there near the stairs, I think."

Josie probably did not mean a thing except kindness, but as it happened Lynn found Hattie sitting on the bottom step of the stairs with a cowboy from Wolf Butte. They had their sandwiches and cake piled on one plate which the cowboy held on his knees, and they were dividing the services of one teaspoon in their coffee. Lynn saw that much before he marched over and roosted on a corner of the table where he could keep an eye on H. LaVerne while he ate.

He was still sitting there when Josie came up and whispered to him that his sleeve was half ripped out of his coat and, if he could dig up a needle and thread, they could sneak into the pantry while she sewed it up. And she added that he wouldn't want Hattie to see him going around looking like that.

Lynn turned and looked at her oddly. "She ain't liable to notice," he said. But he went off and got a needle big enough to sew grain sacks and a spool of shiny No. 10 black linen thread—which made Josie laugh, it was so like a man. However, she made it do—though it took at least twice as long as one would think was necessary.

Two-step, waltz, quadrille, schottische, the dance went merrily on through the long hours after midnight. Lynn danced indefatigably until dawn, but he did not dance with Hattie. Josie was a mighty smooth waltzer, he discovered. He'd bet she could carry a full glass of water on her head all through a waltz and never spill a drop. And when he tried her out with a polka, it was like dancing with cottonwood fluff in a spring breeze. Sure light on her feet, that girl. They schottisched together with a military precision that had the whole crowd watching before they were through. Quadrilles and such he danced with the women who didn't get a good partner very often. After all, these were his obligations as a host. He didn't forget that.

An hour after sunrise he was back at the claim shack with H. LaVerne and the deputy's horse all nicely rested and fed good Rolling M oats for his breakfast. He shouted for the deputy sheriff before he noticed the boot tracks leading away from the shack through the newly fallen snow. He rode about six miles farther toward town before he overtook the deputy plodding sullenly along with wet feet and his big overcoat unbuttoned and flapping as he walked. He turned a red and scowling face over his shoulder as Lynn came loping down the road, driving H. LaVerne before him.

"Good Godfrey but you're an impatient cuss," Lynn grinned as the three horses dropped to a walk just behind the deputy. "Everybody was having such a good time I didn't like to drag your bigamy sharp off'n the table till sunup, anyway. Here he is, right side up with care. And I sure am much obliged for the loan of him."

"You're under arrest!" the deputy spluttered. "You give me my horse and. . . ."

"Come along to jail? Not so you could notice." Lynn slid sidewise in the saddle and grinned down at the deputy with unquenchable good humor. "You couldn't take me in and you know it, not even if you wanted to, which you don't, and I'd bet money on it."

"I'll come back with a posse and a bench warrant!" stormed the deputy. "I'll make you sweat blood for this! I'll . . . !"

"Why, say! You old walrus, if you was to arrest me, I'd make you the big joke of Chouteau County. I'd tell everybody how you glommed the only violin player in twenty miles and took him away from a dance before it had hardly got started. I'd tell 'em where you spent most of the night, and why. Say, everybody in the hull state of Montana'd give yuh the horse laugh, and you know it."

"And when I see you behind the bars, I'll laugh louder'n any of 'em."

"I ain't there yet, you notice."

"Don't let that worry yuh. You will be, about tomorrow night."

Lynn slid back straight in the saddle, untied a small bundle wrapped in a grain sack, and handed it off into the snow thirty feet from the road. "Them's your guns and knife," he volunteered cheerfully. "The shells are loose in the bag, but they're all there. Take your horse and beat it. And don't ever try and bust up a dance of mine again, 'cause next time I'm liable to git mad and do something about it."

He dropped the reins of the deputy's horse, wheeled, and galloped back the way he had come.

"I'll be back . . . and don't you forgit it!" bawled the deputy. "You're under arrest right now! You're an escaped prisoner and will be treated accordin'!"

If Lynn heard, he gave no sign that he did. He was a furred figure riding across new snow in the dazzle of a brilliant morning sun, and presently he dipped out of sight in a hollow and was seen no more by the two who watched him go.

The cattle were wandering disconsolately around over the snow-blanketed feed ground bawling for their breakfast when he arrived. Lynn hitched up the team, threw off the jag of hay that was left after his guests had lavishly helped themselves for their horses, hauled another big load, and scattered it, stabled the team, and went to the house. The place was cold, dismal as a haunted house. Ghosts of gaily-fiddled dance tunes wove intricate garlands of remembered melody within the empty rooms, wraith of Hattie taking pickles and sandwiches daintily from the plate of the Wolf Butte cowboy sitting on the bottom step of the stairs. In the pantry, when he went foraging for leftovers for his breakfast, there stood a phantom Josie, smiling at him, her fine eyes shining with laughter over their simple secret of the mended coat.

Lynn's head ached. His eyes felt as if someone had thrown sand in his face. Two knuckles skinned on Wolf Butte cowboys had turned blue and stiff. He paused in the process of lighting a fire in the kitchen stove, inspected them sourly, and gave them a gentle massaging by using his other thumb. It was when he pulled the big coffee boiler off the shelf where it did not belong that he found Josie's note, written on a piece of wrapping paper with a piece of charcoal and hidden away where he would be sure to discover it.

*It was a fine dance. Hattie and I will come over and help clean up if Pa will let us have the team.*

No use banking on that, Lynn thought, as he crumpled the paper and thrust it in amongst the blazing kindling. Pa Baldwin was an old crank. But it was nice of Josie to want to do it, just the same. Pity Hattie wouldn't have written a word. It was her dance.

He dragged the kitchen table back where it belonged, washed off the marks of H. LaVerne's feet, and ate leftover sandwiches for his breakfast. He wrestled with the heater and its diabolical pipe, got it in place with more skinned knuckles to show for the job, and started a fire to make the place less like a tomb. After that he swept and dragged ungainly pieces of furniture back where they belonged.

At noon he ate again, wound the clock, set the alarm for four o'clock, and went to bed. No use looking for the girls—it was a cinch they wouldn't come. Lynn wasn't at all sure he wanted them to. Not even Josie.

That evening he fed the cattle early and, when they had trailed off to the shed, he hauled four more loads and scattered them on the feed ground in the dark. He hauled a fifth and piled it in a corner of the corral for the team. When that was done, he cooked and ate a prodigious meal, packed what food there was left, rolled his blankets, and stuffed his warbag full of his belongings. A little later he rode away from there, careful to follow the beaten trail left in the snow by the dance crowd. Where the trail divided, hoofprints branching out in various directions, he chose a set headed toward the Sweet Grass hills.

On a far ridge he pulled in Seal and let the pack horse come up alongside while he stared back toward the quiet valley lighted now by the late-rising moon. Just along there, where the creek made a bend, lay the Jameson ranch and the snug winter's job he was leaving behind. He had no illusions concerning the malignant purpose of that deputy sheriff. But that was not the thing that pulled his eyebrows together now beneath his cap of muskrat fur. It was another thought that sent his breath in a white mist between his clenched teeth.

"Darn girls!" he gritted, "and dances too. I hope I never see another one."

He turned and rode on, boring patiently into the white-enfolded hills of the Sweet Grass.

# The One-Way Trail

*Max Brand*℠

☒

*Frederick Faust wrote more than five hundred average-length books (three hundred of them Westerns) under nineteen different pseudonyms, but Max Brand℠—"the Jewish cowboy," as he once dubbed it—has become the most familiar and is now his trademark. Some of the Max Brand titles recently published for the first time in book form include* Sixteen in Nome *(Five Star Westerns, 1995),* Outlaws All *(Five Star Westerns, 1996),* The Lightning Warrior *(Five Star Westerns, 1996), and three collections of short novels and stories published by the University of Nebraska Press as well as the restored tetralogy of the Thunder Moon saga published now as the author wrote it. "The One-Way Trail" first appeared in* Street & Smith's Western Story Magazine *(February 4, 1922). There is action, motion, constant momentum, but the author's concern is not really focused on these but rather on what is most important and most intimate and most meaningful in our lives, what alone ultimately matters. Love, friendship, loyalty, courage are affirmed, yet beyond even these is the prospect of redemption. Like most Faust stories, it is not plot-driven but depends on human character almost entirely for motive and progression—the spiritual capacity for sublimity as well as despair, the potential for decency that exists in every human being, and the possibility even in the outcast, the criminal, the socially and politically disenfranchised, to attain through one gratuitous act true nobility of soul.*

## I

### "FORCED TO FIGHT"

The Shifter picked up a chair from the circle around the stove and, drawing it back a little so that no one could easily pass between him and the wall, he sat down to think. With The Shifter thinking was a process quite unusual. He ordinarily acted first and did his thinking afterward. Thinking was so strenuous a task that he needed utter repose of body while his mind struggled.

Not that The Shifter was stupid. Far from it. But he was only twenty-two years old and, though he had crammed enough action into that narrow span of life to furnish sufficient excitement to a dozen able-bodied men, he had never encountered a problem which could not be solved by the adroit use of his hundred and eighty-five pounds of mule-hard muscle. Or, if muscle alone could not gain the desired end, he possessed sundry accomplishments of wrist, finger, and eye which, in the parlance of the country, were termed collectively "gun sense." Consequently, it was not strange that The Shifter had not overstrained his mentality. But today it was different—very different.

He had come back to his home town of Logan expecting to be received with smiles and open arms as a hero. He had come back that morning after an absence of four years, during which he had not forgotten a single face or a single voice. But the applause which greeted him was so muted as to be almost non-existent. Old Curry, the town loafer, had greeted him to be sure with a broad grin and a request for a five-spot. But that was about the only smile he had encountered. A few minutes later the sheriff had come up to him—Sheriff Joe Brown who had taught him to ride in his childhood. He had been both curt and to the point.

"Now, look here, kid," he had said, "maybe you've come in all ready to light up and celebrate, but my job around these parts is to keep things quiet. You lay to that! And if they's any uncommon trouble starts, I ain't going to ask questions. I'll just start for you, Shifter, and start *pronto.*"

With that, he had turned on his heel and strode off down the verandah. It was this that had made The Shifter go inside the hotel to find a chair and quiet so he could think. They were all against him. That was plain, and gradually he came to see why. They were afraid of him, afraid of The Shifter! He was like a stranger.

When they knew him as Harry French, before he went away, he had been as popular as any youth in the town. Now they seemed to think that he had changed his identity when he was given the nickname. They avoided his eyes; they did not enter into conversation with him; and, when he entered a group, the group dissolved at once and reassembled in another place. He would not have been so surprised anywhere else, but here they ought to know him. They ought to understand that all the stories that floated through the mountains about him were not entirely true. He was a gunfighter only on occasion and by necessity, not by choice. Could not his own people see that at a glance?

He dropped his chin upon his hard, brown fist and pondered. His thoughts flickered out of the hotel lobby, stuffy from the heat of the stove and the closed doors and windows. They danced off to that day, four years before, when he had fought his first fight and won his nickname. It was in the mining town of Ferris to which Harry French had taken the optimism and the fine good humor of an eighteen-year-old youth.

There, on a pay night in the saloon, he had been involved without fault of his own in a sudden hurly-burly of fighting men. Somebody had chipped his ear with a bullet as he strove to get out of the sphere of danger. The moment Harry had felt the sting of the wound, he lost all desire to escape. He had turned back and rushed that crowd, weaving from side to side, smashing out with either hand, bowling over stalwart miners at every punch, until at length a panic took the crowd. They had bolted for the door. The town bully had remained, drawing his gun, and Harry, avoiding the bullet with a side leap, had downed his man with a heavy slug in the thigh.

That was where he had earned the sobriquet of The Shifter because of the restless footwork with which he had gone through the mob. It was an instinct that made him do it. Ever after, when he entered a fight and rushed his man, he came swerving and dodging like a football player on an open field. The result of this swerving attack was that in all his fights he had never been touched with a bullet.

Others of those battles came back to his mind now. Certainly there were many of them—too many! His great consolation was that he had never picked trouble, never forced a combat. Trouble had simply hunted him down and forced itself upon him. And now they looked upon him, even these men of his home town, as little better than a legal murderer who picked fights and then used his uncanny ability to destroy his foes. That explained the cold glances he received. That explained why the little hush had fallen over the circle around the stove since he drew the chair back to the wall.

He raised his head. Every eye was fastened upon him, and instantly every glance turned in another direction. They did not wish to be found staring, for a gunfighter would pick a fight at the very slightest provocation. In fact, every one of those men, hardy fellows though they were, was sweating with anxiety as long as he was in their midst. What fools they were. Could they not see that his one consuming desire was to be friendly with them? Could they not see that he would pay for their esteem with combat?

Tears of vexation and self-pity rose to the eyes of The Shifter, and his scowl grew blacker as he studied the floor, looking down to hide that suspicious moisture. Footsteps entered, paused. The voices which had begun to murmur in conversation were solemnly hushed. The Shifter looked up to find a tall, raw-boned man staring at him with a face deathly pale. His hands were clenched to fists at his sides, and there was a set look of desperation about his face. The lips of the tall man worked a moment before sound came and, when he managed to speak, his voice trembled.

"You got my chair, French!"

Sudden understanding came to The Shifter. Here was Long Tom Cassidy, whom he had known like a brother four years before. Now Long Tom was ready to battle. The reason was perfectly clear. If an ordinary fellow had taken the chair, Tom would never have dreamed of raising an objection, for after all he had no power or right to reserve his seat when he left the room. It just happened that on this occasion, when he returned, he found every chair taken, and in his own recently abandoned place sat a killer of men. That was the reason he stood so straight and stiff. He felt that he would be shamed. He felt that he would be taking water if he allowed this terrible man to preempt his seat. Sooner than be shamed, Long Tom Cassidy was ready to die.

It came home to The Shifter of a sudden, and it made him sick at heart. What could he do? He would rather drive a bullet into his own flesh than shoot down Cassidy. But could he meekly rise from his rightful place and surrender it to another? Might that not be interpreted as disgraceful taking of water? Perhaps Cassidy had built up a reputation for skill with weapons in the past four years. Perhaps he might be capable of putting up a desperate battle, and the others would think that fear motivated The Shifter to make him move.

All these thoughts whirled in a blinding stream through the bewildered brain of The Shifter. He did not want to fight. His heart ached to go up and greet Tom with a hearty handshake, but he could not. Men would as soon shake hands with the devil. They sat about now staring with black brows from one to the other. Then, gradually, they began to shift their chairs out of the line between the two prospective combatants. Their sympathies plainly were all with Tom. At the least provocation they would join him against the gunfighter. The Shifter looked them over with the sad eye of despair and found not a single kindly response to his glance.

"You heard me talk?" Cassidy was saying, his voice gaining in strength and roughness.

"Tom," said The Shifter slowly, "don't be a fool. You ain't got this chair mortgaged, I guess?"

"Look here," cried Tom, "just save your words for them that'll stand 'em. I ain't your dog to be booted out of a chair and then jawed because I want it back!"

A spark of rage was fanned into a red gust of temper in The Shifter, a familiar red blur which had preceded all of his battles. But he controlled himself, leaning back in the chair and running the tip of his tongue over his white lips.

"Cassidy," he said, "you're hunting trouble. Cut it out. I'm not going to fight about a chair, even if you want to."

"Then," said Cassidy suddenly, "get out of it!"

The Shifter stared at the big man for a moment in silence, thinking harder than he had ever thought before. He decided to surrender. It was hard to do. It would bring doubt and some suspicion of cowardice upon him. But at least it would prove to the people of his own home town that he did not wish to force trouble on peaceful men. He leaned to rise.

What happened then was simply misapprehension and bad luck, though unquestionably the first movement of a man leaning to rise from a chair and the first movement of a man leaning to get at his gun are the same. At any rate Tom Cassidy, on edge with excitement, interpreted the movement in the second way and grabbed for his own gun.

That gesture The Shifter noted from the corner of his eye and saw that he would be forced to fight or die. His leap was of a tigerish speed. It carried him out of the chair and far to one side, where he landed with his gun in his hand. In the meantime the bullet from Cassidy's weapon had crashed through the back of the chair he had just left and dug through the wall behind. Long Tom whirled to fire again.

There was one alternative left to The Shifter and that was to run for the door. He would have done so had he not noted the effects of the first fire of Cassidy. The man was a little slow but terribly sure with his bullets. He would shoot The Shifter squarely through the middle of the back as his man went through the door. Flight would not do, then. Reluctantly, holding his fire to the last instant, The Shifter twitched up the muzzle of the gun which had been hanging idly at his side and fired.

## II

### "TO START LIFE ANEW"

In the pause that followed Long Tom Cassidy seemed like a very poor actor on the amateur stage. He did his gestures one by one with foolish awkwardness. The gun dropped from his hand and rattled on the floor. He gripped violently with both hands at his left thigh, and then he sank down on the opposite side.

The others had pressed back against the walls of the room with a shout. For an instant there was only the wail of the northern gale outside the hotel. Then the bystanders rushed in between and surrounded their fallen townsman. A quick examination of his wound showed that the bullet had passed through the flesh only, leaving bone and sinew untouched. He was carried from the room, groaning and cursing, just as the sheriff entered. As he had promised, he paused at the door only to jerk his hat lower over his eyes, then he went straight for The Shifter, a gun in either hand. As for The Shifter, he remained standing idly against the wall with the revolver hanging loosely from his fingertips.

"Stick up your hands, Shifter!" commanded the sheriff. "Stick 'em up!"

Only the muzzle of The Shifter's gun twitched up in return.

"I'll put 'em up when I get good and ready," he said slowly. "You, Brown, keep on the far side of the stove. Understand?"

"I'll make this the last fighting you do, bucko," growled the sheriff, but he remained on the far side of the stove.

The Shifter was white, as always, when he grew wildly angry. "I used to think you were a man, Brown," he said. "But I see you ain't. They don't raise 'em that way around Logan. I come back here ready to act peaceable as a pet dog. First thing I know an idiot starts a fight about a chair. I leave it to the gents standing around here. Did I pick that fight?"

There was no answer.

"What?" shouted The Shifter. "D'you mean to say I started it?"

There was no answer.

"Wasn't I getting up out of the chair just the way he ordered me to do? Wasn't I taking water from him, when the hound pulled on me, and I had to jump to save my neck?"

But still from that circle of dour faces there was no response. The Shifter knew, at once, that he was beaten. He looked back at Joe Brown.

"Well, Sheriff," he said, "I see I get no backing. These blockheads can't see straight. If they do, they can't remember what they see. Point now is . . . what d'you mean to do?"

The doubt was all on the side of the sheriff. As for The Shifter, there was not a shadow of a doubt that he was enraged to the very verge of starting an attack. Many an old tale of his doings in battle floated back upon the memories of the others in the big room. If they wanted The Shifter, they could take him, but the price would be a terrible thing to pay. The sheriff ran his eyes around the circle and wondered. It might be that his reputation as a man-taker would be lost in this affair. But if the fight started, he himself would be the first target for that tall, gray-faced youth. It was a very convincing thought.

"I'll tell you what I'm going to do," said the sheriff, making his voice larger than his spirit. "I'm going to run you out of this town, Shifter. And I'm going to make it hot for you if you ever try to come back. If I had a shade more ag'in' you, I'd lock you up now. But I figure Long Tom Cassidy made a fool play. Anyway, Shifter, out you go and on the run, too!"

The sheriff ran his eyes around the circle of listeners, and his heart warmed. There was an unmistakable air of relief on every face.

"I'll walk, Brown," answered The Shifter. "I was never built for running."

So saying, he deliberately shoved his revolver back into the holster, tilted his sombrero to a more rakish angle, settled his bandanna into a more flowing knot, and slowly sauntered across the floor with his pale-blue eyes wandering from side to side, daring them all, or anyone, to make the first move to detain him or to hurry him. But not a hand was lifted, not a voice was raised, until he reached the door and, with his back turned squarely toward them all, he opened it and stepped out into the staggering gale.

Then, inside the room, a loud buzz of comment rose. The younger men milled together, talking loudly of going after him and bringing him back, and they even went so far as to cast black looks of suspicion at reliable old Joe Brown. But the older men shook hands with the sheriff one by one.

"He didn't do enough for hanging," they assured Joe, "and it'd be a joke to put him behind the bars for anything else."

"He's sure gone bad," said the sheriff wisely, "and, if he shows himself around these parts again . . . well, I'll make things hum for that young man."

But The Shifter had not the slightest intention of ever showing himself within gunshot of Logan again. He was decidedly through. They, his own people, had denied him. They had refused to give him a chance or a hearing. They had set themselves shoulder to shoulder against him and, if he had not been hurt to the very heart, he could have laughed at their folly.

He went straight to the horse shed. A bony, Roman-nosed roan lifted an ugly head and glared at him above the side of the stall. The Shifter tossed a saddle over this unprepossessing beast and dug his knee into the ribs of the big horse as he tugged the cinches taut. Glorious—for that was the name of the homely brute, unless it were shortened to Glory—attempted to catch his master with a rear heel, tossed up with wonderful dexterity on the end of a long leg. Failing in this, he swung his head around but received an elbow in the nose as he attempted to sink his big teeth in the shoulder of the master. In another moment he was outside, bucking like a demon and running straight into the teeth of that terrific north gale.

Inside a quarter of a mile Glorious settled down to a long, easy canter, defying the force of the wind and even pricking his ears into it. In fact, Glorious was never so happy as when he was under way on a long journey and a hard one. His feud with his rider began with every saddling and ended with the first furlong or two of the gallop. For Glorious did not hate The Shifter in particular but mankind in general.

Out of a brief and terrible career as an outlaw in horse-breaking contests, he had passed into the capable hands of The Shifter, and he was gradually settling down. He had been long schooled to detest human beings, but the kindness of his owner was gradually neutral-izing the acid in his disposition. The Shifter had found the long-legged brute invaluable. If there were savagery in the heart of Glorious, there was also uncanny wisdom in his brain. He could tell a rotten bridge by a glance and the first tentative tap of his forehoof. He knew by inborn instinct which stones on a mountainside would give sure pur-chase and which would roll at the first pressure. Mud or snow had no terrors for him. He could have kept his feet in a landslide or have ambled easily on a trail well nigh too narrow for a man. Also, his fierceness was becoming very largely bluff. The Shifter had shrewdly guessed that in another six months, in spite of small eyes and Roman nose, Glorious would be as affectionate and trustworthy a mount as stepped through the mountains.

He drew the big horse down to a steady jog in anticipation of the long and hard trail that lay before them, for The Shifter intended to take the one-way trail across the Kendall Mountains to Vardon City. It was well-nigh a disused route. There were other trails across the mountains. The sole advantage of the one-way trail was that it was the shortest. Running down from the loftier peaks of the Vardon Mountains in the north, the Kendall River cut a narrow trench through the mountains of the same name, a gorge with sides as sheer as the walls of a room almost. Along one side of the gorge a difficult trail had been cut, dipping up and down, twisting in and out. In half a dozen places it was wide enough for passing, but mile after mile it stretched as a narrow little ledge where a man on foot was in danger and where a man on a horse continually risked his own neck and the life of his mount. In recognition of this fact there was an unwritten law that the trail should be used only by travelers from the south to the north to avoid any more head-on meetings such as had, in the early days, been the cause of more than one tragedy.

Ordinarily even The Shifter would not have thought of using this route, particularly now that the north wind was tearing through the gorge, ready to pry between the rider and the cliff wall beside him. But this was not an ordinary day for The Shifter. His mind was in a turmoil of rage, and he welcomed the prospective danger of the one-way trail as a relief. He only wanted to get out of his home town by the shortest and the most expeditious means, and consequently he directed the big, ugly head of Glorious toward the mouth of the gorge.

The wind was increasing steadily, stringing long, pale drifts of clouds across the sky, clouds in such rapid passage from the north that they flicked across the face of the sun in swift succession and dimmed it only momentarily, like a winking light. The Shifter bowed his head to the gathering force of the gale and rode on.

Behind him, about a mile away, came four horsemen, closely bunched and maintaining his own pace. When he halted, they halted likewise; when he cantered, they urged their horses into a gallop. It did not need much penetration to tell that these were townsmen come out to make sure that he was leaving that section of the country. The upper lip of The Shifter curled away from his teeth as he glanced back at them, and for a moment he felt one of those wild, hot impulses to turn his horse and charge back on them. But he restrained himself.

No, his plan for life hereafter was to be free from violence. He would go into a section of the mountains where he had never been heard of, and there he would settle down and carve for himself the repute of an honest, patient, and law-abiding citizen. This idea was strong in his mind as he jogged up the last grade, turned about the shoulder of a mountain, and came suddenly upon the gorge of the Kendall River and the beginning of the one-way trail.

## III
### "A STRANGER IN A HURRY"

It was unlike any other gorge he had ever seen. Though he remembered it well enough from other days, it came upon him now like something seen for the first time. Other things had changed greatly in four years, but the one-way trail along the valley of the Kendall seemed more terrible than ever. The walls went upon either hand to the very summits of the range, as though the chain of the mountains had been stretched from each side until they snapped asunder along a smooth line of cleavage, or as though—to use an extremely old metaphor—a giant axe had cleft through a thousand feet of solid, virgin rock.

He looked down. The Kendall flowed through shadows, save where a shaft of sunlight was here and there reflected from the polished face of a cliff and brightened the water, and in those places he could make out the foam-white surface of that troubled water. When the shouting of the wind fell away from time to time, he heard the call of the Kendall go up the cliffs—wild voices snatched away a moment later in the renewed violence of the storm and blown to shreds. The trail was almost indistinguishable as it wound here and there, climbing with well-nigh imperceptible footings from one jutting crag to another. Sometimes it was merely a distant scratch along the blank walls of stone.

He looked back. The four watchers had bunched their horses closely together and were pointing after him apparently in great excitement. That decided The Shifter. He favored them with a deep-throated curse and then touched Glorious with the spurs. The big horse leaned far forward into the heart of the wind before he could take the first step, and then they jogged out onto the trail, with Glorious pressing close to the wall and snorting his fear of the dizzy fall on his right.

In half a mile he had lost his first terror and was giving himself to his work with consummate skill. The first sharp turn, following the winding of the valley, had proved nearly the death of both of them for, as they went about it, the storm smote them squarely from the inside, and Glorious tottered on the very edge of destruction. Only the quick action of the rider, as The Shifter flung himself violently to the left, gave Glorious a chance to regain his balance, and he found his footing once more. But that lesson did not need to be repeated. Thereafter he negotiated every turn of the trail like a seasoned diner-out approaching an unknown vintage. Glorious literally smelled his way to safety around every corner and then took the turn with his head lowered and his long, snaky neck stretched out. He made such a ridiculous appearance in the midst of this maneuver that Harry French several times burst into laughter. But Glorious merely shook his head and trudged on, regardless of the mockery.

As Madame du Deffand said, when she was told of the martyr who took ten steps after his head was struck off, it is the first step which is the hardest. Within ten minutes Glorious had negotiated all the variety of dangers which the one-way trail presented and had reduced his work to a perfect technique, the chief point being that at all times he kept his long body pressed closely to the wall even when the trail was comfortably broad.

Once his mount had gained this surety of going, The Shifter forgot to a great extent the dangers of the way. Even to the fierce pressure of the wind, now and again falling away and then striking at him with treacherous suddenness, the rider paid little attention. He almost lost himself in his thoughts. They ran, almost entirely, to the new life that would begin at the end of this trail. It was a melancholy series of reflections, taken all in all.

He felt that his past life was behind him, that twenty-two years had been wasted. When a boy reaches that age, he feels that a very great deal indeed has been passed. So The Shifter considered the future with a gloomy sobriety of mind. Out of his past every remembered face was a dead thing; every remembered voice was a ghost.

The Shifter was brought out of these dreary reflections, these grave plans for the future, by a sharp prick of reality. He turned a corner of the trail with his head bowed into the teeth of the wind, and he did not raise it again until he was astonished by the stopping of Glorious. Then he looked up and found facing him a youthful rider on a big, brown horse. And the trail was not three feet wide!

Even two men, in passing, would have leaned in against the wall, so dizzy was that fall which must be avoided. It was impossible for even the most adroit and cat-footed mustang to turn in this space. For horses as large as Glorious and the brown, it was absurd to attempt such a maneuver. Neither could they back the horses to a possible turning place, for behind each was the bend which had just been rounded. If the horses could barely make way around those turns going ahead, it would be an insured fall if they were forced against instinct to back up around them. Besides, it might be a mile in either direction before a more advantageous position were reached.

Both The Shifter and the other sat their horses in silence, drinking in the full extent of the catastrophe, while the animals swayed a little from side to side under the outrageous cuffing of that north wind. The Shifter adjusted himself in the saddle, so that that cunning right hand of his would be perilously near the holster and ready for use, while he studied the stranger. The man was apparently between twenty-five and thirty, perhaps even more. He was well built, rather stocky and broad shouldered, compared to the athletic ranginess of The Shifter, but brown with outdoor life and sufficiently deep of chest to promise unusual power in a hand-to-hand effort.

The head, however, was not so formidable as the body. It was distinctly small, and the face was small likewise, with handsome features extremely regular in cut and oddly contrasted with the aquiline cast of The Shifter. The eyes, too, were set closely together, and in their restless quality they suggested a certain unhealthy cunning that troubled The Shifter.

Yet, whatever the physical possibilities of the stranger, he was now in a blue funk. Never had The Shifter seen a man so obviously in the grip of the frozen hand of terror. He sat in his saddle with mouth agape, staring, his face bloodless. When he attempted to speak, Harry French made out only a meaningless gibberish.

For one thing, it plainly declared to The Shifter that he was the master of the situation. This trembler would make no stern opposition to his will and his ways. But also it was a thing so disgusting to watch that The Shifter blinked and looked away. He was embarrassed also. Some hard-faced, formidable man would have been preferred to this coward, for then they could have fought it out. The better man would have gone on.

"Well," asked The Shifter, "what d'you make out of this business? What'll we do?"

"What do I make out of it?" the other shrilly called back, his face reddening with anger as suddenly as he had grown pale. "What I want to know is what you mean by riding up this trail in the face of a wind like this? Are you crazy?"

The Shifter paused a moment before he answered. He had been vowing, in his inward thoughts of the moment before, that hereafter he would take plenty of time before he spoke or acted. Now he began to act accordingly.

"Seems to me," he said mildly, when he had regained mastery of that treacherous temper of his, "that I'm the one that has the right to ask questions. This here is a one-way trail, I guess. I'm riding it the right way, and you're riding it the wrong way. Got anything to say to that?"

The other hesitated. Then he answered authoritatively: "Plenty to say. I'm in a hurry. I got to get to the end of the gorge. That's why I'm riding this way."

"Same way with me," said The Shifter, his anger steadily rising in spite of himself. "I'm riding this trail because I'm in a hurry."

"In a hurry!" cried the other, and his face swelled with red passion. "In a hurry . . . so you buck into a wind like this! Why, it was all me and my hoss could do to keep to the trail with the wind behind us. In a hurry!"

He regarded The Shifter with a fierce contempt, and the younger man closed his eyes for an instant and commended his heart of hearts to patience. In his entire life he had never met with a man who so keenly aroused his hatred.

"Look here," he said coldly, "they's one thing plain. These two hosses can't get by each other. I'm not saying who's to blame for it. But I'll give you a fair break. One hoss has to die and drop down into the Kendall River. No other way out. The other hoss goes on through, and the gent that loses has to finish his trip on foot. We'll throw a coin, partner, to see who loses and who keeps his hoss."

So saying, he drew forth a broad half-dollar piece and juggled it in his hand. But his heart was by no means as light as his manner. There was not a sinew in the big, ugly, powerful body of Glorious that The Shifter did not love. Only there was nothing else to be done.

"Throw a coin to see which hoss dies?" The stranger sneered as he spoke. "Say, friend, d'you think I'd risk a hoss like The General, here, against a skinny old ramshackle like your roan?"

"You've said a tolerable pile," said The Shifter through his teeth. "And you've said a pile too much. If you got talking to do, try out your tongue on something beside my hoss."

The other changed his manner at once. "In a way," he said with a lofty condescension, "I'm in the wrong, and I've brought this mess about. Well, I'll pay you the price of your hoss. I'll pay you a good price, too."

The Shifter smiled. "D'you think a hoss means just so much money to me?" he asked. "Why, stranger, a hoss is a life, just the way you and me are lives. You can't buy a hoss. You may pay somebody a price, but you ain't paying the price to the hoss. A pile of gents sit the saddles on hosses that they don't own a hair of, because they ain't never taught the hoss to love 'em."

"Bah!" snorted the other. "You talk plumb ridiculous. This is my hoss, got my brand on him, bought with my money. He's just hossflesh. To be used, like soap or oil or coal."

"All right," said The Shifter, breathing hard, "maybe that's all he is to you. I'm sorry."

"For what?"

"For the hoss."

"What d'you mean?" exploded the stranger, pushing his brown horse closer to The Shifter.

But he got no farther in his tirade. The Shifter suddenly swung forward in his saddle, clinging with trembling knees to the sides of Glorious, and his face was gray and drawn. Save for his eyes, he seemed to be in a panic, but the eyes bore an ample assurance that he was in a red fury. The stranger shrank, and his own eyes grew dim and wide.

"Now talk business," said The Shifter. "Shall I throw the coin?"

"All right . . . all right, if it's got to be that way. But lemme get close enough to see the coin fall."

So saying, he pressed nearer, until the head of the brown was near that of Glorious, and on the inside. What was about to come The Shifter had no means of guessing save that, as he took the half-dollar on top of his thumb, preparatory to snapping it into the air, he saw that the hand of the stranger on the bridle rein was trembling and gripped hard.

He snapped the coin high, raised his head to watch its twinkling rise and, just when it hovered brightly at the height, the brown horse was driven at him by a yell of the stranger. He was perfectly helpless. With head thrown up, urged on by the driving of the spurs in his tender flanks, the brown came in with maddened eyes, driving between Glorious and the cliff.

## IV

### "CHARGED WITH CAPITAL CRIME"

There was no time to whip out a gun and shoot, no time to fling himself from the saddle, no time even to throw his weight in toward the cliff to steady Glorious, for the rush of the brown forced the roan straight up and back, rearing and toppling on his hind legs, while the voice of the other rider, yelling with savage satisfaction, urged the brown on. The Shifter looked down. Far below him, with nothing between, rushed the Kendall. The upward and backward lurch of the roan was driving him swiftly to the toppling point. Already, he was clinging fiercely with his knees to keep from pitching headlong out of the saddle.

He saw, to the side and before him, the convulsed face of the stranger as he pressed the brown in and, with his quirt, showered stinging blows over the head of the roan. Glorious, with a squeal of rage and fear and pain, rocked and balanced erect as a bear on his hind legs. The one great forehoof went up, flashed down. Again and again and again! He was fighting as wild stallions fight, not submitting tamely to destruction. To escape that crushing, slashing shower of blows, the brown horse in turn reared, a maneuver which brought a yell of terror from the stranger. The Shifter, at the same instant, flattened himself along the neck of Glorious and gave weight to the rush as the roan drove forward on all four legs and now charged like a fighting dog at the throat of the brown.

Higher the brown reared, to strike with battering forehoofs even as Glorious had done, but Glorious drove in like a savage terrier, and now the weight of his shoulder ground in between the brown and the cliff. There was a shriek from the stranger as the brown reeled back. The Shifter, realizing that their roles had been changed, struggled furiously at the reins to draw Glorious back, but it was like tugging at a stone wall. Higher went the brown, staggered, and, with a terribly human scream of fear, pitched sidewise into the abyss. The Shifter caught a glimpse of a face hideous with terror, the lips writhed back over a shriek which did not come. Then he swayed far out in the saddle, reached with both hands, and with the right he caught the falling man by the shoulder.

The whole length of that arm was whipped through his grip, the sleeve being torn away like cobweb under the terrific force of his hand. But the strain checked, in a measure, the impetus of the fall and, as his right hand caught a firm hold on the wrist, The Shifter flashed his left across and secured a hold lower down. The whole weight of the falling man came with a single jerk—for all of this, of course, happened inside a tenth part of a second—upon the strained shoulders of The Shifter. Glorious, swung over by the sudden side strain against which he could not brace himself, toppled on the very verge of the cliff. Snorting with fear, he fought to regain his balance and, looking down, The Shifter found himself suspended for the second time over the gulf of the cañon. He might throw away his life and the life of his horse for the sake of a man who, he knew, was a treacherous cur. But the sight of that fear-frozen face hanging there a double-arm's length away made him retain his hold. Never had he passed through such a moment. The opening of his hand would save himself and send another human being to death.

Then Glorious, struggling hard, caught his balance again and swayed toward the face of the cliff. In a moment the crisis was over, and the stranger lay senseless on the floor of the trail beside the roan. The Shifter himself was trembling like an invalid newly risen from bed when he climbed slowly out of the saddle and kneeled above the rescued stranger. One pressure of his hand assured him that the fellow lived, though the heart beat faintly and the lungs merely stirred. The Shifter rose, climbed into the saddle again, and pressed slowly on down the trail, speaking in a shaken and changed voice to Glorious. He could not force himself to stay until the stranger returned to his senses. He could not stay to hear thanks from the lips of this detestable coward.

After that the trail seemed as broad and as safe as a high road. What matter if the wind were increasing? What matter if the evening were coming on? What matter even if the rain began to whip out of the sky and rattle against the slicker which he put on? All of this was nothing. If Glorious slipped on a wet stone in the dimness and reeled on the verge of the precipice, it was almost a thing to be laughed at, for The Shifter and his horse had seen the very face of death that day on the trail, and now nothing mattered.

It took more than two hours to do the remaining six miles of the trail, with all of its ins and outs and ups and downs and hardly a place where they could do better than walk. The rain was coming down in streams of stinging force through the dull twilight when The Shifter rode into the muddy streets of Vardon City and heard the downpour drumming heavily on the roofs on either side, while the light from the windows was split into yellow sprays in passing through the torrent of rain. It seemed to The Shifter a harborage and a refuge of perfect peace after the terrors of the one-way trail. He secured a room at the

hotel without difficulty and went up to it at once to lie down to rest—
to rest and to think for, oddly enough, his first step into a life of
kindliness had almost brought him to his death.

He lay on the bed with his eyes closed wearily, and through his
mind passed the picture of what the other Harry French would be
doing at this moment, the other Harry French who had existed that
very morning. He would be down in the lobby of that old building
holding the center of the stage with his stories, with his laughter, with
his mockeries. He would be beating down the glances of quieter men
with his own defiant and bold eyes. After all, was it not better to live
like that, to be feared and respected and followed and admired even
by those who dared not imitate him? Was it not better than to lie
here in the darkness brooding over what the future might hold for
him?

He rose drowsily to answer a soft tap at the door. He swung it
wide. There in the hallway stood a middle-aged man in an immensely
wide-brimmed sombrero and, behind him, solidly packed, were half a
dozen more. Every eye was focused on the face of The Shifter with an
intensity with which he was bitterly familiar. The leader planted his
riding boot inside the door so that it could not be closed. His right
hand rested prominently on the butt of his revolver.

"You're Harry French?"

"Who are you to ask?"

"I got a right to ask questions, son. I'm the sheriff, John Clark."

The thoughts of The Shifter danced away into the obscurity of
strange reflections. Since his resolution to lead a peaceable life he had
been forced into a brawl by a man he tried to avoid, had been driven
from his own home town, had been nearly murdered on a mountain
trail, and now a sheriff with a formidable posse was invading his hotel
room to ask him questions.

Sheriff Clark who, of course, could not follow the trend of these
thoughts was astonished to see The Shifter burst suddenly into ringing
laughter. Then the latter drew back politely.

"Come in, gents, and make yourselves to home. Sorry I ain't got
anything to offer you to drink. But I ain't a drinking man, and I hate
moonshine, anyways."

"Gunfighters and card sharps mostly do," said the sheriff. With this insult on his lips, he kicked the door still wider and strode into the room with his men packed behind him.

As for The Shifter, he saw that a side leap would take him to his gun and belt where they lay on the bed, and then it would be a comparatively simple matter—for him—to jump through the window onto the roof of the shed beneath and so down to the ground and only a few steps from the horses. From the entrance speech of the sheriff he gathered that the visit foreboded him no good. Or were they simply about to invite him to leave the town and ride on?

The sheriff was walking slowly around the room. He reached the gun belt and picked it up.

"I'll keep this a while," he said and drew the gun from the holster.

That is, he made the beginning of a movement to take the weapon, but the gesture was never completed. The toe of The Shifter's boot at that instant connected with the sheriff's wrist, drew a curse of pain and surprise from that worthy, knocked the gun spinning into the air and, when it descended, it fell into the agile hand of The Shifter.

He stood with his back to the wall, with a semicircle of armed men before him, every man ready to shoot. Again The Shifter could have laughed, if it had not been for the fierce and rebellious pain in his heart. For the second time on the first day of his good resolutions he found the protectors of social quiet arrayed en masse against him with their guns in their hands.

The sheriff was nursing his injured wrist with his other hand, still cursing, but he showed no fear, it must be admitted in his favor, and barked forth a steady series of orders to his men. "Watch that window, Bud and Joe. It opens out over the roof of the shed. Block the door, Charlie. And just light that lamp, will you, Pete? We need more light than what we get out of the hall. There's plenty of time to get his gun."

"Sure," said The Shifter coolly. "A sheriff can have my gun any time for the asking but not for the taking."

"Why, you fool," retorted the sheriff, while the flame welled up in the chimney of the lamp as Pete lighted it, "d'you know you've resisted arrest?"

"You lie," said The Shifter almost wearily. "Nobody's told me I'm under arrest. You started to grab my gun, and I kicked it out of your hand. I'd do it again. Keep off there, you with the red hair! You can go as far as the law allows you but, if you take a step farther, I'll singe your whiskers for you!"

This last was addressed to a big man who started to edge in along the wall. His progress was instantly arrested.

"You see?" said the sheriff. "I told you what he was! All right, Shifter. I'll tell you now that you're under arrest."

"That's easy to say," answered The Shifter calmly. "But what's the charge? You can't railroad me, partner."

"The charge is murder on the one-way trail," said the sheriff, his voice suddenly trembling with emotion. "Murder of my son, Jack Clark!"


# V

## "IN THE VARDON CITY JAIL"


The pale-blue eyes of The Shifter narrowed as he stared at the sheriff, but there was no similarity between that brown, hard-featured countenance and the face of the man he had drawn back from the peril of falling into the chasm of the Kendall River.

"Murder?" repeated The Shifter calmly. "Murder of a gent on a brown horse . . . big-shouldered fellow with a sort of smallish head and a . . . a foolish face?"

The sheriff clamped his teeth together. "You hear him, boys?" he said to the others. "He's identified Jack! I've found 'em cold-blooded and steady as iron before but never as bad as this."

There was a murmur of assent from the others.

"He's not dead," said The Shifter. "He's out on the one-way trail."

The sheriff shook his head. "You save that talk for the judge. Meantime, will you give up your gat peaceable?"

"Partner," said The Shifter as calmly as ever, "I never play a game that's sure to be a loser. Here it is."

He handed over the weapon. There was a general sigh of relief from the others.

"Hold out your hands," commanded the sheriff and then, over The Shifter's readily proffered wrists, he snapped the handcuffs.

"What you say'll be remembered for the jury and the judge," he said, "but if you want to talk, go ahead. We'll all listen ... and we'll all remember."

"D'you think," said The Shifter, "that I'd've let you get me so dead easy if I was afraid my yarn wouldn't hold? I'll tell you the straight of it. I was coming north along the trail and at about the middle of it, while I was bucking a hard wind, I come on a gent riding the wrong way. There wasn't no chance to pass, and there wasn't no way of getting to a turning place except by backing one of the hosses about a mile. You know that couldn't be done on the one-way trail with the wind blowing the way it was today. They was only one way out and that was to kill one of the hosses and let it fall over the cliff. By rights, him traveling the wrong way, his hoss had ought to've been killed. But I offered to toss a coin for it and, while I was throwing the coin, this yaller-hearted skunk that you say is your boy rode his hoss at me and tried to knock me over the cliff, and he damned near done it. But old Glorious up and beat him off with his forehoofs and then jumped for the throat of the brown hoss like a fighting dog. I tried to pull him in, but it wouldn't work. He had the bit. And he jammed the brown hoss right off the trail. They fell together, your son and the hoss. ..."

There was a deep groan from the sheriff.

"But I grabbed him as he was falling," went on The Shifter hastily, "and I pulled him back onto the trail. He fainted plumb away from the scare. I made out that his heart was still beating, and then I rode on down the trail. And that, gents, is the straight of the story, I swear it! Either he's in Logan by this time, or else he's still on the trail."

There was something so convincing about the manner in which this story was told, incredible though some of the mentioned incidents were, that the men of the posse looked from one to the other after the fashion of men whose conviction has been shaken and who are willing to hear more reason. But the sheriff, though his eye had brightened, shook his head.

"We'll give you the chance, son," he told The Shifter. "We'll send a man to ride the trail, and we'll wire down to Logan to see if Jack has come in yet. But the fact is that Jack has had plenty of time to have got to Logan long before this. Soon as I had word that the fool boy had took the one-way trail in the wrong direction, I wired on ahead to Logan and asked if anybody had entered the trail from that end. I got back word right off that you were just starting up that way. Well, Shifter, next we heard was that Jack's brown hoss had come rolling and tumbling down the Kendall, all smashed to pieces. But no Jack had come through. Then we see you big as life riding out of the one-way trail. And you didn't have no story to tell till just now. Why didn't you talk out as soon as you come in? Wasn't it worth talking about?"

The Shifter shrugged his shoulders. "Go ride the trail," he said calmly. "You'll find him. You can leave me in the lock-up till he's located. I guess that's square all around?"

Everyone had to agree that it was. They took Harry French—still following him in a compact body as though even his manacled hands were to be feared—downstairs to the street and up the street through the crashing rain to the edge of the village. Here they turned to the left and approached, down a graveled road winding among trees, a house larger than any other which The Shifter had seen in Vardon City. But when he came close under it, he suddenly remembered many things out of his boyhood and particularly this building, so large that it could be seen from the head of the Kendall Gorge, big among the little shacks of the town.

It turned out to be the home of the Clarks which also served as the town jail. The stout cellar wall offered a greater security than any other building in the town and saved the village the expense of a public structure. To the sheriff himself it was a double advantage, for on the one hand he received a generous fee for lodging the guests of the county and, on the other, the fact that he owned the jail was a sort of automatic assurance that he would be reelected to the office of sheriff so long as he cared for the position.

Through a hall of mid-Victorian magnificence The Shifter was conducted to a door which opened on a flight of dark, damp stairs, and down this he was brought to the jail proper. A fencing of steel bars had been constructed like a great netting throughout the cellar and was divided and subdivided into a dozen cells, though more than half of that number had never been occupied at one time. At the present moment there was not a single tenant on any of the little cots. The Shifter was assigned to the central cell which had the advantage of offering him no concealment from spying eyes. Moreover, in case he attempted to break out, he would have two barriers of steel bars to cut through instead of one. All of these facts the sheriff pointed out to his companions who wandered about here and there admiring the interior of the jail with a sort of proprietary pride.

"There ain't any town of our size in the mountains that can show a better jail or a safer jail," they declared more than once, and the sheriff smiled with becoming modesty as he unlocked the door and ushered The Shifter into his place of confinement. One of them came back to The Shifter when the party was about to leave and, leaning against the bars, he nodded wisely to the prisoner from whose hands the manacles had, of course, been removed.

"We know you, French," he said. "We remember you from the days before you got to be known as The Shifter. Maybe you've turned out bad . . . as bad as we've heard. And maybe you ain't so bad, after all. But you can lay to it that you'll get a square deal in Vardon City. Here's wishing you good luck."

The Shifter shook hands heartily through the bars.

"I'll tell you what," he said, "Vardon City ain't through with me. I'm about to settle down, partner, and I've made up my mind that I'll settle down right here. If you folks don't like me to start with, I'll make you like me before I'm through."

The other grinned. Then he whispered shyly: "Don't let the sheriff get you worried so you try to bust out. He's just nacheral gloomy. You see?"

With this word to the wise and a broad wink, the good-natured fellow left The Shifter to his thoughts and retired to retreat with the rest of the party. Alone with the cellar dimly illumined by the light from a single lantern which swung from a rafter in a corner, The Shifter immediately set about examining his surroundings. He had entered the jail in perfect confidence but, when he heard the steel-barred door slam behind him and heard the heavy lock click, his heart had leaped into his throat, as it does when one jumps into cold water. He was trapped, and no matter how harmless his actions had been, the fact that he was helpless was in itself alarming. The size of the lock on the door made him yearn for a key to open it, in spite of his good intentions to let the law take its own course in its own way.

In the meantime his cautious explorations revealed several things of interest: that the bars which surrounded him were new and un-rusted, that they were thick and set close together and resisted his grasp and strong pull, as though each were a wall. Above and on every side he was hemmed in by a resistless opposition. He lifted with ease one of the broad, thin boards which formed the flooring of the cell and found what he had dreaded to find—that the network of steel bars ran under the boards. Truly, he was securely held, and the thought sent a numb thrill of uneasiness into his brain.

Suppose something happened to Jack Clark on the one-way trail? Suppose, in the downpour of rain, his foot had slipped on a wet rock, or in the dimness of twilight he had fallen and . . . ? But here The Shifter's brain refused to work any further with the grim possibility. Upon the known safety of Jack Clark depended his own life. So much was clear.

He had lain down and composed himself for sleep when this possibility entered his mind and brought him bolt upright on his cot. As he sat there with his head in his hands, he was suddenly startled by a feeling that someone was nearby, watching. He looked up with a jerk and found that the sheriff had stolen into the cellar, his footfalls covered by the noise of the storm which still yelled and drummed outside the house. He stood in uncanny silence, his face pressed close to the bars, his eyes on fire with savage hatred. The Shifter, cold with dread, straightened slowly to his feet.

"Well?" he asked, so dry of throat that he could hardly speak.

"We've wired to Logan again," said the sheriff. "Jack ain't there."

"He's on the trail, then," said The Shifter, gripping his hands and steeling himself to fight away the convulsive shudders which were spreading over him.

"We've rode the trail. We've had 'em ride all the way up from Logan. Jack ain't on the trail."

"Then where is he?"

"Down in the Kendall River where you throwed him when you killed him!"

"Sheriff . . . !"

"I'll see you swing for it," said the sheriff slowly. "Aye, I'll see you swing for it. You've sent him to his death. You've sent me to mine. And I'll see that you go down with us. Sleep on that!"

He turned and stalked from the room with a long, slow stride but with his shoulders sagging, as though all in a moment an irresistible load of years had been poured upon him.

# VI

## "A DECISION IS REVERSED"

The stairs from the cellar to the first floor creaked one by one, one by one, under the step of the sheriff. Between every sound his mind rushed through years of life, years of planning and of hope which had been blasted this night by The Shifter. He had built his own future on the future of his son; with his son gone, his own hopes of success were withered at the root. Not that the heart of the grim man was tender for his offspring. He knew the boy for what he was—a coward, a knave by instinct, and something of a fool. But, nevertheless, he had planned to wrest success and wealth from the world through the use of this wretched tool, and he had been on the verge of victory when the tool was torn from his hands. That was why his eyes were fiery when he leaned at the bars of The Shifter's cell and looked at him.

It was an unsavory story, that tale of his life's plans. Ten years before, rich William Chalmers had died and left his daughter and sole heir in the keeping of John Clark as guardian. The fortune which went with her had been tied up in bonds—all but a small sum for her living expenses—and the very interest upon them could not be touched until Alison Chalmers reached her eighteenth birthday. The sheriff had taken the custody of the child with the best of intentions and in all good faith. The gradual wreckage of one business scheme after another did not alter him. Another man would have seen a chance of escape in the fortune which the girl held as her own, but the sheriff was not of that kind of stuff. He had no idea of using the fortune of the girl with or without her will.

True, he did conceive the idea of marrying Alison to his son, but he conceived it without malice aforethought. It is true too that, even as he planned the thing, he knew that his son was really unworthy of the girl, but in Alison he also saw the salvation of Jack Clark. Other fathers had made the same mistake before him.

Although at times he might shrewdly have guessed that his son was a coward and a knave, as a rule he closed his eyes to the truth and strove to make himself think that Jack only needed the passage of time to make him into a real man. He could not be wrong. The boy's mother had been a gentle wife whom the sheriff still loved and looked back on with a deep devotion. The sheriff had never been accused of cowardice or of the instincts of a bully.

More than once the very flesh of John Clark had crawled when he heard or saw evidence of the mean spirit of his boy, but always he shook his head and returned to reasoning and self-delusion to cover up the fact. It was sad, and it was shameful, but, after all, it was natural. He could not despise his own son. Jack must be a good man— in the making. The sheriff would do what he could. When he was done, he depended upon the girl to come to his aid and finish the job.

There was one great, almost insuperable obstacle. Alison hated Jack. More than once this fact had made the sheriff draw back from his plans and shake his head. He wanted the girl to be happy. He wanted to secure her future just as much as her own father could have wished it, but what he could not eventually see was that happiness could never be based upon bedrock if she were to be married to his son. Middle-aged people have a strong predisposition toward believing that the ideas of the young are changeable. Time will tell the tale is too often their creed. And that was the creed to which the sheriff held. Time would change Jack, and time would also change the girl. He himself would oversee the marriage and make sure that Jack treated Alison well. Under his oversight he did not see how matters could go wrong.

He forgot his own youth. He forgot a young man's opinion of marriage. Love was something which he left out of his estimate in the full assurance that habit could take its place. The bitter truth is that men who have loved their wives are too apt to think that a man *must* love a good woman and that a woman can grow accustomed to any man.

All of these things John Clark had pondered upon many, many times. He was struggling honestly to do the right thing throughout. That struggle occupied a great many of his waking hours. There was only one point in his conduct in which he was dubious. That point was whether or not it was right to hold Alison back from communion with other boys and girls of her age. On this subject he debated with himself long and earnestly. His conclusion was wrong, but it was a conclusion honestly reached and honestly maintained. Many and many a time he had said to himself it was fitting that Alison have the right to her own society among the young people of Vardon City, and he knew that she would quickly become popular among them. But he knew also that, pretty as she was, she would be very apt to be impressed with one of the youngsters of the town. This must not be. It was cruel to keep her at home, but by keeping her at home he swore to himself that he was reserving her for an assured happiness when she should marry Jack and when she should achieve the position of head of a happy household under his own supervision.

No doubt this was blind argument. No doubt it was folly. But the sheriff was honest in his conclusions. The result was that he kept her at home, saddling her with household duties above her years. He knew it was painful to her. But he promised himself that in the future she would be amply rewarded for the pain which she now underwent. After the marriage—why, her life would start anew. In the meantime he kept her closely at home. After the days in the public school were finished—and he was glad when they were ended—the sheriff saw to it that she left the house very seldom. He discouraged all intimacy between her and the young men of Vardon City. If he needed an excuse, he found it readily.

"She's not very well," he used to say to people. "You see how pale she is."

All the time he knew that the pallor, the silence, the downward-cast eyes were the result of his own regime which he imposed upon her. The full realization of this struck him when he stepped through the door to the hallway. There was Alison carrying a lamp in one hand and a tray of food in the other for the prisoner. He had not heard her coming. It was characteristic of her, this softness of foot. She stole through the house like a phantom, never lifting her eyes even when she was spoken to, even when she answered.

Bitterly the sheriff realized that this was his work. He saw her now for the first time as he stared at her in the dim hallway. How pretty, indeed! There was a woman who would make some man happy. Possibilities of warmth of soul and of manner were in her. Almost against his will he had checked and changed those impulses. He should have given her freely to the companionship of those of her own age. He had not done so, and for that reason he felt that he had done a hard and cursed thing. Well, now had come the time when he would make amends, most generous amends.

He loved the girl. Many a time he had had to pretend a harshness with her in order to give instructions that kept her at home at her drudgery. But all of those instructions had been for the sake of Jack and, now that Jack was gone, all was changed. Jack was gone, and there remained only one cause for his living. That was to make life happy for the daughter of his old friend. In his sad heart he felt a store of inexhaustible tenderness. How astonished she would be when he began to draw upon that store and pour it forth upon her.

Curiously, sadly, he gazed upon her. She was like a new creature, considered in this different perspective. Yet, he was bothered by those downward eyes. She did not lift them when she saw him but came to a patient halt in enduring silence. Sight of that pale face with the purple-shadowed eyes fell like a whip on the soul of the sheriff. It was his work, and how completely it was his work, only he could tell. But he would make amends, now that Jack was dead and his hopes undone. He would make amends in some way. With that good thought a chain was burst somewhere in his heart. Tears rushed to his dry eyes, tears which the loss of Jack had not brought.

"Alie, dear . . . ," he began.

Her eyes rose. She cast on him a glance of utter astonishment, utter fear, and shrank a little to one side as though to give him more room for passing her. She was used to curt commands, and this caress in his voice startled her. The sheriff turned and stumbled blindly down the passage. He heard the cellar door close behind her as he reached the stairs.

Now he needed quiet to think matters over and rearrange the scattered remnants of his hopes. So he trudged up the stairs to the second story to seek his little private office. He lighted a match as he entered, fumbled until the lamp jingled under his hand, and then lighted it. As he replaced the chimney, his left hand froze about the glass, for he was acutely conscious of another presence in the room. Then he whirled with his hand on his gun and looked straight into the grinning face of his son.

So completely had he made up his mind that the boy was dead that now he blinked in a ghostly fear. Then he straightened, caught Jack by the shoulders, and shoved him with a low cry of rejoicing against the wall.

"Hey!" cried Jack, writhing in that iron grip. "Let go, will you? Let go. I ain't made of leather. What's all the fuss about?"

The sheriff stepped back, still choking with relief and happiness. "We gave you up. What happened, Jack? How come you to get out of the trail? Did you fly? We got a gent down in the cells that I was getting ready to have hung . . . and here you pop up with a dry skin." He laughed, his voice trembling with pleasure.

"A gent on a roan hoss?" asked the son.

"That's the one."

"I wish you'd hang him, anyway," Jack went on surlily. "He was the cause of killing the brown, and he near killed me, too. Tried to ride between me and the wall. He done it, too, and pushed the brown over the cliff. I jumped just in time, but I hit my head against the rock. When I come to, he was gone, and it was getting dark. So I turned and got back here without nobody seeing me. But . . . you don't have to turn that skunk loose, do you?"

The sheriff nodded. "No matter what happened, it was your fault. You had no call to ride the one-way trail south."

"Who'd've thought they was such a fool in the world as to ride that trail north ag'in' such a wind? Anyway, I was in a hurry."

The sheriff sat down, mopping his forehead clear of perspiration, though the room was cold. He said weakly: "It seems all like the insides of a dream. I'm just waiting to wake up. But what made you in such a hurry?"

The eyes of Jack glanced, ferret-like, from side to side. "I told you I had to have that three hundred," he said sullenly. "I did have to have it. It was a matter of life and death!"

"Three hundred!" cried the father angrily. "Where'm I to get three hundred every time you turn around? You spend more'n I do the way it is. What made it a matter of life and death? Whose life and death?"

"Mine!"

The father stared. "Yours? What you been up to? What you been doing, Jack? I know you've played the skunk more'n once, but I never knew you had the nerve to do something that needed killing to pay you back."

Under the stream of sarcastic abuse the lip of the boy lifted and curled with a wolfish malevolence. Like a wolf he could not long look his father in the eye. His head lowered, and he cringed toward the floor.

"It's Kruger. He . . . he cleaned me out of the money with his slick card playing. He just makes the cards talk in a poker hand. I didn't have no chance with him. When I couldn't pay, he wouldn't hear of waiting. Said . . . said that he'd come gunning for me if I didn't show up with the cash. He gave me till yesterday to get it. I tried cards, I tried everything, even you, to raise the coin. But I couldn't, and I didn't want to kill a man because I owed him money, so I decided to slip out and. . . ."

"You didn't want to kill a man!" cried the sheriff, writhing in his chair with shame and anger. "You didn't want to kill a man! Why, you ran to save your skin, and you know it!"

Jack ground his teeth and flashed one evil glance at the older man. "Nobody else could talk like that," he said, "and you know it. I got to stand it from you. But one of these days. . . ."

"Well?" shouted the sheriff. "One of these days what?"

"You'll be sorry for it," concluded the son lamely. "Now, the point is, what'm I going to do?"

"You're going out and face that rat Kruger without the money and tell him he has to wait for it. That's what you're going to do!"

Jack Clark turned a sickly yellow. "He . . . he's a gunfighter!" he said thickly.

His father was even more yellow of face than he. For a moment he gazed on Jack with unutterable contempt, but then sadness succeeded scorn.

"Yaller," he said at last, "and so yaller that I suppose it must have been born in you just that way. Well, Jack, if you won't fight him, you'll have to run again. But I've made up my mind to one thing. I'm going to make a change with Alison. I'm going right down now and bring her up here and ask her once for all if she wants to marry you. If she says yes . . . all well and good. If she says no, then I won't hold her to it."

Jack Clark burst into a stream of protestation. "Good Lord," he cried, "ain't she rich? Can't she be the making of both of us? Are you going to throw a whole fortune away because you're a little peeved at me right now?"

"Peeved at you? Well, Jack, you can call it that if you want. But down I go and get her. She's too good for you. I know that. But I'll. . . ."

He said no more but turned and, striding through the office door, he shut it on the clamorous complaints of his offspring. He hurried down the stairs, fearful of letting the good impulse escape before it should have been turned into a concrete fact. But, when he opened the door to the cellar he stopped, his hand freezing to the knob, his whole body shaken with something akin to fear, so great was his wonder—for from the dim shadows of the cellar below him he heard the melody of a girl's laughter.

## "THE SHERIFF TAKES DRASTIC ACTION"

It must be Alison, and yet—Alison laughing? It was impossible! To be sure, in the old days when her father was alive, she had been a merry little child. But, now that he thought upon it, it was years and years since he had heard her laugh. It was a sufficiently horrible thought, this one that a young girl had not laughed for so long a time that he could not remember, but the sheriff did not dwell on the horror. What chiefly occupied him was wonder at what could have amused her now so heartily.

He slipped a cautious step or two down the stairs and peered below the floor level and through the little forest of upright bars, each faintly marked in place with a sketchy, silver penciling of light from the lantern and from the lamp that Alison had put down. There she was, turned in profile before him, and what an Alison he saw! The fairy godmother had struck her with the wand. The fairy had stripped the drab away and clothed her in sudden beauty. Her fingers were clasped about two bars of The Shifter's cell. She stood with her face close to the bars, her head lifted a little, her eyes bright, the last radiance of the laughter slowly dying from her face. As for The Shifter, he sat on the edge of his bunk with his hands clasped about his knees, teetering slowly back and forth. Certainly he was an amazing young man to sit there so calmly charged with murder.

"But you haven't told me," said Alison, and the quality of her voice was richer and deeper than the sheriff had ever dreamed of hearing from her lips, "you haven't told me why you are here?"

"I'm here," said The Shifter, "because someone disappeared, and they say I'm the cause of it."

Her forehead puckered. Then she started. It was wonderful to the sheriff to see the play of emotion in her. He had known her for so long as having simply a white mask of a face. The chrysalis had been so suddenly broken, and here was a woman before him, young, capable of joy and sorrow, tears and laughter. The sense of her filled the gloomy cellar like a light.

"Does that mean . . . you're accused of . . . ?"

"Yes. But don't say it. It's a hard, black word. It couldn't sound pretty, even from your lips. Well, what are you thinking about? That you shouldn't be down here with a man like me?"

He rose to his feet, more serious than before.

"Oh, no. Of course," she said, and she stretched out her hand toward him with a graceful little gesture of trust. "I know that you are innocent. I know that. I'm only wondering how you can be saved . . . how you can get away."

"By unlocking the door of the cell," he suggested.

"Yes. I think I might be able to get the keys. They're in the sheriff's office."

"And he's the man you're so afraid of?"

"I'd risk it. If it would be any help to you . . . ?"

"No, no!" exclaimed The Shifter. "I won't let you do that! Why, that old devil would make your life a plague. Besides, it wouldn't do me any good."

The sheriff crouched lower against the stairs and gripped his big, bony hands together. It was true. To this youngster he was a veritable devil. He looked at The Shifter with a pang. The makings of a man were in that boy. He had heard enough before of the fighting exploits of The Shifter, and from that last speech he could guess at his generosity and true, quiet courage. Indeed, there were plentiful makings of a man in him, such a man as the sheriff had dreamed once of having in his son. The thought sickened him. He remembered the snarling, shivering man in his office upstairs. Truly, the good angel was close at the side of the sheriff now, pointing out the truth to him.

"Besides," The Shifter was saying, "I'm not going to break away. They can't hang an innocent man. It can't happen. The truth always comes out at the last minute. I've seen it. Looks pretty black for me, I know. I've been tolerable hard. I've done my share and more of fighting. But I'm through with that. I'm going to get out of this mess. Then I'm going to settle down . . . right here in this town, where I've made such a bad start. I'm going to show 'em that I'm all right. I'm going to make 'em like me, just as I've made a pile of others fear me. But making people afraid of you is bad medicine. Look here, you ain't afraid of me, are you?"

"Afraid of you? Why, that's silly!"

"You're a steady one, right enough," said The Shifter, drawing closer to the bars. "You're the sort of stuff a square gent is made of. You'd stick to a friend through thick and thin."

"If I ever found one, of course I would."

"You have no friends?"

"No. They all think I'm queer . . . the people in Vardon City."

"The people in Vardon City are a pile of fools, and I'll show 'em they are! Why, the. . . ." His wrath exploded inwardly, and it made his face a bright red. "I'll tell you what. When I get out of this, d'you know what I'm going to do?"

"Tell me!" said the girl.

How very eager she was, and how close she stood to the bars. The Shifter in turn came close. Their hands were nearing.

"I'm going to get you away from this old scarecrow of a sheriff and take you off where you'll have white folks around you . . . some place where you'll learn to laugh and dance and always have a good time. Understand?"

Her smile was a trifle vague. "I don't know," she said. "I suppose there are such places!"

"Why, right here in Vardon City is such a place. But the point is, would you go with me?"

"Would it be right?"

"I'd make it right!"

"I don't know. I . . . I think I'd have to go, if you asked me to."

"Do you mean that?"

"Yes."

"You'd be happy, then?"

"Oh, don't you see? I've never been happy before, it seems, except just now, talking to you!"

The sheriff saw fire gleam in the eyes of The Shifter, but then the gunfighter drew back a little, drew inside of himself and ground his knuckles across his forehead.

"What's the matter?" she asked tenderly.

"I'm trying to think," he said in a shaking voice. "I'm trying to think what's right for you. That's what comes first. If . . . ?"

The sheriff waited to hear no more. He dragged himself up the stairs and into the hall again, closing the door with trembling fingers. He was so suddenly weak and sick at heart that he slumped against the wall.

Yes, The Shifter was just such a youngster as he had hoped to have in Jack. Honest, clean of mind, clear of eye and heart, brave, kind, reliable. No matter how wild he had been, he would turn out all right. If he took this girl away, he would make her happy as a queen. He would make himself over for her sake. She would have the molding of him. They would work together in the honest partnership which makes a home.

*What would become of Jack?* That was the lightning bolt which shattered the dream. What would become of Jack, the gambler, the idler, the shiftless do-nothing? Jack must be saved. How could he be saved? Only through the girl. It was brutally clear to him. She must not be sacrificed. She must not go down!

So the blasting realization grew on him as he climbed the stairs. His own son—*his own*—was no good. He reached the door of his office. He opened it. Jack was rolling a cigarette with a trembling hand. He started when he saw his father and, as he jumped from the chair, the cigarette was torn to pieces in his fumbling fingers.

The sheriff, as he closed the door, looked over his boy with a glance which for the first time in his life penetrated surely through the exteriors and reached to vital matters inside. He could begin to see the truth, not easily but with a slow and grim grappling. All that he saw made him sick at heart. He himself had made a sad mess of matters, he told himself. He had wasted his money in foolish business ventures. He had done one thing after another wrong in a business sense. But one thing at least could never be said of him. He had never done anything wrong in spirit. In his heart of hearts he had always tried to do right by everyone. The more he thought of this, the more bitter became his insight into the truth of his son. Why had he ever been cursed with such an offspring?

"You're afraid of Kruger?" he said.

"Me? Afraid of him? You see, governor. . . ."

"Don't talk to me!" cried the sheriff in anguish. "Good Lord! A son of mine showing yaller like you're doing . . . well, you've showed it, and that's an end! But I'll tell you this, Jack, you're in worse trouble than you know. If you go down in the village and let folks know that you're alive, and that another gent has been in danger of hanging because of you, you'll get some hard words."

"But I'm not going down into the village," said Jack wildly. "I'm not going to let folks know that I've come back from the pass."

The sheriff started. "You're going to let folks go on thinking that The Shifter killed you?" he asked, repressing his detestation of this man who was his son.

"Why not? What does it matter? Only means that he'll be in jail a couple of days. Anyway, the truth'll come out before he comes to trial. But all I ask is that you don't tell 'em till I get clear of the country. You'll do that, Dad? You won't let 'em know? Kruger would come after me like a hungry dog. And he's a killer . . . a killer!"

He was shuddering with fear as he spoke, and his father shuddered, too, but with a different emotion.

"D'you know what it means to be in a cell under the accusation of murder?"

"I don't know. I don't care. I only know that I got to get clear of this country before Kruger . . . curse him! . . . knows that I'm here."

The sheriff drew a great breath. "What do you intend to do?"

"I'll go up in the hills," said Jack. "I'll take a blanket and a can of beans and go up in the hills. I know where I can find shelter. I'll rest there a day or two. Then I'll strike out."

"You'll leave Vardon City for good?"

"Until you get rid of Kruger."

"I'll never get rid of him. Jack, I've tried you out for a good many years. Listen to me while I talk plain earnest. I've tried you out, and you ain't no good. The Shifter is a real man. Sized up alongside of him, you simply don't count. That's what's opened my eyes. I tell you this . . . you got to get out and stay out. Get out of Vardon City. Get out of my life. I'm through with you. You'd let The Shifter hang, if you could. Well, that opens my eyes to you. Get out and stay out. That's final!"

He turned his back and closed his eyes to the frantic outburst of protestation. He had only one way of closing the mouth of his son. He took out a well-filled wallet and tossed it behind him without looking. Over it he heard Jack whine like a starved dog. Then there was a stream of curses. At length the door closed on the son who was going out of his life.

## VIII
### "SOLICITUDE NOT WANTED"

Left to himself, the sheriff stepped to the window and stared into the blackness until he could make out the tops of the trees around the house swinging to and fro in the full current of the wind, for the night had turned wild again, and the storm struck the sides of the house in rattling gusts and then rushed wailing away across the forest. He turned back, shivering, and took down a heavily lined raincoat from the peg. It would be cold outside in that driving blast of rain. He himself was already cold to the heart.

This, however, could be remedied. From a closet he drew forth a brown jug of ample dimensions and, uncorking it, he poured into a water glass a great potion of colorless moonshine. He was normally a very temperate man, but now he drank it off with a toss of the hand and frowned as he felt the alcohol scorch his throat and burn into his vitals.

He was better for it, however. It numbed the thing which was torturing him. It freed his mind. It was even possible to consider the whole affair without heat. The main thing was to undo the wrong to Alison. For that he must have time for thought. Above all, he wanted to be among friends. He buttoned up the raincoat closely beneath his chin, jammed a broad-brimmed sombrero over his ears, and stepped into the hall. The suction of the wind caught the door out of his hand and slammed it with terrific force, so that the floor shook beneath his feet, and the long, desolate echo rang through the lower regions of the house.

Jack must be gone by this time, and the sheriff thought of the boy shrinking when the storm cut against his face. That was the trouble. He had raised Jack too tenderly. If he had the thing to do over again, he would do it differently. Force was the thing—force, force, force! He dinned that thought into his brain every time his heel thudded on the stairs going down to the lower level of the house. There he paused in the hall. A door had opened somewhere in the rear of the house, and a ghost of song had floated toward him, instantly cut off again by the closing of the same door.

It roused a sense of stern revolt in the sheriff. This night of all nights he wanted to hear no music. He strode back down the hall, opened the end door, and listened again, frowning. This time he heard it clearly as the ringing of a far-off bell, every word distinct:

> *What made the ball so fine?*
> *Robin Adair!*
> *What made the assembly shine?*
> *Robin Adair!*

What a voice sang it! A very soul of joy and tenderness was poured into the music, and for a moment the face of the sheriff went blank. Then he rallied, gritting his teeth, and stepped to the kitchen door. When he jerked it open, Alison looked up at him with a dish in one hand and a dishtowel in the other, looked up with the last note dying on her lips and a smile beginning in its place. The heart of the sheriff was touched profoundly.

"Alison . . . ," he began and paused, horror stricken as he realized how much he had taken from this young life—how much a single, short conversation with a condemned man had restored to her. Then he saw that she was waiting patiently, her head obediently bowed— waiting for him to continue his speech. It was the attitude of a slave— the crushed spirit of a slave—and he had done the crushing. "Alison!" he cried, "I've been wrong! Wrong from the start! Understand that, girl?"

At this she glanced up at him, glanced up with something akin to fear widening her eyes. Plainly she did not understand and, because she did not understand, she was afraid. His thought flashed back to her father, his best friend. Heaven be praised that her father could not see her now!

"What I mean," he continued, making his voice as even as he could, "is that I intend you should be happier, Alison. You need happiness. I've had a wrong idea. I'm going to try to make up to you all the things that I've been wrong in. You understand, honey?"

Her smile was cold and wan. Her nod was one, he could see, of perfunctory acquiescence. "Yes," she said, and her voice had no meaning whatever.

All at once he shrank from her. She was like an incarnation of all his sins. He must escape for more thought. He would go down to the hotel, where the old-timers who knew him would be congregating on this evening of the week. With that thought he rushed out of the house, went to the stables, saddled his horse, led it out, mounted, and rode at a mad gallop down the roadway and into the main street of Vardon City. There he checked the gait to a trot then splashed to a halt under the sheltering roof of the hotel, which projected from the top of the verandah and stretched across an enclosed driving entrance, where a dozen saddle horses and buckboards were already tethered.

He swung down from the stirrup numb of brain and body and, with bent head and sagging stride, he moved slowly up the steps and into the big room which had once been the bar, but where now only soft drinks were dispensed and where the card tables were packed in from wall to wall. There was only a scanty gathering in this social center of the town tonight. But those who had ventured through the whirling wind and the driving rain were hardened old adventurers whom the sheriff had known half his life, men in whom habits had become riveted by long usage. He surveyed their faces for an instant with stern satisfaction. These were men of his own kind. Then he stepped toward the stove and stood before it with his hands extended, until a steam of hot vapor rose from them.

There was a slowly increasing stir among the others. The veterans had greeted him with grunts and nods, after their fashion. Now Bud Morton, still carrying a juvenile nickname through sixty years of hardy action, approached and dropped his hand on the shoulder of the sheriff.

"I sure grieved a pile when I heard what happened," he said. "But what's done is done. Buck up, old man. You still got a long life ahead of you. If it ever comes to a pinch where you need help or a friend, you can call on me." He turned and glanced toward the others. "And here's a dozen more would stand by you, John."

There was a profound hush of sympathy in the room. It was far more eloquent than words. The sheriff could not turn his head. There was only one right answer to this speech and that was to tell them that there was no call for sympathy to be expressed to him. His son was alive and well.

Alive and well! Alive and a self-confessed coward. Far better, indeed, that he should be dead and mourned than that he should be alive and in this condition. He himself—John Clark, known through five states as a fearless man—would rather die than have the shame of his son known, but what could he do? He shrank in all his soul from letting the good men of Vardon City continue to think The Shifter a murderer. Conversely, he dared not proclaim that his son was alive for yonder in the corner he marked the cold, steady eyes of Kruger, the gambler.

In one particular at least Jack had been right. Kruger was a gunfighter. The whole town knew him as such, and the doughty old sheriff would think twice before he invited trouble with the man. He would think twice before he invited trouble, but he would not wait to think even once before he accepted it. That was the difference between himself and his son. That was the difference between courage and cowardice.

He said to Bud Morton, without turning his head: "Thanks, old-timer, thanks!"

Then he scowled down at the stove. How could he explain to them the truth without giving the information to Kruger? Always he felt those cold eyes of the gambler staring at him, probing him from that poker face.

"There's one good thing," said Kruger, "and that's the fact that you got the killer so quick. He'll pay for Jack. He'll pay plenty."

The sheriff raised his head and flashed a glance at Kruger. After all, the man had generous instincts, for otherwise what kept him from telling the sheriff how much was owing to him from his son and demanding payment of the gambling debt, which of all debts is the most sacred? The sheriff remembered how his son had picked up the purse he threw him with a snarl of acknowledgment. What a blind fool he had been to be in ignorance so long as to the real character of the boy.

He must get away from the hotel. These old friends who collected here every week on this day were torture to him. The very fact that he knew them so well was an additional pain. He wanted to be away, aye, in the very midst of the breath and the rain of the storm, so that he could think. He had been an idiot in the first place to come among them.

"Me, too," Bill Culbert was saying. "I've knowed the same thing, partner. I've had my loss, and I've lived through it. Keep your head up, John, and don't figure that this is the end of everything."

Well could Bill Culbert say it. His own son had died a hero's death, saving the lives of men in a mine into which others dared not to go down. Well could Bill Culbert speak, but he, John Clark, was the father of a coward. He turned abruptly.

"Thanks, Bill, old-timer," he said as evenly as he could. "But I'll be riding on. I guess I've had enough of this stove."

He whirled toward the door, strode hastily down the steps, and mounted his horse. Looking through the window, he saw that the men had drawn together, and that they were talking earnestly. No doubt they were talking about his supposed bereavement. Pray heaven that they should never guess at the truth of the matter. He spurred fiercely out into the rain. He must have time and space for thought, and the storm was a fitting accompaniment to the tumult in his brain.

## IX

### "A PROPOSAL OF VIOLENCE"

The moment the sheriff's tall form disappeared through the door, the men in the room had been drawn together and called to attention not by any voice from one of their members but by a clarion call from an unexpected quarter. It came from old Nick, the bartender, who smote his hand flatwise upon the bar and cried: "Gents, line up, stand up! What're we going to do for old John Clark?"

They looked at him in surprise and then muttered to one another. What had gotten into placid old Nick? But there he stood with his face lighted, and not pleasantly lighted at that. He was a formidable figure as to chest and stomach and formidable as to hand, also. It was rather fat than brawny now, though there was strength left in it, and many a man—aye, even of those at that moment present—could have testified to the power which once dwelt in that hand in the days of his prime when Nick, disregarding the threat of guns, had more than once stepped in between brawlers and hurled them indiscriminately through the door to roll in the dust outside.

"Fighting is fine for them that likes it," was one of the maxims of Nick, "but my barroom ain't the place for gents to get their exercise and sharpen up their shooting eyes. If you want a roof for gun play, try the sky."

"Gents," he said now when he found that he had successfully focused their attention upon himself, "I've served drinks in a good many towns and worked behind a good many bars in my day. I've done my turn in towns where the gold was coming from the ground so fast that the boys burned their throats out turning the dust into whiskey and getting it down. But I never seen a town act up so plumb orderly and peaceful as Vardon City. That's why I stuck when I come here twenty years ago. And why was it peaceful? They ain't any doubt about why. It was the sheriff. It was old John Clark. Did I have gunfighters smashing up my furniture in here in a way that would have turned the stomach of an honest man that come in here for a quiet drink? I didn't, because the gunfighters was always scarce in Clark's county. Did I have stick-up artists come along and clean out the money box on me? I didn't, because stick-up artists sure hated the ground where John Clark walked. Did I have slick card sharks come along and trim all the boys that played in my place? I didn't, because old John Clark was always a-sitting right over there in the old armchair in the corner ... that one with the initials carved all over the arms ... and John could spot a card crook a mile away. Well, boys, it's sure a pleasure to serve drinks in a town that has a sheriff like John Clark, and here's what I'm coming to. For the sake of what he used to do, and for the sake of all the drinks that have spun across this here bar, I sure move that we take a job off Clark's hands and finish up this wild young man-killer, this Shifter as they call him. Are the rest of you with me, or are you not?"

There is an accumulative power in words. They build out of nothing. They lead nowhere. But out of them comes an effect. They have, at least, the value of mass. They have the emphasis of quantity. And the emphasis, in the case of Nick, was pointed by a fierce energy which came out of his heart. Therefore, the effect of his words was more than could have been guessed from a hearing of the words themselves, unbacked by all those connotations which spring out of gesture, tone of voice, flash of eye. In the case of Nick there were tremendous flashes of the eye, great swellings of the chest, convulsive poundings on the bar, polished smooth by the innumerable glasses which in the past twenty years he had slid across its surface.

What, above all, gave the words of the bartender point, was that no one in the crowd had even remotely suspected him of containing in his heart such emotion. When one has jested with a man, shaken his hand, and clapped him upon the shoulder for an indefinite period, it is very difficult to take the same man seriously but, when he actually does become serious, the effect is most astonishing.

The effect was, at least, astonishing now as regarded the old and hardened cattlemen who listened to the eloquence of Nick. First they stared at him; then they gasped at him; and at length they glanced at one another as though to check up their own impressions by the impressions of their neighbors. When they found that their neighbors were taking this fellow seriously, they turned back to Nick with corrugated brows which were in themselves an ample token that they meant business. They began to feel, in short, that John Clark was more than a mere sheriff. He was a representative of the whole population of Vardon City and, as such, he was a representative of each and every man in the town. Each man of those within the room remembered how many times in the past the sheriff had stood by him in such and such an emergency. Each and every man was, in his heart, a little ashamed to think that the veteran bartender had outdone him in loyalty to the guardian of the law.

Shame, then, was the bellows from which air was blown upon the fire, and shame is a power well worth taking into consideration. Too few are those who think upon it seriously, but shame is that thing which makes the soldier step out before his mates and dare the impossible. Shame is the spur which the bright spirit doth raise. Indeed, even the stern Milton would probably nod his head in agreement to the misquotation of his great line. At least, it operated powerfully upon the good men of Vardon City, although there was some argument on the matter.

"Speaking personal," said Bud Morton, shaking his gray head from side to side as he spoke, "I always figured that Jack Clark was no more like his father than a half-blood colt of a mustang mare is like a Thoroughbred sire. He's mean by nature, a sneak by training, and a hound by general principles."

Harry Peyton came to the rescue of the Clark family and particularly of its son. "Look at most youngsters," he said, "and, if you look close enough, you'll find that, no matter how well they mean, they ain't no good in practice."

"Now you're talking wise," said Morton. "Anybody here can step out and say that I'm the sheriff's friend. I've proved it with powder and lead, which out-talks words a good many ways, but I'm also here to state that, no matter how much I like the sheriff, I ain't overfond of his son. If the rest of you would dig down into your vitals and talk true, I think you'd say the same.

"I've seen him quiet, and I've seen him loud. I've seen him talking friendly, and I've seen him talking mean. I'm cussed if I ever seen him talk or act the way I like to see a man. He always made me figure that he was only one part a man. At that, I've always give him the best part of the guess. I've always tried to see his father in him. But I ain't never been able to see much of John Clark in Jack Clark. Them two don't seem to string together.

"Why are we figuring to hit this gent they call The Shifter? We figure to go after him because he met Jack Clark on the one-way trail. What are the facts? The facts are that The Shifter was going the right way, and Jack Clark was riding the wrong way on the one-way trail. Well, boys, work it out for yourselves. It ain't hard to do. Suppose you or me was to meet a gent riding the wrong way on a trail when they wasn't room for two gents to pass. What would we do? I ask you that. What would we do? Why, we'd simply up with a gun and get rid of the gent that was superfluous. And this ain't the first time, because there's Hugh Neer. Didn't Hugh Neer take the wrong way of the trail, and didn't he get shot by Billy Jordan, and didn't Billy come into town and boast about what he done, and didn't all of us shake Billy's hand? I ask you that?"

It was a long speech to be made in the name of a defendant not present. Certainly, had The Shifter known of it, he should have presented his thanks to Bud Morton. But as it was, The Shifter was thinking of far, far other things than speeches made in his defense. In fact, he was clinging confidently to a doctrine absurdly old and that doctrine held no man could be lost for a crime which he had not committed.

However, there is no argument so old that it will not meet with a refutation; there is no argument so old that it will not draw out an enemy; there is no argument so strong that someone will not take the opposite side. This is human nature. We delight in opposition. We plague our dearest friends with epigrams. So it was in the present instance. There arose from the ranks of the crowd one who was willing to stake his wits against the wits of all the others, not because he felt that he was inherently right, but simply because he desired to fight the great majority. This is the impulse which drives men to support lost causes. What wonder that it showed itself here, in the person of the gray and venerable Jefferson Smith?

Jefferson Smith was, so to speak, a tartar. In other words, he generally did the opposite of what people expected. Because he was the opposite of their expectations, it is not strange to hear that he was generally detested. What we hate is not, as a rule, what is dangerous to us, but what is new to us. So, to speak plainly, Jefferson Smith was quite generally hated. He was so generally hated that good wives, if one must be perfectly frank, dreaded his shadow over their doorway. He was so generally hated that men cared not at all if their secrets fell into the hands of the ordinary run of mortals, but they cared extremely much if those secrets fell into the hands of Jefferson Smith. Because Jefferson Smith was able to impart to the smallest thing that aroma of the important which may not exist in fact but which is very apt to exist in inference. He was one of those men whose inferences are more important than their statements.

It was this Jefferson Smith, then, who rose in what had been the ancient and respected barroom of the hotel at Vardon City. He rose and looked about him, and by his very rising he called to him the eyes and the attention of the spectators. They turned on their heels, they turned in their chairs, and they beheld Jefferson Smith rise and roll his eyes and tug at his slender beard, for it is not for nothing that in the West a man has shot a five-cent piece at thirty yards and blown its center out. It is not for nothing, either, that a man has killed three hard-fighting warriors of Colt Forty-Five and bronco. So every man in the old barroom of the hotel turned himself toward Jefferson Smith and watched him with the eye of one intent.

Which side would Jefferson take? Both were fairly represented. If not, everyone knew that he would throw himself with the minority. It was generally conceded that by his weight he could determine the whole affair—the life or death of The Shifter was dependent upon the careless malignity or the careless generosity of this fiery old fellow. He allowed them to remain in the dark about his intentions for only a short time.

"Gents," he said, "it seems to me that we're all wasting a pile of valuable time about a mighty small thing. Are all of us going to stand around here and spend the night chattering about a youngster like The Shifter? Bah! I've heard of him. We all have. We've heard him talked about as a man-killer . . . a bad one." Jefferson turned his eye deliberately over the little crowd, and deliberately he picked out his two worst enemies. "Gimme Calkins and Bud Morton to stand with me, and the three of us will take on thirty of such half-baked badmen. I say, boys, that we ought to ride up the hill to Clark's place, take this Shifter out of his cell, string him up to the highest tree we can find, and leave him there flapping in the breeze as a sign to others of what Vardon City does to the badmen who come its way."

He pointed his speech with action as he stepped toward the door. "Who's coming with me?" he said. "Or do you want me to go alone?" And that was decisive.

Alison had not gone to bed. She sat with her face so close to the window in her room that sometimes the pane pressed cold against her nose. Beyond the glass, as her eyes grew accustomed to the night, she could make out vague outlines here and there. Sometimes the sheeted rain was an effective curtain that fenced away the rest of the world. Sometimes it shook away in a change of the wind, and she saw the looming forest. Whatever she saw was noted only in semiconsciousness. Her mind was busy, terribly busy, with the host of thoughts that had been crammed into it this day.

The Shifter—Harry French—was a gunfighter, a known badman. It seemed impossible that this could be the case, but then she was sadly ignorant of men. It might be that she liked him so much simply because he was the opposite of Clark and his son. She admitted this to herself, nodding her head wisely but very sick at heart. She admitted it to her reason, but reason did not satisfy her. If The Shifter were really bad, then she felt that there was no such thing as goodness in the world. The very sound of his voice thrilled her with happiness; the very memory of it was a joy.

"But I don't know much about things," she said to herself aloud. "Most likely I'm wrong, because I don't know much about men."

She had not entirely obeyed the command of her guardian to keep away from The Shifter. She had stolen down into the cellar after she had finished with the dishes, and The Shifter had risen with a smile to greet her.

"Somebody's been talking to you, I guess," he said bitterly when she shrank away from him, watching with frightened eyes. "Somebody's been telling you that I'm a regular snake, eh? Full of poison?"

"I only wanted to know," she answered, "if you'd like to have some books or magazines to read?"

"I'd rather have you to talk to," answered The Shifter at once. "You're a pile better than all the books in the world."

She retreated a little, and yet instinct was singing in her that there was nothing to fear in this man—nothing at all to fear.

"All right," he called gloomily, "if you're going to believe 'em, go ahead and stay away. I'll manage somehow. Good night."

She could not muster courage to answer him. Something was choking her. So she turned and, once her back was toward him, a cold panic sent her scurrying up the steps and through the hall and up again to her room. Here she had been crouched beside the window ever since, harried back and forth by thoughts of The Shifter and his bright, steady blue eyes. She could visualize him so keenly that the eyes of the vision became intolerantly bright and brought her heart up into her throat.

It was at this point that she heard the sound of the knocking at the front door. The sound came dimly up the stairs through the clamoring of the storm. Perhaps the sheriff had forgotten his key. The thought of the sheriff in a passion was quite sufficient to blot all other considerations from her mind. She fled down the stairs like a deer and, panting, pulled open the front door against the drag and suction of the wind. Then the draft nearly drew her out into the night but, as she balanced on tiptoe, she made out that on the porch was not a single figure but a whole group of bewhiskered men glistening faintly through the night in their wet slickers.

"It's the girl," said one voice. "I'd forgot about her. It's the girl. That makes it bad!"

"Who are you?" she asked. "Uncle John is not here. I think you'll find him in the hotel."

Instead of answering, one of the men pushed in. He was a little man, not as tall as she, in fact. He had a sharply pointed little gray beard and glittering little gray eyes. He was withered with the passage of sixty years or more, but he had dried up without growing feeble. He was weather brown. His wrinkled skin looked as tough as leather. His active, gleaming eyes filled her with dread just as she trembled when the eyes of a rat glittered out of a shadowy corner at her. He stared through and through her. He seemed to be poking into veiled corners of her nature. There was nothing that could be hidden from this terrible little man.

Others came in behind him. Some of them were big, all of them were quite old, and all of them had brows wrinkled with knowledge of the world and its men and women and events. The silence with which they trooped in was strange and rather terrible. Alison shrank back toward the wall.

"You can come in, of course," she said. "I'll build a fire for you in the front room . . . and make you some coffee. You must be terribly cold . . . and wet!"

The little man turned toward the others.

"I'll handle this," he said.

Then he turned back to Alison and laid his hand on her shoulder. His voice was smooth and kind. It was wonderful to hear. It sent a drowsy sense of security drifting through her. The hand on her shoulder was light as the touch of an affectionate child.

"Now don't you go bothering about us, honey," he said. "Don't you go bothering to fix up coffee. We'll get along without that. Thing for you to do is just to trot back up to your room and go to bed. We know the sheriff ain't here. But we've come to do something that he'll be glad to have done. We're all old friends of his . . . you see?"

He patted her shoulder lightly as he spoke, and yet it seemed to the sensitive eyes of the girl that there was no reality in his smile. He was not talking to her but around her, just as the sheriff often talked when he wished to keep his true meaning from her. Being a specialist, as one might say, in pain, she recognized the same tactics in Jefferson Smith. The claws were buried not so very deeply beneath the velvet. Yet behind her own blank gaze the wise little man was not able to penetrate to the hidden meanings. She seemed to him perfectly simple, and he gave a little more credence than he ever had before to the tale which the sheriff had spread throughout Vardon City that the mind of the girl was weak. For that very reason he was tenderer and gentler with her.

The other men stepped quietly into the hall and closed the door softly behind them. It embarrassed them hugely to find only this reputedly weak-minded girl as a garrison in the sheriff's house. It was like attacking a helpless woman in a way. They scowled fiercely at one another, those hardy old veterans of the frontier. It would be better to have the sheriff himself present to overmaster and bind before they went after his prisoner.

In the meantime, Jefferson Smith continued to engineer the affair as general of the party. "I'll go upstairs with you," he said. "You can show me the sheriff's office. Can you do that?"

She nodded and turned, passing slowly and with bent head up the stairs, for she was deeply in thought. She knew it was by no means ordinary for a group of men to call in the absence of John Clark and calmly ask to be shown into his office. That office was his sanctum. He hardly allowed Jack, his own son, to step inside those precincts.

What was up? In the guilty, storm-reddened faces of the men she had striven in vain to read the secret. But undeniably there was something fierce behind their attitude, something in the eye of Jefferson Smith which reminded her forcefully of the eye of a cat that sits patiently at the hole of the mouse with steel-like claws ready to strike inescapably. She showed her guest to the door of the sheriff's office.

He paused there with his hand on the knob. "All right, honey. Now you run along to bed. Good night. And happy dreams!"

She looked wistfully up into his face. In spite of his smiling lips, his forehead remained stern. What was going on inside his mind? But all she could do was nod slowly and then turn away down the hall as Smith entered the room. However, she had hardly taken a step when, immediately after the sound of the scratching match and the small flurry of light in the office, she heard the jingle of metal against metal, the unmistakable sound of keys knocking together.

It brought Alison whirling back to the door with her heart a-flutter, for those keys, she knew, were the keys to the prison in the cellar—and there was only one reason for wanting those keys, which was to get at the prisoner—to get at The Shifter. And there, through the partly opened door, she saw Jefferson Smith turning away from the desk with the big, shining bundle of keys in his hand, and on his face an expression of cold and sinister purpose.

The mind of the girl leaped at once to the result. She had heard of lynchings. The absence of the sheriff gave point to her flash of suspicion. She reached in, drew the door to her. Cautiously slipping the key from the lock, she fitted it again on the outside and noiselessly shut the door and turned the lock.

So softly had she worked that Smith, half blinded by the flare of the match close to his eyes, was not suspicious. "House full of drafts," she heard him mutter as he reached the door on the inside. Then came the sound of the turning knob.

There was such a terror in her, now that she had acted, that she could not move but leaned half fainting against the wall of the hall.

"Hello!" she heard Jefferson Smith cry. "What the devil has . . . ?" He wrenched loudly at the door. "Hello! Help!" he shouted aloud. "Hey, boys, the little vixen has tricked me and locked me up here like a rat in a trap."

That brought her to her senses. The shouting of the storm still was louder than the voice of Smith, and there was no rush of footsteps from the lower part of the house, but at any moment it might begin. She turned and fled down the hall.

## XI

### "THE ESCAPE"

Her mind was working with singular precision now. She raced down the back stairs to the tool room behind the kitchen and there, with swift and sure touch, she jerked open the big tool chest in the corner and drew out the steel saw and the oil can. More than once she had seen the sheriff work with it, more than once she had seen him handle stout iron.

Thus equipped, she hurried down to the hall, slipped through the cellar door, and paused a moment before she closed it. There was a sudden outbreak of shouting in the front part of the house. Then came a roar of footfalls on the front stairs. They had heard Jefferson Smith, and they were rushing to his rescue. *How long would the locked door hold them at bay?* she thought, as she tossed the key down the steps.

She ran straight to the cell. The lantern now illumined the big room very faintly, for it was turned low. The Shifter, lying asleep on his cot, was a blotchy shadow among shadows. The girl pressed her face against the cold bars. Her voice shook crazily as she called, and yet she dared not call too loudly.

"Quick! Quick! They've come for you! Wake up!"

The fear in her voice seemed to reach him even in his sleep. One bound brought him to his feet, staring wild-eyed at her.

"They've come!" she stammered. "Here . . . here's the saw. I'll put on the oil . . . !"

"Who's come?"

"Jefferson Smith and a lot of others . . . hard-faced men . . . and they mean to take you away. They've taken the keys in the sheriff's office and. . . ."

She watched his eyes widen, his face turn gray.

"A lynching party!" breathed The Shifter. "Good Lord!"

The saw was snatched from her hand and began its small, shrill song as it cut into the steel bar, until she silenced it with a trickle of oil from the can.

"Hurry!" she pleaded. "Hurry!"

Remembering a vital step which had not been taken, she rushed back to the cellar door and opened it an instant, barely in time to hear a great tearing and crashing sound in the upper part of the house, as though the storm had beaten in a section of the roof. On its heels came a shout of triumph.

They had broken down the door to the sheriff's office with their combined shoulder weight. With palsied hands she closed and locked the cellar door and blessed its solid thickness of stout pine wood as she did so. Then she fled down the steps again and back to The Shifter.

He was working like mad, his face covered with tiny beads of perspiration but absolutely without color, and he acknowledged her return with a frantic rolling of the eyes. Again she picked up the oil can and poured the trickle on the shimmering blade of the saw. It was eating into the heart of the steel bar, but how slowly, slowly, slowly.

"Quick!" she sobbed. "I hear them coming!"

An instant later the body of a man crashed against the cellar door. The Shifter cast the saw jangling on the floor and grasped the bar. It held as though it were a column of stone. The guarding door which kept out the manhunters groaned as they assailed it again. A gun exploded. They were shooting through the lock, but that massive, old-fashioned lock would surely turn their bullets without giving way.

"Once more," cried Alison and, laying hold on the bar, she added her own small strength now made large in her frenzy.

He gripped the bar again. All his strength of body, from head to heel, went into the effort. There was a slight bending, then a gritting sound as of crystal against crystal, and suddenly the bar snapped with a humming sound and bent far to the side. The Shifter flung himself headlong into the gap. He could not go through at once. In fact, his struggles as he was pinned there threatened to tear him to pieces, but finally his hips were through, and then he lay sprawling on the floor at her feet, while at the same instant the cellar door was burst from its hinges and went crashing and bounding down the steps with a flood of yelling men pouring through behind it.

"Get him!" yelled the shrill voice of Jefferson Smith. "Shoot to kill, boys. He's loose!"

She saw a flash of fighting rage come into the eyes of The Shifter. Then he caught up the fallen saw and flung it at the lantern which hung from the rafter a few yards away. The lantern fell crashing, and the big cellar was filled with sudden, thick darkness.

In that darkness she heard the pursuers bang blindly into the bars and shout and curse furiously. Then a hand gripped her.

"Is there another way out? Is there another way besides the one back into the house?"

"Yes . . . yes. If I can only find it in the darkness! Oh, heaven help us!" sobbed Alison.

Deftly she guided him down the alley through the cells and then sharply to the right, until they ran into the rear wall of the house. The hubbub continued in the front of the room, a babel of oaths and frantic callings for a light. Here and there a match glowed, cupped in big hands, but those feeble cups of light were not able to throw a ray into the far corner where Alison fumbled for the old door.

At least, there was a sufficient glimmer of light for her to see that the way was blocked with a big box, and she pointed it out to the prisoner. His hands were instantly on it. It was flung to the side, while the betraying sound brought a yell from the trailers. One thrust of his shoulder and the door went open. Then she stood with him in the freshness of the night, with the wild rain whipping about them.

"Which way?" he asked.

"Here!"

She barely gave him the signal when he was off and she, racing beside him, was able to keep up because of her knowledge of the ground. Twice he tripped and fell headlong over obstacles in the yard and so enabled her to stay near him, and they reached the sheltering darkness of the trees side by side behind the house. The noise of the self-appointed posse now burst out of the cellar and into the storm-ridden night.

"Go back and get lights!" shouted the controlling voice of Jefferson Smith. "We'll run the fool down. He can't get far on foot. Newt Barclay and Saunders, run for the stable and see that he don't get off with a hoss. If you see anything, don't wait to ask questions. Shoot to kill. Jerry, wait here and watch this door so he don't double back like a fox. The rest of you. . . ." His voice died away as he turned back into the cellar.

"Now," said The Shifter grimly to the girl, "you've sure done your share. You've given me a running start, and I'll do the rest of it. Go back to the house."

"Go back and face the sheriff? Oh, I'd sooner die. You don't know him. He'll kill me for this!"

"Is he that kind? But, you can't go with me."

"Shall I go alone, then? I know the ground. I can show you where to go . . . a place they'll never search for you. Only one other person in the world knows about it. And . . . I won't be much in your way. I'll run every step!"

"Lord bless you," said The Shifter. "In the way? After saving me? I'll keep you in spite of everything. If I only had a gun . . . if I only had a measly little twenty-two. But bare hands are better than nothing. Which way, then?"

"Follow me."

She led straight through the heart of the trees, keeping her word valiantly and running ahead over the slippery ground with a sureness of foot and a strength that amazed The Shifter. It was all he could do to keep close to the form which twinkled back and forth as she raced through the trees. In a moment more they came to a stiff up-grade with the trees growing in a more scattered fashion.

"Now we're fairly started," she panted, slowing to a walk. "They'll never catch us before we reach the place."

A gust of wind pitched her into his arms, and he held her close for a moment then whipped off his coat and wrapped it around her shoulders, for her thin house dress was already soaked from the rainfall.

"Come on," said The Shifter. "If they follow us, heaven help the ones I lay my hands on!"

## XII
### "NEW LIVES"

They labored up a weary climb, their feet slipping on the muddy slope, but never once did the courage or the spirit of the girl fail her, so that The Shifter was struck with wonder again and again.

"It's a shortcut," she told him. "They'll never dream of coming this way, and the best of it is that the rain will wash out our footmarks. They won't last till the morning."

"And what of you?" he asked. "What will you do, Alison? Are you going to give up your home?"

"It's not a home," she said. "It's a prison. Oh, if you knew how I love even the rain and the wind because I'm free at last! My whole soul is breaking out and growing bigger. I feel strange to myself, I'm so happy. And I. . . ." She stopped suddenly and caught at his arm. "Listen!"

"Well?"

"Do you hear a wailing?"

"It's the wind. Yes, I hear it."

"No, no. Not the wind. I've heard it before. I heard it when the jail break came last spring, and the two men got away. Jefferson Smith has got out his hounds! Listen again!"

He could catch it unmistakably now, for as she spoke the force of the wind fell away a little, the crash of the rain on the rocks was lighter, and the chorus of the deep-throated bloodhounds swelled heavily up the hillside.

"We're almost there!" she sobbed. "But what good will it do to go into the cave? They'll follow us even there!"

"Will the scent hold in all this rain?"

"Uncle John says that the Smith dogs can follow even the thought of a man. Yes, the scent will hold for them!"

"If we're near the cave, then," said The Shifter, "let's go there and sit down a minute to think. My head's in a whirl in this infernal wind. Come on!"

He helped her up an almost precipitous rise of ground, digging his toes deeply into the mud for footing. They came onto a little shelf of land on the mountainside.

"This is it," said Alison. "At least this cave will give us a cut-off and gain time. It passes clear through the hill and opens on the other side."

"Suppose we cut through it and then block the other end with stones. The hounds may be thrown off."

"Yes, yes! At least we can try."

She led the way, dropping to her hands and knees and crawling through the black mouth of the cave. The Shifter followed and found himself in pitchy darkness. For perhaps twenty feet he crawled on behind the girl, bumping his head when he attempted to straighten. But at length he was able to see her rise to her feet, and he followed her example. The cave had widened to comfortable dimensions. The smell of wet ground was thick around them mixed with another scent, fainter and sharper.

"Alison!" exclaimed The Shifter softly. "There's someone else here! I smell wood smoke. A fire has been burning in the cave."

"That can't be true," she answered instantly. "There's only one other person in the world who knows about it, and that's poor Jack. He and I used to come up here when we were little ones. Jack showed it to me. The wood smoke may have drifted up here and stayed here without being blown out."

"But . . . ?"

He checked himself. There was no time to worry about imaginary dangers, for the voices of the bloodhounds swelled faintly from beyond. The Shifter struck on again through the cave, bending far over to avoid striking his head against any projection. For some ten yards the passage held straight on. Then it veered sharply to the right, and The Shifter, striding blindly ahead, struck solidly against the rock wall.

He recoiled with an exclamation, and on the sound of his voice he was paralyzed with astonishment to have a broad shaft of light flashed upon him.

"Hands up!" snapped a voice. "Hands up, whoever you are!"

The Shifter obeyed.

"If you're hiding out here, partner," he said eagerly, "I'm not hunting you. Matter of fact, I'm in the same boat. And. . . ."

"You!" broke in the holder of the electric torch, and now The Shifter could make out the outlines of the figure and even the glimmer of the revolver which he held in his right hand as he poised the electric torch in the left. "I figured I'd meet you again. But I never dreamed I'd get a chance to get back at you so quick. Now, son, you'll pay me for my hoss you killed, and you'll pay me big!" He added sharply: "Who's that with you?"

"Jack!" cried Alison, her voice ringing out joyously. "Oh, then all the danger is over! Don't you see? It's Jack Clark. He's not dead . . . he's not dead!"

"Good Lord!" groaned Jack, the torch wavering in his hand as he recoiled. "Alison, what're you doing up here . . . with him? What're you doing up here?"

The mind of The Shifter groped vaguely toward the truth. Here was the "murdered" man, after all, safe and sound and lurking like a condemned criminal escaped from the law.

"You'd've hung up here?" he growled savagely. "Stayed right up here while they was holding me for killing you? Clark, you'll pay *me* big for this."

"Will I? And suppose I stop your trail right now? If I catch you running off with a girl, d'you s'pose I ain't got the right to stop you . . . with a bullet?"

The Shifter had been resting one hand against the rocky side of the passage. Now in his blind rage his fingers contracted strongly, and a great chunk of stone came away in them. All caution left him.

"You hound!" he cried and lurched straight at the holder of the light.

The sound of the explosion of the revolver and the mingling wail of the girl rolled faintly out from the cave and reached the spurring horsemen who were driving their exhausted mounts up that hillside on the heels of the dogs, held hard in leash by Jefferson Smith and giving tongue furiously as the scent grew hot.

Up to the very mouth of the cave the hounds dragged Smith. He pulled them to one side, and the others crawled into the black hole. The scent of burned gunpowder was lingering inside to guide them. Far away they heard the muffled weeping of a woman. Morton had found an electric pocket lantern before he left the sheriff's house, and with this he now probed the passage with a dim shaft of light. They turned the corner of the tunnel at a run and so came full upon a strange group.

A man lay sprawled on his face, motionless. Another stood above him, leaning against the wall and staring stupidly down at the stricken. And Alison crouched, weeping, nearby.

"It's me," said The Shifter slowly as they rushed about him. "He tried to shoot me. I hit him with this rock. And . . . and I think this time you got some call to hang me, boys."

Bud Morton turned the fallen man on his back, and a shout of astonishment rose from his lips as he saw the face of Jack Clark. It was a face half muddy and half pale, and from the side of the head a trickle of crimson ran down his face.

"Is he dead?" asked Jefferson Smith from the rear.

"No," answered Morton, his hand lying over Jack's heart.

"He'd better be," said Jefferson in a ringing voice. "Of all the dirty pieces of work I've ever seen or heard of, boys, this is the rottenest. Don't you see it? To get square with The Shifter there, who killed his hoss and maybe licked him fair and square on the one-way trail, this skunk waited up here till The Shifter swung for the job or got lynched. Lynch The Shifter? Why, boys, we'll step up and tell him we're a pile sorry for what's happened."

It required time to bring about the conclusion. In that time Jack Clark, a sadly humbled and humiliated man, went north, far north into a new country, to carve out for himself a new name and a new character. And, since there is possibility of change in even the worst of us, Jack succeeded beyond the dreams of even his father who went with him. There in the north they settled down as farmers in an unknown community, and the letters that drifted south to Alison were all of prosperity, home building, and finally of the marriage of Jack.

They will tell you the story even today in Vardon City, particularly when a stranger is guided through the main street and past the big house at the head of the thoroughfare, its gables barely visible above the surrounding treetops, for Harry French, late The Shifter, and his wife now live in the big house. Their greatest friend is that formidable gunfighter, Jefferson Smith, who takes all the credit for their romance on his own shoulders.

"I smelled a rat from the first," he is fond of saying. "And then I ran it down with dogs. No matter if the name of the rat was not the one I started after. The fact is that I found a rat."

No one cares to dispute Jefferson Smith. Certainly not The Shifter who has laid aside his guns.

# Breaking the Blue Roan

## Honoré Willsie Morrow

☉

*If the name Honoré Willsie Morrow is recognized today, it is most likely as the author of a number of biographical novels, most especially her fictional trilogy about Abraham Lincoln known collectively as* Great Captain *(Morrow, 1930). Morrow was born in Ottumwa, Iowa, and though in her adulthood she visited the West and wrote about the West, she remained an Easterner, closely tied to her New England roots. She was published in many of the slick women's magazines of her day, contributing nonfiction or fictional pieces, some with Western themes. For five years she was editor of* The Delineator. *She married William Morrow in 1923 before he formed his own publishing firm. Morrow's first novel,* The Heart of the Desert *(Stokes, 1913), ran to six printings and is of literary interest because the heroine ends up being happily married to a full-blooded Indian, an uncommon occurrence in Western fiction until the 1970s because interracial marriage was long considered taboo, and one of the partners invariably died before the fade of the story. Morrow's subsequent six Western novels, among them* Still Jim *(Stokes, 1915) and* Exile of the Lariat *(Stokes, 1923), deserve attention because of their often vivid imagery, their concern with women's issues, and their themes of civic duty. "Breaking the Blue Roan" first appeared in* Everybody's Magazine *(December 1921) and has not been otherwise reprinted.*

John Hardy was born in Montana. But he did not grow up to be a sheepman, after all, because when John was a baby his father homesteaded in Wyoming. The homestead prospered and, when Bill Hardy died, he left John five thousand head of Herefords and a hundred or so of range horses. John was twenty-five when he inherited. At thirty-five he still was unmarried, a man of magnificent physique, best known for his taciturnity, his slowness, and his superb horsemanship.

In spite of his many acres and his herds John was not popular with the women of Lost Trail. Some of them said he was too lazy to make love. Some of them said that a man who was soft with horses, like

John, never made a successful lover, others that John was too stupid to find a wife. All of which merely goes to prove that Lost Trail women were poor judges of men.

Quite unknown to the rest of the valley, John was in love, deeply, passionately in love, and had been ever since the new schoolma'am had come to the log schoolhouse on the mountainside. Not that Edith Archer, the schoolma'am, guessed this fact. She would probably have said that one of the Lost Trail girls bred to the saddle and to the bitter hard work of the ranch would be John's choice. At least she would have said this the first few months of her stay in Lost Trail. What she really said later is a part of this story.

Edith Archer was slender and gray eyed, with masses of chestnut hair wrapped around a finely shaped head. Her eyes and mouth were very beautiful, the eyes large, deeply set, and grave, the mouth richly curved and wistful. She was low voiced, an anomaly in Lost Trail where women spoke shrilly, and men spoke softly. She arrived at Lost Trail in September. By May the seven thousand feet of elevation at which the valley was set ceased to make her pant at the slightest exertion. She could stick on a well-broken horse, and she had tooled the Lost Trail school along at a pace unprecedented in the annals of that happy-go-lucky assemblage.

By May most of the eligible young riders of Lost Trail had offered themselves to Edith and had been refused. All but John Hardy and Dick Holton. Neither of these had proposed to the schoolma'am— John, because he did not want to add the pain of a refusal to his general sense of unfitness; Dick, because, for all that he was in love with Edith, he had plans afoot that did not harmonize with marriage. Edith herself looked on marriage as bondage which she had not the slightest desire to enter.

As John was loping past the schoolhouse late one May afternoon, Edith hailed him.

"Oh, Mister Hardy! Would you mind calling for my mail, too?"

John waved his hat and put his spurs to Nelly, who broke into a gallop and arrived at the post office in a sweating lather. A group of riders around the empty stove greeted him noisily. He grinned without losing the quiet dignity habitual to his blue eyes and said to the post-master: "Give me Miss Archer's mail, too, Pete."

"How'd you get on that job, John?" demanded Pink Marshall. "I thought Dick here was on duty. Did you get yours, Dick? Say, I've done formed an ex-Archer club. Come on in, Dick, and Johnny, you'd better qualify!"

Dick, a good-looking man, dark and a little heavy around the jaw, laughed with the rest. "I ain't eligible yet, Pink. You go on with the mail, John. Maybe she likes elephants!"

"I don't know but what you'd better let me take her her letters, Pete," Pink went on. "A guy like John that's too lazy to court Edith Archer ain't got any love in him. And I still like to look at her, even if she don't want me."

"As for me," grunted Art Brown, "I like to listen to her. She's the only woman in the valley that don't bleat every time she opens her mouth."

One of the older men, Hank Lawson, spoke. "I'm going to make a try at breaking the blue roan mare tomorrow. Better come up, John."

"Handsomest horse in the valley. I wish you'd sell her to me, Hank," said John.

Hank shook his head.

"Anybody in Lost Trail that hasn't offered to buy the blue roan from you, Lawson?" asked Pete.

"Everybody's on record but Dick," replied the rancher.

Pete laughed. "Well, some folks has a prejudice against paying money for horseflesh."

There was an awkward pause. Dick had had some narrow escapes from the sheriff, but few people had the temerity to taunt him about it.

Pink came to the rescue. "You'd ought to form an ex–blue roan club, Hank!"

John laughed, lifted Pink by the collar and the slack of his breeches, and laid him across the empty stove, then went out.

Edith was sitting on the log door-step of the schoolhouse when John brought Nelly to her haunches before her.

She laughed. "Were you ever allowed to gallop alone on the enemy when you were in France, Mister Hardy?"

"I was put into the infantry," replied John with a smile.

"They didn't want you to scare the Germans to death, of course."

John's bigness was of bone and sinew. He jumped from the saddle without touching the stirrups, pulled off his hat, and handed Edith her mail. She looked up at him, still smiling.

"Little Charley Banes is watering my horse for me. Will you rest a bit, or must you go on?"

John pulled the reins over Nelly's head and sat down on the log beside the schoolma'am, who did not open her letters but sat waiting for the big rider to speak. Her eyes swept the powerful lines beneath the chaps and the soft silk shirt then paused on the stern modeling of the mouth and chin. Still John did not speak. His eyes lifted from the green-budding alfalfa in the valley to the menacing black saw edge of the Dead Fire range.

"Well," said Edith at last, "I hate to leave it all."

"When do you go?" asked the rider.

"I thought I'd wait for the Fourth of July rodeo," she said. "Shall you ride?"

John nodded.

"Mister Lawson said he was going to ask you to come up to help him with the blue roan tomorrow." Edith looked at John inquiringly.

"Yes, I'll be up there, I guess."

"It must be a wonderful thing to have the skill with horses that you have," sighed the schoolma'am.

"You wouldn't think so if you'd been brought up in Lost Trail, and if you'd been brought up in Lost Trail, you'd have been spoiled."

"Spoiled! My word, man, what was there to spoil? If I'd been bred in this valley, I might have been wild and full of fight like the blue roan, but I'd have been really worth while. As it is, I'm just a soft Easterner."

"The blue roan wasn't bred in this valley. She's a wild horse Hank roped up in the Many Eagles a while back. And I can't see how anyone would want you to be bred in this rough, god-forsaken spot."

"Don't you like it?"

"Of course! But I'm rough and god-forsaken like the country. Nobody like you could put up with it very long."

The schoolma'am stared at the rancher curiously.

"Sometimes," John went on in his low-voiced drawl, "I get tired of it."

"What could you desire more than you have?" asked the schoolma'am.

"Well, even a rider likes something that's beautiful and fine in his life once in a while. The older I get the more I realize that the folks that marry just on cattle and . . . and like cattle . . . don't know anything at all about what there might be in love. There might be something that these Lost Trail folks don't realize exists, you know."

If Edith felt surprise, she did not show it. For long months she had tried to tempt John Hardy to share with her what thoughts lay behind the rugged dignity of his quiet face, and she was not going to stop the unexpected confidence by any show of amazement. She nodded her head. "There should be the same beauty in love here that there is about those ranges yonder, just as subtle and just as enduring. But one would never expect to find it here . . . or anywhere else."

John drew a deep breath. But before he could speak, small Charley appeared with a little bay horse.

"Shall I help you?" asked John.

"If you don't mind," replied Edith.

But John did not offer his knee. Instead, he stepped up on the log, put his great hands around Edith's waist, and swung her to the saddle as if she were a child.

"Shucks!" cried Charley. "You don't have to do that. She can get on as well as anybody."

"That will do, Charles!" said Edith. "You may go now. We'll see you at the ranch tomorrow, then, Mister Hardy?"

"Yes, I'll be along."

John mounted and turned Nelly's head up the mountain. At the turn of the trail he looked back. Edith was still before the schoolhouse door. She waved her hand, and John waved back then rode on with an expression of profound depression on his sunburned face.

Edith boarded with the Lawsons at the north end of the valley.

Their ranch of a thousand acres straddled Lost Trail Creek which tumbled like a liquid green opal past the corrals and down the alfalfa fields. The Lawsons' little log cabin was set in a grove of quivering aspens within easy access of the creek. There was no fence about the house, and cattle, horses, dogs, cats, and chickens inhabited the very door-step amid a litter of saddles, harness, spurs, lariat ropes, and nose-bags.

When John Hardy rode up the next morning about eleven o'clock, two or three riders were sitting on the fence. Mrs. Lawson was established on the hay wagon, and Edith was perched on the top bar of the corral gate, hugging the post. Hank Lawson was standing in the corral, holding a blue-roan mare by a lariat round her neck. John dismounted and tied Nelly to the hay rack.

"You're just in time, John!" cried Mame Lawson. "She's thrown the hull of 'em. She just dumped Dick, and they had to rope her to keep her from climbing the fence."

John lighted a cigarette and threw his long legs over the fence beside the other riders.

"She's sure a bird!" panted Lawson. "But ain't she a beauty? Got some Hambletonian in her, and some Morgan by her head."

"Gord, Hank, you'll be claiming Clydesdale for her yet, just because her mane's curly!" grunted Pink Lawson. "She's just the orneriest unbroke mare in Lost Trail, half Injun pony and the other half wildcat."

John, hunched on the topmost rail, looked from the panting horse to Edith and from Edith to the great white crest of Eagle's Peak which brooded with appalling intimacy over the Lawson ranch then back to the mare. She was about fifteen hands high, a spotless blue roan in color, with the magnificent mane and tail that the open winter range produces. She had the round strong back and barrel so desirable in the mountains, small feet and the lean, wiry neck that spelled ancestry, real if remote. She was panting, and her breast was foam flecked.

"Hard to mount?" asked John.

"Easy as a bolt of lightning," said Pink. "Look at the she hellion with her tail and neck as limp as a rag doll. Wouldn't you think she was stuffed with sawdust? Go to it, John! I hold the record to date. I stayed with her just six minutes. Hank's going to enter her down at Cheyenne Frontier Day as the Great Unbroke. I'd like to see one of those champeens tackle her."

John pulled off his coat and vest and dropped them across the fence. He drew his broad rider's belt tighter, adjusted his spurs, then put on his gloves again. "Who saddled her?" he asked.

"All of us," replied Hank promptly. "Everything's okay . . . new cinch and hackamore. But I warn you, she's got the makings of a killer in her."

Edith cleared her throat. "What's the idea of breaking her, poor thing? I've a queer sort of sympathy for her. You have a hundred horses, Mister Lawson."

Lawson looked from Edith's puzzled eyes to the row of grinning riders. "Well, she's got to be broke, ain't she?"

"I don't see why. You've lots of horses you never break."

"Yes, but she's a beauty, and she's got to be broke. Come on, John!"

John put his hand on the reins. The roan jerked her head high in the air. Lawson now shortened the lariat till he reached the animal's head then, with the mare backing and plunging violently, he loosened the noose and slipped the rope.

"You get on the fence, Hank," ordered John, "and don't make any more noise than you naturally feel you have to."

John had no quirt. With one hand gripping the reins firmly, he lighted another cigarette. As the match flared, the horse tried to rear, and the man jumped aside to avoid her forehoofs. Then he began to talk to her, now and again making a move as if to put his left hand, which held the reins, on the pommel. At each attempt the mare lunged violently backward.

"So, beauty, so! Why worry? Life is always like this. Better be broke by a man than by a mountain lion on the range. So. That's no way to act! So."

Edith, sitting on the gate, tried not to miss a word of the monologue.

"Wait, beauty, wait! You don't know what you've been missing. The best fun in life for horse or man is the saddle. Calmly now. Nobody is going to hit you over the head while I'm around."

Ten minutes of this and then Dick cried profanely: "Get onto the blankety-blank, John! What are you afraid of?"

Suddenly, and without touching the stirrups, John was in the saddle. The mare dropped her head. John established his feet quickly in the stirrups. She drew her legs together under belly; her tail flattened between her hind legs, and her ears lay back on her neck. She quivered, and the great muscles of her shoulders knotted. Then, with a wild squeal, she bucked, and the battle was on. She bucked all the way around the fence, coming down each time with a crack of her right side into the rails in the vain attempt to crush Hardy's leg. She split his boot, but if she hurt his leg, John gave no sign. When she had bucked so long that the spectators had lost track of the number of times she had circled the corral, she ceased her squealing and shot across the enclosure, straight for the gate.

"Get away, Miss Archer!" cried John.

The girl dropped without the gate just as the mare reared, jumped into the air, and came down on her side. John was standing beside her as she lay for a moment, kicking, and as she rose, he was in the saddle. With unmitigated enthusiasm the mare tore across the corral, again reared, and again came down on her side. Edith clambered up beside Pink Marshall.

"Will she kill him?" she asked.

"Shucks! Nobody hardly ever gets killed by horses out in this country," he answered. "You've got to hand it to old John! Sixteen minutes and she ain't budged him."

Edith drew a deep breath. Her eyes swept the glowing beauty of the range then dropped back to the blue roan and the rider whose soft silk shirt was wet with sweat. Again and again the mare, her eyes mad with fear and anger, jumped for the sun and fell back to her side.

"Twenty-five minutes!" cried Lawson.

As if she suddenly realized that she ought to be weary, the mare paused in the middle of the corral, head dropped, legs straddled. John warily lighted a fresh cigarette, but the tense muscles under his wet shirt did not relax nor did his spurs drop from the bloody flanks. His hat long since had rolled under the fence, and his damp yellow hair gleamed in the brilliant sunlight. No one spoke. For a full five minutes the roan stood quiescent; then, agile as a cat, she lay down and rolled. She enjoyed this pastime for several moments, evidently under the impression that she was crushing John into the muck of the corral. But when she regained her feet, he was in the saddle, and once more she resumed the bucking. John's face now was drawn and white under the dripping sweat. Again and again the blue roan threw herself against the fence.

"Fifty-two minutes, and he ain't pulled leather yet," grunted Lawson. "But he might as well quit. I'll send her down to Cheyenne."

"Don't engage space quite yet!" exclaimed Pink. "Watch this!"

The panting horse again was standing in the middle of the corral. John lifted the reins high above her neck and drove the rowels home. The blue roan broke into a gentle trot and slowly circled the corral until John brought her to pause and carefully and painfully dismounted.

"He sure grips 'em!" exclaimed Lawson.

"You'll note that she's spur and not quirt broke," added Pink.

"I ain't seen nothing better, not even on Frontier Day," cried Mame Lawson, "except when Annie Rice, the cowgirl, got killed!"

John walked over to the fence and looked up at Edith. She smiled a little unevenly.

"I'm glad you won," she said, "but I'm sorry for the blue roan."

John nodded. "I didn't hurt her. Not near as much as she hurt me. Maybe she'll live to thank me"—this with a smile that haunted Edith for many hours.

The other riders gathered about the haystack where Mrs. Lawson was dispensing coffee.

"I'd like to ride the blue roan," said Edith.

"You let her alone," John returned slowly, "till she's well broke. And I don't think Lawson can lady break her. Maybe he'll let me do it for him."

"Riding makes me sleep," said Edith. "For a year before I came to Lost Trail, I hadn't had a real night's sleep."

"What was the trouble?"

"Too much teaching and other things."

"A man?" asked John slowly.

Edith smiled. "I've liked many men, but I certainly never would admit that one of them had given me insomnia. And I don't think I'd walk in my sleep or dream queer dreams if I had the skill and courage to fight with the roan every day."

"You let her alone!" repeated John. "Even if you have liked many men, that doesn't teach you to control a wild horse."

Again Edith gave him a quick, inscrutable little smile. "Come and get some coffee."

John returned the smile and followed her to the hay rack.

"Well, Johnny," said Hank, "what are you going to charge me for breaking the beauty?"

"You mean you want me to take her home and get her in saddle-shape?"

"I sure don't! She's good enough for me to start with right now."

"You let me take her home, and I'll lady break her for you for nothing," said John.

"What's that for, Hank or the schoolma'am?" demanded Dick.

"Both," said John coolly.

"Don't you do it, Hank," said Dick. "It would be a shame to have a mare like that lady broke. And don't you think that John's taken the freedom out of her."

The others turned to follow Dick's gaze. The blue roan was standing on the far side of the corral, her head resting on the top bar of the gate. There was something dejected in the droop of the beautiful blue-brown body but something unquenchably spirited in the lift of the head toward the eternal hills. Edith looked from the blue roan to John and from John to Dick.

"I got a good horse that's lady broke that I'd admire to give you, Miss Archer," said Dick suddenly.

"No, thanks!" exclaimed Edith laughingly. "The blue roan or nothing!"

"Aw, she'll be running away the first chance she gets," retorted Dick. "Me, I hope she does." And he strode over to his dapple gray and trotted off.

There was a glorious moon that night. John could not sleep. All the long hours till midnight he lay tossing and thinking of Edith and wondering who the man might be who had given her insomnia for a year. After midnight he gave up the struggle, dressed, and went out to the corral where he talked to the horses and watched the dim outline of Eagle Mountain which guarded the Lawson ranch. He wondered if Edith were sleeping or awake with all the watchers of the moon that send weird calls into the whiteness of the night—coyote, dog, owl, and wildcat. They seemed indescribably melancholy to John, and he was glad when, with the coming of the dawn, the far calls ceased. He went to bed and to sleep.

At noon old Aunty Farmer, who kept house for John, woke him. "They want you to come and help hunt for the schoolma'am," she said.

John jerked on his trousers and strode into the dooryard. Pink Marshall and Art Brown were waiting for him.

"Hank sent word for us to come up," said Art. "Schoolma'am seems to have walked off somewhere last night."

Before he had finished speaking, John was throwing the saddle on Nelly.

"When did they miss her?" he asked, as they trotted out of the yard.

"Not an hour ago. Hank 'phoned to me then," replied Pink. "Said they always let her lie late on Sundays, she was such a poor sleeper. Mame tries to keep the house quiet. But when they went to call her for dinner, she wasn't there. At first they just thought she'd slipped out for a stroll without their noticing. Then Mame sees she hadn't dressed . . . just gone out in her nightgown and slippers."

"Her nerves must be in awful shape," volunteered Art. "How do you suppose Easterners get thata way? Whoever heard of a woman in Lost Trail having insomnia!"

"She'd better settle down here," said Pink. "She takes to this life fine."

"Shall we stop by for Dick?" asked John.

"He went to Cheyenne last night," replied Pink.

No one spoke again until they drew rein at the Lawsons' door. Mame greeted them.

"Hank's following the creek up. He said to tell you folks to scatter."

"Has he tried to put Shep on her scent?" asked John.

"Oh, yes, but you know Shep. He couldn't follow a skunk."

"Are you sure she went away in her sleep?" asked John.

"You just come in here, John," demanded Mame. "Art, you go get Shep. Maybe you'll have better luck. Hank's sort of harsh with dumb brutes."

"I'm better at it than Art," declared Pink, dismounting to collar the trembling collie.

John followed Mame to the door of Edith's room. It was tiny, with plain rough log walls but exquisitely clean. The bed was rumpled. The riding suit that Edith had worn the day before lay folded over the back of the chair. A little white pile of underwear was tossed across the chair seat. John stood with his sombrero in his hand, his quiet lips pressed in a thin line. Mame pulled aside the curtain which made a closet of one corner of the room.

"I know all her clothes, and there ain't a thing gone but her bathrobe and slippers. Besides, she told me that ever since she was a child, whenever anything disturbed her in the daytime, she was apt to walk in her sleep at night."

"What disturbed her yesterday?"

"How do I know? She never tells me what is really going on in her mind. But she's the nicest girl I ever saw, and I love her like she was my own kin."

John turned abruptly. "She must be right near. It's too rough a country for her to have gone far, dressed as she is."

"Why ain't she back then?" demanded Mame. "And there is another queer thing. The blue roan got away last night."

John made no comment. He already was mounting Nelly.

All day long they scoured the country in circles of ever-widening circumference. After sundown, before the moon rose, John returned to his house for a fresh horse and the equipment for living on the trail for a day or two. His arrangements made, he threw himself down to wait for the moonlight. And it seemed to him that he fell into a light doze and dreamed of Edith. He heard her low voice: *"John! Help me, John! Help me!"* He started from the couch with cold sweat on his forehead. "I'm going plumb crazy!" he muttered. "First time I've dreamed of her, though God knows she hasn't been out of my thoughts since she came here."

He pulled on his coat and went out to the corral. He mounted Pete and led Miss Lucky with a light pack on her saddle. The moon was just slipping over the far-flung silver line of the Indian range when Pete trotted out of the gate. John's first stop was at the Lawsons' for news.

"We ain't got a trace," reported Mame, "except one of the children found a little piece of her bathrobe on a nail in the corral. Looks like she must have dreamed of the blue roan."

"Let me see that piece of cloth," said John, following Mame into the kitchen.

The rancher's wife pointed to the bit of blue silk lying among the teacups on the table.

"What kind of a bathrobe was it?"

"One of those Chinese things you see in the store windows at Salt Lake. She said somebody brought it to her from China."

John stared at Mame with widening eyes. "You fix me a bundle of clothes for her, Mame," he said.

When she had done this, he rushed out of the room and put Pete to the lope. At the foot of Eagle Mountain he pulled up while he thought rapidly. He could recall a cañon weathered out of the pink sandstone which composed the chaos that lay between the Dead Fire range and Many Eagles, but it was so inaccessible that it seemed to him highly improbable that Edith could have come upon it. And yet, even as he sat debating with his common sense, he seemed to hear the low voice of his dream: *"John! Oh, John, help me!"*

With a groan he whistled to Miss Lucky and turned into the Many Eagles trail. He knew he was a fool. He knew that Edith must have wakened long before she had come this far, even if this had been her direction. Yet the potency of the dream overcame every protest advanced by his lifelong experience in the hills, and hour after hour he pushed toward the chaotic valley beyond Many Eagles.

It was after midnight when the trail around a mountainside opened into a cañon with sheer sides remotely edged by pines. The sides themselves were barren but in the moonlight of a brilliancy of color that was almost unbelievable. There were many rock heaps on the floor of the cañon. John threaded his way carefully among these, stopping to rest at frequent intervals. The elevation was over eight thousand feet, and the horses were making heavy work of it.

In one of these intervals he heard the dull, thudding tramp of an unshod horse. Before he could start his small cavalcade onward to meet the sound, a figure in a blue robe stumbled into view. It was Edith, and she was leading the blue roan.

When she saw John, she stopped and began to sob: "Oh, John! John Hardy!"

John dismounted and strode toward her. "Here I am, Miss Archer! What in heaven's name has happened?"

"I shot him!" sobbed Edith. "I had to!"

"Shot whom? Are you hurt?" John took the lead rope from her, and she clung to his arm, struggling to control her sobs.

"No, only bruised. Don't speak to me for a minute. I'm trying so hard not to make a fool of myself."

John stood patiently for a moment, then he said: "Suppose you don't try to talk at all until you get into the warm things I've got on Miss Lucky's saddle for you? You put 'em on while I go 'round the rocks here and make us a little camp."

Edith nodded, and John, after giving her the bundle of clothing, proceeded to make a great fire of sagebrush and scrub cedar. By the time the fire was going well, Edith appeared around the rocks in her riding suit, her face white and tense.

"Will you give me a drink of water?" she asked huskily.

John held his canteen to her lips. "Now, I'll put the coffee on to boil and get out the sandwiches Aunty Farmer fixed for me. Then you can tell me about it when you aren't so faint and cold."

"I must tell you now!" panted Edith.

John looked at her keenly. "Let me put the coffee pot on and then you can go ahead," he said. "Sit down here out of the smoke."

"I didn't get to sleep quickly Saturday night," began Edith, "and, when I did, I had troubled dreams. I kept dreaming of the blue roan and that both you and she were hurt. I thought I'd better go to your rescue, and in my dream I went out to the corral, roped the blue roan, and led her away. She was very hard to lead, and she kept pulling me down, and finally one specially hard fall wakened me. I was alone on a strange mountain trail, so cold and with my slippers all wet with dew. And I was so out of breath that I lay down under a cedar tree. While I was huddled there, I heard horses coming. I didn't know who it might be or whether it was just strays, so I didn't call. And then Dick Holton rode by with three horses, and one of them was the blue roan."

"The blue roan! Did you really let her out? I know you couldn't have roped her."

"I must have let her out. I always did dislike him, and he's the last man in Lost Trail I'd have wanted to rescue me. But I wasn't going to let him get away with that beautiful horse, especially as I felt guilty about her. So, after he had gone by, I followed him. I thought maybe he'd put her somewhere for safekeeping and then I could tell Mister Lawson."

"And you followed him? Far?"

"I don't know how far. It seemed a long time. And then I fell and, like a great baby, I cried out, and he heard me and came back. I was sitting against the rock I'd slipped off of, and he just stood and looked at me. I said: 'Where are you going with the blue roan?' and he said: 'I'm going to put her where your friend Hardy'll never glom his big hands on her. She was wandering loose, and she's mine now.'

"And then I saw that he'd been drinking heavily, and I told him I'd been walking in my sleep and that, if he'd tell me the way home, I'd be grateful. Then he laughed and said: 'God, lots of girls have been fond of me, but none of them ever followed me this way!' and he stooped over me, and I struck him as hard as I could, and he struck me back and tried to pick me up and kiss me. And he said: 'I'll fix it so you'll never want to tell anyone in Lost Trail you've seen me.' "

John walked up and down before the fire, his big hands opening and closing.

"Then I fought him and managed to get his six-shooter out of his belt, and I pressed it against him and pulled the trigger. And he dropped and rolled over . . . dead.

"Then I went and got the blue roan's lead rope and started for what I thought was home, and I got lost and I thought you'd never come."

John stood staring at her, cold sweat on his lips. "How do you know he is dead? Did you examine him? Where did the bullet go?"

"I don't know where it went. I couldn't have touched him, could I? I wasn't trying to run away. I am going to give myself up to the sheriff as soon as I get back."

"Give yourself up nothing!" cried John. "If you hadn't shot him, Lost Trail would have made a sieve of him. No one can get away with manhandling a woman or horse stealing on these ranges, even if he is a drunk. But maybe you didn't kill him."

He poured her a cup of coffee and held it to her lips with big hands that shook. She drank it and ate a couple of sandwiches.

"Could you sleep a little?" he asked when she had finished.

She looked at him with horror. "Sleep? No! How could I sleep with his awful voice in my ears?"

"Have you any idea where you were when it happened?"

"No," replied Edith.

"Was there any landmark you could describe? The moon was still high?"

Edith answered carefully: "The moon was just setting. There was a spring with a big tree growing above it."

"Blue Aspen Spring! Edith, you've swung clear around the mountain and aren't two miles from it now. We can get to it by a short cut up the wall yonder."

"Get to it? Do I have to see him again?"

"Edith, I want to see whether you really killed him or not before we report to Lost Trail. You can stay here. . . ."

Edith shook her head impatiently. "No. I told you I couldn't sleep with his voice in my ears."

"Will you do something for me?" asked John gently. "Won't you lie down on my blanket here by the fire and rest with your eyes closed until dawn?"

Edith looked up at him pitifully. "I know you despise me, but I don't dare close my eyes unless you promise to sit by me."

"I promise," said John simply.

He spread the blanket for her and, when she had laid down on it, he sat beside her. She slipped cold, trembling fingers into his and closed her eyes. John sat with his back against the rocks. The moon had set, and the firelight shone alone on the slender, rigid body of the girl, on her pale set face. A half hour slipped by, then John felt Edith's fingers relax, saw the lines between her eyes disappear, and knew that she slept. He tossed more wood on the fire with his free hand and waited. An owl hooted loudly. Edith started and jumped at once to her feet. Then she stared at John while recollection awoke.

"I'm ready to start," she said.

"The sun will be here in a few minutes." John nodded to the east.

Swiftly the dawn was pricking out the fronded tops of the pines far above them. Faintly above the farthest pines rose the gigantic white outline of the Indian range, moment by moment growing more vividly colorful until its splendor paled the prismatic tints of the cañon. They watched the mighty day arrive in silence. When the sun was free of the pines, John turned to the horses. They were pulling restlessly at their ropes.

"These poor brutes are thirsty," he said. "Did you water the blue roan yesterday?"

"Yes, in the afternoon at a little muddy spring. She grazed there, too."

"Did you have any trouble leading her?"

"No! Wasn't it queer!"

"Not so queer," mused John. "Sometimes you find a horse that's like a good dog and recognizes a friend. So, beauty!"—this to the restless blue roan as he approached her.

"Let me lead her," said Edith. "I do think a great deal of that horse."

"Yes?" John smiled a little. "One might not have suspected it. You mount Miss Lucky, and I'll give you the roan's lead."

And so they started. It was a short and not too arduous trip back to the Blue Aspen Spring. It came into view as they rounded the shoulder of the mountain. First they saw Dick's two cow ponies standing by the pool. Then they saw Dick lying by the water's edge. He raised his head at their approach. Edith gave a quick gasp. John dismounted and strode over to Dick's side.

"Where'd she get you?" he demanded.

"Left side and right hip," replied Dick weakly. "I was drunk."

"Bleeding much?"

"Not if I don't move." He lay staring at the sky, ghastly pale and worn.

"I'll leave you some grub," said John. "I'm going back and send the sheriff up here. I am not going to trust myself to touch you, you can bet on that. If you aren't dead by the time he gets here, my advice is that you keep your mouth shut."

Dick's lips set in a grim line, but he said nothing. And so they watered the horses and rode away and left him. Edith did not speak for some moments. The relief was at first more than she could voice but, when after a mile of hard trail John called a halt for breakfast, she said: "It's like waking from a nightmare."

"I know," John nodded. "I'm about as relieved as you are but only for your sake. He deserved more than he got."

The breakfast was on the side of a mountain facing west. Remotely below lay the valley of Lost Trail. As they sat waiting for the coffee to boil, John said abruptly: "I wanted to kill him where he lay."

"After all"—Edith's eyes were on the red mists of Bear Mountain—"he didn't harm me, and I did save the blue roan."

John looked at Edith with something finer than admiration in his blue eyes. After a long pause he asked: "What are you going to tell the sheriff?"

"I am going to tell him the truth."

"You'd better let me say I shot him while I was taking the blue roan and that I picked you up elsewhere."

Edith stared at his grim face, puzzled for a moment, then she exclaimed: "Oh, I see! But I'm not going to let you lie for me. Lies are very difficult. I never have met anyone I thought clever enough to lie. And what about the story Holton will tell?"

"I'll bet Dick tells nothing, and I'll bet he never stays in Lost Trail so long as I'm in it. And Lawson may shoot him up again for stealing the blue roan. He's good for a long stay in Rawlins if he gets well and, when he gets out of Rawlins, or before if I can get at him, I am going to beat him up so his own mother won't know him. But what I have got to do now is to keep the he and she gossips of Lost Trail from bandying your name about. Just leave the story to me, will you, Edith?"

He crossed over to her and sat down beside her, looking into her face with such a depth of earnestness that she said with a little uncertain color flaring in her cheeks: "Yes, if it won't get you into trouble."

"It won't!" He hesitated, then went on: "You haven't asked me how I came to be looking for you in such an unlikely spot." Edith watched his face without speaking, and John went on in his soft drawl: "We were all hunting for you from yesterday noon on. At dusk I went home for fresh horses, and I took a nap while I was waiting for the moon to rise. I dreamed that I saw you in the pink cañon in that blue Chinese thing and that you were calling to me like this: 'John! John! Help me, John!' Did you really call to me?"

"Yes," admitted Edith reluctantly.

"Why?" Edith did not answer. "Did you call to the others, Hank and Pink and Art?" Still she did not reply, and John drew a sudden long breath. "Do you remember that talk we had at the schoolhouse, Friday afternoon, and I said that a man, even a rider, liked something beautiful and fine in his life once in a while. What did you think when I said that?"

"I thought how little the average woman really knows what goes on inside a man's mind. And I've been thinking that ever since. You see, any woman always thinks she's more refined, has more delicate perceptions than any man."

"Lots of 'em have," said John. "Me, I wouldn't know a delicate perception if I met one. Is that all you thought?"

Edith smiled whimsically. "No, I thought that most women were stupid egoists, me being among those present."

"I'm not sure what one of those critters is, but I know you aren't one. What did you really think about what I said, Edith?"

"Well, I thought how blind you were not to see the enchanting beauty of the Lost Trail country, and I thought, as I'd thought so many times before, how strange it was that all of Lost Trail's conversation was in sordid terms of cattle raising when some of it might quite normally be in terms of the most soul-stirring scenery that ever intrigued a poor, futile Easterner."

John stared at Bear Mountain and the glory of the brilliant clouds beyond it, as if he never before had seen them. "All my life," he said, "I have been looking for beauty till I found you."

"Me!" exclaimed Edith. "I'm just a tired Easterner with no nerve."

John grunted with a twisted smile at the blue roan then he said: "Do you remember that I said that maybe there might be something pretty fine about love that we Lost Trail folks didn't know existed? And you answered that there ought to be something as fine here in love as there was in the beauty of the ranges. Edith, will you tell me what love means to you?"

She answered a little hesitatingly: "I thought I knew when I was in my teens, but as I've grown older I've discovered that what I thought was love could never endure. Now I know that, no matter what anyone says to the contrary, the love that endures is a thing of the mind, intangible and permanent and based on the irresistible attraction of soul to soul and not of body to body."

John cleared his throat. "If your mind or soul or whatever it was called across the mountains to us yesterday and only I heard and answered, might it mean that I felt this ... this ... intangible ... oh, Edith, help me! I never would have the courage to say this much if you had not called to me in my dream."

"I called only to you."

"Why?" urged John.

"When I saw you break the blue roan with gentleness, I knew that I could care for you, but I've always hated the thought of marriage so! But . . . but now after this experience . . . John, I guess you've broken me with gentleness, too."

"God!" breathed John. "Edith, could it mean that you would marry me?"

"It might." Her voice was a little uneven.

"Do you think you know how much and how little a man like me could bring you?"

Edith replied slowly: "I know that you are fine and simple and beautiful, like your great hills, and that your inner ear heard me call in my deep need."

John rose suddenly and lifted Edith to her feet. He took her tired face gently between his big palms and looked long into her eyes. Then he lifted her to his heart and kissed her. And she lay quietly, as if, after long wanderings, she had at last come home.

# Shadows of Granite Ridge: At Kunman's Bend

*Vingie E. Roe*

Ⓧ

*Virginia Lawton wrote under the pseudonym Vingie E. Roe. She was born in Oxford, Kansas, but grew up in Oklahoma, where her family moved when she was quite young. She was a tomboy and loved animals and the outdoors. One of the high points of her late teen years was meeting the Oklahoma lawman Heck Thomas. It appears she began writing around 1910, and not long after that she moved to Oregon with her husband. More than sixty stories and some thirty novels were published over the span of her professional writing career of more than forty years, including* Heart of Night Wind *(Dodd, Mead, 1913),* Flame of the Border *(Doubleday, Doran, 1933),* Dust Above the Sage *(Mill, 1942), and* West of Abilene *(Macrae-Smith, 1951). Her Western stories regularly appeared in* Street & Smith's Western Story Magazine *as well as in slick magazines like* Collier's, McCall's, *and* Sunset. *Roe often featured capable and unusual female characters rarely encountered in Western fiction, and her work does not deserve the obscurity into which it has fallen over the years. This is the first appearance in book form of "Shadows of Granite Ridge: At Kunman's Bend," published in* Western Story Magazine *(October 20, 1923), the third of five interrelated stories about Lola Lambert and White Ears.*

**W**hite Ears had taken a journey, a very long journey by land, and then by sea when he had cowered in a dark world that swung and swept from the lower horns of the arctic stars to the upper rim of hell. He would gladly and frankly have died had it not been that his god inhabited this dim world also, coming daily with soft words and many caresses to salve his sickness—for Lola Lambert, his mistress, was on her way to Alaska. And then they had left the tossing ship that had brought them to this far, cold country. White Ears had never seen snow before. In his wild green land of the West Coast hills under the shoulder of Granite Ridge, he had seen it, yes, but never such snow as this that covered all things like a blanket and was solid as the earth beneath.

In a land where the dog is the king of beasts—and the lowliest servant also—he met many of his kind: fierce gray Huskies and dogs from Siberia, all of which served masters of one kind or another for one reason or other. Wild savages they were, all of them, cold eyed and with hair-trigger tempers. They eyed him askance where they lay in their harnesses before the door of the Arkwright House at Devereaux Point. Devereaux Point lay six days from the Seven Flats gold fields and three weeks from the town below where the river steamers stopped.

No matter how the savages of these dog teams looked at him, none had ventured to lure him into a fight, for his formidable size, even in a land where many dogs were monsters, was a strong deterrent. He also lay before the door of the Arkwright House, with his nose on his paws, and gave back glance for glance with his pale eyes gleaming in their narrow slits, and he wondered much about this strange new kin. He was an anomaly, a never-ceasing puzzle to the North-bred dogs of that hard country, for he bore, set in the gray of his rough wolf coat, the badge of an alien service, the broad white collie collar got from his renegade father who had deserted from a sheep camp in the California Trinities. Lola Lambert, bringing him to her out of the wilderness by the alchemy of love, knew that White Ears had inherited far more than just what came from that weakling of a faithful line.

That he was a wonderful dog many another of the motley stream that flowed by Devereaux Point to the Seven Flats was aware. Many a hand went out to him in tentative experiment, for the white collar seemed a sign of gentleness forgotten here, where no man touched another's dogs in carelessness. But though he lacked the ferocity of the malemutes, still none gained a hair's breadth with him, for that same white badge proclaimed him the friend of one master.

Lola had not met Le Brun, who came down from above that autumn, a little journey of a thousand miles or so, and stopped at Devereaux Point. Le Brun was a 'breed, a slim, handsome devil of a man, and cold as the polar floes. He was a study in black and brown—hair, eyes, and skin. He had a name over four thousand miles of territory where it takes something to make a name, and it was not good. He came driving in at dusk one short bleak day behind a team of malemutes that seemed lean to starvation, but had one been able to put his hand upon them he would have found them hard as steel and fit to the last whisper of desire.

As he whirled up to the beaten, snow-packed yard of the Arkwright House, Le Brun's eyes, those seemingly pupilless eyes between their long lashes, in circling swiftly the whole place fell upon White Ears sitting gravely on his haunches by the door. For just one second, as he sat on the sledge, Le Brun's eyes widened in a stare.

"Oh-h!" he said, under his breath. "*Mon Dieu!* That's a master dog!" And he looked to his own huge leader, panting in his tracks. "Thumbs down Kul-luk," he said coolly. "Your day is done. Two inches better at the shoulder . . . and what amazing depth!"

Le Brun stayed at Devereaux Point that night, but he said no words of White Ears, nor did he give him a glance that could draw attention. He saw the tall girl take him out a plate of food and stand by in the still cold air while the dog ate with a deliberate leisure wholly alien. When he was done, White Ears leaned hard against her, and his pale eyes fixed on hers in a silent adoration that gave the watcher a creepy thrill. Lola took the long gray head between her palms and looked back, and it was as if those two communed from their very souls.

Le Brun passed on with the charging stream, but in his own mind he had settled a point that changed his destination, his own fate, White Ears's future, and Lola Lambert's visit at Devereaux Point. He left the common trail at Twin Forks and went east up the frozen tributary to a forsaken spot he knew, where a man might hide forever within reach of his kind. Here he built a camp and awaited the next snow. It took a month of inaction, but he waited—for Le Brun was possessed of a brand of patience that was very high test. He knew when the snow was five days off and made his preparations accordingly, breaking his camp and mushing back the way he had come, though he kept far from the beaten trail. The last night he camped within striking distance of the Arkwright House, and by dusk the snow was falling finely.

Who shall say that our brothers, the beasts, have not the mythical and magic sixth sense? All the early hours of that bitter night White Ears, in his kennel, fidgeted, rose, and lay down, and rose again, sat on his haunches, and peered out at the dim smother with his pale eyes. His sharp nose quested the dull air, and he shifted on his feet. Upstairs, snug between Elsie Devereaux's feather beds, Lola slept in unconsciousness of impending evil. At midnight Le Brun struck.

A whine, wild and luring, brought White Ears in the open to stand like a statue in the whirling smother. A big, light section from a salmon net, flirted and spread with a practiced hand, sailed over him, settled sharply with its rim weights, and with his first instinctive leap—up and high with spread feet—the dog was neatly caught. Caught, but far from conquered. As Lola had said, the attempt to take White Ears was worth watching. It was such a struggle as Le Brun had never known, and it passed in silence, save for the thumping of the great body on the snow, the breath that whistled in White Ears's throat, and the grunts of the man himself, for the dog did not know the use of his voice in fear—had never cried for succor before. Le Brun was a craftsman among dogs. Very swiftly he got a stranglehold of cordage around the broad white collar, drew down, listened to the whistling breath raising its note like a humming wire—pulled tighter yet—and presently he drew away to the waiting sledge a huge, inert bundle. Five hours of heavy snow suavely smoothed out all evidence, and dawn brought a perfect mystery to the Arkwright House.

"Stolen!" said Pete Devereaux. "Stolen, by all that's wonderful! And from under our very noses!"

Lola, looking at the empty kennel, went first red to the edges of her heavy hair and then very, very white. "Very well," she said. "If he's been stolen and not killed. . . . You don't think he was killed, Pete?"

"Not a bit of it. There isn't a man in Alaska who'd kill a dog like that," Devereaux assured her.

"Then, if he's living, I'll get him back if I have to travel every train in the land. I'll start on the first clue."

Devereaux shook his head. "There isn't a dog in the world worth the risk a woman like you would take at that," he said.

Lola looked him in the eyes, and he knew he might have saved his breath.

"Man," she said gently, "he came to me out of the hills and freedom. He met a panther in the air as it leaped for me. He watched beside my bed while I slept in a cabin sixty miles from humanity with the door open. He has never failed me. I *shall not* fail him."

So it was that the great wolf dog of the California coast passed into the hands of that wizard of the trail, Le Brun, the 'breed. Judged by what he suffered in the next three months, it would have been better for White Ears had the tossing ship gone down. Le Brun was a master of dogs as few are in this world, and he set himself to conquer this prince of the breed as only Le Brun could conquer. But from the very beginning there was that between them which sent the blood hot in his cheeks and lent a devilish cunning to his hands. White Ears had never known a man intimately, and he distrusted them all. He had never taken an angry command in life, never received a blow, never known fear of a human. From the first day of his changed estate his education began, and it bewildered him. Weak and sore from the severe strangulation, he was hitched into the team that night and dragged through the heavy hours until dawn. He was tied ignominiously to the sledge with a bite while the others snatched at their food. He was bound in the hateful harness again and dragged until, for very dignity, he ceased his lunges and walked. Le Brun did not beat him but, when he spoke and the others crouched and leaped under the steel of his voice, he watched White Ears for the effect. And that there was none brought his thin lips back from his teeth in a curl.

"Ah!" he said. "We do not fear, eh? But we'll learn."

He proceeded to teach the wild, loving heart of White Ears that most demoralizing emotion. In a month the great gray dog, who had never known let or hindrance, ran in the lead of the savage team as though he had been born in harness. What methods Le Brun had used only himself and White Ears knew, but there was an unhealed scar under the long jaw that used to fit into the palm of Lola Lambert's hand, and around his loins there was an angry mark, as of a tourniquet. But though he answered and obeyed the steel-cold voice, his obedience differed from that of his mates in that it was without the cringing haste that made them so efficient.

Do what he might, Le Brun could never force this new leader to ignominy, could never set his flanks a-quiver with fearful expectancy. And always there was between the two that something that had been there with their first look. Always White Ears's pale eyes met the man's dark ones full, and always they set a mark between himself and his master that Le Brun had never crossed. Time after time the man had raised a hand to deal a murderous blow, and each time the dog had taken a step forward to meet it, ready, waiting, his head low, his white ruff raised, and his eyes like points of light. Each time the hand had dropped.

Le Brun stayed away from the Seven Flats diggings. He ranged far and wide in his restless travel, and everywhere he went he gathered gold, not with pick and shovel in the fire-thawed earth but with those smug and clever tools, the cards, whose every trick he knew as he knew his own devious mind. Everywhere he went, the marvelous new leader of his well-known team drew comment and admiration. Le Brun boasted about him with the swagger of the braggart and made record trips to prove his word—trips that would have killed any other team in the land. They came near killing White Ears, too, at first, for he was new at labor. But he had not run down his prey on the bouldered slopes three full years for nothing. He strained through every deadly journey with the hurry of desperation that he might scan the faces at its end for one. If he saw a woman in the far-flung camps they touched, no hand on earth—not even Le Brun's—could have kept him from investigating her. At this the 'breed always swore under his breath, and it was at these times that he had raised his hand to cross the mark. But with each new disappointment the look of menace in the dog's eyes grew and deepened, and he became more and more aloof.

Kul-luk, the old leader, hated him and was always trying to pick a fight with him. The others hated him too, perhaps for the broad white ring around his neck that made him an alien, and they all waited for a chance to kill him together. Le Brun knew this, and he kept White Ears constantly with him.

The fame of the big dog spread, augmented perhaps by the fact of Le Brun's jealous guard, and several marvelous offers were made for him that the 'breed rejected contemptuously. It was about this time that a rumor began to spread also—a rumor of a woman who had appeared in the places where Le Brun had been, who asked always of him and, finding him gone, disappeared swiftly. She was a young woman, the word went, tall and handsome, and with a calm and determination that were notable. She traveled well heeled, men said, with two first-class teams and a middle-aged Indian and his son from Devereaux Point. She was heard of at Salmon Falls, and then at Kutlow's Landing, three hundred miles above. Always she asked of Le Brun and if he drove an oversized, collie-collared dog. Presently it filtered through the talk that it seemed the dog was first in her eager queries. The speech was long in coming to Le Brun himself but, when it did, his evil eyes lighted with interest and excitement.

*"Voilà!"* he said. "A woman chases Le Brun! That is rare."

When he found that this woman asked always of the white-collared dog, the lighted eyes narrowed, and the hand that held the cards tightened upon them just perceptibly. Thereafter he made heavy journeys and visited far outlying points. But gossip flies fast in the lonely lands, and by spring men smiled at Le Brun in a way that made his blood boil and hinted that he fled from a woman from fear. That crystallized in speech one bleak, blue day at Kunman's Bend, and a dozen sourdoughs laughed in the badman's face.

"It takes a woman, eh, Le Brun, to put fear into you?" said MacDemarra. "And with reason, say I. There must be a strong motive behind such patience and endurance. How long has she been coming, McKendell? When did we first hear of her?"

The old man behind the counter of the store glanced up from his accounts. "Five months, they say. And she's covered every track he's made."

The 'breed raked in a pot from the table before him, having bluffed it out of the rest on a pair of deuces, and spat elaborately at the stove. "Eh . . . a woman! Bah!" he said.

But King, from the Little Pan diggings, leaned across the table. " 'Bah' if you wish, Le Brun," he said, "but if you haven't been running from this same determined woman for the last three months anyway, now's your chance to prove it. She's at the camp below today. She'll likely make it here tomorrow. You've lingered here a bit too long."

Every eye in the room was on the 'breed, expecting they knew not what. But this cool demon of a man had done too many shave-skin deeds, carried off too many situations where the ice was paper thin beneath him, to turn a hair at this. He merely shrugged. "How many?" he asked his neighbor, flipped the pasteboards, and smiled. "I run, *m'sieu?*" he said. "I think you mistake. I stay yet another week at Kunman's Bend."

Presently his sly black eyes glanced cornerwise to where White Ears sat quietly on his haunches, staring at the square of dirty window. The great dog had a peculiar habit of sitting so for hours, passive, motionless, eyes alert, and white-lined ears pricked half forward as if listening for some fine, far-distant sound. And never did he acknowledge his master by meeting his eyes or turning at his voice among the others. When Le Brun wanted him, he spoke to him alone, forcibly, clearly, and White Ears answered in his own dignified time.

All this howling, wind-whipped day the dog had sat so, watching the window, listening, while the roisterers laughed and lost or won at the table covered with dirty, stretched canvas. The sixth sense that had held him fidgeting on a rock in the moonlight, high up in the California hills that long-past night, and had finally sent him down to sniff and pad at the door of Lola Lambert's lost little cabin now held him waiting in a strange excitement that tensed the muscles in his lean body, caused him to breathe lightly. Who shall say that he did not feel her coming out of that infinitude of loneliness and heartbreak that had hollowed the faithful eyes in his thin face, taken the flesh from his bones in silent fret? At any rate he refused the food Le Brun offered him at noon and only shifted behind the roaring stove, while the players left their cards to eat cheese and crackers and canned salmon at the dirty counter.

When they had settled back around the table, he came out again and took up his position where he could watch the high window with its square of gray light. The last big snow of the year would come that night, and the day was desolate to madness. The hours passed monotonously with jest and oath and noisy story over the counter, one end of which served as a bar. The little crowd had grown until it comprised every man at the bend—and then there were barely enough to fill the long room, for the bend had had its fever, recovered, and existed dully without its delirious dreams, but King's words had spread a hint of possible excitement. They welcomed anything at Kunman's Bend these days, from a dog fight to a woman's quarrel.

The hours passed, and those who went in and out in elaborate offhandedness, to search the distances keenly the minute the door was shut behind them, saw nothing on the trail. Dusk fell early with the impending storm, and old man McKendall lighted the big gas lamp. Le Brun had almost cleaned the crowd. There was a heterogeneous heap of wealth before him—gold and silver coins, a few bills, dust in leather pouches, and a little pile of nuggets, duly weighed and valued. King was game to the last ounce, and he was still betting. So was a long, lean boy from Juneau.

Then, all of a sudden, for no visible reason, White Ears sprang to his full height, stood tensely a minute as if strung to the last bearable tension, listened acutely, held the breath in his quivering sides and, flinging up his head, gave tongue to a cry that filled the long room with an avalanche of sound. It was a wild, compelling, savage call, and an old Frenchman sitting by the stove crossed himself swiftly. "That's all wolf!" he whispered.

Twice—three times—the wolf dog put all his heart and his deep lungs into that ringing call to the night and the desolate wastes. With an oath Le Brun got up, took him by the collar, led him to the back room where McKendall kept his stores, and shoved him in among the boxes and barrels. He slammed the door and resumed his seat, but the old door, swelled and peevish, grumbled and edged back a bit along the uneven floor, so that a crack of light split the darkness in the storeroom. White Ears, absorbed in his listening, sat tensely down again.

At the end of another hour the boy from Juneau was done, and King had just laid his last dollar on the dirty canvas. Le Brun reached out a shapely hand to take in the pot—small now—but held it poised in air, long fingers spread. He never took that money. There was the sound of arrival at the door, coming upon them suddenly, and all fell silent. Every man in the room sat as it caught him for a moment, and every eye flew to the face of Le Brun, for the same thing was in every mind. Then old man McKendall came out from behind the counter to open the door but, before he could reach it, it swung in with a strong-handed sweep, and she whom they had expected stood there.

The snow was white on her parka, and she was clumsily wrapped in her furs, but her beautiful gray eyes shone in the light like stars. Wisps of her tawny hair hung down along her cheeks where they had been whipped by the wind of the earlier hours, and they saw, as the rumor had said, that she was very handsome. A moment she stood so, scanning the room. Then she came in and closed the door, and her searching eyes halted on the face of the 'breed by the table—halted, passed on, flew back, and stayed. A long moment they faced each other so. Then the woman walked up to him.

"You're Le Brun," she said in a voice of long-held rage. "Where is my white-collared dog?"

The gambler rose, leaning against the table with his arms folded across his breast. "Does madam not mistake?" he said smiling. "I have only solid grays in my team."

The cheeks of Lola Lambert, reddened by the cold, grew to a dark crimson. "You are not only a thief," she said, "but a liar as well. I have followed you all over this country, and I know you had him a week ago. *Now dig him up!*"

The devil that lived in Le Brun leaped into his eyes. "So?" he said. "A woman would force Le Brun, eh? To blazes with you, madam!"

There fell a slight pause, and in it those in the room heard another sound—a choked, passionate voice that sucked and gurgled in a surcharged throat, a body that fumbled and blundered at the store-room door. Le Brun heard it, and his dark face whitened with cold fury. Lola Lambert heard it and, jerking up her whole tired body, laughed.

"Liar!" she cried again. "He's here, and he's mine."

Lifting her voice, honeysweet and luring now, she called to the faithful heart breaking itself behind the thin partition. "White Ears!" she cried. "White Ears! White Ears!"

A pealing cry answered—a white-tipped foot fumbled through the crack of the door, a sharp nose followed, and the great dog forged through. His eyes were fire in the shadows, and he looked filled with murder, so intense was his joy—wild wolf in all seeming.

"Fiend!" gritted the 'breed between his teeth. "Back! Back . . . !"

With one long, cat-like leap he crossed the space between, snatched a hunting knife from his belt, and raised it high to cross the mark at last in deadly earnest. Few had ever beaten Le Brun—never a woman or a dog. But this time he had misjudged somewhere. He did not know the history of those two years in the California hills when these two had ranged alone, nor the love that was between them. Therefore he sprang forward with the knife lifted.

"White Ears!" shrieked Lola. "White Ears!"

At that call the dog, confronted by this man whom he hated, be-came a fiend indeed. He dropped in his stride and lifted high in the air as he came for Le Brun, curving his body aside and shooting his long head forward. The watchers saw the wide jaws take the man's throat fair, heard them snap with the slashing cut of the timber wolf. It was a clean trick that White Ears had done before on many a plung-ing buck. Le Brun fell in his tracks, the knife clattering on the littered floor, and in a matter of minutes they covered his face and the place where his throat had been. But long before that, White Ears had reached sanctuary—had thrown his great body against Lola's knees and, sobbing, she bent to clutch him in her arms. He could only whim-per like a puppy and tremble as all Le Brun's tortures had never made him tremble.

After a while the girl raised her face and looked beseechingly at the silent crowd. "Gentlemen," she said, "what do you think? Wasn't it justice? The dog is mine, you see . . . and it was life against life. You don't condemn him?"

A long breath escaped from a dozen throats, and King spoke. "It was the high days come back," he said, "when every soul fought for its rights. Your White Ears was the better brute. It was more than justice . . . for we knew Le Brun."

# The Bells of San Juan

## Alan LeMay

☒

*Born in Indianapolis, Indiana, Alan (Brown) LeMay completed his education at the University of Chicago. His short story "Hullabaloo" appeared the month of his graduation in* Adventure *(June 30, 1922). In 1929 LeMay, with the story, "Loan of a Gun," broke into the pages of* Collier's *(February 23, 1929). During the next decade LeMay wanted nothing more than to be a gentleman rancher, and his income from writing was intended to supplement the income generated by raising livestock on his ranch outside Santee, California. In the late 1930s he was plunged into debt because of a divorce and turned to screenwriting, early attaching himself to Cecil B. DeMille's unit at Paramount Pictures. LeMay continued to write original screenplays through the 1940s, and on one occasion even directed the film based on his screenplay.* The Searchers *(Harper, 1954) is regarded by many as LeMay's masterpiece. It possesses a graphic sense of place; it etches deeply the feats of human endurance that LeMay tended to admire in the American spirit; and it has that characteristic suggestiveness of tremendous depth and untold stories developed in his long apprenticeship writing short stories. A subtext often rides on a snatch of dialogue or flashes in a laconic observation.* Spanish Crossing *(Five Star Westerns, 1998) is his first Western story collection. Whiskers Beck was a character featured in stories both in* Adventure *and* Collier's. *"The Bells of San Juan" first appeared in* Adventure *(November 15, 1927).*

**W**hiskers Beck's fan-like spread of white beard was damp and draggled. Above it his mustache stuck out in disgruntled wisps, like the fur of a drying cat. He ran a blue bandanna over his bald head, and his tired hand fell away lackadaisically, leaving the handkerchief perched there in a soggy wad.

From their bench by the bunkhouse door the Triangle R cowpunchers gazed across the broad Wyoming prairie, steaming from its fresh rain. The vapor floated thinly, close to the ground, obscuring the feet of the far mountains. It had been a welcome rain, like a last farewell of the spring that had but a little while ago lost itself to dry heat. It would put fresh power into the grass, add many a hundred weight of flesh to the Triangle R herds, but to Whiskers Beck the downpour had been a vicissitude. He had ridden all day, chilled, coatless, dripping in rivulets. By the time he reached the main ranch again a new leak in the roof had seen to it that he had no dry clothes to put on. Now he sat drying slowly, and thinking of better things. From out in the horse shelter the wheeze of an accordion came through the dusk, accompanying a thin song.

> The bells of St. Mary's er callin', er callin',
> The bells of St. Mary's, tiddly um tum to me. . . .

The accordion's wail suited Whiskers's mood. His mind was turning to younger things, to a place mildly warm where the song of bells really rang over a far dry land. In the smoke of his cigarette he could see a white plain, still sending up heat waves in elusive rainbow shimmerings, even in the twilight.

*A placid expanse of water is held by a dam at the bend of the Pipestone River. Sedges, grass, and willows grow lush at its edge, long after the rest of the land is sere. By the bright water sit the flat-roofed little houses of San Juan, their blue and pink and yellow 'dobe reflected so clearly that it seems other houses are hanging head downward in limpid depths. The little plaza they enclose is shaded by four or five big trees; their twisted arms rise protectively over the tiny town. There is a well in the plaza, its deep waters crystalline and cool. And in the haze of evening the smell of cooking drifts through the village, the steaming aroma of* frijoles con carne *and* chili's tantalizing pungency. . . .

"I don't know what I'm goin' to do with 'Tar'ble Joe'," said Dixie Kane, "if he don't leave off passin' out that cold salt jackfish. Here we come in all holler an' soaked, an' what loud smell brings us up standin'? Damn dead fish again an' not even warm. I never seen such a thing in a cow country. I know the Old Man bought that jackfish cheap an' it's like to spoil, but. . . ."

Whiskers winced and let the sentences drift meaningless past his ears.

*At one side of the plaza stands the ancient mission of San Juan. Its adobe is falling away, revealing the deep maroon of its mortar, the venerable gray of its stone. Its arches are weathered, seasoned, more beautiful with the years. What lost fragment of a Penitente religion is surviving here? Who are the dark-faced, black-robed monks? What are the words of their chanted prayers? A man doesn't recall.*

*At evening the bells of the mission peal in mellow tones. There are only six of them in the squat bell tower, but the man who plays them makes them seem like many more. Some of the chimes are not in key. There is a wild plaintiveness in the songs they sing, a tale of something not quite complete—as if they bear kinship to Indian water drums, Navajo robes at once vivid and subdued, and such almost forgotten things. Sweet bells, though, sweet in the evening twilight. . . .*

"Gosh," said Dixie, "y'oughter see the swell mud in the corral. Tomorrer, if yun see bubbles comin' up to the top, sink a rope down . . . it's me lookin' fer m'horse. I hope it rains all week."

"Amen," said Whack-Ear heartily. "Drizzle, drazzle, squnch, squnch, squnch . . . ain't that music?"

Whiskers, with great effort, dragged himself out of Whack-Ear's imaginary mud. He turned his ears to the accordion, and his mind to far off San Juan.

*In the evening under the trees in the plaza dark-eyed girls stroll arm in arm; and youths in bright serapes, their conical, wide-brimmed hats cocked jauntily, lounge here and there with their cigarettes and watch the girls. A man doesn't remember it all. What were the winged things that lived in the tower with the bells—bats, or owls—or something else? And what were the odd, big-billed birds that nested in the plaza, sending strident bugle tones through the midday heat?*

*There is life, and love, and color in San Juan, to say nothing of the cooking of Madrecito Pasqual. But these things are only decorations for a place of warm peace, where an old man can sit and smoke and rest his rope-gnarled hands. Mornings, no crawling out of bed into the cold dark, no labor stretching ahead to the day's end. Evenings, a chair against a hut by the plaza, a smell of hot food and the song of the vesper bells. They only work when they feel like it, in San Juan. . . .*

A banjo with a tin head, a set of tinware drums, and four galvanized voices suddenly burst into self-expression at Whiskers's elbow:

*Ching lang ling, ching lang ling,*
*Ching la dee dee!*
*Sweet were the words that she hollered*
*at me!*
*Ching lang ling. . . .*

"Holy murder!" Whiskers moaned. Slowly he went inside, where he pulled damp blankets over his aching head. "What I need is a vacation," he told himself. "And by God I'm goin' to take it!"

South, southwest by the clicking rails, south to the *casitas* of San Juan. . . .

⊙

For an hour and a half the little tin car had jounced its way along twisting ruts in a glare of sun but, as Whiskers stepped stiffly to the ground, the sun suddenly completed its drop behind the ranges, and earth and grass merged into a barren of felt as gray as his dust-matted beard. He should have arrived at San Juan earlier, but because of an inaccuracy in his railroad map Whiskers had got off fifteen miles too soon. Since no more trains were due, he had had to travel twenty-four miles by flivver instead of the eight miles expected. For a while he stood there in the dust beside his telescope valise.

At the end of a full minute he said: "Can this be. . . . Oh, I guesso." After two minutes he said: "Seems like I must 'a' kind of fergot this here smell of sheep. Mebbe it won't seem so plumb outstandin', come mornin'." There was a slightly pained expression about his eyes but a fine flourish in his voice as he told himself, *Well, gosh . . . it's great to be back!*

A stir of excitement was animating the figures that lounged against the huts facing the square. They drew together into groups; they jabbered in hushed voices, covertly gesticulating. A ragged youth with a puffy brown face was approaching timorously. Through the Mexican's straggling forelock Whiskers discerned the glint of terror.

*I got a big notion to make a face at him,* said Whiskers to himself, *jest to see him leave his clo'es behind in one clean jump.*

"Ah, *buenos tardes, señor capitán*," the youth quavered huskily. He continued in Spanish: "All is in readiness."

"What?" snapped Whiskers. The dark youth quailed then turned and ran bowleggedly. "Stop!" Whiskers yelled. The young man stopped. "Come back here!" He came creeping back. The groups before the colorless 'dobe shacks had grown swiftly; probably everyone in the village was watching. "Take this valise!" He now took to his half-forgotten Spanish. "Take it to the house of Madrecito Pasqual. No! Pasqual. *Pasqual!* P-a-s-k-o-l . . . Pasqual!"

The valise flopped into the dust again, and bony hands spread deprecatingly. A torrent of frightened Spanish slithered forth. What *el capitán* asked was impossible, Whiskers was told. La Madre Pasqual was dead. Her old man was dead. Her sons were either hanged or run away. Her house was now the jail. He would be only too glad to see *el capitán* comfortable in it, but it was occupied already. But if only *el capitán*. . . .

Whiskers Beck silenced the outpouring with difficulty. "Oh, all right," he conceded, "take me somewheres else."

With something like a sob of relief the youth snatched up the canvas valise and trotted ahead, his bare feet flapping in the dust. Had he been less travel weary Beck would have swaggered. Seldom had he attracted more awestruck attention. As he followed the peon past the huts on the side of the plaza, the inhabitants ahead of him withdrew into doorways, oozed around the corners of walls. He could feel eyes peering at him from windows and doorways ostentatiously vacant. Glancing over his shoulder, he could see the people timorously coming out of hiding to stare at his retreating back.

He whirled in his tracks, and the nearest reappearing group scuttled into hiding again. "Anyway," said Whiskers, "they know who's boss around here!"

They entered the largest of the 'dobe houses, and for a moment Beck could see nothing in the windowless dark. There was a close smell of sweat-drenched clothes baked by the dry heat, a chicken-coop odor from a corner where fighting cocks must have lived for years, and a smell of weak mutton stew that suggested boiled wool. Whiskers gasped for air.

"'Sawful funny how a man fergets smells."

A baggy old woman was before him, bowing and making conciliating gestures. She mouthed bad Spanish with toothless gums.

"Give me a drink," he ordered.

A tin can was handed to him, and he raised it eagerly to his lips. Into his mouth flowed a lukewarm semi-liquid, too thick for water, too thin for mud. It tasted of pond slime and rusty tin. He spat the stuff upon the earthen floor, threw down the can, and booted it into the plaza. The peon who had carried Whiskers's valise leaped for the door and fled. The baggy old woman's apologies became tumultuous, profane. It was evident that she had no other drink to offer, and Whiskers felt ashamed. Silently he went out in search of a saloon.

The clear, lasting light of evening lay coolly on San Juan, revealing none too kindly the hardships worked upon it by careless living. But Whiskers, made angry by his thirst, saw nothing but the thing he sought—San Juan's only bar. PULQUERIA its sealing sign advertised it, and Whiskers strode toward it across the plaza. As he pushed into the room's fetid heat, the reek of raw alcohol, supported by the peculiarly characteristic odors of Mexican liquors, for a moment gave him pause. He scowled redly about the room, fixing a stare of malevolence on each of its dozen patrons in turn. Then his silver rang on the bar.

"Best in the house!"

The white *aguardiente* whiskey scorched its way down his throat, bringing tears to his eyes and starting a small bonfire in his empty middle.

"Gimme another."

He drank a second and a third; then, as he turned to look about him, he discovered that the saloon was empty. At a little square window in the rear mud wall he could see four or five staring heads silhouetted against the evening sky. They immediately withdrew.

"Well, wha-at the hell here?" Whiskers wondered aloud. For the first time he began to notice something odd about his reception in San Juan. He pushed out into the better air of the plaza.

Sauntering, he began a general reconnaissance of this place to which he had chosen to come. As he checked over one after another of the things that had changed, a heavy mood of gloom descended over him with the lowering dusk. For San Juan, somehow, had shrunk. It was only a struggling handful of 'dobe shanties now; and the dusty sterility of the burnt desert had crept in. The gay pinks and blues and creams were gone from the walls of the huts, scoured and blasted to the color of dust by sirocco-lashed sand. The plaza, too, had shrunk in the heat of the years until it was only a sort of dusty yard, a place to throw tin cans, bottles, and old rags. Three of the four trees in the plaza were dead; only broken claws remained of their great, foliated arms. On the last living tree two or three limbs still bore a few handfuls of dusty leaves; the rest were sere. How small and twisted those trees seemed now that they were broken and forlorn! And the big-billed, piping bugle-birds were gone. Beneath the broken trees the clear-water well was filled up, disused, a heap of garbage where it used to be.

Whiskers Beck pressed forward, feeling the urgent need of resting his eyes upon the coolly placid waters of the Pipestone. At first he couldn't find the Pipestone at all. There was, indeed, the dusty bed where it had been, but it seemed that even the Pipestone was now "running upside down." Then, walking along the powdery bank, he came upon all that was left of that bright expanse of water. The dam was broken, washed away in freshets long ago. A few snaggly teeth of drunken stakes, garnished with driftwood, were all that remained. Left unsupported, the broad pond had shrunk to a reeking puddle thick as gumbo. There was still green stuff growing about it—green, that is, in comparison to the parched plains cactus. It grew rank in the weltering mud. From this stagnant mud hole the peons scooped the dull water that they drink. It was wet enough, at least, to breed mosquitoes in swarms and clouds.

"Fer God's sake," said Whiskers Beck. "You could knock me over with a medium-sized axe!"

Scratching his mosquito bites, Whiskers made his way back into the plaza in search of the ancient mission. As he turned the corner of a hut, a ragged, pot-bellied child started up, stared at him, and fled screaming. Beck stopped to scratch his head.

"They's a strap broke somewheres," he told himself. "They must think I've got some disgustin' disease."

Once more, as he strolled before the huts, the lounging groups melted away at his approach to form again, staring, when he had passed. It was beginning to get on Whiskers's nerves.

"Got a mind to make a feint at 'em," he grumbled, "an' have the town plumb to myself."

The little stone building that housed the mission had crumbled away. Its arches were broken, scourged by the sand. Its mysterious windows were notches in disordered stone. Its flagged floors, once worn smooth by the passing and repassing of sandaled feet, were now open to the sky, heaped with windrows of dust. And the people—ragged, timorous, unwashed—where were the swaggering youths who once had galloped in from the plain, the silver decorations tinkling on the bridles of the shaggy, fighting ponies that they rode? Where were the dark-eyed girls who strolled in gay *mantillas* as the twilight fell beneath the trees? They had been beautiful then . . . vanished now, or turned to squat, ugly old women, picking over garbage in the square. And the bells—the bells were gone, as were the ringers, their tower crumbled away with the rest. Gone, gone, the mellow-voiced bells and all the beautiful remembered things, the threads of a vanished dream.

"I ain't goin' to make no statement," Whiskers mumbled, "not tonight. Nossir, not even to myself. But I *will* say, of all the cheap, low-down swindles I ever seen, that railroad ticket I bought to come here was the worst!"

He moped along, dragging his boots in the dust, toward the hut where he had left his valise. Whiskers Beck could not afterward distinctly recall just when or how he became aware that a rifle was looking at him from a window across the plaza. But when he did realize it, there was no room in his mind for doubt. Without seeming to look, he gave that window the careful scrutiny peculiar to men who think themselves likely to be shot. The dusk was thickening rapidly. A gunny sack partly obscured that black hole in the wall across the square. No one could have been certain that anything in particular was visible there. Yet the longer Whiskers studied the opening the more certain he became that he could see part of a face, a bulge of shoulder, a dark-looking something on the window ledge that was hard to account for in peaceable ways.

Every peculiarity that he had noticed in the actions of San Juan's inhabitants returned to him in a tumbling parade. The red grouch that had been growing in him now swiftly cooled. Expecting momentarily to hear the hum of a bullet past his head, yet without quickening his pace, he reached the smelly hut to which he had first been led, hesitated for a fraction of a moment at the door as if he were going to lean against the jamb to rest; then with one quick step put the wall of the hut between himself and the rifle—if that was a rifle—that watched him from across the open ground.

For a moment or two he stood against the hut's inner wall, accustoming his eyes to the new dark. When he had satisfied himself that he was alone, he cautiously peered out around the wooden jamb. At the window which he suspected he could make out even less than before; if anything, the gunny sack had been moved to shield it a little more effectively. No light had been lit in the building in question, or in those adjoining it, and the failing twilight gave his eyes little with which to work. When he had stood there motionless for some little time, a sharp thrill aroused him and, though he made no move, his attention snapped from the window across the plaza to the darkness behind him, within the hut itself. Something had moved there, a rat, a scorpion—or a man. He had no gun, or any other weapon, unless the folding knife in his pocket could be considered such. Motionless, he waited for the sound to recur.

It came again, the smallest part of rustle, the faintest hint of a tread. This time he thought he detected it in a suggestion of weight, telling him that whatever had moved possessed size and mass. He waited, scarcely breathing—waited. Suddenly Beck whirled and grabbed with both hands. His fingers closed on wrists. Then he let go and cursed; for the wrists were flabby and old. As he released them, that horrible baggy old woman sank to her knees on the mud floor and, reaching claw-like hands upward, pleaded volubly that he spare her life, if only long enough for her to get him his supper.

When at last he had got the shaking old woman to her feet, partially reassured that she was no longer in danger, Whiskers wiped the cold sweat off his forehead and demanded his valise. His remaining tobacco was in it. When he smoked again, he thought, perhaps he would be able to eat. He was furious with himself for his nervousness, for the foolish things that the bashfulness of these people had made him imagine. Stepping to the door, he exposed himself full front to whomever might be across the square with rifle or with none and, when no shot came, he mocked himself the more.

"This way, *Señor el Capitán*, in this room here is your baggage, your bed, your supper, everything. Ah, *señor*, we have done our best to make you comfortable and happy. Only walk this way, *señor*."

"Bring a light, *señora*."

"Ah, *sí, sí, señor*, only enter and make yourself comfortable. I will borrow a neighbor's light."

She shuffled out. Whiskers Beck blindly stepped through the door she had indicated into a stuffy room. He was feeling in all his pockets for his matches. A heavy body crushed down upon his head and shoulders with such impact that the tendons of his neck cracked, and he saw an illusory flash of light. He was borne down. His feet were swept from under him, and the floor rushed upward in an attempt to dash out his brains.

Deliberately, when the first daze of impact had passed off, Whiskers took stock of his situation. He was prone on the floor, clamped there by the weight of more than one heavy man. One eye was swelling shut from contact with the hard 'dobe on which he lay, but he believed that he was otherwise unhurt. He could hear congratulatory mutterings above him and, as soon as he had made out that these were in English, he decided to await quietly the development of events. Beck was past the age where men struggle violently without definite purpose in view.

A strong hand jerked one of his wrists behind him, then the other. About each of them clicked a band of steel.

"Put on the leg chains w'ile yer at it," said a wheezy voice.

"What good is . . . ?" said a second voice.

"D'yuh think I wanter get kicked in the eye?"

"Oh, all right."

"What the hifalutin hell?" queried Whiskers Beck in smothered tones. "Yuh think I'm so spooky as all that?"

"We know yer all right," said the breathy voice. "I'll jest set right here in the middle of his back, Ed, till you get them leg irons on. All set? Light the light then an' shut the door."

A goodly glow of kerosene light flared up, revealing nothing to Whiskers except that the floor had not been swept lately.

"Gimme a hand, Ed," the wheezy man said. "Ain't so limber as I useter be. H'ist up! Oomph! Reckon I fall jest as heavy as I ever did though."

With the weight raised from the small of his back, Whiskers twisted his neck to peer upward at the man's huge bulk. "Hope t'see yuh fall heavier," he said.

"What's that?"

"I say," said Whiskers, "I never seen no one fall heavier."

"I reckon not," said the bulky one. "See if you can find his guns, Ed. Darn me if I can find even a bean blower on the cuss. Ain't that queer?"

Lean, strong hands rummaged through Beck's clothes. As they turned him over, Whiskers saw they belonged to a tall young man with a thin, sad face, a face whose defect was a peculiarly earnest expression.

*Don't look real bright*, Whiskers decided. The other man was of bulging oval figure, with a face, Whiskers thought, suggesting a Berkshire pig of political turn of mind. He was growing bald.

"H'ist him up, Ed, onto that bench there. Let's have a look at him."

When the earnest young man had planted Whiskers as directed, the fat one arranged himself in a rickety armchair, placed his fingertips together, and contemplated the prisoner.

"Gosh, Mister Walker," said the man called Ed, "he don't look like such a tough one, does he?"

"He looks more like a man lookin' out of a hay pile," Walker offered. He studied Beck's dust-matted beard disparagingly. "But then, yuh gotta consider that those whiskers ain't his own."

"An' you," said Whiskers Beck, "look somethin' like a cross between a cook wagon an' a balloon. Only I s'pose that four ton of fat ain't yours neither."

"You won't get now'eres that way," said the fat man. He tapped a small nickel star that was pinned to his coatless suspenders. "His guns must be in his satchel, Ed. Crack her open."

They dragged open Beck's canvas telescope, and Ed began listing the contents in a singsong voice. "Bunch of old blue shirts, bunch of old overall pants, bunch of playing cards with a string tied 'round, bottle rheumatiz medicine, bottle of hair tonic, bunch of wool socks."

"Will that hair tonic work?" asked the fat one.

"Bunch of underwear, bunch of pitcher postcards, good light bridle, good pair boots, six-seven pair spurs, three apples, three an a half mouth organs, one boiled shirt . . . ain't clean, old rumpled black necktie, two tired-out high collars, muzzle fer a dog, sewin' outfit in a candy box, gold medal fer ridin', two rat-traps . . . been used, bottle wolf poison, tin thing with a pitcher on it that goes over a stovepipe hole, medium size fryin' pan, skinnin' knife, long piece red ribbon, brush an' comb, bunch of all kinds pipes, one skin off a cat, cigarette papers, mantelpiece clock, about forty sacks Bull, colored pitcher of Niagara Falls, gob of beeswax, bunch of keys, couple dozen loose straps, bag of harness buckles . . . I dunno what this here is . . . two Jew's-harps, twisted-nail puzzle, shoe fer a mule, axe head, piece buckskin, mail order catalog, rattlesnake skin, string of silver *conchas*, sea shell, cigar box of nails, saddler's outfit, Injun pouch full of buttons, china hen's egg. . . ."

"No guns ner dynamite ner nothin'?"

"Nope. Not unless it's dynamite wrapped in this newspaper. Ain't though . . . it's railroad spikes. Extry hatband, curb chain, Spanish spade, double curb, hinge fer a door."

"No use goin' no further," said the fat man with the star, "the valise ain't his."

"Prob'ly stole it," Ed suggested.

"Most like. Not only that but stole it off some pore, dodderin' old man that didn't have good sense. Look at all that worthless junk. Cat skins! Hens' eggs! Useless to anybody not foolish in the head. Ain't you ashamed, now," he addressed Whiskers, "takin' the playthings away from some pore old has-been, prob'ly in his second or third childhood? What do you think yer representin' this time, anyway?"

Beck's old leather face had turned an angry maroon, but he swallowed his temper and answered mildly. It seemed to him that he smelled more *aguardiente* in the room than was accounted for by his own breath. "I'm a cabin boy on a ship," he growled.

The fat one suddenly dropped his ponderously playful attitude. His small gray eyes made a very fair attempt to gimlet Whiskers. "W'ere'd you leave your valise? An' your saddle bags? An' that sack?"

"Refuse to answer," said Beck, "on advice of counsel."

"This here's no laughin' matter," the other rumbled. "Them banditries of yours may be all very neat an' pleasant, but you've went jest a leetle too far. That man you killed happened to be the sheriff's brother. Now look here. You come clean with me an' tell me where the stuff is, an' I'll see that yuh get a fair, square trial. Nobody never made a mistake by comin' clean with Cap Walker. If I'm with you, you got a chance. If I'm against you, yo're in one hell of a fix, mister, an' don't you ferget it. Now you jest better. . . ."

"I don't know who you are, an' I don't give a damn!" said Whiskers. "That ain't all. You don't know who I am an' never seen me before in your life. Mark my words, you better be all-fired. . . ."

Walker waved an incredulous fat hand at Whiskers as he turned to Ed. "Would you believe it?" he demanded. "Jest because he's got some phoney w'iskers on he thinks he's in disguise or somethin'. Jest like we couldn't know him plain by his eyes, an' nose, an' build, an' clo'es. Why, feller, we knew you was comin' here, an' from w'ich way, an' w'en, before you ever started. Every Mex in the town was ready an' willin' to help us . . . they ain't forgot that Verdad affair, not by no means. Well, we'll jest have an end to his hidin' behind spinach, if that's what's holdin' the show back. Off they come!"

Tears of pain came to the old man's eyes—but the whiskers stayed. An amazed, unbelieving look spread over the fat man's whiskey-flushed face. It was followed by a new determination. Walker seized Whiskers's beard with both hands and jerked once, twice, three times, each time harder than before. Then he bent over Whiskers and minutely examined the beard at its roots. Finally he stepped back and sat down.

"Ed," he said wheezily, with the air of one flabbergasted, "they're real. This ain't him at all. We're jobbed, Ed, jest plain jobbed."

Then, suddenly, he swelled like a cinched *burro*. His brief eyebrows went up, his mouth opened, and he burst into soprano guffaws. Slowly, rustily at first, but with increasing celerity, the high cackling laughter poured from him. He rocked in his chair, his face reddened; the tears appeared on his cheeks, and he held himself with flipper-like hands, as if fearful that he would burst. Now and again the laughter subsided to exhausted giggles, only to break forth again in renewed roars.

"The look," he gasped at last, "on his . . . face!"

Laughter again, and more laughter, till he shook like a great weak hooped keg with a dog fight inside. The long lean young man viewed all with a uniform sadness. Whiskers, however, was boiling. The tip of his fan-like beard quivered, and on his forehead the veins stood rigid.

"Leave him . . . loose," gasped Walker at last.

Obediently the youth named Ed unlocked the handcuffs from the wrists of Whiskers Beck and put them in his pocket. Whiskers, his eyes quiet and gleaming now, studied the holstered Colt that sagged from the man's gun belt on the right, noted how the fat man with the star leaned limply against the wall, staying the last of his chuckles as best he could and wiping his eyes with his handkerchief. The young man stooped to unlock the chain shackles from Whiskers's legs. The lock snapped free.

With his right hand Whiskers pressed the man's head down as he brought his own knee up with all his strength. The bony old knee caught the other between the eyes, and he slumped. Beck's left hand had already gripped the butt of the gun at the young man's belt. He changed the gun to his right hand as he sprang across the room.

"Feel *that?*" he demanded, prodding the gun into the fat man's stomach. And the other let his own gun drop back into its holster as his arms went above his head. Whiskers disarmed him. "Now put the handcuffs on yore sorrowin' friend," he ordered harshly, "afore he wakes up. . . . That's good. Got another pair? Fine. Turn around an' stick yore hands back. Now we'll jest harness yore left leg to his left leg with these chain fixin's, so's yo're shore goin' to do a close lockstep if yuh come out of here with 'em on.

"Now, gents . . . I'm right sorry you ain't got no whiskers to pull.

An' I ain't got any paint, ner feathers an' m'lasses, to make you look any funnier'n you do now. So I guess I'll jest leave you here to think over how a pore, dodderin' old man that didn't have good sense come it over the two of you. It'll take three hours to file you two apart, so's I'll be on the train when you leave here. You better foller an' ketch me . . . so's we'll have some real fun explainin' in court how come the two of you was handcuffed an' left behind by a pore old feller without any weapons but two hands an' a knee. I'll leave your guns an' your keys with the ticket agent at the railroad. The tin star, though, I'm afeard I'll have to keep with the cat skin an' the china egg an' such like truck that don't mean nothin'. Now holler yore heads off gents . . . I'm leavin'!"

Mounted on a shaggy burro—the nearest thing to a horse that the village could produce—Whiskers Beck left San Juan. He disdained to fork his ignoble mount. He sat sidewise instead, like a man sitting on a log. That way he could better keep his feet from trailing on the ground. Behind followed a second burro, bearing a Mexican boy and Beck's valise.

"Maybe," said the boy as they plodded past the last house, "I should run back after a bottle of something to drink."

"Not much," said Whiskers, leisurely making a cigarette. He hitched one of his gun belts into a more comfortable position. "Can'tcha see I'm fleein' fer my life?"

As they drew away, Whiskers flung a leg over the burro's rump, so that he sat facing the tail. Here and there a golden light in San Juan was set like a jewel into the dark. Over the village the pitying night crouched low, concealing the scars of time. In the glow of the stars San Juan once more looked as it had many years ago, when its friendly houses beside the Pipestone were beautiful in the dusk. But Whiskers was undeceived.

"Peace!" he spat. "Quiet! Bah!"

# Ghost Town Trail

*Cherry Wilson*

*Although virtually unknown today, Cherry Wilson enjoyed a successful career as a Western writer for twenty years. She produced more than two hundred short stories and short novels, numerous serials, and five hardcover books, and six motion pictures were based on her fiction. Readers of* Western Story Magazine, *the highest paying of the Street & Smith publications where Wilson was a regular contributor, held her short stories in high regard. Wilson moved from Pennsylvania with her parents to the Pacific Northwest when she was sixteen. She led a nomadic life for many years and turned to writing fiction when her husband fell ill. Her first story out was accepted by* Western Story Magazine, *which began a long-standing professional relationship. If thematically Wilson's fiction is similar to B. M. Bower's, stylistically her stories are less episodic and, with growing experience, exhibit a greater maturity of sensibility. Her early work, especially, parallels Bower rather closely in that she developed a series of interconnected tales about a group of ranch hands. There is also a similar emphasis on male bonding and comedic scenes. Wilson stressed human relationships in preference to gun play and action. In fact, some of her best work can be found in those stories that deal with relationships between youngsters and men, as in her novel* Stormy *(Chelsea House, 1929) and short stories such as "Ghost Town Trail" which previously appeared only in* Western Story Magazine *(October 25, 1930).*

## I

"FLIGHT"

Thirty years have passed since the populace of Paradise went "down the hill." And the town—deep in the gulch cut by the swift waters of the Lost Friar—is like a despoiled woman that, grown old and shrunken and unbeautiful, persists in the wiles and artifices of wanton youth. Frowningly the somber spires of the Derelicts and their austere forests view the ghastly masquerade. The Top Notch Saloon, Blue

Moon, and Last Chance still invite with faded signs, though dust is their only offering. The Nugget Dance Hall, Nevada, and Red Front still lure with romantic promise, though only the dead memories of it are within their portals. The seedling ash on the grave of "Nevada" Zoe has grown into a stately thing of silver beauty that graciously shades much of God's Half Acre. Grass grows high in the street bordering the Lost Friar, and the wind makes a strangely human wail through shattered window and gaping door. Mountain marauders howl and prowl within the limits of the town. Yet Paradise is not abandoned!

Three men dwell there, lost among the ruins. The old-timer, Trig Gunnister, whose hand set the seedling ash, who has seen Paradise in birth and life and death. Steve Ross, the somber, loyal youth, for whom he peoples it—so realistically that Steve almost sees it, as Trig does in his "spells," roaring still. And the stranger, who after five years is still—"The Stranger."

No one ever comes to Paradise by actual design. There is no reason why anyone should come. Unless indeed one were curious to view this tomb of buried hopes—one more pitiful human sacrifice to the god of gold. And that incredible mountain grade—up which once toiled an endless string of freight teams to supply the needs of ten thousand citizens and down which was guarded the ransom of many a king in golden bullion—is now crevassed with the washouts of thirty springs and barricaded with the skeletons of pines that have fallen out of the ranks that march in an unbroken line from the dry wastes of Mormon Flats to the ultimate peak of the Derelicts and effectually discourage curiosity.

No one leaves Paradise except Steve. Old Trig has forgotten the world outside. The Stranger would be by the world forgotten—as Steve understands without the telling. And he makes no mention of him on his trips to Toroda where, with the fine gold all three have washed from the poor placer on the Lost Friar, he buys the few necessities of their simple life. So, amid the ruins of what was once the wildest gold camp in the wild Derelicts, they live and little dream that Steve, riding away on his monthly trip for supplies, will bring back instead that which Paradise most lacks—that which will be the death of one, the resurrection of the second, and to the third. . . .

The coppery sun was at its zenith when Steve rode down the last sharp turn of the spiraling mountain trail, and there, as far as eye could stretch, was the desert—the desert whose hot breath had reached him far up the Derelicts. Already his paint pony, Patch, was streaked with dust and sweat. And Jenny—the laziest, wiliest, contrariest old *burro* in seven states—was ready to give up the ghost. Not that this meant much. She usually was. Today the only weight she bore was that of the empty pack saddle and *alforjas*, but well she knew they would be filled on the way home, and being in no haste to burden herself she was lagging far behind.

Pulling up to wait for her, Steve viewed, with strangely eager gaze, that waste of alkali, sand, and sage that stretched north, south, and west. The season was not far advanced, and the sage was still purple, but already the land was like a smoking griddle—in heartbreaking contrast to Paradise with its coolness of lofty heights, of leafy trees, and rich, green grass. A remarkable contrast even for this part of the Southwest—a land of contrast.

But to Steve this purple desolation that would have inspired dread in most men was the gateway to—everything. Across it, twenty miles or so, lay Toroda, a lusty little mining city, the only town of which the boy had any personal knowledge and hence his port of dreams. He was wild to get to town, to be, even for a brief few hours, in the stream of life again. For he was too young and sane to be satisfied with ghosts, with dust that other men had raised, with only the vicarious memory of dead romance. The world called him. Its hunger was on him. His soul longed—and great the longing—for strife, not peace, for life—his own life, self-hewn.

"I want to plow my own furrow," he flared, fired to rare rebellion. "To buck things . . . like other men! To be in the swim! Up there"—his brooding gaze rose to the Derelicts—"that ain't livin'!" Then he remembered, and mutiny died within him. He could never go while. . . . Anyhow, he had these trips to Toroda. They broke the monotony, gave him something to look forward to, something to think over in the long silences. Anxious not to miss a moment of this, he swung impatiently about.

"You ol' slow poke!" he scolded the *burro* that had almost caught up. "Get a wiggle on you! We'll never get anywhere if...."

He saw then that Jenny had stopped and was contemplating the shimmering flats, staring curiously at something on them with unusual animation. Knowing that it took something pretty startling to interest her, Steve shaded his eyes against the sun glare and looked in the direction her long ears pointed, jerking suddenly erect as through the lifting heat veils, far down on the desert, he sighted a moving object—an object that his keen gaze speedily identified as someone on foot, a condition startling in itself in this isolated spot. With rising excitement, he made out that the figure was staggering under a heavy burden and on the verge of collapse. For, as he watched, it fell, rose with difficulty, and took a few reeling steps, only to fall again. This time it failed to rise.

Putting spurs to Patch, Steve raced down the last steep pitch and out on the scorching flats. Slashing through the chaparral that was in places matted and almost impenetrable, he reached the spot where he estimated the figure had vanished but found nothing there. Quickly he beat the sage about with the same result. Had his eyes tricked him? No!—both he and Jenny could not be mistaken.

Widening his search, he came unexpectedly on a dry, shallow wash cut by spring torrents and overgrown with sage. Forcing the paint along its crumbling bank, he was suddenly all but unseated as Patch, with a snort of terror, pitched wildly back. Leaping down, Steve pushed through the matted brush. It was there that his search was ended. For there, in the purple sage almost beneath him, face up to the grueling sun, lay a woman, a young woman—scarcely more than a girl. Her still, sweet face—so white in contrast to the black cloud of her hair—was resolute and revealing of the courage that had kept her going until she dropped. Her dark-blue suit and white blouse—of a texture and cut that marked her, even to Steve's inexperienced eyes, as alien to these parts—were torn by the clutching hands of the chaparral. Proof that she had come through it fast and far—as were her shoes—small wrecks upon her feet. Strangely, though she was unconscious and his survey brief, everything about her suggested to Steve blind, hysterical flight.

Eclipsing his shock to find a woman here, miles from anywhere, he saw the burden she had fainted under—a girl of three or four who clung to her, sobbing: "Mamma! Mamma!"

She shrunk like a frightened fawn as Steve sank down, canteen in his hand, but the instant he spoke, she knew him for a friend and instinctively turned to him for help, piteously telling him: "Mamma won't get up!"

Steve feared she never would—so still and white she was. But he forced a cheerful grin, assuring the baby in his pleasant drawl: "Don't cry! We'll have her well in a jiffy."

Lifting the woman's head, he forced some water between her lips and let it trickle slowly upon her wrists. Wetting his bandanna, he bathed her temples. Then, perceiving signs of returning life, he moved her to a more comfortable position in the meager shade of the sage. Removing her jacket to pillow her head, he noticed that the slender gold chain she wore, holding a small, square locket, had caught in her hair and was tightly drawn across her throat. He loosened it and then turned his attention to the child, relieved to find, when she had drunk thirstily from the canteen, that nothing was the matter with her except fatigue and anxiety about her mother.

"She's tired," the tot reproached herself as Steve bent over the unconscious woman, fanning her with his broad hat. "She carried me. I couldn't walk so much."

Troubled as he was, Steve smiled at that. And there was awe in his eyes regarding her—standing by his knee, gazing up at him trustingly, her big blue eyes all friendliness, her little head a mass of pale-gold ringlets. For he had never been so near a child before. And he was almost afraid to touch her lest she dissolve like the fragile webs mist weaves between wet leaves, or as the petals of a rose fall at a breath. Who was she? Where was she from? He ached with questions but was too much the man to ask her one. The mother was awakening. She would tell.

With a throb of joy Steve saw her eyes open—eyes black as the skies that roofed Lost Friar gulch before the moon came up when only the starshine lit it, big, luminous eyes. He was to his horror filled with fear as they fixed on him, with great, gripping terror that lost its worst intensity when she saw the baby and caught it to her fiercely. Awkwardly Steve tried to reassure her.

"Don't worry. I was just passin' by on my way to town when I saw you. I'm Steve Ross. I'll see you through."

Her black eyes came back to his honest, boyish face, staring and speechless. She made no effort to tell him who she was, or how she came to be here on the long-forgotten Lost Friar Trail. Steve had the curious conviction that she would never tell.

"Take it easy," he advised her. "An' when you're able to travel, I'll take you on to Toroda."

To his dismay that light of terror leaped into her eyes again. "No! No!" she almost screamed, struggling to her knees, clutching the child as if to run.

"I mean," quickly Steve corrected, putting out a restraining hand, "I'll take you wherever you was goin'. Toroda's the only town around, so. . . ."

She fell back from weakness, crying distractedly: "I'm not going any place."

Blankly the boy stared at her. "But you can't stay here," he said, smiling to show he knew she didn't mean that. "There ain't even a ranch for miles . . . barrin' Fool's Acres, an' it's been abandoned for years. Even the buildings are burned down."

She said hopelessly: "So I found," and flashed him a startled glance, as if it were a slip.

But Steve was slow to catch the significance, insisting: "You must let me take you to your home . . . or wherever you came from . . . ?"

The baby put in helpfully: "We came on the choo-choo!"

The train! Suddenly Steve remembered that the railroad crossed Mormon Flats, twenty miles south. But there were no stops. As suddenly he remembered Drake's Tanks! Trains stopped there for water. Had she eluded the crew—who would not be apt to let a woman and a baby off in the desert—and deliberately lost herself in the chaparral? Had she walked the twenty miles from there? For he quickly recalled that she had been to Fool's Acres, several miles beyond. It seemed incredible. Yet the boy knew by her alarm and the quick way she hushed the child that it was true. What was she running from, what terror great enough to drive her to what might have been the death of both of them had he not come along? He thanked heaven he had come. He could take them to safety—to some distant place since she objected to Toroda.

She seemed to read his mind, for bending toward him, laying a hand on his in her earnestness, she said in a determinedly calm voice: "I'm grateful, Steve Ross. But the greatest kindness you can do us is . . . to leave us here!"

Leave them! Steve was stunned. "But can't you see," he protested wildly, "that's the one thing I can't do? It ain't safe! You're strange here. You're used up . . . sick! You'd starve if. . . ."

"I'm hun-gry," whimpered the little one.

The mother turned her face aside with a moan. And Steve, recalling the lunch he had brought along, sprang up and got it out of his saddle bag. Returning, he pressed it on the woman.

"It ain't much"—he apologized, afraid it wasn't good enough for them—"just biscuits an' fried grouse."

"It's manna in the wilderness." Her low-voiced gratitude made him flush.

"It's good!" proclaimed the tiny, blue-eyed miss, happy with a sandwich. "And you're good, too. I hope you stay with us all the time."

Steve's flush deepened. "I hope I can, till. . . ."

"You're kind," said the woman earnestly, her dark gaze fully on his, "and I'm making a poor return. I can't explain. I can't even tell you my name. I can only ask . . . I must insist . . . that you leave us, and . . . forget this meeting."

"But . . . ?"

"Please!" She gave him her hand, and there was in the act finality that checked Steve's protests, gave him no choice. He could not force himself on them. Neither could he take them by force.

Yet he knew, as he mounted Patch and rode away, that he could not leave them. He decided to round up Jenny and give the woman time to collect herself. Surely she would not refuse his help when she realized her plight.

He found the old *burro* hunting Patch, actually trotting to meet him as he rode up in sight. But he kept on until he was some distance from the wash, and there, dismounting, leaned against a boulder to think over his predicament. How could he stay against her will? What could she do, if he rode away as she asked him to? There was no place for her to go. Yet she must have had some place in mind when she got off the train.

Steve remembered again that she had been to Fool's Acres, that she had known the ranch by name when he mentioned it. Then she was not—it occurred to him in a flash—a total stranger to this country. Yet it was ridiculous to suppose Fool's Acres could have been her destination. The ranch had burned years ago, and the queer old desert rat, Ike Ware, who had tried to make the desert pocket blossom from the stagnant water hole there, had long ago starved out and disappeared, his folly wiped from all but the memory of man. Was it this discovery that had stampeded her? No—for Steve could not shake the feeling that she was fleeing from some human menace. And her plight was nonetheless desperate.

His worried gaze went back to the spot where he had left them. From here he could not see them; he could only see the withering desolation, the blinding heat veils lifting, and, in the shimmering blue above, a vulture sluggishly sailing. Black dread fell upon him, and the strained murmur broke from his lips: "She don't realize! She's scared ... loco. I can't go!"

## II
### "TO PARADISE"

Riding back, determined to beg her to accept his help for the child's sake, he found the baby fast asleep, her curly head in her mother's lap, and the woman, to his great relief, looking better, stronger. She had arranged her dress, smoothed her dark hair into some kind of order. Her eyes had a calmer light and her cheeks some color. She seemed singularly unsurprised to see him.

"It's no use," cried Steve, sliding down, "I know this country better than you do. If you won't let me take you away, then . . . I've got to stay."

Abruptly she asked: "Are you from Toroda?"

Astonished by the dread with which she spoke the name, Steve said: "No. I'm from Paradise." He waved toward the hills. "Up there . . . just about five miles."

Her face lighted—with hope, he would have sworn! And he fancied her voice reproached him as she began: "But you said there was no town. . . ."

"It ain't a town exactly," Steve explained, dropping down beside her, thoughtfully turning his sombrero on his knee. "It used to be one, but. . . ."

"A ghost camp?"

He was amazed by her eagerness. "I guess that's what you'd call it," he admitted. "But," grinning at the thought, "ol' Trig would give me plenty if he heard me call it that."

"Trig?" Quickly she caught him up. "Who is he?"

"The oldest inhabitant," said Steve, far too relieved that she was not sending him right off to wonder at her strange interest in Paradise. "He came in with the stampede thirty years back an' stayed when the rest left, because . . . well, he hated to leave Zoe, I guess. An' then . . . I reckon he just forgot to go. When I first come, he used to talk a heap about how the camp would come back bigger than ever. He's still prospectin' for the mother lode he swears is there. But of late he gets spells when he thinks Paradise is like it was in boom times . . . when he sees his old friends and visits with them."

"You mean . . . ?" Her eyes were full of pity.

"He ain't crazy," said Steve stoutly. "He's just queer on that point . . . an', yeah, one other thing. He's jealous of Paradise. Once in a blue moon someone drifts in there by accident, an' Trig goes wild. Just last fall, comin' back from Toroda, I met a huntin' party on the trail riled up considerable. They'd stumbled on the town an' swore someone up there had took pot shots at 'em. I found Trig in one of his spells. He couldn't tell me a thing. But there was smoke in his gun."

"But he let you stay!" she exclaimed—exactly as if they were arguing something and she had scored a point.

"That," Steve slowly owned, "is different. You see. . . ." His eyes fell, and he rooted a boot heel in the sandy soil. "You see, Trig took me there. I was raised up on the Lost Friar. My dad was a trapper. I don't recollect my mother. Dad was caught in a snowslide when I was ten. I struck out over the mountains to get help . . . though it was too late for Dad . . . an' I got lost. Trig found me . . . an ace this side of kingdom come. That was exactly thirteen years ago. I've been with him ever since."

Then he was twenty-three. A year older than she. Surprised for she had felt ages the oldest, she studied him with new interest, seeing a slim, lithe figure dressed in a blue cotton shirt and overalls cinched at the waist by a six-inch riding belt. His hair was tawny and unruly as a schoolboy's. His lean, tanned face was strong, and there was in it a restraint that seemed to hide some nameless hunger. His blue-gray eyes were shy and kind and wistful, as if the hunger were soul deep and they reflected it. He was not good looking, she concluded, in the accepted sense of the word, but—he looked good, as, indeed, she knew he was. And she thought of him, with all his life before him, becalmed in the stagnant backwash of the ghost camp.

"It must be lonely for you," she ventured softly.

"Some," Steve owned readily.

"But you can leave."

"Sure." He admitted that, too. "But I won't. Trig took care of me when I needed him. Now he needs someone to look after him. He'd die away from there. An' I can't leave him with The Stranger."

He saw the unspoken question in her eyes and answered it, telling things he had never mentioned with no more thought than he would turn them over in his own heart. "That's what we call the third an' last citizen. He drifted in one sundown, five years back, an' throwed his pack in one of the cabins. He must have thought it was a sure-enough ghost camp, for he was scared bad when his light put Trig on the warpath an' me an' him went up. 'Who are you?' he kind of gasped, cowerin' back, plumb white. 'I'm half the population!' Trig said, mighty cold. 'An' now you'd best explain yourself!' An' the fellow said, sad-like, after a while: 'I'm just . . . a stranger. A stranger to you . . . to all who know me. A stranger to myself. Just a stranger within your gates who asks sanctuary.' I held my breath, watchin' Trig. An' pretty soon he says: 'Waal, there's room I guess. Your kind ain't no stranger to Paradise.' "

"Trig let him stay!" she pointed out in that same triumph.

"Yeah," nodded Steve, "an' he's still The Stranger to us. We don't see much of him. He lives at the other end of town, an' he's the solitary kind. Friendly enough when you meet him, but he don't go out of his way to meet anyone. He . . . he ain't like Trig an' me. He's been somebody. Talks like a book an' don't let himself go slack. I don't reckon I ever seen a finer-lookin' man. You can tell he's been places."

Idly, to cover the wild thought in her heart, she mused: "A man of mystery," giving Steve the first faint pang of agony that was to live with him. "He sounds interesting. Why do you think he came?"

"I think," replied Steve soberly, "he's died, an' he's buried himself alive in Paradise."

Silence fell upon them both. A fiery breeze swept through the sage, flinging its fragrance over them, filling the air with its murmuring.

Said the mother, her eyes bent on the little sleeper, thoughtfully toying with a silken ringlet: "You spoke of a woman . . . Zoe?"

"Zoe," Steve explained, and she noticed how gentle his voice became, "was a dance-hall girl. She came in with the rush. The prettiest girl at the Nevada House. Ol' Trig . . . he was young then . . . loved her. She died before the camp did, an' is buried up there. It's queer but, when Trig gets one of his spells, he thinks she's livin' an' is sweethearts with him still."

She lifted her dark eyes to the Derelicts, her girlish face growing yet more resolute. Swiftly she turned to Steve, asking in stark appeal: "Will you take me there?"

He cried, startled: "Where?"

"To . . . Paradise?"

Madly his heart beat at the thought. To take her there—how that would alter everything! But as quickly he pushed the thought from him. "You don't savvy! It's no place for a woman. There's no one there . . . just men."

"Just men!" she echoed with strange intensity. "Tell me, is there any better place for a woman in trouble to be than with men?" And before he could reply, she hurried on: "You will take us . . . baby and me. And Trig will give two more strangers sanctuary."

Her appeal struck deeply into his soul, but desperately as he wanted to, he dared not, fearing what old Trig might do.

"I must go," she begged, "not to bury myself . . . no!" Her black eyes flashed. "But to rest . . . to get my courage back. Get strength to do . . . the terrible thing I must! Will you take me, Steve Ross?"

And he, who would have died for her even then, recklessly whispered: "Yes."

He put her on his horse, placing the baby, who she jealously refused to let him carry, in her arms. And himself on the old *burro,* they set off, slowly climbing that incredible grade to Paradise. Foot by foot Steve's fear grew on him. Trig . . . ? He hadn't told her half. Danger might surround her there. But a thousand dangers menaced her here. And there he could guard her—stand between her and trouble.

The sun had just gone down when they entered the dead town. The sky was a fiery lake above. Each austere pine and crag was dyed in its crimson flood. It cast over the ruined buildings a transient, lifelike blush. Their hoofbeats, grass muffled, seemed nevertheless to ring irreverence as they passed The Stranger's cabin, the Nevada House— where once, fairest of them all, Zoe had danced—and on, block on dead block. But nearing the cabin at the farther end, where lived the oldest inhabitant, Steve protectingly forced the burro in advance. He was keyed to expect anything when the sound of his return presently brought Trig running into the street, to stand stricken, his white hair blowing, his warped frame miraculously straightening, his old eyes rapturously staring at the woman riding toward him, wearily weaving, her dark head bent above her burden.

He stared till she was near him. Then he tottered forward, crying with piercing joy: "Zoe!" He cried again, stopping the mustang: "Zoe!"

As slowly she raised her weary head, old Trig lifted a trembling hand to touch her cheek. And Steve, watching in suspense—though sick with the pity of it—was glad that Trig was in one of his spells that he received her so. Tears sprang in his eyes as he heard the old

man beg: "You can't go on like this! You look bad. Zoe, you're tired
. . . sick! Won't you quit the Nevada . . . let me take care of you?"

Then, in Steve's blurred vision, the figures ran together. Would
she understand? Would she play up to his delusion?

"I'm tired," he dimly heard her say. "Please . . . take care of me."

Together they started toward the cabin. Trig, supporting her,
seemed to notice for the first time the child in her arms. "Zoe," and
he stopped short, "who's that?"

Instantly on the defensive she drew away from him. "It's Jacqueline," she said.

"Jac-queline?" faltered Twig, touching a golden ringlet with a finger tip. "Jack? Waal, there's room, I guess."

Letting them enter the place alone, feeling a delicacy about intruding, as if there was something sacred in this meeting, Steve turned
back to unsaddle Patch and wait another day to make the trip to
Toroda. He was bending to the cinch when something drew his gaze,
and he saw that which gave him no less shock than when he had found
the woman in the chaparral.

There, between the buildings, staring at the door through which
she had passed—with the look of one who sees a ghost, the anguish
of one who sees a loved one pass into the tomb—was The Stranger.
Steve had only a fleeting glimpse, for as his eyes recorded that expression forever upon his mind, The Stranger vanished.

### III

#### "I KNOW HER!"

To Steve, also, she was Zoe. Her first night there, seeing that he
was at a loss how to address her, she said with a sad smile: "Call me
Zoe." And the name suited her so well that Steve almost forgot she
had any other.

He had, however, few occasions to address her in that first week.
For exhausted, sick from he knew not what awful trials and fears, she
kept to her own quarters—the cabin he had fitted up for her near the
one in which he lived with Trig. It had been in a fair state of pres-

ervation and, with the best of the battered furnishings left behind in the exodus, it was made surprisingly snug and home-like.

Coming out of it the second morning after her arrival, as Steve was saddling Patch in the deserted, sun-lit street for the delayed trip to Toroda—and, for the first time in his life, loath to go—she gave him a list of things to buy in town and a bill of astonishingly large denomination from which to purchase them. She hesitated then, as if she would make one more request but found it difficult. He waited, thrilling to see her here—so out of place in this scene of ruin yet somehow belonging to it. She had repaired the ravages to her dress. Her white crêpe blouse was daintily fresh, her short blue skirt carefully mended. But watching her—a slight and gallant figure standing so straight before him in those little wrecks of shoes, bravely trying to tell him something—Steve knew that the grief and fear that had inspired her mad flight through the chaparral had pursued her here.

Gently he asked: "What is it, Zoe?"

"That list. . . ." Nervously she twisted the locket gleaming against the white frill on her breast. "There are articles on it . . . things for baby and me. Steve, some question may be raised in Toroda. You may be asked about the woman in Paradise."

He hastened to set her mind at rest. "I'll be careful, Zoe. I'll buy around. I promise you nobody will ever find out anything from me."

Her heartfelt "God bless you, Steve!" sang in his heart all the way to Toroda and back. Nor in that week did he learn more about her former life. One happening had a bearing on it but added to the mystery. This had transpired the night she came. He had made the child and her as comfortable as he could with the means at hand. Then, disturbed by The Stranger's odd behavior, haunted by his look of horror when he had seen her, Steve had gone to his cabin, hoping for some explanation. But he was not in, nor could Steve find him anywhere about the town. This in itself was strange, for there was no place for him to go but the hills and nothing to call him there after nightfall.

Returning to his own cabin, Steve sat down on the porch, shaded even from the moonlight by wild morning-glory vines, fact and fancy running riot in his mind. Old Trig sat beside him, smoking. Both gazed silently down upon the moldering form of the once-live town, unutterably weird and lonely under those soaring, sable hills and flickering mountain stars, with the Lost Friar flashing in its many windings, mournfully babbling of what had been. Here and there through the ruins bats darkly flitted, and the night wind, which seemed to blow here with a strange chill setting every unfettered door a-creaking on its rusty hinges, filled the air with a strange moaning. Shadows filled the street before them, as if the old ghosts of the dead past stirred again, shadows that to Trig had human form and tongue, for his delusion was still strong upon him.

"Zoe's sleepin'?" he suddenly flung into the silence.

Steve's gaze crossed to the darkened cabin, and he said, as one humors a child: "Yes, Trig. She's tired, you know."

"She gets no rest!" fretted the old man. "She looks bad, Steve. She coughs. Dancin', dancin' . . . bits of her life! Dancin' herself to death! I keep tellin' her she's got to quit."

"She's quit," Steve soothed him. "Don't you recollect how she came? Why, you helped me fix her cabin. She's sleepin' there . . . with little Jack."

The old man relaxed in his chair. "That's so," he muttered. "I was afeered, though. I was afeered she'd gone back to the Nevada." Tensely he peered through the dark at Steve in pathetic hope of reassurance. "She's goin' to stay, ain't she, boy?"

"She's goin' to stay," Steve told him. But he remembered with a pang that she was just staying until she got rested, got her strength back, got her nerve up to do—what? What terrible thing did Zoe have to do?

A long silence ensued. Then Trig got slowly to his feet, saying, his gaze once more on the dark street: "The ol' camp's uncommon quiet tonight."

"Yeah," Steve replied but never had it seemed less so. Other nights he had sat here, listening to that moaning, thinking he would go mad—hearing the world calling. But tonight Paradise seemed to hold everything in all the world, to be a world complete. Its very loneliness seemed sweet.

"Nobody's out," Trig mused. "The games must be runnin' high."

And presently, knocking the ashes from his pipe, he pocketed it with the remark he had made every night of his life: "Reckon I'll take a *pasear* downtown an' see what's goin' on."

Moodily Steve watched him shuffling down the dead, dark blocks, pausing at times as if to greet some friend, passing in and out of the empty buildings and on, until he was a shadow no more corporeal than the rest. Every night since he had come here, a boy of ten, Steve had seen Trig make the round. At first as a watchman might, loyally standing guard over the property of friends whom he firmly believed would some day return. Doubtless it was from this fierce sense of responsibility to them that his jealousy of Paradise arose. Now—he was just another ghost. Would he—Steve wondered of himself—in time get queer and see things that were not here? When Zoe was gone—would he see her?

His heart leaped as a light step fell beside him on the porch. He half started up, sure that she had been unable to sleep and that the night had lured her out, but it was The Stranger standing there! A tall, straight, handsome fellow of thirty or thereabouts, with that in his bearing—that air of reserve, poise—which brands a man who has "been places and seen things." But now, as he fell into Trig's chair and leaned forward, his dark eyes on the ghostly scene, his guard was down. Steve was shaken to see him as when he had stared at Zoe a few hours ago and was more shaken when, without the slightest warning, the man turned fiercely on him, hoarsely crying: "In heaven's name, Steve, don't keep me in suspense! Where did you meet her? Why did she come?"

The desperate appeal tied Steve's tongue. It was as if a dying man asked life of him. Seeing it, The Stranger pleaded in a calmer tone: "Tell me, Steve."

Because this man, no less than Trig and himself, would have Zoe and Jacqueline in his keeping, Steve told him everything from the instant he sighted them on Mormon Flats. He was amazed by the awful thirst with which The Stranger drank in every word, his baffled look when all was said, and his inability to believe that it *was* all. "She told you nothing?" he persisted.

"Just that she was in trouble. I think she meant to stop at Fool's

Acres but, findin' it gone, she lost her head and tried to hide in the desert. She's runnin' away from something. Something she's afraid will come. I've got the feelin' it threatens the baby . . . she worships it . . . an' I can't imagine her bein' afraid for herself. But," Steve added gravely, "that's just a guess."

"And a good one," declared The Stranger queerly. "For she's. . . ." A ghastly look overspread his face, and he cried in a strangled voice: "Here . . . alone. What can it mean?"

Leaping to a wild thought, Steve grasped his arm. "You know her?"

He felt the spasm that went through the tall frame. He would know in time how worse than cruel that sudden query had been. Even now remorse touched him, and his hand fell away. But he got his reply—low, unsteadily. "Yes," The Stranger said, startling Steve by the suffering his dark face revealed, "yes," he repeated with a hopeless gesture, "I know her." As the boy sat silently, his brain whirling with this complication, the man said again. "But I swear, Steve, I've no more idea than you of what would bring her. Steve"—he shot this at his companion—"does she know I'm here?"

The boy nodded. "Yes, I told her that. . . ."

"What?" was the hoarse demand. "What did you tell her about me?"

"Why"—Steve was dumbfounded—"I told her there was another man here whom we called The Stranger."

"Of course!" exclaimed the man with a long-drawn breath, "of course, that's all you knew to tell. And that's all she must know of me, until. . . ." Abruptly pushing back his chair, he got up and paced back and forth on the dark porch. "Steve," he said, suddenly stopping by him, "you've known me long."

"Five years," Steve told him.

"Five years!" echoed the man, as if it were his first reckoning of the time. "Five years . . . eternity! Five years I've been shut up in this sepulcher. Five years of intimate contact with you and Trig, yet not once have either of you asked . . . or hinted . . . why I stay here."

"It's none of our business."

"Perhaps not." A dry smile curved The Stranger's lips. "Still, I wonder how many men would respect that? You must have some natural curiosity. You must have guessed there was a good cause. Trig stays here by choice. You're chained by your very loyalty. You must know I stay of necessity. A dozen times I've had it on my tongue to tell you, but, aside from lightening the load on my heart, it would have done no good. Tonight, when it might do good, when I ought to tell . . . I can't. Not until we know why she came." He fell to pacing again. Somberly Steve watched him, troubled, oppressed by a heavy sense of black foreboding. Every shock of the fateful day was multiplied as bluntly the man announced: "Steve, I'm leaving Paradise."

"Leavin'?" the boy cried in astonishment.

"Yes . . . tonight. Steve, if she wonders at The Stranger's absence, tell her. . . ." Grimly, bitterly, in agony, his lips set. "Tell her I've gone on a . . . prospecting trip." For a long time then he did not speak. He just stood, his gaze fixed on the moonlit ruins. Steve waited, the tension growing. His heart leaped when, with a prophetic ring, the slow words came: "Steve, something tells me trouble is rolling down on Paradise."

A tingling crept along Steve's veins. "Account of her?" he asked.

"Because of her, Steve! And if it does . . . if anything happens before I get back . . . Steve, I'm trusting you to look out for . . . Zoe."

Tense, the boy promised: "I'll do my best."

"And remember this," insisted The Stranger, "whatever comes, however it looks at the time, stand by her . . . for she's in the right."

"She don't have to be!" cried Steve.

Again that ghost of a smile crossed The Stranger's face. "But she will be, Steve, because . . . she couldn't be otherwise. And it may help, when things get hot, to know you're in the right."

And it did help when the time came.

Long after The Stranger had gone, Steve sat on, waiting for Trig to come in, and in far, far greater confusion. The Stranger had known Zoe—loved her. Anybody could see that. But instead of rushing to her, when she came in trouble, he was running away. Why? Steve thought of every possible reason, but nothing came of all his thinking but the fierce, sweet joy that he, alone, was to be her protector if trouble came.

As surely as trouble was coming to Paradise, the sun rose that dawn. Just as its first rays touched the eastern crags, Steve was roughly awakened by old Trig—already dressed, his withered face suffused with wrath—bending over his bunk, shaking him. "Steve," he demanded wildly, "who's the woman in Pierson's cabin?"

## IV
### "GONE!"

It is doubtful if old Trig ever got Zoe's status straight. Steve realized all at once just how hazy his mind had become. There had been nothing before by which to measure it. The humdrum affairs of the camp, Trig's placering and prospecting, were so much matters of routine and habit that they required little mental effort. But his inability to grasp this new element that had intruded into his life proved how sadly he had failed in the five years since The Stranger's coming.

Steve was able to allay his wrath, to make him understand—for the time, at least—Zoe's claim upon them, but he was always getting her identity confused. Sometimes she was the Pierson girl come back. Sometimes she was his own Zoe, who slept beneath the silver ash. And sometimes he would look at Steve in pathetic bewilderment, as if he knew he ought to know, and ask: "Steve, who is that woman?" When the boy explained, the old man would say: "That's so. We've got to look out for her." But the baby . . . cloudy his mind, or clear, he had no doubt about her. From the instant he first laid a hand upon her curly head, he was her slave. On her he lavished the thwarted love of his lonely life. He could do nothing unless the child was with him. And she was with him most of the time since that morning following her coming when Steve, carrying breakfast to Zoe's cabin, brought Jacqueline back with him, and she had toddled over the sill, straight into old Trig's arms.

There was something in the picture they made together that brought a lump to Steve's throat, something fitting, poignant—beautiful. Both were frail—but with such a difference. The child with the first flush of strength, the old man with the shadow of it. There was an equality of mind as tragic—she with the unfolding of intelligence, he with only its fading remnants. Together they would set off down the grass-grown street, old Trig with his white bent head, Jacqueline in tiny blue overalls and sandals, her hand firmly clasped in his. Everything they saw evoked in Trig a memory, and he would picture it all for her, as he had for Steve, so realistically that she could almost see.

Right here—in the Blue Moon door—Sheriff Gans had tried to arrest Long Hank, a gun toter from Tombstone and Hank, not being in the mood for incarceration, had made Gans eat the warrant. You bet! Right down like a flapjack. And here—among the crumbling huts and underground warrens of old Chinatown—was the laundry of Yup See who owed his life to Keno's oratory. Keno was a gambler of much sartorial elegance and Yup's best patron. Keno had saved Yup when the boys were all set to hoist him for a minor transgression by a speech that "wrung men's hearts out in tears." Who would do his shirts up? Who could starch a cuff or "stiff a bosom" like Yup? And wasn't cleanliness next to godliness? Must he be as ungodly, draggle-tailed as the rest?

Here—from this old bridge—the maverick offspring of a proud earl of England had committed his sinful being to the stream, sparing his titled kin more remittances and shame. And here—in the Grand Hotel—was where Dan Graw staged his jamboree when he struck pay ore, and an elegant time was had by all. Tales upon tales he told her of the time when the lusty young city on the Lost Friar was roaring its post-natal squalls, when the great stamp mills clacked day and night, when the mountains shook to heavy blasts and drills bored into their very hearts—tales to which the child listened in wide-eyed wonder for, though they were for the most part beyond her comprehension, she was excited by Trig's excitement as he relived them.

Sometimes, returning, they would come to rest beside the mound beneath the silver ash. And he would tell her about that other Zoe, who had danced to doom so long ago. And little Jack's bright face would cloud in sympathy. They spent days in the hills, seeking the lost ledge. Her faith was as strong as his. Gravely she would tell him: "It's somewhere, Trig," and he would assure her with the confidence that had not wavered in thirty years: "As sure as there's balm in Gilead."

She would look about, pointing: "I'll bet it's there . . . under that big wock."

Seriously, as if he were seeking water and that rosy finger were the forked willow branch inclining toward it, Trig would pry up the rock with his pick and prod about, deciding at last with unshaken faith: "I reckon the Lord hid it for us in a safer place."

Her blue eyes would lift to the Derelicts. "I bet He hid it 'way, 'way up."

So they sought their pot of gold under the rainbow and, when home, she chattered of leads and drifts and stringers like any old sourdough. Steve wondered how Zoe could stand this encroachment on the child's affection, the separation—remembering how jealously she had refused to yield the baby to him, even for the trip here. One forenoon while standing with her before the morning-glory vines—where all the little, white, pink-striped bells were open, swinging—watching the old man teaching Jacqueline to ride on the old *burro* that, though stubborn, was gentle as a kitten, Steve expressed something of his wonder.

"She's safe with him, isn't she?" Zoe asked.

"As can be," Steve said quickly. "Safer than with you or me. He's more watchful. Heaven help anyone who offered harm to her! But I meant you . . . I'd think you'd miss her."

Her glance went to the baby now—gaily pummeling old Jenny, who had balked, entreating Trig between shrieks of glee to "push her"—and she said: "I do miss her, Steve. But it's part of what I've got to do. And the hurt steels me to do the rest."

This sharply reminded Steve that her stay was temporary and brought back The Stranger's premonition, two things that he had forgotten in the peaceful days that had passed—the red letter days of Steve's life when Paradise sure enough was heaven. For a week Zoe had stayed in seclusion. Then she had emerged to join them on the porch of evenings or at the river where they were placering. Here she would sit for hours, her dark eyes moodily fixed on the swirling water in the sluices, saying little, deeply thinking. And sometimes Steve would surprise her eyes on Jacqueline with that gripping terror in them and would remark the hungry way she caught the child to her, the defiance and resolution on her face at these times. Wild as he was to know what she resolved, or what defied, he did not ask. And when the little chatterbox touched on subjects that might reveal either, he was as quick to divert her mind when Zoe was absent as when she was there. He was rewarded for his consideration by the ease she came to show in their presence. Long ago he had explained The Stranger's absence—saying, as he had been bidden, that the man had gone on a prospecting trip—and neither mentioned him again.

Sometimes with Steve, more often alone, she went on long tramps, or struck off into the hills on Brownie, the mustang which Steve kept as a second horse and relegated to her use. To Steve's surprise she could ride like a cowgirl and was an expert shot with pistol or rifle. In fact, there were few tricks of woodcraft he could teach her.

"And I thought you was a tenderfoot!" he exclaimed one time when she brought down a hawk on the wing.

"It was just a lucky shot."

Steve shook his head. "It happens too often to be luck," he said. "It makes me feel cheap . . . me so sure you'd get lost that day. And you trailwise as. . . ."

"But I was lost," she told him. "Not in the sense you mean, but . . . *lost!*"

There were times when she forgot the fear that haunted her and laughed with Steve like a happy, careless girl. And there was the time when Steve forgot she was not that. When, drawn by her sympathy— excusably, for he had known such dearth of it—he showed her all his heart. How discontented he had been. How wild to be out in the world and doing. But he would not go and leave Trig. He reckoned it was mean of him even to think of it.

"It's natural," Zoe said warmly. "And it's wonderful of you to stay. You'll be paid, Steve. It will all work out. Some people believe that everyone is in his rightful place. Perhaps God keeps you here for a purpose. Who knows?" A little smile curved her lips. "They say, Steve, that all things come to him who waits."

Huskily then the boy blurted: "It's true . . . you came!"

Her dark glance met his like an unhoped-for caress, setting his blood aflame. Then Jacqueline was between them, and the flame was quenched. For Steve remembered that Zoe could never be anything to him but—a friend. He must halter this feeling that was running away with him. More marked from then was his look of restraint.

What next passed between them was more typical of all their conversations. They were standing on the bald mountain spur above the old stamp mill. It had come to be a favorite spot with Zoe. Day after day she climbed up here, studying for hours on end the panorama stretched below—not Lost Friar Gulch but west, down over the foothills to the desert that stretched and stretched. She was as lost in silent contemplation of it as Steve was in her. She was wearing the garments he had brought her from Toroda. A gray shirt, open at the throat, with sleeves rolled to the elbows, khaki riding breeches, stout shoes that laced to the knee, and a boy's sombrero. Yet, somehow, she contrived to look in this rough dress even more dainty and sweet by contrast. The bracing air of the Derelicts, the exercise, had done wonders for her. Steve noticed the rich bloom in her cheeks almost with regret. When she got her strength back. . . .

"Steve," she pointed, "what's that dark smudge?"

He looked down over the flats, burning in the July sun, marveling at her length of vision. "That's Poplar Springs."

"How far is it from Toroda?"

"Ten-twelve miles." Why was she always asking questions like that? Mapping the whole country in her mind?

"There's something beyond the springs . . . a little south of those dunes. Is it rocks or buildings, Steve?"

"Why, that's Fool's Acres! What's left of it . . . outbuildings and corrals." He waited, half expecting some explanation now.

But she only said "Oh!" And presently: "You say the Toroda road crosses the Derelicts just ten miles south?"

"Yes, Zoe." Why did she want to know? Every time he came up here she questioned him. And of evenings, when ghosts walked in Paradise and the air was filled with that moaning, and the four inhabitants were gathered on the porch, the baby dozing in old Trig's arms, she would continue to ply him with questions, getting the location of every landmark in the country—every trail and ranch and water hole and the distances between—firmly in her mind. Steve knew she was planning something and, in worrying about what it was, he forgot to worry about anything that might arise out of her past. He felt the shadows gathering black about her and wished with all his heart that The Stranger would return.

One night, three weeks after her coming, he awoke in a cold perspiration with the feeling of uneasiness so strong upon him that he resolved to throw delicacy to the wind and beg her to tell him what this fear was that was haunting her, and what she must do to lay it or to let him do it. And then—it was too late for anything. For, while he was at breakfast with Trig, Jacqueline walked in, still in her little nightgown, her sunny head tousled from her bed, her blue eyes woefully perplexed.

"I've come to live with you," she said, stunning them, "till Mamma comes home."

A shock ran through Steve, as though that avalanche of trouble The Stranger had foretold had started rolling. Till Zoe . . . ? On his feet in an instant, he lifted her in his arms, crying: "Where did she go, Jack? When?"

It was little the child could tell him. Last night her mother had said that she must go away for a time and, when Jacqueline awoke, she was to come straight to them. That was all. The intensity of Steve's questions frightened her. And seeing it, he left her to Trig and rushed to Zoe's cabin, threw the door open, and was overwhelmed by the emptiness that swooped out at him. Zoe was gone! Gone, he found, by quick inventory, in her boyish attire—high shoes, flannel shirt, riding breeches, and sombrero. Even then he could not believe that she was really gone but just out on an early ride—a tramp. She wouldn't leave the baby long. Calmed by that thought, he went back to his own cabin. Pausing in the door to smile reassuringly at Jacqueline, he started suddenly. Overlooked in the shock of her announcement was the folded sheet pinned to the pocket of Jacqueline's slip, with "Steve" largely scrawled across the face of it. Fearful of what it held but wildly glad that Zoe had not gone without a word, he unfolded the note and read:

*Steve,*

*I've got to go. Please take care of baby. And don't worry about me. You couldn't help, and you might destroy my last hope—worse. I've added to my heavy debt by taking your rifle and Brownie. I won't try to thank you now for all you have done. God only knows how grateful I am. When I come back—Steve, pray I win! If I don't—Oh, I hardly know what I'm writing! Good bye.*

*Zoe*

## V
### "THE STRANGER RETURNS"

Steve long stood staring at the distracted, tear-stained message, stunned, able only to comprehend that Zoe was gone. Then panic seized him. She might be in danger. She had hinted of some desperate mission, something desperate enough to have driven her to risk her life and the baby's in the desert once before! What could drive a woman to such lengths? Where had she been going the day he found her? If he knew that he would know where she was now. Not Toroda, for the very mention of the town had struck terror in her. Who—what did it hold that threatened her? Where did The Stranger come in? Steve's brain reeled with conjecturings. One thought alone held fast. Jacqueline was here—so Zoe would come back.

Almost unrestrainable was his impulse to follow her, but she had warned him that such a move might ruin everything. He saw the danger of breaking blindly into her game. He had no fear of any natural danger befalling her. She had his rifle, and she knew the country. It was for this that she had been preparing herself.

Nevertheless, Steve picked up her trail, following it over the pass and down to the flats, where it was soon lost in the scab rock. There, looking across the scorching wastes, he decided to respect her wishes—not to risk the destruction of her last hope by his interference. After all, he didn't know if she was in danger.

So he returned to Paradise—again a lonely, looted place—to watch and wait and worry. Having no idea of how long she would be away, he expected her hourly. After hours and days of this, his brain would play him tricks, and he would see her standing before him with her sad smile, then, in his disappointment as she faded, he would curse himself for being as queer as Trig. After three days of this, as dusk crept down the Derelicts and purple stained the sky above, coming out of the cabin, hoping this time to see her coming, Steve collided with someone. He started back with a low cry of relief as he recognized The Stranger.

The man's dark face was deeply lined. He had aged years in the weeks he had been gone. The odor of train smoke clung to him. By this, and by the comparatively fresh condition of his black, trailing reins before the steps, Steve knew that he had left the horse somewhere and gone by rail to some distant point. A thousand questions leaped to his mind but, before he could give utterance to one, The Stranger's fingers bit deeply into his arm, and he demanded in a strangled voice: "She's gone?"

Steve nodded.

"When?"

"Monday . . . in the night. On my mustang. She. . . ."

Hoarsely the man cut in: "The baby? Where . . . ?"

"She's here," Steve said. "Zoe left her." He saw The Stranger start, felt his grip relax.

"Had she told you anything about herself?"

"Nothing. Just what I told you that night. But"—in swift recollection—"she left a note."

He hurried into the cabin to get it, and by the dim light streaming out The Stranger read it, his face changing, as if the hasty lines conveyed to him some special, sinister significance. Coming to the end, he dropped the note.

"I was afraid of that!" he groaned.

"Of what?" Steve cried. He got no reply. The man seemed to forget him utterly. He turned to his horse, caught up the reins. But Steve grasped him. "You know where she's gone?"

The Stranger looked at him, dread in his expression, dread in his tone. "I'm afraid I do! I hope I'm wrong, but. . . ." He swung into the saddle, wheeled, and turned back. "I've got to find her . . . talk to her.

Steve," he said regretfully, "I can't tell you more. Just this . . . I've been to her old home . . . Los Angeles." His voice took on a bitter tinge. "I didn't dare make myself known, but I found out what was behind her flight. I hurried back, hoping she'd still be here. Now. . . ."

He spurred his horse, but Steve seized the bridle. He had to know one more thing before The Stranger went. "You"—he asked tensely as the black plunged—"what's she to you?"

The man's dark face relaxed. Its anxiety was replaced by an exquisite tenderness. "What's she to me?" he asked himself. "She's the only woman I ever loved. But . . . she married my brother. She's my sister-in-law . . . or was, for Jim's dead. I knew he must be that night she came. Else she wouldn't be in trouble and alone. I found he'd died a year ago. She's played a lone hand since. But . . . no more! I'm helping her!"

"An' me!" cried Steve, his heart singing with the knowledge that Zoe was free. "I'm goin', too!"

"No!" was the sharp veto. "Your job is here! She trusted Jacqueline to you. How great that trust . . . you'll know some day!"

Then he rode away.

Steve, staring after him until he vanished in the dusk and still staring, saw a light flare up in The Stranger's cabin. It burned a moment then went out. Then the boy heard hoofbeats ringing up the slope, over the crest, and passing from hearing down the Lost Friar Trail. The Stranger was going to her. And he, who loved her too—he could admit it now!—was as he always was . . . chained here.

From then on time was to Steve a torment, his forced inaction maddening. Bitter anxiety filled the void created by Zoe's absence, this and the hot, fierce pain whose first faint pang he had felt down in the desert when Zoe had found The Stranger's history interesting. Now The Stranger was helping her. They would be together. There was so much between them. What woman could think twice of another man when The Stranger . . . ? Still—and this thought made bearable the hurt—she had known him and married his brother.

To make time pass, Steve tried to work, but he could not. The days were endless, the summer evenings worse. He would spring up at every sound in the dead town, thinking it was her step. His heart would leap at every shadow, and he would start to meet it, thinking it was the girl, or The Stranger come with news of her.

Once Zoe had gone, Trig seemed to forget that she had ever been, to regard the child as his very own. His attitude toward her was possessive in the extreme. And from the first he assumed the entire care of her. To Steve—whose fingers were all thumbs when it came to doing the simplest thing for Jacqueline—it was a never-ending marvel how skillfully, tenderly, Trig did all, and he did not interfere. He knew Zoe had meant it to be so. In the weeks of recuperation she had studied Trig, plumbed his soul to the depths, and found him worthy of this great trust.

But, more and more, as the novelty of living with them wore off, Jacqueline turned from Trig to Steve—not that she gave Trig less affection, but as a child forsakes other children for an adult when trouble comes. She seemed to realize that Steve was the one to tie to, her real guardian. At every opportunity she would slip from Trig and go to Steve, finding him oftenest on the high point above the mill that had been Zoe's look-out. For here—where the girl had sat, fixing the landscape in her mind, forming her nameless plan—Steve now spent long hours, scanning the distant desert for sight of the gallant little boyish figure on his mustang, wondering if The Stranger had found her, praying as she had asked him—more fervently than he had ever prayed for anything—that she would return a winner.

Often, then, he would be surprised to find the tot beside him, watching as intently as he watched, her grave little face as anxious—not talkative, as she was with Trig, but quiet as a mouse, as though fearing to disturb his thoughts which might be occupied with some plan to bring her mother back. Steve's face would kindle with admiration for her fortitude. She never cried for her mother, but she had long sober spells when Steve knew she was thinking of her; and she never went indoors, but she had, tight in her dimpled fist, some memento—a forest flower, a specimen of quartz, a bright-hued feather—that she would lay carefully upon the window ledge to "show to Mamma." Her blue eyes' wistfulness wrung Steve's heart. He could not refuse her plea to be with him, though he saw it hurt Trig and created a rift between them—the first in all their years of companionship. For the old man was jealous. He sought to monopolize the baby in every way.

"Let's go ride Jenny," he would suggest when she was about to leave with Steve. "Jenny's gettin' too fat an' sassy. She'll get too lazy to breathe." But Jacqueline had lost interest in riding. "I'm feelin' lucky," Trig would beg. "Let's go find the ledge. It's out there . . . the mother lode . . . plumb plastered with gold!" But she was too tired, she said. And Trig would complain, with a withering glance at Steve: "Sure you be! He's wore you out . . . draggin' you from pillar to post. He ain't a lick of sense about li'l folks. You stay with Trig an' rest. I'll tell you what"—getting confidential—"we'll make a mulligan for dinner. You don't eat enough to keep a canary alive. A mulligan will fix you up. But," he would add cunningly, "you'll have to help. I'm tired myself."

So she would stay to help Trig, puttering importantly about the kitchen until the savory concoction was bubbling on the stove. Then, losing all interest, she would slip away to Steve. Coming in with him to dinner, she would barely touch the dish, for she had no appetite these days. It would be strange if her repressed worry and grief had not affected it, and it would be a marvel if the two men had not spoiled her somewhat. But, not knowing the perversity which even the most angelic of children sometimes evince toward food, they took it very seriously. There came a morning when she refused to touch her breakfast, throwing old Trig into a panic.

"Jack," he entreated, "you ain't sick?" And when she shook her head: "Then eat somethin' . . . to please ol' Trig. Jist a bite of biscuit an' honey!" But she didn't want any. And when Steve coaxed her, too, she just lay her pink cheek against the white oilcloth and looked pitiful, as if what he asked was physically impossible. "She'll starve!" Trig told the boy, all his jealousy forgotten in this calamity. "She's got to eat."

"She will"—Steve was sure—"when she gets hungry." But when she wouldn't touch her dinner either, he was almost as alarmed, begging her to tell him what she wanted.

The old man pleaded: "Yes . . . tell Trig! He'll cook it. Can't you think of somethin', Jack?"

She could, exclaiming with a promptitude and positiveness that convinced them it was her natural diet. "I want some coconut! Coconut an' . . . an' sardines!"

Above her the men's eyes met in consternation. In guilt, too—for they felt criminally delinquent. Their larder didn't hold—had never held—such items!

"We're great ones!" Trig berated Steve and himself. "Coconut! An' us a-feedin' her beans an' flapjacks! Puttin' our rough chuck in her tender li'l stummick! No wonder it went back on her! Just you wait, Jack. Steve will get it."

For a week Steve had been postponing his usual trip for supplies in the hope that Zoe would come back. He hated to leave Jacqueline solely in the old man's charge. Trig would take the best care of her he could, but his faculties were failing and might desert him if anything usual came up necessitating a quick decision. Now, however, remorsefully sure they had been starving the baby, Steve made ready to go at once. Calling Trig out, the last thing he earnestly warned him: "Don't let her out of your sight. Remember, Trig! She's yours till I get back."

"She's mine!" Trig gloried in that. "Not out of my sight . . . I won't forget."

Steve was nervous when he took the trail and, during all the hot, wearisome miles to Toroda, his apprehension grew. He forced Patch to the utmost and showed no mercy to Jenny, cutting an hour from the journey though he well knew it would only increase by that much his tedious, all-night wait since the stores would have been closed for hours when he got to town, and he wouldn't be able to do any buying until morning.

Arrived in Toroda, too worn out and upset to wander about the streets, he staked the *burro* and paint pony in a vacant lot and stretched out in the cool grass, watching the stars come out in the black velvet arch above, wondering, worrying. Near dawn he slept. He dreamed he saw The Stranger staring at Zoe with anguished eyes and Zoe, with her dark, elf locks and defiant face in as much anguish, staring back. Between them was something bright that Steve thought was Trig's lost ledge but which was resolving itself into a baby's golden head when something jerked him out of sleep, brought him to his feet—a smothered detonation more felt than heard. Standing there in the blackness, trying to collect his scattered senses, to separate from reality the dream, he was aware of a growing uproar in the town.

## VI

### "HE'S NOT RESPONSIBLE"

Most of Toroda's population had been jerked from sleep by that detonation. Boots thumped furiously on the board walks. The dark rang with frantic shouts. Already scores of men were gathering about the office of the Storm King Mine at the upper end of town, and the rest were coming on the run. Here all was indescribable confusion. Now and then a flickering lantern limned a tense, excited face in the living maelstrom through which moved Sheriff Sears—solid, ponderous, self-possessed, not to be budged from his slow, methodical course by the clamoring around him, by the frenzied importunings of Art Jessel, mine manager and the town's big man. What had happened? There were as many versions as there were many tongues.

Proclaimed one in an excited breath: "He got a hundred thousand in cold cash!"

"Rubbish!" another scoffed. "Clark said nothing was touched! And as cashier he ought. . . ."

"Then what's Jessel ravin' about? I heard him tell Sears it was a big loss."

"Must be all of that!" a third confirmed. "When a penny pincher like Jessel hires old Panamint at twenty bucks a day to help Sears trail the kid . . . !"

"Kid?" That description amazed someone. "Why, Jessel says the bandit was big! Tall and dark . . . for he could see black eyes shinin' through the mask!"

This description amazed somebody else who exclaimed with a harsh laugh: "Jessel must have been scared bad! Clark glimpsed him when he run, an' says he was just a striplin'!"

Of only one thing were they certain. The office of the Storm King Mining & Reduction Co. had been broken into, and the safe blown.

The blast that had brought Steve up had aroused the town. Art Jessel, first on the scene, had been held up at the entrance by the bandit, forced into a rear room, and locked in, where Toroda found him—found him foaming at the mouth, beside himself at the theft of he wouldn't say what! Only that its value was great. Certainly his actions bore out his statement. For he showed no reason, no consideration, in upbraiding the sheriff—on the job almost on the echo of the blast—for not getting right off, for permitting the outrage in the first place. As a posse formed and sat their churning horses, waiting, he kept on raving while others acquired and saddled a mount for him.

"What are they waitin' for?" drawled a bystander whose wits still slept. On being tersely told, "Daylight," he said with a glance at the horizon which was fast lighting, its black giving way to a cold, slate-gray: "Waal, it ain't far away."

"Panamint's huntin' sign right now," a voice spoke up. "He'll find it. He's got eyes like a cat."

"Which is Jessel?" Steve asked the nearest man.

The fellow looked queerly at him. *Not know Jessel! Where had he been all his life? Still*—was the man's broad-minded reflection—*there were likely lots of folks on earth who hadn't heard of him.* "There"—obligingly he pointed him out—"nearest the door. On that blaze-faced mare. Givin' Sears 'Hail Columbia!' "

Just then Jessel turned in the saddle, and the light from the office fell full upon him. Steve saw a dark-skinned man of angular frame whose thin, sharp face held more meanness than all the faces he had ever seen. Meanness glared out of his small black eyes. Selfish and cruel was his whole aspect. And—cinching Steve's instinctive dislike—a pathetic excuse for a mustache bedecked his thin upper lip. It was parted in the middle and slicked back. A man must like himself pretty well to take so much care of his mustache. Steve had the strange feeling that he had seen Jessel before—yet he hadn't run into him around Toroda because he wasn't the kind of man you could see and forget.

"He'll get the bandit," muttered the man beside him. "He's that kind."

As unaccountably a chill ran through Steve's heart, the shout went up: "Here's Panamint!"

The boy looked with the rest at the leathery, long-haired old-timer in buckskin now slowly approaching the sheriff. Panamint! He had heard of him—a veteran scout who had sharpened his eyes in the old days trailing Apaches for the government and had kept them keen by just such jobs as this ever since.

"Straight east . . . out of town," the tracker reported to Sears. "He hit for the flats."

"With an hour's start!" Jessel cried and struck his horse.

Watching the posse gallop off, Steve was seized by a wild urge to be gone himself to strike out after them. Only the thought of Jacqueline at home and hungry held him. Almost uncontrollable, this feeling, waiting—ages—for Toroda to get down to business, hearing the citizens in knots on every corner heatedly discuss the robbery, accrediting it variously to a little man—a big man—who had got a fortune in gold—bonds—bullion—who had got nothing.

At last the stores opened. Then Steve bought the things Jacqueline had wanted—everything which he, as a kid, had ever heard of and wanted—glad of the furor that kept the grocer from commenting on his unusual order. With the provisions lashed to the pack saddle on the old *burro*, he mounted Patch and rode out of Toroda. Rode back over the baking flats, his eyes eagerly strained on the jagged rims of the Derelicts, so intolerant of Jenny's funereal gait that he threatened to ride off and leave her if she didn't speed up. Then he forgot his threat in thinking how Jacqueline's blue eyes would shine when she saw this pack. But, he remembered, she wouldn't think much of it. She was used to this chuck, likely had it three times a day in Los Angeles. They were city folks. How had Zoe learned to ride and shoot like that in a city? How had she learned about this country? About Fool's Acres? Was the terrible thing she must do here, or . . . ?

For no explainable reason Steve's mind flashed back to the wild dawn—the uproar in town, Jessel's frenzy to be after the bandit, the conflicting stories about what he'd lost, and unconsciously he urged Patch to a gallop. Realizing it, he reined in. It was too hot to run a horse like that. This excitement had strung him up. That, back there, was living, always something doing—excitement. Some day he would be out in it, doing things, and it would take more than a robbery to excite him.

Around noon, the stifling miles behind, he reached the foot of the Derelicts. Reining from the sage into the mountain road, he jerked up short, staring down, his blood leaping in every pulse. For there, in the forgotten Lost Friar Trail, were tracks—tracks of many shod horses. The posse's tracks! Steve could hardly believe his eyes. That the bandit should take refuge in the Derelicts was logical enough but not in the direction of Paradise. The natural escape would be through one of the passes south where he could cross the mountains and have a choice of routes to one of many towns in the more populous country beyond, but up here, in the highest, wildest stretches, the hills made a tight pocket. There was no way out. This road led to a trap. Didn't the fugitive know that? Or was he going deliberately to Paradise?

Instantly the vague presage of disaster that had been with him since the robbery took color and form—too terrible to look upon! Of all the fearful thoughts it brought, his brain could hold but one. The posse was on the trail to Paradise, men from Toroda—a town whose very name filled Zoe with terror—and Jacqueline was up there, and Trig. . . . Leaping down, Steve studied the tracks more closely, deciding by the freshness of the hoof-torn earth that the posse was not more than an hour ahead of him. Something might delay them. The fugitive might lead them off the road, on a side trail. He might still get to Paradise ahead of them.

Flinging himself on Patch, he urged him up the grade. In his frenzy to be home the climb seemed endless, hopeless. In despair of getting more speed out of the poky old *burro,* he left her to follow and hurried on under the green-arched pines, up the toilsome switchbacks, leaping deadfall and crevasse, until sweat ran down the mustang's flanks, and his sides heaved with his labored breaths. Yet, ever faster, Steve urged him as he neared the pass and those tracks kept ahead of him. On the last steep pitch a sharp crack startled the stillness. Hot on it another—shots! Terror-stricken, Steve hurled himself from his horse and crashed through the fringe of underbrush to the rim overlooking Paradise. There he was rooted to the spot, spellbound by a sight that stifled his pounding heart.

Below him, in the rocks and pines crouched the sheriff's men, their horses bunched in the aspens halfway up the slope. Beyond, under the frowning, austere peaks, in the grass-grown street of the old ghost town, rifle to shoulder, white head bare to the dazzling sun, old Trig militantly stalked to and fro—holding the posse at bay. Even as the horrified boy took this in, Trig sent a bullet into the pines. An answering shot ripped a shingle from the building behind him. The old man brandished his gun, fiercely shrilling: "Come out . . . you ki-yotin' claim jumpers . . . an' fight like men!"

Trig was on the warpath. What about? Was he defending the bandit? No—he was hostile to strangers. Was it Jacqueline? Or was he living in the past again—the old boom times—and under the delusion that they were claim jumpers? Realizing the danger Trig was in, thinking only to explain before he was killed or had killed someone, Steve scrambled down the slope toward the ambushed men—who were too intent on Trig to see him—forgetting his own risk until, almost there, a shot rang past him, dangerously close. He dropped to the ground, crawling under cover of the buckbrush toward the big boulder that sheltered the sheriff. As he reached it, a bullet smashed against the rock. Responsively Sears's gun flashed up.

Flinging himself forward, Steve grabbed the officer's wrist, screaming: "Stop! I tell you, he ain't responsible!"

Wrenching free, Sears stared hard at the boy, relief overspreading his fleshy face. He knew Steve. He had known Trig to speak to in the years before the old man forgot the world. He had heard that the solitudes had "got him." He had quizzed Steve last autumn after that hunting party had complained that someone here had taken pot shots at them.

"Gosh all hemlocks, Steve," he exclaimed, "I'm glad you've come! Maybe you can get him in hand. I know he ain't responsible. That's why we been shootin' high. But he's obstructin' the law. There's been a robbery in Toroda. We trailed the outlaw here. But the minute we hove in sight, Trig started blazin' away at us. Swears he'll shoot to kill if we come a step nearer. An' we gotta go down an' search . . . !"

"Who's this young buck?"

At that strange, hostile tone, Steve jerked around to see Art Jessel behind him, staring at him with black suspicion.

Briefly Sears explained: "Steve an' Trig hold down this town. They've lived up here alone for more years than I. . . ."

"Well," Jessel broke in curtly, "I saw the criminal, and I'll swear it wasn't the old man."

"What are you drivin' at?" Sears ejaculated.

Boring Steve with that hard gaze, the mining man ran a finger tip over the few black hairs on his upper lip. A nervous habit he had and one he was eternally indulging in—as if, Steve thought, he must draw attention to that mustache, which otherwise might be overlooked, or maybe that was how he curried it.

"Just this," said Jessel. "We tracked a man here from Toroda. You say there's just two up here. I say it wasn't the old man. I don't say it was this fellow, but . . . he was in town at the time. I saw him . . . in the crowd . . . this morning."

Sears's face hardened. "That so, Steve?"

The boy admitted it was. "I just come from Toroda. I went in for grub." And when this did not soften the sheriff's expression, he went on in detail, explaining just how he came to be at the scene of the excitement. Then, growing uneasy under their scrutiny, under the curious gaze of the posse, edging as close as they could in safety, he mopped his hot face, gave a self-conscious hitch to his belt, and said, as naturally as he could: "I'll go down an' try to talk some sense to Trig."

He took a step. Gun steel bruisingly pressed against his breast, and Jessel sneered: "Not so fast!"

Angrily Sears interposed: "Not so fast yourself, Art. It just happens that I'm in charge." Turning to Steve, he said harshly: "All the same, boy, you'll have to stick close. You're under suspicion."

"Me?" Steve was mad all through. "Why, you must be loco! I was an hour behind you! If you don't believe it, go back a ways an' you'll find my horse an' *burro*. I come on when I heard shootin'. How could I be the man you trailed?"

"Oh, I ain't accusin' you." The sheriff was noncommittal. "But you'll admit it looks mighty queer that anybody else would sky hoot up here when they might have got clean away in another direction. So you see, Steve, it's to your interest that we find the bandit. An' you'd best help us get on with this search."

Knowing he could not stop them, not daring to increase their suspicion by a sign of reluctance, Steve flared: "You've got my permission. You'll find we're hidin' nothing."

This brought home to him just how much they were hiding. Jacqueline! How could they explain her and not mention her mother? The sheriff would search Zoe's cabin and ask. Vividly he saw Zoe as on that first morn, standing beside him, nervously twisting her locket, beseeching him: "Steve, someone may ask about the woman in Paradise. . . ." And they would find where The Stranger lived, charge him with this, The Stranger whose life was bound up in hers, who lived here on necessity, a fugitive himself!

Responsibility for them bore down upon Steve's brain, crushing thought. Were the bandit cowering among the ruins, he could not feel more trapped. Dully he saw Jessel nursing his mustache, and dully he heard Sears ordering: "Crawl up where you can talk to Trig. I'll be right behind. Explain our business. Mebbe he'll listen to reason an' let us search. If not, we'll have to take other steps."

## VII
### "THE SPARROW HAWK"

Forgetting all else they might find in his dread of their finding Jacqueline, hoping to divert them or find some way to hide her, Steve crept toward Trig with the sheriff right behind. He inched up, screened by leafy brush, to where the old man valiantly stalked, daring the "kiyotes" to "poke a nose out" and punctuating his threats with bullets. He was so occupied that Steve was able to come within a few yards of him.

"Trig!" he called then.

The old man stiffened and swung his gun in that direction.

"Trig!"

The rifle lowered a bit, and the old man faltered: "That you, Steve?"

The boy raised himself up so Trig could see him. When sure that he had been recognized, he went forward, motioning Sears to stay where he was. Trig came to meet him. Through all his worry Steve was struck by the wild light in his kind old eyes.

"Son," cried the old man, keeping a close watch on the pines, "there's mischief afoot! Not out of your sight, you said! I knew there was some mischief up, but it warn't what I thought. It's claim jumpers! I'm standin' 'em off!"

Steve knew that Trig was re-living old times, defending the property of friends long gone but who he firmly believed would one day return. "Trig," he tried to calm him, "you're makin' a big mistake. It ain't claim jumpers. It's the sheriff. The sheriff an' his men. There's been a robbery in Toroda. They think that the crook's hidin' here."

"That's what they told you!" cried Trig, raising his gun. "Oh, but they're the foxy ones."

Steve caught his arm. "I tell you, Trig . . . it is a posse."

A gleam of reason pierced the foggy brain. "Are you sure, son?"

"Dead sure! Here's the sheriff . . . Sears . . . you know him."

Boldly the sheriff walked out of hiding, watching Trig warily, ready for any sign of hostility, but Trig made none. Suddenly he seemed utterly beaten, leaning heavily on his gun, his dazed eyes peering closely at the star on the sheriff's vest and then as closely into his face.

Bewildered, he said: "My mistake, sheriff. But there's mischief afoot. I've been a-feelin' it . . . some worriment. I thought you was it. I'm glad you've come. We'll help you smoke out your man."

"That's fine," Sears said heartily. "Then you ain't seen anyone?"

Steve held his breath. Slowly Trig looked about the place, so godforsaken in other eyes, so stirringly alive in his. "No." Slowly he shook his head. "No, sheriff . . . just the usual crowd."

Sears's eyes met Steve's in comprehension. Then he beckoned to his men. Steve's gaze leaped up the street. Where had Trig left Jacqueline? He was in terror lest she appear, lest Trig speak of her.

He wanted to warn him not to but dared not communicate with him by word or sign.

"That man," rose the shrill cry behind, "why ain't the handcuffs on him?"

He swung to see old Trig, wilder than he had ever seen him, his eyes literally blazing, pointing a shaking finger at the manager of the Storm King Mine, raving to the sheriff: "There's your crook!"

Aghast as everyone was to hear such an appellation applied to the most influential man in the county, Sears protested: "That's Jessel . . . the man who was robbed."

Steve's blood ran cold at Trig's wild laugh. "Robbed? Him? He's the thievin' kind! He's a . . . sparrow hawk! Look at him . . . a-whettin his beak!"

Somebody laughed. Jessel's hand dropped from his lip as if it burned, his eyes glittering like those of the bird of prey he had been named.

"A sparrow hawk!" Trig's voice swelled to a shriek. "The kind that eats livin' prey. He's huntin' it now! Young things . . . but she's sleepin'! I'll keep my eye on him!" While they listened spellbound, little dreaming that tragedy would come out of this delusion—or was it truth, was Trig sanest?—fiercely the old man screamed: "Why, he oughta be hanged higher'n Haman!"

"And you," Jessel grated, his thin face livid, "ought to be put in an asylum."

The hate he had felt at first sight leaped hot in Steve. It was on his tongue when sternly Sears broke in: "Here! This wranglin' ain't gettin' us anywhere."

Under his direction the search began. Trig took no part but stuck like a burr to Jessel, watching his every move. Jessel, in turn, watched Steve. Seeing this, the boy guiltily thought in his very brain: *How could he hide Jacqueline with those hawk's eyes on him? How explain the child in their keeping? The evidences they would find of a woman?* By the wild remark Trig had dropped, overlooked by the posse as mere raving, he knew that the child was asleep in the cabin. She always took a nap in the afternoon. *How could he account for her—suspicious as they were? If he thought of anything, could he depend on Trig to understand and back him?*

Systematically the men scattered out, each group taking a street. Dead blocks woke to the tramp of their feet—which rang like a thousand in the melancholy place. Again the Nevada House embraced armed men. Bats flew blindly from hiding. Old dust was raised. Accidentally or otherwise someone pulled the bell cord on the old fire hall, and a wild, unearthly peal rang over Paradise. The search was thorough, although none believed the fugitive would be found there.

"His horse would be hard to hide here," Steve heard the sheriff telling Jessel. "He's probably gone on through and hid in the hills. I'm sendin' Panamint to circle camp an' see if he can pick up the trail. I'll detail some of the boys to help."

He left on this errand, and Steve, looking around in an agony of indecision, saw one of the men going up to The Stranger's cabin. With a hot, sick feeling in his breast he watched the searcher push the door in, then something attracted the man to the shed beside it, and he went over there. Coming out, he must have forgotten that he had not looked in the house. At any rate he passed it up and went on to the next. But Steve felt no relief. Only a tightening of suspense. This oversight was an accident. It would not happen again. And they were that much nearer Zoe's cabin. When they came to it. . . . Could he say that he lived in it? He visioned the house as it would look to them— as it had looked to him the morning Zoe had gone—with a woman's touch everywhere. No, he could not get away with that. Sears was nobody's fool. And before they came to it, or right after, they would reach his cabin and find—Jacqueline! To postpone that dénouement, to gain time, Steve feigned great interest in the hunt, pointing out spots difficult to search—the old stamp mill with its many levels, boilers, and chutes, the old Chinatown with its subterranean passages on the river bank, but inexorably the search narrowed down. They came at last to the two cabins at the street's end, halting first before the one behind the morning-glory vines.

Said Sears then, turning suddenly to Steve: "This your place?"

Steve nodded, speechless.

"We'll have to look it over," said the sheriff, and for all his apologetic manner he was suspicious. Frankly so when, as he put a foot on the step, Steve cried desperately, "Wait!" He spun to see the boy as white as birch bark. At a loss what to say, Steve looked away, and his heart leaped. "Here's my burro!" he explained, pointing toward old Jenny, grazing down the street. "You'll see I did go for grub. I came up after you. The rider you trailed didn't have a burro."

Already Jessel had the pack off and was going through it. Sears took it from him, tossing the contents out—coconut, tins of canned meat, cookies, candy, jam. . . . "Party truck!" was his dry comment.

"Appetizers," contradicted the boy with a game grin. "I hope there's no law against them."

The sheriff got up. "Well, Steve," he said soberly, "I guess this lets you out."

Again his spurs clinked on the porch. And this time Steve could think of no way to stop him. Seized by a reckless wish to face the worst, he led the way into the cabin, followed by the curious men. Slowly they stalked through the two orderly rooms, so full of betraying things—tiny garments hung on pegs among Steve's shirts, that collection of flowers, feathers, and rock on the window ledge, on the floor a tin cup, half filled with water and sand—Jacqueline's gold pan. All too small to be seen by eyes seeking a man. And there was no man here. No place a man could hide. Silently they filed out.

Sheriff Sears paused on the shaded porch, debating what to do next. Above the town, on the grassy slope pockmarked with a hundred shafts, Panamint and his aides had met in their circling for tracks and were looking down at something, in earnest conference. Across the street Art Jessel, who had preceded them out, had his hand on the latch of Zoe's cabin. Opening the door, he went in, while back in the kitchen of the cabin that had yielded the posse nothing, Steve, with stark despair in his heart, held Trig, gone suddenly violent, struggling like the mad creature he was, raving through Steve's hand, clamped tightly on his mouth. "I left her sleepin'! I tried to keep my eye on him! But he got her . . . that sparrow hawk! Let me at him! Let me at him!"

Hours would pass before Steve could fully appreciate the fortunate chance that took the posse away at that critical instant. He had only a vague idea then of what took place. He remembered Trig's collapse, remembered easing him down on the bunk where he sat, his white head bent, deeply sunk in an apathy from which not even Steve's frantic questions could rouse him, though by sheer force of will he drew coherent answers from him. He remembered rushing out on the porch to see one of the trailers galloping down, yelling that they had found the fugitive's tracks going on through town, and the sheriff and his men dashing for their mounts. He remembered his own shock, keen even in his distress at the sight of Jessel's emerging from Zoe's cabin, wearing a look strangely like the one he had surprised on The Stranger's face when he saw Zoe that night. Yet Jessel's was not the astonished anguish of one who sees a beloved ghost, but rather the startled terror of one who unexpectedly confronts a living, dangerous antagonist!

Then they were gone. He and Trig were again, as in the years before The Stranger came, the only living human beings in the old town. For Jacqueline was nowhere to be found, though he sought her frantically, searching Paradise more thoroughly than ever the posse did. Steve was in panic as the sun slowly sank. Thinking she must have wakened and wandered off to hunt him, he sought in every spot where she had ever found him and, finding her in none, he thought of all the places that could engulf a toddler. He thought with horror of the Lost Friar. Up and down the banks of the stream that wound through the town he ran, his eyes bent in sickening dread on the swift water, his heart leaping to his throat a dozen times at sight of a bit of cloth on a snag far in the swirling depths, or something like the drowned gleam of a white face or golden head. Then, as the sun dropped behind the Derelicts, he rushed back to the cabin to question Trig again, desperately hoping to draw more from him.

"Quit naggin', son!" the old man moaned. "I tell you . . . we prospected all forenoon. Then we got dinner. She et some. Then . . . like always . . . she took her nap. I left her sleepin' an' got the water bucket an' went to the creek. Comin' back, I seen them men ridin' down an' run back for my gun. She was still sleepin'. Then you said it was a posse . . . an' we all come . . . an' she was gone!" That was all. Not even of this was Trig longer sure, for he looked up at Steve, imploring, pitiable. "She was here, wasn't she?" he asked weakly. "I didn't dream her?" On being told she had been, he muttered: "Of course. But I had to ask. 'Pears like I'm wrong so many times." Feebly he got up then and reached for his gun. When the boy demanded where he was going, he said with frightening gentleness: "Out. To find that sparrow hawk."

Steve held him, forcibly took the gun from him, and, going out on the porch, thrust it under the boards. Then he forgot the old man, for night was coming on, and Jacqueline was gone. Standing there, he looked despairingly up to the hills, so grandly sunset-flushed. Each tree and spire was tipped with fire. The gulch was fast filling with mountain purple. Its haze was on the long slope above, pock-marked with shafts—the shafts! Black holes, water-filled and deep, pitfalls for little, unsure feet. In more terror even than when he had searched the river, Steve ran up the slope. From shaft to shaft, shudderingly looking into each black mouth, searching for the drooping lip of each for a tiny sandaled track, he was peering fearfully into the last when the ring of hoofs drew his gaze down the ridge, and he saw the posse coming back. In the van, leading his horse, head bent, came old Panamint, slowly following a track that led back over the very ground they had trailed the fugitive in on. Beyond him rode Sears, chagrined out of his habitual calm, and Jessel, nervously worrying his mustache, his eyes darting down at the dead houses in nervous flashes, his sharp, cruel face still wearing that apprehension graven on it in Zoe's cabin.

Starting forward with some wild idea of confiding all to the sheriff, something restrained Steve—some instinct warning that to do so would not be serving Zoe. And he substituted: "What luck?"

"The deuce's own!" Sears complained. "He doubled back when he saw the trap. Looks like he come around town an' out. . . ." He broke off staring at the boy leaning against the ancient windlass of the shaft, his bronzed face as white as if he had been ill, and his own hardened in that first suspicion. This feeling was in his flat comment: "Funny you didn't see him."

Steve felt Jessel's eyes dart to him. He feared what was behind them. Jessel must have found sign of a woman, must have kept it to himself, else Sears would have investigated. Puzzling over this strange twist, Steve absently replied to Sears: "I just came up. He could have ridden by here a dozen times and me not see him."

"Are you blind?" Jessel sneered. "Or didn't you want to see him?"

Steve said abruptly: "I wasn't lookin'."

"Waal," Sears grumbled, "I wish you had been. Might have saved us a lot of trouble. We dropped his trail on that rocky ledge up there. Lost us an hour. Just by luck one of the boys picked it up on this side. How he could get over an' not leave a track beats me. He must 'a' flew. Reckon by now he's halfway down to the flats." He looked at his men, bunched around, tired, hungry, cross grained, then up at the darkening sky. "Waal, Art"—he turned to the Storm King man—"I reckon we'd best camp here tonight an' get a fresh start in the mornin'." And to the boy, who was frozen by that decision: "Can you give us a hand-out, Steve?" A quizzical gleam was in his eyes. "Reckon we don't need them appetizers."

"Camp . . . here?" raged Jessel before Steve could answer. "What are you trying to do? Give him an all-night start? Come on . . . let's get out of this . . . I mean, keep the trail hot. Sears, you've been cold on this job from first to last!"

Nettled, Sears snapped: "We can't trail in the dark. An' once we get in the timber, goin' down, it'll be black as a stack of. . . ."

"We'll go as far as we can."

An angry muttering rose among the men. Swinging around, Jessel faced them. "I'll pay ten bucks," he cried, "to every man jack who can stay with this trail till sunup!"

Fatigue and resentment were wiped from each face. This bonus would go far to brighten the night. And they all remembered that the moon would be up when they reached the flats. The sheriff shrugged and gave in. The cavalcade was in slow motion. With wild impatience, Steve watched until they were over the crest that dropped to the desert, then he went on searching until the Derelicts lost their sharp edge and merged, and his eyes played tricks, and he heard from the gulch below the faint echo of frantic shouts.

Storming down, torn between hope and fear, he found old Trig in the cabin door, holding—Jacqueline! "I went out," he was babbling, holding her tightly, "an' I come back, an' . . . here she was!"

And that, for him, was enough. That was enough for Steve just then, trembling in the reaction from the long strain. Enough to have Jacqueline home safe and sound. And Trig was his old self again—or as near his old self as he would ever be or had long been. It was as if the blue-eyed baby, laughing at Steve from his arms, was light for his blinded mind.

Not until all now hidden was made known did Steve fully understand Jacqueline's mysterious disappearance and return. She told them what she could, and fantastic it was. She said a man had carried her off. What kind of a man? Oh, a nice man! As big as Steve? Yes. As Trig? Bigger! And his eyes were black. Tall and dark . . . then, Steve remembered, that had been one description of the bandit. He had put her in a tunnel. Which one? It was a "new" one. She could show them. Up back of the mill? Yes, it was. Behind the bushes. He had hidden her there and told her to be still or badmen would find her. And he had watched the men until they were gone, and he carried her back, through the old mill to the cabin. That was Jacqueline's story, and she stuck to it—proved it, for as soon as ever the sun came up next morning, she led them straight to a tunnel that Steve had not known was in existence. In all his boyhood explorations he had never seen it. But Trig recalled when it was driven, and that it had been bored completely through the ridge, the work being done from the other end and all ore taken out there, leaving no dump or visible sign of its presence here. The timbers that framed the mouth had long ago caved in, and the opening was entirely overgrown.

Exploring it with a miner's lamp, they found tracks of a horse on the damp floor. The bandit's escape was made clear and also why Panamint had failed to find the tracks when he doubled back. The rock ledge, approaching the tunnel from the other end, had left none. The bandit had not flown over the ridge, as Sears had grumbled he must have, but had done something almost as unexpected—he had come through it! And from this leaf-hidden opening, overlooking town, he had had a full view of all that had gone on. Standing where the outlaw had stood, Steve reconstructed his movements. He had ridden through Paradise, making a trail to decoy the posse, then twisted back over the rock ledge to this old tunnel, come through it, and watched his chance to carry off Jacqueline, no doubt doing that while Trig was holding the posse back. Then, when his trail was found, while the posse was scouring the hills behind, he had restored the child and escaped from town down the road he had come up.

What had been his object? Had he meant to hold her as hostage if his refuge was found but, seeing a way out, restored her rather than be encumbered by her? How had he known she was here? Only one man besides Trig and himself knew that—The Stranger! The Stranger might have found this tunnel in his years at Paradise. He would be interested in keeping Jacqueline out of sight. It came to Steve with a shock, that if it had been The Stranger, then—The Stranger had robbed the Storm King Mine. *But he's straight!* the boy thought—The Stranger's sad, dark, handsome features flashing to his mind. *He's straight . . . I'd stake my life on that! Even if he has to hide . . . has buried himself alive . . . he ain't no thief! He's a gentleman. He's Zoe's kind! An' he's gone to help her. He wouldn't be holdin' up a mine!* And if he had, why would he make straight for Paradise, leaving a trail a blind man could follow, risking the posse's finding the baby when he could have escaped in some other direction and not been put to the dangerous necessity of spiriting her away? It looked to Steve as though the man, whoever he was, had deliberately led the posse to Paradise, that it might look over the place, and then led it away again for some mysterious reason.

More heavily weighed the mystery as the days passed. It hung like a pall over Paradise, smothering the very life out of Steve. Sinister now was the silence that had been so lonely before Zoe came and afterward so sweet, sinister and threatening, for he never felt safe about Jacqueline. Whoever had taken her might take her again and fail to return her. It might not have been The Stranger.

The nights, with their almost human wail, seemed more than he could bear. Their thousand natural disturbances resolved themselves into sounds like Zoe's voice, like her step, renewing his hope, only to break it, until his spirit was more bruised than the souls of all the thousands who had forsaken this place of broken hopes. It seemed to Steve that he must go. It seemed he had dreamed Zoe, that he had gone crazy, as he used to think he would when the world was on him, its lure pulling the very heart from his body—chained here by loyalty. Yes, he had gone crazy and dreamed of Zoe, dreamed he had found her where the sage was purple, dreamed all those happy walks and talks—when sometimes she would forget the terror that stalked her and be a carefree, laughing girl—dreamed she had said that day when he had shown her his heart: "Steve, all things come to him who waits," and the light in her dark eyes when he cried: "It's true . . . you came!" Had that been a dream? But she had left her baby with him—loving little token that she would come again. Then Steve's heart would almost sing. Then questions would leap and burn, and he would strive to throw off the black cloak of secrecy that was smothering him.

Trig found nothing amiss. He had forgotten the events that had shaken Paradise. He lived once more in the past. He had resumed all care of the baby, and Steve, who had watched him closely since his breakdown, wondering if he was not putting too much trust in the failing mind, could not detect the slightest faltering in his vigilance, his dog-like devotion to her.

It was the third night since the posse's visit, a moonless midnight. Steve had not waited up for Trig, out patrolling his dead beat, but had gone to bed to stop the everlasting whirl in his brain. He was lost in sleep when something pierced his unconscious, and he came back to the awareness of the pitch-black cabin, of blind, hasty steps before the gun rack, of an alarming metallic click.

He cried out: "Trig!"

"Hush!" hoarsely whispered the old man, groping toward him.

"Trig, what are you doin'?"

"I'm a-loadin' up! There's prowlers about!"

Instantly Steve was alert. "Who, Trig? Where?"

"In Pierson's cabin!"

Wildly the boy's heart leaped. Zoe had come back! He caught Trig's arm in the dark and struggled up. "It's Zoe, Trig!"

He felt the old man start. "Zoe?" he echoed confusedly. "No," he said with conviction that sunk a dagger in Steve's breast, "Zoe's dead."

Dressing in mad haste, the boy remembered that Trig was speaking of his own Zoe—dead so many years ago. He knew that if Trig realized that she was gone, then he was in his right mind, and this was no imagination.

"It's someone," Trig swore savagely, "who ain't got no right here! Some snooper! I heard him there when I made my rounds, an' I come for my gun."

## IX

### "THE VISITOR"

Fumbling beneath his pillow, Steve found his revolver, and with it in his hand he groped with Trig out on the porch. With difficulty restraining the old man, Steve pushed back the vines and looked across to Zoe's cabin. So dark was the night that he could see only the outlines. Tensely he listened but heard nothing. Had Trig been . . . ? He started. Through the window over there had flared a tiny beam! It flickered an instant and was gone so soon that Steve doubted having seen it. But just as he was convinced of this, he saw it again. The ray of a flashlight playing over the room. Could it be Zoe come home, or The Stranger come to get something for her, or neither? Hope and dread at death grips in his heart, he turned to Trig.

"I'll run him off," he whispered. "Go back and watch Jack!" Old Trig jealously protested his right to deal with the intruder, and Steve was forced to resort to craft. "Go watch," he said tensely. "It might be that sparrow hawk!" The mere suggestion was enough to send Trig back to Jacqueline. For his instinctive distrust of the Storm King man—the feeling that Jessel menaced her—was one thing Trig had not forgotten.

Alone, then, Steve stepped noiselessly into the street and crossed over to the cabin. He stood beside it long moments, listening, hearing stealthy movements within, seeing that light intermittently flash off and on. Then, as cat-like footfalls came toward the door, he backed to the corner of the building and crouched, waiting, his gun ready, his blood tingling. Slowly the door opened, under such a careful hand that its rusty hinges gave no sound, and a figure stepped forth, indefinite in the darkness. For a moment it stood looking about, then hugging the black wall it stole silently along the cabin toward the spot where Steve crouched.

Waiting until it was almost opposite, Steve stepped suddenly out, thrusting his gun into a nebulous face, with the old, cold, compelling command: "Hands up!"

The figure stopped dead in its tracks. The hands went up. And in the act, the flashlight gripped in one came on, sweeping Steve's face in its rising arc. In a bound Steve had seized the flash, turning it full on the face of his captive, staring at it, joy dead within him, dread rampant, for the face before him was not Zoe's, nor The Stranger's, nor yet—as he had a wild idea it might be—Art Jessel's. It was the last face he expected to see at midnight in the ruined town—the sun-seared, time-seamed, wind-browned face of old Panamint—Panamint, who had won fame in the old days trailing Apaches for the government, who had kept in practice ever since. Panamint—in Zoe's cabin, on her trail!

"You?" His tongue was thick with dread. "What are you doin' here?"

"My duty!" the old trailer said calmly, and his face in that bright spot of light was strangely unabashed.

"Your duty?" flashed Steve, bitterly, furious at what he thought that duty was. "Breakin' into private property? What right . . . ?"

"If you'll pull my coat back," suggested Panamint, not arguing the point, "an' flash that light inside, you'll see my authority."

Steve did so. His startled eyes fell on a star such as the sheriff wore.

"The badge of a special deputy," Panamint defined, lowering his hands now that his credentials had been shown. "A special deputy . . . that's what I am. Duly sworn in an' authorized to poke my nose in suspicious places."

"Then why sneak in like a coyote? If Paradise is suspicious, why didn't you come in daylight?"

"An' get perforated by that ol' lunatic?" rejoined Panamint dryly.

"No, siree! Not unless it's necessary. I ain't wishful to make any trouble except"—and menace rang in this—"as concerns one party."

Tense, Steve asked: "The robber?"

"Mebbe," evaded the old trapper.

"Then he shook you off the other day?"

"Temp'rary."

There was in this laconic admission an assurance of ultimate triumph that so fanned Steve's helpless rage that caution was powerless. He thought of this man prying into Zoe's secret, stalking her unaware, watching her with his cat's eyes. "You sure got a noble duty!" he blazed. "A fine business for a man to be in . . . makin' himself a human bloodhound."

Surprisingly Panamint agreed with him. "It is," he allowed, "for a fact. It allus went plumb ag'in' my grain to trail a feller man. Barin', of course, the brute beasts in human form. But every *hombre* has his price. Mine is a stake that'll keep me in my ol' age an' forever free me from houndin'. An' Art Jessel sure offers it."

"That snake!"

"Waal, somethin' on that order," conceded the trailer—and it was a singular way for a man to speak of his employer. "Bein' robbed didn't humanize him none. It's almighty strange how he takes on . . . an' why he won't say what he got robbed of!"

Boyishly Steve flashed: "You'd think it was his mustache!"

Night hid the old trailer's grin and, when he spoke, there was no hint of mirth in his tone. "What Jessel lost that time," was his grim reflection, "sure put the fear of God in him. An' what he lost last night throwed him into several consecutive an' aggravated conniptions."

"Last night! What do you mean?"

"Jessel," said Panamint, "was robbed again. His home this time."

There was no sound then, that is none of their making, though around them the thousand voices of the night were speaking—the wind wailing in the pines, rattling the moldering bones of the old town, a coyote mourning, the stream's sad singing. All were saying that ruin was the end of everything; that happiness was a dream, and despair the reality; that mean-hearted snakes like Jessel were created to wreak ruin, and the courage of one slight girl could not prevail against them. Strangely, then, Steve bowed down before the things the night was saying only to feel Panamint's long arm about him.

"Speakin' of bloodhounds . . . ,"—the old trailer's voice was strangely kind. "Boy, there's times when they're handy critters to have around. Many an' many's the lost soul that's been restored to friends by a . . . bloodhound."

Then he was gone, and Steve was alone in the dull, dark, dreary place, to pace the night out with chaotic, frantic thoughts. Crushingly the black mantle of mystery now lay upon him, but its fullest weight was borne. Soon tragedy would rip off the last smothering shred. Already its fateful hands were on the folds. Steve scarcely realized when it began to lift, in his horror of a happening that was not mysterious. The next afternoon, while down at the river placer, working at the sluices—forcing his hands, at least, to something constructive—sudden sounds startled the stillness, frenzied footsteps, shouts. Leaping up the bank, he saw old Trig running toward him, his face like parchment, with something terrible written upon it.

"Steve," wildly he called, "come . . . quick! Jack's sick!"

# X
## "FOR THE DOCTOR"

To anyone experienced in handling children Jacqueline's sickness would have been no mystery. Zoe would have foreseen it. She would have looked with horror upon the scene that took place the evening following Steve's last eventful trip to Toroda. Still giddy with relief at Jacqueline's safe return, and in a remorseful desire to make up to her for having "starved" her, the boy arranged on the shelf the packload of delicacies he had brought—everything he had ever wanted when he was a kid, everything any child could want—and triumphantly held her up, inviting her to pick out her own supper. Long she had stared in wonder at that shelf. Then, turning dazzled eyes back, she had looked from Trig's smiling face to Steve's, asking with babyish incredulity: "Can I have anything?"

"You bet you can," Steve had grinned.

And Trig had jealously amended: "Just all you want."

Jacqueline had wanted a little bit of everything, blissfully spreading a frosted cookie with jam and sprinkling coconut on the sardines until Steve's face turned green just at sight of the mixture.

"That mess," he had shuddered to Trig, "would make me sick!"

"An' me, I reckon," the old man had admitted. "But one *hombre*'s food is another's poison. Ours sure didn't agree with her. She knows what she wants. Let her pick."

And pick she had! Indiscriminately the first meal or two, then more fastidiously subsisting entirely on candy the first day, and the next on gooey little cakes, and on this—the third, having lost her appetite for sweets—she had reached instead for the tins of highly flavored meats. In consequence she woke from her nap that afternoon screaming with pain. Frightened out of his wits, old Trig ran for Steve.

Frantically they applied every remedy at hand, but these seemed only to make her worse. Spasm after spasm convulsed her, and she was burning up with fever. Frightened, helpless, they bent over the cot on which she tossed, her fevered cheeks so dry and hot, her big eyes filmed with pain, her delirious little tongue wailing all her repressed longing for "Mamma! Mamma!" until tears shut her from Steve's sight, and he turned away.

"Son," old Trig moaned, lifting an agonized face to him, "son, I'm afeered it's ptomaine!"

Steve went white to hear his own fear put into words. Ptomaine! The scourge of wilderness men who must, of necessity, live so much out of cans. They had seen it strike the strongest down. How easily it could take a baby! And there was nothing they could do. In their secret fears, they had long ago done everything they could do if it was ptomaine, but a doctor might do something. She must have a doctor— quickly. Quickly? With thirty miles between? Bitterly Steve cursed their isolation. To take her to town was out of the question. She was far too sick. But he could bring a doctor to Paradise. He did not realize that this would disclose all they hoped to hide. He thought of nothing then but to get help as fast as ever heaven would let him. Crossing to the window ledge to get his sombrero, he went suddenly blind, looking at the little heap of dead petals, bright pebbles, trifles that Jacqueline was saving.

"Mamma!" the suffering little voice wailed on. "Oh, Mamma, why don't you come?"

Blindly Steve recrossed the room. "Trig," he said earnestly, "take care of her. I'm goin' for the doctor as fast as I can,"

The old man's eyes met his, straight—sane. He said simply: "Make time!"

With one last swift glance at the little stricken figure, Steve rushed out. Saddle in his arms, he tore down the path to the meadow by the creek where, since the other horses had gone, he had picketed Patch to keep him from straying. There he stopped short, rooted in the waving grass. . . . For Patch was down! He had got tangled in the stake rope and been thrown. And the unnatural position in which he was lying, the almost human appeal in his eyes as he turned them on Steve, and his plaintive whinny told the boy only too plainly that fate had dealt yet another cruel blow to them. When the rope was cut and Patch had struggled up, he was barely able to stand; his shoulder was so badly sprained that he was useless in this crisis. And there was not another horse in miles! There was only old Jenny, . . .

"Make time!" The plea mocked Steve. Make time—with the old *burro*, slow as death—slow—death! Of all the locoed talk! Death was fast! Right now it might be galloping. . . . Make time? At least he lost none, rounding Jenny up, saddling her, and heading down the Lost Friar Trail. She seemed to sense the need for speed and responded. Slipping, sliding, stumbling under the cathedral pines, down the winding, washed-out road, now dim as the mountains hid the lowering sun. She did her best, but nature had not made her fast, and her best was maddening when a life might hang on time.

Never had Steve felt so hopeless, so desperate, never had his brain been so active. It was painting pictures—as he lashed, spurred, coaxed, and cursed the old *burro*—pictures of Jack as first he saw her, appealing to him to help her mother, as he had seen her last, tossing on her cot, wanting her mother, and torturingly as he might see her next. He could not bear to look at that! "It ain't fair!" he cried brokenly. "She's so little!" And he saw Zoe come back. What could he say to her if anything had happened to Jack? "She trusted me!" bitterly he told the old burro, his sole audience. "When she asks me for her baby . . . what can I say?"

Ages of this! Then he was down the grade and out on the desert, still hot but veiled with the first lavender mists of dusk, out on the flats, smooth and rolling, faster going—no! his heart took a sickening plunge—for he felt Jenny slowing. Not in rebellion, for she tried to respond, but her race was run. She was too old—too soft—to stand this pace. Frantically he tried to hold her to it, but he could not. Losing hope of maintaining anything like it, Steve prayed for help. And, like an answer to prayer, he saw—far over the chaparral, here miles from anywhere, in a spot so forsaken that in years of traveling to and from town he had met almost no one except Zoe and Jacqueline—a rider! But it was not the rider that made his heart rebound. It was that rider's horse. With it he could make time! He could make it in two hours or less and start the doctor back on the fastest horse obtainable.

Covetously he watched that horse, as sure of it as if he were on it, cutting the wind right then. In this country one could commandeer a horse in emergency. The rider would either loan it, or ride on for help himself once he learned the need of it. Thus, flashingly, Steve thought—entreating Jenny to keep up—he saw, to his despair, that the rider had changed his course, had swerved south, toward the wash at the foot of the Derelicts. And in terror lest he pass without seeing him—for the amazed boy saw he was riding like the wind, lashing at top speed, as if he too were running a race with death—Steve shouted with all his might: "Stop!"

Seeing no break in that headlong gait, he waved his hat about his head to attract attention, shouting like a madman: "Stop! Stop!"

The rider heard, for his head turned toward Steve, but he did not stop—nor slow up even. Instead, more furiously he spurred his horse. He was almost to the wash. Once in it he would be lost. To Steve it was as if he saw all hope for Jacqueline going. He must have that horse at all costs. In the recklessness of desperation he drew his gun. Somewhere he had read that ships at sea sometimes fire across the bows of other ships to stop them. So he was inspired to fire across the path of this flying rider—to warn him that an emergency existed. Rising in the stirrups, he leveled the gun well above the rider's head. His finger tightened on the trigger, then simultaneously three things happened. Fumble-footed old Jenny stumbled, the gun crashed, and the rider slumped. Steve saw him reeling, slipping, then—just as the horse took the plunge—topple from the saddle.

Realizing with horror what he had done, Steve let Jenny slow to a trot, to a walk, seeing as he neared the rim of the wash the horse he had so coveted struggle free and, whirling, stare, eyes rolling white, down at the motionless form that but a moment before had been upon his back. Then the old *burro* saw it and balked, scared. Steve saw it and with far more terror got down and went slowly up to it—a slight, boyish figure in flannel shirt, riding breeches, and high-laced boots, crumpled face down on the ground. His blood freezing, his very soul dying within him, Steve turned the body over. As he did so, the sombrero fell off, revealing a mass of soft black hair that framed a face. . . .

Here, in this very place, perhaps beneath this very sage—purple then with bloom, gray now as ash, gray as the brow of death—Steve had stared into that same still, sweet, senseless face! Dazed, he gathered the girl in his arms. And there in the gray sand, the gray sage all around, the gray sky watching, he held her close—her dark head on his breast, his crazed eyes fixed in fascination on the awful scarlet pattern forming on her gray blouse—its scarlet ravelings running down his hands.

## XI

### "THEY'RE AFTER HER"

In Steve's preoccupation with that dreadful scarlet pattern he did not hear the hoofbeats thundering toward him—though the earth shook with their drumming, though they crashed into the wash—almost plunging upon him. A foam-lashed horse slid to a stop so close that its hoofs threw gravel in his face. It stood with heaving sides, nostrils wide, and eyes distended, as it saw, or scented, that fearful red design. The rider who leaped forward with the stiff step of one who had ridden far and fast saw the boy with stark amazement, saw with anguish his sad burden, and—that pattern!

"Steve!" he cried in horror. "What's happened to her?"

Dumbly Steve looked up. It was The Stranger, but he felt no surprise. He was beyond it, almost beyond the power to answer. Soundlessly his white lips worked, finally achieving the dull words: "I killed her!"

"No!" The Stranger groaned. "Oh, heaven, no!" He dropped on his knees beside Zoe, not wondering how or why or when but only wildly seeking to disprove his claim.

"I didn't know who it was." Dazedly the boy muttered his dazed thoughts. "I had to have the horse. I called for her to stop. She ran away. I meant to shoot high. But old Jenny...."

"She's living!" cried the man, heedless of Steve and his mutterings. And in mad haste—as though with this decided, he had, strangely, more pressing things to do—he pulled the girl's blouse back where it was reddest, exposing the bullet wound just beneath the right collar bone. Whipping out his handkerchief, he folded it into a small, compact square and pressed it to the wound. Then, without a second's loss of time, he ripped the sleeve from his own shirt and bound the compress on. This done, he sprang up the bank and looked back the way he had come—back over the dusky sea of chaparral.

"Steve," he said swiftly as he leaped down again. "We've got to get her away from here! They're after her!"

"After her...?" echoed the boy dully.

"After her, Steve. The posse! Not two hours ago Zoe held up the mail stage out of Toroda! The posse's on her trail...!"

Again that dull echo: "Zoe held up the mail...?"

Finally The Stranger seized him, shook him to rouse him from this nightmare, crying: "Steve, pull yourself together! I need your help! She does! She held up the stage. But she didn't get away with it! While the driver was throwing the sacks down, a passenger slipped out on the other side of the coach and covered her. She made a break ... got in the rocks. They had her cornered. I got there in time ... opened fire on them and yelled for her to run. She got away. So did I. They rushed back to town and got a posse. They'll be here any minute, and

. . . don't ask me anything!" he entreated as Steve seemed about to break in. "Just listen! It's the truth! I haven't time to explain. But there's a conspiracy against her, Steve. A big estate involved. Jessel's back of it. It was she who robbed his office and his house. She had a right . . . they're hers! I've been in Toroda . . . shadowing Jessel. I knew anything she planned would be against him. That night she robbed the mine I watched her. She doesn't know it, but I helped her escape. Then I lured the posse on my trail. I had to take refuge up there . . . the only place I could outwit them. I hid Jacqueline while they searched the town. . . ." He ran up the bank again to look and listen.

Steve, into whom these words had dug like rowels rousing him, tore his eyes from Zoe to watch The Stranger—up there scouring the plateau—and listened. He heard only the wind in the dry sage, the crunch of brittle grass beneath the feet of Zoe's horse grazing on the rim of the wash, and the labored breathing of old Jenny and The Stranger's mustang.

"Steve," went on the man, returning, "I learned about this fiendish plot in Los Angeles and hurried back to help, knowing she was desperate. I was afraid of this . . . or worse. I was afraid she would kill Jessel. She'd be justified in it. I don't know yet what she hopes to gain by all this, but we must get her away from here . . . quick!"

A shock ran through Steve, hearing without the need to listen the far drum of horses coming.

"Quick!" cried The Stranger. "Get on my horse! I'll lift her up." He stopped, staring at Steve who was on his feet, holding the slender, unconscious form, fresh agony on his somber face as suddenly he remembered. Sharply the man asked: "What is it?"

"Jack," the boy gasped, "she's sick! That's why I shot her . . . to get a horse to fetch the doctor!"

In a few clipped sentences he told The Stranger all. What Jack had been eating, her symptoms, their fear of ptomaine, what they had done, while louder, louder hoofs beat out their iron song on Mormon Flats. The Stranger, summarizing the situation in a flash, made his swift decision.

"Steve, I don't believe it's ptomaine. You've upset her digestion. You don't know how sick a child can get . . . and get over it quick. I think you've done all a doctor could do. She's probably better by now, but we've got to risk it. There's a chance for her mother if.... Steve, take Zoe to Paradise. I'll draw the posse off!" He had caught his horse and now supported Zoe while Steve swung on, then lifted her to the saddle before him, pausing to take his hand, though the galloping orchestration was so plain that ears trained on it could pick out each separate instrument. "Stick to the wash!" he said coolly. "They can't see you. I'll take her horse. I ought to lose them in the dark. But if they catch me, I'll confess to everything to give her time. Steve, I don't know when I'll see you again, so tell her about me. Tell her Lance is not dead ... but here ... helping her! Lance ... don't forget! Tell her I'm going to explode a bomb under Jessel that will shake the very Derelicts! So long, Steve."

The boy cried huskily: "An' luck ... Lance."

He saw the tall form spring out of the wash, run toward Zoe's horse, and swing on. He heard shouts as the posse saw the fugitive, glimpsed him up there, galloping down the rim fully in their sight and, with them baying at his heels, turning south for the easy route through the Derelicts. Then, free from all danger of pursuit, Steve rode slowly up the wash. Zoe in his arms, the old *burro* trailing behind, he began the long, long climb to Paradise. Carefully he rode, not trying to guide the horse but letting it pick its own way, while he watched the road closely to anticipate any slip or jolt to spare Zoe all he could. Slowly the long dark miles dropped beneath them. His arms were numb from her dead weight, his body ached from the strain of his position, but his heart was on the rack, and he did not feel it.

He thought of the first time he had made this ride with Zoe. How she had looked ahead to Paradise—a sanctuary. What sort of refuge had it been for her? For the baby? Up there Jacqueline was fighting for her life, wanting her mother to come. Here—on the Lost Friar Trail—Zoe was coming! Remorse quickened Steve's brain to everything that increased self-accusation but deadened it to the many rays of light pierced in the black cloud of mystery by this night's revelations. He did not wonder why The Stranger—or Lance, as he now knew him—had left that night of Zoe's arrival without talking to her, finding out her trouble, and so saved himself that trip. Nor why she should think him dead. One revelation all but paralyzed his power of thought—Zoe was the bandit! He could not believe it. And yet he asked his tortured heart, climbing now in the utter dark, was it any more odd than that he, who would have died for her, had shot her?

The stars were out, jeweling the jet-black night with a million lances. A white glow lit the steep trail except for long stretches where the trees canopied it. And by this light Steve stopped often to make sure Zoe was breathing. Half way up the grade he felt her move in his arms and looked down. Her eyes were open—big, black, luminous, with the terror he had first seen in them, but it passed, and she smiled pitifully. "Steve! It was . . . you?"

His lips quivered. "God knows I didn't mean to, Zoe!"

And he wanted to explain how he came to do it, knowing she would absolve him, but he checked himself. At least he could spare her that—that worry about. . . .

Anxiously she whispered: "Steve, how's Jack?"

How was Jack? Steve would give the world to know! He managed to evade. "She's up there, Zoe."

He wished she wouldn't talk, or think—would save her strength. But her pale face, so near his own that it thrilled him through all his torment, was thoughtful, fearful. "The posse . . . ?" She raised herself, whimpering as pain tore through her.

"Gone, Zoe. Miles away by this time. Lie back . . . rest."

But her frantic gaze had fallen on the laboring shoulder of The Stranger's black, and she struggled in Steve's arms. "Oh, Steve," she panted, fighting for strength of utterance. "Stop! We must go back! There's something in my saddle bags! Something I've got to have! It's . . . it's worth more to me than all the world!"

"It's safe," he tried to quiet her. "The Stranger took your horse to fool the posse. They never saw it was a different rider. Anything of yours is safe with. . . ."

"The Stranger?" She was wilder than ever.

"He's The Stranger to me, Zoe, but he ain't no stranger to you. He said to tell you not to worry. He's got a scheme to help you. He said you think he's dead. But . . . he's been buried alive in Paradise." He felt her trembling, saw with what wild, incredulous hope and joy her eyes fixed themselves on him. "He's been helpin' you all along. He helped you get away at the mine. An' tonight. . . ."

"Lance!" she breathed. "Oh, I thought so! I thought it was his voice! God hasn't deserted me! It seemed . . . it was Lance, wasn't it, Steve?"

"Yes," said the boy wearily, "it was Lance."

She relaxed in his arms, her face more peaceful now than he had ever seen it. He might have been the wounded one, so drawn with pain was his own.

"Steve," she whispered earnestly, "don't think of it. It's . . . all right, Steve."

What wasn't he to think about? What was all right? Oh, everything. Lance was alive!

Another deeper, darker mile had dropped behind before she spoke again. Her eyes were wide and brave and filled with dread. "It . . . hurts," she gasped. "Oh, I've simply got to rest."

"We're almost there, Zoe." He hated to stop now. Every moment added to her danger. She must have care. That wound must be cauterized and. . . .

"I can't . . . can't stand it!" she moaned. "Steve, put me down!"

He drew rein and, easing her to the ground, carried her to the side of the trail beside the frothing Lost Friar. As he lowered her to the thick, springy couch of moss, she lapsed into unconsciousness. He ran to the stream for water. Stooping to dip some in his hat, a chill ran up his spine, the primitive warning of an unseen presence—an instinct strong in wilderness men. Whirling, gun in hand, he saw— with rage as primordial—a long dark form slip from the shadows and bend over Zoe. A form that entered upon the scene with a cunning for silent motion that had eclipsed the cunning of the fierce Apache. A form he had once seen in light more dim. The old bloodhound— Panamint!

# XII

## "A FRIEND"

Why he did not shoot there and then, did not pile tragedy on tragedy, Steve was never able to understand, so crazed was he to see Panamint—Art Jessel's hireling—standing over his helpless quarry, so sure then that the posse was behind him. But something stayed him, made him fire first the warning: "Stand back, Panamint! I'll kill you if you touch her!"

The old trailer seemed not to hear, seemed not to see the boy advancing with cocked revolver. He seemed to be mesmerized by the girl's face, so gleaming white in a jeweled shaft of starlight as he muttered under his breath: "It's her! I'd know her anywhere! It's Joan . . . a woman!"

As the bowstring snaps into place, its arrow sped, so Panamint jerked up. And with a glitter in his eyes no night could hide, and an ominous ring in his voice that struck through Steve's grief, he demanded: "Who done it? Boy, did the posse shoot her?"

Bitterness blotting out all else, Steve told the bitter truth: "I shot her!"

Panamint must have guessed that a tragic mistake lay back of it, for his face softened, and he said with a gruff pity: "I'm alone, Steve. I'm a friend. You sure need one. And she does worse. Put up that gun an' hold this light till I see how bad she's hurt."

Not understanding, or trying to, sensing only that Panamint was an ally, Steve took the flashlight which the old plainsman had drawn from one of the capacious buckskin pockets. He held it while Panamint drew Zoe's blouse back, removed the compress, and bared the wound. Steve did not look at it but searched instead Panamint's dark face. He was in despair as he saw it grave with, he thought, fear of the worst; he was near collapse when it cleared and the old man muttered: "Shot through. High, though. No bones touched. An' we'll take precautions ag'in' that. Fetch me that kit outta my saddle bags. My hoss is back the road a piece."

Steve found the horse and ran back with the kit, thanking heaven for having sent help tonight to this wild mountainside. Help of no mean kind, for Panamint was skilled in rude surgery. He knew exactly what to do and did it as gently as a woman, talking all the time. "Poor lass!" he murmured as if Zoe heard him. "Little we know what's around the bend. Little I dreamed I'd see you this way, be trailin' you!"

"You've tracked her down!" flashed the tormented boy. "You'll get your price . . . soft livin' the rest of your life, at the cost of . . . !"

"Don't!" said the old man huskily. "Forgive, boy, as you want to be forgiven. We've a heap to regret . . . both of us."

Steve was shamed to the quick. "I didn't mean it, Panamint. I'm just . . . out of my head."

"Sure, son. Now hand me that iodine." Oh, Steve was glad that Zoe was not conscious then. "I ain't in Jessel's pay no more," cried the trailer. "Money couldn't hire me to track her . . . ol' Treff's girl! As soon as I found it was Joan, I told Jessel I'd lost my knack. Told him I couldn't find anything in Paradise that night, that my eyesight had gone bad. An' he fired me outta hand. Which suited me to the ground . . . considerin' all I did find." He looked around. "Now, Steve . . . that gauze."

Steve handed it to him. "What did you find, Panamint?"

But the old man, absorbed in his bandaging, stuck to his own trail of thought. "That day we tracked our man in Paradise, Jessel snooped in that cabin . . . the one you found me in three days later, doin' the same thing. Next day he 'most knocked me cold by callin' me in an' tellin' me a woman was back of the robbery. Said he'd found out she was stayin' in Paradise an' knowed who she was. Said he didn't want the sheriff to know it yet but would have him make me a deputy so I could go up an' investigate, an' if she was there, to bring her in. Not to Sears but to him! Said he wanted to deal with her himself. But before I left, he showed me what he'd found in that cabin. . . . Thar!" he exclaimed with a certain pride. "That's done! An' a mighty neat job. 'Twon't come loose on the way up an' hemorrhage none."

Drawing the blouse over the bandage, he buttoned it and peered into Zoe's face, cursing under his breath, cursing Jessel, cursing himself. Then he got to his feet beside Steve, who leaned against a pine, praying that this was a dream, wondering what Panamint had found.

"When I seed that," pursued the old man, "I'd 'a' quit the case right then, only I figgered it best to learn all I could, if I was to help. It was a locket that...." Zoe's locket! She had left it. Jessel had found it, identified her by it! "A gold one ... with two pictures in it. One of Treff Valle ... my pard of early days ... with his baby on his knee. His baby Joan here ... who was just like a daughter to me. The other was of a purty woman who anyone could see was the baby growed up. I tell you, Steve, it give me a shock to run across her like that. An' I knowed if Treff's girl was robbin' Jessel, she had mighty good cause. An' well she might have ... considerin' ol' Treff found an' owned the Storm King which Jessel is manager of. An' I made up my mind I was goin' to find out what it was an' help her if I could. Same as Treff would do for one of my girls ... if he wasn't dead. She's all right, Steve."

For the boy had bent over Zoe again, to be sure she breathed.

"Can't you see," Panamint exclaimed, "she's restin' easy?"

"Too easy!" Steve groaned. "She could go on ... restin' like that ... just as easy as not. She might never wake up. Just rest ...!"

"Boy, hang onto yourself! She's in no danger now. The test will come later. But the Valles are a hardy breed. She'll make the grade. She's goin' to need you, Steve. Hitch your mind to that."

Steve tried to, but his brain kept whirling. Joan Valle! That was her maiden name. He liked it—Joan. But he liked Zoe better. Would she let him call her Zoe when ...? It didn't matter. When she got well, she'd go—with The Stranger.

"Lissen, Steve. We've got to get together on this. I've assembled all the pieces to this puzzle but the key ones. Mebbe you can furnish 'em. What I want to know is how, if Joan robbed the Storm King, it was a six-foot man we follered to Paradise?"

"How do you know that?" the boy cried.

"Why, you see, I was up there quite a spell before you found me in the cabin." Closely, through the gloom, Panamint watched Steve. "An' it would take a big *hombre* to fill the footprints I found in that ol' tunnel, Steve. For I found your tracks in it, an' Trig's ... an' a li'l track that has me guessin' yet." He paused for a moment, hoping for an explanation, but Steve made none. Panamint reproached him:

"Don't trust me, boy? Waal"—looking down at the senseless girl—"I can't blame you. I got my surmise, though. After hearin' the bandit described two ways . . . as a big man by Jessel, an' just a kid by Clark . . . I come to the conclusion there must be two of 'em, a big one an' a little one, that the big *hombre* had drawed pursuit to hisself deliberate . . . so the little one could get away. He left a trail a blind man couldn't miss to Paradise an' out . . . though he could throw dust in our eyes whenever he'd a mind to. An' it come to me why he done that. The woman was the little bandit. Joan . . . Treff's girl! I knowed Treff had trained her to ride an' shoot, an' that she had the family grit, so she could carry it out . . . particular with a man helpin' her . . . as foxy as that *hombre* is. An' tonight. . . ." Tonight! Steve tried hard to concentrate. "Tonight I come down town to find it sizzlin' with news of the stage hold-up. Two men done it, they said . . . a tall man an' a kid. I was sartin sure it was the same pair. I trailed the posse out an' over the flats, till I come to that tangle of sign in the wash an' was stumped bad, but finally I got it straightened out. Someone, I see, had been hurt an' took away by another somebody who rode a hoss an' trailed a *burro*. The posse was after somebody else ag'in . . . likely the big *hombre*, repeatin' his old tricks, while the party with the mule was helpin' the girl escape. I figgered it was you an' come. Now, boy, I've showed you my hand."

Again he paused expectantly. Again Steve said nothing.

"Don't trust me yet?" Panamint reproached him.

"I sure do," Steve said warmly.

"Then why are you holdin' out on me?"

"Holdin' out?"

"About the big bandit. Who is he?"

"Panamint, don't ask me! I can't tell you . . . yet. Mebbe when he knows you're a friend. . . ."

"I savvy." The old trailer nodded. "But, Steve, why did you shoot her? What was you doin' down thar? Can you tell me that?"

Steve did. He was going to need Panamint's help. It was bound to come out. Briefly he told him about Jacqueline, her sickness, his need for haste, and his desperate act.

"Uh-huh," mused the old-timer. "Baby . . . that's what I thought. Baby sick . . . mother hurt . . . both in need of nursin'."

In his wild impatience, Steve broke in: "Then prove you're a friend! Get a doctor . . . quick!"

"Doctor?" Panamint was shocked. "Want to kill 'em? Besides, if the truth comes out, this li'l girl may go to prison. Boy, I'm a-goin' home to fetch my ol' woman. Contrary to most of her sect, she's close mouthed. An' she's plumb healin'. I'd sooner have her a-doctorin' me'n a whole flock of M.D.s. An' she's had a sight more experience with gunshots. An' babies. . . . Say, she'll fetch that young 'un around in no time. She's raised a baker's dozen of her own. Here, let me help you get off. Then I'll make tracks."

In a moment Steve was mounted again. Zoe was laid in his arms. Oh, it was good to have her there, even like this! Panamint, stiff as a dried hide, took his hand and said: "Steve, the worst is yet to come. I don't mean just with her but . . . sparrow hawk! Trig had him right. Boy, Jessel's got a bunch of toughs from the mine guardin' his property since the last hold-up. He's plumb loco about what he's already lost. He'll come to Paradise ag'in backed . . . not by a sheriff's posse . . . but by his hoodlums. There's goin' to be a hot time in the ol' town."

Then he was making tracks down the grade, and Steve was renewing his toilsome grind. The pain of the motion brought Zoe to consciousness, only to faint again, and be brought back to more pain. She was unconscious when they won the last discouraging pitch and rode, by dead of night, into the dead town.

Again the sound of his horse too soon returning brought Trig to the porch to see, by the lamplight streaming out, the boy and his burden. Tottering down the illumined path, he peered, stricken, into Zoe's still face then, trembling, he turned to Steve. "Son," he quavered confusedly, "she looks . . . like my Zoe. Like my Zoe, when . . . they said she was dead. They carried her up the hill . . . prayed over her. . . ." And then, looking back at the girl, the time of which he spoke seemed the reality, and he touched her cheek, pleading heartbreakingly: "Zoe . . . wake up! Look at me! Girl, you're jist a-foolin' me! Wake up, Zoe! They're goin' to put you away."

To bring him back from the day, thirty years ago, when they had laid his Zoe away, Steve cried sharply: "It's *my* Zoe! She ain't goin' to die!"

The old man raised his anguished face and brushed a hand across his bewildered eyes. "Your Zoe," he muttered. "That's so," and he turned away wearily.

"Trig!" It took all Steve's nerve to ask. "How's Jack?"

Trig's mind, cloudy on all else, was clear on this. "She's mendin', Steve. She's been askin' for you. I told her you'd come tomorrer. She's restin' now."

Words choked in Steve's throat. He carried Zoe into her cabin and laid her on the bed. When Trig, who had lighted the way for him, had left, the boy bent over her, his dark face strangely steady. *Jessel's comin'*, he thought to himself. *He's bringin' his thugs. He wants to deal with you hisself.* Aloud he said: "Girl, you just lie still . . . rest."

## XIII

### "HE'S GOT HER!"

Close mouthed—Panamint's wife? Not so you could notice it! Except, perhaps, on secret things—which was most likely what Panamint meant. But she sure was healing! Five minutes from the time she yanked her sunbonnet off, tied her blue-checked apron on, and took her patient in hand, Zoe said she felt as if she was in heaven. After a dose or two of tea made from the herbs Panamint's wife brought with her, Jacqueline was as good as ever and happy as a lark to be with her mother. Steve blessed the ground Panamint's wife walked upon.

Always at the beck and call of anyone in trouble, she was never happier than when she had both strong and capable hands full. She was a typical frontier woman, and she looked exactly as Panamint would if you put petticoats on him. She was tall, brown, and lean, every bit as sun seared and time seamed. And Steve, who was much at a loss what to call her for he did not know Panamint's real name and felt he could not just call her, as the old trailer respectfully did, his "ol' woman," naturally addressed her at first as Mrs. Panamint.

"Lawsy!" she exclaimed, her brown eyes snapping. "That sounds fine. But it takes too much time. Ma's plenty, son."

So she was Ma to everyone—barring old Trig who had been suspicious of her from the first, a feeling Ma returned with interest. Trig was jealous because Ma wanted to do everything for Jacqueline.

"You tell that ol' woman," he would grumble to Steve, "to let Jack be. I can tend to my own baby. I had her all cured up. Then she comes along an' takes the credit . . . her an' her tea."

And Ma was as outspoken. "That ol' man," she'd complain to Steve, "gives me the creeps. The way he eyes me . . . lawsy! I was givin' Jack some pennyroyal, an' he jumped on me like I was poisonin' her. I don't see how her mother puts up with it. If that child was mine. . . ." And she would tighten her lips to show where Trig would come in under those circumstances.

Steve tried to reason with Trig, but Trig had little reason left. New things had been coming too fast for him. He could not assimilate them, and he gave up trying. He gave up his mental grip on everything but Jacqueline. He clung to her with every failing faculty. Steve foresaw tragedy when Zoe took the baby away. For that matter he saw nothing but tragedy—in the constant threat of Jessel's coming, every inkling of which he had kept from Zoe, in the chance that the sheriff might decide to look over Paradise again, in The Stranger's continued absence, in Zoe's worry about him—worst of all, he saw it in the lawless things Zoe had done. What would be the outcome? Sheriff Sears was slow but nothing stopped him when he got going. There would be a reckoning. Look where he would, Steve saw trouble coming, and he could do nothing to avert it—could only wait.

On one point, however, his mind was at rest. He had told Zoe how he came to do what he had done that night, and she had said that he did just right. He had done the one thing he saw at the time to do for Jacqueline. Zoe had cried with tears in her eyes: "Steve, you've been my rock of refuge."

He knew it was not true. Lance had been that. But he wished he could be yet, wished Zoe trusted him enough to tell him what it was all about, so he could put up a fight. Boyishly he wished he could rout Jessel and all his hoodlums single-handed. Together he and Panamint—who had stayed on, occupying The Stranger's cabin—discussed the advisability of hiding her in the old tunnel, but Ma vetoed that. She put her foot down flat. Put a sick woman in that damp, drafty hole? Not if she knew it! It would be the death of her—that, or the pack-rat smell. So, overruled in this, the men left Zoe where she was and, to guard against surprise, took turns watching from the high peak that had been Zoe's look-out. Every daylit hour found Steve or Panamint on guard there. Yet their vigilance would be of no avail, for who knew the advantage of a lofty perch better than the sparrow hawk?

On the second day Panamint, making a record trip to Toroda, brought word back that The Stranger had completely eluded the posse that night. Steve was there when he told Zoe, and her joy at the news hurt, though he was glad too and knew that part of it was relief that Sheriff Sears had not got whatever she had in her saddle bags.

Often, in his lonely watches, Steve wondered what this was. What had she taken from Jessel that he was so afraid for her to have, that he wouldn't let the law help him get back but must deal with her himself? And, if she had it, what was her reason for holding up the stage? Not money! She had plenty. She had been poor when Panamint had known her. But her father—just a wandering prospector, then— had discovered the Storm King and had made a fortune from it. High in the Derelicts, on that bald spur where he had often sat with the girl, pointing out the landmarks to her, wondering at her questions, Steve often thought of the day—now two months past—when he had found her, of her terror when he offered to take her to Toroda. He knew now that it was fear of Jessel, who—Lance said—was in a plot against her. He often thought of the way Zoe's eyes flashed when she told him she wasn't going to Paradise to bury herself but to get strength, rest, to do the "terrible thing" she must. She had meant these robberies that had so infuriated Jessel. It seemed to him that fate must have led her here—straight to Lance, whom she had for years thought dead but who still cared enough to be risking his life for her. Where was he now? Was he planting his bomb under Jessel? Steve wished he would come—end Zoe's suspense, though the coming meant tragedy to him. His brooding gaze was fixed on the desert in as much eagerness for The Stranger as in dread of Jessel. When Panamint sat there, watching with his cat's eyes, and Steve was free to look in on Zoe, he would see her disappointment and reproach himself for not being Lance.

Yet for all the threat, pain, and strain, life went on smoothly under Ma's regime. The threat of Jessel had not the power to dim the blaze of August sun or stop the Lost Friar from running along—dimpling in its shallows, frowning in its still waters—or mute the bird songs in the willows that overhung its grassy banks, nor did vestige of his shadow fall upon the oldest and youngest inhabitants. Again Trig and Jacqueline, hand in hand, went rambling, hunting the mother lode, she assuring him in perfect trust: "It's somewhere, Trig," and he quavering in unfaltering faith: "As sure as there's balm in Gilead!" Nor did any of the awful threats, locked within her own heart, retard Zoe's recovery. Ma declared she had never seen "a body" make such headway with a gunshot wound. And Zoe smiled, giving Ma's hard hand a grateful squeeze as she said: "But see who my nurse is!" Steve thought there was a lot in that. You couldn't keep your mind on trouble, seeing Ma bustling around, so sensible and sane, and listening to her cheerful chatter.

The morning of the fourth day Steve was about to leave for the look-out to relieve Panamint, on guard since dawn, when Ma came in and said Zoe wanted to see him. Steve went over and found Zoe looking so well he just stood twisting his sombrero and staring at her as she lay there, the soft cloud of her hair blue black against the pillows, her sweet girlish face, pale and thin but hauntingly beautiful in the golden trail which the morning sun was blazing over the white-and-purple Indian blanket. He thought she did not look much older than Jacqueline and as sweet and innocent—the little bandit!

"Sit down, son." Ma shoved a chair under him. Then, on the plea that she had to "rinse out a few things," she bustled out, leaving them alone. Steve waited, wondering what Zoe wanted, unable to think of a thing to say. There was so much he couldn't touch on—where she didn't trust him.

To put him at his ease, Zoe said: "Jack tells me she's going prospecting this morning."

"Yeah," Steve grinned. "Trig had a dream about the ledge last night. They're goin' to find it . . . just like that! Trig ain't got a doubt in the world it's there. All he's got to do is to find out where."

Said Zoe after a while: "That's the only way, Steve. Just go straight to your goal. You won't get far if you don't think it's there." And he knew she was not thinking of Trig at all. Suddenly she said, with a sad smile: "I've been a safe blower, committed a hold-up, and I don't know what all, to gain mine."

Tensely, his blue eyes fixed on her face, Steve asked: "Have you gained it, Zoe?"

She did not speak for some time. "I . . . I think so," she said then, "but . . . it's in my saddle bags . . . with Lance. Steve, do you think he'll come soon?"

Steve did not know. He hoped so. He said earnestly: "He'll come as soon as he can, Zoe."

Looking out the open door, he wondered if he ought to tell her that they feared Jessel might come too, that Jessel had found the locket, knew her to be the bandit, and had learned that she lived in Paradise. But he could not bear to pile more worry on her, and everything was so peaceful. . . .

"Five years!" Zoe cried in wonder. "Think of it, Steve! Five years Lance was buried alive in this place." Steve did not think that was so much. He had been here many more himself. "Five years!" Zoe couldn't get over it. "Not knowing what was happening to those at home. Living with the knowledge of the pain he'd caused them. I don't see how he stood it, Steve." Her dark eyes went out to the crumbling town, up to the frowning Derelicts, and suddenly turning back to him she said swiftly: "I've done wrong, Steve, to keep you in the dark. I didn't like to unload my troubles on you, but I can't keep things shut up! I want to tell you about myself."

He said in his downright way: "You don't have to, Zoe . . . unless you think it will help." Her just wanting to was enough. She *did* trust him. Wildly happy, he could hardly wait for her to begin, but she was watching the scene in the street.

The prospectors were getting ready to start out. Sleepy old Jenny, drooping as if she needed a prop, viewed the preparations in disgust. Jack, in her blue overalls and sandals, was helping Trig hunt his pick, which he swore he'd put right there by the porch and which couldn't "take legs an' run off," and he had a mighty strong suspicion where it had gone. That old woman had hid it on him.

Zoe turned back to Steve, dark memories crowding her face. "I hardly know where to begin," she faltered. "There's so much. I can only pick out the highlights. But to make a start . . . it was my father who discovered the Storm King."

"I know. Panamint told me. He talks by the hour of Treff Valle an' you."

"Oh, I remember him, too!" The girl's eyes lit with a warm light. "But I never thought of him when I came back. The only friend I could think of . . . the only one who could give me shelter, so I wouldn't be seen in Toroda . . . was Ike Ware who took up Fool's Acres. He was another of Dad's old partners. I went to him, only to find that. . . . Steve, all my early life was spent in the wastelands. I've prospected with Dad from the Canadian to the Mexican line. But after Dad discovered the Storm King, things changed. Having made his strike, he lost all interest in mining. I was fifteen then. He wanted me to have advantages. We moved to Los Angeles. And Dad, not even wanting the responsibility of operating the Storm King, had a mining brokerage firm incorporate it for him, turning over to them a majority of the stock . . . almost as a gift because he wanted James Grayson to handle it. Grayson was the head of the firm. He had two sons . . . Lance and Jim. Among the assistants in his office was a nephew of Missus Grayson's, Art Jessel.

"Yes," she smiled mirthlessly at Steve's sharp start, "enter the villain! Few people had any use for him. But because he was a favorite with Missus Grayson . . . her only surviving kin . . . he was given a place of trust. James Grayson and my father died within a month of each other. Some time before his going, Dad had sold the firm his remaining interest in the Storm King, but we had kept up our friendship with the Graysons. In fact . . . after that I made my home with them. You see, I was only seventeen, and all alone. Like you, Steve, I don't remember my mother."

Again she paused—to pick out the next highlight, or to watch the procession starting out, Trig with his pick—which Ma hadn't hidden on him, after all—leading the old *burro* on whose fat back Jack was perched, her golden ringlets gleaming in the sun, brighter than the mother lode they hoped someday to find. Then the street was empty again.

"James Grayson's death"—Zoe continued rapidly—"gave Art Jessel his chance. He played up to Missus Grayson, won her full confidence, and gradually assumed management of the entire business, including the Storm King. But soon . . . either through neglect of it for the mine, or because it suited his selfish ends . . . he ran the firm into bankruptcy. The doors were closed, pending the appointment of a receiver. And in this interval, a hundred thousand dollars in Liberty Bonds, held in the firm's trust, disappeared. Only three people had access to the vaults . . . Jessel and the Grayson boys. Jessel, of course, proved an alibi, showing that he was out of town at the time. Jim was arrested. Little by little they forged a chain of evidence against him. We were engaged then, were to be married within the month. They brought the case to trial, and . . . Jim was convicted. And then. . . . Oh, Steve, the sacrifice of it! Lance came forward and confessed. He was sentenced to San Quentin for ten years, but he never reached prison. While crossing on the ferry, he escaped the guard and jumped overboard. He was wiped from the records as being legally dead. But through everything, Mother Grayson . . . she was my mother by law now, and a real mother to me . . . never lost faith in Art Jessel. The Storm King was saved from the crash, owing to the fact that James Grayson had left it as a separate estate to his wife. She kept Jessel on as manager. He moved to Toroda where he could devote his whole time to it, and. . . ." Imploringly she threw a hand toward Steve. "Summon all your faith in me!" she cried tremulously. "I'm going to strain it."

"Not mine, Zoe!"

Tears sparkled in the smile her dark eyes flashed him. And she hurried on, as if to get it all over and done with: "Steve, the next summer I was in the hospital in Los Angeles. Mother Grayson was in Toroda at the time but, when she got Jim's wire, she started right home. Jessel accompanied her. Their train was wrecked a few miles out of Los Angeles, and Jim's mother was fatally hurt. She died in the hospital where, a few hours before, Jack was born. But in a will made on her deathbed, she left the Storm King to Jack. Then . . . as if fate must help Jessel in his wicked ambitions . . . a year later Jim passed away . . . pneumonia . . . and then I. . . ." It was not the old grief that swept Zoe's face that made Steve's heart go out to her, but that fear he had first seen on it—a great, gripping terror. "Before I got over the shock, a woman cropped up out of nowhere and claimed my baby was hers. I thought she was crazy at first. But she . . . Sadie Kurtz . . . brought her claim to the court. She proved by the perjured evidence of two nurses . . . bribed by Jessel, I know now . . . that she had been in the hospital at the same time I was, that Jim had come to her, told her that our baby had died, and that the shock of knowing it would be too much for me, that he paid her a thousand dollars to substitute her child for ours. And Art Jessel . . . oh, I can see him now, so convincingly reluctant, testified that he had loaned Jim a thousand dollars at the very time the Kurtz woman had sworn that Jim paid the money to her."

Zoe's eyes closed on their black bitterness, and she lay back white and spent. Steve waited, his whole being tense, hate for Jessel consuming him and pity for Zoe—only twenty-two—put through such torture.

"Oh, I made a fight," wearily she assured him. "I showed them how . . . with Jacqueline out of the way . . . Jessel, as Mother Grayson's only heir, would inherit the Storm King. I told them Jack was mine . . . that a mother knew. But nothing I did or said had much weight. I kept it in the courts a year, but Jessel had laid his plans too well. I lost. Before they could take Jack, I ran away. I knew I couldn't hide her forever. But I intended to take refuge at Fool's Acres, and from there put into execution the plan I'd formed. You know what happened. How I found Ike Ware gone . . . the ranch burned . . . I lost my head then. I didn't know what to do or where to turn to. But . . . you found me, Steve. You gave me a home, gave me time to get my bearings."

Her eyes flashed as they had flashed that day in the blossoming sage. Well, Steve now knew the meaning of that defiant blaze. Every mother fights for her young. Zoe was fighting for Jacqueline.

"I had to get evidence against Jessel. Steve, I'd fought him fair. Now I didn't care. I'd never give Jack up. And out of court . . . up here . . . home again . . . I wasn't a defenseless woman. I could use a gun. I could, if I had to . . . and I did . . . use dynamite. I blew Jessel's safe. I didn't find what I wanted, but . . . well, wait till Lance gets back!"

Her eagerness couldn't dispel Steve's firm conviction that nothing would stop Jessel from coming—with all that to bring him. Fiercely his eyes went to the street, hearing steps. But it was only Trig, who had forgotten something and come back to the cabin. Watching him go in, Steve relaxed. Panamint was watching, too.

"Keeping straight toward my goal," Zoe ended, "I broke into Jessel's house. Luck was with me this time. I found the canceled checks he had given his witnesses for their perjured evidence, his correspondence with Sadie Kurtz. It was almost conclusive, but I was as insatiable as he. I knew he was terrified. I felt sure he would write to her. One night, watching his house, I saw him writing. I watched him post the letter. I resolved to have it at all costs. I held up the stage. . . ."

She started up from her pillow, shaking like a leaf as Ma rushed in, screaming to Steve, who pushed past her, his face dead white. "Oh, I told you so! I told you that ol' man was crazy as a loon!"

And Trig was. Halted there on the porch, his eyes blazing up the street to where he had left Jack, he was yelling like a maniac: "He's got her! That sparrow hawk!"


## XIV

### "CORNERED"


As Steve burst out of the cabin, the child's screams pierced his ears, while Trig rushed by, mumbling demented things. His eyes, flashing up street, fell on a sight that sent him pounding after Trig, almost as wild as he. For in front of the old Nevada House, two blocks up, Art Jessel was lifting Jacqueline from the *burro's* back. Overstrung as he already was by Zoe's recital, Steve would have shot Jessel there and then, but as his gun leaped into his hand, he realized that he dare not shoot lest he hit Jack. And it flashed to him that he would be doubly handicapped in this showdown. Trig was unarmed. He would have to watch out for him as well as for Jacqueline.

Sharply he yelled, rushing by: "Get your gun! Your gun, Trig! I'll watch him!"

The old man understood and, without the loss of a single motion, turned and ran back. Running on, it struck Steve that Jessel was showing strange unconcern, making no move to get away, just walking, watching, holding the struggling baby. He knew he was safe behind her—the coyote! But as he dashed across the intersection and into that block, Steve learned the reason for Jessel's contemptuous indifference to his hostile approach. For when he was scarcely forty paces off, Jessel's hand went up in a signal. At the act, half a dozen men burst out of the Nevada House, every one with a gun in his hand, and every gun fully on Steve.

"That's far enough!" Jessel called. As Steve stopped, he added: "I just wanted you in earshot."

Hotly the boy's gaze passed over the men—a hard-faced, wicked-looking lot—to rest on Jessel, none too gently restraining Jack who was fighting like a little wildcat. "You drop her!" blazed Steve, his blood boiling. "Take your paws off her or. . . ."

"Or . . . what?" broke in the Storm King man with an insulting laugh. "The first crooked move from you will be your last. Do you know you're breaking the law up here . . . harboring a kidnapper?"

"You liar!"

"Go easy!" warned Jessel, his mean face twitching. "Maybe you don't know it, but that woman you're hiding up here is a kidnapper! The courts say so. I've got the law back of me. And," he said superfluously with evil triumph, "I've got the kid! I'm taking her to her lawful mother right now, if. . . ."

"If what?" Steve took him up, nervily feigning contempt himself.

"If," Jessel bargained, black with rage, "that she-thief don't give back every paper she took from my safe!"

Steve's angry heart thrilled exultantly. Jessel was scared badly, far worse than they had ever dreamed. He wanted to make terms! The boy did not know what to do. He was determined not to let Jessel see Zoe. He knew Zoe would promise anything on earth to get Jacqueline.

She would be crazy now, for she must have heard the baby scream. Undecided, desperate, he looked at Jack, whose big blue eyes were begging him to come to her aid. He looked at Jessel, cruel, implacable, and at his hired thugs, who would shoot at a word. And he knew Jessel would give it if. . . . Irrevocably, then, the matter was taken from his hands. For Trig rushed by, rifle half raised, as powerless to shoot as Steve had been, but with that in his face which brought a cry of terror from Jessel.

"Stop . . . you fool!"

But Trig did not hear nor did he see the threatening guns between him and the sparrow hawk who had his destroying clutches on Jack. A gun roared! Steve saw Trig stumble—fall—before his eyes, then a red mist swam, and whirling on the wretch who held the smoking gun, he fired point-blank. The man fell, clutching his shoulder, but he regained his feet as Steve charged straight at the rest.

"Get back!" The boy's words had the cutting force of a lash. "Get back, you rats, or I'll drop the bunch of you!" he cried, so taking them by surprise, so awing them by the promise of death in his voice, his flaming eyes, that they fell back before him, taking shelter in the Nevada House.

Before they could recover their wits, Steve had reached Trig, who was struggling up, and helped him into the Blue Moon opposite. They were safely inside when a leaden hail ripped across, splintering the rotten casements, tearing holes in the wood. Harmlessly the storm went on while Steve held Trig, trying to find out how badly he was hurt.

"It's nothin'!" the old man raved. "Just a scratch . . . in the leg! There . . . see for yourself! It's just a scratch!"

To Steve's relief that's all it was, but it was not Jessel's fault. All at once Steve saw the seriousness of the situation.

"Let me go!" Trig was as violent as he had been that day of the search. "He's got Jack!"

"An' he'll have her!" It took all Steve's young strength to hold him. "If you go out there, his men will kill you! He'll have Jack then!"

Trig ceased to fight at that and ran to the door, which Steve had slammed behind him, not to open it but to throw himself on the floor, thrusting the muzzle of his rifle through the missing lower panel, blazing away at the Nevada House, exhorting Steve: "Pour lead into 'em! Melt 'em!"

Steve, carried away by the thrill of battle, by the sting of gunsmoke in his nostrils, kicked out a board nailed across a broken window and emptied his gun. Then he cursed himself for wasting ammunition. He knew that he hadn't hit anyone, wasn't likely to. All the cartridges he had were in his belt. Shoving shells into the empty chambers, he looked into the street, hung with blue wisps of smoke, and saw Jessel, stunned at the turn things had taken, backing into the Last Chance, adjoining the Nevada, holding the frightened child as a shield before him. Trig, too, saw. He was already up, had yanked the door ajar, and was recklessly exposing himself to the fire that, all this while, had kept up over there. In a bound Steve reached him, pulling him back just as a volley struck.

Then things seemed at a deadlock, one that could not long endure. Trig was almost beyond control. Steve was desperate—for Jessel had disappeared. No telling what the man might do. He could get out of the Last Chance by the rear, escape through the ruins behind, and get away, or go to Zoe, while his thugs kept Trig and Steve penned here. How had they got by Panamint? Jessel must have slipped in during the night and been hiding all morning, watching his chance.

"Let ... go ... of ... me!" Trig raved. "I. . . ."

Then he was transfixed by a scream wilder than his own, one that curdled Steve's blood. They heard shots that did not rip into the Blue Moon, a torrent of imprecations not aimed at them and, looking out the window, they saw Jessel's men bursting from the Nevada. Not out front did they come, taking chances on being dropped by them, but through the windows opening into the alley between the Nevada and the Last Chance.

Wondering at the cause of their sudden evacuation, determined to keep pace with them, Steve and Trig crawled through the side windows of the Blue Moon to take shelter in the next building. They saw, as they dropped down—as another blood-curdling whoop came to them—a wild figure in the alley over there, a terrifying figure with long hair blowing wildly, leathery face fixed in a ferocious scowl, gun blazing in almost a steady flash, emitting war whoops that must have been utterly unnerving to Jessel's thugs. Panamint! He had heard the shooting and come to aid them. Steve's spirits rose as if the newcomer were a regiment.

"We've got 'em betwixt us!" the old trailer yelled. "Go after 'em!" And he ducked around the rear of the Last Chance.

They heard his gun barking in the back, and they blazed away in front. They dared not shoot into the Last Chance, for Jacqueline might be in there, but the noise they made helped rout the men from this building into the next. Steve and Trig kept pace, firing constantly, and Panamint kept to the alley, finding the most unexpected places from which to rake the interior with fire, routing them out again, carrying the fight on down the dead blocks.

Paradise, stark in the blazing sun—old, despoiled, all her many shrunken, misshapen imperfections sharply drawn—was having one last fling, one moment of fierce life equal to, exceeding, any of her wanton youth. The austere spires, the somber forests, frowned on the unseemly sight. Panamint, veteran of a hundred skirmishes, was in his element. It was enough to scare a man to death to look at him! To hear him yelling that nerve-breaking war cry of the dread Apaches struck demoralization into Jessel's men. The house-to-house retreat became a rout until, reaching the shack at the street's end, too cowardly to take to the open and inspired by the courage that animates a cornered rabbit, they made a feeble stand. But here Steve and Trig and Panamint came together and, from the shelter of the building the thugs had just left, riddled the shack, forcing them out, sending them fleeing for their very lives up the hill to the old stamp mill. There, among its many boilers, chutes, and levels, they were safe for the time, for the defenders dared not follow them in, nor did they want them. They wanted Jessel.

"I saw him a minit back," Panamint yelled to Steve, crawling toward him, wiping the dust from his eyes. "He's makin' for the pass. Steve, go after him! I'll hold these hired guns."

Steve was off before the words were fairly spoken. The pass! Then Jessel was making a break to escape with Jack, to get her to a safe place where he could dictate terms. Streaking up the ridge, Steve wondered where Trig was, remembering that he had seen him, a moment before Panamint spoke, cutting back for the Last Chance where he had last seen Jack. He thanked heaven Trig wasn't to be in on this. He must catch Jessel before he reached his horse—most likely cached somewhere in the thick timber on the ridge. He had a terrible fear that he was already too late but, rounding a bend in the steep trail, he sighted Jessel disappearing around another bend a hundred yards on and Jack's terrified face, looking back as she bobbed up and down in his arms.

"Stop!" the boy shouted.

Jessel whirled. The gun in his hand belched, and a bullet sang past Steve's head. As Steve took to cover in the brush bordering the trail, hardly losing a motion in his headlong pursuit, Jessel held the child in front of him and backed to the crest, just a few yards on. Now Steve sighted the saddled horses waiting in a dense clump of trees beside the trail. In his desperation, as Jessel seized the bridle of the foremost one, he left the sheltering brush, plunging openly after him. Seeing that he was too late, he was frantically planning to risk a shot when he saw Jessel spin about, his face blank in utter bafflement. Following his gaze, he saw four riders sweep over the pass, wheeling to a stop beside Jessel. Steve recognized them in a blend of joy and despair. For it was Sheriff Sears, two of his deputies, and—The Stranger. He saw Sears, bulking big in the saddle, coolly cover Jessel with his gun, his face sterner than it had ever been. He saw Jessel staring at The Stranger as at a ghost.

"You!" he gulped panting, trembling, craven.

Coldly The Stranger smiled down on him. "Yes, Art . . . it's I."

Suddenly, seeing them together, Steve knew why Jessel had struck him as familiar. It was his likeness to The Stranger, a similarity of build and complexion—though Jessel resembled The Stranger only as an imitation resembles the real thing. He saw the glitter of inhuman hate in Jessel's eyes as, recovering from the shock, he faced them, trying to bluff Sears by asking: "Do you know who this man is? He's a fugitive! He's. . . ."

"I know all about it," Sears said evenly, "but you don't seem to. I'd better wise you up. You're under arrest."

Wildly Jessel laughed. "Under arrest? That's good! For what?"

"Waal," Sears drawled, prepared for the least quiver of motion in Jessel's gun, "you can take your pick . . . perjury, bribery, embezzlement . . . most anything you want. We've been keepin' the wires hot for a week, an'. . . . But your cousin, here"—indicating Lance—"can tell you a heap better than I can."

"He can't tell me anything!" Jessel foamed. "I tell you he's. . . ."

"Art"—Lance moved his horse up a step, and there was something almost like pity in his face—"you might as well give up. You've run out your string. It's been a long one . . . thanks to your treacherous soul that let you betray every confidence placed in you, betray your own flesh and blood, thanks to your miserly spirit and, yes, thanks to luck. For it was lucky for you that I took the blame for stealing those bonds when you fixed suspicion on Jim, otherwise you wouldn't have had a chance to plot for the Storm King. You see . . . heaven forgive me! . . . I thought Jim was guilty. He was so young and reckless. I confessed to the crime because I knew he and Joan . . . I wanted to see them happy."

Now Steve knew why The Stranger had buried himself. He had loved Zoe enough to clear the way for her to marry his brother. Steve's heart swelled with admiration—lost half its sting.

"You're crazy!" Jessel's face was pasty, and his bravado was deserting him fast.

"If I'm not," Lance flashed, "it isn't your fault. Look down there." He pointed at Paradise at her worst, spent, shattered. "I've put in five years there. Five years of torture. The best years of my life. Years when I should have been building. But"—grimly his face swung back to Jessel—"they're well spent if they held me here to write finish to your career."

"You will?" Jessel's lip went up in a wolfish sneer.

"It'll do you no good to bluff, Art." The Stranger was relentless. "I've got evidence enough . . . right in this saddle bag . . . to send you up for a good long stretch. When Joan came . . . when I found out how you'd plotted to take Jim's baby from her, to beggar the whole family, get everything into your selfish hands . . . I resolved to risk imprisonment for your crime on the chance of exposing you. So I went to the sheriff and laid everything before him. We've been working on the case a week, but Joan gets the credit. It was she who got the bonds Jim was accused of stealing from your safe. She must have remembered the numbers and denominations . . . else she wouldn't have taken them. They never did you much good, did they, Art? You didn't have the nerve to dispose of them. Still, I suppose you got a lot of pleasure from just fingering them. And it was Joan, too, who got the canceled checks you gave for perjured evidence. And your correspondence with Sadie Kurtz. Money mad! Well, you won't need any money where you are going. Sears will tell you that."

"You're dead right!" the sheriff snapped.

Jessel turned on him like a trapped thing, whining: "It's a frame-up! You can't prove it. I'm fighting this to a finish, and"—his grip on Jacqueline tightened as he turned back to his horse—"I'm taking this child to Sadie Kurtz, and whoever. . . ."

None of them ever knew just how it happened. It was all over in a second. The others were intent only on Jessel but, through his raving, Steve heard a rush behind him and saw Trig plunging past in a determination that would not be denied. He saw Jessel drop the child, terror glittering in his eyes. He saw Jessel's gun quivering in a sharp explosion, and Trig stagger back from the terrific impact. Trig reeled, with difficulty holding himself erect, and swayed during one second of awful silence in which Steve had two impressions—that a bird was singing and that he had never seen on Trig's old face such a look of absolute bewilderment.

Then, while they watched helpless with shock, the old man, with a mighty effort, steadied himself and raised his gun. It crashed smoke and flame, and the sparrow hawk dropped to the Lost Friar Trail. Trig sank slowly, his hands instinctively grasping a seedling pine that was precariously rooted in the rocks. He tore it out as he crashed and, with his other hand outflung, clutched at the rocks where it had been. Steve, running to him, lifting his head in his arms, saw that Trig would never need him again. He could leave Paradise any time. There wasn't anything holding him now.

Utterly unnerved, he had but a vague idea of what went on—of Jacqueline's grief-stricken cries, of the last gloating cry of the sparrow hawk, writhing in the dust: "Luck's with . . . me . . . yet! No stripes for . . . Art Jessel! Sure . . . I took the bonds . . . didn't want to . . . sell them! God . . . full value! I've had . . . five years of . . . your life. Five years . . . I've had . . . Storm King. Not bad . . . for . . . the . . . poor relation. . . ."

Death stopped him then.

Through his tears Steve saw Trig's hand on the rocks. He lifted it—tried to brush the dirt off. Then he saw something grasped in it. Gently opening the fingers that held it so tenaciously, he saw a fragment of rock and on its freshly broken edge the dull, unmistakable gleam of free gold.

## XV
### "THE GOAL"

Again Paradise is roaring. Only thirty days have passed, but the old town is wondrously transformed. Once more she is young and strong, and the more intriguing for all she has undergone. The Blue Moon Saloon, Top Notch, and Last Chance invite with bright, new signs, though gold is the real intoxicant. The Nugget Dance Hall, the Nevada, and Red Front lure with romantic promise—and live up to it. Dust lies thick on the streets bordering the Lost Friar. Through the gulch the wind still wails, and the river mourns, but human sounds drown their song. And the somber Derelicts, eternal, indestructible, frown down. For this, too, will pass in time, and they will again view its ruins. Graciously the silver ash now shades another mound. For Trig has been "carried up the hill" and laid to rest beside Nevada Zoe. And in that faraway land, where there is no delusion, she is again, perhaps, sweethearts with him.

The faith to which Trig clung so unswervingly in life was, in death, dramatically fulfilled. For the gold-flecked rock that Steve clasped from his dying hand proved to be the fragment of a rich vein which Trig bared as his last struggle uprooted the sapling pine. Trig had found his ledge—as sure as there was balm in Gilead!

No one denied Steve's claim to the find. And while he was still overcome by grief, Sheriff Sears, Lance Grayson, and Panamint attended to the filing, to every legal detail, making the claim secure against the gold-mad horde that stampeded into the district as soon as the news leaked out. Though they asked for nothing, Steve saw that every one of them shared his good fortune, so that Sheriff Sears now saw his way clear to buy the ranch that had been his dream for years and to which he will retire as soon as his term is up, and old Panamint found his old age provided for far beyond anything he hoped to get from Jessel, far beyond his wildest dreams.

"I'll scalp the *hombre*," fiercely he told Ma—who couldn't forgive herself for "abusin'" Trig—"who tries to sic me on another track!"

And so again an endless string of freight teams toils up that mountain grade—where every wash-out has been filled and the last barricading skeleton of a dead pine removed. Again the Derelicts tremble to heavy blasts, and drills bore into their very heart. And the old stamp mill—under repair, waiting for new machinery, now on its way across the flats—will soon clack again. For with the influx of prospectors and the revival of interest in the camp many of the old mines, so long abandoned, have been found to contain rich ore, overlooked in the mad haste of the first rush. Though the Gunnister—for Steve named his mine after its discoverer—is the big mine of Paradise. And today Steve is, in point of residence, the oldest inhabitant.

Coming out of his lonely cabin just as the sun sank behind the Derelicts, Steve felt old—old and used up. He could not get over missing Trig—hated to profit by his death. He was rich, he guessed, but what was the use of money unless you had someone to spend it on? Just responsibility. Right now there were a thousand things he should be doing. But instead of doing them, he sat down for a moment to rest behind the morning-glory vines. Their leaves had felt the nip of frost up here, for it was early September and would soon be fall. Nor would they be missed. They had given shelter from the blasting sun.

Now the sun was to be sought—not hidden from. They would dry and die, but they had served their purpose.

Something of this passed through Steve's mind as he looked across to Zoe's cabin. His blue-gray eyes were shy, still, and kind but not wistful. The hunger was gone. Every hope they ever had held had been abandoned. Zoe was still here, but every day she stayed prolonged his torture. Yet—how could he bear her going? He had not seen her often since Trig's death or, rather, he saw her constantly—with Lance. They were busy, he knew, with their own plans. He had not gone to see her. No need to make it harder.

There wasn't anything he could do for her. She was well now. Better than ever. She didn't have a thing to worry her. The only thing against her at all had been the attempt to rob the stage, and Sheriff Sears said that the law, as he interpreted it, was meant for the uses of justice; and he was interpreting the law in this neck of the woods, "by heck!" and didn't see any justice in persecuting a distracted mother who had only done what any woman worthy of the name would do. So she was free—to go. She would soon. She had not been able to see how Lance could stand. . . .

"Hoo! Hoo! Steve, see me!" came the childish hail.

He smiled to see Jacqueline riding by on the old *burro*. The streets were alive with wagons now, but old Jenny was watching out for her. He thought how deeply she had mourned for Trig and was glad she could forget.

His heart leaped as a step fell beside the porch, but it was only Lance. As he dropped into the chair that had been Trig's, Steve saw how eager his dark face was and understood his happiness. Together, for a long time in silent communion, they looked down at the roaring gold camp, as active at sun's set as at its rise. For whoever watched the clock in a gold strike?

Abruptly Lance turned. "Steve," he announced, "I'm leaving Paradise."

When he could trust his voice, Steve asked: "When?"

"Tonight," Lance rejoined. "On the stage. I've just stayed on until Zoe got well. She's fine now. She's able to paddle her own canoe, but she'll never have to again. She'll have me to . . . Steve, I'm taking over the Storm King Mine. Oh, you don't know what it means to be a man again!"

Steve said earnestly: "You've been that all along."

"To be free, I mean!" Lance cried, joy breaking down his reserve. "To be able to come and go . . . to think ahead. I. . . ." He checked himself, asking with real interest: "But you . . . Steve, what are your plans?"

Steve looked away. "I . . . I ain't got any," he confessed. "I used to make a lot. I used to be crazy to get away from Paradise, to get out in the world. Now . . . I don't care. The world's come here."

They said good bye after a while, not a real good bye for with Lance in Toroda they would be meeting often. But Zoe—that would be a real farewell, one Steve could not bear. To escape it he saddled Patch and struck off to the hills, going wherever Patch willed, until purple stained the sky above, and he found himself back at the lookout above the stamp mill, his eyes straining down to the desert which the stage must cross. Zoe would be half way down the grade by now. Now she'd be—a searing mist blinded his eyes. He moaned her name aloud, and through his heart shot all the concentrated joy of the universe as behind him, sweet and low, and softly, a voice said: "Steve!"

He started up, and there she was, with her big, dark eyes and black elf locks.

He faltered: "I thought you'd gone!"

"Me . . . go?" No music ever stirred Steve's heart like Zoe's low laugh. "No . . . I'm not leaving Paradise. Oh, Steve, I love this. The excitement . . . it's in my veins. I'm a prospector's daughter, remember?"

He didn't give a hang whose daughter she was, but—"Lance . . . ?" That was as far as he could go. It was far enough.

"Lance," Zoe smiled, color flooding her face, "left on the stage. He's going to look after the Storm King. It's Jacqueline's, you know. And he's been appointed her guardian."

Steve didn't give a hang about Lance's relation to Jack. Tensely he asked: "Zoe, what's he . . . to you?"

Steadily her dark eyes gazed on his. "He's what he always was," she said, "my best friend. Or," she qualified with a glow that set his blood aflame, "my next best, I guess, Steve."

And then he had her in his arms. And Paradise sure enough was heaven. Lance had gone—and she had come to him.

# Wagon Wheel Exile

## Cliff Farrell

◙

*(Alfonso) Cliff(ord) Farrell was born in Zanesville, Ohio, where earlier Zane Grey had been born. Following graduation from high school, Farrell became a newspaper reporter. Over the next decade he worked his way west by means of a string of newspaper jobs. He would claim later that he began writing for pulp magazines because he grew bored with journalism. His first Western stories were written for* Cowboy Stories *in 1926 and his byline was A. Clifford Farrell. By 1928 this byline was abbreviated to Cliff Farrell and this it remained for the rest of his career. In 1933 Farrell was invited to contribute a story to the first issue of* Dime Western. *He soon became a regular contributor to this magazine and to* Star Western *as well. In fact, many months later he would have a short novel in both magazines. Farrell became such a staple at Popular Publications that by the end of the 1930s he was contributing as much as 400,000 words a year to their various Western magazines. His earliest Western fiction tended to stress action and gun play, but increasingly his stories began to focus on characters in historical situations and the problems faced by those characters.* Fort Deception *(Doubleday, 1960),* Ride the Wild Country *(Doubleday, 1963), and* The Devil's Playground *(Doubleday, 1976) are among the best of his twenty novels. The story that follows first appeared in* Ace-High Magazine *(June 1937).*

## I

### "BANISHED"

**A**t the edge of the blackjack thickets Bill Carmack squatted on the heels of his ragged moccasins. Wonder grew in his sunken, bloodshot eyes as he peered out at the scene on the open flat. The plains sun beat scorchingly on a canvas-sheeted Mitchell freighter. Yoke-scarred oxen wallowed in the mud flats along the sluggish river. A fish hawk, wheeling lazily overhead, shrilly challenged the toiling boy who wielded a shovel in the rock-impregnated sand. The boy was digging a grave. A silent form, wrapped in a tarp, lay beside the high-wheeled wagon. The boy, rusty-haired, freckled, lanky, could be no more than fourteen. He was making slow progress with the short-handled spade. Often he brushed at his eyes with the back of his hand. The sleeves of his faded butternut shirt were rolled high on his arms. A length of packing rope served as a belt for his worn, linsey pants.

Bill Carmack was bare to the belt, having used his shirt to reinforce his moccasins. His buckskin breeches were shrunken and ragged. His ribs could be counted, and his long jaw and cheekbones framed an unshaven, drawn face. He was starving, half mad for the food that he scented on the wagon with the avidity of a wild thing, but he paused there a moment, watching. Off in the distance Carmack could see the ragged scar that snaked through the barren sand hills. That was the Smoky Hill Trail, over which thousands of the Pike's Peak "busters" had gone that summer. Four hundred miles or more along that wheel track to the east were the Kansas settlements. More than two hundred miles to the west the trail terminated in the frontier camps called Auroria and Denver City. Except for Bent's Fort, the old trapping rendezvous on the Arkansas, a week's journey through the buffalo range to the southwest, there was no other white man's stronghold in all the plains and prairie country.

All this weight of loneliness seemed to bear on the toiling boy. Pity for the poor kid brought a lump to Carmack's throat as he stepped out. At first glimpse of that ragged, bronzed figure, the boy leaped to the wagon, to seize a muzzle-loading Sharps.

"I'm a white man, son," Carmack called.

The muzzle drooped, solemn eyes stared incredulously, and then the boy began to sob. He turned away in an attempt to control this show of weakness. Carmack came up and threw an arm around his shoulder.

"Don't be ashamed to cry, son," he said. "There's a time when tears help."

"Paw told me not . . . not to waste strength mournin' him," the boy choked. "But I can't help it."

"Your dad?" Carmack asked. "It wasn't Injuns, I reckon, or you wouldn't be here, either. What happened?"

"Paw fell under the wagon this mornin' as we side-lined down a steep. He ... he didn't live long."

Carmack shuddered. The wagon's tires were buried above the felloes in the gritty earth. The big, dead-axled Mitchell carried a crushing load.

"I'm Denny McCoy," the boy explained. "We're five weeks out of Leavenworth, bound for the Cherry Crick camps. In another two weeks we'd have been there. Then this has to happen."

Carmack picked up the spade. "I'll take care of the diggin', Denny. I'd be obliged if you'd rustle a bait of that buffalo hump I see hangin'. My backbone is jammed against my belt buckle."

The freckled youth manfully mastered his grief and for the first time carefully appraised his visitor. "Where's your pony an' horse, Mister?" he asked wonderingly.

"I've been afoot for more than a week," Carmack shrugged. "I was down to the point of eatin' rattlers raw ... but I couldn't even find one. I've lived on wild plum an' gooseberries, but they don't stick to your ribs."

"Injuns?" Denny whispered with respect.

A sultry grimness gathered in Carmack's eyes. "Not exactly. I came from Denver City. Was aimin' for the Kansas settlements. Maybe we can throw in together on the backtrail."

Denny shook his head. "I'll outfit you for the trip, mister, but I ain't goin' back. There's forty barrels of flour on that load. They say flour will bring a hundred dollars a barrel in the diggin's this winter. It ain't worth eight a barrel back in the settlements."

"Was your dad workin' for Harmony and Leffler?" Carmack asked sharply.

"Yuh mean the big tradin' company? Nope. Paw an' me was aimin' on doin' our own tradin' in the camps." The boy looked closer at the gaunt man. "Why did yuh ask that, mister?"

Carmack began digging. "Better turn back with me, Denny," he advised. "The Cheyennes an' 'Rapahoes are on the scalp trail between here an' the mountains. They'll lift your hair."

"My mother is back in Leavenworth," Denny said grimly, "with four kids younger'n me. Paw mortgaged the homestead to load this flour. Now that he's gone, she'll need the money worse than ever. I'm goin' on. I'll travel at night an' keep my hair."

"You've got guts, kid," Bill Carmack commented. "But it ain't only Injuns that. . . ."

His gaze lifted, and Denny turned to stare. A rider had appeared on the trail beyond the sand flat. He came slowly over a swell. Then, as though rising from the earth in his wake, the tilts of lumbering bull wagons hove above the sand hills. More wagons, rolling three abreast, rose up against the hot sky, moving majestically westward toward the mountains, which lay like a low, purple bank of clouds against the horizon.

"A bull train," Denny breathed. "Headin' for the mines. I don't need to be skeered of Injuns now."

He ran wildly toward the caravan. The wagons came lifting against the plain until two score of them broke the monotony of the land like a fleet of white-sailed ships at sea. Denny waved his arms, and the plodding oxen came to a stop. Riders and men on foot swung out to meet him. A Concord mud wagon turned out of line and followed them. Many of the wagons had painted on their tops the initials of Harmony & Leffler, the freighting and trading company that was waxing fat on the business created by the discovery of gold in the Rockies.

Carmack's haggard lips tightened. He did not move as he watched a man on a big black stallion swing up and curtly question Denny. The rider was bare headed, and his mass of thick, curly black hair glistened oilily in the sun. He was big, superbly proportioned. He wore the blanket trousers, gaudy shirt, and red sash typical of the French-Canadian freighter. A knife and gun were thrust in the sash.

Carmack turned and took from the wagon seat a holstered gun and belt that had once belonged to Denny McCoy's father. He belted it around his lean hips. With Denny in their midst a score of armed freighters came hurrying toward the Mitchell, with the sash-clad giant making impatient gestures. The mud wagon swung up behind them, and Carmack noticed that it carried only one passenger—a woman. A linen duster protected her crinolined traveling frock, and a dust veil shielded her face.

The big man dismounted, cast a glance at the tarp-wrapped body and the inadequate grave. "The grave, it is ready," he said. "Quickly we will bury him then push on. It will delay us less than I had feared."

Bill Carmack spoke. "You're in too much of a rush, Big Pierre. It's customary to bury white men deep in this country so that wolves and Indians won't dig them up."

The gaudy Canuck whirled. For the first time he took full cognizance of the lean, ragged man. His big hands went to his hips, and he rocked on his heels, smiling insolently.

"So!" he sneered. "It is *M'sieur* Carmack who left Denver City so suddenly with but a canteen and the clothes on his back."

"Yeah," Carmack said softly. "I was canteened out of camp, if you want to put it that way, though I don't remember having the canteen. My freight sheds and wagons were burned . . . and my oxen stolen. I was turned out on the trail without even a knife to defend myself. You never expected to see me alive again, did you, Pierre? Nor does Jared Leffler."

"You speak with a bold tongue, my frien'," Big Pierre returned silkily. "White men who trade with the Indians deserve the noose. It is not too late to remedy that."

"Indians?" Carmack was holding his temper admirably. "I traded only with white men, but Harmony and Leffler didn't want honest competition. Their warehouses are filled with flour, and there are twenty thousand men scattered along Cherry Creek who'll need that flour to live through a Rocky Mountain winter. They can't eat gold. They'll have to eat Harmony and Leffler flour and sandy beans and moldy sowbelly. And they'll pay a dollar a pound for it. They'll pay it or starve. By spring, Harmony and Leffler will own all the gold in Denver City and Auroria. It's a pretty picture."

There was a little gasp of indignation and a swish of skirts. Carmack found himself confronted by an angry girl. She had leaped from the mud wagon, throwing back her veil. "Coming from a ragged tramp that hardly deserves answer!" she blazed. "It's a lie, and you know it. Harmony and Leffler would not stoop to such methods. If your equipment was destroyed, it must have been an accident."

She had lustrous, dark chestnut hair, cut in modish bangs over her forehead. The hot, dry winds of the plains had made little impression on the creamy softness of her cheeks.

Big Pierre glared at Carmack. "You have cast the insult on the *mademoiselle*. For that, you will feel the bite of the lash. Seize the dog and bind him to a wheel. Bring Pierre the long whip."

Bill Carmack stepped back, and the octagonal-muzzled six-shooter was now in his hand. A wicked smile twisted his lips as the forward surge of freighters stopped suddenly. "Come on!" he rasped. "Or does it make a difference when a dog has fangs? The night you burned me out to die on the plains you didn't give me a chance to bite back. You jumped me in the dark, sandbagged me, and left me on the trail with the buzzards circling over me at dawn. Come on! I'm ready to bite back now."

The girl leaped in front of his gun. "No," she said imperiously. "This is no place for bloodshed. Have you no respect for the dead? There is an open grave here."

"This is as good a place as any," Bill Carmack gritted. "There's room for many graves here. My only regret is that Jared Leffler isn't here to fill one."

She stared, appalled, anger building in her eyes. "You brute!" she breathed. "Do you know who I am? My name is Alice Harmony. I inherited a partnership in Harmony and Leffler from my dead father. Jared Leffler, the man you are so eager to kill, is my friend and adviser as well as my business partner."

Carmack had lowered the muzzle away from her lithe body. He eyed her icily. "When you see your partner, tell him that Bill Carmack is still alive and will some day come back to Denver City," he intoned. "Tell him that I'll bring more wagon loads to trade with the miners, and that I'll continue to make only an honest profit. Tell him that I'll live to stamp the name of Harmony and Leffler from the trails of the West."

Proud resentment burned in her cheeks. She tried to stare Carmack down but failed. With a scornful shrug of her tall, graceful body she presented her back to him. "Deepen the grave, Pierre," she commanded. She placed an arm around Denny McCoy and walked away with him.

Big Pierre's deep chest swelled. His fingers hooked in a significant gesture. "You are fortunate, my frien'," he murmured, with a nod at the girl. "But for her, you would be called to answer me, Pierre LeDoux."

"Maybe it is you who are runnin' in luck, Pierre," Carmack countered. "They say you've whipped as many as three men single-handed and that you like to break their backs with your arms. The miners know they're being robbed at the H. and L. trading posts, but they've learned that, if they protest, you or some of your Canucks will stamp in their faces with hobnails. But some day you an' me are going to lock ourselves in a room. Only one of us will walk out."

Big Pierre licked his thick lips greedily. "I will 'wait that day with great impatience, *m'sieur*," he promised.

With Big Pierre urging them, the freighters hurriedly completed the grave. Denny McCoy stood, with clenched fists and locked lips, staring dry eyed as Pat McCoy's body was lowered. Alice Harmony, bare headed, her hair rippling in the arid wind, recited the Lord's Prayer. Denny's hand crept into Carmack's palm, and he turned blindly away as the freighters began to cover the grave.

Alice Harmony approached. "You will go on with the caravan, of course, Denny," she urged.

Big Pierre moved up, shaking his head. "May I suggest, *ma'mselle*, that the camps are hardly the place for a boy without kin. I have arranged to send five good men back to the settlements with his wagon. They will deliver him safely home."

"What you mean, Pierre, is that his load of flour is not welcome in the camps," Carmack said scornfully.

Alice Harmony flushed but ignored Carmack. "Pierre is probably right, Denny," she remarked. "He just came from Denver City, bringing an armed guard to escort the wagons through the Indian country. He knows conditions there. You should turn back. You can be home in a few weeks, safe and sound."

Denny drew abruptly away from her, his young eyes cold. "I reckon we can take care of ourselves," he stated.

"We?" the girl questioned sharply.

"Bill Carmack an' me," Denny nodded. "We're pardners."

"I regret your choice," she warned. "What do you know about this man?"

There was a boyish admiration in the glance Denny cast at Carmack. "I never seen him 'til an hour ago," he admitted. "An' I didn't know his name before it was mentioned here. But every trail man has heard of Bill Carmack. He's a damned good fightin' man, a buffalo hunter, Indian scout, an' the best blasted bull whacker that ever popped a lash over a team on the Overland or Santa Fé trails. I'm damned proud to know him."

Alice Harmony appraised Carmack with a new, sharpening interest, and there was something like doubt in her eyes. She turned without comment and went to the mud wagon. She overlooked Big Pierre's offer of assistance and mounted lightly into the high-wheeled vehicle. Carmack caught a glimpse of her unveiled face looking back as the driver swung the mules toward the waiting caravan.

## II

### "MIDNIGHT RAID"

Carmack and young Denny McCoy watched the Harmony & Leffler wagons dwindle away among the sand hills. Loneliness clamped down over the high plains once more. A cooling breeze carried a promise of distant mountains, but the sunset had a brassy tinge as though the world was on fire beyond the horizon.

"We'll span up after dark an' hit the backtrail, Denny," Carmack proposed. "Indians might have spotted this camp."

Denny's face fell. "I didn't figure you'd advise me to take the load back to Kansas, Bill," he muttered accusingly.

Carmack grinned. "Not the load, Denny. Only you. We'll hide the wagon in some basin and corral the oxen in a *coulée*. I'll go with you a ways. On the short grass prairie we're bound to find buffalo hunters or a caravan that'll see you safe to Leavenworth. I'll come back an' take your wagon through to the mountains."

Denny considered that gravely. "What about Big Pierre?" he asked. "What about Harmony and Leffler?"

Carmack touched the holstered gun at his side. "I'm borrowing this from you, Denny. I'd never have started down the trail if I'd had a gun or even a knife. I'm ready to go back to Denver City now. I'll sell your flour there, son, and I'll send the money to your mother."

Denny arose and extended a freckled hand. "Shake, pardner," he said with mature deliberation. He spat impressively in the sand. "You're Bill Carmack, all right. If there was a doubt in my mind, it's gone now. I'm headin' West with you."

"Listen, Denny . . . ," Carmack began to argue.

The boy's chin came up. "Paw wouldn't let any man go where he was skeered to go himself," he stated. "Neither will I. We both go ahead . . . or we both go back."

Carmack framed an objection then set his lips against it. He glanced at the grave. "I reckon Pat McCoy will sleep easy there, Denny," he said softly. "He's proud of you."

They spanned the five yoke of oxen at dusk and hit the trail before the moon ballooned above the prairie. Carmack had shaved and clothed himself from Pat McCoy's warbag. There was fresh buffalo meat on the wagon. Topped off by beans, biscuits, spuds, and scalding tea, this food had revived him, and the haggard hollows were already fading from his face. They had burned brush over the grave and driven the outfit over it. Denny did not look back. He set his face westward as he trudged along by the wheelers, sounding his lash.

As they plodded through the night, Carmack too was silent, thinking of other lonely graves that he had left behind, from Independence to Sacramento, from Leavenworth to Santa Fé. He had thought that after fifteen years of out-trail tragedy he was hardened to it, but every time he looked at the sturdy step of the boy he had to swallow hard. Carmack recalled that he had been no older than Denny when he marched on his first wagon trip over the long trail to California. Fifteen years of whacking bulls, fighting Indians, hunting buffalo, trapping—of starving, sweating, struggling. He had returned from California penniless, for it was not his luck to find gold in the earth. He was a freighter by instinct and destiny, and the Pike's Peak rush had opened what seemed a clear path to financial success.

There was money in freighting to the mountains—as well as hardships and danger. With three wagons he had earned enough in his first year to lay the foundation for an ambitious trading and freighting company. Those plans were nothing but charred embers now. Harmony & Leffler, backed by St. Louis money, had brushed him aside, destroyed him as they would an insect. They had the mountain trade monopolized now. As Bill Carmack, penniless, wearing a dead man's clothes and a dead man's gun, swung the bullwhip, he thought of Alice Harmony's velvet brown eyes, her aristocratic ways, her high pride, and her evident background of breeding and wealth.

The wagon, with the oxen moving like a multi-legged serpent, lurched over the sand hills which were rippled billows of silver in the moonlight. At midnight they cleared the sand hills and crawled down to the dark flats adjoining a Smoky Hill ford. There, the blackjack brush closed in as though hopeful of choking the trail that men had cut for their ponderous vehicles. Moonlight struck streakily on the wagon and plodding oxen as the deep wheel ruts converged in a single wagon road. It was an ideal place for an ambush, but that thought did not occur to Carmack in time.

Like animated shadows forms spilled from the blackjack, swarming upon the wagon. Carmack caught a glimpse of Big Pierre's swart face, flashing in the moonlight. Evading the sledge-hammer swing of Pierre's fist, he leaped back clawing at his holster, but there was another man at his back. A gun barrel thudded on Bill Carmack's head. He reeled dizzily. Vaguely he heard Denny's wild, angry shout of alarm. Then Big Pierre was upon him, pinning his arms. Blood streamed from his scalp, and his muscles were numb and futile. More arms wound about his knees, and Big Pierre's knuckles drove hard against his jaw. Carmack sank slowly to his knees, the world spinning.

Dimly he felt them lift him and drag him off the trail. As he fought back the painful daze, he saw Denny, his wrists bound, in the hands of two grinning, sharp-featured Canucks. They set Bill Carmack on his feet. His arms and ankles were laced tightly with hide thongs. Big Pierre loomed up, smiling broadly, and slapped him with a wide, hard palm. Carmack felt the inner flesh of his cheek shred between his teeth.

Denny McCoy uttered a choked cry of wrath. "Let him alone, yuh yella-gutted son!" the boy spat. "Hittin' a man who's hands are tied! He'd beat yuh to a pulp if he had an even chance."

Pierre slapped the boy, knocking him into a clump of brush.

"Lay off the kid, Pierre," Carmack gritted. "Take out your grudge on me. I talked him into headin' west instead of goin' back to the settlements."

"Gladly!" Pierre snarled and knocked Carmack down.

Carmack, bleeding, pulled himself to his knees in spite of the bonds. "Better finish the job, Pierre," he advised hoarsely. His eyes had a metallic glitter in the moonlight.

Big Pierre knotted a fist for a blow that might easily have killed the bound man, but he mastered his lust for punishment, and his smile flashed venomously. "Some other time, *m'sieur*," he growled. "Pierre is not yet ready to kill you. The *patrón*, *M'sieur* Leffler, wants you to live so that when you go back to the settlements you will carry the word to other fools that the company does not mean to be trifled with." Pierre turned, pointing, with a guffaw. "This is what happens to traders who seek to compete with Harmony and Leffler."

Bull whips were popping. The Mitchell freighter lurched ahead. Canucks, wielding goads and whips, shouted like madmen, and the oxen broke into a lumbering, snorting stampede. The approach to the graveled ford lay a few rods ahead, with the river glinting murkily in the moonlight. Just above the ford was deeper water, guarded by a low, clay cutbank. The Canucks swung the frenzied lead yoke off the trail and down through the scant brush toward the cutbank. Carmack's jaws clamped. The lead team made a belated effort to swerve at the brink, but there was a downgrade there, and the weight of the wagon swept the outfit irresistibly on into the river. The cutbank caved under the heavy wagon, toppling it in on the bawling oxen. There was a long, churning splash—and the gruesome, half-human sound of drowning animals. Then, except for the slithering sigh of the current, silence came.

Big Pierre smiled. "Forty barrels of flour will be worth but little at the bottom of the river," he remarked. "No, *m'sieur*?"

Carmack looked at Denny McCoy. The boy's face was gray and

drawn. He was thinking of his mother with four young children and a mortgaged homestead back on the Kansas border and of the wagon and ox team that had been their only means of livelihood.

Pierre slapped Carmack again savagely. "Do not forget that it is Big Pierre who has permitted you to live a little longer, my frien'," he said. "*B'nuit, m'sieur.* Again I look forward with anticipation to our next meeting. But perhaps I am too optimistic. Only tonight our scouts reported a Cheyenne war party to the north of the trail. But even the Cheyennes do not have the courage to attack a caravan guarded by Big Pierre and his brave ones. You will not be as fortunate, I fear." Pierre drew his knife and, with a sweep of the blade, freed Denny's wrists. "Let it not be said that Big Pierre leaves bound men to die in the hostile country," he guffawed. "Come, my comrades. We return to the caravan, where the beautiful *mademoiselle* sleeps peacefully, not knowing that Big Pierre's protecting hand is far away."

They waded the river. Carmack heard them mount in the brush beyond and ride away as Denny set to work on Carmack's bonds. The boy was sobbing in helpless rage. "The crawlin' snakes!" he kept gritting.

Carmack arose and shook the rawhide loops from his ankles. He walked to the cutbank and looked down into the muddy current. All that showed above the surface was the curve of a wagon tire around which the muddy tide gurgled. Big Pierre had taken the six-shooter, but Carmack remembered that the Sharps rifle had been in the wagon bed along with the pouch and powderhorn. He stripped off his clothes and dove repeatedly until he retrieved them. He also brought up a bag of jerky and a quantity of soaked beans. The watertight horn had protected the powder. He cleaned the gun with strips from the tail of his shirt then loaded it and rammed the charge home.

"Where we goin'?" Denny asked quietly as Carmack shouldered the heavy weapon.

Carmack, his face swollen and discolored, looked at him. "To Denver City," he spat. "Where else? We'll collect payment from Jared Leffler and that Harmony girl. They'll pay starvation prices for that load of flour, and they'll pay for that wagon and team."

Denny slapped a fist into a palm. "An' I want to be there when you make Big Pierre pay for maulin' us around, Bill," he insisted. "I'm followin' you, pardner . . . to hell, if you lead."

They camped before daybreak in a *coulée* a dozen miles to the west. They had the flint and powder for a fire, but Carmack ruled against it, lest the smoke attract Indians. They breakfasted on tough buffalo jerky and muddy water. During the afternoon, hidden by the brush, they watched half a dozen Cheyennes, in breech clouts and war paint, ride down the plain in the distance, heading for some rendezvous to the south. Fresh scalps dangled from their lances. One was that of a blonde white woman. Denny's cheek took on a sallow, sickly tinge as he watched it swing in the hot sun. Afterwards his young eyes seemed older and harder.

"We're not far from the Platte stage road," Carmack commented tersely. "Some poor devils will never see Denver City or the Kansas settlements again. Skin your eyes from now on, Denny. If the tribes are raidin' the stage trail that means red hell has broke loose all over the plains."

That night they resumed their journey westward, deeper into the Cheyenne country.

### III

#### "GOLD TOWN'S PAYMENT"

Denver City, sprawling and unlovely, sent its lights defiantly against the twilit loneliness of the high plains. In the background the mountains reared up like a black, impenetrable barrier under the fading final glow of day. Bill Carmack and Denny McCoy, sheltered in a dry wash a mile out on the sage flats, waited for full darkness. They were gaunt and footsore, their clothes and boots showing the ravages of two hundred miles of travel. Twice they had narrowly escaped discovery by war parties of Cheyennes and Arapahoes. Only the previous morning they had sighted the smoldering ruins of a Platte River stage station, and Denny had not forgotten the mangled, staked bodies in sight near the embers.

They walked unmolested in among the scattered, outlying tent shacks. Denny, peering down crooked side lanes, caught alluring glimpses of lights. He hung back to watch the flow of humans moving along the crowded sidewalks. The sound of revelry in Blake Street called to him, accentuating the solitude of the plains from which he had come. The raucous hurdy-gurdies and the sing-song voices of monte cappers must have sounded to Denny like music from heaven. The camp was like a feverish pulse beating on the brink of the unknown, set there against the mountains on the shore of a sea of plains and prairie that painted, fighting Indians claimed as their own. Carmack thought of the arrogance and reckless pride of white men who had the wild temerity to drink and gamble while they failed even to place sentries over the tiny foothold that they had gained in this hostile land.

He turned into a muddy lane of log and mud houses that he knew to be Larimer Street. He paused in the deeper shadow of a shack, watching in silence a pretentious dwelling a pistol shot away. It was a big log home with glass widows, circled by a deep verandah and flanked by a drive way, carriage shed, and horse stable. Lights glowed around the draped windows. Denny caught a glimpse of a crystal chandelier glittering on a ceiling, and it was enough for him to visualize a dining table set with snowy linen, rich silver, and shining goblets.

"Jared Leffler's mansion," Carmack said briefly, and Denny stiffened.

They drew back as the scuffle of hoofs turned into the street. A woman, riding a side-saddle, handling a spirited horse with firm hands, swung down lightly at the buggy step. She turned the horse over to her companion, who was in the rough garb of a hosteler. He led the two horses to the saddle barn. As the big stained-glass door was opened, they saw that the woman was Alice Harmony. She was greeted by a spare, hawk-visaged, elderly man garbed in the knee-length broadcloth coat of a wealthy merchant. Then the door closed.

Carmack said, "Stay here, Denny!" and started in long strides for the house. "That man was Leffler."

He mounted the verandah, walking on his toes with little sound, and tried the ornate door. It was not locked. He stepped into a narrow, beamed reception hall. He heard Alice Harmony's voice from a lighted door off the left rear. The response of Jared Leffler came in a harsh, assured voice.

Carmack moved to that door, stepped through. The girl had removed her riding bonnet. Her hair was drawn into a soft roll at the back that revealed her ears, small and aristocratic. The room was fitted as a man's study, book lined, with game pelts on the floor. Jared Leffler, lean, spare, thin lipped under a waxed, graying mustache, sat at a big polished desk. Leffler's lined, yellowish face froze as he saw the ragged, unshaven figure stalk in. The girl turned. She recoiled a step with a gasp as Carmack crossed the room. Leffler pushed back his chair violently. His bony hand flashed to the breast of his coat. Carmack's fingers bent crushingly around Leffler's wrist, and he snatched the half-drawn cap-and-ball gun away. He cocked it as he backed to the center of the room.

"I came back, Leffler," he said softly. "I trust that Miss Harmony brought you word that I was comin'."

Jared Leffler, superintendent and partner in the prosperous firm of Harmony & Leffler, came to his feet. "What do you mean by breaking into my house like a common desperado, Carmack?" he rasped.

Carmack cast a glance at the girl. Except for that first start of dismay she had not moved. She had lost a shade of color, but there was no fear in her—nothing but haughty scorn.

"I came to present a bill for immediate payment, Leffler," Carmack remarked. "You're indebted to a boy named Denny McCoy for forty barrels of flour and a five-yoke bull team as well as a lynch-pin Mitchell freighter. I'll set the total amount at eight thousand dollars. Dig deep, Leffler. I want it in gold. Dust or hard money is equally acceptable, as long as it's yellow. Not a cent less and not a cent more."

Jared Leffler's hand crept toward a bell cord. At that Carmack's lips peeled in a mirthless smile. "I'll blow your fingers off it if you touch it, Leffler," he promised.

Leffler's hand jerked away. "You fool!" he grated. "You know what will happen to you if my freighters find you in camp. They gave you one chance to get out of the country alive. You won't escape so easily the next time."

"You're fritterin' time away, Leffler," Carmack snapped. "There's a safe behind you. Open it. I'll weigh out the dust myself. I'll make sure of an honest count."

"You're insane," Leffler shrugged. "I know no one named Denny McCoy. And certainly I owe him no such sum. This is merely a ruse for bare-faced robbery."

The girl said, "You forget, Mister Leffler, I spoke of the McCoy boy. He is the one whose father we buried on the trail."

Leffler frowned and shrugged. "No difference. The person is entirely unknown to me."

Carmack's lips curled. "Both Miss Harmony and Big Pierre probably also told you about the load of flour in the McCoy wagon. And they've no doubt told you that the wagon and its load are under ten feet of water in the Smoke Hill River, along with the drowned oxen. It'll never compete with you in the Denver trade now."

The girl's lips lost their scornful quirk. There was a sudden alarmed question in the glance she turned briefly away from Jared Leffler. "Carmack," she said swiftly, "what are you driving at? Denny McCoy's wagon was in no danger when I last saw it."

Carmack studied her suspiciously. "Are you tryin' to tell me that you didn't know Big Pierre and his frog-eaters jumped us that same night at the ford and ran the wagon and team over the cutbank?"

Alice Harmony stared at him, her slim body growing slowly rigid. "That's a lie," she breathed, but there was a rising doubt in her eyes.

Carmack moved to the desk, caught Jared Leffler by the coat, sent him spinning violently toward the big iron safe. "Open it, or I'll pistol whip you within an inch of your life," he commanded. "I'm not collecting this for myself. Pat McCoy left the gamest kid that ever walked the trail. And he left a wife and a family back in the settlements who need the money a damned sight worse than you or this high-nosed girl. Pay up, or I'll make you wish you had never hired snake-blooded Canucks to do your dirty work."

Leffler had a certain type of courage. "I'll see you in hell first, you scum!" he spat. "I'll give you two minutes to clear out of here. Then I'll put them on your trail."

Bill Carmack stood an instant, the knowledge of defeat riding him.

With a savage growl, he swung a fist—and knocked Jared Leffler cold. The trader fell against the safe then to the floor. Carmack blew on a bruised knuckle. "Scream," he spat at the girl. "Yell your damned head off. I can't hit a woman, but I'd like to take a squaw pole to you."

Alice Harmony's quiet scrutiny baffled and angered him. "It *is* true," she murmured suddenly, and there was something akin to shame in her tone. "I knew Pierre and his men were away from camp that night. But I never dreamed that. . . ." She turned to the safe. "Wait!" she said imperiously.

Carmack had turned to leave. That order held him. Frowning suspiciously, he watched her handle the combination and open the heavy door. She delved into the maw of the safe, brought out a balance scale. One by one she produced four fat pokes of gold dust and weighed them. She extracted a portion from the final poke then pushed them across the desk.

"Eight thousand in gold, Carmack," she stated. "Harmony and Leffler's debt to little Denny McCoy is paid."

Carmack looked at the pokes. The savor of this triumph had suddenly eluded him. More than once in the past ten days he had pictured Jared Leffler groveling at his knees, weighing out dust with supplicatory speed. The matter-of-fact acquiescence of this girl robbed him of the taste of victory. He moved to pick up the dust. As he did so, her head lifted—and he saw her expression shift to fear.

"No!" she screamed. "Pierre!"

Carmack whirled. Some wildling instinct at the same moment sent his body curveting aside. He glimpsed the cold flash of thrown steel, heard the hiss of the blade. The knife bit deeply into the solid pine wall behind him. Big Pierre stood poised in the hall door, his beady eyes already mirroring dismay at his miss.

Carmack's gun covered the big man. Pierre seemed to shrink and draw in his deep chest, as though to lessen the shock of the bullet that he expected. Carmack did not pull the trigger. "This looks like the day for which you waited, Pierre," he said. "Step in one pace then turn and stand while I make sure you'll have only your fists to fight with."

Big Pierre's slack lips took on form again, and he settled his big head incredulously down on his thick neck. "You do not mean that you will fight hand to hand with Pierre, *m'sieur?*" he growled hoarsely, and an avid flame leaped into his eyes.

Carmack glanced around. A door, ajar, showed a linen or cloak closet opening off the room. He backed suddenly to Alice Harmony's side. Clamping his free arm around her waist, he carried her bodily across the room.

She saw his intention and suddenly began to struggle. "No!" she panted. "You can't fight Pierre. He will kill you. He's too big, too strong."

Bill Carmack's eyes had a queer, marble hardness. He did not seem to hear her. He thrust her into the closet, closed the door, and turned the bolt.

"Carmack!" she called frantically. "Please!"

Carmack moved to where Big Pierre stood, grinning expectantly. He searched the massive Canuck, relieved him of a second knife and his six-shooter. He slid them under the desk, out of easy reach, then pushed his own weapon in with them. Then he closed the door leading to the hall—and dropped the heavy bolt. He was caged in the room with Big Pierre.

The Canuck laughed and came at him, leaping nimbly high. His powerful legs drove his moccasins in the *savate* at Carmack's head. Carmack faded aside. He caught one of those thick ankles in mid-air and turned with a twisting wrench. Big Pierre struck that whipsawed plank floor with a jar that shook the house and squeezed a groan from his lips.

"*Sacre!*" the big man panted. He came to his feet like a great, ruffled cat, his lips peeled back, his square, yellowish teeth clenched. He moved in on Carmack, cursing in the jargon of the *voyageurs*. His heavy arms were spread in a gorilla-like posture, and his thick fingers were hooked and eager to gouge and maim. Carmack stepped in close, and his fists shattered the Canuck's teeth. Then the big man's arms closed around him. Carmack felt the python-like strength of his opponent. He could see the red, murderous blood-lust in the man's glaring eyes. "Now, *m'sieur*," Big Pierre gasped, "I have you! So!"

Carmack laughed hoarsely. There was naked, primitive savagery in that sound. He slid his arms up, and his thumbs sank deeply into the Canuck's neck below the tip of his ears. Carmack could feel flesh and sinew giving. With a scream of agony Big Pierre slacked his grip and broke away, staggering back, his bleeding lips twisted in agony. Carmack followed him. They traded punches, toe to toe. Big Pierre's nose seemed to vanish in a bloody, smashed welter under the power of Carmack's fists. The bulky Canuck uttered a hoarse, strangled cry and backed away from that exchange. He dove in again, his fingers seeking Carmack's eyes, but Carmack smashed him back with driving knuckles. Again the Canuck ploughed in. He brought his weight to bear, seeking the back-breaking grip that he had used to snap the spines of more than one opponent. Bill Carmack's wintry laugh came again, and he deliberately allowed Pierre to wrap those heavy arms around his waist. Then Carmack, with volcanic, glazing fury, broke that grip, pushing Pierre away from him.

"Now, *m'sieur!*" Carmack taunted, and devils danced in his eyes. He was breaking the Canuck's nerve and spirit. Big Pierre backed away. There was the knowledge in his mind that he had met a better man. He kept backing away from the relentless advance of the shaggy man with the glazed, gray eyes, but the room was too small now. He was caged in here with Bill Carmack. He turned, at bay, and Carmack slashed him to ribbons with fists that never seemed to tire. Pierre staggered blindly around the room, sobbing hoarsely, seeking escape. Carmack cornered him, and his fists thudded with fearful impact. Big Pierre's battered bulk sank limply down . . . and he lay still.

The fight had been heard. Men were in the hall, shouting and battering at the bolted door. Carmack walked unsteadily to the desk and thrust the pokes of gold inside his tattered shirt. He armed himself with the two six-shooters and Pierre's knife then cast a look at Jared Leffler, who was sitting up now, fingering a bruised jaw and staring at him glassily.

Carmack turned and opened the door of the linen closet. Alice Harmony came out slowly. There was incredulity in her wide eyes as she saw Big Pierre. She recoiled from Carmack. Though he was hardly aware of it, Big Pierre's fists had left their bloody marks on his face.

She made no attempt to stop him as he went to a window and knocked out the glass with a sweep of gun muzzles. She watched him leap into the outer darkness.

Jared Leffler came to his feet and staggered to the window. "Stop that man!" he bawled. "A thousand dollars in gold for him . . . dead or alive! He robbed me."

There was confusion and shouting in the dark streets, and Leffler rushed out. After a time gunshots *spanged* raggedly in the town. More uproar welled up but faded slowly away.

Leffler came back, sweating and furious, and found Alice Harmony waiting. "They stole horses and got out of camp," he raged. "The fools! I'll post a reward for them in every border town. If they get through the Indian country, they'll find themselves in prison."

"They?" the girl questioned.

He nodded impatiently. "There was a boy with Carmack . . . the McCoy whelp, no doubt."

"Leffler!" Alice Harmony cried sharply. "Is it true that you burned Carmack's freight sheds here in Denver City? And that Big Pierre and his men ran the McCoy boy's wagon into the river?"

Leffler's temper was raw. "They knew better than to buck the company," he snapped. "They brought it on themselves."

"And you *do* intend to charge starvation prices for food when winter sets in?" she persisted.

He eyed her sharply. "Business is business. Things like that are part of the game."

"Not when my father was alive," she said.

Leffler's lips curled. "Your father wasn't a business man. He thought only in terms of pennies. That's why Harmony and Leffler never progressed far when he ran the company. We owned only ten wagons and were always on the ragged fringe of failure. Look at the company now since I've had complete control."

"Yes," she repeated dully, "look at it. Hiring brutes like Big Pierre to terrorize boys and to fight in packs against lone men like Bill Carmack. Look at it!"

"It's rather late for you to moralize, my dear," he grated. "For three years you've lived in ease in Saint Louis, enjoying the luxuries the company furnished through my efforts."

"I didn't know," she breathed, and there was tragic self-reproach in her manner. "I didn't know that it was blood money. But I'll take no more of it. Leffler, I'm ending this partnership. Tomorrow I'm heading back to Leavenworth. I'll let my lawyers see about dissolving the company. From now on I refuse to let you smirch the name of Harmony. What you do with your own name is none of my concern."

Leffler glared at her. "Do you think I'll let you pull out now? You own two-thirds of this company, but I've made it what it is. I won't let you ruin me after the way I've slaved to build it up."

She turned away coldly. "I'm leaving tomorrow," she said. "I would appreciate it if you would have a coach ready."

"That's impossible," he sneered. "Don't you understand that the tribes are ... ?" He paused, suddenly veiling his resentment, and bowed. "Very well, my dear. I'll have the Concord ready, and I'll send an adequate escort of armed riders with you since you seem determined to undo my work."

She eyed him, a sudden chill in her heart. She had not missed his reference to the tribes. She turned slowly and went to her room. She had heard much talk about the Indian war, but it had seemed a remote thing. She had seen no sign of hostiles while crossing the plains with the big, heavily-armed caravan. She decided that Jared Leffler had at first intended to frighten her into remaining in Denver City until spring where he could bend her to his will, but something had caused him to abandon that argument. Had the hope sprung into his mind that the Cheyennes would ... ? She refused to think that of Leffler who had been her father's partner for years. It was fantastic. Surely there could be no danger on the main trails.

She began packing the trunks which she had opened only the previous day. She was listless and discouraged. She kept thinking of Bill Carmack, ragged, haggard and bloody, leaping through that jagged window and fleeing like a hunted animal into the vastness of the plains with only a boy as his companion.

# IV
## "CAPTIVE WHITE WOMAN"

Carmack and Denny slowed their horses to a walk. The lights of Denver City were ten miles behind them. The stars were hazy through a misty sky, and the darkness of the plains was almost tangible in its density. The horses, which they had taken from a tie rail in their flight from town, were shaggy Spanish ponies, fit for what lay ahead. Carmack had retrieved the buffalo gun from the *coulée* in which they had cached it. He carried Big Pierre's six-shooter in his belt, and Denny now proudly packed Jared Leffler's expensive cap-and-ball gun.

"We can make Leavenworth in two weeks on these ponies, Denny," Carmack declared. "We're shy on ammunition for the side guns, but the rifle will keep the pot full. Our hair is still fastened to our topknots, and we'll do our damnedest to keep it there."

Denny was elated. He kept talking about the trouncing Carmack had given Big Pierre, which Denny had watched through a window. Carmack did not mention the black doubts that lay in his own mind. He knew that Harmony & Leffler wielded powerful influence in the Kansas border towns. Carmack had a hunch that prison might await him in Leavenworth. They camped at dawn. There was no pursuit. Carmack could have told Denny that white men were not venturing far from their strongholds now with the tribes riding the warpath, but he did not mention it.

During the day they took turns standing guard over their *coulée* camp. Late in the afternoon, far to the north, Carmack saw a slowly moving wisp of dust pass down the Platte River stage trail. It was the only sign of life on that normally busy route. It looked like a Concord mud wagon escorted by four saddle guards. He shrugged, remembering the ruins of the stage station and the mutilated bodies he and Denny had seen on that trail.

"Travelin' in daylight," he muttered. "They must be new to the Indian country."

Carmack and Denny pushed on that night, also following the course of the Platte trail. It was longer than the Smoky Hill route, but he believed it would swing them clear of the hotbed of the Indian trouble in a week's time. As they drew off in the brush of a creek at dawn, Carmack's head lifted. He stood like a statue, listening intently.

"Imagination, I reckon," he muttered at last to Denny. "I fancied I heard gunshots . . . far off."

They broiled buffalo steaks over a masked fire, but Carmack was preoccupied and kept walking to the lip of a nearby cutbank where he could peer through the brush out across the open plain. Suddenly he ran back and stamped out the fire. "Stand by the ponies," he ordered. "Prairie dogs holin' up out there. Somethin' comin'."

He returned to the cutbank and peered over the lip. The prairie dogs had all gone to cover. Then, against the dawn skyline, rose a wild horde of mounted Cheyenne warriors. They came pouring over the swell in a flood, a hundred strong. Carmack saw bloody scalps on lances. Young warriors were chanting their boastful stories of victory. Carmack's long muscles went wire taut. Through the dust he glimpsed a white woman, tied to a pony. She was Alice Harmony! Her dress was torn and her dark hair streamed loosely. There was despair and resignation in the droop of her shoulders. Carmack stared with hard eyes as the painted braves, with their hideously daubed faces and feathered equipment, passed by in barbaric pageantry. The roll of the plain swallowed them.

Denny was at his side, quivering. "We got to git her away from them devils, Bill," the boy panted. "She's a white woman."

Carmack arose, and they ran to the horses. Denny learned more about Bill Carmack that day. He learned that there was something of Indian cunning and the wild instinct for concealment in the lean, sandy-haired man. And, too, there was a relentless bloodhound quality that kept them on the trail of the war party as it crossed the open plains without themselves being discovered. That uncanny skill did not fail Carmack even when, toward mid-afternoon, they came to a point where the war party had split into a dozen bands of eight or ten braves each. Trails fanned out in varied directions. Carmack spent nearly half an hour choosing between them. Then he picked a tiny fragment of muslin thread from a sagebrush and said, "She's with this bunch. Eight warriors, by the pony tracks."

After nightfall, with Carmack leading the way, they wormed an inch at a time through willows and chokecherry brush until at last they could look down at the camp the eight warriors had made in a watered swale. The Cheyennes had killed an antelope. They were eating raw liver and toasting thin steaks of spitted meat over a small fire. Alice Harmony, tied hand and foot, sat huddled beyond the fire, in the shadow of a cottonwood deadfall, her hand drooping on her breast. A six-foot Cheyenne chief, with a blood-tipped feather in his oily, braided hair, prodded her roughly with a moccasin. He grasped her loose hair and brandished a scalping knife. The girl looked up at him without fear or shrinking, but her face was a colorless oval in the fireglow. Denny, his teeth set, lifted his six-shooter, but Carmack caught it, his thumb blocking the manner in time.

"Wait!" he breathed.

The Cheyenne chief, tired of terrorizing her, went back to the business of gorging himself. With a gesture to Denny to remain there, Carmack wormed away. In ten minutes he was back with the buffalo gun they had left with the ponies out in the open swales. Once more they wriggled through the brush, circling half around the camp. They inched down through heavier thickets to a point that brought them within sound of the warriors' guttural voices. Carmack lay like a stone man, marking out the rifles and bows and lances that the Indians had placed near at hand.

Into Denny's ear he finally whispered his plans. "I'll drop one of 'em with the Sharps and then run in shootin'. They may take to the brush, thinkin' they've been jumped by a bunch of white men. You hold your fire until I get the girl free, then open up on any that show fight."

Carmack waited. The tension rasped Denny's nerves. Feathered shadows danced against the brush as the warriors passed across the glow of the fire. Carmack waited, watching the Cheyennes, seeking a time when the majority were out of quick reach of their weapons. At last, slowly, deliberately, he lifted the buffalo gun. Denny saw the hardness of his eyes as he laid a sight. The roar of the black powder charge beat like a cannonball in the stillness. The Cheyenne chief, who had been taunting the girl again, broke grotesquely at the waist and fell with a strangled screech. Then Carmack was up, running into the camp with the six-shooter in his hand. The warriors leaped to their arms like startled cats. Carmack opened up. His first bullet sent a brave, scarred by the tortures of the sun-dance, staggering headlong into the red embers of the fire. He fired again, and a stocky, painted Cheyenne reeled back.

One Indian had snatched up a rifle and crouched on a knee, pulling a bead. Denny McCoy saw that it was time to take a hand. He used a deadfall as a rest for the long-barreled cap-and-ball gun. He drove a bullet squarely through the chest of the kneeling brave. From the brush Denny's gun roared twice more at the flitting, howling forms. Four Cheyennes were down. The remaining four, convinced that they were in a trap, broke for shelter in the thickets.

Carmack jerked the scalping knife from the hand of the dead chief and slashed Alice Harmony free. He threw her bodily over his shoulder as he turned for the darkness where Denny waited. The body of a dead brave smothered the fire, reducing visibility. An arrow buzzed, and he felt the hot pain as a barb burrowed deep in the calf of his right leg. The force of it sent him to his knees, but he arose and staggered on into the brush.

"I can walk," the girl panted. "Put me down."

Carmack set her on foot. He broke off the dangling arrow shaft, and the three of them raced away through the brush. Frenzied war whoops followed them. Denny, turning, saw an Indian outlined against the dim red embers. He fired but missed.

Their ponies were fighting the picket pins in the swale beyond the creek brush. Carmack tried to lift the girl into a saddle, but the strength suddenly ebbed from him, and he went to his knees.

"He's wounded," she panted. "Denny! Help me! We've got to get him on the horse."

The surviving Cheyennes had estimated the numbers of their attackers now and were racing to harry them from the brush.

"Ride," Carmack mumbled. "I'm all right."

"And leave you here to be scalped?" the girl screamed.

With Denny helping her, she dragged him across a saddle. She leaped astride behind him, holding him there as she pounded the pony's flanks with her heels. Bullets followed them as they swept away into the darkness, and Denny answered with the last load in his gun.

"Come on, yuh bloody devils!" the boy screeched back defiantly. "We'll wipe yuh out if you trail us."

The Indians had no desire to follow these fighting whites. There was no pursuit as they galloped away beneath the glittering stars. Carmack sluggishly pulled himself astride the horse. Alice's arm was around him, steadying him, and she could feel blood on her hand.

After a time Carmack thickly ordered a halt in a buffalo wallow. "Make some twists of grass for light, Denny," he requested haltingly.

Alice set her teeth against a sob of sympathy when she saw the broken arrow shaft jutting from his leg and the well of blood from his ribs.

Carmack still had the chief's keen-bladed scalping knife. "Better not watch this," he told the girl curtly. "I'm going to take out that barb."

She knelt beside him and took the knife. "Let me do it, Carmack," she said.

Carmack took a grip on the ground and made no sound during that ordeal. The girl's hands were sure, and she removed the arrowhead swiftly. She ripped strips from her dress and made a tourniquet. Then she contrived a bandage for the angry crease along his ribs. She finished the task then looked into Carmack's gray face. Suddenly her steely calm broke. She placed her hands on his unshaven, battle-scarred cheeks. "Carmack!" she breathed brokenly. And she kissed him on the mouth. She lifted his head and looked at him, and there was shy wonder in her eyes.

"Why did you do that?" Carmack asked hoarsely.

"I don't know," she breathed. "All I know is that I don't want you to hate me, Carmack. I was a vain, careless fool, letting Leffler run the business in his selfish way. I only realized the truth the night you came to the house. I started back to Leavenworth to dissolve the partnership. The Indians attacked us at dawn, killed the men Leffler had sent as guards . . . and captured me. I know now that Leffler had sent only green, inexperienced men." She still had her warm hands pressed against his cheeks. "Please don't hate me, Carmack," she said.

It was Denny, with youth's penetrating wisdom and scorn for such emotions, who spoke, "Aw, kiss her, Bill. It's plain she's loco about you. She ain't worth much on the hoof, but I reckon you could make a purty good squaw outta her."

Carmack saw the shy color deepen in her face. She said bravely: "I'm afraid he's right, Carmack. At least I'll need a man like you to operate the business. We'll call the new company Harmony and Carmack."

☻

A company of U.S. cavalry, escorting a supply train over the Platte River trail, found three white people mounted on two horses waiting beside the trail at dawn. One was a gaunt, ragged man. The girl who rode with him, holding his arm around her waist, was beautiful in spite of the mud and dust and dried blood that soiled her torn garb. And there was a tousled, rusty-haired boy of fourteen with a heavy buffalo gun slung across his knees. He spat in the grass and disdained any show of joy at sight of the column of uniformed dragoons.

"I don't know what he needs first, a doctor or a marryin' parson," Denny stated to the captain, indicating Bill Carmack with a jerk of his thumb. "He was a damned good fightin' man until today, but it looks to me like his ramblin' days are ended. A petticoat has got him."

# The Quickest Draw

## T. T. Flynn

⊘

*This story marked T. T. Flynn's second appearance in Street & Smith's Western Story Magazine. The editor, Jack Burr, remarked in "The Roundup" in the issue dated April 4, 1939, that "since the publication of the December 10th issue ... we've had so many inquiries concerning the author of this yarn, which made such an outstanding hit, that we decided to find out a bit more about him." Born in Indianapolis, Indiana, Flynn was the author of nearly a hundred Western short novels for the magazine market, some of the finest of which have been gathered in* Rawhide *(Five Star Westerns, 1996). His novels, including* The Man from Laramie *(Dell First Edition, 1954) and* Night of the Comanche Moon *(Five Star Westerns, 1995), are no less notable. He moved to New Mexico in 1927 and spent much of his time living in a trailer while on the road, exploring the vast terrain of the American West. His descriptions of the land are always detailed, but he uses them not only for local color but also to reflect the heightening of emotional distress among the characters within a story. The psychological dimensions of Flynn's Western fiction came increasingly to encompass a confrontation with ethical principles about how one must live, the values that one must hold dear above all else, and his belief that there must be a balance in all things. The cosmic meaning of the mortality of all living creatures had become for him a unifying metaphor for the fragility and dignity of life itself.*

## I

### "PRODIGAL'S RETURN"

**P**res Morehead came home from his Argentine ranches on the 10:20 train, and no one in the crowd around the weathered little Cottonwood Springs station recognized the tall man in the expensive gray suit and hat whose tanned face was alert and eager with anticipation. Holding his cowhide bag, Pres Morehead stood there on the platform putting names to faces, names he'd remembered for eleven years. And suddenly it struck him that it wasn't like what he had thought it would be.

Those two weather-beaten cow waddles sitting on the baggage truck must be Sandy Stevens and Jerry, still down for forty-a-month-and-found on some ranch pay roll. That listless man piling express packages on another truck was Bat-Ear Johnson. You couldn't mistake those ears. The brisk-looking *hombre*, fat around the middle, diamond ring on a pudgy finger, who brushed by to get on the train had to be Jonas Ridgway whose father had been president of the bank. Looked like Jonas headed the bank now, fat and easy off his loans and discounts.

*¡Madre de Dios!* Pres thought with dismay as he glimpsed a portly young woman holding a candy-smeared baby. *Martha Peters!* Something hungry and eager that had lasted through the years drew back in Pres Morehead, and he spoke to none of them.

The hotel seemed peopled with strangers. On a whim, Pres signed the register as John Emory. Time enough to make himself known after he'd seen Tom Morehead and Phil Morehead, his father and brother. At eighteen Pres Morehead had been a ranch kid who had taken it on the run after a minor shooting scrape over a dance. Not bad trouble. His father could have easily settled it for him. But there had been other brawls, and Tom Morehead had been increasingly exasperated. And, anyway, the great horizons had been calling to restless youth.

Now, at twenty-nine, Pres Morehead rode a livery horse toward the Bar Z as he had left home, in riding boots and overall trousers he had changed into in his hotel room. Later there would be time enough to tell about those square miles of Argentine grassland, herds of fat cattle, the great hacienda house which he shared with a partner.

You could reach the Bar Z by the long pass around to Turquoise Creek, or you could take the shorter cut up Bearhead Cañon, up the narrow switchback trail over the cañon rim, and down through the steep balsam and pine slopes to the head of Turquoise Creek. Pres Morehead rode up Bearhead Cañon as he had many times in the past. A thousand feet deep, Bearhead Cañon slashed down from the mountains, and the trail up the side had dangerous caved-in spots. Twice Pres dismounted, testing the trail himself. His movements sent pebbles plunging hundreds of feet into space. Near the top the trail edge caved without warning. One hoof of the claybank flew off into space. The horse plunged forward, scrambling madly to safety. When it was over, Pres rested in the saddle, eyeing the sheer drop to the boiling current of Bear Creek, far down.

"Close," Pres said aloud and grinned ruefully as he shook his head. The vast flat Argentine pampas got you out of the habit of this sort of thing.

Pines and fir clung to the cañon walls, and the high air had a heady bite. The years rolled away, and Pres Morehead was eighteen again, whistling lightly through his teeth as he rode over the rim of Bearhead Cañon and down through the green mountain grass and trees of the long northern slope. This was Bar Z land, from the rim of Bearhead Cañon to the foothill flats far beyond Turquoise Creek. Old Tom Morehead had homesteaded on Turquoise Creek and leased and bought until he had the Bar Z as he wanted it—summer pasture on the high slopes, winter grass in the lower lands—not a big ranch but a good ranch.

Pres Morehead's eyes softened as he thought of the gruff-voiced, bull-headed old cowman who was his father. They'd never exchanged much affection, but it had been understood. It would be there, Pres knew, when he rode in after eleven years. Down into the cedars above the grassy flats of Turquoise Creek Pres rode at a lope. None of the details had changed. The picture was the same. Here was what he had hungered for in the years of exile.

The sudden, whip-like scream of a bullet, the shock as it tore the pommel leather off, was no part of that picture. Pres reined sharply. Someone had shot at him with a rifle—someone on the Bar Z! He could think of no possible explanation for such attack. The gunman came galloping through the cedars, and Pres watched with narrowing eyes. This wasn't Phil, his older brother, or old Tom Morehead, or any man he knew. A saddle scabbard showed that the stranger's repeating rifle traveled with him. Crossed cartridge belts supported business-like gun holsters. The man wore chaps and a weather-beaten old hat. In the early twenties he had a hard, young roughness that held no welcome.

"Maybe that gun went off by mistake," Pres suggested curtly.

"How come you're on Bar Z land?" the gunman questioned brusquely, studying Pres with cold, inscrutable eyes.

"You a Bar Z rider?"

"You hit it."

Pres smiled faintly. He'd met a hundred such young men, tough, hard, whose guns were for sale to handle any trouble if the pay was right. "Must be something wrong," he guessed aloud. "The Bar Z didn't used to need gunhands."

"They're riding now." The young gunman had been looking beyond Pres suspiciously. "Anyone with you?" he demanded harshly.

Pres was beginning to enjoy the situation. "I didn't see anyone," he answered gravely.

"Where'd you come from?"

"Up Bearhead Cañon from Cottonwood Springs. I'd like to visit the Bar Z, if there's no objections."

"Got business there?"

"You might say so."

"Know how to get to the ranch house?"

"I'll take a chance on finding it."

The rifle motioned him on. "The ranch house, stranger. No place else."

Funny when you thought about it—this welcome cold as a winter norther off the high peaks—but the brusque efficiency of the young gunman was sobering. Pres knew his father wouldn't hire such men if the provocation weren't great. He took the down slopes at an easy gallop, the young gunman close behind him.

They came to Turquoise Creek, far down, where the cottonwoods were tall, and Pres pointed the way to the wide draw off Turquoise Creek where the corrals, windmills, and ranch buildings brought the past flooding back. There in the afternoon sunshine was the log-and-stone ranch house. There, too, in the warm sun was a girl galloping past an outer corral to meet him. Pres pulled to a walk, eyeing her in half consternation. She wore overall trousers, riding boots, a loose, free blouse. Her hat hung to the saddle pommel, and her brown hair was free in the wind. Her voice, clear and young, had a ring of authority as she called to the young gunman.

"What is it, McAlister?"

There had been no women on the Bar Z. Phil Morehead must have married, and well and luckily, Pres thought. This girl had a tense, proud face and a fire of energy that fed from the spirit.

Behind Pres the young gunman replied: "Found him alone this side of Bearhead Cañon. Says he came up the cañon from Cottonwood Springs, heading here to the ranch house. So I brought him in."

The girl stopped a horse's length away. Pres noted her dark eyes, warily questioning. He smiled, but there was no answering smile for him. Her saddle carried a scabbard and rifle, her belt holster a pearl-handled gun. Her voice was cool when she spoke again.

"I don't know you. What do you want on Bar Z land?"

Pres gave her a broader smile. "I just dropped in to talk to Tom Morehead and Phil. You might let 'em know they've got a visitor."

Now the antagonism leaped from her, puzzling but open and direct. "Do you live around here?" she asked coldly.

"Not now," said Pres. "I used to. When I got into Cottonwood Springs today, I rode over for a talk."

"You've had the ride for nothing," she said clearly. "My brother and I own the Bar Z now. We bought the ranch from Tom Morehead."

"I hadn't heard," Pres said slowly. "Where can I find the Morehead men, ma'am?"

At the question he would have sworn that an additional barrier came up between them, that the fire inside her flamed and defied him. "You won't find them," she said. "They're dead."

The wild, roistering years young Pres Morehead had put in on the hot, feverish lands of South America had brought iron control, but he felt the shock of that cold announcement slow his heart, and for a moment he was frozen. Then he found his voice, and surprisingly he could still speak calmly. "I hadn't heard that, either. No. It's news, ma'am. A surprise."

The girl said nothing. She sat stiffly in the saddle, watching him. After a moment she reached into a trousers pocket and brought out a gumdrop. She bit the gumdrop in two and chewed it slowly, her eyes still on him. For some reason that bit of candy fired cold anger under Pres's sudden grief. The two dead Morehead men didn't seem to bother her in the least. She was indifferent and coldly antagonistic.

"How did they die?" Pres asked evenly.

"Phil Morehead was killed in a gun fight last year. His father was shot by someone shortly after he sold the ranch. The sheriff has made no arrests in either case."

Now there was no doubt of her unfriendliness. Pres nodded impassively. "I'll ride back to Cottonwood Springs. Sorry, ma'am, that I bothered your gunman."

"They're hired to watch," she said briefly. "You're not the first. The Bar Z is closed to strangers."

She put the other half of the gumdrop into her mouth. Pres Morehead wheeled his horse with unnecessary violence and rode away without a civil parting.

## II
### "DOCTOR'S ADVICE"

The livery-stable man was named Bratley, and his voice rasped in the thickening twilight inside the barn. "Never mind about that busted pommel. It don't matter. But who shot at you does. How'd it happen?"

"A gunman on the Bar Z gave me a stranger's welcome," Pres explained briefly.

"Might have known!" Bratley said violently. "Those damn' *Californios*! It's a wonder you didn't get a bullet in the back like old Tom Morehead did!"

Pres's hands froze on the cinch strap. His voice was brittle as he asked: "These people on the Bar Z shot Tom Morehead?"

Bratley evidently realized he had spoken out of turn. He spat and asked gruffly: "How'd you happen to be on the Bar Z?"

Pres pulled the cinch strap out of the ring. His answer was curt. "I used to know the Moreheads. Hadn't heard they weren't around here any more and rode over to the ranch to see them."

The livery man snorted. "If you'd said something, I could have told you it was a waste of time." He paused. "Did you know 'em well?" he asked shrewdly.

"Hadn't seen 'em in years," Pres managed carelessly. "These people on the ranch have some quarrel with Tom Morehead?"

"Can't tell you," said Bratley. "You hear things. Folks talk sometimes when they ain't sure what they're saying. I never paid much attention. Guess there ain't anything I can tell you. Going to be riding out tomorrow?"

"I don't know," said Pres and walked out.

The town hadn't changed much—the same dusty main street, a few new buildings with false fronts. None of it mattered, nothing mattered here in Cottonwood Springs now with Tom and Phil Morehead dead. Then Pres noticed a familiar little white building with a sign. PAUL WINTHROP, M.D. A lamp had been lighted inside against the growing dusk. On an impulse Pres turned in. His impulse crystallized when a short, active man with a gray mustache came out of the inner room to greet him.

Doc Winthrop was older, but his cheeks were still red-veined and cheery, his eyes twinkling, his manner courteous as he said: "Something I can do for you?"

Pres smiled thinly. "I'm Pres Morehead, Doc."

Doc Winthrop put his whiskey glass down on the back-room desk and shook his head in amazement. "Never would have known you, Pres. You've changed. Not only your face. Something inside has changed, boy. You don't look like . . . Cottonwood Springs."

Pres gave him a wry grin. "Maybe I helled around too much before I drifted down to the Argentine and hooked up with a partner."

"Do all right?" Doc Winthrop had found another glass. He poured whiskey into it and handed it to Pres.

"We made out fair."

"Your father never said."

"He never knew," said Pres. "We didn't know ourselves whether we'd be bigger the next year or broke. My last two letters home weren't answered, so I thought I'd come back before they forgot all about me."

"Married, Pres?"

"No."

Doc Winthrop hesitated. "Better go back and enjoy life, boy. There's nothing around here for you any more."

Pres drained his whiskey glass and asked the question that was hanging between them. "Who killed my father and brother?"

Doc Winthrop sighed. "How do I know, Pres? Your father never knew why your brother was shot. Phil had been a little wild, had been hanging around some wrong 'uns over at Corkscrew Flat. It looked like Phil feuded with someone who put a bullet in his back that night. Your father gave up then, Pres. Sold out to this brother and sister from California. He aimed to go to the Argentine and be near you. I guess he didn't tell anyone but me. The sheriff never got any good sign on his killer. Your father being the last Morehead around here, it's kind of drifted along. There's been rustling going on, and one thing and another to keep the sheriff busy."

"What might 'one thing and another' be?"

"Sheriffs have been drifting in here hunting the Sugar Kid and his bunch, Pres. It kinda looks like they've holed up in the mountains through here somewhere, but they haven't been smoked out."

"Who might the Sugar Kid be?"

"A sweet name for a poison package," said Doc Winthrop. "Oregon, Idaho, and Montana were his stamping grounds. Things got too hot, and he pulled out with every sheriff for five hundred miles itching to get him. His bunch was almost cornered over in the San Juan River country. They fought out and vanished."

"Any reason for thinking they're around here?"

"A Montana sheriff went over to Corkscrew Flat to look around and never came back," said Doc Winthrop. "Paddy O'Leary, kingpin over at Corkscrew Flat, says the Montana man didn't get there."

"O'Leary's word carry weight?"

"His guns do," said the little doctor. "Our sheriff hasn't spread it around, Pres, except to me, but Paddy O'Leary's been buying a heap of gumdrops lately. Corkscrew Flat never was partial to gumdrops before. Those northern sheriffs all brought the same story. Find a gunman with a pocketful of gumdrops and chances are you've got the Sugar Kid. Not much sense to it but they do say every man's got a weak spot. I'm betting gumdrops'll hang the Sugar Kid yet." The doctor reached for the whiskey bottle. "Take my advice, Pres. Go on back to the Argentine. You can't do any good around here. You might get into trouble if word gets out you're Pres Morehead."

"Gumdrops," mused Pres. "Funny . . . damn' funny, ain't it? Who are those people who bought the Bar Z?"

"Two stubborn young fools who haven't got sense enough to run for their lives," said Doc Winthrop wryly. "Any day I'm lookin' for one or both of them to be hauled in on a wagon bed . . . or worse. The girl is too pretty for her own good, out there away from town on the Bar Z, and too near Corkscrew Flat."

"Tell me about them, Doc. Or do you know?"

"Better than other people around here," said Doc Winthrop. "I'm doctoring Bob Brady. They talk to me."

"Folks always did," nodded Pres.

"Kathleen Brady and Bob Brady grew up on a ranch and went to the cities. San Francisco, mostly, I take it, and Bob Brady studied some in Europe. He's an artist. The doctors told him he'd better get out of the city. He and his sister had enough money to buy the Bar Z from your father. They paid twelve thousand cash and took over the mortgage your father owed the bank."

"I didn't know the Bar Z was mortgaged."

"We had bad years, Pres. Anyway, your father took the cash from the bank, mostly big bills and a little gold, put it in a money belt, I guess, ready to leave for the Argentine. A few days later he rode out to the ranch to see the Bradys. They say he got there and left. It was about a week before he was found in the bottom of Bearhead Cañon, near his horse. The horse had been shot. Tom fell with him."

"And the money?"

"Gone," said Doc Winthrop reluctantly. "I hate to say this, Pres, but maybe you've already heard it. There hadn't been any rains. Old Injun Steve, who can track a shadow, showed where your father had ridden up the Bearhead Cañon Trail to the ranch . . . and then where he came riding back to where his horse was shot. And then another horse had come down the trail, over those tracks, and gone to the body, and then climbed back up the trail again. Injun Steve followed the tracks down to Turquoise Creek and lost 'em where cattle had been driven over the road. The sheriff did what he could, but there wasn't any proof he could pin for certain. Bob and Kathleen Brady took it pretty hard, and . . . well, you know how folks can get to talking about strangers."

Pres said nothing.

Doc Winthrop paused, and then continued slowly. "The Bradys had made a good buy from your father. There wasn't any trouble between them. And the Bradys aren't the kind who'd kill a man in cold blood for his money. But the dust from all that was still in the air when rustlin' trouble hit the Bar Z. Bob Brady wounded a rustler. Since then Bob Brady has been shot at. And instead of getting some sense and pulling out, those two have put up no trespassing signs, hired gun-packing hands, and put out word they'll run the Bar Z until hell freezes over, and all strangers are warned to keep outside their wire and stay healthy." Doc Winthrop sighed wearily. "Folks still had their back fur up over your father's death. They took the gunhands as proof that the Bradys were tough and looking for trouble. There hasn't been much sympathy for them. And if you ask me how it's going to end," added Doc Winthrop with a worried frown, "I don't know. But my idea is that Bob and Kathleen Brady have got a grizzly by the tail and they're going to get clawed before it's over."

"Are the Bradys friendly with anyone at Corkscrew Flat?" Pres asked slowly.

"Hell, no!" said Doc Winthrop. "They're hiring gunhands to keep out the rustlers. That ought to answer that."

"I rode out to the Bar Z today," said Pres. "I got shot at by a gunhand and told by the Brady girl I wasn't wanted around there."

"Can't understand that," Doc Winthrop said. "They'd be friendly to you."

"She didn't know who I was."

"That's why."

"Matter of fact," said Pres, "no one but you, Doc, knows I'm back. I registered at the hotel as John Emory."

"Any reason for that, Pres?"

"Not at the time. Just an idea." Pres stood up. "But I'll stay John Emory for a time, Doc."

Doc Winthrop's eyes did not always twinkle. Now the little doctor was almost sober, almost stern as he got out of his chair. "You're not fooling me, Pres. You're looking for trouble now."

"I'm not trying to fool you, Doc. I'm just telling you not to say I'm back."

"Telling me?"

"Asking you."

The little doctor sighed and shook his head. "A doctor learns to keep his mouth shut, Pres. Sometimes the things he has to hold in are hard and hurtful. Many's the time he has to wonder if he's done right. I'll be hoping you keep out of trouble."

## III

### "KINGPIN OF THE FLAT"

Night had clamped down by the time Pres Morehead bought a .30-30 repeating rifle, three boxes of shells for the rifle, and two extra boxes of .45 shells for the old bone-handled side gun that had come out of his suitcase in the hotel room. On the way out of the hotel he had stopped in the dining room to wolf a quick meal. Now in the hardware store he added a saddle scabbard and a pair of blankets to his purchases.

Outwardly he was calm; inwardly grief scorched like blazing fire. Thought of Tom Morehead's drop to the bottom of Bearhead Cañon fanned the flame. A few hours before Pres had felt the cold, sinking feeling of helplessness as his horse scrambled uncertainly on the edge of the drop. Old Tom must have felt the same hollow feeling under the belt as his bush-whacked horse launched into space, down, down, to the water-smoothed rocks far below. Phil Morehead's death was different some way. Maybe he had earned a little of it. You couldn't tell what feuding Phil had touched off at Corkscrew Flat. He had always been headstrong, high tempered. But Tom Morehead hadn't deserved cold-blooded murder for the stake it had taken him a lifetime of hard work to earn. Doc Winthrop was a level-headed man you could listen to—kindly, too kindly for his own good sometimes. Too quick to back up people he liked. You could bet Doc Winthrop hadn't seen the Brady girl eating gumdrops.

The livery stable had been left in charge of a lean, red-necked hosteler who kept up a running fire of talk as he helped saddle a fresh horse for Pres. "Yuh must be fixin' to travel with them blankets. I hear someone took a shot at yuh today. That scabbard an' rifle looks like yo're aimin' to burn back a little if it happens again."

"I hear rustlers are riding in these parts," said Pres shortly. "I'll feel better with a rifle."

Inwardly Pres damned himself for talking about the Bar Z gunman when he came in. The story would be going around town now. News of the rifle and the side gun would quickly be public property. Strangers would be wondering about the man called John Emory who had tangled with the Bar Z and ridden out of town armed. But he hadn't known about Tom Morehead until it was too late to avoid the talk— and gossip about John Emory would be nothing compared to the talk if it became known that Pres Morehead was back, riding the night trails heavily armed.

Corkscrew Flat was the half-way point. Once there had been mining activity in the rocky heights behind the flat and along the placer washings of Corkscrew Creek and the side cañons that slashed back and up into the mountains. Then Corkscrew Flat had been a riproaring center for the district. But the placers had worked out. Cattle and sheep outfits had pushed up to the mountains, grazing high on the succulent summer grasses. Corkscrew Flat had little left but whiskey, gambling, and dancing. You went to Corkscrew Flat when towns like Cottonwood Springs were too tame or too far away.

Now, tonight, under a thin moon Corkscrew Flat hadn't changed. The same ramshackle old plank buildings and cabins clustered at the upper end of the flat. Half a dozen separate little rivulets still brawled across the boulders and gravel. Willow brush along the water was thicker, if anything. Lights burned in some of the cabins. The Corkscrew Bar was lighted. It hadn't been dark a night since it opened, Pres guessed.

The old trading store and bar had been built side by side, connected through the partition. The saloon had a dance floor, rooms at the back for gambling, a bar where forty men could line up. Tonight a generous dozen horses and several *burros* were at the hitch rack. Twice that many men were inside, Pres noted as he entered, cowmen, prospectors, miners, a few whiskey soaks. It was any man's guess where the rest were from—out of the gulches and mountain valleys, the grazing lands lower down, a little town or two this side of the mountains. But they were at Corkscrew Flat to drink and dance and gamble. The noise of it beat out into the night. Half a dozen girls had dancing partners, and one of the men whooped drunkenly above the music as Pres entered.

Eyes settled on him in quick, wary scrutiny. Strangers did well to walk softly here until they'd proved themselves. That Montana sheriff hadn't been the only man to disappear around Corkscrew Flat. A Mexican was playing a guitar and a giant Negro sawing on a fiddle. A pallid bartender with skin stretched like paper over his face bones set out whiskey and made change from an open cigar box on the back bar.

"Ain't seen you before," he remarked.

"I'm looking for Paddy O'Leary," Pres said.

"Paddy!" the bartender called.

Pres sensed he was being watched by the other men nearby. They watched furtively as O'Leary came leisurely from the end of the long bar. The man was short, fat, with a big pinkish face running up to the smooth expanse of a broad bald skull. He lacked even eyebrows. He might have been an overgrown baby, bland and cheerful. The two guns in open holsters under his arms seemed incongruous. Then, suddenly, Pres noticed that the pink face merely lacked expression. Even the pale blue eyes looked vacant as they ran over Pres. "I'm Paddy O'Leary, mister." The voice was soft, high-pitched, like a woman's voice.

"I'm looking up some old mine locations," Pres said. "They tell me in Cottonwood Springs you know these parts well."

The pale eyes considered him, then Paddy O'Leary smiled until his eyes seemed to sink in crinkles of fat and humor. "If I don't know, I can find out. You hunting old mines with a rifle, stranger?"

"Never can tell what you'll be hunting with a rifle," Pres smiled.

O'Leary seemed to think that hugely funny. "That's something to think over. Come back in my office. I'll do what I can for you."

The office was at the back, off a passage from which other doors opened. Poker chips rattled on a table behind one of the doors. An old roll-top desk and half a dozen wooden chairs furnished the office. A wall lamp threw yellow light over old calendars, pictures, reward notices, tacked one on top of another on the walls.

O'Leary waved his visitor to a chair. Pres waited a moment and said bluntly: "No use beating around the bush, O'Leary. What will you do for five thousand dollars?"

O'Leary blinked. The old wired desk chair creaked as he dropped into it. "Cash?" O'Leary questioned.

Pres nodded.

Eyelids closed slowly down over the pale-blue eyes. When the eyes opened again, O'Leary asked: "Got the five thousand dollars on you, mister?"

"When I bring five thousand dollars to Corkscrew Flat, it'll be earned first," Pres said deliberately.

A shadow of disappointment passed over the pink face. Looking at Paddy O'Leary, Pres could understand why he was kingpin of Corkscrew Flat. His blank bulk seemed to spread an uneasy threat over the dingy little office. "Five thousand cash will buy a heap of anything, stranger. What mine were you thinking of?"

"Call it the O'Leary mine," said Pres coolly. "Maybe it's never paid dividends because it's never been worked right. I'm wondering if five thousand will bring pay ore out of it."

O'Leary's high chuckle shook his fat body. "That's a smart way to mine. What kind of ore are you lookin' for?"

"Who bushwhacked Tom Morehead?" Pres asked.

The wired chair creaked, and Paddy O'Leary leaned forward, blank faced, staring. "Who are you?" he asked abruptly.

"Not a lawman," said Pres.

"No," O'Leary agreed. "The law ain't puttin' up five thousand to find out about Morehead." The fat cheeks screwed up as he squinted. "Five thousand is easy to talk."

"I'll show it to you in the Cottonwood Springs bank tomorrow if you can deliver."

"Only someone close to the Moreheads would throw away five thousand like that." O'Leary's eyes closed. His voice dropped until he seemed to be speaking to himself. "I heard there was a son who went away years ago. . . ." The pale eyes snapped open, staring at Pres.

Pres stared back. "John Emory is the name. You'll find it on the Cottonwood Springs hotel register."

A big, soft hand lifted off the chair arm in a slight gesture. "Never mind the hotel register. I'm wondering why you rode out here to Corkscrew Flat to see me."

"I had an idea you might save me a heap of trouble. It would be worth five thousand."

"Set a thief to catch a thief?" asked O'Leary.

"If you want it that way."

The fat man's chuckle shook him again. "I like to do business with an honest man. No misunderstanding that way. You always know where you stand. An honest man with five thousand to spend. . . ."

"Well?" said Pres after a moment. Inside, he was like a stretched fence wire. He'd gambled heavily in tipping his hand on Corkscrew Flat like this. O'Leary might be tarred with some of the guilt himself. Another dead Morehead to end the matter might be worth more than five thousand to O'Leary. You could bet that if Pres Morehead had guessed wrong, hell would be popping before long. But if he'd guessed right, he would have knowledge the sheriff couldn't get, knowledge he himself might not be able to trace down in years. Cheap at the price— cheap at any price when he thought of Tom Morehead taking that long fall to the cañon rocks.

O'Leary nodded, squinting again. "Interesting. I'd have to know. . . ." The rattling doorknob brought O'Leary's bulk out of the chair with a quickness that was revealing. The big man could move with amazing lightness. "What is it?" his high-pitched voice cracked out sharply.

The bartender answered through the door. "Feller to see you, Paddy."

"Tell him to wait!"

"Says he's in a hurry. Got someone outside to see you."

"Coming," said Paddy O'Leary. He stood for a moment, considering. He caught a coat off a nail and shrugged into the sleeves, moving his arms to make certain the holstered guns were free and easy to get at. His pale eyes wandered about the room. "I'll be back," he said and walked lightly out and closed the door.

Pres stared at the door a moment and drew the gun from his holster to make sure it was ready for use. Then he checked the rifle. He'd felt this way before, with his nerves crackling tension. You couldn't read O'Leary, couldn't tell what he was thinking, what he was going to do. But you could be sure the man was dangerous, tricky, cold blooded, calculating, ready to kill if it suited his purpose.

Pres stepped into the passage—and as quickly stepped back into the doorway, pulses hammering. He'd been able to see across the dance floor to the front half of the bar where O'Leary was meeting a man, turning to the front door. One look at the crossed cartridge belts, the leather chaps, the weather-beaten hat had been enough. A side view of the face had been final proof. McAlister, the man had been called by Kathleen Brady, McAlister, the hard young gunman riding for the Bar Z.

A harsh voice rose in the gambling game across the passage. "I'll raise yuh twenty! Gonna string along?"

Couples were dancing again. The wild rhythm in the Negro's fiddle sawed at Pres's nerves as he thought of the gumdrop the Brady girl had eaten. And now one of her gunmen had shown up on furtive business with Paddy O'Leary of Corkscrew Flat!

There would be a door somewhere at the back of the building, Pres knew. He went back along the passage and was outside in the night a moment later, listening hard as he strained his eyes to the dark. The loom of the building took shape beside him, then one of the nearby cabins, the shadows of the brush clumps scattered across the flat. Moving carefully, Pres stepped around the corner of the building and edged toward the front. Somewhere ahead in the night

O'Leary would be talking to the Bar Z gunman. And what O'Leary might be saying might mean a bullet in the back for Pres Morehead.

The window shade of O'Leary's office had a half inch of space at the bottom one could look through. Pres made sure the office was still empty, the door closed. The night seemed empty ahead. O'Leary might be returning to the office. If he found his visitor gone, any man's guess was good as to what might happen.

The wailing fiddle, the throbbing guitar, fell silent outside. Now the night noises were more audible. A horse stamped at the hitch rack in front. The water brawled softly in the little streams that threaded the rocky flat. Then a horse moved on the rocks off to the right. A moment later the impatient lift of a woman's voice came through the night quiet.

"You didn't say that before, O'Leary!" O'Leary's reply was too low to be understood, but Pres knew who had spoken. That cool, clear voice belonged to Kathleen Brady. She was angry. Her voice lifted again. "How much more money do you think you'll get?"

They were behind the nearest clump of willows—O'Leary of Cork-screw Flat and the Brady girl whom Doc Winthrop had worried about because she lived nearer the flat than Cottonwood Springs. Thick as thieves, the two of them tangled in the same business, tarred with the same stick. Pres went over the rocky gravel toward the willows. He'd heard enough to damn the Bradys. He had to hear more now. Money wouldn't buy the truth of this from Paddy O'Leary.

Behind Pres a stone turned against another stone. He swung around, too late to escape the sharp order: "Stand still, you skunk!"

Pres was already pulling his gun. He'd taken a chance and lost. Caught now, he'd get short shrift. A gun licked red at him, blasting against the night quiet—two shots while he fired once. Then the top of his head seemed to explode, and he plunged down on the water-worn stones.

A kind of consciousness lingered. Pres could just about make out Paddy O'Leary shrilling furiously: "Get the hell back in there! Drinks on the house! This is a little private business that don't need attention!" Steps ran to the spot. O'Leary's high voice sounded again: "Is he dead?" A foot kicked Pres, and a rough hand closed tightly on his

wrist. Then a match flared. "Hell, no! Only creased him! Who is he?"
And that was the Brady gunman speaking. O'Leary swore angrily.
"Don't know him. He walked in saying he wanted to ask some questions about old mines around here. I didn't have a chance to hear
what he wanted to know. Did that Brady girl leave?"

A fog was closing down. Pres tried to fight it back. From a vast
distance the young gunman snarled: "What do you think she did, with
a gunfight under her nose? You ain't lying to me, O'Leary?"

"Why should I lie to you?"

"This fellow eased on the Bar Z today over that old cañon trail.
I headed him off, and he claimed he was looking for the Morehead
men. Now he turns up asking about old mines! Somebody's lying.
What's he . . . ?"

Then pain-filled fog blotted out their voices. . . .

## IV

### "DEATH'S TESTIMONY"

The next thing Pres heard was a man moaning, groaning, whimpering. The sound pushed the fog back, and he opened his eyes. A
faint, flickering light threw wavering shadows on a low ceiling. Pres
stirred and found himself in a bunk. Something familiar about it, too.
He had a quick, groggy feeling that he'd lain in this bunk before,
looked at the same ceiling, the same rusty, old stovepipe over there
in the corner, the same big nails driven into the logs by the door, and
that big split log butting into the left side of the window, chinked in
the split with mud. . . .

The shock of remembrance wiped his mind clear, brought back
the past with a rush. This was the old Bar Z line cabin up the shoulder
of Grizzly Mountain. The cabin Tom Morehead had built for his winter riders who watched this end of the ranch for blizzard-trapped cattle. Many times young Pres Morehead had stretched in this bunk.
Every detail of the room was etched on his mind. The moaning, the
whimpering, had not stopped. Pres turned his head and saw no one.
Trying to sit up was an effort. He almost groaned at the pain hammering under his scalp.

A candle end on the old sheet-iron stove gave off a flickering light. And on the dirt floor a man was lying, a fat, bald-headed man who stirred with restless pain, who weakly clawed his fingertips into the dirt, who groaned and whimpered. Paddy O'Leary's coat was gone. His guns were gone. His shirt hung in tatters. And the big man had been beaten, mauled, manhandled until he hardly looked human above the chest. Life still flickered in him, but the man had been broken cold-bloodedly and cruelly.

Pres swung his legs down and sat up. The room swam dizzily. As he tried to control his whirling senses, the door opened on creaking hinges. The lanky young man who entered wore a six-gun and carried a rifle. He was thin lipped, weak chinned, and his careless swagger was half sneering.

"Decided to look around, huh?"

Paddy O'Leary cringed from the voice, moaning as he tried to inch back over the floor. Pres felt sick at the sight. No man deserved to be tortured into a wreck like that. "Who did it?" Pres jerked out.

"Good job, ain't it? He won't strut so big on Corkscrew Flat after this, the dirty snake! Take a good look at him. How d'you like it?"

"Want to know what I think about it?" asked Pres grimly.

"I asked you."

"Gut-shooting's too good for the men who did it!"

The man was still grinning as he spat tobacco juice against the cold stove. "He's lucky. We might have built a fire an' roasted him a little. Don't take any time to build a fire. Got sticks ready outside the door."

"What was the idea?"

"Caught him lying. He was seen cookin' up something in his office with you. We brought him over here to think it over. Take another look at him."

"What was he cooking up?"

A wolfish grin preceded the answer. "We'll let you tell it. What O'Leary got ain't but a caution to what you'll get if you don't come clean on what you're up to around here. Look at him good if you think you're tougher than he is."

Pres stared at O'Leary. So they hadn't broken the man. They'd wrecked the thick body, but they hadn't broken O'Leary's spirit. He had evidently kept his mouth locked.

"How about it, Emory? Feel like talking?"

Pres moistened his lips. O'Leary hadn't told them that a Morehead had come offering five thousand for information. And he wondered why O'Leary hadn't told and saved himself. "Did the Bradys order this?" Pres questioned harshly.

"Curious about the Bradys, ain't you?"

"That," said Pres, nodding at the floor, "would make anybody curious."

"Now ain't that nice?" grinned the lanky young man. "You're on Brady land, Emory. I'm on the Brady pay roll. You was caught sneakin' up on the Brady girl at Corkscrew Flat tonight. Figure it out, if it'll do you any good."

Pres stared at the man and turned his head to O'Leary, whimpering there on the floor. He thought of the Brady girl nibbling candy while she callously told of Tom Morehead's death and fury burned out the weakness in his body. The beat and hammer of the anger throbbed in the bullet furrow across his scalp. Doc Winthrop had been blind. Little Doc Winthrop—the one man who might have gotten at the truth by being shrewdly close to the Bradys—had been fooled by cool talk, by a woman's face. Tonight Doc had been back there in Cottonwood Springs, worrying about Kathleen Brady's safety, while she had ridden furtively over to deal with O'Leary, while her men were callously doing *this* to O'Leary. There had to be a reason for it. The answer seemed plain enough. The Bradys were afraid. A stranger asking for the Morehead men had made them wary. The same man caught talking with Paddy O'Leary had made them afraid. You had to be afraid of something to do this to a man. And they still must be afraid, for the stranger they still knew as John Emory was being threatened with the same treatment they had just given Paddy O'Leary.

"You've got your chance to talk now, Emory," the lanky young man drawled. "What about it?"

"What do you want to know?" Pres muttered.

"You ain't deaf! I asked what yo're after around here! What was you after from O'Leary?"

"Mines," said Pres. "Old mines."

The wolfish smile broke out on the young man's face again. He drew his six-gun lazily. "That all you aim to say?"

From the edge of the bunk Pres gritted: "What would you like to hear?"

"The truth, damn you!"

"What," asked Pres, "would sound like the truth?"

He was watching that fading, wolfish smile, watching for the gun, the hand that held it, trying to think of something in the cabin that could be used against the gun.

Tight lipped, threatening, the man grated: *"You're a lawman, ain't you?"*

"No," Pres denied, watching the gun. He wasn't afraid of a killing shot if he didn't answer right. Not at first. Maybe a shot to wound him, to lame him, make him helpless; but he wouldn't be killed until there was nothing more to be gotten from him. Paddy O'Leary was proof of that.

"Damn it, you *are* a lawman! I'm gonna make you admit it! Wolfing around on the Bar Z like you did an' then sneaking to Corkscrew Flat! Yo're a damned lawman an' you got a hold on O'Leary!"

"What kind of a hold?" Pres countered.

The weak-chinned face was tightening with anger. "Don't sit there firin' questions at *me*! Are you gonna admit it?"

The candle was burning low. Little gusts of wind through the door made it flicker badly. The dark shadows danced and crawled on the walls, but there was enough light to shoot a man, torture a man. There was enough light for Pres to see the slow, convulsive movements of Paddy O'Leary at the back of the room. The Brady man moved a step nearer the bunk. His back was to the stove, to Paddy O'Leary. He lifted the gun muzzle suggestively like a club. Lips drew back over his teeth in the beginning of a snarl.

*"How about it, feller?"*

Paddy O'Leary had stopped whimpering, had lifted his head

slightly. That mashed, gory caricature of a head that hardly seemed human was coming up out of the black shadows which clung to the floor. . . . Pres dropped his eyes lest the truth be mirrored in them by a flicker of attention. He had to keep the other's attention on himself.

"Looks like you aim to have your own way," he said dully. "You got me cold."

"So you *are* a lawman?"

Behind the lanky young man two eyes opened in the gruesome head. The bulk of Paddy O'Leary pushed up on his hands, up to the length of his arms. Only the heart of the man, deep in that wrecked body, could know what the effort cost. O'Leary's big arms were tense, trembling, shaking with the effort. He quaked and swayed with weakness, so that Pres felt the strain of it drawing him tight and breathless as he stared at the floor.

"I'll tell you what I came here for," muttered Pres heavily. "If it's got anything to do with the Bradys, I can't see it. I'm expecting to walk out of here on my way afterward. How about it?"

"Sure," agreed the other with a tight grin. "All I want's the truth. If it ain't got anything to do with the Bradys, you're in the clear. We'll forget all about it."

Paddy O'Leary got to his knees with another terrible effort. His great, puffy, gory lips made a convulsive movement that might have been a grin. O'Leary turned on his knees, without a sound. His shaking arm reached out toward the stove, to the flickering candle end. His big hand slapped down on the flame—and the cabin was plunged into instant blackness.

The gunman whirled toward the stove as the light went out, and Pres launched himself from the bunk, reaching for the other man's gun arm. The lanky young man cursed loudly as Pres crashed against him and caught his wrist. He tried to jerk free. They struck the stove and knocked it over. The stove pipe tumbled over their heads. A savage twist turned the gun toward Pres. Two crashing shots spat red fire close to his face, deafened him. The bullets just missed his arm and shoulder. Pres got his other hand back of the gun and swung the muzzle away.

Out of the darkness, a hand clawed against his face, found his eyes, tried to gouge out an eye. The sharp agony in Pres's eye socket was like fire burning into the brain. Sick with helplessness, he caught at the hand and hurled the other man away as, with a twisting wrench, he jerked the gun free from his grip. The jump, the twist to one side, saved Pres from the roaring shot that sought him in the blackness.

He tripped over a piece of the stovepipe, rolled across the floor as two more shots crashed out of the corner. Then he found himself up against the wall opposite the bunk. The shots had missed him—and as he came up to a knee, the quiet of death shut down inside the cabin. Five shots had been fired, he figured. The six-gun might hold another, or it might be empty if the gunman had been carrying an empty shell.

Seconds passed while Pres hugged the wall and his shot-deafened ears returned to normal. He heard a faint, metallic click. Then a handful of empty shells scattered over the floor near the door. The thin, gritting voice of the lanky young man knifed from the corner. "Now, damn you! I'll get you now!" A piece of stovepipe clattered softly as a foot struck it. The gunman swore softly.

Crouched there against the wall, Pres desperately balanced the odds. He might dive through the door before a bullet cut him down, but that would leave Paddy O'Leary with the Brady killer. Pres slid his hand along the floor. Somewhere nearby was the rifle the gunman had dropped. Pres touched an old packing box that had been used for a seat. It came up soundlessly in his straining grip. He threw the box and rolled across the floor as it struck.

The gunman yelled, the box smashed down on the stove, and the gun blasted lead through the darkness again. A cold shock went through Pres's leg as a bullet found him. And his groping hand found the wooden stock of the rifle.

The gunman was shouting furiously. Low down in the corner, the gun blasted again and again as Pres came up to his feet with the rifle. The Brady man was floundering against the stove. He fired again as Pres jumped to the spot, clubbing the rifle by the barrel. The gun stock struck a body, struck it again, and the Brady gunman cried out. Pres clubbed savagely at the sound. He felt the wooden stock smash against a yielding object. A foot struck his leg, quivered, and lay still.

Pres dropped to his knees, groping. He felt the overturned stove, and his hand came against the motionless figure beside it. They'd left matches in his pocket. He scratched a match against the stove, and the scene leaped at him. The Brady man sprawled there with his jaw battered out of shape, blood crawling over soot-blackened skin. He still gripped the six-gun. Paddy O'Leary lay there, too, one arm stretched out above his head, and the big hand still clamped in a viselike grip about the Brady man's ankle.

Everything was suddenly as plain as if the cabin had been lighted, and Pres had witnessed the moves. Paddy O'Leary had fallen back to the floor with the candle stub in his hand. The candle lay there beside him. But down in that mashed, mauled head, Paddy O'Leary had been thinking while the gun crashed and the fight raged in the dark. Paddy O'Leary had known what was happening, had known when the Brady gunman reloaded that Pres Morehead faced odds too great for any man. In the darkness O'Leary had reached out and gripped the gunman's ankle. Grimly, desperately, O'Leary had held that ankle while lead smashed into his already-mauled body. Dying, Paddy O'Leary had held on grimly to give Pres Morehead his chance.

Bullet holes were there in O'Leary's half-naked torso. One just above the belt, the other high up on the chest. Little round reddish holes from which the blood was reluctant to come. They hardly looked dangerous. Pres caught up the candle, lighted it with the dying match, and held it in his left hand and felt for O'Leary's heart. The faint flutter and beat of that heart was almost impossible to feel, but Paddy O'Leary felt something, sensed something. A quiver of life ran through O'Leary. He stirred.

Pres tried to loosen the fingers clamping on the gunman's ankle. He could not pry them free. "It's all right, O'Leary," he said. "All right now! Let's go!"

O'Leary stirred again. The monstrous puffed lips, bloody, frothy now, moved in what might have been a smile. He released the ankle, and his eyes opened and stared at the candle. He lay motionless, as if dead, but the bloody froth on his lips bubbled slightly.

"Can you understand me, O'Leary?"

The fat man moved his head and then began to choke, gasp. After long moments the blood cleared from his throat, and he lay with his mouth open, gasping. He was in a pool of blood, dying fast. Pres spoke clearly. He had to make the man understand.

"He's done for, O'Leary. You did it. But he shot you. There's nothing I can do for you. Understand?"

O'Leary's head barely moved, but it was a nod, clearly a nod.

"You never told me who killed Tom Morehead," Pres said. "This is your chance, O'Leary. If there's anyone you want the five thousand to go to, I'll see that it's paid."

The warped smile on the puffed, battered lips was plain now. So was the slight shake of O'Leary's head.

"No one you want the money paid to?"

Again the negative.

Hot candle grease slid down Pres's fingers as he bent lower. "Tell me, O'Leary. I'm going after the men who did this to you. I've got a hunch it'll be the same outfit who killed my father. Listen, the Sugar Kid is mixed in it, isn't he?"

Now blood swelled up in O'Leary's throat as the man strangled and gasped again. When the spasm passed, O'Leary looked like a dead man, but his eyes were still open.

Pres tried again. "Is the Sugar Kid mixed up with the Bradys?"

O'Leary's head barely moved, but it was a nod.

"And they're the bunch who killed Tom Morehead?"

O'Leary nodded again. His mashed mouth tried to say something, but the words were only a mumble that broke off into another spasm of choking. This time the attack did not stop. On and on it went until blood was gushing from O'Leary's mouth. And suddenly the big man shivered and lay limp and quiet. This time his eyes were closed. Now there was no heart beat, no life left.

## V

### "MEETING AT THE BAR Z"

Shaking from the strain, Pres got to his feet with the candle. Now he knew. No court of law, no jury would hang a man on what he could tell. In life Paddy O'Leary might not have convinced a jury, but in dying he had convinced Pres Morehead. The Brady gunman's jaw was smashed. He might be unconscious all night. Pres buckled the man's gun belt around his waist, reloaded the six-gun. The rifle was useless.

On a sudden thought Pres knelt down and searched the Brady man. He found a fat leather money belt next to the skin. The belt pockets held gold coins and bills—two five-hundred-dollar bills and several hundreds. Pres looked at the money. His hand began to shake; his eyes grew moist. A ranch hand would not be carrying five-hundred-dollar bills. No cowhand, no gunman would have them when he could get smaller money. Only a man like Tom Morehead, drawing thousands from the bank to carry in a money belt, would get bills like this. Tom Morehead had been carrying this money—and it was his blood that stained the edges of the bills so darkly.

Pres shoved the money into his pocket, blew out the candle, and walked outside. The gunman's horse was tied to the silvery trunk of a small aspen.

Pres mounted and started the horse down the slope of Grizzly Mountain, on the trail he had often ridden as a boy, to Turquoise Creek and the Bar Z ranch house. His watch was gone, so he could not tell the time, but the thin moon had dropped far down on the sky. Long hours had passed since the guns had roared on Corkscrew Flat. But the night had still more hours, and another day lay ahead, and the savage anger that rode now with Pres Morehead would last until this business was finished. The money weighted down his pocket with bitter reminder. Blood was soaking the inside of his left riding boot. The wound was beginning to hurt. The bullet had scored deeply in the calf muscles of the leg.

The Brady gunman had smelled of liquor. Hidden in one of the saddle pockets Pres found a half-empty pint bottle of whiskey. He poured the liquor into the wound then took a long gulp before he finished tying up the leg. He soaked the bandage with what was left of the whiskey. The drink brought some strength as he rode down through the thinning trees to the lower range. More Brady gunmen might be on his trail tonight, heading for the line cabin to see what had happened to Pres Morehead. But only the night wind in the pines, the hoofs of the horse, the creak of saddle leather, and the rustle of brush broke the night quiet.

Down off Grizzly Mountain, through the foothills to the little bluffs along Turquoise Creek, Pres followed the familiar trail. Half a mile from the bluffs the horse threw up his head. The moon was gone, but there was enough starlight to see the pricked ears, the horse testing the wind. Pres reined up and tried to read the night. He thought he heard the faint, far-off call of a man then the bawl of a cow. He rode on cautiously. After a time he was sure he heard cattle.

He reached Turquoise Creek bluffs, a hundred feet high, with the creek shallows rippling along the bottom, and the ranch road following the other side in the long bend the creek made with the curve of the bluffs. Then he tied the horse a hundred yards back from the bluffs, went forward on foot, and looked down into the black drop with wary amazement.

Down there on the ranch road cattle were moving. Not a few cows and steers. Not a small bunch. A trail herd was strung out down there for a quarter of a mile by the sounds, cows, calves, and steers. The point men had long passed. The drags were moving abreast when Pres reached the bluffs. A match flared across the creek as a drag rider lighted a cigarette. A moment later another match flared. Pres heard the faint sound of their voices as they exchanged comments.

Bar Z cattle were on the move, but not to pasture, not trail herding this way in the middle of the night. Uncertainly, Pres stood there, trying to fathom the mystery. Brady cattle moving hurriedly, steadily toward the ranch boundaries. Doc Winthrop had spoken of rustlers working on the Bar Z and other ranches. Against that threat the Brady gunmen had been riding the Bar Z fences. Now where were the gunmen?

If the men down there were not rustlers, then the Bradys were sending their own beef off the Bar Z furtively, hurriedly, in the night. That meant fear. And it would be fear of Paddy O'Leary and the man who called himself John Emory, fear of a lawman getting close to the Bar Z, to the Bradys, to the proof of Tom Morehead's murder, to the hiding place of the Sugar Kid and his killers. O'Leary's dying nod had said the Sugar Kid was on the Bar Z with the Bradys.

Pres walked back to the horse and followed the trail upstream to the end of the bluffs and down across the creek to the road. There he hesitated. The cattle had passed beyond hearing. The road was empty. If the Bradys were clearing the beef off the Bar Z, they'd be moving out of the ranch house, too—and the Cottonwood Springs bank would have land and fences and buildings and nothing else for its mortgage on the Bar Z. Pres pointed the horse toward the ranch house and the Bradys.

He met no one. Half a mile from the ranch house he swung off across the range, circling wide and coming through the scattered brush to the draw where the ranch buildings lay. Now dawn was not more than two hours off. The stars were bright; the air was sharply cool. Down there in the flat the bunkhouse was dark; the corrals seemed empty. Only a house window showed light.

Pres tied the horse at the edge of the draw and went down the slope on foot. He came up behind the corrals, and they were empty. So was the horse corral. The bunkhouse door was half open. No one snored or moved inside. Gun cocked, Pres stepped silently inside and struck a match. The flare showed him empty bunks, a careless litter on the floor as if men had gone through their warbags hastily and discarded everything not needed.

Tight lipped, Pres moved to the friendly log-and-stone house that had been a part of his boyhood. The window was still lighted. A saddled horse stood out in front. Behind that window lay the big main room, to the right of the center hall. A murmur of voices came from inside.

Clearly enough a man said: "Gimme that bottle again, as long as it's free."

And somebody else said: "Deal the cards, Pete, if we've got to sit here."

Pres did not need light to find the latch and ease the door open. His feet moved unerringly in the dark hall to the closed living room door. Thumbing back his gun hammer, he shoved the door open and stepped inside.

"Hoist 'em!" he bit out.

Hands flew up.

"Hell! *Now* what?"

A lamp burned dimly in a wall bracket at the end of the room. Five men had been playing poker at the center table. Pres scowled at their strained, questioning looks. Grizzled Ed Safford and Hi-Low Kenny sat there with unreadable faces. Fifteen years back they had been riding for Tom Morehead. The next two were younger men, cowhands—and the fifth was Doc Winthrop.

"Well, Doc," said Pres as he approached the table, "you fooled me."

Doc Winthrop looked unhappy. He was pale. His voice was thick and husky as he said: "Just take it easy now."

"Shut up!" Pres said through his teeth. "I'll find out damn' quick what you're doing here. Stand up!" Pres ordered the nearest young man. "Back to me! Got a money belt?"

"Nope," denied the young man uneasily.

Pres made a quick one-hand search, did the same thing to the other young cowhand. Neither man seemed to be carrying cash.

"Sit down," Pres told them. Bitterness made his voice shake. He took the paper money from his pocket and showed it to them. "I took this off one of your riders a while ago. It's all I needed to know. Where's that Brady girl and her brother?"

"We don't know where the Bradys are. Take it easy," Doc Winthrop urged.

"Your talk about the Bradys," Pres said bitterly, "maybe you didn't know this cutthroat outlaw called the Sugar Kid had been training with them. Maybe you didn't know the Brady girl made night rides over to Corkscrew Flat to see Paddy O'Leary. Maybe you don't know the Bar Z cattle are being moved off tonight. You've got a hell of a lot to explain."

Doc Winthrop looked like an old man now, and his voice was dry and weary when he spoke. "There's nothing I can do. I didn't know all that . . . and you haven't done any good telling it. Don't move! Look there in the kitchen door behind you!"

*"It's buckshot, brother! 'Don't move' is right!"*

The speaker had been sitting there beyond the dark doorway behind Pres, invisible unless you looked closely. Now he was on his feet, thick chested, beefy, white teeth gleaming in a short black beard as he enjoyed the moment.

"Pitch that smoke iron down on the floor!" he ordered.

"Don't try anything wild, Pres," Doc Winthrop begged. "He'll cut you in two with buckshot. Throw down that gun like he says."

The shotgun was cocked and ready. Silently Pres tossed his gun on the floor.

Grizzled Ed Safford sighed with audible relief. "Thought you was gonna get it sure," the old Bar Z man said.

Pres eyed the group bitterly. "I didn't think I'd catch you in anything like this, Safford."

"Me, neither," Safford retorted. "I ain't sure what it's all about, but do you figger I'd be settin' in the living room playin' cards at this time of night, if a gun wasn't keeping me at it? Or Doc either? You just cold jawed yourself in on a stewpot full of hell an' made it worse."

The bearded man came leisurely into the room, cradling the shotgun. His finger cuddled the trigger, and he was grinning unpleasantly. "You've got a hell of a lot to explain," he said to Pres. "Where'd you get that black all over yore face and hands?"

Pres noticed then that soot had smeared his hands and clothes, his face too, he reckoned. "Knocked over a stovepipe," he said briefly.

"Gimme that money." The bearded man looked at the bills, shoved them into his pocket. His smile turned ugly. "So Slim let you get away? He must be dead then. Serves him right for lettin' it happen. An' you know all about the Sugar Kid an' O'Leary an' who kilt that old codger in Bearhead Cañon, an' yo're on the warpath to do something about it?"

Pres watched the man closely. The unpleasant grin grew broader.

"And you got a line on these men, too, an' got it all figgered out. All you need is the Bradys now an' the Sugar Kid, an' you'll be all set."

Pres stood silently. Some of this made sense, some didn't. But the buckshot gun made sense—and the bearded man was working up to something.

"The Bradys," he told Pres, "have lit out an' won't be back. The Kid and the rest of the boys have gone with 'em. I'll be tailin' along after I hold this bunch here for a day or so. But you're the skunk who caused all this upset. You come lookin' to raise hell, and I'm gonna give it to you with a load of buckshot."

He meant it. The glint of it was in his look, in the tense curl of his finger over the shotgun trigger.

"Going to butcher me without giving me a chance at a gun?" Pres asked slowly.

"That's right. Get down on your knees an' beg if it'll make you feel better!"

Ed Safford's sudden yell filled the room like thunder.

*"Look at this!"*

Ed's hand had already hurled a fistful of poker chips off the table. He was diving sideways off his chair behind the table as he yelled. And Pres, on a hair-trigger waiting for the shotgun to bellow death, jumped sideways as the bearded man looked toward the table and his head jerked as the poker chips struck his face.

The shotgun's roar shook the room as both barrels went off. Wadding and part of a shot charge tore the side of Pres's coat. The heavy recoil drove the bearded man back a step. He hurled the gun at Pres and jumped backward, swearing as he clawed for his holstered gun.

The empty shotgun half numbed Pres's arm as he knocked it aside in the air and dived for the man, but the six-gun was streaking out of the holster and the bearded man was leaping back out of reach. Then shots from the table behind Pres came deliberately and evenly spaced. Two bullets hit the bearded man in the chest, one centered on his face. His hands flew up helplessly as he sprawled back through the kitchen doorway and lay there.

Ed Safford got up from his crouching position behind the table and blew smoke from the muzzle of the gun Pres had tossed on the floor. "Didn't think I could make it," said Ed laconically. "But you was a goner anyway, Pres. I made the gamble."

Pres looked at his hand. It was unsteady. "I feel shaky that way," he admitted. "Some gamble, Ed. But how come? He might have got you, too."

Ed's reply was brusque. "Think we could 'a' sat there an' watched Tom Morehead's boy get butchered like a barbecue beef? I seen Hi-Low inchin' a fist toward the whiskey bottle an' knowed he was aimin' to chuck it. An' the doc was gettin' stiff in his chair like he was goin' over the top of the table. I jest happened to beat 'em to it."

"Just happened," said Pres. "Ed, *I'm* ashamed. Doc . . . Hi-Low, I'm apologizing."

One of the young cowhands, still pale and shaken, pleaded: "What'n hell is it all about?"

"You heard," said Pres.

Doc Winthrop nodded. "We heard, Pres, but we still don't know much. I got to worrying about you tonight and finally hitched up my buggy an' drove out here to see the Bradys. Some gunmen met me down the road, took my team and buggy, and brought me to the bunk-house, where these *hombres* were being held under guard. After a time we were brought into the house here and left with that man watching us. We were told we'd be held here a day or so, and anyone trying to get away would be shot."

"It was those damn' gunmen the Brady woman hired," Ed Safford grunted. "We'd turned in at the bunkhouse when this McAlister rode up an' called a couple of 'em outside. Next thing the four of us had guns stuck in our faces an' were told to be quiet an' not ask any questions. Are the Bradys really skinning out, Pres?"

"I'll tell you what I know," said Pres and did.

They listened silently, with hardening faces.

"I c'n understand some things now," Ed Safford said. "It was plain to us she hired those gunfighters herself. Her brother was kinda puny an' didn't stir out much. She give 'em orders . . . mostly through this young McAlister. Told us regular hands to go on with the work an' the new men would look out for rustlers an' help us when they were needed. We never did know where she hired 'em. They was a close-mouthed bunch. But we figured she must be on the right track. There wasn't any more rustlin' after they started riding the fences." Safford spat, shook his head. "An' all the time she was thick with O'Leary over at the Flat."

Hi-Low was a lean-jawed man with a slow way of talking. Now Hi-

Low's voice had a hard, rasping edge. "I knowed there was talk about Tom Morehead's murder, but I couldn't figure the truth of it layed here with us. They figure on two-three days' clear start. Are they gonna get away with it?"

Doc Winthrop had been listening in troubled silence. "Men," he said heavily, "I'm only a country doctor, but I've brought folks into the world and closed their eyes on the way out. I've talked to folks when their hearts were breaking and when the fear of death was on them. I've heard their secrets, their sorrows, and their happinesses. None of you has ever had reason to think me a fool."

"Hell, no, Doc," agreed Hi-Low awkwardly. "Who said so?"

"Then don't call me a fool for saying Kathleen Brady and her brother aren't guilty of all this," said Doc Winthrop simply. "I sat by young Brady's bed while he told me of the things he meant to do after he got well here on the Bar Z. I heard the truth of it in his sister's voice when she walked outside with me and asked for me to hope that their ideas would work out. Tears were in her eyes. That girl never would have let a man be tortured as this man O'Leary was tortured. Pres, Hi-Low, Ed . . . go easy. Those two aren't guilty of all this."

An embarrassed silence followed. Pres broke it slowly. "Then who is guilty, Doc?"

"I don't know," Doc Winthrop confessed.

"They're gone," reminded Ed Safford.

"I know," Doc Winthrop nodded. "I'm just asking you to go slow in your judgments until you're sure."

"That oughtn't to be hard," Pres said. "We'll find the lot of them, and the truth will be there. How many of these gun artists did the Bradys hire?"

"Seven," said Ed Safford.

"Including the man I left up on the mountain and this one?"

"Uh-huh."

"Which leaves five, unless they've picked up more. They've got their hands full of cattle and making time. They're not looking for trouble yet unless they sent a man to that line cabin and found me gone . . . which I don't think happened."

"Five," Ed Safford said grimly. "And five of us, leaving out Doc."

Ed looked at the two younger hands. "Joe, Sam, you two ain't said much. How much fight you got left?"

Sam was a tanned, open-faced young man with a quick likable grin. "Plenty fight," he said. "But how about guns? They took ours."

"We've got a shotgun, two six-guns, and there's a rifle back there in the kitchen. Ought to be some more guns if we search the place good."

"The horse corral is empty," Pres said. "They took everything. My horse is tied on the rise behind the bunkhouse. There's another out front. And that's all."

"Joe," said Safford, "how about that bunch you run out of the east flat today? Can you and Sam haze four-five back here a-burnin'?"

"If they ain't too hard to find in the dark."

"Git goin' then. There ain't been time to clean out this ranch. They just were lucky we'd been working the cattle into the home pasture for a count an' cut. Or maybe it wasn't luck," Ed growled. "Maybe it was planned. Sorry, Doc, I can't help thinking out loud."

"I don't blame you," Doc Winthrop said. "I'm just hoping the gun sights stay off Kathleen Brady and her brother until you know what you're doing. There was a gun hanging in the bedroom closet. It may still be there."

They had the ranch house and outbuildings to themselves in the search for guns, cartridges, extra saddles. Doc Winthrop noticed Pres limping and insisted on examining his leg. His doctor's kit had been taken with his buggy, but there was a medicine chest in the house. He cleaned and bandaged the leg and the furrowed scalp, and Pres took time to wash himself. A rifle, two gun belts, and several boxes of shells had been overlooked in the bunkhouse. More guns and cartridges were found stored away in the ranch house. Saddles and bridles had been left in the saddle shed.

"All we need," said Ed Safford, "is horses."

Ten minutes later drumming hoofs brought them outside with guns ready, then running to guide the rush of a full dozen horses into the waiting corral.

"Had luck and found 'em at this end of the flat near the water," Joe said.

" 'Bout time we had some luck!" Hi-Low answered, slamming the gate. "Somebody light that lantern while I hang a rope on one of these ornery broomtails."

Minutes later, when they were mounted, Pres said: "Doc, why not ride back to Cottonwood Springs and tell the sheriff?"

"Tell him the Bradys are moving their cattle off their land?"

"Tell him about O'Leary, and the money I found, and this outlaw the Bradys are running with."

Doc Winthrop's answer was heavy. "If a Cottonwood Springs posse thought it had proof the Bradys caused your father's death, Pres, the Bradys would be damned right then. I'll not be the one to ride for the sheriff before I know the truth. I want to see the Bradys first."

"I guess we all do," said Pres. "Let's go."

## VI

### "THE SUGAR KID'S FINISH"

The cold faint light of the new day found them riding hard beyond Bar Z land into the foothill country that sloped to the northwest toward the Parrados River, two days' ride away. At a short halt to breathe the horses, Ed Safford scowled over the cigarette he was rolling.

"This don't make sense, Pres. They're leaving a trail a kid could foller. A couple of days this way an' they'll be in the Parrados Valley, smack near the Parrados sheriff an' other ranchers an' the railroad."

"And the railroad shipping pens and cattle buyers," Pres said. "The Bradys have a legal right to drive their cattle to Parrados and sell every head for the best money they can get. For cash money that'll leave them free to travel."

"Cottonwood Springs would be nearer."

"And hostile to them. Questions would be asked. The bank might have something to say about it. In Parrados," he pointed out, "they can sell and leave quick. The Bradys warned the public off the Bar Z. Their gunmen got folks out of the habit of coming around. Cottonwood Springs folks don't get over on this side of the mountains much. A gunman stayed on the ranch to make sure you men didn't carry word away, and another stayed to find out from me what trouble they could expect. They've got plenty of time to sell and travel before the word gets around."

"Chances are they'll grub and water and grass a little when they reach Porcupine Creek," Hi-Low guessed. "They won't want to ga'nt the critters down too much. We'll ketch 'em down there in a couple of hours."

"An' chances are," Pres added, "they'll be watching the backtrail. We'd better cut off to the left and hit the creek lower down."

The rest agreed. They circled off into the higher foothills and rode down through the broken country toward Porcupine Creek. The sun was high and bright when they watered the horses and turned up-stream beyond the creek.

"Scatter out, so one man just sights the next," Pres said. "I'll take the point nearest the creek and pull my hat off if I see anything. The rest of you do the same."

A mile farther on they had scattered until Ed Safford was the only man in sight, and Ed was hard to keep track of, riding well off to the left and behind. In this broken country one could not see far. And sound did not carry. Suddenly Pres topped a swell of land and looked down a slope onto a big grassy flat where a trail herd was grazing. He had not realized the Brady herd could be so near. There was a chuck wagon, a two-horse buggy, and two riders circling the cattle. The rest of the crew was afoot by the chuck-wagon fire, evidently eating. And keen eyes were watching, for the nearest rider yelled something toward the chuck wagon and pointed his horse toward the slope of the rise. A moment later another rider swung up on a horse by the wagon and came galloping.

Pres watched with narrowing eyes. His face was set, hard and bleak. The rider coming from the chuck wagon was a woman. It was the Brady girl, coming of her own free will to look the stranger over. Bitterness that had been building up against Kathleen Brady and her gun crew held Pres motionless, watching her. He deliberately left his hat on as she approached. This was Pres Morehead's quarrel now, and only the Brady girl and one rider were coming.

Half way up the slope the rider waited for her. They exchanged a few words, and the man came on ahead of her. He was grinning and near enough now for Pres to see that it was not McAlister but a younger man, double gunned, carrying a rifle in his saddle boot to match the rifle by Pres's leg. The Brady girl wore a buckskin riding shirt, short jacket, small sombrero. Even at a distance it seemed to Pres that the sleepless night had left her weary, tired, had dulled the fire that had blazed out from her spirit only yesterday.

"Howdy!" her man called.

"Howdy," Pres said curtly.

"Live around here?"

"Riding through."

"Alone?" the man asked as he rode up.

"More or less," said Pres. "I wasn't looking for a trail herd."

The man didn't know him. The night had left Pres Morehead an unshaven, soiled range rider, but the Brady girl would know him quickly enough. Pres sat loosely, watchfully, waiting for her recognition. Her man was speaking as she came to them.

"We're moving some beef to the railroad. The lady runs the Bar Z brand over against Grizzly Mountain. She says grub and coffee are hot down at the chuck wagon if you feel for a bite. Ain't that right, ma'am?"

She reached them in time to hear the last. Pres felt his nerves tightening to the explosive point as she looked at him stonily and nodded. "If you're hungry," she said.

"I'm not," said Pres.

Her white throat moved as she swallowed. She knew him. The hand she rested on the saddle horn trembled. Pres noted the men down at the chuck wagon watching them. The Brady rider was eyeing him narrowly, and his smile had thinned.

"Ride down an' talk with the boys, stranger. How about it . . . ma'am?"

"We'd . . . we'd like to have you," Kathleen Brady said.

Pres met her glance squarely for an instant. The fear that leaped at him was so poignant and startling that Pres sat there shocked and puzzled. But from the corner of his eye he saw the young gunman touch a spur to his horse and move carelessly over to the right.

"Nice horse you've got," the man said.

Pres nodded, and saw the man trying to read the brand.

*"That's a Bar Z horse, ain't it?"*

Pres had been expecting the streaking draw that started now with no other warning. His own hand slapped to his gun butt and whipped up, triggering lead with equal suddenness. Amazement flashed on the Brady man's face as roaring lead knocked him sprawling from the saddle. His horse squealed and bolted like unleashed lightning. Kathleen Brady cried out as if her own flesh and blood had been shot. For an instant her words failed to make sense to Pres.

"You've killed him!" she cried. "You've killed Bob! Oh, why did it have to be this way?"

The gunman rolled over on the ground and lifted his gun. Pres spurred hard to get out of the way. It was hard to shoot a man sprawled out and dying. And the second Pres hesitated was too long. The gun crashed twice—and the horse under Pres stumbled down to his knees as Pres swept the rifle out of the boot and jumped. The Brady man was through. The gun had dropped from his limp hand, and his eyes were closed, but he was dying with a snarling smile of satisfaction on his young face. Grimly Pres ended his horse's suffering with a bullet and whirled on the Brady girl.

She sat there, pale and frozen, as Pres gritted at her: "That your brother?"

"That man?" Her voice broke. "My brother's down there with the rest of them! A prisoner! And they'll kill him now as they said they would!"

She had come without guns. There was no danger from her. Pres was looking toward the chuck wagon. Down there men were already spurring horses toward the trouble.

"Nobody's getting killed down there!" Pres said coldly. "What are you trying to tell me?"

She was dismounting, dragging her horse to him. "Take this horse and ride!" she begged huskily. "They'll kill you! Maybe I can make them believe you took my horse. They'll . . . they'll *have* to believe me."

"Aren't you the boss down there?" Pres bit out.

"Do I act like I'm the boss?" she cried. "Are you blind? They took over the ranch last night. They're driving our cattle off to sell. They're taking my brother and me along to sign the sale papers. We're helpless! I had to ride here and ask you down there so they could see who you were. They're holding my brother. They told me I'd better bring you back."

"Get on that horse and ride like hell!" Pres snapped at her. "I'll hold them."

"No . . . no! That isn't the way! I'll go back to the chuck wagon. It's the only chance I've got to help Bob. They need us both until the cattle are sold. Oh, please! Don't stand there making it harder!"

Cattle were scattering before the gunmen spurring across the flat, four men—and they came with rifles out and their purpose plain. Two of them started to circle out to the right, and one swerved off to the left, and one came straight on. You could see they meant to surround the dismounted man and cut off his escape. Pres caught the dying man's six-gun off the ground and took the reins from Kathleen Brady.

"If I don't see you again," Pres said, "Doc Winthrop will tell you who I am. And if I don't see Doc again, tell him I was wrong and he was right!" Pres swung onto her horse and grinned down at her. "I wish I had time to tell you myself," he said as he thumbed fresh cartridges into the guns.

He holstered one gun and kept the other in his hand. She cried out in protest as he put her horse into a gallop down the slope toward the chuck wagon and the gunmen coming for him. The man riding straight at him was the hard-faced young gunman called McAlister. Somehow Pres had expected that. He had been increasingly certain as to who McAlister must be. Paddy O'Leary would have known. Pres thought of O'Leary and Tom Morehead as he cocked his six-gun and spurred hard down the slope.

The other riders were swerving back, but they were too far away now. They would not be there when Pres Morehead met the Sugar Kid. Dust was rising above the milling herd as the outside cattle began to break away toward higher ground. McAlister reined to an abrupt stop and threw up his rifle. Pres heard the close scream of lead. Then a second bullet came still closer. Now he was within six-gun range and, as he opened fire, McAlister slammed the rifle into the scabbard, drew both his hand guns, and came on, firing with rapid precision. A fear-maddened steer bolting close made McAlister's horse shy. Pres shoved his emptied gun inside his belt and snatched out his other weapon.

A bullet clipped across his shoulder. Another smashed into his left arm. With guns roaring, they rushed together. The snarling grin on McAlister's face was plain. No fear there. A killer was working at his trade and taking his chances. Then one of McAlister's guns flew through the air as his arm went limp from a grazing bullet. Three shots left! Pres held them until the last moment—and fired them in a roaring burst that carried the memory of Paddy O'Leary and Tom Morehead. McAlister snatched desperately at the saddle horn. He was clawing at the air and falling, as his horse swerved aside and Pres flashed past.

Pres awkwardly tried to reload as he rode through the stampeding cattle to the chuck wagon and Doc Winthrop's buggy. He could barely use the wounded arm. Now through the dust haze and thunder of cattle hoofs bullets were shrilling as the other three riders closed in, working their rifles. Clutching his rifle, Pres made a flying dismount at the chuck wagon.

One look was enough to place the thin, pale, young man struggling there on the ground with wrists and ankles that had been tied with pigging strings. Bob Brady bore a striking resemblance to his sister.

"Keep down!" Pres yelled.

Using the back of the chuck wagon for a rest, Pres sighted the rifle carefully on the nearest rider. The man was fair in the sights when Pres squeezed the trigger. As he threw another shell into place, Pres saw the rider slide out of the saddle. Two gunmen left—and they suddenly seemed to realize that the chuck wagon made a perfect fort for an expert rifleman. They swung sharply around in the dust haze and bent low as they rode for cover.

Pres sighted on one man, missed, tried again and got the horse. The rider staggered up from the fall and broke into a limping run for the higher ground. Then he stopped as other riders burst over the rise and raced down the slope. Caught by surprise, the last rider whirled his horse toward the nearby brush along Porcupine Creek.

Pres stepped out from the chuck wagon and watched two horsemen race across the slope at an angle to cut the man off. The crackle of gunshots came faintly through the last of the stampede, and the outlaw's horse plunged into a rolling fall. The rider got to his knees, to his feet, with his hands high in the air.

Pres found a butcher knife on the chuck wagon and freed Bob Brady. "I guess it's over," he said as he cut the ropes away. "Your sister's all right. I'm Pres Morehead, and I'll be obliged if you'll help me get this arm tied up. Are there any more of these gun artists around that you folks took pleasure in hiring?"

"No," said Bob Brady huskily. "And they're the last we'll ever hire. Kathleen had a wild idea she could find who killed Tom Morehead by buying information from that whiskey seller at Corkscrew Flat. He made her believe he could get the truth if she paid him money to hand to the right men. And then when rustlers got at our cattle, it seemed logical to have O'Leary get us some men who were ready to use their guns and keep strangers out. O'Leary sent us these men, and the rustling stopped. Yesterday Kathleen told me that a man had come asking for the Moreheads. She thought he was a law officer. I didn't know she was so worried that she'd ride over to Corkscrew Flat last night and ask O'Leary if he had information for her. He wanted more money. Kathleen took McAlister for protection on the ride, and there was a shooting outbreak while she was talking to O'Leary. Kathleen galloped home alone. She hadn't been home an hour when McAlister came to the door. Instead of explaining what had happened, he told us he was clearing out with his men, and we were going along to sell the Bar Z cattle for them."

Bob Brady paused and continued ruefully: "McAlister told us he and his men were all on the run from the law, and O'Leary had been hiding them out and helping them dispose of cattle they rustled. O'Leary told them we would hire them, and they'd be safer inside our fences drawing pay than hiding out. So they worked for us and left our cattle alone. Last night O'Leary double-crossed them in some way, and they decided to move on and take all our stock . . . and make us sell it for them." Bob Brady licked his lips. "I didn't like the way

McAlister looked at Kathleen all this morning. It's . . . it's pretty terrible to be helpless to protect someone you care for."

"I'll bet," agreed Pres. "But she's all right now. Doc Winthrop snagged her a horse. Here they come."

But Ed Safford was there first, complaining loudly as he leaped off his horse. "Pres, why didn't you shuck yore hat when you seen trouble? You done us dirt an' stole the fight!"

Pres grinned as he stepped away from the chuck wagon to go meet Doc Winthrop and Kathleen Brady. "I'll tell you later, Ed," he promised. "Right now I've got other things to tell. I was too busy to think of them when I left the lady, but they're coming back to me now."

Ed Safford didn't get it. Wise old Doc Winthrop probably wasn't fooled, judging by the way he was smiling. As Pres limped forward, something hungry and eager that had stayed with him through the long years of exile went to that meeting with Doc Winthrop and the Brady girl, sitting her horse with the proud fire that was the expression of her spirit. Nothing that had happened in this terror-filled day had been able to quench that fire. Nothing ever would, Pres knew.

# Valhalla

*Conrad Richter*

✪

*Born in Pine Grove, Pennsylvania, Conrad Richter was the winner of both a Pulitzer Prize and a National Book Award. His novels,* The Sea of Grass *(Knopf, 1937) and* The Lady *(Knopf, 1957), remain enduring classics; so too are the short stories contained in his collection,* Early Americana and Other Stories *(Knopf, 1936). It is the simplicity and beauty of his style that belies the demons he fought and the tremendous anguish he experienced throughout his career as a writer. Although he began writing in 1913 and had one of his short stories chosen as the best for the year in 1914, his career did not bear the fruit of its true promise for nearly two decades. The early thirties were some of his most difficult years. Between 1931 and 1933 Richter, who had been writing for the slicks in the 1910s but who had met T. T. Flynn in Santa Fe and become a client of Flynn's agent, Marguerite E. Harper, wrote for the pulps in order to make a living, his stories appearing in* Short Stories, Western Trails, *and* Blue Book. *Years later Richter credited this experience with teaching him much about plotting. "Valhalla" was the short story that convinced Richter he should try to get back in the slicks since the story was considered, although finally rejected, by* The Saturday Evening Post *before it was purchased by* Blue Book, *appearing in the December 1934 issue. The story exhibits Richter's uncanny ability to conjure haunting characters and images that stay in the mind far past the first encounter with them.*

Young Peegy—P. G. Bishop, Jr.—always remembered him by the smell of burning cedar wood. Down here along the border you had to burn mesquite. Its wood was a dark bitter brown and its smoke smelled damp and musty, like the odor when you leaned over a hand-dug well at a Mexican *jacal*. But last Monday Anselmo had driven supplies to the herders in the low mountains to the west. Yesterday he had come back with red cedar in the truck body. And today blue incense drifted in lazy layers around the ranch house.

Bathed in the smoke, the boy saw the stranger for the first time, a bent figure moving up the wheel tracks that led from the world. He was on foot, but he wasn't a Mexican. Little and stiff and very old he looked to Peegy as if he had been dried up by a hundred years in this desert air but, when he came closer, the boy saw an unshrunken hooked nose. The bleary old eyes grew suddenly blue as they focused on the child.

"'Mawnin'," he drawled. It was late afternoon. "You Bishop?"

Peegy, in new overalls with a red Spanish flare at the cuffs, stiffened with pride. "Dad!" he shrilled, but his eyes remained buttoned on the old stranger.

In town, where they lived nine school months of the year, he saw plenty of people. Down here on the ranch the nearest neighbors lived eleven miles away. They were Mexicans. The nearest railroad was at Deming. You grew tired of looking at yucca and cactus—of trying to catch lizards. You got hungry to see people. The sheep were off on the range. The sand hills were rounded ovens that sent up their wriggling heat-waves all day long. Those far blue hills lay in Chihuahua. Anselmo said that when you rode up to them, they weren't blue, and they weren't cool.

The boy heard his father come out of the ranch house. There were times in the lambing season that P. George Bishop spent weeks on end away from the town house. When the boy first saw him after that, his father seemed a kind of stranger—a big stranger with a clipped red mustache from cheek to cheek and a ram's head, wide at the bottom, with jaws and jowls and cheeks that buried the ears behind them. And then the boy understood why the Deming and El Paso papers called him the sheep king of Luna County.

Peegy was watching closely to see what the old man would do. Most men, he had noticed, flinched before his father. All the Mexicans and some of the Americans took off their hats. But this shrunken old stranger did not change.

"You George Bishop?" he drawled. "I heard in Columbus you needed Mexican sheep herders. Now, I'm not a Mexican, and all my life I hated sheep, but I reckon I can tend 'em good as a Mexican."

Peegy had never heard any man talk to his father that way about sheep. He saw his father glance over the shabby visitor coolly, so coolly that even in the hot late-afternoon sunshine everything seemed to freeze and stand still.

"I don't think an old cowhand like you would get along with the sheep. I advise you to stick to cattle."

The misty old eyes fastened on George Bishop. "I wouldn't be passin' my hat to a sheepman, but I got a bad disease . . . a kind of rawhide constitution. It's kept me eatin' the hen that scratches on my grave till I'm too old for chousin' cattle. But I'm lucky to have a disease that's curable. And I figure sheepherdin's a quick way to do the curin'."

"You couldn't herd sheep with your rheumatism," P. G. Bishop said with bluntness.

"Who's got the rheumatism?" the old fellow demanded, stiffening. "For fifty years, summer and winter, I've worked all the ground they is between Chihuahua and Kansas. I've slept out in the snow and when she was rainin' heifers horns foremost. I've swam all the rivers between the Rio Grande and the Platte. And I've drunk 'em when they was that muddy you had to chew before you could swallow. And no piggin'-string's tied me down yet."

A shadow fell across the boy. He looked up and saw Dick Wight, his father's foreman. Still young, with a lean, hard body, a coppery face, and derisive black eyes, he was a handsome and reckless figure on a horse, and one of the few men Peegy knew who was utterly unafraid of his father.

"We might use a man helpin' Anselmo sack fleeces," Dick suggested. "It'd give him a little stake till he hits the trail again."

The bleary eyes of the hook-nosed stranger had brightened as their gaze rested on the young foreman. "I'll be glad to help you out, pardner," he said, and added glibly: "I don't savvy much about wool, but I reckon I can catch on. Back in 'Eighty-Three I didn't savvy much about law, but I got an *amigo* out of a shootin' scrape. They was holdin' court in Tom Talley's saloon in Chloride. I knowed the old judge liked to h'ist 'em some. I was kind of swingin' a wide loop in those days, and I stood at the window and plowed some lead in a couple of whiskey kegs. The juice started to spout, and court was adjourned till them present could save the whiskey from a sandy grave. The judge got plumb asphyxiated at his bullet hole, and by the time he got sober enough again to hold court my *amigo* and me had jumped the country."

Peegy saw his sister, Nan, on the gallery looking amused. She had come out to listen. Down here on the ranch she was always running after Dick. Up in town it was Dick who ran after her. Last winter his old car, burnt-orange with sand-hill dust, had been a familiar sight parked at their curb in Deming. Only yesterday he had driven to the ranch with the latest, shiniest model to reach the border.

"Your new hand can tell some stories to Peegy, anyhow," George Bishop in a dry voice told his foreman.

"I ain't much of a hand to make 'em up," the old stranger said apologetically. "But I can tell plenty of true ones."

☺

Peegy was in bed that evening when he heard the hoofs. After Nan had put him to bed and had left the room, he always raised the shade by his bed to the top. He liked to wrinkle his eyes half shut until the dancing beams of light came right down out of a star into his dark room, but he didn't like the scent of the greasewood that drifted through the open window. It smelled like an antiseptic and took him back in memory to the hospital at El Paso where his mother had died.

All he heard at first tonight was the radio from the living room and the dull throbbing undertone of the gasoline engine that ran the dynamo. Then he sat up in bed at the window. Dim forms were riding up to the ranch in the starlight. He heard Dick go to the living room door to listen, then his father's heavy tread, and Nan's sharp heels clicking across the polished floor.

Peegy slipped out of the hot sheets. The darkness outside the hall door felt cool and sweet. He could see only one of the horsemen. The light from the living room window streamed like a broad belt over the rider and his gray mount. Peegy saw it was an American who lived at Five Stars.

"Sorry to trouble you tonight, Mister Bishop." His deferential voice held an inner excitement. "Did you know old Joe Sandoval was murdered today?"

Peegy threw a convulsive look into the shadows behind him. When he turned, the man on the gray horse was talking again.

"Pablo Garcia stopped at Joe's about two this afternoon. The old fellow didn't answer, and Pablo looked in the window. He saw Joe lyin' on the floor with a knife stickin' out of him. So the boy rode home, and his father came over for me."

Nan at the living room doorway said: "*Oh!*" and Peegy felt a shiver run up his spine. With admiration he saw in the light from the doorway that his father's face had not changed. It was calm as if some neighbor had ridden up to ask if he could water his herd at one of the Bishop tanks.

"I'm listening, Hodge," he said.

"Bein' I'm deputy sheriff down here," the rider went on, "I got a few men and rode over. Whoever done it had dug holes all over the floor. You know the money Joe got from you for sellin' his water, Mister Bishop. The Mexican people say he had it buried somewhere around his place."

"I heard that," George Bishop said. "I think Dick told me."

"Whether the murderer got the money, I don't know," Hodge continued. "But I saw where a herd of sheep passed south of Joe's place today. We followed the trail and found the herder was Ricardo." The speaker hesitated a moment. "He said some funny things when we cornered him. I thought we better bring him up to talk to you. Pablo stayed with the sheep."

Peegy saw his father reach out a hand. The boy had just time to save himself from being ordered to bed. He dodged under a low tamarisk at the edge of the gallery. Then the big electric bulb on one of the gallery posts flooded everything with white light.

Peering out through the feathery foliage, the boy saw five grim riders and in the middle sat one of his father's herders, Ricardo Anaya. The yellow Mexican pony he rode looked like young Pablo Garcia's. The herder's hands were tied behind his back, and a lead-rope tethered the yellow pony to the horn of a posse man's saddle. The boy saw the wide shoulders of his father move among the horses until they came to the yellow pony. The older herders were often abject in front of George Bishop, even before Nan or Peegy, but this one belonged to the younger generation. Scarcely more than a boy he wore no leather *chaleco* but cheap American clothes that fitted his back and shoulders like a glove. He was a white Mexican and sat the yellow horse of Pablo with disdainful eyes.

"What do you know about this, Ricardo?" George Bishop asked.

The young herder shrugged. "It was not me who kill José. I tell this *hombre*, but he don't listen. It was like this way, *patrón*. You know even from the yucca on the hills the sheep can smell the water of José. I walk in front with my arms out like this, to keep them back. On the last hill I can see the water and the house of José, and a horse tied to the acacia tree. Then somebody runs out of the house. Soon I can't see the man and horse for dust."

"A stranger?" Bishop asked coldly.

"No, *patrón*. Often I have see him before."

"Who was it?" The only emotion George Bishop showed was the narrowing of his eyes.

The Mexican youth's eyes glittered. "It is a little far from the hill to the house of José, *patrón*. Maybe I make a mistake on the man, but the horse I know. It was a dun, and I could see plain a big mark on the left hip."

In the shadows Peegy felt the foundation of his world shake. His father owned a dun horse with a great splash of brown on his left hip. Anselmo called him Pistolero because the mark was the shape of a holster. Nan claimed it looked more like Africa. Peegy himself had seen Dick riding the horse today.

The boy glanced rigidly at the foreman; he was standing under the flood light with an unreadable face. He did not move or speak, but George Bishop's powerful face had darkened. The deputy sheriff seemed to notice it. He coughed painfully.

"I don't like to have to say this, Mister Bishop, but I saw where there'd been a horse tied to Joe's acacia tree today, like Ricardo says. He had a broken hind shoe. You understand," he stammered, "I don't think for a minute that any of you did it. And the best way to clear you of this herder's story is to let me look at the hind shoes of that dun with paint on his hip."

"You'll find him in the corral," George Bishop said shortly.

"Wait a minute!" called Dick. He was very cool. "You don't need to look at him. He's got a broken hind shoe. I was at old José's today. I went inside and talked with him for twenty minutes."

There was a strained silence. Peegy saw his father stand perfectly quiet. The herder's eyes burned. Nan, her face white, crossed the gallery.

"This is ridiculous!" she said, and her voice trembled. "What would Dick do a terrible thing like that for?"

All the mounted men except the herder grew extremely uncomfortable. Peegy saw several of the riders turn their heads to gaze silently at Dick's new car. The paint shone through a thin coating of dust. The nickel mountings sparkled in the flood light like silver. After a moment Nan glanced at the car then looked swiftly away.

Peegy's bare toes were squeezing the sand when he saw the bent figure of the old stranger move out from the shadow of the adobe warehouse. His pipe was in his hand. The pale blue eyes telegraphed a look of encouragement to Dick.

"Maybe I can hold up a lantern till you read this brand straight," he drawled. "I reckon I come by this dead Mexican's place today. It must've been the place, because it had a 'dobe house and plenty of water. I soaked up some of the water, rode my legs a ways, and laid down under some yucca. I was still there when this fellow came along on a dun hoss with paint on his hip. I seen him stop and go in the house." He nodded toward Dick, and Peegy felt cold. The old fellow drew several times on his pipe, but it was out. "The rider of the dun come out after a while and rode away," he went on glibly. "The old Mexican come out with him . . . he sure acted mighty spry. About that time I seen sheep comin' down the hill. The herder left the sheep fightin' for water and went into the house. Pretty soon I heard a screech. Then it was plenty quiet a while." The speaker sucked audibly on his fireless pipe, while his eyes strayed to Dick. "About that time I figured I better be movin'."

Peegy felt a surge of relief and gratitude to the old man. Now everybody would know that Dick didn't do it. But somehow the vindicated foreman looked strangely uncomfortable. So did Nan on the gallery.

"If you heard him yell," the deputy said slowly, "why didn't you go in and help him?"

"Got any tobacco?" the old stranger asked. The finger of one hand that was all veins and tendons tamped down his pipe, while his pale blue eyes flickered around the circle. "Much obliged. . . . I'll tell you. I never interfere with other people's business, especially Mexicans'. One time in the Big Bend country, around 'Eighty-Three, I heard a woman screamin'. I run in a house and seen a drunken Mexican draggin' her around by the hair. Every time he passed the door, he give her a beat with the bootjack, to keep track of the rounds. The woman was young and good lookin', and I threw my gun down on him and busted the bootjack out of his hand. I walked in and started to read off a text, when the woman jumped me. If I'd done her a favor, she didn't know it. I figured for a minute that a panther was clawin' my shirt. I lit a shuck out of there, and I haven't mixed up with Mexicans since."

The men on horseback were staring cynically at the old stranger. The deputy exchanged a glance with Peegy's father. "May I ask this man some questions, Mister Bishop?"

"Fire away!" the old stranger invited, holding a match to his pipe.

"This has gone far enough," George Bishop interrupted quietly. "Hodge, I want you to take Ricardo to Deming and have him locked up. Tell Judge Gunthorp I'll have enough evidence to hang him before the month is out."

The deputy blinked. "O.K., Mister Bishop," he said respectfully. "We'll run him up tonight in my car."

The young herder's face had gone livid. Staring fascinated, Peegy saw the Mexican's eyes burn toward George Bishop. Black knives with tips of flame were there. "So you hang me?" he panted. "You want to save your *caporal* because he marries your girl. So you hang an innocent one like me. I don't forget this, *hombre!* Maybe you forget I have friends? You can hang me, but my friends don't sit down and see an innocent one hung. I swear you now, what you do to me, my friends do to you. But they don't stop then. They do it to your baby in arms, and to the old people with canes! Many times you will be sorry you hang an innocent one like me."

In the shadow of his tree Peegy shivered. He saw Epifania's face white at the kitchen window, as if already she had seen the whole family wiped out. But his father's face had not changed. When the little cavalcade had become blurred shapes riding beneath the stars, George Bishop turned. His new hired hand was drawing on his pipe in the quick short puffs of an old man.

"You say you came from Columbus?" Bishop asked in a peculiar deadly voice. "How did you happen to pass Joe Sandoval's place? It's seven miles off the trail."

"Sure it is," agreed the old cowhand placidly. "I never stick to trails if I can make better time crossin' country . . . especially if I can smell water. I was born with a compass in my head like a hoss. The first time I helped drive a herd up the trail to Ogallala, Nebraska, the boss died. I brung his body to Palo Pinto alone, drivin' two hosses in a Kansas wagon and sleepin' nights by the copper coffin in the wagon box. I kept off the trail to miss the Indians. It took me forty-one days, and most of that time I had nobody to ask directions of except the man who was ridin' in the wagon box. But I fetched up at Palo Pinto straight as a hungry calf findin' its mammy in the herd . . . the fall of 'Eighty-Three."

"All right, 'Eighty-Three," George Bishop said. He turned and threw his young foreman a look. "You better keep your windy friend away from Deming, or they're liable to hang you."

Back between his hot sheets, Peegy puzzled over that. The whole scene passed again before his eyes in the darkness: the grim-faced riders, the cool control of his father, the squinting expression of the old stranger. But what he remembered most were the burning sulphur flames in the black eyes of the herder. They were like the eyes of a wild animal he had seen once from the car at night. His father had said it was a coyote or dog, but Peegy was sure it had been a wolf or a mountain lion.

He awoke next morning feeling that something exciting had happened and wasn't over yet. It was like knowing you were going to El

Paso, or that Epifania and Nan were baking chocolate cake. Then he remembered: old José had been murdered.

He saw Nan at breakfast. The shadows of a poor night's sleep lay under her eyes. It brought back to the boy how queerly everybody had acted last night when the dried-up old stranger was talking.

Peegy smelled the wool before he came to the open warehouse door. The warehouse was a long adobe building with a dirt floor. It was piled high with rolled and tied fleeces. Usually the wool was sacked as sheared, but this year the sheerer outfit had come before Anselmo had hauled the sacks from El Paso. In the center of the room a huge sack, three feet square and seven feet high, hung from the frame. Anselmo was tossing a cataract of fleeces into the maw, while in the sack, invisible except for the contortions of the burlap, someone moved about. Peegy climbed up on the platform until he could look down. There in the giant sack, tramping down the wool into a suffocating cloud of fine dust, the sweat pouring from his parchment face, was old 'Eighty-Three.

He looked up and saw the boy. "'Mawnin', Bishop!" Then he called: "Anselmo, turn off that danged Niagara a minute!" He took down his red bandanna and wiped his face. His old eyes squinted up through the dust. "Bishop, the Good Book says you don't go to Hades till you die, but the Lord must've changed His mind since He wrote it. Everybody aft and sassy in the house?"

Peegy nodded then shook his head. His eyes buttoned very clear and direct on the old cowhand. "Why will Dick get hung if you go to Deming?"

Old 'Eighty-Three was thoughtfully combing wisps of wool from his face with his fingers. "Well, for one thing," he said, squinting, "I ain't a-goin' to Deming. I'm that embalmed with the smell of sheep that no self-respectin' hoss would take me. Even a cow wouldn't drink out of the same river with me. Maybe you haven't read in the Bible, Bishop, but Noah sure made a mistake when he didn't hire a cowhand to round up his herd for the ark. The first critters a hand that knowed his business would have left out would have been the sheep. Does that kind of answer your fire?"

Peegy shook his head, and the old fellow abstractedly pulled down

**Conrad Richter 307**

a fleece that had been caught in the nails of the frame. The wool looked white where it had been next to the skin, but the rest was brown and all heavy with oil.

"You figure your paw's got something buttoned up in his vest about Dick?" he drawled. "I don't reckon, Bishop. People just naturally ain't happy, like the old days. When I was a boy, I seen a family get nearer to heaven hewin' the logs on one side of their cabin and puttin' in a puncheon floor than one of these oil kings that builds hisself a state capitol to live in. Why, all I needed as a boy to make me bump my head on a cloud was a gun!"

"My father," Peegy announced, "said he doesn't believe you ever had a gun in your hands."

"I ain't lately," 'Eighty-Three agreed solemnly. "Times is changed. It's not like the old days any more. Even the stars look kind of tarnished. Grass don't get so green. The fences killed off the range. Everything's kind of gone to seed. Right where the courthouse stands in Amarillo, I killed a lobo wolf once." He took off his hat, shook the wool from it, and went on: "You can't tell where you're at any more, Bishop, with all the roads and bridges. When you crossed a river in the old days, you knowed that river next time if it was midnight and darker than a Negro ridin' ahead of a snowstorm. Now you hop over the Arkansas or the Red like a jackrabbit over an arroyo. Most the people in this country don't know they got rivers. I buried a couple Comanches once on the Canadian, and, if I could find the place today, they'd sure be a garage settin' on one of them skeletons and a beauty parlor outfit on the other."

"Who killed the Comanches?" Peegy had pricked up his ears.

'Eighty-Three sat down on the soft wool, and into his old pale blue eyes there came a faraway look. "I reckon I done it to the ones I buried. We were camped on the south side waitin' for the river to go down to cross. We had a trail herd for Wyomin', and I'd took along my night hoss, Pompy. He could see better'n a cat in the dark. Clem Tomkins tried to buy him and, when I wouldn't sell, he rawhided me into shootin' targets. I put up the hoss, and he put up the twenty dollars he was gettin' after we hit Cheyenne. I was that worried over losin' Pompy I shot too high and kind of grazed the target. I knew

Clem could beat that. He threw up his gun. About that time I told him to look up. He looked and seen a passel of Comanches ridin' for us like a prairie fire. Well, Clem missed the target by a mile. And then, Bishop, the real shootin' match started."

Peegy retold the story at the supper table. He saw Nan glance at her plate, and Dick sat stiffly in his chair. As a rule supper was the big sociable meal of the day, with Peegy's father and Dick back from the range, the radio going, lots of talk, and beef steak or mutton swimming in chili.

Tonight the radio was going, and the aroma of supper was there, and yet it wasn't there. Oh, they talked, and now and then one of them laughed, but they didn't fool Peegy. Underneath he could feel a sort of strain. He couldn't exactly put his stubby finger on it. But he noticed that when everything grew too quiet, his father talked, chiefly about Donaciano, the herder he had seen that day. It was Donaciano this and Donaciano that, and Donaciano quartering the sky with his staff and predicting rain—which wasn't like George Bishop at all.

Two weeks passed and now Peegy knew for a certainty something was wrong. Supper had become an ordeal. Nobody mentioned José's murder any more. Nan had begun to visit friends in El Paso and Deming and Cloudcroft. Twice she stayed away for several nights. Dick hardly spoke a word except to 'Eighty-Three. The foreman's face was like tanned leather. His eyes might have been two pieces of obsidian swept up out of the dust.

The day before the trial George Bishop drove to El Paso. He said he wanted to close a deal before he became tied up in the courtroom at Deming. Nan rode along with him in the car. All morning the peculiar smell of the Southwest was in the air, that indescribable desert scent of raindrops—Donaciano's rain—on thirsty sand. Earlier, Anselmo had taken Mita in the truck to see her mother who was sick with cancer at Coyote Springs. Epifania was taking care of baby Ethel for the day. In the warehouse old 'Eighty-Three was trying to find enough to do so he could stay for another week.

At lunch Peegy tried the radio. Sunny days you had trouble getting Albuquerque. Peegy's father said the sun made sparks on the sand and that was why, if you touched a wire, sometimes you felt a shock.

But today, except for an occasional snap and bang, it came through very clear. A man was talking. Peegy looked bored. At twelve o'clock, and again at six, KOB in Albuquerque broadcast its radio newspaper.

He ate glumly. From time to time the words *London, England, Washington, D.C., New York City* rang in his ears. Of a sudden he straightened. He had heard the words *Deming, New Mexico.* Deming! Why, that was home where he went to school in the winter time.

*"Deming, New Mexico,"* the rapid radio voice rattled off. "Ricardo Anaya, sheepherder accused of murder, killed his jailer here today and escaped with two Mexicans, believed confederates. The men visited Anaya in the county prison this morning and are thought to have smuggled a revolver through the bars. With Sheriff Gleason and his deputies out, Anaya shot the jailer from his cell, and his confederates released him. A curious crowd watched them flee in an old green car without a top, carrying an arsenal of weapons and ammunition from the sheriff's office. Check of the El Paso–Phoenix highway revealed no such car, and they are believed to have taken one of the many lonely trails for the border. . . . *Hollywood, California . . . !"*

Peegy hastily finished his lunch. The warehouse was empty, but the open door of the camp house revealed the hook-nosed and ancient parchment face of 'Eighty-Three on the other side of a makeshift table with a blue oilcloth. His bandanna was tucked in his neckband for a napkin.

"Want some sheepherder biscuits?" he asked, squinting.

A little ashamed of having run, Peegy shook his head. After what he had judged a manly interval, he stammered out what he had heard on the radio. The shriveled parchment face did not change. Old 'Eighty-Three went on calmly dipping a biscuit into his coffee.

"The sheriff'll get 'em," he said confidently. "Probably has 'em back in calaboose right now. Reminds me of a little story . . . but I can't tell it right without a gun in my hand and a few ca'tridges . . . just to give it some long hair and woolly leggin's."

"We have guns at the house," Peegy informed eagerly.

'Eighty-Three took his time about pouring out the rest of the coffee. He drank it black. Then he wiped his mouth and lighted his pipe. At the doorway he stopped, and his bleary old eyes strained down along the wheel tracks that led to the world. He stood a long time, but all Peegy could see was a speck on the cloudy horizon.

"What you want, coming in here?" Epifania bristled suspiciously when Peegy brought the old hand into the ranch house.

'Eighty-Three paid her no attention. He took down a repeating rifle from the mule-deer antlers above the mantel. Epifania retreated into the kitchen, and Peegy chased back into the hall. He reappeared presently from his father's room, dragging a heavy cartridge belt that George Bishop wore when he went for deer in the Black Range. The old figure fitted a cartridge into the barrel then filled the magazine.

"I reckon I can use the gun to tell the story," he decided. "But they's no gun for a young fellow like the cap-and-ball Long Tom I learned to shoot with. You had to get game on the first shot or lose it. If they had guns like that today, men would be better shots. Shootin's got to be easy as gettin' married. You don't need to pull down your sights any more. You always get another chance. That's one reason the country's in the shape she is."

"You don't call that a story?" Peegy scoffed.

"I'm scaffoldin' up my hoss right now," 'Eighty-Three promised. "But you got to get in the fireplace. This story's got Indians in it and, when they was Indians around, the kids always had to get in the fireplace. It was a kind of religion."

He lifted Baby Ethel from her cushioned chair at the table and stood her in the wide stone mouth of the fireplace. Baby Ethel could stand erect, but Peegy's tow head was quickly streaked with soot. He couldn't hear the old man. Stealthily the boy stepped out. He found 'Eighty-Three standing at the door. Framed between him and door jamb lay a far stretch of wheel tracks. And bumping along the distant trail came a queer-looking car.

"You kids listenin'?" the old fellow began without turning around. "It was the first time I went up the trail with a herd. I was only a button, but everything went smooth as old britches on a new saddle till we got to Kansas. That night the Indians shot and screeched around the beddin' ground, and we couldn't hold the cattle. Next mawnin' I found myself plumb alone except for eleven steers. I drove 'em all day and didn't see hide nor hair of my outfit. That evenin' I come on a dugout with nobody to home. You kids savvy what a dugout is?"

"Sure," Peegy said, his eyes fastened on the approaching car. He could see now that it was green and looked as if it didn't have a top.

"Well," 'Eighty-Three went on, "it had a little stove and a big bed, and bein' I was tired and only a kid, I hobbled my hoss and crawled down in bed. It was kind of dark in the dugout, and I slept till I woke up and found I had a long-horned steer in bed with me. He was big as an elephant and red as your nose in January. He'd figured the sod roof was grass and come bustin' through. And dang if he didn't kick me out of bed."

A ripple of gurgles came from Baby Ethel, her face, hands, and dress now smudged with soot.

'Eighty-Three turned around. "Get back in your corral, boy!" he ordered sternly.

Peegy hated to go because he could see three men in the car. Even in the fireplace he could hear it coming closer. There was a knock in the engine every so often, like Anselmo pounding in the shop, and a rattle like when you jumped up and down on the cots in the camp house. The car sounded as if it were turning around. The rattling stopped, but the sound of Anselmo's hammer kept on just outside the front door.

"*Oyé, patrón!*" a mocking voice called. "We want to see you a little!"

The boy peered around the edge of the fireplace and instantly knew that a terrible thing was about to happen. Across the dining table in the next room he saw Epifania standing in the kitchen doorway. She was crossing herself, and her wrinkled face was the color of unwashed wool.

Stiff with fear Peegy looked at 'Eighty-Three. The boy caught a glimpse of thin jaws closing like a vise and of a shriveled parchment face grim and expressionless as a piece of old leather. The old man seemed unconscious of everything except what was waiting for him outside. One hand worked the bolt of George Bishop's rifle. Then with his hooked nose pointing the way, he stepped through the open doorway.

Before 'Eighty-Three had set foot on the gallery, the boy saw him throw rifle to shoulder. The discharge was drowned in a roar like some of Donaciano's thunder. The boy saw a piece of San Ildefonso pottery on the living room table crumple to pieces and a great flake of plaster fall from below the picture of the Organ Mountains at sunset.

From that moment everything for Peegy was a little confused. He had a blurred impression of Baby Ethel throwing herself on his neck, of 'Eighty-Three's rifle speaking again sharply, of the sudden roaring exhaust of the car. When the boy reached the gallery, he found old 'Eighty-Three, pale blue fire in his eyes, watching the top-less green car that swayed crazily down the wheel tracks. As Peegy stared, it swung off the trail, turned in a wide circle, and plunged out of sight in the arroyo. After a moment a single figure appeared on the farther bank, running in the direction of the blue hills in Mexico.

"The Good Book tells you to love your enemies, Bishop," 'Eighty-Three said in a peculiar voice. "But it's kind of hard to do when they're shootin' at you."

Only when the old man turned did Peegy see that above the teeth-bitten pipe stem protruding from 'Eighty-Three's breast pocket the shabby tan shirt was blotched with red.

✪

Dick rode in at a gallop soon afterward. He said he had heard the shooting from Ignacio's herd on Kelso's Ridge. It was late after-noon when George Bishop and Nan arrived home from El Paso. Be-fore they were out of the car, Peegy and Epifania and Baby Ethel, still streaked with soot, were on the running board, all talking and crying at once. A grave young figure came up slowly from the camp house. His black eyes looked somber.

"So that old-timer," he mocked bitterly, "never had a gun in his hands?"

Peegy saw his father's face go faintly red, but Nan stood up and ran from the car into the foreman's arms.

"Oh, Dick!" she begged him.

✪

**Conrad Richter** **313**

It was hard for Peegy to fall asleep that evening. The sheets had never felt so hot. He knew that Epifania was still in the kitchen. The scent of cedar smoke drifted through the open window. When he smelled it, Peegy could hear in his mind the drawl of old 'Eighty-Three after Dick had carried him down to the camp house.

"You know, Dick," the triumphant old voice had said, "some folks figure, when they die, they're a-goin' to a city with streets of gold. Maybe they are, Dick, but I ain't. What I kind of see is plumb green like the old days when we'd round up in the spring. The skies is brighter'n you can see 'em, pardner. The air's sweet, like she used to be. And they's no wool to stomp down in a greasy sack...." He started to cough.

It was here that Dick, with a silent gesture and stricken face, had sent the boy out of the camp house.

# A Storm Comes to Crazy Horse

## Tom W. Blackburn

☒

*In the decade between 1939 and 1948 Tom W. Blackburn contributed more than three hundred stories of varying lengths to the magazine market. Also during the 1940s he worked as a screenwriter for various Hollywood studios, a circumstance that prepared him to adapt his own Western novels as screenplays, beginning with his first,* Short Grass *(Simon & Schuster, 1947). Blackburn's longest affiliation was with the Disney studio, where, for a time, he was best known for having written the lyrics for* The Ballad of Davy Crockett, *a popular television and then theatrical series based on the exploits of this legendary frontiersman. Perhaps his finest achievement as a novelist is the five-part Stanton saga, which focuses on the building of a great ranch in New Mexico from the Spanish period to the end of the nineteenth century and is currently being reprinted in hardcover editions by Chivers Press in the Gunsmoke series. Tom W. Blackburn's Western fiction is concerned with the struggles, torments, joys, and the rare warmth that comes from companionships of the soul, the very stuff that is as imperishable in its human significance as the "sun-dark skins of the clean blood of the land" that he celebrated and transfixed in shimmering images and unforgettable characters. "A Storm Comes to Crazy Horse" first appeared in* 10 Story Western *(November 1940) and has not been previously collected.*

Apache Valley was a glacial hell and the slopes of Crazy Horse the heart of it. A howling norther was booming down the vast sweep of the San Luis, funneling through the pass at Wolf Creek and exploding on Crazy Horse, a wind-driven, merciless ram of snow. In the lean-to back of the schoolhouse Bert White hunkered close to the cheery glow of his stove. Behind him, on a table and covered with a cloth that lifted occasionally at one corner as a sliver of the blast outside knifed through the room, were his unwashed supper dishes. The water pail behind the door was nearly empty. No pump on earth would prime in the temperatures abroad in the night. The dishes could wait.

A shabby *Swinton's Fourth Reader* rested on Bert White's knees. A white sheet of paper half covered with school examination questions lay at his elbow. But his mind had drifted from both reader and questions. It was on the storm. There would be no class tomorrow and no one to question. A blizzard did that in Apache Valley. A blizzard stopped everything but life and a man's thoughts—and the schoolmaster of Crazy Horse had no love for either.

Thus, when a hand knocked heavily on the lean-to door, it seemed Providence, long unkind to a quiet and lonely man, had relented. Bert White was startled, knew even a brief moment of fear, but he raised the bar and opened the door. Three men stood outside in the storm-blown night. The first man stamped into the room, shaking off the snow and the cold which had blackened his face, as impatiently as a terrier shedding water on a river bank. The other two men were in bad shape. They seemed to live only because wills of iron demanded they cling to life as long as their bearded, rock-hewn partner. The three drew near to the stove without a word to the man in whose home they had found the shelter they so desperately sought. The weaker men sprawled down on the floor. The leader flopped into Bert White's chair. For a time it seemed their numbed bodies sucked in the warmth of the stove so eagerly that the rest of the room grew chill.

Bert knew this to be only imagination—one of those strange thoughts which come and go in the heads of men who live alone. Bert knew, well enough, the reason his whole body had gone suddenly cold. There would be no mistaking the identity of these three men. Hundreds of law dodgers describing them were posted the length and breadth of Apache Valley. Thought of these dodgers made Bert White cautious.

Two framed pictures stood on the table. As though straightening the cloth-covered dishes also there, Bert's hand brushed one of the frames so that it tipped forward, face down. The likeness of a young and lovely woman stared out curiously from the frame he left untouched.

For a time that could have been counted by the measured beat of a clock, there was no movement in the room save the labored breathing of weary owlhooters and the hammer of a timid man's heart. Then the bearded leader pushed off his cap, eased his feet out of stiffened swamp-boots, and shrugged free of his thick wind-jacket.

"Coffee!" he said.

Bert White looked at him, shoved his coffee pot onto the stove, and took three tin cups from their nails. In a little while the coffee began to simmer. Bert squatted down by the nearer of the two men on the floor. Bubbling foam from frosted lungs was on the fellow's lip. Blood darkened his face as congested circulation slowly throttled him to death. Bert fumbled with the stiff, thawing clothing. He tried to loosen it, tried to chafe and rub the dying man, but the leader's broad foot in a stinking, half-rotted sock, prodded him away. Bert stood up. The big man pulled his foot back. His eyes were blank, but he shook his head. Bert would have continued his attempt to ease the frozen man on the floor, but the leader stirred irritably.

"Too far gone!" he said flatly.

Bert measured the words carefully in the methodical way his mind was trained to work, but he couldn't quite understand. A partner is a partner. Hell and high storm should serve to bind trail comrades only the tighter. Yet this was not so among these three. The big man continued to look at Bert steadily. After a little while Bert backed away.

Not long after that the man Bert had tried to help died. He put up a pathetic, frantic struggle before he went under. Bert looked at the bearded man again. The fellow nodded and stood up, stretching the joints of his great frame. He bent above the stove and poured himself a cup of coffee. He kept looking down into the dead man's drawn, frosted face as he sipped the coffee.

"Joe won't last long, neither," he said. He jerked his head at the stove. "Keep the fire up. I'm floppin'!"

The man moved down the room and sprawled on the bunk at the far end. Bert could see a gun butt pressed into the hair of his belly. A thick, sagging money belt was around his waist.

The big leader went into a light, cautious sleep. Bert White sat back down in his chair and began thinking. The second man on the floor died about midnight. Wrapped tightly in the clothes he had worn in the storm, he passed on much in the same manner as the other. And so Bert was nearly alone again—as alone as he had been in the early part of the night. His mind was turning toward the woman whose picture faced him across the littered table. A lot of thoughts came into White's head at sight of that picture. And these thoughts connected with the many reasons folks in Apache Valley said Bert White was crazy. First off—and there was still a little raw spot in Bert about it—when he'd come from Denver to take the school on Crazy Horse, he'd let his whole name out—Ethelbert Anson White. Folks had ribbed hell out of him because of that handle, all saving one girl who thought it was a fine name for a teaching man. But folks knew, too, that a young schoolmaster on his first job is apt to step off awkwardly at first. They gave Bert credit in their way and sort of forgot the bow-tie handle, especially after he married Lola Barton and worked away at the old place her folks had left her until it was decently on its feet again.

Apache Valley was flinty hard, cut off, and forgotten deep down in the hills. But folks measured a man pretty high who could do what the young school man did with his own hands and a woman's help. Then Lola White, returning from Denver on the paymaster's stage, was shot to death at Reservation Point the day Indian Yarrow's crew took thirty thousand Army dollars from the strongbox in the boot and got away clean. A lot of people aside from Lola White died that day. Bert was never sure what happened to him after that. It hit him hard, but he had kept it all in, had never even told why Lola had gone to Denver. But the news got around after a while from someone who had seen the same Denver doctor Lola had.

Bert became more and more like a recluse. Sometimes he tried to fight the loneliness, and sometimes he didn't. Usually it didn't seem to make much difference. After a while it got so friends made him sick with their kindliness, and he began to keep out of their way. He wrote to Leavenworth and got a prison picture of Yarrow. He dug up all the dope on how Yarrow had looked when he escaped and with whom he ran and about everything anybody knew about the man. He framed this picture and stuck it up beside Lola.

Once in a while word from the outside world came to him through the kids. Some folks got to thinking about a crazy man teaching their youngsters, but there was nothing they could do about it. Kids in Apache Valley were bred of a hard strain to a hard life, and more than one big-boned rancher found he couldn't whip his boy for size long before the young one was done at Bert White's school. Bert could handle the biggest and the hardest of them all. Why, he didn't know. Maybe because they liked him. They were fools about that. They'd bust their heads learning for him, and they'd ride twenty miles of a Saturday, when there wasn't any school, to talk with him. They fed his soul, these kids, so that he couldn't die like he sometimes wanted. And he had to wait.

Not that he ever quite knew what he was waiting for. It was just that something kept him on Crazy Horse, something that bothered him through the dreary years. That something was strong tonight. There was a storm outside, tearing the heart out of the hills. There were two dead men on his lean-to floor. And there was a live man asleep in Bert White's bunk. A thought without shape kept coming back through the haze in Bert's mind. Somehow—and even about this he wasn't quite sure—he had a feeling that he was about through with waiting.

❍

The man on the bunk stirred and sat up. He looked at Bert, sprawled out in his chair, and he looked at the cold stove. His eyes got mean. "You been sleepin'!" he grated irritably. "The fire's down! I've had my belly full of freezin' for one night. Keep it up!"

Bert White pulled himself up out of his chair and nodded toward the second man on the floor. "He died," he said quietly.

The bearded man on the bunk grunted. "Sure! We rode the lights out of the horses comin' through the pass when a man couldn't stand against the wind and blazin' hell couldn't have made steam in a thimble! But it was their risk, same's mine. I rode it out. They didn't. Sixes and sevens, mister. My belly'll be the fatter for it!"

The man's stubby fingers passed across the loose front of his shirt where Bert had seen the money belt. Flinty satisfaction pulled at the fellow's mouth. He rolled over and burrowed down again on Bert's blankets. He spoke over his shoulder.

"Drag Joe and Benton outside. The wind won't hurt 'em now, and they've been trouble enough already. It's a cold night. You keep that fire up, feller! Next time she dies down, I'll load you outside with them two."

Bert didn't mind the job so much. He moved pretty fast with the men on the floor. All the heat the little room held would dissipate swiftly through the open door on a night like this, so he was careful and made two trips. After the second he stood outside himself. It was a fine, smashing night for sound, a kind of big music a man could feel if he wasn't afraid of the cold. He looked at the dead men he had laid in a corner drift. He didn't feel anything but the storm and the music. It didn't seem such a bad night for even killers to die.

Back in the lean-to he was restless. He puttered around the room. The fire had to be kept going. He was full of feelings he couldn't name. He needed help, and there wasn't any, just Lola's picture and a lot of things that went with it, half a hundred little knots and ties that bound him to her through the bare and lonely years—a comb and a cracked mirror in a fancy shell hand rim, a little reed basket where she'd kept her sewing, and a box of fingered photographs. He got them out again. Funny about trinkets like that! A man usually wouldn't have such junk around. Then he meets a woman and marries her, and she dies. Then he'd hardly rest overnight without those trinkets right at hand. That stuff hadn't meant anything special to Lola, yet he treasured it.

There was a clear space on the floor by the stove where the two dead men had been. He put his box of junk down there. It made a little pile. He looked at it. Then he opened a scarred chest and emptied clothes and bedding and faded linens on top of the box of junk. The bearded man's cap and boots and jacket were in a corner. He kicked them onto the heap. He poked around for more loose stuff. This search turned into a kind of pointless game, with the pile of junk on the floor growing bigger all the time.

For an hour he kept quietly at it, stoking the fire and piling everything he owned and everything that was loose upon the floor. Once in a while he'd stop and look at the pile, at the intruding jacket and cap and boots in its midst, and he'd think maybe he was a fool. But he knew he wasn't.

Finally he was tired and about everything was moved so that the heap was nearly as tall as the stove. It was a big pile now, clear against the wall on one side. Bert White smiled a little to himself.

Sometimes, when he wanted oil, there was a little pressure on the kerosene tin, so that when he took the lid off, the sides sort of caved in and made a sharp, rattling bang of sound. But the lid came off quietly this time. He tipped the can with care, so that the stream came out only about half the opening in the top and didn't gurgle. He soaked the pile and the floor until the tin was empty.

It was a long wait, and it got sort of uncomfortable because the big man was heavy in his sleep. The fire was dead, and Bert's breath a plume of vapor every time he exhaled, but he was patient.

Finally the man on the bunk sprawled over as though he'd forgotten something important. He sat up. Bert eased back in his chair until he leaned against the corner of the table by the lamp. The man on the bunk kept looking for him, his eyes dilating. A furrow ran down from his brow to the tuft of hair between his eyes. Suddenly he came off the bed like a cat, staring at the heap of stuff on the floor, but he didn't say anything. Bert didn't say anything, either.

Bert remained silent until the other pulled awkwardly at his shirt-tangled belt, as though his mind wasn't on what he was doing. His motion was a sort of second-nature reach for the comfort and blunt dominance of the gun against his belly. All Bert did then was to move his arm a little. The lamp fell off the table and rolled on the oil-soaked floor. The flame split the room in half, separating Bert from the bearded man. The big one howled unintelligibly and, when Bert didn't move, he seized the water pail and flung its shallow contents into the flames. Even the steam was swallowed. He stopped his yowling and knifed a keen, desperate glance at Bert.

Bert smiled. To him the scene was beautiful. The storm was outside; an inferno was within. Bert White didn't move. The big man seemed to understand. He pulled out his gun and fired across the room. Bert didn't hear the report, didn't think the bullet hit him, but he sat down anyway. The bearded one tried once to reach a blanket in the center of the room but, when the flame puffed out and charred the sleeve of his shirt, he spun and plunged out the door, slapping madly at his burning clothing.

Bert saw him go through the door. It was funny. The man left the door wide behind him, so that the full force of the storm poured into the room, carrying the flames away from Bert. But Bert White kept on getting warmer until he was sleepy. The thought came to him that this one night, after countless ones of bitter wakefulness, he would sleep well.

☻

The fire on Crazy Horse was wild—wild as the storm that fanned it. Far across the valley one of Bert White's kids saw it through the snow, a red glow in the fitful lapses of the blizzard. It was closer to the center where there was help, so he rode there, but it took him all night and half of the next morning in that storm to get word to the sheriff and the others. The storm dropped that night, and with sunup a lot of men were in the saddle. But one man could have done all there was to do. The sheriff, maybe, understood better than most, because he'd been wanting to meet up with Indian Yarrow a long time himself.

He pottered around in the ashes of the schoolhouse on Crazy Horse, and somebody found two fully-dressed dead men in a drift near where the door had been. A quarter of a mile off they found another, face down—a madman caught in that frozen night without boots or jacket or cap. The sheriff knew all three of the dead men. So after a while he came out of the ruins and got all three bodies loaded up behind saddles and swung up himself. All the time he thought curiously of the grim patience of the quiet man who had waited through the years for his chance to die on Crazy Horse.

# Three-Way Double Cross

## C. K. Shaw

*Born to a long line of ranchers on a homestead in the Cherokee Strip, C(hloe) K(athleen) Shaw grew up in eastern Oregon, where, she once observed, the "mail arrived according to the conditions of the road, likewise your doctor and your law." Her forte was an ability to create interesting casts of characters through whom and between whom she was able to develop a suspenseful and unpredictable interplay. She was a highly polished and talented writer who, like many women Western writers, probably fooled the majority of her readers as to her gender. Her career spanned more than two decades and her stories appeared in many of the best-paying pulp markets, including* Dime Western, Western Story Magazine, Lariat Story Magazine, *and* Star Western. *More times than not a C. K. Shaw story would be headlined on the front cover. Although she did write stories in which women figure prominently for romance Western pulps such as* Rangeland Love Stories *under the byline Kathleen Shaw, in the majority of her Western stories the woman's point of view is notably absent and often there are no female characters whatsoever. She seemed naturally drawn to characters living on the fringes of the law and frequently her stories are about outlaws as depicted in this story, "Three-Way Double Cross," which appeared in* Western Story *(June 13, 1942) and has never before been collected.*

**O**ld Ab Haines seemed to hear voices in the howl of the wind. He walked to the little square window with the rags chugged around it to keep out the icy air and scratched a peephole in the frost. But he couldn't see anything, for snow was plastered thick on the outside of the window. Walking back to the little sheet-iron heater, old Ab listened to the snapping of the pine knots in the stove. A fire on a winter night was a lot like a gun talking. Yeah, a lot like the voice of a gun. He looked across the stove at Two-Button Lewis. Two-Button would not be hearing the snap of those guns. He had always been without a scrap of imagination. When the three of them had been young bloods—Ab was including Rockrib Burton, of course—they had cut some fancy figures on the rim of hell. All three had been born to swing, and yet here they were living out their days peacefully in the winter-bound Rockies of Colorado.

Ab half regretted their peaceful ending. The three of them had had some grand high-tailing days, gunned to a queen's taste, spitting in the eye of anyone who stepped on their toes. Again Ab looked across at Two-Button, his lips shrunk in tiny pleats over his empty gums. Two-Button was not regretting the peaceful ending of those smoky days. Ab recalled the day he and Rockrib Burton had seen a slim youth shoot the head off a rattler and announce proudly that the snake had ten rattles and two buttons. He had slipped a cog on rattlers and since had been known as Two-Button. Rockrib had noted the way the young man handled his gun and had offered him the spot as third man in a gold-hunting expedition. Ab remembered telling Rockrib that the youth had no imagination, but Rockrib said Ab had enough of that for ten men.

What had appealed to Rockrib was the way Two-Button had handled his gun and the way he had kept on handling it through fifty-one years. The Battle of Bull Run would not have been a special treat for anyone who had seen Two-Button in action. When he started triggering a gun, things fell apart. And through it all his eyes were as lonesome as a deer's and his voice tucked up in velvet.

Looking at Two-Button now, no one could have known that there sat a great warrior. You would have thought he was a burned stump if a few nettles had been growing beside him. Lifeless, no imagination. You would never have believed he had once laid his hand around a gun with no effort, balanced it, twirled it, fanned it, and through a thickening screen of smoke pulled the same fast, steady trigger. Any ninepins he was shooting at was the same as dead timber. He did not miss because there was nothing to excite him. If there had been a little flourish to Two-Button, he would have been one of the long-haired boys of the smoke trail, but he did his shooting so mildly that nobody thought to tag him as deadly. It was talk at more than one bar that Two-Button Lewis had taken a bad step by throwing in with tough *hombres* like Rockrib Burton and Ab Haines. For fifty-two years

Ab Haines had been doing the imaginative work for Two-Button, just as he was tonight.

"Two-Button," he said, his voice a little squeaky, "if we'd got caught as we tried to make Bloody Pass when that posse was crowdin' us, I reckon our bones would've been well bleached by now."

Two-Button lifted his deer-like eyes. "Thirty years does a tolerable bleachin' job, yeah."

"And we'd be right well situated in hell by now, know our way around and. . . ."

"But we wasn't caught," said Two-Button. "Say, Rockrib is plenty late, and this is a he-wolf of a night."

Ab scratched the frost for another peephole and again plastered snow was all he saw. He lighted the lamp. It was a he-wolf of a night, as Two-Button had said. A bad night to be abroad if there was rheumatism in your joints. Old bones drew more cold than young ones. Rockrib would be stiff as a poker likely and head into the winter with one of his bad cases of chilblains. A horse came into the yard, its hoofs echoing on frozen earth. The shack was on a hillside, and the space below and to the front was as bare as the palm of your hand.

"The ol' son of a gun made it!" cried Two-Button.

Ab looked at him with disgust. Two-Button was expecting their pard, so any horse that entered the yard had to be Rockrib's. Not a speck of imagination. Ab opened the door, and the wind slapped his pants around his legs and whirled snow in his face.

"Hello!" came a strange voice from the dusk.

A big man slid from the saddle with a hitch-like movement that told of frost-numbed muscles. Ab told Two-Button to take the pilgrim's horse into the lean-to which was handier than the barn on nights like this. Ab hurried the stranger inside so he could close the door. Then he helped the big man off with this coat. The stranger hitched away when Ab went to unbuckle his silver-studded gun belt.

"Leave her rest on my hip," the man said in a thick voice. He cursed the night, the country, and everybody that lived in it.

Ab agreed that it was a bad night for humans to be abroad and set out some whiskey that helped more than the fire to take the kinks out of the stranger's tongue and muscles. The man stood turning his great bulk before the stove. Ab looked at the unlined face, the icy ash-blue eyes that neither heat nor whiskey thawed. Boots with the Lone Star of Texas burned into choice cowhide were on his feet, but there was none of the slow soft South in his big voice. The studded belt sagged with an ivory-handled gun. Ab saw the tip of a metal star cropping out above the stranger's vest and glanced at Two-Button who had returned from putting the horse away. Two-Button hitched at the ribbed drawers rolled over the top of his pants, sat down, and took off his worn boots so his toes could warm faster. Feeling Ab's glance, he lifted his mild eyes then fell to rubbing his chilled toes. He had not caught Ab's signal for alertness.

"How about a bait of beans?" Ab asked the stranger.

The man nodded and kept rubbing his muscles. He was most interested in his right arm and hand. When Two-Button had the beans hot, the stranger sat down to the table and spooned them up hungrily. He laid a thick slice of onion on a cold sour-dough biscuit and took huge bites. After each swig of coffee, he wiped off his mustache. When he was finished eating, he moved his chair near the stove and tipped back against the wall. The heavy homemade chair creaked under his weight. The stranger took out wrapping paper, folded into cigarette-size oblongs, and tore one piece off carefully. He held this in his lips while he shaved some tobacco off a plug into his palm. Over the oblong of paper sticking to his lip he studied the three old-style rifles hanging in straps on the wall. He rolled his smoke, struck the match on the stove to light it, then he examined the newspapers pasted on the walls.

"You must've been some time in Arizona," he remarked.

Ab kicked the gunny sack against the door where the snow was blowing under in a thin drift.

"Uh-huh," Two-Button answered the stranger.

"Nope," corrected Ab. "A friend just come through and left them Arizony papers, and since the shack needed fresh paper, we pasted them on. It's been two years since that roll of papers was left. You can tell by the date ... Eighteen Eighty-Six."

Ab's mind had flashed to the time a couple of years back when they'd left southern Arizona in haste. Rockrib had been in difficulties, of which it was better that the badge-toting stranger knew nothing.

Ab glanced at Two-Button, but the old fellow was still hunched, thinking over the lie that had been told. After fifty-two years Ab could read Two-Button like a book, and he could see that his pard was not taking the stranger seriously. A house had to fall on Two-Button before he sparked up.

"What was the name of the friend that left these papers?" the stranger asked.

Two-Button looked at Ab accusingly. He always claimed that lies got you tangled up and might land you at the end of a rope. Ab had no such feelings. He had handled lies by the bushel and had never ended up with rope trouble yet, unless you counted the time that Rockrib and Two-Button had ambled up just before the jerk.

"I don't recollect the name of the feller that left them," Ab said. "I don't recollect things as well as I used to."

The stranger snorted. "I ain't just askin' for my health. Two years ago Rockrib Burton killed a man around Tombstone. Murdered him!"

Two-Button stiffened. "Rockrib didn't murder that feller! He give him his choice to give up the claim he'd jumped or go for his gun. The feller chose wrong."

The stranger whittled a toothpick out of a match, his eyes like two spots of cold ashes. "Rockrib Burton was a tough hand of the early 'Fifties," he said slowly. "I reckon this is his shack, and you two are Smoky Haines and Two-Button Lewis."

Two-Button saw too late the ashy look in the stranger's eyes. He rose carefully so as not to get a crick in his back. "Are you the law?" he asked.

"With a diamond-studded badge and a smoking pistol!" the stranger answered. He drew his ivory-handled gun and spun it neatly. "The law, Grandpap, and a special kind of law. The man Rockrib killed was connected with money. Two years ain't long for a rich pa to spend hunting down the murderer of his son. On top of my wages he's giving me one thousand dollars as a plum for bringing in this old jack's ears. Don't look so sad, Grandpap. If you stay where you are and don't make no palsied reach fer one of them rifles on the wall, I'll let you live out the rest of your moth-eaten years."

Two-Button's sad eyes were as blank as a set of false teeth floating in a horse trough. He looked at Ab. Both of them knew that Rockrib was due to ride up to the door any second, and here waited a stranger cocked and primed to mow him down. And it would be like slaughtering a lamb, for Rockrib would be wooden from the cold. But he would go down fighting; old Rockrib had ridden too many tough jobs to a standstill to fold up on this one. And they had taken the stranger in, warmed speed into his gun arm, put beans in his belly, and given him the information he was after. Two-Button hung on to Ab's glance, begging him to do something. Ab had always said that Two-Button's saving grace was knowing he had no imagination. He never raked up something to pass for it and thereby gummed the works for a real artist.

"So you're after that reward, *too!*" Ab quavered. "Sheriff Harry Nassey has kind of figured Rockrib was a good gent and. . . ."

"Nassey! Does that ol' has-been know there's a price on Burton's head? Is he tryin' to beat me out?" The stranger was all hound now, his stomach pulling in, his nostrils quivering.

"Sheriff Nassey's been holdin' off," Ab explained. "He knew the feller that was killed was a no-good, claim-thievin' snake."

"Holdin' off, has he!" The stranger loosed a laugh. "He's lost himself a neat spot of cash by that play."

"Has he been holdin' off?" asked Two-Button in a puzzled tone.

" 'Til today," Ab answered. "I tried to get Rockrib not to go to town today. I told him the sheriff was weakenin', beginnin' to fall under the spell of that reward, but Rockrib wouldn't listen to me. Now he ain't home . . . probably in jail."

"Naw, sir!" Two-Button cried. "Harry Nassey couldn't never jail Rockrib."

The bounty hunter was suddenly like a caged wolf. He was so big that, when he began striding, he crowded the table to the wall and jarred the stovepipe so far out of joint it began to smoke. The weak board in the center of the floor gave dangerously. Bull-sized and boiling with anger, the stranger left small space in the room for Two-Button and Ab. He began to tighten his muffler.

"I'll ride into town and take that jail apart," he rumbled.

Ab helped him get ready, his hands shaking. If he could just get the stranger back into the night ... but his haste was his undoing. The lawman's lips curled away from teeth that gleamed like the prongs of a pitchfork.

"So that's your game, Grandpap?" he said. "Tryin' to get rid of me!" He came close to cuffing Ab's ears with his great palm but, when Ab did not dodge, changed his mind. "Tried to outsmart me," he roared. "No busted-down batch of brains like yours can outthink Chuck Kelerton!"

"Suits me to have you stay here," said Ab indifferently. "Have another cup of coffee, Chuck?"

"With strychnine in it? Your eyes wasn't tracking when you asked me, Grandpap!"

"When you get seventy-one, your eyes don't track so good," Ab replied.

"Just the same I'll not have any more coffee, and I'll drink my own whiskey."

Kelerton pulled a bottle off his big frame. He had planned on saving his whiskey for some other cold night, but there had been a gleam in Ab Haines's eyes that warned him of foul play. The three men sat down and remained seated until the beat of hoofs was heard on the wind-swept hillside before the shack. Ab glanced with a start at Two-Button to see if he had caught the quality of those hoofbeats. He opened his mouth to speak, closed it.

"What's wrong with them hoofbeats?" snapped Kelerton.

Ab turned, realizing that the bounty hunter had gotten the message he had tried to send to Two-Button. "Them beats?" he asked. "Them beats comin' into the yard, you mean?"

"I don't mean none other!" Kelerton's voice was like wind roaring down the side of a mountain.

"Yeah, what's wrong with them beats?" asked Two-Button, aroused by the bounty hunter's curiosity.

Chuck Kelerton's hand settled on Ab's collar. "Speak up!" he ordered.

Ab listened another second. "I know Rockrib's Buck horse as well as my own," he said. "He clicks his sharp heels down like he means business. He don't set them down like he's a stumbler and knows it . . . like the sheriff's black."

"You mean that's the sheriff?" Kelerton asked.

Ab looked at Two-Button. "It's that double-crossin' Harry Nassey," he said. "He's after Rockrib."

"After Rockrib?" cried Two-Button. "But Rockrib went to town."

"And the sheriff tried to arrest him, and Rockrib didn't stand hitched for it. You know ol' Harry Nassey ain't lettin' the snow freeze on his mustache for nothin' less than a mighty rich plum. He likes to toast his shin bones on cold nights, but that reward was too much for him. Now he's trailin' Rockrib. That reward is considerable, ain't it, Chuck? I mean without the part you get personal for fetchin' in the ears?"

"Vultures," Two-Button said in a velvety voice. Age had not seamed his voice as it had Ab's. "Two vultures ready to tear at Rockrib's carcass so's to split the head money!"

"There won't be no split," Chuck Kelerton snarled at him.

Opening the door, Ab stood with his hand protecting his eyes, his elbow poking through the gunny-sack patch on his jacket sleeve.

"No split?" Two-Button asked of Kelerton. His eyes were sad and moist. "Rockrib would want the sheriff to have half of that money, 'cause him and Nassey are friends."

"He would?" Kelerton growled. "He would, huh?"

"The buzzard!" cried Ab. "I'd rather a stranger had it than a friend that turns on you. The ol' spavined turtle! The ol' ring-boned centipede!" The wind shook Ab's thin frame. "You poisoned hunk of coyote bait!" he called under the whine of the storm. "Comin' out here after Rockrib, after him helpin' you tail up your cows when they was frosted down last winter. After me and Rockrib both set up with you when you had pneumonia, and after the way Rockrib rode fer the doctor when your son got busted up by a fallin' bronc. Then you come a-huntin' his scalp!"

"Give your tongue a rest," snarled Kelerton. "I'll talk to the sheriff from now on."

He caught Ab by the collar and skidded him out of the way.

"Come in, Nassey," he called. "S'pose you don't like the night no better than me."

Sheriff Nassey had never had the reputation of blowing smoke from his ears, but for twenty years he had met trouble and wiggled through. He could swing a gun if he had to but hadn't been especially speedy even in his younger days. Therefore he never carried a chip on his shoulder. He had a deputy who was noted for his draw, but when the deputy was home in bed that did not help the sheriff. He entered the cabin without any bluster.

"Sheriff," Kelerton said, "I'm here to get Rockrib Burton, and I don't need your help. Warm yourself and hit back for town."

The sheriff stamped off some snow, took off his cap with the fur-lined ear tabs, and shook it. He pulled off his mittens, unbuttoned his coat, and stepped over to the stove. He wore a gun belt over one thigh, but it lopped at a bad angle and was not studded with silver that gleamed in the lamplight. Lined up against Chuck Kelerton, he looked pretty sorry. Badger-gray from seventy years of hard living and a little stooped, the sheriff was not much of a threat. His big nose was blue from cold, and a red line weaved across his cheeks where the skin hugged the high bones. His eyes were washed back in his head like two pools of water on a dry mesa.

"What you buttin' into my territory for?" he asked Kelerton. There was bluster in his voice.

Kelerton's big rumpy frame bristled and his young voice rolled with power. "I'm a special man hired to bring in Rockrib Burton, and I aim to bring him in."

"He gets an extra thousand for fetchin' in his ears," Ab put in, seeming to relish the tough spot in which the sheriff found himself.

"I should've grabbed Rockrib sooner," the sheriff said. "But he was a friend of mine, and this weather has been such a he-wolf to get out in. I never thought about a special man bein' sent."

"You know it now, and I'm takin' Burton back with me."

"You mean after you ketch him," the sheriff said. "Mister, I tried to take Rockrib when he rode into town, and he shot the gun out of my hand, cracked me on the head, and kicked me after I was down. I follered him, but I never chanced the cut off. He could've saved three hours by takin' her, but them miles stand on end and there ain't footin' fer a mountain goat. But he's a he-wolf fer stuff like that. I recall the night he went fer the doctor when my son was. . . ."

"Three hours!" Chuck Kelerton bellowed. "That would have landed him here before I arrived!"

Ab Haines had listened to the sheriff's words with pride. Rockrib had not let down the rep the three of them had built up by fifty years of tough going.

The sheriff took a pine knot from some wood stacked against the wall and jammed it into the stove. "These knots make a good fire," he said, "but they're hard to work up."

Chuck Kelerton's prime-grade cowhides shook the cabin as the big fellow picked them up and set them down. He barged up to Two-Button and grabbed him by the arm.

"Which way did Rockrib go?" he barked.

Two-Button's eyes were deadly serious. "No feller can make that cut off on a he-wolf night like this, even Rockrib," he declared.

"He'd make it," the sheriff said. "He's come and gone." He unbuckled the overshoes he wore over his boots and pulled his pant legs free to let the heat circulate.

Sheriff Nassey looked at the table where there was a cold plate smelling of beans, crumbs of bread, and a slice of onion. "Don't bother with Two-Button Lewis," he said to Chuck Kelerton. "Ab Haines is the likely one to question. He prob'ly slipped Rockrib on his way without ever wakin' Two-Button out of his doze." He poured himself some coffee and dished up some beans from the pot on the heater. "I'll figure a way to make Ab talk when I've put something under my belt."

He talked as he ate. "This bunch we're dealin' with ain't regular run-of-the-herd stuff, Kelerton. Ol' Two-Button Lewis yonder is a mild *hombre* that likes to tend the horses and sweep out the shack and set and oil his gun, but I never come out here and saw Ab Haines a-doin' anything but settin' a-thinkin' up some reason for why he shouldn't make a trip to town on a day like this. That's why I knew Rockrib would be the man to come to town fer the regular supply of tobaccy. Smoky Haines . . . Ab was known as in his younger days, accordin' to my reports. You'll recollect, Kelerton, the three of them has records, not posted fer head money, but records. Rockrib is the only one of them that's worth a plug nickel, though. I've looked into it thorough."

"You double-crossin' ol' horn toad!" Ab Haines cried as the sheriff rattled his front teeth.

"I knew Rockrib would be the one to come to town today," the sheriff went on. "Ab always swells up and tells how tough he is, but he leaves the rough jobs like buckin' a blizzard to Rockrib Burton."

"Which is a bare-faced lie!" yelled Ab.

"So in rode Rockrib," the sheriff snapped with a jerk of his head at Ab which said he had proved his point. "But Ab Haines is the ramrod of the gun workin'," the old lawman conceded. "He wasn't called Smoky Haines for nothin'."

"I thought Two-Button Lewis was the gunny," growled Kelerton.

"In the young days the records show he was passin' good, though Ab Haines and Rockrib Burton was the tough *hombres*. Now all Two-Button does is oil his gun and wonder which end is which."

Chuck Kelerton leaned toward Two-Button with a fierce stare. The old man's soft brown eyes showed tears at the corners, and his shrunken lips puckered. Kelerton swung away from him in disgust. "I ain't carin' about no more past history," he snapped. "Let's make Haines talk."

The sheriff hitched at his chair. "Ab Haines will be a tough customer, but a hot poker on the bottom of his feet should start him talkin', or bendin' his arm backward till it snaps square off at the pit, or hangin' him by his thumbs. We might have to use all three. Ab's a tough hand."

"*Was*, you mean. He's empty as a last year's snake skin now."

The sheriff lifted his gaunt form off the chair. He had put away half the pot of beans and four sour-dough biscuits, but he still looked hungry. He wiped his mustache with a bandanna and glared at Chuck Kelerton. "You've got fire in your blood and power in your muscles now," he growled, "but it'll get frosted out sooner than you think. Then you won't be half as chipper as Ab Haines."

"Are you goin' to make that feller talk, or shall I?" demanded Chuck.

"You can have the job if you want," the sheriff snapped. "But 'fore we start, understand you're not high-kneein' it into my territory and packin' off my reward. You get that special thousand, an' that's all."

"Go ahead and make him talk," Kelerton rumbled.

The sheriff blinked. "Maybe I'll split with you," he said thoughtfully.

"Yeah, maybe. Get Haines to talking. You know him and can tell where he's shellin' out the truth."

"I reckon he won't try to lie to me," the sheriff said. "He was with me the last time I made a gent ante up. . . . I depytized him and Two-Button both. I stood the gent against the wall and I. . . ." He became so interested in drawing a knife from beneath his shirt that he let the sentence trail off.

Two-Button rose from his chair. "None of that on Ab!" he cried.

"Come on with your toad stabber," Ab challenged. "Cut my ears off so close to my head they'll never grow again. I've had 'em seventy years and I'm 'most finished with them anyhow."

The sheriff drew the blade with loving care. It shimmered in the lamplight, nine spotless inches of steel. The lawman pulled a hair from the tuft over his left ear, held it to the light, and snipped it off with the knife.

Ab cackled. "I saw you try that on the other feller."

"And 'fore I finished, the other feller talked," the sheriff replied. "Which one do you favor? I'll take the weak one first. Seein' we've been friends and you've done me a few good turns, I'll leave you the best one." He spoke to Kelerton. "I never knew a man to stand for both ears."

Kelerton was still growling like a grizzly, but he had grown a little white about the gills as though his beans were not resting well. Two-Button shrank back a step, the horror of Ab's fate in his eyes. The wind caught the hinged window of the lean-to and whanged it back and forth. Chuck Kelerton spun about, cursed the wind, and looked at Two-Button. The old man's face was like a snow-locked plain, all but the eyes. They had the anguished look of a dog that had been kicked by one whom he trusted.

Kelerton faced the sheriff again. "Get to carvin'," he ordered. "We're wastin' valuable time."

The sheriff pulled another hair, and this time he split it. Ab's cackle grew thin. He turned from the hard stare of the sheriff and drew Chuck Kelerton's glance. "I'll look funny without ears," he squeaked. "Nothin' to hold my hat up."

Two-Button weaved back to the wall, his sock feet making no more noise than the snow drifting under the door. Inspiration was in his moist, brown eyes, and he went for his rifle faster than you would figure old bones could move.

Chuck Kelerton felt danger and heaved about. "Drop her!" he bellowed. "Drop her!" He dug for his ivory-handled beauty.

Two-Button had no more idea of dropping the rifle than he had of buying fish. He wheeled the old girl into position so fast she was a blue streak and pulled the trigger. A pellet of lead kicked Chuck's gun from his hand and tore the flesh of his wrist. He let out a roar that outdid both the report of the rifle and the whanging wind. The sheriff looked up from his business of splitting a second hair.

"What's this dad-blamed talk of cuttin' Ab's ears off?" Two-Button croaked at him.

"Now you've done it," the sheriff accused Chuck Kelerton. "You've let this toothless ol' windmill get a gun in his claws. You've let him draw your fangs, and now I'm lookin' down the wrong end of a rifle!"

"Arrest him!" snarled Kelerton. "He's got the gun on me, not you!"

"But he could turn it mighty fast," the sheriff pointed out. "Ol' Two has a rep as long as your arm."

"Get that gun away from him 'fore his shaking sets off another blast."

"What's all this talk about cuttin' Ab's ears off?" Two-Button quavered. His misty eyes repeated the question again and again.

Chuck Kelerton thought this was a good moment to go for his under-arm holster. His right hand was wounded, but he was almost as swift with his left. His reach was smooth and swift, but as his fingers dived from sight, Two-Button's rifle quaked the shack a second time. This shot also took, and Kelerton fell back against the wall with a wounded shoulder.

The sheriff stood a second in disgust, then he returned his knife to its sheath. "So you're the gent that horned in on my territory, huh?" he asked Kelerton. "Rode all the way from Tombstone to help me mind my business. Got a shot at a pair of thousand-dollar ears and muffed the job! Let an old man ride you down! Turn your face to the wall while I take that under-arm gun off you. I'm not splittin' my reward with no four-flusher like you!" Suddenly his voice rasped: "I said stick your face against the wall!"

Kelerton's youth, which had been standing out in smashing vibrancy earlier, lost its advantage. His fire and strength had been leveled by an old-style rifle in quaking hands. Even his growl was weak as he turned his face to the wall.

"I'll give you a hand in emptyin' his holster, Sheriff," Ab said.

The sheriff did the tying up himself, and Ab looked on with pride. "I never seen but one man do a better job," Ab said when the work was finished. "That was Rockrib Burton. He tied a sheriff up in Salt Lake once, and I reckon we was in New Mexico 'fore that badge toter got loose. Likewise our trail was so cold he never struck it."

"It's a tolerable job," the sheriff admitted. "Now, Ab," he said, "we'll strike out to ketch Rockrib. As long as his ears is worth a thousand dollars, we'll each take one."

Two-Button laid down the rag with which he was cleaning his gun. "Leave out this carvin' talk," he said. "Stuff like that makes the shivers run up my back. I never seen a man carved up yet that it ain't spoilt my supper."

"Get ready to ride," Ab ordered.

"In that he-wolf of a night?" Two-Button asked accusingly, but he shuffled about collecting warm socks, coats, and mufflers.

When the three of them left the shack, they found the storm had quieted.

"Blizzards have a funny way of lettin' up," Two-Button said. "They just give their tails a last switch and roar over the mountains. Then the stars come out, and the snow starts to shine."

"Recollect that blizzard that caught us when we was in the Bitterroots of Idaho?" Ab asked. "If we hadn't rode blind into that ol' shack, we'd've wound up spendin' the winter and most of the spring under seventeen feet of snow. If that'd happened. . . ."

"But it didn't," Two-Button said. "I'll be glad when we get to a warmer climate."

Daylight was over the white land when they met a man joggling along on a black gelding. The black was settling its feet carefully, as though it was a stumbler and knew it. The rider took his mittened hands from his pockets, lifted the bill of his cap, and drew rein.

"Howdy," he called. "I heard a buzzard from Tombstone was in the county for to collect hisself some head money, so I rode out to warn you. I see I'm late."

Ab nodded. "Yep, Sheriff, but ride on to our ol' home. There's a feller there that might be gettin' cramps. Rockrib is a he-wolf at tyin'."

Sheriff Harry Nassey settled back in his saddle and laughed. "I heard this *hombre* was a wind splitter with the hardware, how come you don't show no battle scars?"

"Ol' Two handled him neat as a fiddle," Ab Haines replied. "Two was kind of slow to ketch on, him havin' no imagination, but when Rockrib thought of how Two hates carvin', why, things was hunky-dory."

Two-Button Lewis wiped tears from his eyes with the back of his mitten. "I sure didn't know what gag them two fellers was tryin' to pull," he said mildly to the sheriff, "but when they started to talk about carvin', I figured the joke had gone far enough."

# Spawn of Yuma

*Peter Dawson*

⊘

*Jonathan Hurff Glidden was born in Kewanee, Illinois, and graduated from the University of Illinois with a degree in English literature. In his career as a Western writer he published sixteen novels and more than 120 short novels and short stories for the magazine market. His Peter Dawson novels are noted for their adept plotting, interesting and well-developed characters, authentically researched historical backgrounds, and stylistic flair. Jon's first novel,* The Crimson Horseshoe, *won the Dodd, Mead Prize as the best Western of the year 1941 and ran serially in Street & Smith's* Western Story Magazine *prior to book publication. After the war, the Peter Dawson novels were frequently serialized in* The Saturday Evening Post. *One of Jon Glidden's finest techniques was his ability, after the fashion of Charles Dickens and Leo Tolstoy, to tell his stories via a series of dramatic vignettes that focus on a wide assortment of different characters, all tending to develop their own lives, situations, and predicaments, while at the same time propelling the general plot of the story toward a suspenseful conclusion.* Dark Riders of Doom *(Five Star Westerns, 1996), a story collection, and* Rattlesnake Mesa *(Five Star Westerns, 1997) are among his most recent book publications. "Spawn of Yuma" first appeared in* Western Story Magazine *(May 11, 1940) and has not previously been collected.*

## I

### "A JAILBIRD TAKES WINGS"

The man who lay belly down and half covered with snow at the lip of the *rincon* looked dead but for the thin fog of vapor that betrayed his breathing. His curly, straw-colored hair was powdered with snow, and his outfit—light canvas windbreaker, brown vest over thin blue cotton shirt, Levi's, and boots worn through at the soles—was made a mockery by the below-zero wind. The bronze of his lean, beard-stubbled face showed two colorless spots along his high cheekbones, a clear sign of frostbite. His lips were blue, and his long-fingered hands, one clenching a sizable rock, were clawed in a stiffness that suggested death. His brown eyes, squinted against the wind-riding particles of snow, were very much alive. They stared unwinkingly into the fading light of dusk, regarding a rider on a roan horse threading his way through a sparse growth of timber seventy yards below. A wariness was in the eyes, the wariness of the hunted animal. Once, when the rider reined in at the near margin of the trees and looked directly above, the hand that held the rock lifted an inch or two out of the snow.

That gesture and that weapon, feebly menacing when compared to the Winchester in the saddle scabbard of the horseman, remained fixed until the rider had disappeared into the snow haze. It gave a small hint of the dogged energy that had driven Bill Ash these last four days and three nights. The fact that he now laboriously thrust his body up to a crawling position and started dragging himself toward the dying coals of a fire at the bottom of the *rincon* was further evidence of it. He knew only that the fire's warmth meant life to him. And he wanted very much to live.

Stark singleness of purpose had brought Bill Ash in those four days and three nights the two hundred and twenty-seven miles from Yuma's mild winter to the equally bitter one of these Wild Horse Hills. He had walked off the penitentiary farm and escaped on a bay gelding stolen from the picket line of the fort, regardless of the knowledge that he was unarmed and that his outfit was too light to warm him against the weather into which he was heading. Last night, when the gelding had thrown him and bolted, the compelling drive that was bringing him back home hadn't weakened. He'd thrown up a windbreak of cedar boughs and built a small fire, gambling his luck against the fierce beginnings of a blizzard.

Somehow he had lived out the night. Today he had crossed the peaks afoot. This was the sixth fire he had built to drive out the pleasant numbness of slow death by freezing. As he crawled to the fire and held his stiffened hands to within three inches of the coals, Bill Ash knew that it had been worth it. For, three miles to the south and out of sight in the gathering night and the falling snow, lay the town of Rimrock, his goal. The blizzard that had so nearly claimed his life would in turn work to save it now. The gelding would be found and identified. The snow would blot out his sign. No law officer, even if he were interested, would believe that a man unarmed and afoot had been able to outlive the storm.

It took Bill Ash a quarter of an hour to thaw his hands enough to move his fingers, another thirty minutes before he felt it was safe to take off his boots and snow rub the circulation back into his frost-bitten feet. The pain in his feet and legs was a torture that dispelled some of the drowsiness brought on by cold and hunger. An hour and ten minutes after crawling back from the edge of the *rincon*, he was walking over it and stumbling down the slope toward the trees where the rider had passed. The roan's sign wasn't yet quite blotted out, the hoof marks still showing as faint depressions in the white snow blanket. Bill examined the tracks out of curiosity, remembering something vaguely familiar about the roan but still puzzled as to who the rider might have been. Well back in the trees where the wind didn't have its full sweep, he found the sign clearer. And at first sight of it he placed the horse. The indentation of the right rear hoof was split above the shoe mark. The roan had once belonged to his father. He wondered idly, before he went on, who owned the horse now and what errand had brought the owner up here into the hills at dusk to ride into the teeth of the blizzard when any man in his right mind would have been at home hugging a fire.

Two minutes after dark, ten minutes short of seven o'clock, Bill Ash stood in an alley that flanked Rimrock's single street and peered in through the lighted and dusty back window of a small frame building. The window looked into an office. Two men were in the room. Bill Ash knew both of them. Ed Hoyt, whose law office this was, sat back to the window in a swivel chair behind his roll-top desk, arms upraised and hands locked comfortably behind his head. He was smoking an expensive-looking Havana cigar. The cigar and the glowing fire door of the stove across the room were the two things that made it hardest for Bill to wait patiently, his tall frame trembling against the driving snow and the cold. The other man, old Blaze Leslie, was wizened and stooped but every inch the man to wear the sheriff's star that hung from a vest pocket beneath his coat.

Neither man had changed much in the last three years. Ed Hoyt was, if anything, more handsome than ever. His dark hair was grayer at the temples, Bill noticed, a quirk of pigmentation for Hoyt had barely turned thirty. The lawyer's broadcloth suit and the fancy-stitched boot he cocked across one knee were visible signs of affluence. Ed Hoyt had obviously done well at practicing law. But aside from this new-found prosperity, he was the same man who had defended Bill three years ago and tried to save him a term at Yuma. Blaze Leslie was as unchanged as a slab of hard rimrock, his grizzled old face wearing a familiar harassed and dogmatic look. Bill couldn't hate him, even though it was Blaze who had arrested him on the false charge that sent him to prison.

About twenty minutes after Bill stepped to the window, the sheriff tilted his wide-brimmed hat down over his eyes, turned up the collar of his sheep-lined coat, and went out the door onto the street. Bill waited until Blaze's choppy boot tread had faded down the plank walk out front before knocking at the office's alley door. He heard the scrape of Ed Hoyt's chair inside and stood a little straighter. Then the door opened, and he was squinting into the glare of an unshaded lamp in Ed Hoyt's hand. He felt a rush of warm air hit him in the face, its promise so welcome that the sigh escaping his wide chest was a near sob.

He said, even-toned: "It's me, Ed . . . Bill Ash," and heard the lawyer catch his breath.

Hoyt drew back out of the doorway. "I'll be damned!" he muttered in astonishment.

Bill stepped in, pushing the door shut behind him. He did not quite understand the set unfriendliness that had replaced the astonishment in Ed Hoyt's face. Ed was clearly surprised and awed, but there was no word or sign of welcome from him.

Bill said uncertainly, trying to put an edge of humor in his voice: "Don't get to believin' in ghosts, Ed. It's really me."

Hoyt moved quickly across the room, reaching back to set the lamp on his desk and wheeling in behind it to open the top drawer. His hand rose swiftly into sight again and settled into line with Bill. It was fisting a double-barreled Derringer.

"Stay where you are, Ash!" he said tonelessly.

It took Bill several seconds to realize that this was really the man he had once considered his best friend, the man who had defended him at his trial. His hands were thrust deeply into the pockets of his canvas jacket, and he clenched them hard, the only betrayal of the bitter disappointment that gripped him.

"I'm cold," he said mildly. "Mind if I soak up some of your heat?" He stepped obliquely across the room, putting his back to the stove's friendly warmth. Only then could he trust himself to add: "I didn't expect this sort of a howdy, Ed."

Ed Hoyt's round and handsome face hardened. "Blaze just left," he said. "He's got the word from Yuma. He never thought you could make it through the storm."

"I had to," Bill told him, then nodding toward the Derringer that still centered on his chest: "Do you need that?"

"There's a reward out for you. I'm a law-abiding citizen." The statement came flatly, without a trace of friendliness.

Bill's brows raised in a silent query. He was able to stand quietly now, to keep his knees and shoulders from shaking against the chill that had a moment ago cut him to the marrow. The stove's heat was warming his back through the thin canvas.

"And you were so sure I was innocent!" he drawled.

"It's been three years," Hoyt reminded him. "I haven't found a shred of proof that you didn't kill that man, that you didn't steal your father's herd."

"You made it convincing enough at the trial. They didn't hang me."

"If I had it to do over again, I'd do it differently! You were guilty, Bill. Guilty as hell!"

Bill's mind was beginning to work with its normal agility. The first thing, of course, was to put Hoyt in his place. All at once he knew how he was going to do it. He said: "Ed, I've got my hand wrapped around a Forty-Five." He nodded down to his right hand thrust deep in his pocket. "Want to shoot it out or will you toss that iron across here?"

The change that came over Ed Hoyt's face was striking. His ruddy skin lost color, the eyes widened a trifle and dropped to regard the bulge of Bill's pocket. Then, after a moment's indecision, his nerve left him and the Derringer moved out of line. He dropped it. Bill, stepping across to kick the weapon out of the lawyer's reach, said dryly: "These ladies' guns are tricky. You're lucky it didn't go off." He stooped to pick the weapon from the floor, reaching with his right hand and smiling thinly at the ready anger that crossed Hoyt's face on seeing his hand emerge from the pocket empty. As he straightened again, he nodded toward the chair behind the desk. "Sit!" he ordered curtly. "I've got to know some things before I leave here."

Hoyt lowered himself into the chair, sitting stiffly under the threat of Bill's right hand that was once more in his pocket but now armed. A change rode over him. His anger disappeared, and he said ingratiatingly: "I didn't mean it, Bill. Your steppin' in here like that set me on. . . ."

"Forget it!" Bill cut in, irritated at the show of hypocrisy. "Tell me how it happened, how he died!"

"Your father?" Hoyt asked.

Bill nodded. "I read about it in a Tucson paper. That's why I'm here, why I busted out to get here."

"They found him below the rim near your place," Hoyt said, adding: "Or rather, that's where he died. The rim was caved in where he went over. They dug until they found the horse and saddle. The saddle was bloody. That was enough proof."

Bill's lean face had shaped itself into hard predatory lines. His voice held a thin edge of sarcasm when he next spoke. "Looks like the Ash family travels with hard luck. The paper said the old man and Tom Miles had had an argument and that Miles was missing. Any more evidence that he did it?"

Hoyt showed a faint surprise. "I thought you knew. They arrested Miles three days ago. He claims he didn't do it."

Inside Bill there was an instant's constriction of muscle that gradually relaxed to leave him weak and feeling his exhaustion and hunger. The thought that had driven him on through these four bleak and empty days had been the urge to hunt down Tom Miles, his father's killer, the man he suspected of having framed him with murder and rustling three years ago. To find now that the law had cheated him of a meeting with Miles, of the satisfaction of emptying a gun at the man, was a bitter, jolting disappointment. He leaned against the edge of the desk, his knees all at once refusing to support his weight, as Ed Hoyt went on: "Miles was tried yesterday. They hang him day after tomorrow."

Bill's face shaped a twisted smile. "Saves me the job." There was something more he wanted to know about his father's old enemy. "What evidence did they have against him?" he asked.

"All they needed. He and your father were seen riding toward the hills together that afternoon. They'd had an argument a couple days before. Something about whose job it was to fix a broken fence. I don't believe Miles was guilty. I defended him." He raised his hands, palms outward, in a gesture of helplessness. "I couldn't convince the jury. Your father was a big man in this country. People wanted to see his murder paid off."

There was a long interval of silence, one in which Bill felt the keen disappointment of not having been able to deal out his own justice. Abruptly he thought of another thing. "What about Linda?" he asked.

The mention of that name brought a frown to Ed Hoyt's face, one that reminded Bill of the nearly forgotten rivalry that had existed three years ago between himself and the lawyer. It had been a strange thing that Bill should love the daughter of his enemy, now his father's killer, and stranger still that his best friend, Ed Hoyt, should be Tom Miles's choice of a son-in-law and that their rivalry at courtship had never interfered with their high regard for each other.

"Linda's taking it pretty well," the lawyer answered. "We're . . . we're to be married as soon as this is over."

A stab of regret struck through Bill, yet he could speak sincerely: "You'll make her happy, Ed. It's a cinch I couldn't . . . now."

Linda must have known then that waiting for his parole from

Yuma was as futile as trying to get her father's permission to marry an ex-convict. He had written her a year ago telling her as much. His letter had been casual, intended to convince her that he no longer loved her, that she wasn't still his one reason for wanting to live. Gradually, through this past year, he had put her from his mind. It had changed him, hardened him, this realization that the one thing in life that really mattered was being denied him. But it had seemed the only fair thing to do, to remove himself from her life when to remain a part of it would have been too great a handicap for her to endure. "What about Miles's ranch?" he now asked in a new and gruffer voice.

"I'll run it, along with my business." Hoyt leaned forward in his chair. "That brings up another thing, Bill. Have you heard about your father's new will?"

Bill shook his head. The lawyer reached over and thumbed through a stack of papers on his desk, selecting one, a legal form, and handing it across. "That's a copy. Your father had it made up two days before he died. The original's temporarily lost. Blaze Leslie's going to try and find it at your layout once this business is over. It must be somewhere in your father's papers."

Bill read through the two pages, not believing what he saw the first time and going over it again. Here, in black and white, was an indictment that aged him ten years. First came old Bob Ash's blunt statement that he was disowning his son. He gave his reason. In the three years since Bill had been in prison, he'd been convinced that his son had betrayed him by stealing his cattle and killing one of his crew. In his father's own salty language was written the details of disposing of Brush Ranch in case of his death. A value of five thousand dollars, less than a tenth of its worth, was set on the outfit. The buyer was named as Ed Hoyt. The reason, bluntly given, was that Ed Hoyt had performed loyal services in trying to save his, Bob Ash's, son from a deserved death. And for that loyalty Ed Hoyt was to be given title to the ranch on a mere token payment. The five thousand was to be divided equally between three members of the crew who had seen long service on the Brush spread.

The names of these three men wavered before Bill's glance. He realized abruptly that tears of anger and hurt were in his eyes. He crumpled the paper and looked away until he got control of himself.

Ed Hoyt must have detected this emotion in him for he said: "I'm sorry to break it to you this way. Now you know why I think the way I do, that you were guilty, after all. Your father convinced me."

"But his letters would have said something about it!" Bill argued. Then he saw how futile that protest was. He tossed the wadded sheets onto the desk, giving way to the bitterness that was in him. "I'm headed out, Ed." He nodded to indicate the alley door. "I'll keep an eye on you through this window for a few minutes to make sure you don't head up the street to send Blaze out after me."

Hoyt's face blanched. "I wouldn't turn you in now, Bill. You deserve another chance. I won't give you away."

"No?" Bill said dryly and let it go at that. The one word was eloquent of his distrust and bitterness. As he stepped to the door leading out to the alley, he paused a moment. "Tell Linda I'm wishing her luck." Then, catching the lawyer's sober nod, he was gone out the door.

He stood for several seconds outside the window, watching that Ed Hoyt didn't move out of his chair. He turned up the collar of his light jacket and put his back to the drive of the wind, feeling the cold settle through him once more in a wave that completed his utter misery. No longer did he have the will to move, to fight, even to live. He knew he should get away from here, put miles between him and Rimrock tonight, for Ed Hoyt couldn't be trusted not to go to the sheriff once he thought the fugitive gone. Yet it didn't seem to matter now what happened. The law had cheated him twice now, this time of the one thing that mattered, his chance to exact vengeance on Tom Miles, his father's murderer. In two more days the law would call Tom Miles to answer for his crime at the end of a rope.

Strangely enough, it gave Bill little satisfaction to think that the man was to die this way. Miles and old Bob Ash had been bitter enemies since they had come to this country. First there had been a long feud over the boundary that divided their outfits. Then, after years of fairly peaceful neighborliness, had come the matter of Bill's and Linda's feeling for each other. Bill's father hadn't minded, but Tom Miles had, forbidding his daughter to see the son of his old enemy. Suddenly, in swift and unalterable succession, had come Bill's arrest on the charge of stealing his own father's cattle and murdering a Brush crewman, the trial and Ed Hoyt's inspired defense that had saved Bill from the hangman's noose and instead sent him to the penitentiary for life. Then the three long years at Yuma. Bill had always suspected Tom Miles of the frame-up as the surest means of keeping his daughter from marrying an Ash. Now that the law had finally caught up with Miles, he was sure of it.

## II
### "LINDA MILES'S STORY"

Bill Ash could never afterward quite explain the half-insane impulse that prompted him to turn abruptly away from Ed Hoyt's window and stride along the alley in the direction of the jail. He knew only that a moment before his right hand, reaching into his pocket, had touched the cold steel of the Derringer. He had a weapon, a weapon that could kill a man at short range. He knew that a small window was set in the rear of the jail's single cell and that Tom Miles deserved to die without a chance.

He came abreast the low stone jail. A rain barrel sat under a downspout within three feet of the high-barred window. Faint light showed through the window, which meant that Blaze Leslie was still in his office that occupied the front half of the building's one long room. That didn't matter, nothing mattered but this chance of seeing Tom Miles, defenseless, die by a hand he had betrayed.

Bill climbed onto the barrel, feeling its weight of solid ice hold steady beneath him. He leaned over and looked in the glass of the window as he was reaching for the Derringer. The bars of the cell's front wall drew a lined pattern half way up along the narrow room. Beyond the bars sat Blaze Leslie, boots cocked up on his battered desk. He was reading a paper with a lamp at his elbow. On this side of the bars was outlined a cot and a figure lying on it. Tom Miles was stretched out on his back, knees up, arms folded across his chest. Bill's face took on a sardonic grin as he raised the Derringer and swung it down, about to break out the glass and take his careful aim at Tom Miles. At the precise instant he caught a whisper of sound behind him. He pushed back from the window and turned his head in time to see a shadow darker than the snow-whipped night moving in toward him. Then, suddenly, a weight drove in at his legs and pushed him off balance.

He was falling. He reached out with both hands to break his fall, dropping the Derringer. He lit hard, one shoulder taking up his weight. A figure moved in over him as he tried to roll out of the way. A glancing blow struck him on the head and stunned him for a moment. Then the cold muzzle of a gun was thrust into his face and a low voice said, "Quiet! Or I'll kill you!"

Bill recognized the voice instantly. He forgot the gun and the slacking off of tension brought a reaction in him that started every muscle in his body trembling. He was coldly sane once more and ashamed of the impulse that had guided him here.

He was about to speak when the voice said again: "Get onto your feet!" He obeyed. Then: "Your hands! Keep them up!" He raised his hands to the level of his shoulders.

The figure, a full head shorter than his own, moved around behind him. The thrust of a gun nudged him in the spine in a silent command that started him walking along the alley. When he had taken three strides, the pressure of the gun moved him over toward a slant-roofed woodshed behind the store that adjoined the jail. The voice said: "Open the door and go in!"

He reached out, loosened the hasp on the door, and stepped inside. It was warm in here. The air was heavy with the reek of burned coal oil. The hard pressure of the gun left his spine, and he heard movement behind him. The door hinges squeaked, and the cold draft of the wind abruptly died out. The flare of a match behind threw his shadow across a stack of split cedar in the shed's far corner. Then the match's flare steadied and the voice said: "Turn around! Keep your hands up!"

As Bill turned, he had to squint against the glare of a lantern held at a level with his face. Beyond the lantern he saw a face, and a yearning suddenly leaping up to him made him breathe: "Linda!"

He caught the quick changes on her oval, finely chiseled face. Disbelief and wonderment widened her eyes. There was a flash of recognition and then that, too, disappeared. "How do you know my name?" Linda Miles demanded flatly.

He was held speechless a moment, groping for understanding. Finally it came, and he laughed uneasily, realizing how Yuma and these past four days must have changed him. His face was gaunt and bearded, and his hair, long uncut, gave her no clue to his identity. Three years at hard labor and a diet only sufficient to keep him alive had thinned him down to a wiry toughness that made him a shadow of what he had once been. Before he could answer, she said again, sharply: "How do you know me?"

"Look again, Linda."

Once again his voice prompted that flash of recognition in her. He could see it come to her eyes, die out, and then flare alive again, this time more strongly. She said in a voice barely audible: "But it can't be!"

"It is, Linda."

The lantern lowered slowly until it rested on the floor. Now he could see her better. The heavy gun she was holding lowered to her side. Her hazel eyes were wide, tear filled, as she finally understood what his being out there at the jail window had meant. Suddenly, choking back a sob, she cried: "Bill! Bill, he didn't do it!" He made no answer. She came close to him, her two hands taking a strong grip on his arms. She shook him fiercely. "I know, Bill! You must have faith in me."

Her nearness, the fragrance of her hair, made him want to take her in his arms. He didn't. He was remembering Ed Hoyt, knowing that what had been between himself and this girl could never come back. But still he couldn't trust himself to speak.

Her look gradually changed to one of alarm. "Bill! You're half frozen! You're thin! You're sick!"

He shook his head and smiled down at her. "Not sick any more. Just a little hungry. Tired, too, maybe."

Her hand came and ran gently over his beard-stubbled face. "I didn't think I could ever be this happy again," she murmured. Then, before he could grasp the depth of emotion that lay behind her words, her hand ran down over his thin jacket, and she said: "You've been out in this storm, in this?"

"I'm all right now," he told her.

"You're not!" Abruptly she reached down and moved the lantern to one side, indicating a pile of gunny sacking on the floor closest to the wall that faced the back of the jail. A board had been pulled loose near the floor.

"I've spent the last two nights here," she explained. "Watching, hoping I'd catch someone sneaking into the jail. I thought you were the man I was after, the man who had framed Dad." When she caught the look of disbelief he couldn't hide, she said: "Never mind. I don't expect you to take it all in. But lie down there and rest, and we can talk later when I get back. The lantern will warm you."

"Where are you going?" he asked as she turned to the door.

"To get you the best meal in town," Linda answered as she went out.

He sat weakly down on the improvised bed. He moved the lantern closer, relishing its warmth. As he lay back on the gunny sacking, he realized how implicitly she must trust him to leave him like this, within striking distance of her father. He closed his eyes. The knowledge of having lived out his dream of seeing this girl once again was a tonic that calmed the riot and confusion in him. He no longer felt alone. He was asleep in less than ten seconds.

An instinctive awareness made him open his eyes at the sound of the door hinges grating against the moaning of the wind that whipped the corners of the shed. Linda came into the light. She knelt alongside him, laying a tray covered with a cloth on the floor. "I'm thankful to have a friend or two left," she said. "Charley won't talk." She was speaking of Charley Travers, owner of the lunch room. She added: "You didn't tell me you'd seen Ed. I met him on his way to the jail to tell the sheriff you were in town. I made him promise he wouldn't." She smiled in a way that showed him a deep hurt that lay within her. "He . . . he told you we were to be married?"

Bill nodded. "He's a good man, Linda."

She shrugged lifelessly. "Good enough, I've decided. Or rather, Dad has. I'm going through with it for Dad."

Bill knew that much must be left unsaid between them. To hide his own thoughts, he reached down and took the cloth from the tray. "You never know how good food is until you've gone without it, Linda," he drawled.

She had brought him a bowl of bean soup, steak and potatoes, and a generous pot of steaming coffee. He tried to eat slowly, knowing that his stomach would rebel at this full meal after having gone so long on next to nothing—his last meal had been the hindquarters of a tough old jackrabbit scorched over the flames of a fire made of wet wood. He ate the steak first, drank half the soup, and then had his first cup of coffee. Pushing the tray back, he said: "The rest can wait."

"I didn't forget this, either," she told him, and took a sack of tobacco from a pocket of her wool jacket.

He had built his first cigarette in four days and was taking in his first satisfying lungful of smoke before she spoke again: "You came back to kill Dad, didn't you, Bill?"

He nodded, reminded once again of the gulf that had widened between them in these three years. "I had a gun," he said, deciding not to tell her how he came to have the Derringer and of Ed Hoyt's strange action.

His honest answer brought a look to her hazel eyes that implored him to understand and believe. She said softly: "I know, I know exactly how you feel. But I know Dad didn't kill your father, as surely as I know he didn't frame you three years ago. The reason I know is that I was with Dad that afternoon your father died. I had ridden over to the Hansens' to take their new baby some things. I met Dad and your father on the way back, there at the fork in the trails. Dad and I watched your father ride on. Then we came home. Dad wasn't out of my sight that whole afternoon and evening until Blaze Leslie came to arrest him that night."

As she spoke, Bill's long frame went rigid. He searched her face now, loathing himself for the brief moment he had thought he could read deception in its strong clean lines. No, Linda Miles would never lie to him. Too much lay between them to make that possible. Suddenly a full understanding came to him. It left him weak and uncertain. For an instant he felt lost, as though blind and groping for a solid footing that had been swept from under him. Linda must have read what lay behind the dogged set of his face, for she went on: "I was going to write, to try and explain. This is better, your hearing me say it. I tried to tell them at the trial, but they wouldn't listen." Her head came up in a proud look of defiance. "Now I'm trying to make you believe."

Bill heard himself saying: "I do believe it, Linda. You'd never lie to me."

A wave of emotion swept over her. Gratitude and tenderness were in the look she gave him. "You *do* believe me?" she said humbly. Then she choked back a sob and buried her face in her hands. "Nothing else matters now, Bill."

Because this girl had been denied him, because he remembered Ed Hoyt in this moment, Bill didn't reach out to touch her as he longed to. Instead he said flatly: "Then who pushed my father over the rim?"

Her face tilted up to him again. She visibly restrained the tenderness that had been in her a moment ago, seeming to realize the force of will that was guiding him. "I've tried to find out," she answered. "I've spent a week trying. I've traced down the whereabouts of nearly every man within fifty miles on that afternoon. It wasn't as hard as you'd think. I'm sure of all but three men who matter. And only two of those ever had even an argument with my father. Only one of that pair ever had serious trouble with him."

"Who are the three?"

"Fred Snow, Phil Cable, and Jim Rosto."

Bill placed two of the three. Fred Snow was his father's cantankerous old ramrod. He'd always argued bitterly over the management of the outfit with Bob Ash, never meaning half of what he said. He had always stayed on beyond threats of leaving to do as fine a job as any man could. Bill ruled him out immediately, knowing that behind Snow's truculence lay a sincere and deep regard for Bob Ash. Phil Cable was president of the bank. Long ago he and Bob Ash had mutually agreed to have nothing to do with each other. Their trouble came over Cable's refusal to loan Bill's father money when he was making his start. Old Bob Ash had always banked at Pinetop, a town thirty miles farther west. Bill couldn't place the third man and asked, "Who's Jim Rosto?"

"He's the one I meant when I mentioned serious trouble. It happened after you were gone, Bill. That fall your father was short of hands and hired Rosto, a stranger, for roundup. Your father caught him abusing a horse one day and had him thrown off the place. He made him buy the horse and take it with him, saying it ruined the animal. Rosto threatened to come after your father with a gun. Nothing came of it, and their feeling died down. Then, the following year, someone talked Blaze Leslie into taking on a deputy. I think it was Ed Hoyt who decided it. He said Blaze was too old to be doing all the work and suggested Rosto for the job. They say he's been a good law officer."

"And you can't place Rosto on the afternoon of the murder?"

Linda shook her head, frowning thoughtfully. At length she gave an uneasy laugh: "It probably isn't important. Rosto left town the day before your father was killed, so he couldn't have done it. He took a rifle and enough food for two weeks and said he was going over into the Whetstones to hunt deer. They say he had that roan horse of his carrying twice as much as any man. . . ."

Bill stiffened. "A roan? Was that the horse my father made Rosto buy?"

Linda nodded, puzzled at his interruption.

Bill leaned closer to her. "That roan gelding with the split hind hoof?"

The girl thought a moment then all at once nodded. "Yes, now that I think of it! I've noticed that split hoof. But why is that important?"

"I saw Rosto just before dark, up in the timber. He wasn't packing anything on his hull, and he was headed away from town."

Linda's look showed plainly that she was only puzzled. "Then you think . . . ?"

"The first thing is to see Blaze and find out if Rosto's back from his hunt," Bill interrupted. "If he isn't, then we know he's holed up somewhere else, don't we?"

"Hiding?"

"You say he had a run-in with the old man. He left here the day before the murder, saying he was headed across into the Whetstones, sixty miles away. He was to be gone two weeks. Yet, with only a week gone, I see him riding a blizzard, heading away from town and with no grub."

She saw what he meant now and said in an awed voice: "Then he didn't go across into the Whetstones?" Her eyes widened. "Bill! He could have done it!"

"Not so fast," he cautioned her. "He may have a reason for being back. If he does, Blaze will know about it. That's your job, to find out about Rosto from Blaze without his suspecting that you're after information."

Linda stood up. "I'll do it now."

"Careful," was Bill's last word to her.

Ten minutes later, when Linda returned to the shed, she found Bill asleep. She didn't have the heart to wake him. She knelt beside him and for long minutes looked down into his face, seeing that sleep had wiped out the bitterness and frustration that was, to her, the most terrible change these three years had made in him. Food and rest would fill out his gaunt strong frame, but she wondered what it would take to rid him of the deeper wound these years had kept open deep within him.

She went across to her room at the hotel and returned with a pair of blankets. She spread them over him. Her last gesture before turning down the lantern was to bend down and gently kiss him fully on the lips. She had to have that to seal the memory of what they had once meant to each other, to help her through the trouble she knew lay ahead. For Blaze Leslie wasn't expecting Jim Rosto back for another week.

## III

### "A KILLER'S BACKTRAIL"

The next day seemed endless to Linda. The blizzard was at its height, and the needle-sharp pennants of snow that rode the wind and cut at her face as she walked down the alley toward the shed at daylight seemed to fit her mood. She must be cautious in dealing with Bill, in telling him about Jim Rosto. For she understood the unbalanced desire for revenge that was driving him. She could be thankful for only one thing—his hatred was no longer centered on her father.

But when she sat in the shed, talking with him, she saw that she was powerless to head him off from trouble. When he heard that Rosto hadn't been seen in town for better than a week, he said ominously: "That means we've run onto something. I'll want a horse and some warm clothes and a gun, right away."

"Why, Bill?"

"I'm taking a look at that old Forked Lightning line shack up Snake Cañon. If he's hidin' out near where I saw him yesterday, it'll be there."

"But the storm, Bill!"

He smiled thinly. "It'll help. I won't be seen."

She had to give in to him finally and an hour later watched him ride away into the fog of snow. He rode a horse jaw-branded Sloping M, one of Tom Miles's regular string that Linda had taken from the feed barn. He wore a sheep-lined coat and Stetson belonging to Charley Travers, the restaurant owner. Thonged low in a holster at his thigh was a gun, the one Linda had last night rammed in his back. It was her father's. She had carried it since the night he was arrested.

Seeing him ride out of sight, afraid at the thought she might never see him again, was only the start of a day crowded with disappointments for Linda. By three that afternoon, when she waited at the shed and saw Bill's tall figure coming back along the alley, her feeling of defeat was so complete that her thankfulness he was alive and safe couldn't out-balance it.

The first thing she saw as he stepped into the shed and closed the door was the small tear in the left shoulder of his jacket and the stain of blood that ringed it.

"Bill!" she cried. "Your arm!"

He moved his left arm stiffly, his eyes surface-glinted and hard. "He was up there, Linda. Waitin' down the cañon a quarter mile short of the shack. I'll go back again tonight. This time I won't give him as good a chance at me."

"Someone shot you, Bill?"

He nodded. "I was lucky. It's nothin' but a burn."

She insisted on looking at the wound. It was more serious than he had admitted, but the hole through the bunchy muscle that capped his shoulder was clean and he had bandaged it well.

Presently she was calm enough to tell him: "Bill, I have had news. It wasn't Jim Rosto who shot at you. He rode into town this morning at eight o'clock! He's here now!"

His hands reached up to take her by the shoulders. There was a wild light in his eyes. His grip was so vise-like, so hard, she gave an involuntary cry of pain. That brought back his reason. He took his hands away.

"I'm sorry, Linda," he said quietly. He was silent a long moment, then shrugged and gave a long sigh. "Now what? I'd hoped we could take what we know to Blaze Leslie. I'd even give myself up to him if it'd make him wait a few days and look into this."

"We'll have to go to him tonight. He's away today, has been since early morning." She smiled without a trace of amusement in her eyes. "That's something else. People here were all so anxious to see Dad tried for the murder. Now their tempers have cooled off. They're remembering that they were his friends once. Blaze can't find anyone to act as hangman tomorrow morning. He's ridden over to San Juan to see if he can pick up a Mexican who'll do the job for ten dollars. He won't have any luck. They're friends of Dad's."

Had Bill been conscious of it, the caustic, bitter quality of her voice would have shown him how close she was to the breaking point. But something she had said took his attention so forcibly that he didn't recognize the near hysteria that lay behind her words.

"Blaze left town early this morning?" he said incredulously, turning something over in his mind. "Then *he* could have done it!"

"Done what?"

"Taken that shot at me up the cañon."

"Bill! Not Blaze!"

"Why not? Rosto was here, so someone else was up there near the line shack."

She said lifelessly, numbed by this new development: "Then we can't count on him for help."

He shot a sudden, seemingly irrelevant question: "Does Mart Schefflin still run his freight wagons through here?"

"Yes. But...."

"And today's Thursday, isn't it, the day Schefflin's due?"

She nodded. "But in this weather he...."

"Mart Schefflin never let weather stop him, did he? If he hasn't already come through, this will work!" She saw a new excitement and hope flash into his glance. "Linda, I'm going to get that job Blaze is offering!"

"You ... you're going to hang Dad?" she said incredulously.

"I am! Only I promise you he won't hang."

"But ... but how, Bill?"

"I don't quite know," he answered truthfully. "But I'm going out the trail beyond town and wait for Schefflin's wagon. I'll hop a ride. I'll be seen coming to town that way. I'll be a stranger. From there on I'll have to trust to luck."

"And if you're caught?" Her deep concern for him was in her eyes.

He shrugged his wide shoulders. "I won't be," he drawled and wished he could believe he wouldn't.

Blaze Leslie stomped into his office at five that evening, his gray longhorn mustache frosty and his narrow hawkish nose blue with the cold. Jim Rosto sat in the chair at the desk back by the cell. His move in coming up out of the chair was cat-like and lazy, its smoothness holding an economy of motion that seemed to fit the rest of his makeup, his dark and saturnine face and his black eyes.

"Any luck?" he asked easily.

Blaze was surprised at seeing his deputy. He pulled off his sheepskin, threw it onto a nearby chair, and stepped over to the stove to warm his hands. "Not a damned bit!" he growled in disgusted answer to Rosto's question. "How come you're back?"

"Game's all yarded up over in the Whetstones. Then this blow come along. I decided it'd be healthier under a roof."

From the cell at the back of the room Tom Miles's booming voice called: "You should have taken my word for it, Blaze. A hundred dollars couldn't hire a San Juan man to spring the trap under me. What'll you do now?"

Blaze stared back into the half-light of the cell. "I wish to hell I knew, Tom!" he said acidly.

He was a thoroughly beaten old man tonight, worn out, discouraged, hating his job. For thirty years he and Tom Miles had been friends, real friends. Circumstances he still couldn't trust called for him to be the witness to his friend's death at sunup tomorrow morning. All day he had thought of Tom and Linda and Bob Ash. Things like this just didn't happen. But they had. And, unless he could find another man, he himself would be pulling the trap that started Tom Miles on the ten-foot drop that would break his neck tomorrow morning.

Big, gruff, hearty Tom Miles was taking it the way Blaze had expected he would. When asked, Miles insisted on his innocence. But Blaze had never once detected a trace of fear in him. The rancher's stolid bearing was maddening at times. Blaze would have preferred a cringing, half-mad victim for his hangman's rope.

His dark thoughts were jerked rudely to the matter at hand as Rosto drawled in his toneless voice: "I think I've found your man, Blaze."

The old lawman wheeled on his deputy. "Who?" he demanded.

"A stranger," Rosto told him. "Rode in this afternoon on Schefflin's freight outfit. Tramp lookin' for a handout. He spent a dime for a beer at the Melodian and stuffed his mouth at the free lunch counter until Barney told him to lay off. Then he had the gall to ask Barney for a job."

Blaze only half heard what Rosto said. He was staring at Tom

Miles, catching the smile that slowly came to the rancher's broad and rugged face.

"It looks like this is it, Tom," he said in apology.

Miles shrugged. "No one's blamin' you, Blaze. Go on over there and hire him."

Blaze sighed and nodded to Rosto. "Get him!"

The five-minute wait before Rosto came back with the stranger was a trying one for Blaze Leslie. He started to tell Miles how he'd hoped all along that something would save him. But words right now were pointless, more so because no shred of proof existed beyond Linda's loyal testimony at the trial. Blaze, like everyone else, believed that the girl had committed perjury to try to save her father.

His frowning glance sized up the stranger who came through the door ahead of Rosto. The scrubby beard hid a face that was lean and strong looking. The man's thinned-out frame looked steely tough. There was a sag in his left shoulder, a tear in that sleeve, high up toward the shoulder. But the beard and the unkempt hair, the red-rimmed brown eyes and the outfit, much the worse for wear, convinced Blaze that he was looking at a saddle bum. No flicker of recognition showed in his eyes as he sized up Bill.

"Did you tell him, Rosto?" he said brusquely and caught his deputy's negative shake of the head.

He eyed Bill so belligerently that Bill said: "Any law against ridin' a wagon in out of a storm, Sheriff? Or have you trumped up a charge against me?"

"No one's arrested you yet, stranger. What are you doin' here?"

Bill jerked his head to indicate Rosto. "Your understrapper said you wanted to see me."

"I don't mean that!" Blaze said curtly. "Why are you in town?"

Bill shrugged. "One town's as good as the next when it comes to lookin' for work."

"Any particular kind of work?"

"No. And I'm not particular." Bill smiled thinly at his twisting of the sheriff's words.

"I've got a job if you want it. Ten dollars for three minutes of work."

Bill frowned. "That's easy money. What's the catch?"

"We're hangin' a man tomorrow morning. We need a hangman."

Bill shook his head. "Huh-uh, mister! Not me!"

"I'll make it fifteen dollars," Blaze said in a grating voice.

A shrewd look came to Bill's eyes. "How about fifty?"

"You go to hell!" Blaze snarled. Then he seemed to think better of it. A long gusty sigh escaped his narrow chest, and he said: "Fifty it is. Half now and half afterward." He took out his wallet, thumbed out five bills, and handed them across.

As he took the money, Bill looked hesitant. "I once saw a hangin' that turned out to be stranglin'," he declared. "I don't aim to see this one the same kind. I'll take your job if you let me tie the knot myself to make sure it's right."

"Go ahead," Blaze said lifelessly and stepped over to sit down in his chair. "Be here half an hour early in the mornin', at six."

"A man's fingers can't work in the cold at six in the mornin'," Bill asserted. "Get me the rope now and I'll take it with me tonight and tie it like it ought to be. Where's your gallows?"

Blaze nodded irritably to the street door. "Show him, Rosto. And buy him the rope."

As he and Rosto went out and along the walk, lowering their heads against the knifing wind, Bill said: "Salty old gent, ain't he?"

Rosto laughed softly. "Plenty. You're savin' him some gray hairs, stranger."

They made a stop at the hardware store where Rosto bought a twenty-foot length of new hemp rope. Two doors below they turned in at the feed barn and walked to the corral out back, where Rosto showed Bill the crude platform of new lumber two carpenters had nailed together that afternoon. The protruding beam that was used to hoist hay into the feed barn's loft was to be the gallows. The platform, twelve feet high and braced by a scaffolding, was nailed to the side of the barn below the loft door and had a crude trap cut through it directly under the beam. The trap door was unfastened now, hanging downward on its shiny new hinges. Bill saw that it was sprung by a notched two-by-four pivoted in the platform.

Rosto pointed to the lever. "All you got to do is give it a good kick. Fifty bucks ought to be good pay if you don't happen to hurt your pet corn." He laughed.

"You act like this was a weddin'," Bill said dryly.

Rosto froze immediately. He held out the rope, drawling: "You ain't bein' paid for your talk, stranger. Remember that! Be here at six in the mornin'." With that he turned and walked back up the barn's runway and to the street.

Bill spent forty minutes that night working by the light of a lantern in the loft of the barn. Once he went down to borrow a tallow candle and a knife from the hosteler, explaining that the rope would slip through the knot better if it was slick. But anyone watching would have seen that he had an added use for the tallow and that he used the knife for purposes other than trimming the end of the twelve windings of the knot.

At nine o'clock he was satisfied. He had secured the end of the rope to the beam and carefully measured its length so that he judged the loop would fit over Tom Miles's head as he stood on the platform and still leave eight or ten feet of slack. He ate a leisurely meal at Charley's place and smiled faintly after Charley had spent ten minutes talking to him without recognizing him.

Linda had said that she would be in the shed behind the jail at ten. He went there before the hour and found her waiting. As he entered the shed, he had a moment's panic at seeing a tall figure standing behind the girl's. Then he recognized Ed Hoyt.

"Ed wanted to speak to you, Bill," Linda said. "I have his word that he won't give you away."

Ed cleared his throat nervously. "This is a fool idea, Bill," he began. "If I'd been at the office this morning when Linda came to tell me what you were doing, I'd have stopped you. Instead of riding up there into the hills, you should have gone to Blaze...."

"How much have you told him, Linda?" Bill cut in.

"All there was to tell, Bill. He wants to help."

Bill eyed Hoyt bleakly. "He wanted to help last night, too," he drawled.

"I was keyed up last night," Hoyt defended himself. "Didn't realize what I was doing. Linda has convinced me that her father's not guilty . . . not that I need convincing," he added as an afterthought. "What I want to know is what you plan for tomorrow morning."

"Why?"

"I'm one of the four men who's to be there. I could help."

"Who are the others?"

"Blaze, Jim Rosto, and Judge Morris."

Bill didn't show his relief. He had hoped that the witnesses to the hanging would be few. This meant that there would be, at the most, two men against him, Rosto and Blaze. Ed wouldn't interfere and old Judge Morris was physically harmless. He wished he could be sure of Blaze, but the sheriff's absence from town this morning had undermined the faith he'd always had in the lawman.

As he hesitated, Hoyt said once more: "How are you going to work it, Bill?"

"I don't know yet," Bill lied. He couldn't bring himself to trust Ed Hoyt completely after last night's reception in the lawyer's office.

"But you must have some idea," Hoyt insisted.

"It all depends on what happens, who brings Miles up to the loft, who stays with him on the platform." Once that last statement was out, Bill immediately regretted it. No one but he and Linda had the right to know exactly what was going to happen.

He was irritated at Ed Hoyt's being here, for tonight would see the end of his and Linda's meetings alone. If he succeeded in getting her father away, he might never even see her again. She was promised to another man, and he begrudged sharing any of these last minutes with her.

"Linda, I want you to stay," he said sharply. "See you in the mornin', Ed."

There was an awkward moment's silence, one in which Ed Hoyt ignored the blunt invitation to leave. Then Linda said: "I'll go back to the hotel alone, Ed. It was good of you to come."

She and Bill stood silently a long quarter minute after the lawyer had gone out the door. Then Linda said: "You don't like him, do you, Bill?"

"I must've been too busy thinking about this other thing," he told her, neither admitting nor rejecting her accusation. Then, to change the subject, he said: "Here's one more thing for you to do. I'll want two horses on the street, as close to the feed barn as you can leave them. You might have Charley pack up some grub for us to take along."

"Where are you taking Dad?" Linda wasn't voicing the possibility that her father's escape might not succeed.

"To that line shack the first thing. After that . . . ," he shrugged.

That seemed to be all there was to say. The minutes dragged by for them both. Bill realized that his antagonism toward Ed Hoyt had brought a strained feeling between them. He was sorry to have hurt Linda's feelings yet was stubbornly unwilling to admit that he was wrong.

"It's late," she said finally. "I must be getting back." On impulse she reached out and took Bill's hand. "I . . . some day you may know how grateful I am, Bill."

"I'm doing it for myself as much as for you." He took her hand, clasped it, and took his hand away immediately.

"I know. But you are doing it, which is what matters. I wish things could have been different, Bill."

He tried to read a meaning into the words. He was finally sure it wasn't there. There was a tenderness in her glance, but that was gratitude alone.

She turned abruptly to the door and said: "Good bye, Bill," and was gone.

He stayed on for another ten minutes in the shed, his thoughts bleak and empty. Beyond seeing Tom Miles free, he had no plans for the future. He might head for the border or go East to lose himself in one of the cities. He didn't much care.

Later, as he stretched out on the hay in the feed barn loft, he was an embittered man, alone, without hope, knowing that the last page in this chapter of his life was about to be closed, never to be opened again.

## "A DEAD MAN TELLS A TALE"

In the hour between six and seven the next morning, while he waited in the loft for Blaze to appear, Bill Ash smoked cigarette after cigarette, telling himself that the tobacco tasted stale because of his own inner staleness. He wasn't hungry, although his stomach felt empty and dry. He was nervous. Three times he examined the six-gun he had thrust through the waistband of his pants. Three times he saw that the cylinder was loaded.

Relief came when he heard the sound of men coming slowly along the runway below. In another ten seconds Blaze Leslie's doggedly set face was rising into sight up the loft ladder.

Blaze was alone. "Let's get on with it," he said curtly.

They swung the hinged loft door outward and looked down into the feed barn's corral. Three men stood down there. Tom Miles's heavy erect frame topped Ed Hoyt's by half a head, Judge Morris's by a full one. Ed and the judge were standing with their backs to the wind, stomping their feet calf-deep in the heavy blanket of snow, hands thrust deeply in overcoat pockets. Tom Miles seemed unaware of the wind or the snow but more interested in what was going on above.

His steady upward glance must have rubbed raw Blaze Leslie's nerve for, as Blaze let the rope with its noose fall out to hang from the beam, he grunted savagely: "To hell with this! I'm going down there and stay. I'll send one of the others up with the prisoner."

It was Jim Rosto who followed Tom Miles up the ladder into the loft half a minute after the sheriff had gone down. Miles's wrists were bound with a length of rawhide, and he no longer wore his flat-crowned Stetson. When Rosto took him by the arm and started leading him across to where Bill stood, alongside the open door, he jerked away. "I can make it alone, Rosto!" he said irritably.

For a moment Bill was afraid that Miles might throw himself from the loft door, preferring to die that way rather than at the end of a rope. But the rancher calmly followed him down the short ladder out of the loft door onto the platform. For about ten seconds they were alone there while Rosto was climbing down.

In that brief interval Bill stepped close to Miles and said in a low voice: "Miles, I'm Bill Ash! Linda sent me. Don't ask why but, when you fall through that trap, stiffen your neck. When you hit the ground run through the barn for the street! You'll find two horses at the tie rail. Ride east out the street and cut north beyond town. I'll be right behind you!"

"What the hell's this all about?" Rosto's slow drawl said behind Bill.

Bill turned slowly to face the deputy. "I was askin' if he wanted anything over his eyes."

For a long moment Bill thought the suspicion would never leave the glance Rosto had focused on Tom Miles. But finally the deputy's dark face broke into a twisted smile.

"Him cover his eyes?" He laughed stiffly, callously. "Not Tom Miles."

He nodded to the noose swaying in the wind below. "Do your stuff, stranger!" Then, suddenly, his right hand pushed back his coat and dipped to the holster at his thigh. He added ominously: "I'm right here to see that you pull the knot tight behind his ear!"

Bill tripped over the end of the two-by-four lever as he stepped over to reach for the rope and pull up the noose. The lever held and didn't let the trap down. Rosto pushed Miles over onto the trap and stood close while Bill lowered the noose over the rancher's head, tightening the knot until it hugged Miles's right ear.

As the knot closed, Rosto reached over Bill's shoulder and ran his hand along the tallowed rope. "What's the idea of this?" he growled suspiciously.

Bill knew then that Rosto had learned in some way of the part he was playing here. The knowledge settled over him in a wave of dread that finally washed away to leave him cool and nerveless. He turned to face Rosto. "That's so it'll tighten faster," he answered easily. "Are you doin' this, or am I?"

"By damn, I am!" Rosto snarled. He lifted the heavy .45 from his holster and rocked it into line with Bill. "Step back, stranger, and see how it's done."

From below Blaze Leslie's voice rang out harshly: "What's goin' on up there?"

Bill glanced down. Blaze stood at the foot of the ladder, looking up. Ed Hoyt and the judge were farther out, their glances also directed above.

Then, before he quite knew what was happening, Rosto was muttering behind him: "You'll damn' soon find out!"

Bill wasn't ready for what happened with such startling suddenness. One moment he felt the platform quiver under the thrust of Rosto's boot as the deputy kicked the lever. The next, as he whirled around, he was in time to see Tom Miles shoot downward through the trap opening as the door banged solidly beneath the platform. The rope came taut, whanged, and curled upward loosely. Ed Hoyt's voice sounded in a shout of alarm from below. At that exact instant Rosto stepped over to line his gun down through the trap opening.

Bill lashed out hard, throwing all his weight behind his arm. His fist caught the deputy behind the ear a fraction of a second before the .45 exploded. Rosto sprawled downward to his knees. Bill jumped over him and through the opening. His breath caught as he plummeted down the twelve-foot drop, sweeping his coat aside to snatch the .38 from his belt.

His weight struck hard against the frozen ground. He went to his knees and fell sideways in a quick roll. Two guns exploded simultaneously, one from above, one from beyond the foot of the scaffold. The burn of a bullet scorched Bill's left thigh. As he rolled, he had a quick glimpse of Ed Hoyt standing thirty feet away, a smoking gun in hand. Then his bewildered glance lifted to the trap opening on the scaffold above him. Rosto stood there, rocking his gun down on him.

Bill came to his feet, dodging aside as he threw a snapshot at Rosto. Their guns blended in a prolonged burst of sound. A geyser of snow puffed upward an inch out from Bill's right boot. He whirled in through the barn doorway and ran up along the passageway between the stalls. Half way he wheeled in behind a bale of alfalfa and thumbed two swift shots out the maw of the back door. Ed Hoyt, running in through the doorway, stopped suddenly and lunged back out of it.

Bill came into the street in time to see three men running down the steps of the hotel, four doors beyond, and Tom Miles, astride a rangy claybank horse, swinging away from the tie rail. He ducked under the tie rail, pulling loose the reins of the other horse, a black. He vaulted into the saddle as three warning shots exploded hollowly from inside the barn. Bending low in the saddle, he wheeled the black out into the street and kicked hard at the animal's flanks with his spurless boots.

As they left the end of the street, swinging immediately north, Bill drew even with Tom Miles. They rode hard, silently, Bill looking back after they had gone on a full minute. He saw that the slanting cloud of wind-racing snow had already hidden the town from sight.

They put two more miles behind them before Bill tightened his reins to slow his black. Tom Miles pulled in and let Bill come alongside. The rancher's glance surveyed Bill critically an instant before his blunt face broke into a broad smile. "I wouldn't have given a nickel for my carcass when Rosto kicked open that trap," he said. "But my neck didn't even feel it. How did you work it, Ash?"

"Cut through most of the rope and tallowed it. The cut was hidden by the knot when I had it tight."

"Rosto knew what was up?"

Bill nodded soberly. "And Ed Hoyt gave me this." He ran his hand along his thigh, and his palm came away blood smeared. When he saw the look of concern on Miles's face, he added: "I'm glad I got it. It proves a thing or two I've been wantin' to know."

"What?"

"Last night Ed Hoyt wanted to help me get you away. Linda was there. This morning he tried to cut me down. You figure it out, Tom."

He went on then, started briefly to tell the rancher what had happened in the last thirty-six hours. He was interrupted by a muted nearby hoof mutter riding the toneless scream of the wind. He kicked the black into a run as two shadowy figures loomed up out of the snow haze behind. A gun spoke once, its explosion whipped away by the rush of wind. The bullet had a concussion of air along Bill's cheek. He called: "Ride, Miles!" and bent over in the saddle, cutting off to the left.

Linda had made a wise choice of horses, particularly in the claybank. Even with Tom Miles's heavy weight, the claybank more than matched the black's speed. Gradually those dim shadows behind faded from sight, and once more Bill and Miles were riding clear.

Bill purposely made a swing to the west, knowing that the posse—if there were more than two men on their trail—would follow sign. Two more miles brought them to a broad and high shelf of rock. It stretched for a hundred yards to each side of them, its surface swept clean of snow by the wind. Bill right-angled to the north, thinking that the posse would waste perhaps a full minute in picking up the sign.

He rode point for the line shack in the cañon where the rifle had yesterday come so close to taking his life. He paid close attention to the horses now, slowing down out of a run to a stiff trot when the black gave signs of tiring. In these brief intervals he finished telling Tom Miles what had happened.

"We'll have a look at that shack and then go up the cañon and over the peaks," he finished.

"Over the peaks!" Miles blazed. "We're stayin' on here! I'm goin' to finish this thing!"

Bill smiled broadly. "I was hopin' you'd say that."

Today Bill rode straight up the narrow, twisting cañon, unmolested as he crossed the open stretch where the rifle had caught him yesterday. Beyond the widening in the high walls he caught the smell of burning cedar wood and knew again that his hunch on the line shack had been a shrewd one. A few seconds later he caught a glimpse of the sod-roofed shack through the trees. A thin haze of blue smoke drifted lazily up out of the chimney.

They left their horses there and approached the shack by working in from tree to tree. When they were close, Bill motioned Miles to wait and made a quarter circle of the cabin before he went any closer. The snow deadened his footfalls as he crept up to the shack's single side window. He took off his Stetson and stood erect, looking in. He peered squarely across the small room at a blanketed figure lying on a bunk against the far wall. To his left, on the rear wall, was a huge stone fireplace where red coals glowed dully. He left the window, rounded the corner of the log wall to the front, and motioned Tom Miles to join him.

As Miles was coming up, Bill cocked his gun and reached out to pull down the rawhide latch string. He felt the latch raise and threw his weight against the door, wheeling in through it and lining his gun at the bunk. He stood there for two seconds, three, while Tom Miles came up behind him. The figure on the bunk didn't move. Bill walked over to the bunk and looked down into the gray-bearded face of the man lying there with closed eyes. Then, as his eyes focused to the light, he gasped and the gun fell from his hands. He went to his knees alongside the bunk and reached out, taking a rough hold on the sleeper's shoulders and shaking him hard. "Dad!" he cried. "Wake up! It's me, Bill! You're all right now!"

Tom Miles stared incredulously at the scene before him, Bill Ash there on his knees beside the bunk, his face drained of all color, calling hoarsely to his father. Finally, when Miles knew he wasn't looking at Bob Ash's ghost, he reached out and laid his hand on Bill's shoulder.

"Can't you see he's sick, Bill?" he said, his voice awed. "Take it easy."

Only then did Bill's reason return to him. He stared up dully at Miles, and tears came to his eyes. He breathed in a voice raised barely above a whisper: "He isn't dead, after all. He's alive."

It was Tom Miles who caught the hint of sound at the door. His big frame jerked around, stiffened. Slowly his hands came up to the level of his shoulders.

"Bill, we've got visitors!" he said quietly.

Bill turned away from the bunk and glanced toward the door. Ed Hoyt stood spraddle-legged in the opening, a leveled .45 in each hand. Jim Rosto's dark face was peering in over Hoyt's shoulder. The lawyer caught Bill's look of utter confusion and laughed softly.

"I thought you'd have a last try at comin' up here!" he drawled. "I won't miss this time, like I did yesterday."

Comprehension was slowly coming to Bill. He stayed where he was, there by the bunk, looking across at Hoyt for five long seconds.

He said in a flat and toneless voice: "You're the one who framed me into Yuma?"

Hoyt nodded. "Linda was worth trying for," he said blandly.

Tom Miles caught his breath. "Damn your guts, Hoyt! You'll never marry her now!"

"No? And what's to stop me?"

"I will."

Hoyt laughed again. "They claim the dead rise up out of their graves. I've never believed it. But you can try, Miles."

As the rancher's face went slack under the threat of Hoyt's words, Bill said: "Why didn't you finish the job, Ed?" He nodded down to his father's inert shape in the bunk.

"A last detail that wasn't cleared up, Bill. You see, he still refuses to tell me where he put the copy of his will. I'm not even sure he signed it."

"You could have forged his signature to the one you have."

"Blaze saw my copy. He'd know it if he saw it again."

As Ed spoke, Bill had reached out to lay a hand on the top blanket in the bunk. As his hand moved, his father breathed a low moan. "What have you done to him?" Bill said sharply.

"Drugged him. Rosto brings him to once or twice a day and works on him. He's a stubborn man, Bill. We ripped off one of his thumb nails last night. That nearly did it. The other one comes off tonight. We'll break him in the end."

Ed Hoyt was getting an obvious satisfaction out of telling his story. Bill, staring into the twin muzzles of the pair of .45s, kept a firm check on the riot of hatred that was boiling in him. "How did you get him here?" he asked.

"Rosto brought him. In fact it was Rosto who roped him off his horse that day up on the rim and pushed the horse over. I gambled on that, thinking no one was going to take the trouble digging through a hundred tons of rock to prove your father had. . . ."

As Hoyt spoke, Bill's hand suddenly tightened on the blanket. He threw his body in a dive toward the door, swinging the blanket out over his shoulder and rolling into Tom Miles's legs. The blanket flew squarely at the lawyer, opening out. The double explosion of Ed Hoyt's guns beat the air of the room. Tom Miles fell heavily backward across Bill's legs, catching his breath with a groan that told Bill one of Hoyt's bullets had found a mark.

Bill's fury steadied to a cold nervelessness. His right hand streaked out and closed on the gun he had dropped by the bunk two minutes ago. He swung the weapon up into line as the blanket dropped to the floor, two feet short of Hoyt. The lawyer's guns swiveled down. Bill's rocked into line, and he let his thumb slip from the hammer. The gun's solid pound traveled back into his shoulder. He saw Hoyt stagger backward, Rosto wheeling out of the door behind him. Then Hoyt's guns were slashing flame at him. A bullet gouged a splinter of wood from a floor plank. The splinter scratched Bill's face as he was shooting a second time, looking across the .45's sights.

Ed Hoyt coughed thickly as the bullet pounded into his chest. He went to his knees, his lips flecked with blood. Behind him Rosto stepped suddenly into the doorway, his guns swinging down. Bill was all at once aware that Tom Miles no longer lay across his legs. Then, suddenly, from behind him sailed the smoldering end of a cedar log. Rosto saw it coming squarely at him and dodged. That split-second hesitation of the deputy's was ended as Bill's gun exploded again. His bullet and the log end drove Rosto over backward, screaming. The deputy's body stiffened in a head-back arch. He lit that way in the snow beyond the door, his hands beating the ground wildly in a last convulsion that stiffened suddenly. Then his body went limp, and he lay without moving.

In the next hour much happened that Bill was never to forget. Blaze Leslie and half a dozen others rode up to the shack, their horses badly blown in the ride that had brought them up here following the sign of Hoyt's and Rosto's ponies. Linda came later, in time to hear old Bob Ash tell what little he knew of what had happened during the last week. Strong coffee and a stiff jolt of whiskey had deadened the effects of the drug he had taken.

Bob Ash's glance clung fondly to his son as he told the men gathered around him: "Rosto met me up the trail on the rim that afternoon. Tied me and then drove that bay mare of mine over the drop-off. He brought me here. Hoyt came up that night, and they started work on me. Funny thing about that will he wanted me to sign. It was his idea from the first that you were guilty, Bill. I led him on to thinkin' I didn't have much use for you, just to see how far he'd go."

"But you've been here a long time. What's happened?" Bill asked.

His father shrugged and sighed wearily. "Nothin' much that I can remember," he said. "Two days ago I was ready to sign anything they gave me. But the drug was so strong I couldn't talk or even move my head. So it's Hoyt's own fault he didn't get away with this. Whoever gave him those knock-out drops didn't tell him how to use 'em."

It was another hour before Doc Selden rode up from town and took care of the flesh wound in Tom Miles's side and the bullet crease on Bill's thigh. As Selden strapped the bandage about Miles's ample waist, the rancher looked across at Bob Ash and at Bill and Linda sitting at the foot of the bunk.

His face reddened, and he said: "Bob, you're a cantankerous old mule, but so am I. Suppose we call it quits." He stepped over and thrust out his big hand.

Bill's father tightened his lips to hide a smile. Then he frowned. "What good's shakin' hands? It'll take more'n that to make me forget you're so damn' bullheaded!"

Miles muttered a curse under his breath. "Supposin' I say I'll let Linda marry into your family."

"Don't know as I want her," Bob Ash insisted stubbornly.

"As if that mattered," Linda said, looking up at Bill. "Does it, Bill?"

He shook his head. Before he kissed her, he caught the sly wink his father gave Tom Miles.

# Marked Man

## Eli Colter

◙

*Born in Portland, Oregon, Eli(za) Colter at the age of thirteen was afflicted for a time by blindness, an experience that taught her to "drill out" her own education for the remainder of her life. Although her first story was published under a nom de plume in 1918, she felt that her career as a professional really began when she sold her first story to* Black Mask Magazine *in 1922. Her style clearly indicates a penchant for what is termed the "hard-boiled school" in stories that display a gritty, tough, violent world. Sometimes there are episodes that become littered with bodies. Over the course of a career that spanned nearly four decades, Colter wrote more than three hundred stories and serials, mostly Western fiction. She appeared regularly in thirty-seven different magazines, including slick publications like* Liberty, *and was showcased on the covers of Fiction House's* Lariat Story Magazine *along with the likes of Walt Coburn. She published seven hardcover Western novels. Colter was particularly adept at crafting complex and intricate plots set against traditional Western storylines of her day—range wars, cattlemen versus homesteaders, and switched identities. Yet, no matter what the plot, she somehow always managed to include the unexpected and unconventional, like the cold-hearted murders of women in* Outcast of the Lazy S *(Alfred H. King, 1933) and* Cañon Rattlers *(Dodge, 1939). Colter's work has never been anthologized. "Marked Man" first appeared in* Western Story *(August 1948).*

Craine stood without moving, repressing an impulse to flinch a little inwardly, listening to the low whine of the bullet dying away. It had come close, too close for comfort. He repressed, too, an impulse to run headlong down the trail, up the steep rocks, anywhere to find retreat clear of pursuit. Was it always going to be like this, he wondered, running, hiding, afraid of every shadow, every sound? Was he to live out the rest of his life hunted—for a thing he had not done?

It seemed absurd that the notice in the post office would refer to him:

WANTED FOR MURDER
WARREN CRAINE
HEIGHT SIX FEET AND THREE INCHES,
WEIGHT ONE HUNDRED AND NINETY-FIVE POUNDS,
HAIR DARK, EYES BLUE.

The next line was nothing less than ludicrous. CITIZENS ARE WARNED: THIS MAN IS DANGEROUS. All Arizona should laugh at that.

"Still," Craine thought, "I might learn to be dangerous . . . if this keeps on much longer."

He turned and looked down at the town far below at the foot of the bluff, easily visible through the boughs of the drooping pine tree which hid him. A shot at random that had been. They couldn't have seen him. But still it had come too close. He was too near the town; he'd better be moving on. His whole body slumped a little at the thought of continued forced flight. If they'd only let him alone for a little while, give him a chance to rest. But a fugitive wanted for murder wasn't supposed to rest, not until they had him in a cell, and then only until they got the noose ready for him.

Craine laughed aloud with sardonic relish. If Haley could only see him now: good old Mac Haley, who had loved him like his own son, bluff, acid-tongued old Mac, who had tried to pound some sense into his reckless young head. Mac who had said: "You damn' young fool, Warren! You're goin' to wind up at the end of a hangman's rope if you don't settle down and stop actin' wild as a locoed colt." Mac wouldn't see anything humorous about all this, but he'd jump at the chance to say, "I told you so," if he were still alive to say anything. Craine laughed again.

From the brush somewhere behind him a voice said, "What's funny about it?"

It wasn't a voice Craine had ever heard before. He couldn't easily be deceived about that. Other men might never forget a face—Warren Craine never forgot a voice, not if he'd heard it say half a hundred words. He answered without turning: "Not a thing. Not a danged thing."

"Ain't you even interested enough to look and see whether or not I got you covered?" the man in the brush asked curiously.

"No," Craine answered wearily. "I take it for granted that you have."

He was wondering whether he could duck around the pine tree fast enough to escape a mortal wound. Possibly he could, but it was too risky. Any wound might prove mortal. Infection might get him if the slug didn't. And he had to stay alive. He had to stay alive, and free, until he cornered the man who had killed big Mac. He had to find out who the killer was first.

The man made a little noise, coming from the brush into the small clearing in back of Craine and beyond the drooping pine, a snapping of twigs, a swishing of branches. "You ain't got nothing to fear from me, if you're on the dodge," he said. "We belong to the same brotherhood. What did they want *you* for?"

Craine turned then and eyed the stranger sharply, a man of average height, with a wide, heavy build, his angular face half hidden by thick brown whiskers that matched his long hair. The man's eyes were clear brown, hard and wary. Right now they seemed slightly amused. "Who are you?" demanded Craine.

The bearded man smiled wryly. "If you expect to keep on dodgin' them that's after you, you want to learn to guard your rear a little better than that, Craine. I was down to the post office day before yesterday, saw your picture and description. They don't know me around here with all this hair on my face. I wanted to see if I was posted too. I wasn't. So, I asked a silly question, didn't I? I know what they want you for. Only, I wasn't sure till you turned around. I seen you once, down in Bluerock, half drunk and shootin' the lights out. I never forget a face. You didn't see me."

"No, I didn't. Who . . . ?"

"Names don't mean much," the bearded man interrupted smoothly. "Just call me Mac . . . that's part of it." He smiled again at Craine's visible start. "Yeah. The man you killed was named Mac, too, wasn't he? Big Mac Haley."

"I didn't kill him," Craine said. "He was all the father I ever had. Why would I shoot him?"

"What happened to your own father?"

"He died before I was born. My mother died the week after I was born. Big Mac brought me up. Anything else you'd like to know?"

Mac shook his head. "You got any idea who *did* shoot Haley?"

"No. If I had, do you think I'd be here?"

"Where's your horse?"

"Shot from under me by a posse that nearly got me too."

"Where's your gear?"

"Cached in the brush about ten miles from here."

"Hmm." Mac shrugged and gestured to the steep slope above and behind him. "Come along. I can give you some grub and another horse. You ought to have more sense than to be hangin' around this close to Bluerock, Craine."

"I'm not hanging around here. I doubled back this way to escape capture. I couldn't get far afoot. I was going to try to swipe a nag somewhere tonight. I think I'll stick to my original plans. Thanks all the same."

"You'll do what I tell you to!" Mac drew and leveled a long barreled black gun with phenomenal speed and ease. "I've got use for you. Been lookin' for you ever since I seen that notice in the post office. Try any funny business and I'll wing you, enough to tame you. You'd better go along under your own steam. Take the lead. Go straight uphill along that red outcrop. I'll tell you when and where to turn."

Craine obeyed. There wasn't much else he could do until he had an opportunity to down the bearded man and get away. The chance was bound to come sooner or later. He started up the steep hillside beside the outcrop, the bearded Mac close behind.

They continued up the hill almost to the summit where they came upon a rock formation common to the desert hills, great leaning boulders of weird, eroded shapes tilted and piled upon one another. Three of the stones, roughly the size of a cabin long enough to contain two rooms, reared upright in a nearly perfect triangle. A great massive slab, weather eaten and moss grown, lay across the tops of the three upright boulders, like a domed room. The entire rock cluster looked to be a solid formation from any angle, even if a man stood close enough to touch the towered walls. The opening was completely hidden behind a clump of brush and scrub pine.

"Go around that thicket, right up to the wall, and then turn left," Mac said. "You can see where I go in and out from there."

Craine walked up to the wall and turned. He saw a narrow passage between wall and brush—man made, since the brush had once grown tightly to the wall. Moving on along the passageway, he came upon the slit of an opening—less than three feet wide at the bottom, narrowing to a mere chink eight feet above—where the angling boulders came together.

"Go on in," Mac told him. "This is where I live."

Craine walked warily into the opening. It became a kind of low tunnel—dipping so that he had to bend his head at the end of it—some fifteen feet long. Then he stepped out into the cavernous room formed by the three upright boulders and the huge slab fashioning the roof. From five different openings at the top, where the slab failed to fit down tightly, light came in sufficiently to illumine every corner of the natural stone room.

The room was a good thirty-five feet in diameter between the points of the triangle. Directly under one of the overhead openings a stone oven had been built against the wall. Two skin rugs and an old square of carpet lay on the floor. Three homemade chairs stood around a rough plank table. Several boxes, made into cupboards, and a meal barrel with a ham and a slab of bacon lying on top of it were on either side of the stone oven. Three pole bunks were built along one wall, all of them covered by thick gray blankets. On the middle bunk a man lay.

Craine stared then walked slowly toward the bunk, fascinated. The man lay quite still, on his back, staring at the stone ceiling. Only his eyes moved to look up at Craine as he stopped beside the bunk. The man made no attempt to speak. He was a young man, in his late twenties, about Craine's own age. He was covered by one of the gray blankets, but it was easy to see that he would be about six feet and two or three inches tall. He must weigh in the neighborhood of a hundred and ninety pounds. His thick, curling hair was dark brown, almost black. His eyes were a light clear blue. His features . . . ? Craine shook his head incredulously. The man on the bed looked enough like him to be his twin.

Behind him he heard Mac saying: "That's my son, Danny. He was paralyzed . . . by a bullet that was meant for me. I reckon maybe you can guess what I brought you here for, now. Big Mac Haley shot him."

"No," Craine said. "I don't see why you brought me."

"Well, you look like him, don't you?" The bearded man's eyes were on his son's expressionless face. "You two're as like as peas in a pod. You can see that, can't you?"

"Yes. So what?" Suspicion had begun to grow in Craine's gaze, and bearded Mac read it aright.

"And I didn't kill Haley because he shot Danny, so you can forget that right now," Mac said. "I didn't kill him, but I'm glad he's dead. If ever a man deserved killin', Mac Haley did. We won't go into that now . . . you wouldn't believe it. Haley shot Danny in the side, and the bullet came out at the back, done something to the boy's spine, left him like this. Soon as he was well enough to move, I brought him up here."

"How long ago did this happen?" Craine asked curiously.

"Nigh onto a year ago. I been prayin' Dan'd get better, but I dunno." Mac bent over the bunk. "You want anything, son?"

Danny said a little thickly: "No. Nothing, Dad." His gaze went back to Craine. "So . . . this is him."

"This is him, Danny."

The gentleness in the older man's voice struck sharply into Craine's divided attention. He was seeing pictures in his mind, the long, toiling journey the older man must have made, slowly lugging the helpless Danny to a horse, bringing him up the steep mountain to this rock nest on the summit. He was seeing the days afterward, Mac's tending the stricken boy, bringing him food, keeping him company. He began to feel a growing sympathy for the bearded man.

"Has a doctor seen him?"

Mac nodded. "Yeah. After it first happened. He said there wasn't much any man could do, said Danny might just get better as time went on. He *is* gettin' better, too. He can talk better, and he can move his hands a little now. Show him, Danny."

Danny raised both hands from the blanket, until the arms were almost upright from the elbow, then dropped them limply again, smiling up at Craine, an odd eagerness in his gaze. "I can even feed myself now," he said, "if I do it slow. I'm a lot better."

"That's good," Craine told him, "you keep right on getting better." He said to Mac: "What do you want of me?"

"I want you to do some fighting, Warren Craine," Mac answered. "Not with guns, maybe . . . though that might come into it, too, before you're done with it. I want you to do some fighting to get back what's your own."

Craine frowned, puzzled. "My own? I don't have anything that's my own, since my horse was killed. What do you mean . . . my own?"

"I mean the Diamond M Ranch and everything that's on it, lock, stock, and barrel," Mac said grimly. "That's what I mean. It's yours by rights."

Craine blinked in astonishment. "Because Haley took me in and raised me, you mean? But that doesn't give me any right to the ranch and other property he left! I wasn't any relation to him. I know he was a hard, rough man in a lot of ways, but he was always good to me. I appreciated it . . . but he didn't owe me anything. The shoe was on the other foot. I owed him everything I ever had."

Mac sat down on the bunk by Danny's feet. "That ain't what I mean, and it ain't so. What did he do for you? Fed you, clothed you, and give you a little spending money. But you always worked as hard as any hand on the ranch. You paid for everything you ever got from Haley, personal. As long as he was livin', there wasn't no man could do much about it. You believed what you was brought up to believe, and there wouldn't be much hope of clearin' the whole thing up without your help. You ain't sittin' pretty as the foster son of old Mac Haley now. You're a marked man, wanted for the killing of Mac Haley, and not daring to show your face until you can prove you didn't do it. You're in a spot to listen to me now. *That's* why I brought you here."

Craine stood silently for a moment, studying the old man's face. Then he pulled over one of the homemade chairs and sat on it, facing the bearded Mac. "Just what are you talking about?" he demanded.

"Things you wouldn't've heard, son . . . because it was old stuff as you was growin' up. The inside story wasn't knowed by many men, and they figured it was a sight better to mind their own business. Old Mac Haley came to this part of Arizona before you was born. The country was wild, and there was lootin' and robbin' on every hand, so much of it that many a man made his stake any old way he took a fancy to, and such tricks was too common to cause much commotion. Usually the man grew respectable as the years went on, and people forgot how he made his pile. Maybe you know that . . . I reckon you've heard it."

Craine nodded. "Of course, but it didn't concern me, and I never paid much attention to it."

"That's where you're wrong . . . it *did* concern you. Haley came here with a partner. The partner had money, plenty of it. Haley didn't. The partner bought a ranch, a damn' good ranch, and stocked it. He had money left, still plenty. That was why Haley froze onto him, though his partner didn't realize that till later. He trusted Haley, only so far . . . but too far, at that. You following all this close?"

"I'm following you," Craine said curtly.

"But you ain't believing me, eh? You will! The partner moved onto the ranch before he bought it because his wife thought they'd better see if they liked it first. They rented it for three months before they decided to buy it. The partner had given Haley a job as foreman and kind of turned errands over to Haley. He sent Haley into town to pay the rent. He sent Haley in to bring supplies. Haley kind of got to be regular errand boy, because he played for it and offered to do things. And the partner's wife was poorly so he was glad to stay close to the ranch and look after her. You beginnin' to see daylight, son?"

Craine frowned. "No."

Mac's voice turned sharp. "You are, too. You just don't want to admit it."

"Go on, what happened?"

"The partner kept all his money in a little iron safe, about as big as that rock over there," Mac went on. "He couldn't be bothered with banks and such. It was a perfect setup for a dog like Mac Haley. When the partner decided to buy the ranch, he sent Haley in with the money to do the business end of it. The wife was down sick, her time was on her, and he wouldn't leave her. He knew she was bad sick. She was. She died leavin' her baby behind. Didn't I tell you it was a setup for Haley? Can you guess what he done?"

Craine stared into the older man's eyes, his face a shade lighter in color. "You tell me."

"I'll tell you first what he *had* done. He had paid all that rent in his own name, representin' himself to be a moneyed man. He had bought that ranch in his own name and had the deed made out in his own name. The partner was too stunned over his wife's death to think of business right then. After the wife was buried, Haley and his partner drove off from the ranch one night in the buckboard. Haley came back in the mornin' and give out that the partner had given up ranching and gone away, too broke up over his wife to want to stay. He said the partner had asked him to bring up the baby boy. Can you guess what really had happened, son?"

Craine said again, grimly: "You tell me."

"He shot the partner and left him in the woods for the coyotes. What was one picked skeleton more or less in them days? Nobody questioned Haley's story. The ranch was his. The money in the safe was his. He was set for life. That ranch was the Diamond M. The partner's name was Jacob Craine. The baby boy's name was Warren Craine. You're victim of a big wrong that's got to be set right, son."

"And where do you come in?" Craine demanded skeptically. "If all this is true, how do you know so much about it?"

"I was workin' right there on the Diamond M, son. I was the cook. I slept in a room off the kitchen. I heard things. There was only four rooms in the house then. Haley built it up since, with your dad's money. From the room where I slept anything said in the kitchen or the other two rooms could be heard clear."

"You *heard* Haley say he had done all this, about the ranch, the deed in his own name, and so on?"

"I sure did. He was right cocky about it, feelin' his oats. He was proud of how slick he had been. He'd even been feeding the ranch hands a cock-and-bull yarn about how it was him had all the money and his partner just wanted to make a good impression on the wife, so he allowed it and didn't mind. He boasted of that, too."

"I'm beginning to believe you may be telling the truth," Craine said slowly. "It sounded awfully wild at first. It doesn't seem so wild now. When I was a kid and some of the old hands were still around, I heard them tell how my father and mother were pretty down on their luck . . . how Haley had money and bought the ranch and kept my folks till my mother died. But I was told that my father died before I was born, *not* that he went away."

"More of Haley's lies," the bearded Mac said harshly. "He give it out that was what he was goin' to tell you as you grew up . . . said he was afraid if you knew that your dad just went away you might feel he'd deserted you and it might make you bitter. Everybody agreed with him, thought it was right sympathetic and kind of Haley."

"But why did he keep me then?" demanded Craine. "Why didn't he get rid of me, too?"

"He had a use for you, son! Folks knew a baby'd been born in that house . . . the ranch hands knew it. If Haley made any attempt to get rid of you, it'd turn 'em against him. It turned 'em against the father, to think he could go off and leave his baby like that. Nothin' much could have made Haley solider with everybody than to keep you and bring you up, talkin' about how sad it was you bein' abandoned that way, and how it was all he could do for his partner's sake, and how he couldn't blame his partner none, seein' how broke up he was, and the baby would be a sad reminder. Oh, Haley was slick as greased lightning, son. Anyone that tried to bring him to cases wouldn't have a leg to stand on. Craine had been a quiet feller, never talkin' much about his business. Haley had talked plenty, planting his own story, havin' the whole thing all plotted from the beginning. And that's the heritage old Haley left you, son. It's a mighty crooked mess, and you're the one to straighten it out and claim your own."

Craine sat silent for a long time thinking. Then he said slowly: "How did he get his partner to go away with him after he'd spilled all this about what he'd done with the money?"

"Easy enough, son. Haley was a lot bigger than Craine. Craine was shocked, sick at heart, dazed. Haley just knocked him out, tied him up, and carried him out to the buckboard, makin' sure nobody saw him. He drove off with him, came back without him, and spread his yarn. Four or five skeletons was found in the brush and rocks that year, buried where they lay. Who was to say one of 'em was Jacob Craine or wasn't? I've heard of some slick schemes, son, but I reckon Haley pulled about as smooth a one as I ever knew of. He didn't figure any man could ever bust his bubble. How could they, when nobody even knew about it but him . . . and *me*?"

"And he found out that you knew!" Craine said. "Or guessed it, you being right there in the house. Why didn't he kill you, too."

"He tried to, son. But he wasn't the best shot in the world. I got away from him, and left him to do his own cooking. I went clear out of the country. But I never forgot you, boy . . . I never forgot how all your father'd left you had been taken away from you. I figured on comin' back and helping you to square things some way. And I had my own boy to look after. Danny didn't have nobody to look after him but me. I come back here a few years ago, figurin' Haley wouldn't know me if he saw me."

"The beard?"

"Partly. Other things too. I'd been slim in them days when I was on the Diamond M. Putting on weight makes a lot of difference. And my hair had been red. As I grew older, it turned sort of sandy brown, the way you see it now. I *don't* look like the same man. I tried to figure some way of proving how Haley'd cheated you, but I couldn't. There *wasn't* no proof. Only my word against his. I took to hangin' around, trying to get a chance to talk to you. Haley run into me, and he did recognize me. He guessed what I was up to and took a shot at me. The slug hit Danny. Since then I just been layin' low, waiting a chance, believing it had to come, that the right had to win out. My chance came when Haley got killed, and you had to run. Now I'm askin' you . . . just what do you know about Haley being shot?"

Craine drew a long breath and sat, staring down at Danny's quiet face. "Not much. Haley and I were riding range, and somebody shot him from the brush. I shot back, but I didn't hit anything. Haley fell off his horse, but he wasn't dead. I took him in. I told the boys what had happened. They believed me. Everybody believed me. They'd have gone right on believing me, if Haley hadn't come to just before he died and said it was me who shot him. He died raving about what ingratitude he'd got for taking in an orphan and raising him. I didn't blame him too much. He was shot in the back. I was riding behind him. Maybe he did think I shot him. Maybe he was *meant* to think I shot him."

"I wouldn't doubt it none. Well, son, where you goin' to start?"

Craine gazed steadily into the older man's intent brown eyes. "I don't know whether I believe all this or not, yet. I have to think it over. It's so plausible. It could have happened so easily. Wilder things than that happened in this country before I was born. But, if it *is* true, if that ranch really belongs to me, again I'm asking, where do you come in? You made a point of calling my attention to how much your son and I look alike. You're horning in on this for more than the mere desire to see justice done to your one-time boss' son. Danny's resemblance to me has something to do with it. Spit it out."

"I don't mind," Mac said quietly. "I'm gettin' old. Danny may never be much better than he is now. When you come into your own, I'm asking that you take Danny and me with you. I'm asking that you let us live in the house with you, and you and Danny share alike. You can give out that he's a relative of yours ... a brother, if you like. You could easy be took for brothers. And I won't make a nuisance of myself. I can earn my way. I'm still a good cook."

Danny said, the eager look in his blue eyes again: "Would you? Dad and I ... we never had much of a home. I might get well enough to do things to help. I'd try not to be too much trouble."

Craine got abruptly to his feet, feeling confused and shaken, not knowing what to believe. Was all this story a sly and clever yarn on the old man's part, an attempt to work out a soft spot for himself and Danny, all built on Danny's striking resemblance to him? The resemblance *was* striking, Craine realized that, but it wasn't such an unusual thing. He'd seen other instances of it. He'd seen two men in a saloon once, one looking so much like the other that he had jestingly told the older man he could never deny his son. And they hadn't been kin.

They had been total strangers. In fact they had never seen each other before. He stood looking steadily at the bearded Mac. If a thing like this was true, there must be some proof of it somewhere. Surely no truth ever existed without its just proof, but Craine didn't say that.

"I told you I have to think it over," he said. "I have to see if I can't find something to bear out what you say. But if it *is* true, if it all happened exactly as you've told me, nobody could deserve more to be taken in and made a home for, as Haley took me in." He turned his gaze on Danny. "You wouldn't have to worry about being any trouble, Danny. I've always missed having folks of my own. You and your dad could kind of take the place of the folks I never had. *If* I work this out, *if* what your father says is true, the Diamond M will be your home from then on."

"Son, there *was* proof once," Mac told him. "I don't reckon it still exists."

Craine said quickly, "That old iron safe's still there, if that's what you have in mind."

"No!" exclaimed Mac. "A safe box that locks with a big iron key that's got the words 'Meecham Safe Company' on the front of it, and a picture of two deer, one lyin' down and one standing up."

Craine stared at him. "That's it." But he warned himself: *That doesn't mean anything. He could have been to the ranch house and seen the old safe. He could even have been the cook there, as he claims, and all the rest of it could be a smoothly trumped-up lie.* "It's in the old part of the house, off the kitchen, in a kind of little niche in the wall. Haley used the room for a kind of office."

"Then there may be proof. I mean, it still may be there. That room used to be my bedroom. I had a bureau in that niche. I know that safe. I was trusted, son . . . I been sent to take things out or put 'em in more than once. In the bottom of it is a little false drawer. You'd never know it was there. You just press on the back of the bottom, hard, and the drawer lifts up. There's just a chance Haley never knew it was there, never found it."

"What's in it?" Craine demanded sharply.

"There was once in it some papers that could prove your rights, son. Your dad had a habit of scribblin' little notes down so he wouldn't forget dates and would be reminded of little things he wanted to keep a record of. He kept his papers in that drawer. Your parents' weddin' certificate is there. Your birth record's there. I know . . . I put it there myself, at your mother's request. I mean, them things is still there, if Haley never found 'em. That's all you got to do to prove whether I'm lyin' or not. Look in that drawer."

"And if nothing is there, you can still say it's only because Haley found the papers and destroyed them," Craine said evenly.

"That's right, son. I don't blame you none for doubtin'. It must sound like a right wild story to you. But it's God's truth, and may you find it out."

"Well, first I have to find out who killed Mac and clear myself . . . if it can be done," Craine pointed out. "You made some crack about being on the dodge when you first spoke to me down there above the bluff. What did you mean by that?"

The bearded Mac smiled wryly. "I lifted a couple of Haley's horses, son. Could be he had me posted for it, if he happened to find out it was me took 'em. I ain't taking any chances on it or on getting my neck stretched for stealing a couple of knotheads."

"Oh," Craine said thoughtfully. "You said you've a horse I could use. One of them?"

"That's right, son. You'll find 'em tethered in a little brush-fenced pasture back of this rock nest. Gear in the lean-to. Help yourself. But take care of yourself, son. Anything I can do, let me know."

"I'll let you know," agreed Craine.

"You'd better eat before you go, boy."

"I'll eat at the Diamond M."

A slow smile lifted the mouth under Mac's thick, sandy-brown whiskers. "I figured you'd head there. 'Luck, son. And watch your step."

Craine went out of the big rock room, through the long narrow passage and along the wall behind the thicket, thinking hard. He moved on around the outside of the huge upright stones, found the brush-fenced pasture and the three horses in it. Two of the horses were branded with the Diamond M, common stock horses that had been loose on the range. He saddled one of them and rode away down the steep trail that descended tortuously through the brush and trees, still thinking.

Away from the bearded man and the helpless Danny, Craine could begin to sift things a little more clearly now. *Was Danny so helpless*, he wondered, *or was that supposed paralysis part of the scheme? Did the old man and this Danny expect him to make some kind of wild play to gain possession of the Diamond M?* He had to think that over. It was a story that would stand. It was a story no one could prove untrue.

"Slick," he muttered. "Mighty slick. And if I *could* prove myself innocent of Mac's murder, and if I could make that story stick and take over the ranch, and if I did take old whisker face and Danny in, would Danny suddenly have a miraculous recovery from his paralysis? Hmm. And what am I bet, if I succeed in sneaking into the house without being caught, open the safe, and the drawer is there . . . what am I bet that I find the drawer *empty?* Maybe he's just a little too damned slick, him and his Danny. There isn't a loophole through which I can pin him down anywhere."

But he knew he would go on. He would slip into the house and investigate the old iron safe. It was as familiar as his own room. It had been there as long as he could remember. He'd opened it, taken things out and put them in, a thousand times. But he'd never seen any sigh of the hidden drawer, and Haley had never spoken of it. The next involuntary thought gave him a jolt. If all that should come to pass, someday maybe there'd be a shot in *his* back, out on the range, and he'd be buried deep. Then old whisker face and the man who looked so much like Craine could spin another slick story. They could say that the helpless Danny had been sent away to some big doctor in the East for an operation that might make him well. Only Danny would never come back. He would die from the operation. And the supposed Warren Craine who remained there as owner of the ranch with old Whiskers for his cook would in reality be Danny, and the real Warren Craine would lie rotting under six feet of dirt.

Craine cursed aloud. "Got it! And, by Jupiter, it *is* slick! So slick it almost worked. They almost sold me. I won't waste time looking around in any empty drawer. The drawer's probably there, all right. And Mac likely was the cook. That's where he got the idea in the first place. That Danny's no more his son than I am . . . he's no more paralyzed than I am. Whiskers picked him up somewhere because he looked so much like me, and the two of them got their heads together and cooked up the whole smart plot. Well! The first thing I do is ride straight for the sheriff."

No more running now! Nothing to be afraid of any more. Once he could bring forth the man who'd shot big Mac Haley, the sheriff and everybody else could easily believe that what he had said was true. Haley honestly thought Craine had been riding in the rear. The shot that got Haley had sailed almost over Craine's left shoulder. What else could Haley think?

"Jiminy?" Craine muttered in mounting excitement. "It grows slicker and slicker. Whiskers did it. Of course he did it! He figured I'd shoot back, as I did. He figured I'd run to see how bad Haley was hurt and give him a chance to get away . . . which I did. He figured Haley would accuse me of the shooting, and if Mac Haley died, I'd be on the dodge and give him a chance to pick me up and pull all this show with his 'paralyzed son.' And I almost fell for it. Phew! Get along, horse! We've got business with the sheriff."

His mind turned to other things, now relieved of a little strain, eased of the fear and worry attendant on his own flight and the reason for it. Sheriff Blaylock would find ways of making old Whiskers talk. He wasn't taking the law into his hands, Craine told himself, and making things all the worse for his own case. Whiskers and Danny wouldn't run away. They'd be lying holed in right there in the rock nest, waiting for Craine to take over the Diamond M.

Maybe, after Whiskers and Danny had been brought in, and Craine himself proved in the clear, there might still be a place for him there on the Diamond M that had always been home to him. Almost certainly there would be. The ranch would go to Haley's cousin, now . . . Lester Haley, big Mac's only living kin. Craine remembered with a smile the day, four months ago, when Lester had come to the ranch, a big bluff and hearty man much like big Mac. Mac had been overjoyed to see him and had spent hours reliving boyhood days with Lester, telling Craine of the pranks he and his cousin had played, the two of them roaring with laughter at the recollections. Craine sighed. Maybe big Mac hadn't been any saint, maybe Lester wasn't, but Craine and Mac had got along, and he and Lester Haley would get along, once Lester was convinced that Craine hadn't killed big Mac. Craine realized suddenly that he was dog tired. He couldn't get to Sheriff Blaylock and have it all over any too soon to suit him. He prodded the horse to a faster pace.

Craine rounded the next turn in the trail and came face to face with Lester Haley. Haley was sitting his horse directly in the middle of the trail, gun drawn, waiting. Craine hadn't a chance in the world. He drew his own mount to a halt.

Haley's face was hard set, his eyes cold and dangerous. "I *thought* it was you I shot at up there on the bluff, Warren," he said. "So I hung around, waiting for you. Stick your hands up and keep 'em there."

Craine obeyed. He had no more choice than he'd had with old Whiskers, he thought bitterly. "What are you intending to do with me, Lester?"

Haley laughed. "What would I do with the man who killed my cousin? Take you down and turn you over to the sheriff? Huh uh! Too bad you *would* try to get away, and I had to gun you down. But I want witnesses. We'll go on down to the ranch, where some of the boys can look on and back me up."

Craine thought: *a silly argument. The boys would back him up, anyway. He's got some other reason for letting me live that long.* He made no answer, asked no useless questions. What Haley had in mind would show soon enough.

Haley backed his horse off the trail, the gun still leveled. "Now ride ahead of me and keep your hands up. First funny move out of you and you get it right where Mac did . . . which would be kind of fitting, at that."

Craine rode ahead, his hands held level with his shoulders. He kept that position all the way to the Diamond M, and five of the cowboys came out into the lane to watch stony-eyed as the two riders came to a halt in the side yard. Haley ordered Craine to stay put while one of the men disarmed him. Slim Peele vaulted the lane fence, walked up, and took Craine's gun, thrusting it under his waistband.

Haley ordered Craine to get down, and Slim Peele stepped back. Slim looked straight into Craine's eyes, as if he had never seen him before. Craine slid off the horse.

"Get in the house, fast," Haley ordered. "We've got a little pow-wow on. Then...." He glanced at Peele and at the other four cow-hands in the lane. "Then this sniveling ingrate is going to try to get away. I'll have to mow him down. *Then* the sheriff can have him, after it's too late for him to bust out of a cell and take to the woods again. Move along, Warren."

Craine turned toward the house, remembering with bitterness that Slim Peele had once been his close comrade. Neither ever went to town without the other. They rode range together, roped and branded together. Now, by Slim's own decree, they were strangers. Craine went ahead of Lester into the house, and Lester, gun still drawn, commanded curtly that he head into the office and sit down. As they went into the little office room where the old safe sat, Craine heard a horse go racing down the lane and along the road.

"I could have downed you on the trail," Lester said. "The boys would have taken my word. I preferred to get you here before I told you what I want of you. Mac had some cash and a couple of pretty important papers. I can't find 'em, and I figure you'd know where they are. He always had plenty of cash on hand. It'd be wherever he kept them papers. They ain't in the safe. I've looked. Where are they? And don't start stalling. You'd know."

Craine thought fast—probably in that hidden drawer which big Mac Haley must have discovered long ago. He shook his head. "I wouldn't know offhand, Lester," he answered. "I never poked my nose into Mac's private business." Time, he thought. He must play for time and for a chance to get the jump on Lester. "There are any number of places around the house where Mac could have kept the cash. I didn't know about the papers. I'd have to look."

"Well, get busy and look, then," ordered Lester. "And keep right on lookin' till you find 'em."

Craine got to his feet, acutely aware of the gun pointed at him, following his every move. He started looking. He dug into every kind of recess he could think of in the office—excepting the safe. Then they went into Mac Haley's bedroom, and the search continued. Craine knew well enough that Mac had always kept two or three thousand dollars around the house, and he knew just where the money would be. It was so exactly the kind of place where a man would hide money, it was odd that Lester hadn't thought of it. Big Mac had an old bureau in his room here, a heavy old thing that had once been topped by a large rectangular mirror. The mirror had been broken. When the mirror frame was removed, there was an opening down the back of the bureau where the long ends of the frame support had thrust down. Big Mac had trimmed a long flat piece of the frame to fit and had laid it in place across the top of the hole. He had never even screwed it there. In that hole he had kept his household cash, but he hadn't kept any papers there. Craine had taken money out of that hole at Mac's request too many times to be mistaken about that. No papers were ever there. Nothing ever was there but the money. He wondered what important papers Lester meant. He did not go near the old bureau in his search.

Lester was growing impatient now. All this poking about, looking into and under things, had taken well over an hour. A few minutes ago Craine had heard horses outside. He hadn't paid any attention to them. There were usually horses moving about outside. They were starting out of big Mac's room, Lester scowling and angry enough that for an instant his thought lagged, his attention was astray, before Craine saw his chance. They moved to leave the bedroom and search elsewhere, Craine in the lead. Craine did a little lagging himself— not too much—to bring Lester's thoughts sharply back to attention— just enough to bring himself closer to that drawn gun than Les Haley had ever intended. Then Craine's left hand shot out behind him, gripping the gun barrel and shoving it down. In the same breath he whirled, bringing one up from the floor with his right fist. The blow landed squarely on Lester's jaw, the whole action so swift that Lester had no opportunity to fend it. As Haley went down, Craine jerked the gun out of his hand. The revolver roared, and the bullet went whining past Craine's thigh.

Craine stepped back, pointing the gun down at Haley, recocking the gun with his thumb. Haley was dazed but not unconscious. He glared up at Craine, beginning to curse in fury. Before Craine could make any other move, he heard feet running across the yard toward the house. He backed to the wall, the gun still covering Haley.

The front door burst open, steps rushed down the hall, and the cowboys from the lane crowded into the room. In the lead were Slim Peele and Sheriff Blaylock. At sight of the leveled gun, they all stopped.

Slim drew a sigh of relief. "I was afraid it was the other way around. Put up the gun, Warren. I went after the sheriff." He said to Blaylock, "Take him in, Sheriff. I don't figure there's a thing to be said in his defense. But . . . if there is, I want him to have a chance to say it. That's why I came for you."

"I won't put up the gun," Craine said curtly. "I had started after the sheriff myself. I wasn't thinking very straight, but I realize now that if I let you take me in, no matter what I tell, you won't believe it. What I *could* tell sounds too wild. I'll just have to prove it. I know who shot big Mac. The killer shot from behind me. He intended Mac to think I was the one who fired. I think now that he was an expert marksman and knew just what he was doing. He intended Mac to live long enough to accuse me."

"And who are *you* accusing, Warren?" asked Blaylock.

"You wouldn't know him," Craine answered. "If I told you why he shot Mac . . . well, like I told you, it's so wild you wouldn't believe it. But, if you'll go with me, and not give him any hint that we know he's guilty, just let him talk and listen to the story he spins, I can make you see his motive fast enough."

"Where is this supposed killer holed up?" Blaylock asked curiously.

"In a rock nest on top of Cougar Hill."

Blaylock laughed. "And you think I'm going on any wild goose chase like that with you, Warren, and give you a chance to give me the slip or maybe put a bullet in *my* back?"

Craine whitened. "You're going. All of you. The man's there. Two of them are there. The older one killed Mac. You'll have to see for yourselves just what the setup is. Then you'll believe. You take me to jail now, and they'll get wind of it and light out. You're all going up

Cougar Hill with me. Hang it, how much chance would I have to pull anything and get away from six of you?"

"About as much chance as a celluloid dog in hell," Slim Peele answered tersely. He said to Blaylock: "I said I wanted him to have his chance, Sheriff. I'm still saying it."

Blaylock pursed his lips, frowning. "All right. Hand over the gun peaceably, Warren, and we'll go with you. But you'll ride in the middle and Slim will lead your horse."

"Suits me." Craine lowered the gun, let down the hammer, and handed it to Blaylock, butt first.

All this time Lester Haley had remained on the floor, sitting up now, listening intently to every word. He spoke for the first time since the sheriff had entered the room. "Maybe I was a little hasty. I agree with Slim, of course. If there's anything to be said for Warren . . . if there's really some other man who did kill my cousin, I'm for learning the truth right now. Let's get moving."

Craine looked at Blaylock. "Sheriff, may I see you for a few minutes alone? Will you come to the office with me?"

Blaylock nodded. "I don't see why not. Lead the way."

Craine led the way into the office, Blaylock at his heels. The others moved into the hall and waited there by the front door. Craine got the big iron key out of the desk drawer and opened the safe, while the sheriff stood watching. Nothing of any importance was in the safe. Craine pulled boxes and papers out and laid them on the desk. Then he got down on one knee and reached into the safe, feeling along the bottom of it. At the back he pressed down. Nothing happened. He pressed harder. The hidden drawer lifted and came forward about half way. Craine pulled it the rest of the way. The sheriff was close now, gun in hand, looking over Craine's shoulder. In the drawer were no more than eight or nine folded papers, tied together with a string. Nothing else was there. The top paper was instantly identifiable as a receipt, signed by Mac Haley.

Craine thought grimly: *I might have known. Those valuable papers of Mac's that Lester wanted. We'll go into that later. But Mac knew about the drawer all the time, of course. Probably it was his own safe in the first place.*

Craine took out the small packet of papers and shoved it into his pocket. He pushed the drawer back, and it dropped into place. "That's all, Sheriff," he said, getting to his feet. "I just wanted to get these. I'm ready to go now."

"Hmm," Blaylock growled. "What's so important about some of Mac's old receipts?"

Craine shook his head. "I don't know yet. They're what Lester was trying to make me find, as well as Mac's house cash. We'll look at 'em later. They might help cinch the killer, though I doubt it. Shall we go?"

They rode up the hill in a long file, two of the cowboys in the lead, Craine next, with Peele leading his horse. The sheriff came behind Craine, with Lester Haley and the other three cowboys behind them. They kept that formation all the way to the brush-fenced pasture behind the rock nest. They left the horses there, and Craine led the way into the big rock room, Blaylock close behind him with gun drawn.

The bearded Mac got quickly to his feet, beside Danny's bunk, his eyes lighting with surprise then widening in amazement as the other men followed Craine. Mac's gaze fixed on the drawn gun in the sheriff's hand, went to the sheriff's badge, then came back to Craine. "Was there anything in the drawer, Warren?" he asked quietly.

"Some old receipts of Mac's, is all," answered Craine.

Bearded Mac's gaze went beyond Craine and Blaylock to Lester Haley and to the cowboys back of Haley, near the entrance to the room. "There's your killer, Sheriff," Mac said harshly. "Not this boy! That's the man who killed Haley. I didn't know he was in Arizona! He's the one who would have wanted Haley dead."

Blaylock didn't turn, didn't take his gaze from the bearded face. He said mildly: "Yeah? Who are you talking about?"

"Lester Haley, of course! He's always been a killer. He killed before, long ago. He and Mac Haley were a pair of killers. Big Mac had his signed confession to a killing that Mac was supposed to have done. Mac held it over him. Lester would have been after Mac long before this, but he's been in prison. When he got out, it must have taken him a little while to trace Mac. Mac was the only one who knew he was a killer, who could hold that confession over him. Why wouldn't he shoot Mac and frame the boy, so he'd get the ranch and be sitting pretty?"

Blaylock did turn, then, to stare at Lester Haley. Haley was gaping at the bearded man with bulging eyes. His face was bleached to the color of dirty paper. He gasped three words: "Jumpin' Jehoshaphat! You!"

The bearded man smiled thinly. "It's me, all right. You'd better take your man, Sheriff."

"There's something queer here," Blaylock said curtly. "Did you kill your cousin, Haley?"

Too shaken to muster any defense, Haley slumped like a man about to fall. "Yeah, yeah, I killed him. All he said was . . . is true. You can prove it fast enough. That paper is with those receipts. I was tryin' to make Warren dig it up. Mac swore he didn't have it, hadn't had it for years, but I knew better. I couldn't find it. But Warren did. I can see it in those papers he found somewhere. Besides, this man here knows me, and I know him!"

"Hang on to him," Blaylock said to Peele. "Better tie him up." He turned to Craine. "Take a look at those receipts, Warren. The confession's got to be with 'em."

The bearded Mac said in sudden excitement: "This killer says it is! If those receipts are old enough, the confession was in that drawer. I put it there. Haley asked me to keep it for him. Hang it, son, can't you be a little faster?" He crowded close as Craine took the papers out of his pocket and slid off the string.

Craine's eyes widened, "Why, hell! This receipt is for rent money entrusted to Mac Haley's care. It was signed by him twenty-nine years ago."

The bearded Mac put out a hand that was shaking. "Then Haley never did find the drawer! I put that receipt there, too. Look at the next paper, quick."

It was a bald confession to a murder that had been committed by Lester Haley, intended to frame Mac. It was signed by Lester Haley. Craine unfolded the next paper. He was conscious of men crowding at his elbows now, Slim Peele close, and all of the others except the one holding a gun on the bound Lester Haley. The next paper was another receipt, signed by Haley, for money entrusted to his care with which to purchase the Diamond M Ranch as proxy for Jacob Craine.

Sheriff Blaylock said sharply, "Here! Wait a minute! Then Haley pulled a fast one. Warren, that ranch really belongs to you!"

Craine didn't answer. He was unfolding the next paper, a wedding certificate made out for Jacob Craine and Sarah Weston. The old man was gripping his arm now, the excitement of them all so tense that no one paid any attention to Danny. Danny was sitting up in his bunk, crouched a little forward, watching them all with burning eyes.

Craine unfolded the last paper. It was thick parchment, decorated with little scrolls and cupids, forget-me-nots, and pink roses. At the top in Old English type were the words: OUR BABY'S RECORD. Craine's gaze went down the double sheet, and he stood rigid, unbelieving. The words blurred and danced before his eyes, but he read them accurately.

*Born this day to Sarah Weston Craine and Jacob MacLeod Craine, twin sons, named Daniel Marvin Craine and David Warren Craine.*

Sheriff Blaylock said, "What in thunder?"

Craine raised his eyes to old Mac's bearded face. "*MacLeod.* Jacob *MacLeod* Craine. Mac! You . . . you're . . . ?"

Jake Craine said softly: "That's right, son. Big Mac didn't kill me. He thought he had. He left me there for dead, and little Danny. He didn't do a thing to Danny, just left him lying there by me. What chance would a week-old baby have? But Danny's cryin' brought me out of it. I had to fight for life, for the two of us. And I wasn't lyin', son. I *was* the cook. I was a mighty good cook. Sarah was doing so poorly."

"*You* are Jacob MacLeod Craine, this boy's father?" Blaylock said incredulously. "And that man is his twin?"

Jacob Craine drew himself erect. "That's right, sir." His gaze went to Danny. His voice rose almost to a shout. "Danny! Danny! You're sittin' up!"

Danny blinked and looked dazed. "Why, I didn't even notice it, I was so excited. All these years you've been promising we'd get our own back . . . we'd find my brother, David. I was just so damned excited I forgot what I was doing."

Blaylock wheeled. He said roughly. "You cowhands! Get out of here. That goes for me, too, and my prisoner. We'll all get out of here. We've got a job to do, all of us . . . spreading it fast all over the country that Warren Craine isn't a marked man any longer."

They all crowded toward the outlet from the stone room, Blaylock herding them.

"Slim," Warren called. "Come back here."

Slim shook his head, smiling. "Time for all that later, pal."

Jacob Craine laid his arm across Warren's shoulders. "Reckon you could get used to being called Davy, son? That's what me and Danny been calling you all these years."

"Used to it!" Craine echoed. "I can get used to anything! Great Scott, Dad! Let's rustle around here and get Danny down the mountain."

Danny grinned and swung his feet to the floor. It was a little difficult for him, but he got them there.

"Uh uh! Danny will get himself down the mountain. Dad! For gosh sake! Think of it. We . . . we're all going home!"

# Night Guns Calling

*Steve Frazee*

Ó

*Born in Salida, Colorado, (Charles) Steve Frazee began in the late 1940s to make major contributions to the Western pulp magazines with stories set in the American West as well as a number of North-Western tales published in* Adventure. *Few can match his Western novels, which are notable for their evocative, lyrical descriptions of the open range and the awesome power of natural forces and their effects on human efforts.* Cry Coyote *(Macmillan, 1955) is memorable for its strong female protagonists, who actually influence most of the major events. In* High Cage *(Macmillan, 1957), which concerns five miners and a woman snowbound at an isolated gold mine on top of Bulmer Peak, the twin themes of the lust for gold and the struggle against the savagery of both the elements and human nature interplay with increasing intensity.* Bragg's Fancy Woman *(1966) is about a free-spirited woman who is able to tame a family of thieves.* Rendezvous *(1958) ranks as one of the finest mountain-man novels, and* The Way Through the Mountains *(Popular Library, 1972) is a major historical novel recently reprinted in a mass merchandise edition by Leisure Books. A Frazee story is possessed of flawless characterization, the clash of human passions, credible dialogue, and often almost painful suspense. The story that follows first appeared in* Fifteen Western Tales *(September 1948) and is now collected for the first time.*

**B**raley Hodding sat in his rawhide chair on the porch and damned the excitement. He wanted to slip away into that semi-dozing condition in which images and events from days that would not come again were warm, sharp, and far more vivid than when he sat fully awake and tried to being memories back to life. But how could a man do that with all the uproar?

People were gabbling like magpies around the porch at the new house. It had been the "new house" to Hod for twenty-five years. He saw Baxter, his oldest boy, open the door of a blue sedan and shake hands with the driver. Sunshine ricocheted off the shoes of a big man in a gray suit when he got out of the automobile and walked with Baxter toward the magpie crowd at the new house. Sons, grandsons, and great-grandsons were flopping around like chickens with their heads cut off, working their jaws, laughing, shaking hands with strangers, having a big time. Even Baxter's prize bulls in the white-painted corrals were catching the excitement and getting uneasy. These days you couldn't tell what would happen when you started out to do a little private something. People from all over had to horn in, even those shiny-shoed men from the capital who had been around a month before.

Hod looked up at Signal Point, three hundred yards away. At the end of a long sage-covered mesa that ran like a ramp toward the sky the mass of jumbled, naked rock stood high above the intersection of two valleys that were Hodding land for mile on mile. Three hundred yards was a long way to see clearly without his glasses, but he'd be damned if he'd put them on with all these strangers around. He could see the white canvas covering the statue on the point. The three big blurs must be automobiles. Even before the sun had made his chair inhabitable, squawking noises, shrill whines, and some young idiot counting *one, two, three* had come from up there. They even had a flag pole, a long bull pine that could have been used better in a corral on one of the upper ranches—up where there was no need for white planks and posts to impress fools who went by so fast on the highway that they couldn't tell what they were passing anyway. Well, let them make their talks, run up flags, and have themselves a time. One of these days, tomorrow, maybe next week, he'd go up and have a look at that statue.

Sunshine flashed in his eyes from the shiny parts of another string of automobiles turning in at the big white gate. Hod damned them and closed his eyes. After a time the noises around him began to level into humming constancy. The sun was warm on his face. His head leaned toward his right shoulder. . . .

*The train came in at Bluebell Siding. . . . Young Braley Hodding had never seen the sky so blue or so much gold in the frost-nipped aspens. For mid-September it was much too warm to be natural, but the perspiration on his back and neck felt cold when he twisted to look at Bob Armitage lying beside him. His breath came back hot against his mouth from the bandanna that covered most of his face. Skinny Bob Armitage's brown eyes generally were leaping with humor. He usually had a smile on his wide mouth. Now his eyes looked scared, and you couldn't see what his mouth was doing.*

*"Vrain says when the fireman pulls the spout down over the manhole." Armitage was gripping his rifle hard.*

*"I wish we hadn't . . . I'm scared." Hod hoped the engineer would take the train right past the water tank without stopping.*

*"So am I," Bob Armitage said.*

*Steel ground on steel. Steam hissed and the engine stopped just ahead of the red tank. Little streams of water were jetting onto sunshine from the leaky wooden structure. The fireman went back over the coal pile.*

*Hod let his breath out in a long flutter against his mask. It wasn't so bad when they began to run down through the sliding yellow dirt of the cutbank. Hod took one coach, Armitage the other. Slender Jim Vrain, whose dark eyes and small hands were always moving nervously, stood on the bank above the locomotive and told the engineer and fireman what to do.*

*Little red-headed Ray Jacks, who laughed a lot and covered his mouth each time with two fingers to hide rotten front teeth, and tall, gaunt Jay Woodson, whose racking cough had caused Vrain to curse savagely while the five men were waiting for the train, went toward the express car on the run.*

*It all went too easily to seem real. Hod and Armitage held the passengers in the coaches without trouble. Jacks and Woodson caught the expressman just leaving his open car to get a drink of water. Vrain made the engineer get out of the cab. The fireman sat down on the coal pile and cursed.*

*Jacks shot twice, the signal that he and Woodson had the sacks. The third unscheduled shot near the engine worried Hod at first, but he had little time to think about it, between keeping the passengers quiet and wondering when Vrain was going to get the train started on up the pass.*

*Jim Vrain really was smart, Hod thought. Without water the engine couldn't make it to the top of the pass where the telegrapher was. The engineer would go until he worked up nerve to stop and back down to the tank again. The water* spout would be tied down to a rail, and the tank would be empty. The train began to move.

Hod and Bob Armitage jumped off. Little Ray Jacks and stooped Jay Woodson were standing by the sacks near a switch stand. As the express car pulled away, Jacks waved at the expressman and laughed when the latter cursed sullenly.

On sun-warmed cinders with the gold of the aspens about them they divided the payroll of the Chief Mine. Six thousand, two hundred and fifty dollars in gold to each of four men, ten thousand to Vrain as leader. Bob Armitage and Hod had nose bags in which to carry their shares.

"What was that shot at the engine?" Armitage asked.

Vrain grinned. "The fireman gave me some lip. I bounced one off the sand dome to scare him up." He began to strap new saddle bags.

Bob Armitage and Braley Hodding rode away together, their backs to the peaks, the gold-lined, twisting furrow of Branch Creek Valley far below them. At sunset they separated.

The blizzard came at dusk. Fine, dry flakes twisted and tossed before the wind, obscuring everything. Hod shivered beneath his ragged blanket coat. He should hole up and wait it out, he knew. But by now the train had tipped over the summit. The telegrapher had done his work. Men and horses would be moving on both sides of the range. Through the cold stiffness of the slicker around his pack beneath him he felt the solid burden in the feed bag and urged the reluctant horse to keep moving.

In the dark of restless snow the little gray walked straight into a prospect hole with both front legs. Cold as he was, Hod whipped his feet clear. He was thrown through whirling gloom into utter darkness. When he came back to snow and cold, he was draped in the broken snags of a fallen yellow pine. His left shoulder was useless. His chest seemed broken, as if the cold had made it brittle. The little gray was jammed head down in the narrow, shallow hole, with a broken neck.

The nose bag made a heavy weight on his good shoulder when he stumbled away into the night. Cold nibbled his ears, pawed at his bones, and his aching chest was hell's fire with every breath. The snow and cold were living things that jeered at him.

Seventeen-year-old Braley Hodding saw the sullen dawn through streaks of black pain while he sat with his back to a tree, the nose bag heavy across his legs. It was snowing at a gentle slant now. The flakes no longer danced and *whirled. They came down sticky and clung to his legs, made his hat brim droop. He fired his pistol once before it jumped out of numbed fingers. Snow attacked the metal gleefully. His head went toward the terrible pain in his chest, and he was glad to sleep.*

☼

"Dad! Oh, Dad!"

Hod came out of his semi-stupor by saying, "Yes!" irascibly and opening his eyes. First he glanced toward the wicker rocker, next to his chair, then at Baxter. The oldest boy was a fine figure of a man, except for those damn' glasses he thought he had to wear. Beside him was a big man in a gray suit.

"Sorry to wake you, Mister Hodding," the big man said.

"I wasn't asleep! I never sleep in the daytime!"

"Dad, this is Mister Harrison. He's head of the State Historical Association," Baxter said.

"I'm glad to know you, Mister Hodding," the big man said. He smiled. "After all you've done for this part of the state, I should say it was high time I knew you."

Hod grunted. Anyway, the young idiot hadn't tried to crush his hand the way some did. Damn 'em anyway! Twenty years ago he would have put any man to his knees if he tried that knuckle-popping stuff.

"We're hoping you'll feel like coming up to the ceremony," Harrison said. "I think my car will make that hill, and you can sit. . . ."

"Not today," Hod said curtly.

Baxter grinned. "They're only going to have it one day, Dad."

"To hell with it!"

Harrison looked at the wicker rocker. "I'm sorry David Ballard couldn't have lived to see this tribute to Shawano. It was Ballard, you know, whose testimony convinced the local chapter of our association that his uncle actually is buried in the rocks on the point."

Hod grunted again. He pulled his black hat a little lower toward his hawkish nose, but still he couldn't see Signal Point distinctly. He could see a few more dark blurs that must be automobiles and that big pile of canvas over the statue he'd ordered for the final place of Chief Shawano, great leader of the Utes, friend of the whites, uncle of half-breed Dave Ballard. "Dave wouldn't give a damn about this stuff," Hod said.

"He lived here a long time with you, didn't he, Mister Hodding?" Harrison asked.

"Fifty-nine years. Glad I met you," Hod replied.

He closed his eyes. He opened them again when he heard the two men walking away. Baxter looked back with a grin. Good boy, Baxter, but those damn' glasses he always wore . . . !

The last of the magpie crowd went gabbling up the hill. The young idiot with the loudspeaker counted again. Hod closed his eyes and shrugged against the pillows that took the hardness from the rawhide chair. What the hell would Dave care about speeches and statues? Hod grinned and began to doze. As a reader skims to resume his place in a book he has laid aside without marking, so Braley Hodding slipped deftly down the long trail of yesterday.

☒

*The train came in at Bluebell Siding. . . .*

*"You walk! You walk!" The dark face with a strip of blanket tied under a hat kept shouting at young Braley Hodding.*

*A hand went under his sore shoulder to help him up. He cried out. The hand lifted under his other shoulder. Hod came to his feet, dragging the nose bag. He tried to use his left arm to strike when the man started to take the nose bag. Hod gasped with pain. The man let him keep the bag. He walked through snow, cursing the dark face that told him to walk. Cold air burned his lungs; snow was wet on his face; more snow tried to trip him; the canvas bag was unbearably heavy.*

*Hod woke on a thick mat of pine needles under a lean-to, with blankets over him. The world he could see was painfully white. He smelled smoke. His left arm wouldn't move at all. He began to drowse again and felt better.*

*When Hod saw light again most of it was blocked by men standing in front of the lean-to.*

*"How long's he been here, Dave?" a deep voice asked.*

*"Since we come from Custer . . . one week."*

*"With you all the time?"*

*"His horse fell the first day we were here," Dave Ballard said.*

**Steve Frazee  403**

"Who is the kid?" a new voice asked.

"Hell, you've seen him! That Hodding kid. Him and that skinny young Armitage helped hay around Custer this summer. I saw this one start out a week or more back with Dave here to go trapping."

Hod closed his eyes. He'd ridden from Custer with Dave Ballard. Everybody thought he was going trapping with Dave. At Signal Point Bob Armitage had joined them. Dave had neither known nor asked where they actually were going.

"Maybe Dave and this kid were in it together," a slow, cold voice suggested.

The deep voice laughed. "With Dave's braids hanging past his ears? Any descriptions mention that?"

"He could have had 'em shoved up under his hat," the cold voice insisted.

"Yep! Maybe he had those slit-reared buckskin pants and that eye-busting red shirt and coat shoved under his hat, too!" the rumbling voice derided.

Everybody—there must be five, Hod thought—laughed; but the slow, cold voice was still doubtful. "Isn't this the kid . . . him and that skinny Armitage . . . that led Dave and staked him to gamble after haying season? Maybe Dave's lying. . . ."

Hod opened his eyes when grunts, curses, and feet scrapings sounded. He saw a rawboned blond giant struggling with a small, wiry, blue-eyed man who was trying to get at his gun. Two others were holding Dave Ballard, who had drawn a knife. Ballard didn't struggle long. His eyes were black and shining in his broad face as he watched the small man. "He said I lied." He was speaking of a terrible accusation.

The blond giant's shout carried volume without losing depth. "Everybody take it easy!" he bawled.

His size and the smash of his deep voice forced order. When he glanced into the lean-to and saw Hod with his eyes open, the giant squatted and grinned. "Little argument about a train robbery, but Dave says you were here, and I say Dave's word is good enough."

"Train robbery?" Hod whispered the words. He tried to sit up and couldn't make it.

The rawboned blond's look was sympathetic. "Better take it easy, kid." He scratched through shaggy blond curls under the side of his hat. "Yeah, five men got the Chief payroll at Bluebell Siding two days back. One of 'em killed the fireman in cold blood."

*Hod tried to sit up again, until the pain of broken ribs forced him down.*
*A black-bearded man squatted beside the giant. "How you feeling, button?"*

*"Awful," Hod whispered and closed his eyes. That gold. That dirty, bloody*
*gold. He'd never touch it!*

*Two days later he took the gold with him after Dave brought it from the*
*trees someplace. "I said you should not ride." Dave shook his head solemnly.*

*Hod rode slowly through melting snow on Dave's under-sized, mean-eyed*
*Indian pony. His chest and shoulder were thumping agony when he reached the*
*mouth of Branch Creek Valley that night. They were brutal, flaming pain when*
*he tied the scrawny horse to a sagebrush and went toward Signal Point at dusk*
*the next night. The nose bag was a terrible cross to carry over scrambled slabs of*
*rock where snow still lay on the north side of the point. More snow was just*
*starting to fall.*

*Hod slipped while moving rocks with one hand to seal the opening into*
*which he'd dropped the sack. He fell against his wrenched shoulder and got to*
*his feet only after the pain had made him vomit. When he got back to the pony,*
*he realized that his hat was gone. He tried to rest his head on his arms against*
*the horse to gain strength to mount. The hard-eyed brute shied away, tore its rope*
*bridle reins loose from the sage, and started briskly up the valley. Hod cursed*
*numbly and watched the horse go.*

*Snow began to whirl around him again. Soon it was blinding. Eight miles*
*down the valley was a ranch. Then he was off the trail, bumping into sage, and*
*falling over it. Jaw slack, he cursed and stumbled on, wondering if there wasn't*
*some way he could tear his shoulder and chest from the rest of him and be free*
*of the pain. The eighth or ninth time he fell, scattering pain from the back of*
*his skull to his hips before it collected again in his chest and shoulder, he knew*
*he wasn't going to make the riffle.*

*He got up and went on. Defiantly he began to sing, hymns he thought he'd*
*forgotten, parts of ribald songs, anything that came to mind. More and more he*
*began to think he was wandering in the blizzard the night after Bluebell Siding.*
*Though he had no sack to carry, each time he got up he thought he was dragging*
*the heavy bag of gold with him. Then he did not get up. He crawled as far as*
*he could. With his head lying on his right arm, he still tried to sing. Snow*
*hissed down softly on him there in the stage.*

"All right, Hod, quit your faking!" a husky voice said.

Braley Hodding jerked his eyes open. Instinctively he glanced at the battered old wicker rocker beside him. Then he looked at his great-granddaughter, black-haired, dark-browed, strong and smiling. She was the only girl in four generations of Hoddings.

"What the hell do you want?" he grumbled.

"What the hell do you think?" She tapped a spoon against a bottle.

He argued a little for fun. In the end he gulped, spat on the porch, and cursed. "That decrepit old horse doctor can't outlive me fair, so he's poisoning me off."

Ann slipped the bottle and spoon into a hip pocket of her dungarees. She deftly buttoned three buttons of his denim jacket before he slapped her hands away. Down was quilted in red nylon inside the lining of that jacket, but only he and Ann could talk about the open secret. She stood back and smiled. "When are you taking me fishing, Granddaddy?"

"Hod, by hell!"

"When are you taking me fishing, Hod?"

He grinned. "One day after all these jaybirds get out of here, we'll ride away up on the headwaters of East Elk, a place where Dave and me. . . ." He glanced at the wicker rocker and let his pretense mutter into silence.

Ann looked toward Signal Point. After a while she said: "You miss Dave all the time, don't you, Hod?"

"All the time," he said quietly. "Dave saved my life twice. Once when my horse busted its damn fool neck in a prospect hole and once not two miles from here, when I let a mangy Indian pony outsmart me, and Dave was trailing me on foot because he figured that's what would happen."

The crowd on Signal Point covered a long stretch of the steep-sided mesa. They were hunched heaviest around the high point of slabbed rocks where the shrouded statue reared.

"Doc will probably be out today," Ann said. "I thought he'd be here before now."

Hod jumped a little. He'd thought she was gone. "He ain't missing a thing." He grinned at the girl. "Bet he don't catch me asleep."

She smiled. "I'll bet he doesn't, either." Ann looked back at Signal Point. "I saw that statue when the truck was trying to get through the north field."

"Good one?"

"Fine!" She was silent so long Hod thought again that she'd gone. He opened his eyes just as she said: "Grandma told me lots of times about the man who stopped here the same day he crippled Dave Ballard in that fight when Baxter was a baby."

"Huh! Martha talks about a lot of things she don't know much about."

Dave Ballard had been dead four months, Martha for fifteen years, but lately Hod had begun to talk of her in the present tense. "But don't you let me hear you ever say a sassy thing to Martha!" Hod warned.

"All right, Granddaddy."

"Hod, by hell!"

Ann smiled and walked toward the new house. He shrugged against his pillows and glared at the dim spectacle on the point. Then his hawkish features relaxed. Four generations—hell, it was worth waiting ten for a girl like Ann. A loud voice startled him into a curse.

"People of Hodding County and visitors, we are gathered here at an historic site to pay belated honor to a great friend of our forefathers. That we are a little late in paying our respects is no fault of. . . ."

So the young idiot who couldn't count over three finally had got that loudspeaker thing to working. Hod tucked his hands against the warm lining of his jacket. He shouldered against his pillows with impatient little jerks. The voice from the point droned on, sending words that gradually became mere sounds above the green alfalfa in the north field, over the white sheds and corrals, to the unheeding care of Braley Hodding, pioneer. Hod leaned his head toward his right shoulder. His hands slipped loosely inside his jacket. The sun was warm on his face.

*The train came in at Bluebell Siding. . . .*

*Something about the way the man sat his horse caused Hod to put eight-*

*month-old Baxter back into his crib quickly and go into the yard. Martha's words followed him until the plank door chopped the sentence in half. "Why do they always ride in at mealtime, and when we have scarcely . . . ?"*

*The sky was sick and gloomy. Dry snow lay in little pockets on the frozen ground, but the rider had no shawl or scarf around his ears. Under his trim white hat his face was dark from cold. Before he swung off the horse, he looked at the one-room log house, the bare stubble of a tiny alfalfa field below the point, the big log barn and the new corral, still a-building.*

*"Jim Vrain!"*

*Vrain's fancy gloves were out at the fingers. His face was stubbled with dark beard. Under the expensive saddle the horse was a bang-eared brute fit to be skidding poles for Hod's unfinished corral. Vrain's smile was fluent, but it had lost its charm for Hod.*

*Vrain put the glove back on the hand that Hod had not received. "What's the matter, Hod?"*

*Hod held his voice low. "You killed that fireman because he cursed you, Vrain."*

*Vrain smiled easily. "Ease up, Hod! He recognized me and said so. I had to take him quick." He kept smoothing the fingers of his ragged gloves, and his eyes moved alertly.*

*Hod stared hard at Vrain's face, reading the fine marks of moral decomposition that he hadn't seen the day a handsome rider swung off his horse to talk friendly and easy with two youths loafing in front of the Custer livery stable after haying season.*

*"He called you what you are, Vrain," Hod said.*

*Vrain's face went a little darker, but his easy smile held. "Hard talk, Hod." His dark eyes moved carelessly around the ranch. "Hard talk, coming from a man who's getting quite a little start, family and all."*

*"I never used one cent. . . ." Hod cursed himself.*

*Vrain raised his eyebrows. "No? Go ahead, Hod."*

*"This place is clean, Vrain. It stays that way."*

*"Why not?" Vrain said. He glanced at the window. Yellow lamp light was warm on the crib by the stove. "For a man with a place like this, a family and all, that's the thing to do. The very thing."*

*"That's twice you've mentioned my family. Spit it out, Vrain!"*

*The slender man smoothed parts of split leather over one finger. "I'm busted,*

Hod. Hard luck in Texas. You know how it goes. Can you stake me to a thousand?"

Hod stared. Anger made hard lumps inside him.

"Just a thousand. You said you never used. . . ."

"Get out!"

"Or . . . if the place is clear, like you say, the bank in Custer would go a thousand on a ranch like this." Vrain shifted to another split glove top.

Hod started for him.

"Easy does it!" Vrain jerked his head toward the window. Martha was peering out. "I don't suppose she knows." He nodded toward his horse. "Look at that chunk of coyote bait! Look at these gloves and boots. I'm in a bad way, Hod, so bad it doesn't matter much about me . . . but you, a family man and all. . . ." He got into the saddle with springy grace. "Say, three days, Hod? Remember what happened to that little Jacks? It could happen to any one of us. Like I say, it doesn't matter much about me, but you. . . ." He smiled and shrugged. "See you in Custer, Hod."

Vrain tipped his white hat to Martha at the window and rode away over the frozen ground. "So long, you pioneer!" he called. Hod heard him singing before he went from sight.

After a while Martha opened the door and called. "Were you and that man quarreling? I couldn't tell for sure. He smiled so much and tipped his hat when he rode away."

Hod walked toward the barn. Rage and despair were heavy weights rolling around inside him. The hopeless, awful pain was worse than broken ribs had ever been.

"Hod, your supper!"

"Eat by yourself, damn it!"

For a long time Hod stood behind the barn, looking at the point. Little Ray Jacks. . . . Two weeks after Bluebell Siding, Jacks had been standing on the station platform at Granite, joking with a miner. An expressman passing by had stopped a moment just to listen to the little red-headed man's laugh and watch the accompanying gesture. Jacks had no gold, nor did anyone ever know what he had done with it. A mob led by the dead fireman's friends took Jacks from jail that night, with the sheriff's help. They hanged Ray Jacks from a long tie laid from the cab top of one engine to the cab top of a locomotive that had hauled a murdered fireman back from Bluebell Siding.

*Six times a thousand dollars lay under the rocks on Signal Point. Hod would never use it. Maybe Vrain would take the thousand and ride away for good. Hod shook his head and smiled to himself. A thousand now, next month or a year from now another thousand, all of the gold, then the ranch. One backward step from Vrain, and the man would torment him forever. Still—the gold was just lying there.*

*Mechanically Hod saddled a horse. Without hat or coat he rode over frozen ground, tortured with indecision, his mouth bitter with the taste of Bluebell Siding. When he returned to the cabin, Martha was a shadowy figure in the yellow light leaking from the stove.*

*"Tell me, Hod. Maybe I can help."*

*He shook his head. The sight of plates in the warming oven made him wonder if he could ever eat again. Before his fingers quit stinging from the warmth of the room he cleaned a gun he'd seldom used since one blizzard-driven night when it had jumped from senseless fingers while he sat against a tree.*

*Martha's face was tight and drained and little Baxter was crying for no reason at all when Hod rode for Custer the next morning. The baby's heart-broken wails rang prophetically in his ears long after he was out of sight of the cabin and the quiet woman standing by the door.*

"Snap out of it, Granddaddy Grumpy! Doc is coming!"

"Hod, by hell!" he grunted before he opened his eyes to glance unconsciously at the rocker and then at the dark-browed girl.

"Hod, it is, you profane old pirate." Ann buttoned another button on his jumper before he slapped her hands away.

From the hill the loudspeaker was saying: ". . . and to Braley Hodding, one of the last surviving pioneers of the Shawano Valley, we are indebted for a great deal of authentic history of this county. To him we are indebted. . . ."

"For a terrible stream of profanity," Ann said. She got another button before he knocked her hands aside with a grin.

Doc was coming from the car. His great-grandson was angling toward the new house. The youth waved to Hod and called hello. Hod raised one hand shoulder high and wagged it a little.

"Spank him, Ann, if he won't keep his jacket buttoned around his miserable old carcass!" Doc called. "I used to have to do it every week."

"One of Baxter's bulls is on the bum!" Hod yelled. "Think you can do anything for him, Doc?"

Doc came up the little rise slowly and stopped in front of the porch. He pursed long, thin lips that seemed crumpled at the corners for lack of space. "After working on you, a fine, intelligent bull would be a pleasure. When are you going to die?"

"Any time after you, you skinny, dried-up bag of bones!" Hod laughed. "And don't think I didn't see that skinny descendant of yours sneaking toward the new house so's he could talk to Ann."

The girl was dragging a chair from the cabin. She put it close to Hod's. "Granddaddy, Great-granddaddy!" she flung as she walked away.

"Hod, by hell!" The old man laughed till a fit of coughing stopped him.

"Thank you, Ann," Doc called. He glanced at the wicker rocker then sat down in the chair beside Hod.

The loudspeaker on the hill was still at work: ". . . appall the average doctor. No blizzard was ever too severe, no homesteader's shack too far away. Day or night he never turned down a call for help. Many of us here right now were brought into the world by him. Bankers, ragged prospectors, prostitutes, or whatever you were, he never asked. . . ." The voice ended on a note of embarrassed realization. Laughter that at first sounded like excited shouting swept down from the crowd on the point.

"That's Baxter talking . . . about me," Doc said.

Hod hadn't recognized the voice. "Huh! He sure is careless with his compliments." He scowled. "Nobody told me he was going to talk."

"It was on the program, you know." Doc smiled. "Lose your glasses, Hod?"

"What glasses?"

Baxter's voice and more laughter came from the hill: "What I meant to say is. . . ."

"How old is Baxter, Hod?" Doc asked.

"The boy? Oh, sixty-some, I guess. Why?"

Doc was silent for several moments. "Remember the day we rode up this valley a long time ago? The willows were brown from frost over there where that big alfalfa field is now. We each tried to shoot a mallard out of the air with our rifles, and Dave said we were crazy."

"I remember. When you start looking back like that, you're growing old."

Doc said: "Who's denying it?"

Irregular clapping came from the point. A new speaker took over the public address system. "Today we are honoring not only a great leader of Indians, the heroic Chief Shawano, but in a measure all those pioneers who were the first to set foot. . . ."

"Sam Worsham died this morning, about an hour ago," Doc said.

Hod was half dozing. He roused to say, "The hell he did," in the manner of one for whom death no longer evokes fear or respect, then he tucked his hands inside his warm jacket once more. He shrugged against his pillows and closed his eyes. The loudspeaker was a hypnotic mumble, growing fainter and fainter.

*The train came in at Bluebell Siding. . . .*

*Young Braley Hodding was lying in Dave Ballard's brush lean-to with a wrenched shoulder and five broken ribs. A rawboned blond giant squatted in front of the shelter and said: "Better take it easy, kid. Dave says you were here. I say his word is good."*

*Then Hod was meeting big, rawboned, blond Sam Worsham two miles down the valley from Signal Point when Hod was riding over frozen ground where dry snow lay in little pockets.*

*"Hello, Hod." Worsham leaned to one side and blew his nose toward the ground. He rubbed a rough blue mitten across his upper lip. "Little trouble in Custer last night."*

*"Yeah?" Hod said, his mind on other matters.*

*"Dave Ballard and a stranger named Vrain got into it over a poker game. Dave killed him, but this Vrain got Dave twice from the floor. Dave was dying last night. Guess he's dead by now, Hod."*

*Dave Ballard was not dead when Hod reached Custer. Everybody but Hod* and young Bob Armitage, who was working in Santee's pharmacy and helping old Doc Santee with cases now and then, said Dave couldn't last another day. Doc Santee was up at Sawmill Forks with seven pneumonia cases and wouldn't be back for several days at least. Doc didn't return at all. Along with five of his patients he died at Sawmill Forks of pneumonia.

So Bob Armitage did what he could for Dave Ballard. He couldn't help the bullet-smashed hip much. He was afraid to touch the thumb-thick piece of lead lodged in the heavy muscles near Dave's spine, but Armitage said with a scared grin that he was going to leave the stomach wound open for a while instead of sewing it up tight. People said Bob Armitage was a damned young fool and that Dave Ballard would die for sure now. But what was one less half-breed, even if a few people like Sam Worsham, who had known old Chief Shawano, did trust Dave Ballard and say he was as good as any man?

"We'll have to have a doctor for him," Armitage told Hod. "I've still got all that gold. After I found out about the fireman. . . ."

"I've got some too," Hod said.

With a thousand dollars he rode over the range that night. Other towns had their troubles too, and doctors were scarce. The two he might have got said to hell with a half-breed Indian even if he was Shawano's nephew. Hod came back a week later without a doctor. He returned the thousand dollars to the nose bag on Signal Point after learning that Dave Ballard was still alive.

Some people said a white man would have died a long time ago, especially considering the idiotic way young Armitage handled things. When Dave could be moved, Hod brought him to the ranch on a mattress in the back of a borrowed wagon. Martha tightened her lips and said that money was scarce. For several days she said very little at all to Hod. He said little himself. He was busy building another room on the cabin.

❂

"Wake up, Hod," Doc said without raising his voice. "They look like they're getting ready to unveil your statue."

"I wasn't asleep," Hod grumbled. He looked at the wicker rocker then squinted at the hill. "Guess they are, at that."

Doc smiled. He nudged Hod's arm. "Here."

Hod didn't put the glasses on. "Damned snoop," he grumbled.

"Picking a man's pocket like that." He peered hard at the point. "Does it take all that canvas to cover a man's statue, even with a war bonnet?"

"There must be a lot of staging." Doc smiled.

"Do they bust champagne on its head?"

"No, they just talk till sunset."

"I'm going to look at that thing one of these days," Hod said. "Better be just what I had Baxter order."

"I think it is. I looked at it just before they swung it up on that concrete base," Doc said.

"Where was I?" Hod demanded suspiciously.

"Asleep." Doc grinned.

Hod stared balefully. "I'll cut that Ann girl out of my will, so help me!" He grinned. "Someday. . . ."

Doc stared critically at the point. "No, I guess there's going to be more gabbing."

They listened to the loudspeaker for a while: ". . . the inner fraternity of Ute warrior chiefs tenderly bore their beloved leader to this then-secluded and remote place among the rocks. In the gentle dusk of evening. . . ."

The crumpled corners of Doc's wide mouth twitched. "Did Dave know where Shawano really is buried, Hod?"

"Hell no! Nobody does."

The speaker buried Shawano all over again, while a crowd whose forefathers had cheated and murdered the Great Leader's people listened intently to the dramatic, if somewhat inaccurate, account. Words changed to sounds and worked their soothing hypnosis. Hod began to doze again, with the golden sunshine of distant years warm on his face.

☼

*The train came in at Bluebell Siding. . . .*

*Hod's mind whisked its way through the years. There was a long, lean stretch of time after Dave came home with Hod. As soon as he could hobble on crutches, Dave went out and tried to build a lean-to against the hill. Hod found him where he had fallen and carried him back to the cabin. "No good, Hod," Dave said. Nor would he stay in the cabin. He slipped out as soon as Hod's back was turned. After Hod hid the crutches, Dave Ballard crawled outside.*

*Hod began to build another cabin, the one where he and Doc were now sitting. Two children were clinging to Martha's skirts when she came to where he was working.*

*"He knows how I resented him, Hod," she said quietly. "Whatever the bond is between you two, it is too strong and unselfish for anyone to break. I'll try to be his friend from now on." She helped Hod build the cabin.*

*Bob Armitage had gone East by then. He came to the ranch the day before he left and told Hod and Dave: "An operation might help that hip ... or it might make it worse. If I make the riffle, I'll know more about it when I come back."*

*A year later Dave Ballard disappeared in the night. He came back eighteen months later, limping along the lane from Hodding Station on the brand-new railroad that had been extended down from the mining camps. His hip was much better then, and he began to do a thousand tasks around the ranch, necessary, endless, and routine chores that had little to do with riding and cattle. His hip improved even more so that he could ride on slow, gentle horses.*

*Little Baxter and his two brothers dogged Dave Ballard's footsteps. He laughed with them as he did with no one else. With patience and skill that amazed Martha and Hod, Dave taught the boys practical aspects of ranch life, things that Hod himself was learning the hard way. Martha's face was grim and worried when all three of the children wanted to sleep in Dave's cabin. He winked at her and told the boys with frightening solemnity that he'd scalp fast if he ever caught them in his cabin without their mother's permission.*

*One bad year wiped out more than half of the small ranchers in Shawano Valley. Something happened to the price of beef. Snow came a month early on the range. Spring blizzards decimated the calf crop. Native hay went to forty-five dollars a ton with the range still snow locked. The next year was even worse. Hod had to mortgage.*

*A day came when he knew he couldn't meet the note, due in a month. He looked at Signal Point a long time, arguing where duty and honor lay. He decided to go down honestly, standing tall with as much honor as he could salvage from Bluebell Siding. A week later he told himself that it was Vrain's fault alone that the fireman had been killed. Yet, Hod didn't want to touch the gold. But— just lying there, what good was it? Where was right and wrong now that nothing* could bring the fireman back? "I'll never use it," Hod told himself, wondering whether he could make good his vow.

Dave Ballard disappeared. Two weeks later he came back with his pockets full of notes crumpled and dirty as if from much handling around a gaming table, with much silver heavy in a buckskin money belt. He gave the money to Martha and then went to his cabin to sleep for two days and nights. Braley Hodding met his note. Someone told Hod that Dave Ballard had been gambling day and night at Aspenedge, a new mining camp sixty miles away.

Six years after he'd gone east Bob Armitage returned to hang out his shingle in Custer. People were skeptical, remembering how he'd handled Dave Ballard, but soon the word was passed that young Doc Armitage would go anywhere at any time help was needed and never send a bill. Some even began to recognize that Bob Armitage was a good doctor.

Several times Dave Ballard disappeared when Hod needed money badly— once when Martha had to have an operation that Bob Armitage said he could not perform, again when Hod overstretched himself in buying land and faced ruin, once when cattle died by the thousands in blizzards. There were few small ranchers left after that.

Years fled. Hodding was a solid name wherever men talked cattle. Hod no longer had to look at Signal Point with cold speculation twisting in his brain. There came a day when he realized that he had known for years that there always would be Hodding land and Hodding substance. Now Baxter's prize bulls brought as much as forty thousand dollars each. The taxes Hodding paid in one year were enough to have bought all the ranches in Shawano Valley at the time Hod was married. But he paid respect to gold on Signal Point. It had always been there to take. Since that night he'd returned the thousand dollars to the nose bag, he'd never gone near the rocks. Thanks to Dave Ballard he had never been forced to the final inch of hard decision; but deep in his secret conscience he knew that six thousand, two hundred and fifty dollars in tarnished gold had given him a bulwark that others lacked. True, he'd worked as hard and as shrewdly as any man; he'd faced the gamble of weather, prices, and other factors that he could not control; and in the end he had emerged with land and riches, while some of the others had failed along the way.

Bob Armitage had spent his money wisely in becoming a doctor. Nobody knew what had happened to Ray Jacks's share. Jim Vrain had squandered his. Hod had never heard of Jay Woodson again after Bluebell. Whatever the others *had done with their gold, Hod knew he couldn't gloat over what he had not done with his.*

✪

Dr. Robert Armitage roused Hod from his reverie. "You know something?" Doc asked.

"I know a hell of a lot of things!" Hod said testily. "Enough not to disturb a man when he's thinking."

Doc laughed. "I've been thinking too, but I don't do it with my eyes closed." He looked at Signal Point. "They'll talk till moonup, I'll bet." His long mouth twitched at the corners. "I'd just as well tell you now."

"Tell me what?" he asked.

"Dave Ballard sent me to medical school, Hod. After the first three months I knew I'd never make it, trying to work and study at the same time. Right then he began to send me money, just as if he'd known or as if I'd written him for it. For five years he sent me the darndest mixture of soiled bills and silver you ever saw. Most of the time the packages weren't even insured. I can see that sprawling handwriting yet, the same they taught him those few years they had him trapped in a mission school when he was a little boy. He asked me never to say anything about it, never to write him. I never did."

Hod glared. "What'd you do with the Bluebell money?"

"Never went near it after I hid it . . . the second time."

They listened to the sounds from the hill: ". . . and so, as president of the local chapter of the State Historical Association, I have been given the honor of. . . ."

"What did you do with yours?" Doc asked.

Hod grinned wickedly. "It's smack under that damn' statue's base."

"So's your hat," Doc said. "I jammed it down there myself." Hod pulled away from his cushions and stared. Doc's wide mouth smiled. "After I moved my bag from Red Steer Creek, I put it way down in the rocks on the south side of the point, along with your hat that I found on the north side. I could even see the leather bottom of your nose bag, so I slipped in a few more rocks to help you out." Doc

**Steve Frazee   417**

Armitage yawned. "The concrete they poured for the base was supposed to seal Shawano's tomb solid. It ran down through the rocks and covered both sacks pretty well, according to the way I remembered things when I looked last week."

"Why, Doc. . . ." That was all Hod could say while he grinned.

Doc Armitage wore a far-away smile as he looked up at Signal Point. "Dave sent me exactly fifty-five hundred dollars," he said gently.

"Fifty-five hundred . . . ?" Hod repeated the words absently. In the little account book that he hadn't ever known Martha kept, until her death, she had recorded fifty-five hundred dollars received from Dave Ballard. Hod told Doc.

"You know," Doc said, still smiling, "I've been thinking. That receipt Baxter found in Dave's things, the one that showed Dave spent fifteen hundred dollars for an operation the time he was gone from you a year and a half . . . say, you take half of fifteen hundred . . . ?"

Hod began to laugh.

"He was a pretty fast gambler," Doc said, "but not that fast."

Hod's laughing shook his insides and made little sound except when he tugged for air.

White canvas flared in the sun. The crowd shouted.

Hod fumbled for his glasses, found them where they had slipped between his legs on the chair. He began to wipe them on his denim sleeve.

Perhaps Doc was thinking of frost-brown willows and two boys trying to shoot ducks from the air with rifles when he said: "Folks think that chief up there looks a whole lot like Dave."

Hod's skeleton hands fumbled to get the hooks of the glasses over his ears. "It had better . . . or I'll send for that sculptor!"

He looked at Signal Point. "How'd that happen!" Hod yelled. "That damn' Indian is on a horse. I never told no one to put him on a horse!"

Doc was still smiling. "I did, and Baxter agreed. It's just a mean-eyed, scrawny Indian pony, but it will take Dave riding over these hills on moonlit nights when no one is looking." His eyes were filmed with distant memories.

For several moments Hod left his frail, earth-bound, dying body along the cushions of his chair and raced through moon-silvered hills to overtake a friend.

"Of course, too, it takes a whole lot more concrete to pour a base under a mounted statue," Doc said. "At the time I hadn't guessed...."

❂

Sixteen-year-old Bob Armitage looked from a window of the new house. Ann was standing beside him. "I wonder what those two old characters have to laugh about like that?" young Bob asked.

# Brother Shotgun

## Jeanne Williams

◉

*Born in Elkhart, Kansas, Jeanne Williams is held in high esteem for her historical novels set in the West, for which she has won several Golden Spur Awards from the Western Writers of America. Along with T. V. Olsen and Elmer Kelton, she got her start writing Western stories for the pulp Western magazines in the 1950s and was among the last of a new generation of Western writers still able to learn their craft in the short story magazine market before it disappeared. Over a twenty-year period Williams published more than seventy Western, fantasy, and women's stories in pulp and slick magazines. Her Western stories appeared in* Ranch Romances, Thrilling Ranch Stories, *and* Real Western Romances. *In many of these stories Williams displayed a sensitivity to women's concerns and issues. It was this interest in presenting a female point of view as the focus of her stories that led her in the direction of the historical novel, although she was met with resistance from publishers until the highly successful publication of* A Lady Bought with Rifles *(Coward, McCann, 1976). Some of her best work is found in* The Valiant Women *(Pocket, 1993) and* The Longest Road *(St. Martin's, 1993). "Brother Shotgun," which appeared in* Ranch Romances *(2nd June Number: June 14, 1957), is one of Williams's own personal favorites, collected now in book form for the first time.*

His name was still Johnny Chaudoin when he hitched his gray nag in front of the two-story frame building. It was the only house in this town that both showed a light and looked as if it might have room for a stranger. A day's ride in the raw March wind had made his bad leg so stiff it didn't want to hold him up. He cussed it in French, Spanish, and English. He would've cussed it in Cherokee, too, if there'd been swear words in that language. His Indian grandmother claimed there weren't. He stamped till the blood came alive beneath the knee a Minié ball had smashed and went on to the house. It wasn't till he'd climbed the steps that he could make out the lettering on an old card tacked to the door.

ROOM AND BOARD
INQUIRE WITHIN

The board probably wouldn't amount to much, the way this part of West Virginia had been raided and counter-raided in the war but, as far as Johnny was concerned, he wouldn't enjoy a man's meal anyway till he was settled down to a rib of freshly killed buffalo. Buffalo—a sea on the plains, huge-shouldered, small-flanked, with enormous heads bent to crop the sweet, curled grass. How many nights in camp with the Eighth Kansas had he chewed on corn bread and cow peas and closed his eyes, trying, if only for a flash, to see the herd and sniff the wind with them? The Reb Minié ball had put an end to that. Johnny had been able to earn a stake working in a coal mine—they were glad to get even kids and cripples this fourth year of the war—but his soldiering days were finished. Now he was going home.

He knocked, his chapped knuckles cracking against the splintered door. Laughter came from inside, then there was scurrying and the impact of bodies hitting the panel. He had time to think—*sounds as if all the boarders have ten kids apiece*—and then the door swung inward. Johnny stood looking at more children than he'd seen since he ran away from home and his own ten brothers and sisters, forty years ago. Or at least it seemed that way. The boy in the door was redheaded. Above his blazing thatch leaned a black-eyed girl with the copper skin of an Indian. A blonde baby had pushed under the boy's arm and was staring up at Johnny with a finger in her mouth. Behind these three others crowded—all ages, all sizes.

Johnny, in spite of an addiction to minding his own business, wondered what the parents of this bunch could look like. He was a mixture himself, with a French-Spanish father, an Irish-Cherokee mother, but at least he and his ten siblings had all possessed black hair and eyes. Anyway, they used to have. His hair was streaking now, and he guessed his two older brothers would be white-headed—if they were still alive.

There was a flutter. A tall girl had come up, gathering the kids back, effectively yet without fuss. She looked at Johnny half smilingly, half questioningly, and he saw that her eyes were the gray silver of the underside of a cottonwood leaf. She had funny colored hair, too. It reminded Johnny of the shine of yellow moonlight off an aspen— almost white but warmed with gold. You could say she was tow-headed, but Johnny had lived with Indians and did not lump shadings as white men did.

He took off his hat. "I wonder, ma'am, if I could put up here for a day or two?"

Quite frankly she looked him over. He was in his buckskins. There was no way for her to know which army, if any, he had fought for. Was she for the Union, or did she believe in the Confederacy as many people did in the young state of West Virginia?

Her question startled him. "Can you pay in greenbacks?"

Johnny blinked. With Yankee money almost ten times as valuable as Confederate that was a sound question. Yet—well, he had her mixed up with moonlight and cottonwoods in his mind. "I can pay greenbacks," he said and reached for his money pouch.

She flushed. Her eyes flickered down a second before they came back to his. She said in a distinct tone: "If my husband's alive, he's in a Yank prison. But it takes money . . . real money . . . to buy shoes and food. Come on in, mister. We've just sat down to the table."

Johnny looked at the kids. The Indian-looking girl was in her teens. The girl with the gray eyes could not possibly be the mother of all the others—but, if you don't ask questions, folks'll tell you more than if you do, Johnny believed, so he bowed and backed out the door. "I'll join you directly, ma'am, but first I have to take care of my horse. Is there any hay in that stable out back?"

"There hasn't been for the past three years, but my neighbor, Eli Stricker, who sells me milk, keeps cows. I don't imagine he'd mind selling you some of their hay." She turned to the redhead. "Timmy, run over to Mister Stricker and ask him if he'll fork some hay over in the lot for this gentleman's horse, please."

The boy ducked past Johnny, making for the house to the right, and the girl's lips curved in either amusement or contempt. "No use asking Eli to *give* anything. I pay for milk and get blue-john. You can come in the back way when your horse is tended to."

She swept the children in front of her, back to the lamp-lit kitchen. Johnny unhitched the gray and rode it around to the fenced lot surrounding the stable. A stocky red-faced man was already levering a pitchfork of hay over into the lot. Johnny met his curious stare.

"I guess you're Stricker."

"You'd guess right." Stricker twitched up another forkful, making sure all the clinging wisps fell off before he tossed the central mass over in the lot. "Danged raiders burned off most of my field last fall. I hardly had enough to help my own stock through the winter. Afraid I'm going to have to charge you a Yank dollar for this fodder."

Johnny, lifting off his cobbled saddle, rubbed the gray's sweaty back and withers with the saddle blanket. It was an old horse with its teeth worn off smooth from years of grinding, but it was about the only four-legged critter Johnny had been able to find after the surgeon decided Johnny was through soldiering. At first, remembering fast Indian ponies, untiring hounders of the buffalo, Johnny had been wild at this beast's shambling gait, but days before he had reached the mine where he'd worked out his stake his impatience had turned into a feeling of kinship. He was getting old, too. Some days he felt nearer seventy than fifty. *I want just one more hunt*, he thought. *One more season.*

He led the horse over to the trough that the spring spilled into and left it drinking while he moved back clumsily—for the day's ride had left his leg still numbed—to Stricker. "I figure on resting up here for a couple of days. Fork over hay for my horse in the morning, and the next day, too, and you're welcome to the dollar."

Starting to protest, Stricker's gaze tangled with Johnny's and fell. He tossed over another forkful of hay then put down the fork with the air of a job well done. "All right, stranger. I'll do it as a favor to Luanne, to keep her from losing a boarder. You're the first paying guest she's had in three months."

Baffled though he was at the set-up, Johnny didn't care to hear this man talk about the girl. But neither did he want to rile her neighbors, causing her unpleasantness that would linger after he was gone. He nodded to Stricker. "I'm much obliged for the fodder, mister. Guess I'll go up to the house and get me some food, too."

Stricker's voice floated after him. "Better hurry or the orphanage will have gobbled it all."

Orphanage? Johnny shunted his saddle into the stable, first untying the tarp that held his extra socks and camp stuff, and taking his shotgun out of the scabbard. There was an Indian flute in the trap, carried through all the war and these last months at the mine. Johnny wondered if the kids and Luanne might like to hear him play it. He would kind of like to do that—leave them a song before he went West to the buffalo. Mingled shrill voices, the sound of chairs scooting back, and the rich smell of stew hit him all together as he stood at the back stoop a minute, listening, before he opened the door.

The stew was tasty, even though it was short on meat, and there was pan bread. Except for the three youngest children, none of them over two, everyone drank sassafras tea. Johnny had dreamed about coffee, but sassafras tea was better than some of the roasted acorn brew you got nowadays. Johnny squinted at the milk in the three babies' cups. It was thin, a transparent blue around the edges. He said to Luanne, who had properly introduced herself by now as Mrs. Benton: "Ma'am, that milk sure looks as if it had been skimmed. Good cow's milk is bad enough, but that's sickening."

"Eli has the only cow's milk left in town," she said wearily. "He scrapes off the cream and sells it to people who can afford it. Anyway, what do you mean 'good cow's milk is bad enough'?"

"Goat's milk is way ahead, ma'am," said Johnny, expounding his pet theory. "What can you expect from folks who eat hogs and sheep and chickens, who drink milk from critters that're so dumb they have to be fed and sheltered through the winter?" Johnny thumped down his fist. "It stands to reason that what you eat makes up your body. If you eat helpless, stupid, feckless critters, it'll affect your nature, too."

Luanne smiled. "I think we're safe, Mister Chaudoin. Raiders have pretty well gotten off with all those animals. The meat in our stew was from a squirrel Timmy killed today with his sling shot."

"Squirrel's good meat," Johnny approved. "They's smart creatures. They store up food against the winter and live free in the woods." Timmy glowed as Johnny nodded at him then listened with his thin face pushed forward as Johnny went on. "A man who lives on wild game has to be quick and silent and has to depend on himself. He eats venison from swift deer and the tongues of buffalo who can scent a storm coming. Bear makes him strong, and he gets speed from the antelope, and cunning from the sage rabbit. Freedom is in all of them, in their flesh, to thrive again in his flesh. The Comanches know this. They won't eat a turkey unless they're mighty hungry. They figure the meat will give them chicken hearts so they'll run from danger."

"Are you telling the plain truth, mister?" squeaked Timmy, his blue eyes sparkling.

"So help me," Johnny affirmed. He leaned over and roughed up the boy's carrot-colored hair before he turned to Luanne. "Goat's milk would be the thing for these youngsters, ma'am. It'll make 'em quick, sure footed, and independent."

A smile teased at Luanne's mouth. From the way it settled into natural lines, he could tell she'd never lost the grace of humor in spite of the war, and whatever had happened to her husband, and Stricker's blue-john. "Even if it wouldn't do all those things, Mister Chaudoin, it'd be nourishment. But we might as well pine for strawberries in cream."

"Seems it'd cost less to buy a goat than to pay for milk."

"I don't pay in cash." When Johnny frowned, Luanne explained. "This was my parents' home, and mother had some lovely furniture . . . a chair from France, a pianoforte, marble tables, that sort of thing. Eli's wife has always wanted to be a social leader. By owning my mother's things, she must hope to acquire mother's character."

"You traded that furniture for milk?"

Luanne shrugged. "My parents are dead. They won't feel any grief over it. And you can't eat marble and wood."

"Then why in sam hill didn't you trade the stuff for a cow?"

"Eli wouldn't agree to that. He says the cows furnish his living. No one, in these days, is going to trade a milk animal for furniture.

Eli's wife, fortunately, wants the things enough to barter milk for them."

Johnny's mind hummed with questions. She ran a boarding house. Didn't she get any money from it? Where did the kids come from? Was she paid for their care? Would they be on her hands till they grew up? What would happen when the furniture was traded off? Johnny coughed and pushed back from the table.

He was on his way home. This was none of his business. It was three years since he had crept up on a buffalo, careful of the wind, wrapped in a hide. It was three years since he feasted on hump rib and lay in his blankets, settling into that deep, sensuous sleep that came as the rich flesh was absorbed into his own blood and bone and muscle. He thought: *just one more season, God—one good hunt.* It was the prayer that had sustained him through the war and the Minié ball and the weeks in the coal mine. He had hated the mine. It wasn't right that a mine should be down deep, with no sun or wind. He didn't want to be buried underground even. When he thought of it, he hoped his bones would bleach out pale in the prairie grass, with the wind over them and the buffalo sniffing all around.

A hand on his knee brought him back to West Virginia. The blonde baby girl had come up to him. Rosy mouth puckered over her finger, she watched him with calm interest.

"Mustn't suck your finger," Johnny said, bending down and lifting her to his good knee. "It'll make your teeth grow crooked, missy."

She giggled, and he saw her teeth. They were the shade of the transparent edge of blue-john. And her body on his lap seemed to weigh no more than a huddle of bones with the marrow gone. Oh, hell! Ought to be able to get some kind of milk critter without blowing too much from his stake. Of course he'd wanted to buy a rifle. You had to get up too close with a shotgun, and many a hunter had been gored to death by the buffalo he was trying to kill. He'd need another horse, too. Even if the gray could stand the trip to the plains, it sure couldn't chase a herd. But the little girl was so danged scrawny!

Johnny said to Timmy: "Suppose you dig into that tarp of mine and fetch me the flute."

He played them songs and then let the Indian-looking girl try to make tunes, while he sang "Las Mañanitas," "Green Grow the Rushes, Oh!," a chant his grandmother told him the Cherokees used to sing, and "Frère Jacques" to commemorate his French blood. But Timmy didn't know French.

"Frère Shotgun!" he cried. "By grannies, I finally puzzled out a word from those *dor-may-vooz* and *sona-lay matinas*."

"Hold on," Johnny said. "That just means Brother John."

"Well, your name is John, and you have a shotgun, too," Timmy said. "The song's about you. Teach it to us!"

Johnny did, while Luanne smiled, and the black-eyed girl fluted. Even the baby girl caught the spirit and tried to sing. By the time Johnny went to bed, his name was Shotgun.

Next morning Johnny found out a lot. While he searched the town and visited a few farms, he let it be known he was boarding at Luanne's. At that nearly everyone he met burst out talking. Though he hadn't been able to abide the hypocritical concern of Eli Stricker, Johnny listened to these others. He had to know the answer to the questions that had pestered him last night, the answer to Timmy, and the baby, and the Indian-looking girl, and the other five children. Johnny talked mostly to old men and women.

The providers, the earners, the young men, were nearly all off to war, some for the Union and some for the South. Johnny saw that what Luanne had said about raiders looting the country was true. Fields lay charred and black from being burned the summer before. Poverty crushed hard on nearly all the people, though a few had chickens or a cow or a pig. The Strickers were probably more prosperous than anyone in the little village. The one store didn't have much merchandise. The owner had been killed by marauders, and his widow either couldn't or wouldn't stock even staples. Luxuries nested beside tallow and flour and maybe what you wanted was there, and maybe not.

"Luanne's a fine girl," the widow told Johnny as he paid for the candy sticks he was getting for the kids. "But she got in over her head, taking in those youngsters. She can't buy food for 'em much less shoes.

Her father . . . he was a doctor . . . left her the house but precious little cash. And the last she heard from her husband, he was a prisoner up north among those damyankees."

A girl, with her parents dead and her husband gone to war, had decided to run a boarding house to bring in cash and keep herself from sinking into self-pitying uselessness. And then, instead of paying guests, the place had filled up with children. Timmy, a cousin of her husband's, had been beaten savagely by his stepfather and had run away from him. Sara, the dark girl, who was sure enough half Indian, had lived off in the brush with her crazed father till his death a year ago. Luanne, gathering berries in the woods, had found the girl and brought her home.

The blonde baby girl with the bluish teeth had been left, along with an older sister, by a young couple who had stopped at the boarding house last spring. The man and woman had fussed a good deal, and they seemed worried. It turned out later that the man had deserted from the army, and the sooner he could get to California, the better he'd like it. The woman had seemed to love her children, but she was the kind who is plain crazy over her man, worthless and mean as he may be. Luanne woke up one morning to hear the babies crying and to find the parents were gone. The woman left a note and a little money she must have begged from the man. She said he wouldn't fool with the children and that she couldn't live without her husband. Luanne was so kind, wouldn't she take care of them and not let them know what kind of a woman their mother had been? She'd try to send money. But she never had.

And the other four children? Oh, a young farmer got killed in the war, and his wife sickened and died that same winter. The wife had no close kin, and her husband's folks wouldn't have the kids because their father had fought on the Union side. How had Luanne managed to get by? Well, she still had an occasional boarder, though she had surely finished what money her father, the doctor, had left. She was a marvel with knitting and made sweaters for a shop in Charleston. When they could, people helped with what they had—a few eggs, cast-off clothing, fruit, and vegetables. In summer Luanne and the children made a big garden. But it got a little harder all the time to stretch her tiny resources. She was just doing the best she could, trying not to think about the morrow, hoping the war would end and her husband would come home.

Johnny pieced it together. When he had, he knew he had to get a goat or at least a cow. He had no luck that morning. But after more stew for dinner, Johnny went forth again, riding his horse because his leg was paining him, and he figured he might have to cover a lot of ground. It was at a cabin back on a wagon road that he found the goats. After some argument, and the production of his greenbacks, Johnny persuaded the old man who owned them that the kids of one nanny could be weaned or bottle fed with the milk of the other "fresh" female. Poorer by fifteen dollars (which was two dollars more than he'd been paid for a month's service in the Army), Johnny led the goat home.

Luanne protested. But Johnny, fixing up a milking block in the stable, finally turned to her and said grimly: "Look, ma'am, I want to go West and enjoy my hunt. I couldn't do it if I left these youngsters drinking that blue-john."

"But you. . . ."

"I'm crippled some," Johnny finished for her. "I'm not so young, either. I fought for the Union . . . on the opposite side from your husband. But you see, I'm a man. And a man's supposed to help feed children."

Her eyes had grown cold when he named his army. "Are you trying to salve your conscience?"

He thought of the buffalo and the rest of his greenbacks. "Maybe, but not the way you mean. I never could relish the idea of any man's belonging to another. That's why I fought."

She looked at him, and he looked back, and after a few moments the tenseness left her muscles. "Well, you must take your board and room free, then, as long as you stay. I thank you for the goat, Shotgun."

He grinned and went back to his work. "She'll be thrifty, ma'am, and will forage for herself. Her milk'll make the babies strong and able to walk the edge of a cliff without falling over. And, see, with this block you can milk her and not have to bend to the ground."

"I'll learn to milk," Timmy said, "if you'll teach me, Shotgun."

Shotgun rumpled the red hair. "Sure. Sure, I will."

What were a few more days of staying here? The horse could use the rest. But the few days became a week. The stable, now it had an occupant, needed patching up, the fence had to be mended, and a heavy storm caused leaks in the roof. Johnny spent several more dollars on these repairs. It seemed ornery not to attend to them when, while they didn't cost a lot, it was more money than Luanne could scrape up. Tim could milk Nanny now as if he'd been doing it all his life, and Sara was getting to play a smart tune on the flute. The kids could chant in Cherokee and sing snatches of French and Spanish. Johnny felt kind of pleased. It was a strange new feeling to know that after he'd gone on, and maybe even after he was dead, these kids would sing the songs he'd taught them and teach them to their children. Johnny had always passed through life as traceless as the wind, except perhaps for the bones of animals he'd killed and the ashes of his fires. He had never left his trace on human hearts. Now he was leaving his songs in the minds of these children and rich milk in their stomachs.

But it was a long way West, and the buffalo were sniffing some Kansas breeze. He was old. It was time to be going. Early one morning he put his things in the tarp. The flute he held a minute then laid aside. It had been his grandmother's. Now it would be for Sara who played it with love. He counted his money. Each bill represented hours in the black earth and the pain in his leg. The bills had been earned to get him home and to buy the rifle, a horse, and supplies for that hunt, which had to be good since it might be the last. But now the bills took a different shape—shoes for the baby, a pair of whole pants for Timmy, bright red cotton for Sara, medicine if a child fell ill and coughed till its life was rasping out, an easing of the worry lines in Luanne's face. The buffalo wouldn't be at their best now anyway. They would be scabby and mosquito bitten and muddy from their wallows. He wouldn't relish the meat at all. Of course he wouldn't. Funny it should be so hard to leave the money there on the bureau.

He went back to the mines without telling Luanne or the kids good bye, except in the note he left instructing Luanne how to use the money. If it had been hard in the mines before, it was twice as bad now. Starting all over for the second time, the day when he'd have enough scraped together to leave seemed mighty far off. His leg raised the devil with him till he could hardly sleep at night, and his dreams were full of buffalo, spread out over the plains for miles. He kept track of the time by thinking what the herd would be doing now.

April. May. June. Little yellow calves were dropped and ran beside their mothers. Buffalo rubbed themselves raw trying to get away from the flies and the gnats. Johnny began to have a funny feeling in his heart sometimes as if a hand had lifted it and held it high and pulseless for a second before dropping it back in place.

July. August. September. Bulls fought and took the cows. By now Johnny was sure there was something the matter with his heart. He wondered what would happen when the hand kept hold of it and didn't let it slip free.

In October he left the mines. His homestake was meager, but he guessed he'd better head West while he still had a hope of seeing the plains again. The gray horse had aged even in these months, and Johnny rode slowly. The hand squeezed his heart now. Sometimes it hurt so bad he thought the blood must be plumb wrung out. It bothered him especially when he climbed up or down from the saddle. Still, he felt glad to see how much better the children looked. When he stopped in front of the boarding house, as he had done seven months ago, Timmy was chopping wood.

He dropped the axe, yelling: "Shotgun's back! Luanne, Sara, it's Shotgun!"

They all came out, the little blonde baby girl hugging his knees, Sara waving the flute, saying: "I play it so well now, Shotgun, you must hear!" The other kids hung on to his sleeves while he led the horse out back to be sheltered and fed.

He lifted the baby—she weighed a good bit now—and was swept into the house. There were beans with ham hock and dried peach pie for supper. The milk in the children's cups was rich and white. When the children were shooed off to bed, Luanne came over to Johnny.

"I just don't know how to thank you," she said. "The money you left bought clothes and shoes for the children who needed them most, and when Timmy had pneumonia, it paid for his medicine. It got wool so I could make more sweaters for sale, and . . . Shotgun, I was at the end of my rope last spring. But we didn't know where you'd gone, and I was afraid you'd given up all your savings. You did, didn't you? . . . or else you'd be chasing buffalo right now?"

"No matter," Johnny said. "I have another homestake, and I'm purely glad you're doing better. Don't the baby's teeth look nice? Don't you fret, Luanne. I'm going home. Glad I could help you on my way."

She wasn't the crying kind of woman, but the gray eyes were extra bright as she went over and brought a red bundle from a shelf. She shook it out. Johnny got the scent of the rose leaves she must have put in it to keep the bugs out, and then he stared at the long-sleeved, hooded red sweater. It was made with a black stripe at hip level and two others at the chest. It was knitted of warm yarn.

"It's yours," she said. "And I made you a pair of black socks and a pair of red. I thought surely someday I'd learn where to send them."

Blindly Johnny took the sweater and pressed it with his callused hands. No one, no woman, had made him such a garment, sewn with love, since he was a child. He said: "Why, it's the fairest thing I ever saw."

When he went up to bed, he had to stop on the stairs twice as the hand clutched at his heart, but he held the red wool as if it was medicine, and the spells passed. Johnny was tired, but it was only for the gray's sake that he stayed at the house four days. If you had time, this was good—singing with the kids, holding the baby, watching Luanne looking brighter than he had ever seen her. But Johnny had no time.

With the instincts of the beasts he had lived among and hunted, he felt death in his flesh and bone. He felt it in his heart. If he wanted to see buffalo again, he must travel fast. This was the best time of the year, the time it would be when he got home, late in November. The calves would be fat and brown, and the insects would trouble the herd no more. It was the fat time of the buffalo, the rich time for hunters. He had to go. His tired horse, ruined knee, bad heart wouldn't get better. If they were to carry him home, they had to do it now.

He packed his tarp on the morning of the fifth day and put on the red wool sweater. He went down the stairs to find Luanne crying in the kitchen. She couldn't stop even when she saw him. He thought at once, her husband. "What's wrong, Luanne?"

She said: "Shotgun, my husband got exchanged, but he was so sick in prison, they're going to let him come home. But he hasn't any money and can't get paid, and you know they don't get good care in army hospitals." She shook her head back and forth as if she were driven wild. "If I could go take care of him, bring him home . . . ! If he dies now . . . !"

Johnny said, with a great tiredness and a great peace settling on his soul: "There's no need for crying. I can lend you the money, Luanne."

She gazed at him. "Your stake?"

"No," he lied. "I can give you the money and still have enough to get out West."

"Are you sure?"

"Of course I am!"

She put her face against his shoulder and cried. "Here," said Johnny, patting her arm, "you'd better get ready to go to your man."

When she was gone on the train, Johnny told Sara, who was to care for the children, good bye, and he told Timmy and the others not to forget the Cherokee prayer or "Green Grow the Rushes, Oh!" or "Las Mañanitas."

Timmy said: "We'll remember 'Frère Jacques,' too, Shotgun. Send me some buffalo horns, will you?"

"If I don't," said Johnny, touching the boy's head, "you go out in a few years and get your own. Sara, mind you play that flute pretty."

He mounted up, with the hand on his heart clutching. He waved with his hat as he rode off, and the baby girl ran after him crying, till Sara caught her.

For a good way Johnny could hear them calling: "Shotgun! Shotgun! Good bye, Shotgun! Shotgu-u-un!" He waved again, at the edge of town, and turned his face West.

He was in pain now. The hand gripped. But he sat as straight as he could and directed his intention and his will. If he was going West with all his desire, might not his spirit keep on after his body stopped? Might not his direction be so strong that the flesh couldn't stop it? If he fixed his mind on the buffalo—was that drumming their hoofs? Was that their dust obscuring the way in front of him? He strained to see. But the soft hills were falling away, slipping back. The hand lifted his heart and squeezed and squeezed and squeezed. He was slipping. He felt the earth. Then there was the sound of a great herd. He was running after them, West, to the prairies—West, to the hunt. The meat would be good and the sleep sweet.

# Bonaparte McPhail

### Robert Easton

✪

*Born in San Francisco, California, Robert Easton always identified strongly with the history of his native state. His first book,* The Happy Man *(Viking, 1943), is a portrait of California ranch life in the 1940s that earned him wide critical acclaim. It consists of a number of wide-ranging vignettes that in the words of veteran editor Harry E. Maule in his collection,* Great Tales of the American West *(Modern Library, 1945), suggest "most of the people, even on the headquarters ranch of the streamlined El Dorado Investment Company, have the stamp of the old West on them. Tradition dies hard." In his later Saga of California, Easton undertook an ambitious series of interrelated novels, each dealing with a different period in the history of California, from the coming of the Spanish to the present day. He is presently at work on* Blood and Money, *the third novel in this saga to be published as a Five Star Western, whereas the two earlier volumes are now available in mass merchandise paperback editions from Leisure Books. Easton is also coeditor with his wife, Jane Faust Easton, of* The Collected Stories of Max Brand *(University of Nebraska Press, 1994). "Bonaparte McPhail" first appeared in* Collier's *(August 26, 1944) and has been slightly revised by the author for its first appearance in book form.*

**W**e used to walk away and leave him talking to the empty air and, when he was alone, he would talk to himself or the cattle and tell them his ideas. We used to talk *about* Bonaparte McPhail. His name was a joke. Sitting in the cookhouse at meals or after supper in the bunkhouse around the potbellied stove, we would carry on, spitting to hear the hot iron sizzle—Derringer, who was top hand, Sammy Lee the cat skinner, Jacob, and the rest of us—amusing ourselves with the boners Bonny McPhail had pulled.

For instance, one time he was working at a place, and they told him to go out and burn the stubble, so Bonny ties some sacks on a wire and the wire behind a wagon, lights those sacks, and just drives around the field. This works fine for a while, and Bonny is about as proud as Thomas A. Edison until he sees a bunch of heifers in the grain field next door, in where they had no business being because that was prize grain and would make thirty sacks to the acre if it made a pound. So what does Bonny do? Why, he gets right over there, wagon and all, and wagon and all he puts those heifers out of that grain—something three men on horseback couldn't do.

Of course by then he's burnt up eleven thousand dollars' worth of barley which is why Bonny came to California to change his luck and was working on the cattle ranch of Jed Elkins when I knew him, forty-nine years old, drawing a dollar a day and his board, still waiting for his advancement and still thinking too much about Napoleon, Shakespeare, and Thomas A. Edison, who had got him in trouble before. So we carried Bonny as a joke and used him to pass the time until one day—and this is what happened.

Jed Elkins's place is up three thousand feet. His valley is a cup inside a rim of mountains that looks to be made of gold. The sun was just coming over those mountains, making them all shiny at the edges like big nuggets, when I walked into the blacksmith shop and interrupted Bonny who was busy at the anvil.

" 'Morning," he said, as though he never had seen me before, kind of glaring through his glasses the way an inventor does who's been interrupted, and kept right on hammering a bar of some kind he had heated in the fire.

Now Bonny was not what you'd call beautiful. He looked more than anything like one of those bandy-legged apes that walks like a man, short-legged, long-barreled, tail stuck out, and his blue jeans always were three sizes too long and his dirty gray shirts overlapped them all around by six inches. He sported a felt hat, city style, that looked as if it had wiped up the floor of some big city garage, and a cigarette holder, and a brown seep of tobacco juice from the corner of his mouth, that was a style all Bonny's own.

I said it was time to go feed our cattle. Bonny hammered on. He was shaping one of those pinch bars made of iron three feet long, common to every ranch and carpenter's shop in the country, with a pry on one end and a curved pinch on the other for pulling nails. Bonny was building something that looked like a hammer head on the outer curve of this pinch. All of a sudden he stopped, picked the bar up, and went through some wild motions meant to indicate the pulling of a nail with the pinch and the pounding of one in with the hammer.

"Think it'll work?" he asked, handing me his invention.

I made a few passes myself. "Sure it'll work," I told him. "All a fellow needs is an arm and shoulder of iron, and he wouldn't mind using this thing at all."

Bonny took back his bar the way a mother takes her baby from a stranger. "Maybe," he said. "We'll see what the board of directors thinks about that . . . yessir," he continued, when we had loaded our pickup truck with sacks of rolled barley and cottonseed and were heading up the valley, "yessir, I wouldn't be surprised . . . it's been five days now. I wouldn't be surprised to get a letter today from the chairman of the board of directors of the Atlas Steel Company in San Francisco. It's been five days since I wrote and diagrammed him the idea and, when I'd done that, I went on to explain how there was hundreds of thousands of these pinch bars in daily use throughout the United States, and not a one of 'em but what you had to put it down and pick up a hammer every time you wanted to drive a nail.

"I begged 'em . . . yessir. I begged 'em outright . . . to consider the hours, days, even the years spent and wasted by all the working men multiplied by all the pinch bars every time that they're laying down and picking up occurs. It's a shocker . . . ! As I said," concluded Bonny, "that was five days ago. 'Course a board of directors don't meet like you and I. And with ideas like mine there's patents to look up and papers to clear. Oh, it might take a week, maybe longer."

We drove east toward the mountains. The sun was just rising over the highest peak of all, one somebody of an academic turn had called Olympus, and the name suited because that mountain was a ranch by itself of golden cloves and wild oats, marked with lines of green where the sycamore springs ran down and made good growing for the oaks. Jed Elkins turned three hundred head of weaner calves up there each autumn and let them run till they became cattle. They were well on their way now, and Bonny and I had the job of helping them along daily with a little rolled barley and cottonseed and, when I wouldn't listen, Bonny would talk to them.

"Tell me," he said, and I knew he had got an idea somewhere, "you remember bringing them little cattle off Olympus Labor Day for the dehorning? It took four of us all day. Now, if I do the same in an hour, aren't I doing four men's labor?"

"Sounds like you are," I admitted.

"So I do the labor of four men," continued Bonny, "aren't I entitled to the wages of them four?"

"Reasonably speaking," I said, "you might be so entitled. Yes."

Bonny's cigarette holder worked up until it nearly set the brim of his hat afire, a sure sign his mind had hold of something big. "I'm hittin' Elkins for a raise," he said. "You watch . . . you just watch me now, and I'll show you."

The place we fed cattle was a hollow in the side of Olympus where a cañon widens and a number of washes come down through the rock. The walls are pitted by the weather into caves where owls live. That hollow itself might be an acre across, and it held, as usual, about a dozen white-faced calves waiting for us.

Bonny got excited as soon as he saw them. "H-o-o-o-o-o-o, babies!" he cried the old greeting, and they replied in kind, and he answered them: "C-o-m-e, babies! H-o-w's my babies?" and they answered with one voice, crowding all around the pickup: "H-U-N-G-R-Y! H-U-N-G-R-Y!"

This was the conversation Bonny carried on with cattle, along with a lot more that only he and the cattle could understand. Yet I have been riding through a field, or come over a ridge when he did not know I was around, and watched and heard him talking to those little cattle, stopping his fence mending or errand running or whatever he happened to be doing at the time, to go and talk with his babies. And they were his babies. Bonny had laid his hands on every one of them. He helped them be born. He cut, marked, vaccinated, and docked their tails. And when the time came for them to leave their mothers and grow, he would climb the shoulders of Olympus and dig out the springs and fix the leaky troughs with redwood slivers that swell with the water, so that his babies might have something to drink.

Now he got out of the truck to give his general call. He did this like an opera singer, by resting one hand on the fender brace of the truck and swelling up and letting go with a giant's version of what he had been saying: "C-O-M-E, babies!" And the babies answered and came. From the brakes and gullies, off the slope, up the cañon, from everywhere they came until the sides of Olympus ran red with cattle. This always made Bonny shake with excitement. "See, they know me. They know me!" he would explain. And yet these were but a small part of the cattle, just the lazier ones who stayed near, waiting to be fed.

"Now," said Bonny, when we had put out our feed into the wooden troughs, "you come with me and I'll show you. Just imagine you're the boss."

He led the way up one of those washes that pitch down as steep and bare as the slides in a school yard. We had to lean forward to climb. The rock was of sandstone at first, and then it changed to something harder and darker. Bonny felt his hand along the wall and said, with a prospector's smile: "Granite." We climbed, and again he felt the wall and said approvingly: "Granite. Joshua could have done the job alone if he'd had this."

We had come to a place that was like a chimney in the rock, leading to the sky and a bright patch of Olympus fringed with trees that you could see away up there like a splash of sunlight. The sight made Bonny tell me the story of the two kings and the cloth of gold. These two kings met one time in a meadow with all their people to declare friendship. They spread a pillow and a gold cloth, standing for Virtue. Then the first king took a glass of wine standing for the blood of his country, and the second king took another standing for the same, and they dumped those wine glasses on the cloth of gold till the wine mingled together and ran down. Bonny said that was how the sides of Olympus would run with cattle when he shouted.

"I'm a-gonna do it here," he said determinedly, glancing around him like a murderer.

"Go ahead," I told him, and he did. He inhaled. He expanded, and then he made the sound, and it was a sound. It flushed the white owls screaming from their caves. It peeled off the face of the stone and sent it crumbling into tiny avalanches. It brought a rock as big as an egg splintering onto the floor of the wash between us, and I shouted: "Bonny, that rock might have killed you!" and he grinned back: "What do you think of my idea now?"

"Fine," I said, still shouting because the echoes kept coming back, "fine, you've convinced me!"

He was going to try it again when I stopped him. There had begun to be a rumble in the wash. The sound was as though a train were coming far away, or perhaps as though water had broken loose somewhere farther up. It grew; it sharpened; it became three express trains ready to burst out of a tunnel. I went for one wall and Bonny for the other. There was no climbing—a lizard could not have climbed from that wash—so I had to turn and watch the leaders of the cattle come around the bend, pour around that corner in the rock, and begin talking and trying to stop as they saw Bonny, fail to stop, be shoved on down still trying and, in their effort, widening that freshet of cattle till the churning feet were beside my feet, and I could have touched the nearest steer. Then they broke on by and were gone in a rumble down the wash. I knew I had started to sweat and that my belly was a pad of dampness.

Then here they came again, and again, and again, seeing Bonny, trying to stop for him, then breaking and passing on down like so many loads down a coal chute. At the end there was Bonny grinning and trying to tell me: "This ain't nothin'. This here holler granite's like a pianer scale. You'd oughta see me play her a hundred yards higher!"

"Never mind," I said. "I'll take your word."

He walked and slid down to the feed troughs. There was a churning acre of calves, and it took some tall explaining from Bonny to tell them why no cottonseed was in those empty troughs. But at last he made himself clear, and we were in the pickup driving home. "You know," he said, "those little cattle are sure fond of me. I wisht I had a couple hundred like 'em to get a start with Verna."

Verna was Bonny's widow woman. He had met her through the Lonely Hearts Club. He had written and asked them for a promising widow woman in a mind to marry, and they had sent him two addresses, one in Santa Ysabel, one in Oakland. He had tried the Santa Ysabel one first. The answer had come right back. He and the lady had quickly discovered an interest in getting married and agreed to meet one Saturday afternoon in the park. At four o'clock Bonny was there, in his best new suit and tie. He waited an hour and forty minutes by the goldfish pool and the only living creature he saw was the large colored lady on the bench opposite. "She made as if she was gonna approach me, once," he told us afterward, "but it was just scratchin'." But when we kidded him about it, he flared up with genuine regret: "I should 'a' spoke to her. She probably was lonesome in her heart just like I was."

When he had written to the second address, Bonny had asked for a picture and when it came, signed: "Love, Verna," he showed it around the bunkhouse, and we agreed she must be a widow, all right, because no man could stay married to a face like that and live. Bonny thought she was fine. They met downtown in Oakland. She was needing some new stockings at the time, so Bonny bought her those. Then it was a new bridge, so Bonny arranged that with the dentist. Finally there were one or two items of insurance to settle, and the wedding day was set for Christmas, which was the day Bonny had in mind now, as he told me: "We'll take a herd of heifers, borrow, and calf 'em out to pay the loan. I'll find some city youngster with a rich old man ready to set him up in the cattle business, and he and I'll go partners. Backing's all I need. I got the woman that can put me over . . . really polite, you know, appreciative of them eight-thousand-dollar homes, them beautiful terraces and the rest. Oh, she'll make it easy, as a woman can . . . or she can be ornerier'n buckskin. Cross her once, maybe give her a black eye, and sure as hell she'll go to town shopping the next day, just to get even. Tell me, now, honest," he said, "how much is that steel company gonna give for my pinch bar?"

"Why, I can't guess, Bonny," I told him. "I haven't any idea."

"I figure ten thousand," said Bonny. "Shucks, what's ten thousand dollars more or less to them big fellers? They don't skimp, that's why they're where they are. And just to show 'em I play the game square, I'll drop the first two thousand right back in their company. And then I'll drop a couple in Standard Oil, that's a good company. But the bigger part I'll save . . . it'll start Verna and me with about three hundred little cattle, like them we've left back there."

And so we pulled into the yard just at noon, when Tim, the old China cook, was ringing his bell. That dinner bell always made Jingo, the blue Australian shepherd dog, howl miserably, and this gave Bonny an idea so that he broke off what he was saying, thought an instant, and then explained to me: "Know why he howls? Jingo's part Saint Bernard . . . see? . . . and he thinks it's them monastery bells a-callin' him home."

It had come just before lunch. When Bonny arrived, we were all eating, and there it was propped against his coffee mug, the letter. Bonny ignored it and sat down.

"See you've got mail," said Derringer after a minute. He was top hand. He and Bonny never did get along because Bonny talked with cattle, and for a bronc stomper out of Arizona and a master of his art that is like going to church without your pants—it just ain't done.

"Read us your letter, Bonny," urged Sammy Lee. "I'll bet Verna has to have a new pair of shoes by Saturday."

"Now, all of you are wrong," said Jacob, the irrigator. He kept Jed's alfalfa wet, an old Mormon out of Salt Lake City, and he said: "Nawsir, it's from the chairman . . . the chairman of the board. And they're all gonna make Bonny vice-president, and we'll have to call him 'Mister.' "

So the talk ran, and Bonny put his face into his plate and let it go, but he didn't touch the letter. Not until Sammy Lee passed him the coffee. Without thinking, Bonny picked up the letter to get at his cup and, once he had it in his hand, he couldn't set it down.

"Read out," was the word. And Bonny did. He read out loud and clear and steady as a judge:

*Dear Mister McPhail:*
*In receiving your last letter, I note the smell of liquor on the flap of the*

*envelope where you licked it. After what happened to my late husband, I told you before I never could marry a man who drinks. Believing you have done this to other women, I am returning your ring by parcel post.*

*Verna H.*

Bonny folded up the letter and continued his meal. There was silence. Then one by one the boys started filing out and finally Old Jed, the boss. Old Texas Jed was a kind man. He had the face of a gourd a hundred years old, and he said gently as he passed, "You fellers burn the upper pasture this afternoon and clear out them brush piles so we can plow."

Then Bonny and I were alone, with only the chipper of Tim out in the kitchen talking Chinese to the cats. The clock on the shelf ticked. Bonny looked up for the first time, and I thought of faces of animals I had seen go silly and out of shape with pain as he said, baring his teeth in a silly old grin and shaking a fist at the walls and the world outside: "The combat deepens! On ye brave!" This was not a new saying of Bonny's. I'd heard him use it before. It was his version of what the knight, Roland, had said at the battle of Roncesvalles.

✪

The field we burned in that afternoon was summer-fallow land running up against Olympus where some woodchoppers had worked the year before and left their piles of trimmings, brown now and ready for burning before we could plow. Bonny and I carried out gunny sacks and old crankcase oil in our pickup, dipped and fired the sacks, and spread them through the piles. Toward mid-afternoon a breeze came up the valley from the ocean and made the fires leap. Soon we were going around in the early winter dusk, and I had not seen Bonny for some time when I met him at a big pyre, leaning on his pitchfork, watching the figures leaping in the flames that live only for a second and are gone. I joined him and looked, too, and finally he said, without turning from the fire: "Michael Archangelo . . . he was a great painter, but he never made statues like those," meaning the figures in the flame, and then very thoughtfully: "Women has got to be whole hog

**Robert Easton  443**

or none. . . . Bob, women has got to be like Caesar's wife: out of the question." That was the most Bonny ever said to anyone on the matter of the letter.

He and I worked together afterward, while the wind freshened from the sea, turning colder and putting a lid of clouds over the valley. We rounded off and covered the fires against the wind, loaded our tools, and started home with the wind rising beside us through the dark trees in a way that made both wind and trees alive—a kind of edging and building toward something cold and wilder. Then we turned the corner, and I could look back and see the string of red dots shining like rubies in a belt around Olympus. "Our fires, Bonny," I said. "The wind brought them alive. We'd better go back."

We stopped the truck.

"Gee, ain't them pretty fires?" said Bonny.

"We'd better go along back," I told him.

The fires kept winking on and off like fireflies, while we watched, and Bonny said that was soldiers passing between us and the fires, though it was only the wind freshening and dying. Finally the lights went out. He waited another ten minutes and drove home.

✪

The last I remember was the sound of Bonny cleaning his teeth on the bunkhouse porch where the wash basins were. The next I knew I'd overslept. There was light in the room and voices outside. I got to the window barefoot. There was the light coming in the east, just as it should be, but it wasn't daylight, it was fire. The ridge of Mt. Olympus hung up there in the sky like a huge rainbow of flame.

Two minutes later I was meeting Derringer and Jed Elkins by the corner of the barn and Derringer was saying, as he watched the fingers of that fire take and run: "Not with a horse, you can't," but Old Jed was answering him: "We can try, we sure can try to get those little cattle out."

Bonny arrived. He was short of breath, missing his hat, and his shirt was not tucked in at all. He took a good look and went off running as though the devil were behind him.

"Where's he going?" Jed demanded.

"Crazy," said Derringer.

"Let's get out the horses," said Jed.

The three of us hit the barn together, and three more came and added to the confusion in the dark, till horses we had known for years were rearing and pulling back and threatening to knock the barn down. There was no rope that would untie, no bridle that fitted, and if we had forgotten how to swear, we should really have been lost. As it was, we got through.

Somehow we gathered outside, everybody, even Tim in his China-black slippers and beanie-hat, saying over and over in a terrible sing-song: "Missa Jed. Missa Jed . . . cattle burn all up?" And just as we gathered there at the barn door a vehicle shot by in the darkness, going at least sixty miles an hour, and we had the briefest, wildest glimpse of the face of Bonny McPhail, his hair flying, his fist clenched and shaking, and his fighting words: "The combat deepens! On ye brave!" We moved out then.

Bonny was gone faster than the wind, but we did fairly well. These were the smearing gusts. They caught us like a squall does a row of trees, and you could feel the clothes flattened to your back and your hat smashed down and even the lacing of the horse's tail about your thighs, and then the gust dropped you and did the same to the man ahead. The fire had traced out the main ridge of the mountain. Now a long pincer was nipping out along the farming land, breaking over into one fresh ravine after another where it would take with the draft, like a match set to a jet of gas, and go running clear to the summit. Olympus was being cut into ribbons of flame.

The fire sounded almost alive. You could hear it above the wind, spitting like a big cat on the prowl, mean and ugly and muttering along, until it found a patch of brush it liked and could lick over and relish a minute. Then it would go right up to heaven in a snarl. It smeared suddenly on the grass, where the wind hit hard. It left behind the glowing skeletons of trees. It lit everything with a hellish yellow light and roared and muttered and talked among its different parts like a monster, and yet over and above all this you could hear something, a human sound. It came from the shoulders of Olympus. It might have been old Jove himself up there, calling to hand the thunder and telling the waters to be still. Because you could hear him. You could hear Bonny above all the wind and fire, going out and echoing between the summer fallow and the dark sky. "H-O-O-O-O-O, babies! C-O-M-E, babies!"

"By golly," I heard Jed say, "it's Bonny!"

I did not try to tell him it was the general call.

Then we rode. The long pincer of that lower flame was pouring over the ridges, hesitating on each crest, gathering like a big snake and then pouring on over with a lunge and a snapping to ride with the wind. Before we tried to race it, we were beaten. In the cañon where Bonny and I had fed the cattle it sent a jet skyward that made Olympus echo and shake, but over it we heard the general call: "C-O-M-E, my babies! T-H-I-S way, babies!"

Then the voice went off short as though a knife had cut. We stopped riding without knowing why we did. The fire went on across the mountain. Then it began, a faint sound like the rushing of many wings. Then it was a deep, positive rumble close to the ground as though a dam of water had broken loose. Then here it came in a ragged line breaking through the fire, of shapes of cattle, falling and crying and pressing on, some burning, some already charred, some falling and skidding and showering sparks. They came down lunging out of that fire like shapes in a dream. They were unbelievable. Their noise was like the cry of terrified children first in pain; and they went by and would have run us down, if we had not moved, in endless driblets that were agony themselves, dropping off a dead one here and there, smelling bitterly of charred flesh and hair like a thousand corrals at branding time, and so on down into the flat land, a long mass that glowed with its own burning and marked the way.

Far below in the farming ground the herd drew together and circled in a radiant wheel that cried aloud and broke apart gradually to extinguish itself, a section at a time. Derringer blurted out as if he were in pain himself: "Why don't they git apart? Why don't they git apart?" But Old Jed answered, as calmly as though he'd seen it every night of his life: "They're rubbin' ag'in' one another. They're rollin' in that plowed land."

At dawn the wind swung into the east and turned the fire back.

We watched it die on the ridges and fade away on the slopes where the cattle in October had grazed off all the grass. We heard it whimpering out in the cañons when we set Sammy Lee and Tim rounding up the little cattle that roamed the summer-fallow land still crying, though it was like moaning now—the sound little children make long after what hurt them has gone.

We rode into one cañon with the sun, toward the hollow where Bonny and I used to feed cattle. The fire was still burning in the fallen trees, and the walls held and multiplied the heat like metal. We rode over lumps in the trail that had once been cattle. The rising air had killed the owls, too, and they lay dead along the bluffs. A hundred yards up the wash that pitches into the hollow as steep and bare as a slide in the school yard we found what was left of Bonny. The fire had not touched him, only the loving feet of his babies. And there he was.

"He'd nearly made it," muttered Derringer. "The poor fool."

"Well, he had an idea," Old Jed said thoughtfully.

Jacob added his: "Them city's walls come down, all right, as in the Bible days, but they come down on top o' Bonny."

You see, none of them knew you can play a hollow granite wash like you can a piano scale, if you have the knowledge. And they never will believe me when I tell them, though they handle Bonny's name differently now. In fact, they have changed the name of Mt. Olympus and called it after him.

# The Girl Who Busted Broncos

### S. Omar Barker

⊙

*Born in a log cabin in Beulah, New Mexico, S(quire) Omar Barker first started to write in 1923 and had several animal stories accepted by* Adventure. *"I came to write Western fiction for several reasons," he commented to us in a letter in 1978 (when he was, as he put it, eighty-four and a half years old). "Born and raised on a small mountain ranch, I . . . knew more about cowboys, cattle, and ranch life than anything else, and have always considered cowboys and ranch folks a very special and admirable breed, worth writing about both in the past and the present. I consider the . . . old-time cowboy . . . a folk-hero, a proud, traditional legend, not a myth. The practical reason for my writing Westerns is . . . the Western pulp fiction magazines were a wide open market, not only for fiction but also for fact and for verse, of which I wrote a great deal as well as stories." In the course of his career as an author and poet he wrote about 2,000 poems, about 1,200 factual articles, and approximately 1,500 short stories and short novels published in around 100 magazines. Although he wrote several juveniles, he produced only one adult novel,* Little World Apart *(Doubleday, 1966). His brand was the Lazy S.O.B. "The Girl Who Busted Broncos" first appeared in* The Saturday Evening Post *(December 16, 1950) and has not been previously collected.*

**H**ackamore Higgins was sitting on a stump, blow-sucking "My Darling Nellie Gray" on a mouth harp when Mr. Ignatz Head-of-a-Cow and Mr. Joe-Mary Morning Star rode up on a pair of Diamond Dot ponies. These two Spanish-American gentlemen of the saddle had been christened Ignacio Cabeza de Baca and José Maria Lucero. The translation had been Hackamore Higgins's idea. Ignatz was a skinny little rooster in a big black hat. His eyes were small, black, and humorous. Joe-Mary was a fat little *hombre* in another big black sombrero. His eyes were big, brown, and innocent.

The harp player on the stump was a gray-eyed *gringo* with red-blond hair and the long, lean back of a rider. He wore frizzledy cowboy duds and a curled-silk, rusty-red stand of two-months-no-shave. There was the look of a cowboy about him, but the axe, grubbing hoe, and team of twitch-tailed jack mules were plainly implements of land clearing, not of cowpunching.

"Hallo, keed!" Mr. Ignatz Head-of-a-Cow flavored the Mexican accent of his English with a buckaroo breeziness as cheerful as the chirp of a cheek-full chipmunk. "Whassamatta, you playin' lovesick *música* to the mules?"

"Go to hell, too," said Hackamore Higgins.

"*Señorita* Smeeth have quit hees job an' goned to Denbar," offered Ignatz, batting his eyes.

"Let 'er go gallyger," said the cowboy.

"The boss got new teacher for the keeds," went on Ignatz with a gleam in his shiny black optics. "Named Phibby Marteen. She is a horsewoman."

"My cousin got one horsewoman," bragged Mr. Joe-Mary Morning Star, "weeth the nize mule colt!"

"Thas not a horsewoman, stupid!" Ignatz corrected him scornfully. "Thas a woman-horse! *Caballo mujer!* Whassamatta, you don't spik corrected English!"

"Hah!" Joe-Mary passed his companion's scorn right back at him, with some to spare. "A dog spik better Spanish than those!"

"So I am a dog, eh?"

Instead of wasting more wind on words, Mr. Ignatz Head-of-a-Cow proceeded to yank Mr. Joe-Mary Morning Star's hat down over his eyes, jerk out his shirttail, and give his horse's tail a twist, apparently all in one motion. The startled cow pony bucked a couple, but the little matter of a sombrero down over his eyes didn't keep the dumpling cowboy from staying on top. He spurred the pony around and came back to snap the popper on the end of his quirt about half an inch from the thin, eagle-beak nose of Mr. Ignatz Head-of-a-Cow.

"Hey, no fights!" Hackamore Higgins barged in between them in time to prevent the ruckus from roostering up into a sure-'nough quirting match. Or maybe it would not have, anyhow.

In the days before a combination of woman and horse trouble had made him blow up his job as bronc peeler for the Diamond Dot, Hackamore Higgins had stepped in to prevent these two wagglewits from quirting the hell out of each other more times than he could count. Only he never knew for sure whether it was really necessary or not. One minute they might be snarling and waving their quirts at each other like hell wouldn't hold 'em and the next leaning on each other to sing a duet.

"*Zás!*" exclaimed Joe-Mary, giving his quirt a whack on his worn leather chaps for emphasis. "If I get mad, I wheep somebody two inches from his life!"

"Sure," agreed Hackamore Higgins. "But as long as you ain't mad right now, maybe you'll tell me what you two sheep thieves are up to. You sure never rode all the way up here just to sweat your horses!"

"Maybe we camed looking for estray horse," said Joe-Mary.

"The boss still ain't hire no broncs peeler on your place," said Ignatz.

"The fimmale Miss Smeeth have gone back to Denbar," said Joe-Mary.

"The new keeds' teacher got beeg-size nose, tooths like a wolf, shape like a bromestalk, a wobble of the jaw. She don't make no eyes to the man," said Ignatz.

"She is a woman-horse," said Joe-Mary.

"No danger to fall in love weeth thees one," said Ignatz.

"So what?" inquired Hackamore Higgins sharply.

"Thas what you theenk!" Ignatz shrugged and waggled a lean brown finger at him. "I bet you joost bustin' to come back to the job of broncs busting for the Diamond Dot, same like before!"

"You're wastin' your wind, pals," said Hackamore Higgins. "When I got throwed by a bronc and throwed over by a gal all in the same day, I figgered it was time to lay aside my young and foolish ways . . . an' done so. I swore off both broncs an' women, drawed my time, an' come way off up here in the hills to clear me a little bean patch where a man can ponder in peace. If you two sheep thieves think you can come belly-bustin' up here an' double-talk me into goin' back to bronc peelin' for the Diamond Dot just because the gal that give me the mitten has been replaced by a wobble-jawed woman with an outsize

nose, you're both just as crazy as you talk. Because I ain't a-goin' . . .
you savvy?"

The two Diamond Dot riders swapped eye-batting glances.

"Hah!" said Ignatz.

"Hah!" echoed Joe-Mary.

" 'Hah' hell!" snorted Hackamore. "I meant it, boys! Come on up
to the shack, an' I'll steam up the coffee pot."

As they stepped into the one room of Hackamore's unfinished log
cabin, the two cowboys stared at the unheard-of luxury of a water tap
and a sink.

"By jeengs!" exclaimed Ignatz. "You feex thees place for a
woman!"

"In hees house," said Joe-Mary, "my cousin also have one
keetchen stink, but he don't got no woman . . . joost hees wife!"

Hackamore whipped up a hospitable snack for his former fellow
cowpokes, but it was eaten in strained silence. The visiting cowboys
understood and appreciated the fact that they had ridden the forty
miles up here for the sole purpose of persuading him to give up this
homestead foolishness and come back to his old cowpunching and
bronc-peeling job on the Diamond Dot. But he didn't aim to go. On
that point he had his neck bowed for sure.

He also surmised that they might not be above hurrawing him a
little over the circumstances under which he had suddenly sworn off
bronc busting—and women. Hackamore had just been fixing to ride
a snorty sorrel bronc its first saddle when Miss Adele Smith came out,
apparently to watch him. Black-haired, petite, the Dodson kids' private teacher was plenty pretty. Maybe looking at her had made him
dizzy, or maybe he had tried to show off too much because he knew
she was watching. Anyhow the sorrel colt had bucked his hat off, the
second jump, and sailed him after it, the third—so high that his shirttail flapped like a cow-camp towel in a blizzard. And Adele Smith,
whose flirtatious smile in the two weeks she had been at the Diamond
Dot had got him so razzle-dazzled he didn't know straight up—this
city gal who didn't know any more about bronc riding than a hog does
about Sunday—had stood and laughed at him for getting thrown.
Galled to the gizzard, but still badly smitten, Hackamore Higgins had

got up and, without even picking up his hat, vaulted over the fence and caught the girl by both wrists.

"Listen here, little lady!" he had busted out angrily. "I don't allow no gal to laugh at my bronc ridin'... unless she's goin' to marry me! Now how about it?"

Then was when she laughed, sure enough. "Marry you?" she had giggled. "That's even funnier than your bronc riding!"

That was the first time he had ever suffered the double temptation of wanting both to kiss a woman and to kick her, but he found himself just a little too much of a gentleman to do either. Instead, he had abruptly turned his back on her, caught, unsaddled, and turned the sorrel bronc loose. It was the first time in his life that he had ever failed to climb right back on any horse that had spilled him. Then, before he had time to cool off, he had gone to old George Dodson and asked for his time.

Now Joe-Mary and Ignatz smacked their lips loudly over his biscuits and gravy and glared at each other solemnly.

"If somebody say that Jáquima Higgins got scared to ride some bronco because one time he fall off," observed Ignatz, "I knock him onto the middle of nex' week."

"One time," said Joe-Mary, "my cousin keeck a pig on hees back porch, turned out it was a bear!"

"Her name," said Ignatz, "is Phibby Marteen. She...."

"Hah!" broke in Joe-Mary. "Bears don't got no name!"

Gloomy silence fell also upon his visitors, broken only when they were once more a-straddle of their cayuses, ready to ride away.

"Well, good bye, keed!" Ignatz shrugged a sigh. "I forgot to told you Miss Phibby Marteen trying to beat the broncs, by jeengs, herself!"

"Hey, hold on a minute!" exclaimed the *gringo* cowboy. "You mean ol' George is lettin' a woman...?"

But already Mr. Ignatz Head-of-a-Cow and Mr. Joe-Mary Morning Star were galloping off down the draw in a fog of dust.

✪

Hackamore Higgins didn't ride his mule on up to the house. Out here in the corral there didn't seem to be anybody around. Evidently the Diamond Dot crew was all out some place on cow work. Yet here in the round bronc corral were six glossy four-year-olds, switching and stomping at flies. It had taken Hackamore a week to make up his mind—and then not for sure. Anyhow, here he was, back at the Diamond Dot.

He unsaddled his mule behind a shed out of sight of the house, carried his saddle inside the bronc-corral gate, and began letting out a loop in his rope. It felt good in his hands. He had forefooted and thrown a sleek little bay gelding and was fixing to slip a hackamore on its head when a voice, throaty but definitely feminine, spoke behind him at the corral gate.

"You could have caught him easier with oats," it said in a tone of mild reproach.

Hackamore managed to resist an urgent impulse to see what the owner of such a voice looked like.

"Go 'way," he said.

"Hmm!" said the voice. "You must be that crazy Hackamore Higgins I've been hearing about."

"I ain't Daniel Boone," grunted Hackamore, still without turning.

"If my whiskers were pink," said the voice, "I'd borrow somebody's sharp axe and chop them off."

Guitar music—soft. Thrumming guitar music—that was what the voice reminded him of. He could feel it doing things to the inside of him that he'd better put a stop to, right now. Doubtless this was the homely horsewoman governess Ignatz and Joe-Mary had told him about. Since ignoring her didn't seem to do any good, maybe the best way to get rid of her would be to talk plumb rude. He remembered Ignatz's description.

"Whiskers," he said, "are a heap easier to keep out of other folks' business than a great big nose!"

Whatever effect the rude remark might have had was spoiled by the fact that at that moment the bronc got back enough of his knocked-out wind to jerk his head free, bunch his muscles, and get up, neatly upsetting the cowboy as he did so. Hackamore listened for a laugh or a giggle that he could get good and mad about and actually felt disappointed that he didn't hear any. The bay colt joined the other broncs, circling the corral with the rope still dragging from one front foot. The cowboy got to his feet, still stubbornly avoiding a direct look at the owner of that disturbing voice, and started after his rope. Out of the corner of his eye he glimpsed a tall slender figure in faded blue denim coming out into the corral, a pan of oats in one hand, a hackamore in the other.

"Wait a minute, Pink Whiskers," she said. "Let me catch him for you."

Then, before he could have said tiddle-my-tucker, she had the bay bronc timidly nosing the oats in her pan. He watched her gently slip the hackamore on his head. Then she turned and came across the corral toward him, the bronc trustfully following her now whether he wanted to or not. But one glance was all it took to make him want to. Instead of the "beeg-size nose, tooths like a wolf, shape like a bromestalk" that Ignatz had mentioned, what he saw was a pertly upturned little nose, the tantalizing, demure smile of as perfectly toothed a mouth as he'd ever admired, a softly rounded chin, warmly golden-brown hair, and a figure that looked about as much like a broom stalk as the letter S does like an I.

"I will be damned!" said Hackamore.

"I've been working with them for nearly two weeks," explained the girl. There was a sparkle of amusement in her warm brown eyes. "I can catch all but one in this bunch the same way."

"I . . . I didn't mean about you ketchin' the bronc," gulped the cowboy. "I mean . . . why, hell, you're plumb pretty!"

For an instant the girl's friendly smile froze into a frown, then she laughed, and a puckish, impudent look came with the blush over her face. "As a teacher it has always been my policy to reward little boys who talk nice," she said with mock gravity. "Would you care for one of my kisses?"

"Ugmm-wmph!" said Hackamore, tricked by surprise into swallowing his wind. "I sure. . . ."

Before he could say "would," the girl pulled several candy kisses wrapped in waxed paper from her pocket and gravely held them out to him. "I always carry them," she said sweetly. "Get a couple of these stuck between your teeth when you climb on a bucker, and it keeps your mouth from flying open. Only the way I gentle them first, most broncs don't pitch much with me anyway."

"I can see why they wouldn't," said Hackamore. He finally found a grin big enough to show a little through his whiskers. "Are you by any chance Miss Phibby Marteen?"

The girl frowned. "So Ignatz and Joe-Mary did ride up to try and lure you back, after all!" She spoke stiffly now. "Yes, Mister Hackamore Higgins, I'm Phoebe Martin, and if you think you can come back here and beat me out of riding these colts after all the trouble I've taken to gentle them, you've got another think coming."

"I like spunky gals, all right," said Hackamore, stiffening up a little his-ownself, "but bronc-bustin' ain't. . . ."

"I am not in the least concerned about what kind of girls you like, Pink Whiskers! All I'm saying is. . . ."

"A bronc corral, damn it, ain't no place for a lady! Just because you've got these colts eatin' out of your hand ain't no sign. . . ."

"Broncs are just like men. They tame awful easy for a little food and currying! Besides. . . ."

"Ain't no sign," broke in Hackamore stubbornly, "that they won't throw you a mile high when you climb on 'em. Fu'thermore. . . ."

"From what I hear, you ought to know about that," said Phoebe Martin sweetly. "At least when I get thrown I. . . ."

"Quit interruptin' me, purty woman," interrupted the cowboy, who knew he was getting hurrawed and wasn't right sure yet how he aimed to take it. "Sure I've been throwed, but what bronc peeler ain't?"

"At least when I get piled," said the girl, "I climb right back on again . . . instead of running off to the hills to raise beans and pink whiskers!"

"Somebody around this place," said Hackamore Higgins, "is a blabbermouth. Wait till I get my hands on them two wobble-jawed Mexkins! I'll . . . !"

"Don't call Ignatz and Joe-Mary 'Mexkins!' They're good, honest Spanish-American cowboys!"

"Honest?" snorted Hackamore. "Those guys told me you . . . well, never mind!"

"Please . . . what did they tell you?"

"They told me you had a long nose, tooths like a wolf, a shape like a bromestalk, a wobble of the jaw, an'. . . ."

"Why . . . why, the doggone Mexican fibbers!" exclaimed the girl, flushing all the way to the edge of her brown-golden hair.

"If they hadn't," said Hackamore, "I wouldn't never have come back here."

"Why?"

"Because," drawled the cowboy, batting his eyes and deliberately reaching for the makin's of a smoke, "I know what a sucker I am for purty teachers."

To Hackamore it looked as if the girl's naturally uptilted nose actually turned itself up a notch higher. "Fortunately," she sniffed, "I know of one teacher who is not a sucker for pink-whiskered cowboys."

"I could put 'em to soak a few days an' shave . . . if it looked like it might be worth the trouble."

"I wouldn't bother if I were you! And now if you'll kindly let me have the corral, maybe I'll have time to saddle this bay colt and give him his first ride before the children's next lesson period."

Hackamore shook his head. "You've got it backwards, purty woman. I come here today a-purpose to take my old job back, an' I'm fixin' to uncork a few myownself . . . just to prove that I still can. Shoo!"

The tall girl didn't shoo. She shrugged. "All right, then . . . we'll both ride one."

"An' if you get your purty neck busted, it'll be your own dang fault! Which one of these broncs did you say your oat-pan pettin' hasn't tamed down any to speak of?"

"The buckskin with the black points. I'm afraid he really will buck. If you'd rather ride one of the gentler ones . . . ?"

"I'd sure hate for you to make me mad, purty woman," said Hackamore. He was already shaking out his loop, but he held it. "I'll help you saddle yours first, anyhow."

That high-chinned her again. "Now you're trying to make me mad. I was raised saddling broncs by myself."

"Suit yourself," he grinned. "An' by the way it's the horn end of the saddle that goes in front!"

Squatted on boot heels against the fence, smoking his brown cigarette, Hackamore Higgins couldn't help admiring the quiet, sure-handed way she got the young bay saddled without a tussle. Doubtless she'd had the saddle on him before, but just the same it was plain she had a way with horses. Whether she could keep the bay from bucking or stay on top of him if he did buck was another question. If she should happen to get hurt. . . .

"All right, Pink Whiskers," she called to him, leading the surprisingly docile bay toward the gate. "If you need any help saddling the buckskin, just holler!"

"Whenever I need any help gearin' up a bronc, I'll shoot myself. Hold on a minute, Miss Martin. If you're fixin' to climb on that colt right away, I'll come hold him."

"I thought I'd let him soak till you're ready with the buckskin," said the girl sweetly. "Then we can both climb on at the same time . . . and see which one stays longer."

There may have been moments when Hackamore could have used a little help all right, for the buckskin showed off pretty salty, but he didn't call for any. It added an extra inch or two to his grudging respect for the girl that she watched him from outside the fence without comment or suggestions. The buckskin didn't pitch with the saddle, but there was a four-hundred-dollar hump in his back, and he kept his tail down tight. Ordinarily Hackamore would have given the bronc his first saddle ride inside the corral, but if a girl whose business was teaching a batch of kids how to spell could ride outside so could he. Phoebe Martin swung open the gate, and he led the buckskin out, surprised at how little the bronc set back on the hackamore reins.

"I can see somebody's been teachin' this baby to lead," he said.

The ground outside was a little sandy and damp from a recent rain. They led the broncs a few yards away from the fence.

"You better let me hold him while you get on."

The cowboy spoke matter-of-factly, trying to keep the anxiety he felt out of his voice. But the girl, with a lift that was as graceful as it was fast and sure, was already up in the saddle. The bay colt moved out, stiff-legged and uncertain, but he did not buck.

Hackamore cheeked the buckskin, got a firm foot in the stirrup, and eased himself into the saddle with one swift motion. Maybe he could have kept the bronc from pitching if he had tried, but he didn't. The buckskin was big, long-legged and limber, with the salt-and-vinegar of rebellion in his soul. He bucked high and hard and snaky, with Hackamore's long legs combing him every jump. The cowboy could remember being thrown by horses no harder to ride than this one—especially once with a girl from Denver watching him—but he didn't aim to be thrown this time, and he wasn't. It took about thirty wild seconds for the buckskin to decide he was wasting his wind and break into a shambly lope. Out of the corner of his eye Hackamore could see the girl following—and the bay colt still hadn't bucked.

"Take it easy, big stuff!" Hackamore gave the buckskin's sweaty neck a firm-handed pat and tugged back on the cotton-rope hackamore reins hard enough to slow him down. Maybe there was just a hint of well-earned brag in the grin he gave Phoebe Martin as she came alongside. "Looks like we got us a couple of saddle horses," he said. "As soon as we work a little of the wobble out of 'em!"

"I'm sure glad I didn't have to ride that one," said the girl. Something about the way she said it made Hackamore feel good.

"Maybe he wouldn't have pitched with you," he said. "You've got magic." *Of more kinds than one*, he added under his breath, unable to cope with a sudden bashfulness that wouldn't let him say it aloud.

Suddenly both broncs threw up their heads, ears pricked sharply off to the right where two riders came loping toward them over a nearby rise. Expert horsemen both, it was the custom of Mr. Ignatz Head-of-a-Cow and Mr. Joe-Mary Morning Star to make their every approach a galloping, free-reined, arm-flapping parade entry, and this was no exception. Hackamore could feel a spooky nervousness tense the bronc's muscles under him.

"Hallo, keed!" Ignatz's buckaroo breeziness sounded more irrepressible than ever. "Don't I told you *Señorita* Phibby Marteen ees a very fine woman-horse?"

He punctuated the compliment by sweeping off his huge black sombrero in a gallant bow to the *señorita*. The bay colt thought he saw the big black thing coming at him and suddenly swallowed his head. So did the buckskin. Hackamore survived the whirl-around—just a little off balance. Maybe he could have got back in the middle and stayed there, if anxiety for the girl hadn't split his attention. As it was, the buckskin's next jump threw him high and far, smack into a mud puddle left by the recent rains. He landed sitting down, and his right hip struck on a rock out of sight in the puddle. When he tried to get up, the numbness in his leg made him splash and flounder around like a shallows-caught water dog. He saw that the bay colt had quit bucking, and Phoebe Martin was still on him. He realized how funny he must look and listened for a laugh.

What he heard instead was something like a gasp: "Oh, Hack!"

He had somehow managed to get to his feet and start limping toward where Ignatz had caught the buckskin by the time the girl had slipped off the bay and come hurrying to him. "Please, Hackamore! You're hurt! Don't get on him again!"

That made him feel good. So did the touch of her hand, but he shook it off and reached for the buckskin's reins that Ignatz held out to him. Instead of its usual grin, the thin brown face of Mr. Ignatz Head-of-a-Cow wore an almost comic look of guilty anguish. "I am the son of a burro!" he cried. "Nex' time I wave some hat on the face of a bronc, I hope somebody kick me in the pants!"

"I knowed I was on a bronc," said Hackamore. He cheeked the buckskin, got a firm foot in the stirrup, and swung his numb leg across the saddle. "Now scatter your marbles, big stuff," he said, and the buckskin promptly obliged him.

Maybe he was glad it didn't take long this time to smooth the buckskin out, but he didn't say so. He gave the sweaty neck a friendly slap and swung him around. Phoebe Martin was astride the now docile bay colt again, schooling him to rein. The grin that broke out through Hackamore's mud-smeared whiskers was comradely—and maybe a little more.

"Purty woman," he said, "I see you know how to ride!"

The smile she gave him made Hackamore Higgins forget the pain throbbing in his hip. "You did all right yourownself, Pink Whiskers," she said.

Now Ignatz also ventured to grin. "Thees bronc peeler," he chuckled, "he also know how to fly an' to swim!"

"One time my cousin go swimming in the reever," said Mr. Joe-Mary Morning Star, "but not from purpose. He theenk hees wife poosh heem!"

The girl was the first to laugh, and Hackamore had a hunch that maybe it wasn't just Joe-Mary's comic comment on his cousin that she was laughing at. Like as not she was remembering how funny a long-legged buckaroo had looked, both on the wing and splashing around in the mud. But now it was all right. Now was the time to laugh. There was a twinkle in her warm brown eyes. "I've just been wondering . . . ," she said and stopped.

"Wonderin' what, purty woman?"

"If you and I could handle this bronc-busting job just as well without those darn whiskers!"

Hackamore sensed that she wasn't just joking now—and that was all right, too. It made him feel good, just the way a man ought to feel about that kind of a girl.

# Mule Tracks

## Dwight Bennett Newton

*Born in Kansas City, Missouri, Dwight Bennett Newton went on to complete work for a master's degree in history at the University of Missouri. From the time he first discovered Max Brand in Street & Smith's* Western Story Magazine, *he knew he wanted to be an author of Western fiction. What makes Newton's fiction so special is the combination of characters who seem real and about whom a reader comes to care a great deal and Newton's fundamental humanity, his realization early on (perhaps because of his study of history) that little that happened in the West was ever simple but rather made desperately complicated through the conjunction of numerous opposed forces working at cross-purposes. Yet, through all the turmoil on the frontier, a basic human decency did emerge. Among his finest novels are* The Avenger *(Perma Books, 1956), now reprinted under the restored title* Lone Gun *in a hardcover Gunsmoke edition from Chivers;* Crooked River Cañon *(Doubleday, 1966);* The Big Land *(Doubleday, 1972), which is available in a full-length audio version from Books on Tape; and* Disaster Creek *(Doubleday, 1981). This story first appeared as "Peaker Kid" in* .44 Western *(November 1953), but Newton changed the title back to his own when it was reprinted in* Bad Men and Good *(Dodd, Mead, 1953), the first Western Writers of America story collection.*

**S**ixty years, you would think, ought to dim out on a person, yet everything about the start of this story I'm going to tell you is as clear today as it ever was. I can close my eyes now and picture up that street in Kansas City, jammed with gold-crazy Peakers and in the midst of it a sick kid with the bottom dropped out of his world. I can feel the way the sun smashed down and just how the dust stung your nose—awful hot and dry for that time of spring. Everybody east of the river seemed bound for the diggings—by stage if they had the tariff, which few did, otherwise by any means they could find. There were horsebackers and people in wagons. Here and there you'd actually see some pilgrim afoot, toting his belongings in a handcart or wheelbarrow or even on his back. Far as I was concerned, though, Kansas City looked like the end of the line.

And then, needing a friend the worst of all my life, I found old Tom Bolling. Rather, he found me. All of a sudden he was there, an old man with snow-white hair but, I was to learn, tough like cured leather. "What was your trouble, lad," he asked me, "with the redhead on yonder wagon?"

"It's my wagon!" I said. "Drove clear from Illinois. I met a couple fellows said they'd split expenses for carrying them to the diggings and, when I left them with the outfit a minute, I come back and found they'd sold it and run!"

"Can you describe them?"

I did, as best I could, but he only shook his head. "You'll hardly find them again in such a jam. Nor could this man who paid good money for the team and rig be expected to hand it back."

I knew that. I was grateful he'd even let me fetch some personal belongings from under the seat—or at least what those two crooks hadn't made off with. I still had my case knife with the broken horn handle and a Bible my mom gave me which I'm afraid didn't show much sign of use. But my dad's big turnip watch was missing, the one that had a winding key to it and a fob with a little picture of my folks worked in. It wasn't worth nothing, didn't even run a month at a time, but losing it was the last straw. When my folks died, I'd had nothing else left of them except the wagon and team, salvaged from loss of our farm two years before in the panic of '57 and which I'd been figuring would get me to the mines. Now rig and watch were both gone.

Well, the watch is right here by my elbow, as I sit scratching all this down on paper. How I come to get it back is part of the story I'm telling you.

Tom said: "I'm real sorry, lad. Wish I could help. Would you be interested in a job?"

"No, thanks," I answered. "I'm just a no-good Peaker, I reckon, but I'm going out to those diggings if I have to crawl there on my hands and knees!"

He smiled. "No need of that. This job will get you to the mines . . . if you know anything about mules, that is."

"I've rassled one or two."

"Good profits in packing supplies to the gold fields this season with either a freight outfit or animal train. I've got a string ready to leave, but there's just my boy and me and I druther have another hand along, especially if he knows mules. Trip would last maybe two months. Grub and expenses and fifty dollars cash when we get there. What do you say?"

Just so it would help get me to the mines I'd've said yes to anything right then. I was husky for my age—though you mightn't think so looking at me now, in 1918, and I got no tintypes to prove it by. I told him I figured I could make a hand for this mule outfit of his. So Tom Bolling took me to where he had them penned, and I met his boy, Chuck—a gangling fellow a few years older than me.

Tom said: "We'll start packing directly come sunup. I suggest we turn in early."

But somehow I didn't sleep much that night. Too excited, maybe. After all, tomorrow I'd be on my way to the diggings—Pike's Peak or bust, fellows! When I did sleep, it was to dream about those crooks and my dad's watch they'd stolen. I woke up wondering if I'd ever run across them again, and what would happen if I did.

In early gray dawn we picked our first victim and tried our hands at packing an ornery, half-broke mule. We hemmed him in a corner, and I took his head, while Chuck came with the wooden saddle. Soon as he saw it, his ears went back, and then he was out of my hands and trying to climb straight up the rails of the pen. Immediately all the others, seeing the trouble their friend was in, begun bucking and tearing around, raising the dust, and their heels looking big as fry pans.

"Open the gate!" screamed old Tom. "Get him out of here before they murder us!"

So Chuck lowered the bars while I clamped onto the hackamore like grim death, knowing if I let go we would just be shy a mule. Once safe from those heels, we finally got the saddle on and cinched down tight, and for some reason the old boy quieted like a lamb. Tom yelled: "He knows when he's licked! Now, quick . . . load him up!"

Our trade goods were done in bundles, ready to go, so it wasn't hard to throw them on the crossbar and batten them in place and cover the works with a tarpaulin, lashed tight. Our first mule was packed but, as we mopped our brows and stepped back for a look, he flew to pieces. In five good jumps he had the pack scattered to hell and gone with all to do over again. And eleven more mules in the pen.

Well, we done it but only after a crowd had gathered to lend a hand. The dust really flew. It took as many men as could crowd around, and even then we had to choke some of those critters nearly unconscious to get the saddles on them. About five in the afternoon we had the last one ready. I could have collapsed, but old Tom's eye had a determined glint.

"Fetch the horses, Chuck!" he ordered. "Let's hit the trail!"

We made three miles that first day. It began to look like the hard way to Denver. After Tom managed to cook a little something for dinner, we sat around the fire and ate in silence. That first night on the prairie, with a black sky pressing down and no other humans anywhere near us—except for Kansas City, of course, three miles east—I think it kind of come over me, the size of the thing we'd tackled.

Tom asked quietly, "Still set on Pike's Peak, lad?"

"Just hope we get there before the claims run out," I told him grimly. "I'm going to make my fortune in the diggings. And not driving mules, either!"

"I was in the rush to California," Tom Bolling said after a time. "Right in the midst of it. Took a steamer from New York, waded through the malaria swamps of Panama, and caught another boat heading north along the coast. Of course, I was ten years younger then."

"Gosh!" I said. "Did you find any gold, Tom?"

He hesitated. "No. Not very many did. I got my eyes full, though. Seen things I wish I never had. . . ."

"Like what?"

"Well, in the gold fields, son, men live sort of on the raw edge. Take some decent fellow that used to read his Bible and loved his mother when he was back home in the States . . . out there the lust for gold can turn him into a killer. I've seen men strike down their partners over a bag of dust. I'm hoping you and Chuck won't be running into nothing like that."

His talk sobered me. Dead tired as I was, I lay a long time worrying as I listened to the prairie breeze and picket chains dragging as the mules and horses drifted around. All at once I found myself clutching the Bible in my coat pocket. Maybe I hadn't read it as much as I should. Starting tomorrow I'd dig into it some every day. And I loved my mother too. Any man was a liar said I didn't. Lying there in the night, I could see her face plain against the stars—clear and fresh in my mind as if she hadn't died five years ago. With daylight, though, things looked different. I remembered my silent promise to break the Bible out, but just then there wasn't time. We had a quick breakfast and then rounded the mules in and fell to work.

Maybe they were getting docile, or we were just learning something about handling them. Anyway, wasn't much after noon when we had the last pack strapped on. We covered eight miles that second day, and our spirits were good when we made camp. We picketed our string along a creek where wild plums grew, and the moon came up and, although we were still in easy walking distance of the Missouri River, it looked like we were on our way. I was just dropping off when I thought, sort of drowsily, of the Bible I hadn't taken out of my pocket. Tomorrow sure, I thought.

Two more days and we had things down to a system. We could load and be on the trail inside an hour. The mules had learned their places in line, and of a morning they'd go and stand over their packs, waiting, with a fast kick for any other mule that tried to nose in where it didn't belong. Our lead animal was a smart little critter named Betsy. We tied a silver bell onto her, and the rest would jog along after, mile after mile, pretty as ever you please. By and by we began making time, passing up wagon outfits now instead of the other way around. We went up the Kaw, and the Spring got greener and greener. One evening we trailed into a little settlement, about where Abilene stands today. Wasn't much to it in 1859—couple of dugouts on the far side of Mud Creek, a sod building that was swing station for the stageline. The big daily coach had gone dusting past us a couple hours before sundown, passengers hanging to every square inch and hollering and laughing as our mules scattered out of the way. Now it stood in front of the station, getting a new team hooked on maybe, with all the people inside the building taking on beans and coffee and dried apple pie.

We splashed across the creek, found a place on the heights where the long-beaked mosquitoes wouldn't be so thick, and made our camp. Down to the settlement, lights glowed in windows and behind blankets hung over the dugout entrances, and there were voices and a dog yelping and someone beating music out of a harmonica. Friendly sounds across the quiet prairie night. I said: "We going down?"

Old Tom was settled back against a tarp-covered pack saddle, legs crossed, an old corncob pipe fired up. "You and Chuck can. I druther stay here and watch the stuff."

So we mounted and jingled our horses toward the settlement. Men were tinkering on the big coach by lantern light, and Chuck asked one of them: "Hot box?"

"Only wish it was," he growled. "Busted a thoroughbrace. Might be laid up here all night, and we hoped to make the next station."

"Tough," Chuck agreed. "Glad I got nothing worse than pack mules to worry about."

We rode around the building where there was a rope corral among some trees. And now I got to tell you what happened to me there, because it was about the most important event of my life. And I ain't really proud of my part in it, either, though it turned out all right. The back half of the station was a kitchen—I remember how the sparks was streaming out of the stove pipe, straight as the stars, like a fountain. Somebody was working with an axe at a woodpile by the door. We tied, and Chuck started on, but I delayed a minute to see did my horse have a rock under his shoe—he'd been limping some. Well, wasn't nothing wrong, so I turned to follow Chuck, and as I did something went streaking past me and hit the ground good and solid. I leaned and found it—an axe head! It just wasn't funny, how close I'd come to having my skull split open. I did some cussing, I'm afraid, and then I turned and stalked back toward that woodpile. Out of the shadows a voice whimpered: "I never meant to, honest! It just sort of flew off."

I said: "I ought to just sort of wring your neck for you! Be careful, can't you?"

Which is how I met my wife. Of course, I couldn't be supposed to know the future. If anyone had told me right then I'd some day marry this thing with the big dark eyes and no brains apparently, I'd've knocked him down. Still, this wasn't no way to talk to any girl, and it started her crying.

"I was only splittin' some w-wood for the stove."

I jerked the axe handle away from her and shoved the head on. It fit loose. I told her: "No wonder!" and hunted till I found a couple of chips the right size. I shoved them in and upended the axe and pounded it on the ground to settle them. "All right!" I told her. "Stand aside. Watch somebody that knows what he's doing." And I fell to and really made the chips fly. When I'd split everything in sight, I threw the axe down and said: "Now, where do you want it toted? Speak up, while I'm in the mood to do your work for you!"

She sobbed out: "You don't have to tote it nowhere! I never asked you. . . ."

"In the kitchen?"

"Yes."

I gathered up an armload, and she hurried to open the door for me. In the light she looked sort of pretty, in a faded calico dress and brown eyes wet and reproachful looking. But I was too sore to look at her. I dumped my armload into the box, and I said: "Don't see why you need more wood on *that* stove. Somebody'd think you was sot on burning the place down!" I reached and shut off the damper and then turned around and marched out.

Just before the door slammed she managed to get out a couple of words. She said: "Th-thank you. . . ."

And, somehow, that made me feel bad all of a sudden. This girl should have thrown dishes at me, rude as I'd been, but saying that instead kind of worked in under my skin. Otherwise I'd likely forgot about her in ten minutes. So you see, I guess those were the two most important words I ever had spoken to me, if you want to look at it that way.

I was thinking about her as I went around the station toward the front. I had just reached the corner when two men strolled into sight, wiping their mouths on their sleeves like they had been inside and finished eating. And I knew them—the last two I would ever have expected to meet here.

I had assumed they'd started for the Peak after stealing my wagon and team and selling them. Yet here they were and hard to tell who was the most startled. Doc Prine, the red-faced one with the eye-glasses, looked just a bit scared, but the one who called himself Big Jim Madigan only smiled broadly. "Well! A real surprise, kid!"

"Where's my money?"

"Got it right here, son. You didn't think we meant to steal it, did you?"

"What was I supposed to think?"

"Why, there was this game. All I needed was a stake to get the three of us to the diggings in style and not limping along in that damned wagon. But when we wanted to give you your share of the winnings, we couldn't find you."

"Looked all over," Doc Prime told me.

I said: "Well, let's have it now!"

Madigan had brought out a fat wallet, and I saw the money that stuffed it. "Let's step over a little ways. Don't want those toughs on the stage to see how much I'm carrying."

That was reasonable. I let him lead me and Doc a few yards from the station where there was brush and it was darker. "This do?" I asked him.

"Yeah," grunted Madigan. "This'll do fine!"

I never knew what they hit me with, or how long I lay there. It was Chuck found me, after a bit, and I was back in our camp on the hill when I come to. I can still feel that headache, pretty near! I groaned and I cussed, and then I started for the tarp that had our guns and ammunition under it. Old Tom said, sharp-like: "Don't be a fool, lad!"

"Let him alone," said Chuck. "He can't do any harm."

His tone made me look around. "Why not?"

"Stage has already pulled out half an hour ago. They got the thoroughbrace fixed."

Well, that was that. I went back and dropped down by the fire, so far in the dumps nothing anybody said could cheer me up. My head kept hurting worse, and finally I just turned my back and went to sleep. Dawn was running a silver line of brightness around the rim of the prairie when a noise woke me. I lay listening, trying to place it. Then I did—broad, iron-tired wheels, and six sets of muleshoes, starting up yonder at the settlement. That brought me out of my blankets in a hurry, but it was too late. I could only stand listening as the stagecoach faded into the distance.

Chuck and his dad were awake now. I turned on them, trembling. "You lied to me! You said they left last night!"

"Please, Ned!" Chuck begged me. "You'd just have gone and got yourself killed!"

"Then leave me get killed my own way!" I retorted. We come nearer to fighting, then, than in all the rest of the way to the Peak— or in all the years I was to know them afterwards, for that matter. But it blew over, though I didn't speak to Chuck Bolling for almost a whole day. Pretty soon we had the train packed and headed down through the trees and past the dugouts and the station which looked bleak enough by daylight.

All at once I remembered the girl, and on an impulse I told them: "I'll catch up!"

Gray smoke was trailing out of the station chimney, and on the slab step a towheaded kid was wriggling his toes in the dust and playing the harmonica I'd heard last night. I dismounted, stepped over him, and went into the main room that had long tables and benches where the stage passengers ate their meals. And there, barefooted, in her blue calico dress with brown hair coming down free around her shoulders, the girl paused in sweeping the dirt floor and stared at me, kind of frightened. I walked up to her, and I said: "I come to apologize!"

We were alone—I never met her ma and pa till later than this—

and we just looked at each other a minute. Out in the sunshine the kid with the French harp had started in on "Barbara Allen" and somehow the music that come in through the open door got all mixed up with this girl. It tangled into the shine of her hair and the brown of her eyes, and ever after I was never going to be able to separate the girl from the tune, or think of one without the other coming into my mind, and like as not tears into my eyes, too. I swallowed and twisted my hat around, and I said: "You must figure I ain't worth the spit to hold me together, the way I talked last night. I'm asking you to forgive me."

Her warm brown eyes kept going back and forth as though they were looking first into one eye and then the other—a little trick she had. "But I 'most brained you with the axe head," she pointed out. "And then you helped me, and I said, 'Thank you.' "

I nodded, miserable. "That's just it! You said 'Thank you.' "

"Well, of course I forgive you. . . ."

I wanted to leave—I had to leave—but I just couldn't yet. Suddenly I blurted out: "My name's Ned Cady, and I'm a mule freighter, and I'm headed for the Peak to make my fortune. Next time we meet maybe you'll know I ain't so bad as I acted last night, and you'll try to like me a little. I hope so, anyway. Good bye!"

"Good bye, Ned," she told me. "I'll be waiting for next time."

I was already out of the building and in saddle again, and my face felt red as fire. But looking back, I could see her watching from the doorway, and at the last minute she put up a hand in a timid sort of wave. I waved back.

And the kid with the harp was still playing "Barbara Allen," and I took that tune with me as I went, and I wore it right inside my heart. And not even knowing what her name might be, I took the memory of the girl and the song with me all the way to the diggings.

✿

The Kansas you see today from a train window, plowed into fields and spotted with towns and chopped up by roads and section lines, ain't much like the prairie we pushed across that late spring of '59. Then grass brushed your stirrup leathers and, except for the ground wind running the waves across it and maybe the song of a prairie plover or the sound of some animal cutting off with his belly hugging the ground, there wasn't no noise, only what you made yourself. Each morning the sun rose behind us, and at night it dropped in a splotch of purple and red in front. And every day that sun got stronger, and the land around us turned dryer.

We'd been warned that the Smoky Hill route was a dry one, but this was something more than we'd expected. The river became a meandering bed of white sand, lined with starved-looking cottonwoods. We were packing water by this time that tasted brackish after a few hours in the canvas containers. And we were seeing things. Mirages. Strange, to have a herd of giant antelope go racing across the sky on long, toothpick legs stretched out of shape by the shimmer of heated air. I can't begin to describe it.

One evening, sweating and tired, we shoved our string onto grass near a spring where there was another of the stage stations. Riding over, Tom and I seen three plots of turned sod that couldn't been nothing but graves, and we asked the agent about them. He looked like the desert had cooked all the juice out of him and burnt him nigh to a crisp. "Peakers," he told us. "Week ago the east stage come limping in shy a pair of mules and with three dead passengers. Cheyennes got 'em."

I felt my stomach crawl. Tom said: "I thought the reds was peaceable this year."

"They are. This was a party of a dozen or so that some pilgrim riding the coach saw skylined and, just for sport, took a shot at. Knocked one out of the saddle, and the rest put up a fight, natural enough. They were driven off."

Tom cussed. "That's the way half our Indian troubles start! I just hope the skunk started the shooting was one of them you buried."

The agent shook his head. "Don't often seem to work that way. The rest of the people on the coach wouldn't let him go any farther with them. They kicked him out, here at the station . . . and what did he do but steal a horse off me and cut his stick during the night. We should've strung him up!"

I went to the window and took a long look at the flats, and the brassy sky, and the meanders of that dry river. I felt a little sick, thinking about the people in the stage. And then something on a shelf by the window caught my eye. I picked it up with a trembling hand.

I said: "Where did you get this watch?"

"Off one of the gents we planted. It's no good. Don't run."

"I don't care if it don't. It was my dad's! See, here's the fob with his and mom's picture worked in." Then I saw the gold-rimmed spectacles lying beside the watch. "Did those come off the same man? A little, baldish fellow?"

"That's right. Couldn't see no point burying something might be of use to a live man. If you want the watch, take it!"

"Thanks!" I swallowed. "Didn't see anything of a tall, tough gent . . . mean eye, and a lopsided nose?"

"That sounds like the one did the shooting, the one swiped a bronc from me!"

Old Tom must have read the look in my eyes then. He said: "Easy lad! It was a week ago, remember? This Madigan would be a far piece by now."

"Sure," I grunted. I couldn't help, though, but feel that Doc Prine at least had got no more than was coming to him.

Next day, we sighted buffalo—only ones we laid eyes on during that first trip of mine across the Plains. From a rise we watched them drift by in a great brown cloud of woolly bodies, their passage making a low rumble like the mutter of the sea, the dust built into a cone-shaped yellow cloud as their knife-sharp hoofs dug up the sod and tossed it over their shoulders. Must have been a small herd, by buffalo standards, but seemed to me it stretched to nowhere across the flat horizon. I remember wondering what in the name of time we'd do if our mules should get caught in a herd that size. But it turned out that was one thing we needn't have worried about.

A couple evenings later, when we had made camp, I went hunting firewood at a place where I'd seen a few scattered cottonwoods. I thought there might be water, though I doubted that. We hadn't seen anything wetter than our own sweat for days. Precious little for the mules to eat, too, and those critters were getting fined down, and it wasn't improving their tempers any. All of us were on a raw edge and ready to argue over any fool thing, just to be arguing.

Well, there wasn't any water—just a dry bed. I dragged myself out of saddle and started gathering down branches the sun had bleached white. I was stooped over, one arm nearly full, when something hit my back and sent me rolling. It was a man I saw when I had my feet under me again, a man that looked like he had been made out of old bones strung together and covered with cured rawhide. He came at me again, eyes glaring, weaving on his feet, and though a head taller than me he was too far gone to make any real trouble. I didn't even give him all I had in my right fist. I held the punch, and he staggered into it, and I laid him out in the sand.

Big Jim Madigan was hard to recognize now. His clothes hung in rags. His hair was tangled and matted and so was his beard, and his eyes were sunken places in the sun-blackened face. I could've killed him with a very little pressure of my bare hands around his throat. Was a time I'd've liked to. Instead I fetched the water can off the saddle of my hollow-ribbed bronc and got some of it down him. After a bit he started coming 'round.

He had no gun, but his wallet was still stuffed with greenbacks. As he opened his eyes, I was counting out a sheaf of them. "For my team and wagon," I told him. The rest I threw back to him, and the wallet landed in the sand, and he just stared at it. He was so far gone I don't think he knew me at all. When I helped him to his feet, he didn't weigh anything. I got him onto my horse and so into camp, where Tom and Chuck started throwing questions at me.

"This is Madigan," I said. "Him that robbed me and shot the Indian and got the others massacred and stole a horse from the station agent. I guess the horse died or bolted, because he's been wandering for some time in this desert. I druther left him die, but . . . here he is!" And I turned and walked away to get my eyes as far from the man as possible. I hated him that much.

That night, before bedding down, I loaded a gun and shoved it into my waistband under my shirt. I felt some better then. But Big Jim was a plenty sick man, apparently too far gone for mischief. When he could talk, he told us something about losing his bronc and being stranded without water and no gun to kill him any food. I hadn't said anything about him jumping me from behind, but he must have known what I thought of it. We didn't have much to say to each other.

Tom took charge and fed him up, and after a day or two he could sit a saddle and even help a little with the mules. Somehow I didn't care to see him do it. We had pretty valuable cargo in those packs. I tried to warn Tom and Chuck not to give him too much leeway, and they promised to keep an eye on him. But it seemed to me they thought of Madigan as being too weak and nigh gone to be any real danger to a healthy man.

One day we sighted a low purple line against the sky ahead. Chuck said: "Look at those clouds, Pop! It's going to rain!"

"Where's any clouds?" retorted old Tom, grinning like at a secret. "All I see is mountains!"

The mountains! We gave a whoop when we heard that, for it meant we were almost there. But the enthusiasm flickered a little when another day passing didn't seem to bring the purple line any closer. And that afternoon we met the first eastbound wagons. There were three of them and kind of weird to see them crawling toward us. I think we had got to feeling that wagons were built to roll only in one direction—westward. The canvases of these were dirt-brown and everything looked as though it had seen a lot of wear. The men on the seats had the same look.

Tom, gone sober, said: "You boys swing the mules wide. I'll talk to them."

He was gone a long time, until after we had passed and the wagons were mere specks seen through our dust. When he caught up again, he was pale and worried. Tom said: "It's this way, boys. Looks like a false alarm. According to these folks, the big strike at the Peak was only empty rumors. Those that can still get home are pouring out of the mountains by the thousands. Only ones left are the stone broke and the dead. There's no gold . . . never was any!"

We all sat our saddles not saying a thing. The mules, forgotten, broke line and went wandering for graze. The sun poured down. It was the blackest moment in my life, I think.

Chuck said: "What about all the stuff in our packs?"

His dad shrugged. "In Denver, according to this fellow, you can buy a good pickaxe for ten cents. If you've got ten cents."

We camped early. Seemed little reason to push on, and all we could do was sit staring at the fire and listening to the mules grazing, and figure our losses. I hadn't anything to lose, myself, but it made me sick all over to think about Tom and his boy and those pack saddles loaded with worthless merchandise.

Chuck suggested once, in a hollow voice: "Maybe it's a mistake."

But the next two days we met more and more of the same beaten look. All told the same story. On the dirty canvases where "Pike's Peak or Bust" had been painted, there was just one word now—"Busted!"

Yet we still headed west, bucking the traffic. We had formed the habit. Besides, it was only a few days more to the mountains, and we wanted to see for ourselves. The mountains got bigger ahead of us. At last we limped into Denver on the tail end of a day, with sunset painting the sky above the ramparts of the Rockies. She looked like a ghost camp—half-deserted streets and log buildings and tents that already had that long-empty look. We made camp in a brush clearing where we could see the lights and hear what noise came from there. Despite I had looked forward to this day so long, now I didn't even want to go into town. I'd heard enough from the people we had met—about men going hungry because they couldn't pan out fifty cents' worth of gold a day, about town lots selling for the price of a meal, and all the rest.

I told Chuck and Tom: "I'll watch the mules. You two have a look if you want."

Chuck said all of a sudden: "Hey! Where's Madigan?"

We saw then he'd slipped out on us while we were talking—taking along the horse Tom had loaned him. A fine show of gratitude, after saving his life, and it was just one more thing on top of all the rest. I managed to keep from saying: "I told you so!" It would not do any good.

Full night came, and my friends mounted up and rode slowly over to the camp. For a long time I stood looking at the distant lights, and listening to the night breeze, and getting lonesomer and bluer every minute. I was thinking of that girl at the station, of how I'd said I was going to make my fortune at the mines and then come back. I could forget that now. Finally I broke out my blankets and rolled up in them, and looked at the jut of the mountains against the stars, and so went to sleep.

A distant gunshot woke me, and then there was some more firing, like a lot of different guns popping at random. I threw off the blankets. I could hear a confused yelling, now, and seemed to me it came from the direction of the town. Someone came running past, and I sang out: "Hey, partner! What's happened?"

He yelled back the news: "Fellow named Gregory's just struck it, up Clear Creek. Everybody's going . . . !"

He left me gasping. After the first, wild, heart-thudding minute I had my doubts. I didn't want to be taken in twice in a row. But then, as the noise from Denver kept coming across the darkness, I realized I had no need to be suspicious. You couldn't fool those people twice. They knew all right what they were cheering about this time.

Maybe you think I didn't go crazy! I took my hat and threw it in the air and yelled, and then a kind of frenzy hit me. I had to get in there before all the claims were taken—before those other goldseek-ers beat me out of mine. I dragged my hat on, running. I took my horse off the picket line and slung the saddle on him. I was just tight-ening the cinches when I remembered. I'd promised to stay and guard the mules and the trade goods! It was going to be valuable again, now. Even the stuff we'd seen strewn along the trail, east of town—stoves and mining equipment and all kinds of discarded junk—would be worth plenty since a boom meant boom prices.

But here minutes were ticking away that might mean the differ-ence between me staking a bonanza and somebody else getting it. I got so worked up I pounded my fist against the saddle, and maybe I even cried a little. I caught myself thinking: *What's this junk to me? For all I know Chuck and Tom could be on their way to the stake right now, leaving me here to rot!* After which I hauled the saddle off, and dropped it on the ground, and went over and sat on a rock, and made myself calm down. Chuck and his dad knew I wanted to get to the strike. They'd be back in a minute. I would wait.

I felt better, sort of cleaner inside, when I'd made that decision. In fact, it's one of the few things I ever did that I'm proud of. Because you'll see shortly what would've happened if I hadn't stayed. I was sitting there—I remember I had just lifted an arm to sleeve the sweat off my face—when I heard a slithering sort of sound behind me. A voice said: "Don't move, kid! Except to get both hands up over your head!"

My whole body started to tremble. I did as I was told, and then Big Jim Madigan come out of the brush. I could see the gun in his hands. I remember wondering who he had stole it from. He said: "You're alone? All right, kid, just be good, and I won't hurt you."

I got shaking to my feet. "What are you going to do?"

"Wait till the old man and his son get back and put them out of the way. Then you and me will pack these mules and load the stuff into town and sell it. It'll bring me a nice pile of dust."

"No!" I shouted and, not thinking, I made a lunge for him. He stepped back, and I saw the gun come down, and I dodged. It took me a glancing blow across the ear. The ground swung up and hit me solid. I landed on my side, the blood from the torn ear running hot across my face—I still bear the marks of that tear. But I wasn't more than half knocked out, and suddenly I remembered the hogleg inside my shirt, digging into my belly where I was laying on it. I rolled. I got both hands on the butt, and I dragged it out, and half blind with fear and rage I pushed the heavy muzzle up at Big Jim, and it felt like I near squeezed the trigger through the guard. The gun roared, splitting open the whole night, and it bucked like a kick in the stomach. And I lay there panting and shaking all over. There was a bubbling sort of scream, and something fell heavy across my legs. It was Madigan, and he was dead.

At the touch of him I think I started to babble, and I kicked and fought until I was free of him. Even then I couldn't stand up. I just kept pushing away from him frantically until a rock against my back stopped me, and I lay panting and sick and staring wide eyed at where

I thought his corpse must be. I never had seen a man killed before, and here I had killed one! All at once I came aware of the gun still in my hand, and I threw it from me. Old Tom said later that when he and Chuck come tearing in, at the sound of that shot, they found me there by Madigan's body having something mighty close to convulsions. He had to slap me good and hard to bring me out of it.

Well, I'm telling this the way it happened, even if the truth ain't anything to brag about. And killing Big Jim Madigan changed the course of my life—saved me, probably, from becoming one of those hopeless derelicts that follow the gold strikes endlessly in search of the stake they never find. Because, lying there weak and exhausted, with old Tom's arm around me and his voice soothing in my ears, it come over me what he'd said that first night on the prairie—about California and the killings he'd seen for a poke of gold.

Because I had killed, too! Not for gold, but to save the lives of my friends. Still, I had killed with hatred in me, and there'd been an awful eager sort of pleasure when the trigger gave under my finger, and I knew I had Madigan targeted, and that he would die. It was there, in me, despite the terror. And I didn't ever want to feel that thing again. So I said to old Tom, and the words came out hard because I couldn't control the sobbing of my voice: "You were right! I ain't going after gold. I don't want no part of it . . . not ever!"

Finally old Tom got me quieted. He said, real gentle: "It's all right, son. Me and Chuck, we owe you a lot. You're to have a share of what we clear on the train of goods. You can get a start in life with that for a nest egg."

"No, Tom," I said. "You owe me nothing but the fifty dollars I signed on for." I was thinking straight now, and I told him the thing I had figured out for myself. "I'll buy me a rig and team and head back along the trail and pick up some of that stuff we seen lying around where people threw it away. I'll bring it to Denver and sell it, and I ought to make some good money. But I won't go near that Clear Creek strike! I don't want any part of . . . of what you saw in California!"

And that's how the Cady Freight Line was born, which is the story I started out to tell you. I wasn't thinking so far ahead as that, though, the night the news of the Gregory Gulch strike reached Denver. It would be hard to explain all the things that were going through my head as I sat with Chuck and Tom and heard the noise of the celebration in town drifting across the wind. But the minute of killing Big Jim Madigan, I think, was the dividing point in my life. Beyond that moment I wasn't to be a kid any more. I was to be a man, knowing how a man thinks and how he feels. Now I had a program to follow through. And for the first time in a long spell I could hear again—somewhere at the back of my mind—the ghost of an old French harp, faint and sweet, singing "Barbara Allen."

# Ride the Red Trail

*Wayne D. Overholser*

○

*Recipient of four Golden Spur Awards from the Western Writers of American, Wayne D(aniel) Overholser was born in Pomeroy, Washington, and attended the University of Montana, the University of Oregon, and the University of Southern California. He began writing for Western pulp magazines in 1936.* Buckaroo's Code *(Macmillan, 1948) was his first Western novel and remains one of his best. In the 1950s and 1960s he would publish as many as four books a year under his own name or a pseudonym, most prominently as Joseph Wayne and Lee Leighton.* The Violent Land *(Macmillan, 1954),* The Lone Deputy *(Macmillan, 1957), and* The Bitter Night *(Macmillan, 1961) are among the finest titles under the Wayne D. Overholser byline. Many of his novels are first-person narratives, a technique that tends to bring an added dimension of vividness to the frontier experiences of his narrators, and frequently, as in* Cast a Long Shadow *(Macmillan, 1955), the female characters one encounters are among the most memorable. Almost invariably his stories weave a spell of their own with their scenes and images of social and economic forces often in conflict and the diverse ways of life and personalities that made the frontier so unique a time and place in human history. The following story first appeared in* Fifteen Western Tales *(May 1954) and has not been previously collected.*

**I**n San Fernando at the foot of the mesa they said the old one had never been born. She had always been there, for evil is as old as man. She had been buried, or so it was said, but it must not be true, for she had never died. Perhaps the truth was that young Dick Starr and his bride Lennie had buried someone else. It was foolish to believe that evil can be removed from the face of the earth by the simple process of burying a human body. No, she must still be up there, the old one, hiding in the scrub oak or aspens by day and roaming the country by night, or standing on the edge of the mesa and looking out across the valley while the wind plays with her long, white hair. And it was equally foolish to think of the devil as a man. The devil was Mary Starr. Make no mistake on that.

Lenore Smith was not a pretty girl. She was tall and big-boned and strong. Her nickname was Lennie. She had the ample breasts and wide hips of a woman who was born to have babies, and she had the kind of heart that had room to love one man and only one man. The man was Dick Starr, old Mary's grandson, and all the others who wanted to take Lennie for a wife were just wasting their time. The others were mostly Mike Starr, Dick's cousin, who rodded Starr Ranch and fancied himself a tough hand in the best of the Starr tradition. He kept telling Lennie that Dick would never come and, when old Mary died, Lennie was marrying Mike, and she wasn't to make any mush talk about love. That was for soft heads like Dick.

This morning Lennie had a song inside her that wanted to be sung because Dick was coming back, and he was coming today. Mike and old Mary were going to get the surprise of their lives. But she didn't sing the song. No one who lived on the mesa ever sang, not since Lennie had come there to work.

She hurried with the dish washing, one eye on the window to judge the time by the shadow of the lone cedar in the yard. It would be hours before Dick arrived. She hoped it would be after dark. Still, she kept glancing out of the window at the shadow, and the minutes dragged out until Lennie thought she could not wait through the day. The dishes weren't done when she heard the clang of the triangle from the upstairs room where Mary lay. With a sigh Lennie wiped her hands on a towel and went upstairs. You never knew what Mary wanted. She should have died a week ago, or even a month ago, and how she kept on clinging to life was a mystery to Lennie. Sometimes Lennie thought the talk in the valley about Mary being the devil was true. How else could anyone explain the fact that she was still alive?

Lennie stood beside the bed looking down, waiting, and Mary stared up at Lennie, her black eyes the only thing in the hide-and-bone face that seemed alive. It had been months since she'd got out of bed, but she still ate well and, when she wanted something, she could make a terrific clatter with the triangle that hung at the head of the bed. Lennie could hear it from anywhere in the house or out in the yard.

"Sit down, Lennie," Mary said.

So Lennie pulled up a chair and sat down. The dishes could wait. Mary kept right on looking at her. Lennie doubted the old woman knew she was dying. Up until she'd been thrown from a horse seven months ago and got a spine injury, she had never been sick a day in her life. As long as Lennie had been working there, Mary had lived as she pleased, not giving a damn about anything. Lennie wasn't sure how many of the stories they told about Mary were lies. She was a hell-cat for sure, if even a small percentage were true. Some said she'd killed three men, and others claimed it was six, but Lennie knew a lot of folks doubled a figure every time they told a tale.

There wasn't any doubt about Mary's drinking talent. When she'd been on her feet, she could have put any man under the table by swapping drink for drink, and that included young Mike Starr. There was no doubt about her poker-playing prowess, either. More than once Lennie had seen Mary come back from San Fernando with a pocketful of gold that she'd slap down on the table and then laugh like a fool when she'd tell Lennie that all a woman had to do was to let a man think he was good, then he was as easy to whittle down as a chunk of rotten cottonwood.

She had a wicked tongue that had more sting than a bullwhip, and a vocabulary that contained some words most mule skinners had never heard of. She'd cursed Lennie more than once and on one occasion had slapped the girl on the face. Only one time, though, for Lennie started toward the front door. Mary ran after her and apologized, probably the only time she had ever apologized to anyone in her life. But Lennie was the best girl who had ever worked for Mary, and Mary respected her and even liked her, if there was any room in her tough old heart for affection.

Lennie would have left a long time ago, if she hadn't fallen in love with Dick. Mary's two sons were dead, worn out, folks said, by working twice as hard as any man should work. The grandsons were the only blood kin Mary had. Lennie never heard where the boys' mothers were. Probably they'd just run away. It was hard enough to live with Mary now that she was an old woman. Twenty years ago it would have been impossible.

The grandsons were so different it was hard to believe they were related. Mike was Mary all over again, in a man's shape, or at best he thought he was. A hard drinker, a wicked fighter, a woman chaser, Mike was a reasonable facsimile of what Mary would have been if she were a man. On the other hand Dick sneaked into the family through the back door, and Mary, on the surface at least, was ashamed of him. Slender, handsome, soft voiced, Dick was the kindest and most considerate boy Lennie had ever met. Dick was a fighter, though. He had that much Starr in him. Mike should know. One day he had Lennie backed against the wall trying to kiss her when Dick came in. The fight laid Mike up for a week. He still had a scar on his right cheek, a reminder that Dick would have killed him if Mary hadn't got there in time to pull Dick off.

Lennie was remembering all this as she sat beside Mary's bed, and she couldn't help wondering what Mary was thinking. In some ways the old woman had two faces. Lennie thought Mary liked Dick better than Mike, although she would never have admitted it if Lennie had asked her. But whether she liked Dick or not, they just weren't made to live on the same ranch. One day Mary told Dick to run a squatter off Hannah Creek and to kill the ornery son if necessary, but Dick said that wasn't his way, that there was plenty of room on the mesa for the squatter and Starr Ranch, too. So Mary told him to get the hell off Starr Ranch and stay off until he learned to follow orders.

Dick rode away without even telling Lennie good bye, and Mike had done the job for Mary. Two days later someone found the squatter's body in a ditch not far from San Fernando and, although the townspeople figured Mary or Mike had done the killing, figuring was all they did. This happened before Mary was hurt. Dick had been gone more than a year, and it was Lennie's guess that the old woman never thought Dick would take her at her word. But in all this time Mary had never once asked about Dick, although she may have known that Juan Perez who cut and hauled wood for Starr Ranch mailed Lennie's letters to Dick and smuggled Dick's letters to Lennie.

The minutes ticked away, and finally Lennie could stand it no longer. She said: "I'd better get back to work...."

Mary said: "Stay there," and let go with some of her choice cuss words. "What's so damned important about work this morning?" Lennie didn't answer, so Mary grinned. It wasn't much of a grin, just a crazy uptwist of her liver-brown lips. She said: "Lennie, you sure are a fool. You could marry Mike today. But no, you're in love. You're soft, Lennie, as soft as a gob of fresh mush, and so's Dick. What're you hanging around here for if you don't want Mike?"

That was a good question. Lennie blinked and didn't say a word. There was no use to lie to Mary. She'd catch you every time. The truth was Lennie figured Dick had a right to half the ranch and, if she stayed, maybe she could help him get it. That was why she'd finally written, asking him to come back. Mary couldn't go on this way forever and, according to the lawyer from San Fernando, she had left everything to Mike. Lennie wasn't quite sure that was true. Mary never said anything about it either way, and Lennie figured the lawyer might be lying. Just the same it seemed time for Dick to get back. Lennie thought Mary might change her will. If the old woman liked Dick better than Mike, and if Dick was on hand, well, there was a chance for him at least.

Finally, with Mary's question hanging there unanswered, the old woman said: "I know all right. You've been waiting on me hand'n foot ever since that damned horse dumped me. You think I'll leave you something when I cash in, don't you? Well, I still say you're a fool. You got your wages!"

Lennie rose. "I've got to finish the dishes...."

"Sit down, damn it," Mary bellowed. She didn't have much body left, but there was nothing wrong with her voice. When Lennie obeyed, Mary went on: "That's better. You want to know why I called you up here. All right, I'll tell you. Mike got it out of Juan that you've been hearing from Dick. Not that I give a damn, but I'm curious. What's he been doing?"

"Riding for Saul Yeager in Baca County," Lennie said.

The ghastly grin came to Mary's lips again. "Well now, I know Saul. He'll make a man out of Dick, or he'll kill him."

"Dick's always been a man," Lennie flared. "And if you had any decency in you, you'd see he got half the ranch after you . . . you . . . !"

"After I kick the bucket? That it? Well, the way I figure, he don't have nuthin' coming after he pulled out and left me like he done." Mary's eyes closed, and she took a long breath. "So you think I'm not decent. I reckon I ain't. Never had much truck with decent folks. I dunno what's wrong with Dick. He's decent, and I ain't. Maybe that's the trouble." She opened her eyes and stared at Lennie again. "You're a good, strong girl. You'd make a good wife for either one of 'em. Which one you gonna marry?"

"Dick."

"But he's in Baca County, and you've stayed here with Mike. If Dick ever does come back, he'll have nothin' to do with you, not after Mike tells Dick what you'n him have been doin'." Mary grinned again. "You sure are a fool, Lennie."

Lennie got up, trembling. "Dick will marry me. You'll see. Come morning, I'll be gone. Dick's going to be here today sometime."

"If you're gone, you'll be riding alone," Mary said contemptuously. "I'd best tell Mike that Dick's coming. Not that I think he will. Or that you'll be leaving, neither. Mike's got his rope on you and, if you run with it, you'll be laid flat like a calf at branding time."

Lennie stood there, still trembling, shocked by what she had done. If Mike knew Dick was coming, he'd hide in the scrub oak along the trail, and he'd drygulch Dick. Lennie whispered: "Don't tell Mike. Please. I didn't intend to . . . !"

"Go along," Mary said maliciously.

Lennie stumbled out of the room and down the stairs. She looked at the cedar's shadow, then she finished the dishes and looked at the shadow again and knew it was time to start dinner. Mike and the crew would be riding in before long, within an hour or so, and if the meal wasn't on the table, he'd get ornery. And he'd be ornery if the meat was tough, or if the biscuits weren't light and fluffy, or if the coffee wasn't strong enough to suit him. It seemed to Lennie that Mike was ornery most of the time. She'd had enough of him. Come morning, she was leaving. Maybe Dick wouldn't show up, and maybe she'd be riding alone as Mary had said, but she was leaving.

Lennie had dinner on the table when Mike came in, his spurs jingling, the crew trailing. Red faced and sweaty from being over the stove, Lennie poured the coffee, ducking back quickly when Mike reached out to put a big arm around her waist. "You've mauled me around for the last time, Mike," Lennie said. "I've told you before. You'll get this coffee right in your ugly mug if you keep pestering me."

Mike laughed. He winked at Lud Barlow. "Hard to get now, ain't she, Lud?" Mike sat down and speared a steak from the big platter in the center of the table. "Well, they tell me the harder they are to get, the sweeter they are once you do get 'em."

Lennie moved back to stand beside the range. She wondered what Mike would do when Mary told him Dick would be here today. But it wasn't anything to wonder about. For all of his size and loud talk and jackass laughter, Mike didn't really have a man's guts. He wouldn't wait here at the ranch and smoke it out with Dick when he rode in. No, somewhere along the trail he'd bushwhack Dick. That was the first thought she'd had after she'd blurted out to Mary that Dick was coming. Now, staring at Mike's wide back, she was more certain than ever that was what would happen.

She glanced out of the window and saw Juan Perez sitting under his wood wagon, eating dinner. If she could get Juan to go to town now. . . . Quickly she got a plate and spooned beans onto it. She forked a steak from the frying pan to the plate, laid a biscuit beside it, and ran outside, half expecting Mike to ask her what she was doing. Then, half way across the yard to Juan, she heard the triangle in Mary's room. She didn't go back. Mike could answer. Afterwards he'd grumble and remind Lennie it was her job to wait on Mary.

"I've brought you something hot to eat," Lennie said.

Juan looked at her, surprised, for she had never brought him anything to eat before, but he took the plate.

She said: "Dick's coming home today. Mary knows, and she'll tell Mike, and Mike will wait for him along the trail and shoot him. You've got to go back to San Fernando now and watch for Dick when he comes through town. Tell him to wait until dark and take the back trail."

But Juan shook his head. He didn't say a word. He just shook his head. Everyone in San Fernando was afraid of Mary and even more afraid of Mike. Taking letters back and forth was one thing, but quitting work at noon to warn Mike's enemy was something else, and Lennie knew she'd been crazy to even think Juan would do it.

"I can't go," Lennie urged. "Mike would know what I intended to do. He'd tie me up, or lock me in the house, but you can think of some reason to quit work. One of your horses is lame or something."

Juan shook his head again. He was an old man with a wrinkled face and a scar on his chin where Mike had struck him once. Now, looking at his brown, worried face, Lennie knew she was wrong to ask him to risk his life for her or Dick. She said: "All right, Juan, I'll have to figure out something else."

She went back to the house and waited at the door while the crew streamed out. Mike wasn't with them. She went into the kitchen and was fixing a plate for herself when she heard Mike come down the stairs. She got a butcher knife from where she had left it on the warming oven and sat down at the table, the knife across her lap. She didn't look up when Mike came into the room. He walked around the table and came toward her. He put a big hand on her shoulder and squeezed it. He said angrily: "You damned . . . !"

She had been sitting with her body slack one moment, leaning forward, then she came out of her chair sideways in a quick turning motion, right hand gripping the wooden handle of the butcher knife and bringing the blade upward in a savage thrust that would have disemboweled Mike if he hadn't jumped backward and stumbled and fallen, his head banging against the wall. For a moment he lay there, blinking, scared, and then angry. Suddenly he grabbed for his gun, and Lennie had no doubt he would have killed her if she hadn't lifted the knife above her right shoulder.

She said: "I'd rather kill you than not, Mike. You pull that gun and I'll let you have this knife in the belly." Her eyes displayed her hate.

She had never thrown a knife in her life, but Mike didn't know that. He dropped the half-drawn gun back into holster and got up and backed away around the table, his eyes that were as black as Mary's filled with a wild, insane hatred. "I'll tame you good. I've gone easy on you on account of the old devil upstairs, but she ain't gonna last much longer. And if she was telling the truth about Dick's coming today, he won't last, neither." His voice gagged with rage.

Mike stalked out, giving her his back, and she laughed hysterically, thinking of the fear that must be crawling up into his belly and prickling along his spine. He was making a show of being unafraid, but it was just show. He glanced around before he reached the door then bolted through it and went on across the porch, and she knew she was right.

She sat down at the table again, but she couldn't eat. She heard Juan's wood wagon leave the yard, heading back up the slope toward the timber. She couldn't blame the old man, and yet she had clung to a faint hope that he would think of a reason for going to town. Now even that ghost of a hope was gone.

She stared unseeingly through the window at the cedar, and she thought about what Mike had said. He'd left her alone because of Mary. Well, that was smart enough, all right, with Mike wanting the ranch and knowing that Mary liked Lennie and wanted her to stay. But if Mary died, and Dick was killed . . . ! Lennie picked up the butcher knife. A poor weapon. If she just had a gun.

There was a Winchester in Mary's room, leaning against the wall at the head of her bed. Maybe, if Mary took an afternoon nap as she usually did, Lennie could sneak the rifle out of her room. Lennie got up and washed and dried the dishes. The cedar's shadow gradually lengthened as the sun moved westward. And Lennie, who had never really been afraid for herself before in her life, was afraid now. It had never occurred to her that her safety depended on old Mary's life, old Mary who might die at any moment.

Lennie, working feverishly washing and drying the dishes and putting them away, understood exactly how this was. She couldn't count on any help from Lud Barlow or the rest of the crew. They were Mike's men. The ones who had been Dick's friends had been fired within a month from the time he left. She wiped sweat from her face with her apron, and then, still holding the butcher knife, she went into the sitting room, a wild thought occurring to her that, if she made a run for it and got shot, Dick might be close enough to hear and be warned by it. But it was no good. She knew that at once. Dick might still be miles from the mesa.

She stood in the doorway, her eyes on the corral, and it came as a shock to her that Mike and the crew had not left. The horses were still out there. She didn't see any of the men, but it seemed a reasonable guess that they were hiding, waiting for Dick to ride in. Mike knew she would be watching. That was like him, she thought. He wanted her to see Dick cut down now.

Lennie must have stood there for an hour. She wasn't thinking of anything except Dick who was coming, now or within an hour, or two hours, or three, riding into a death trap. She was still standing there when she saw Lud Barlow come barreling out of the timber beyond the barn and corrals, cracking steel to his big roan at every jump. Mike ran out of the bunkhouse. A couple more riders appeared from the barn, another from a shed. Barlow swung down, jabbing a forefinger toward the mesa hill. "He's coming," Barlow said. "He'll be here in a minute or two. Dunno how he got to the rim. I was watching the road, but he must've come up Hannah Creek. He. . . ."

"Put your horse away," Mike shouted. "Don't stand there gabbing about it. We don't want him to see nobody but me." He wheeled to the other men. "Get back to where you were. What the hell's the matter with you? You knew what I told you to do."

A minute or two Barlow had said. Lennie looked at the butcher knife, and she thought of the Winchester upstairs. There was only one thing she could do. She had always been afraid of Mary. She wasn't afraid of what Mary would do to her. But there was Dick and the will and the ranch which should be his. And there was the wild talk in San Fernando about Mary's being the devil. Lennie had never done anything she knew Mary didn't want her to do, but now she had no choice.

Lennie went up the stairs on the run. She banged into Mary's room. The old woman's eyes had been shut. Now they snapped open. She shouted: "What in hell are you . . . ?"

She stopped. Lennie grabbed the Winchester from where it leaned against the wall and ran to the window. She saw Dick coming, and she saw Mike standing there in the yard, waiting, and she knew the others, Barlow and the rest, were all hiding so that the instant Dick made a move toward his gun, he'd be killed without a doubt. Lennie knocked the glass out of the window and yelled: "Drop your gun belt, Mike."

He turned, but Barlow yonder by the corner of the barn was quicker than Mike. He threw a shot at Lennie that knocked splinters from the casing. Lennie was no hand at throwing a knife, but she was a crack shot with a rifle. If she hadn't been, Barlow would have killed her with his second shot. As it was, he never fired a second shot. She got him through the stomach and, before he fell, she turned her rifle on Mike, jacked a shell into the chamber, and shot him directly through the head. By that time Dick was there with his six-gun in his hand, and the other three, probably thinking Lennie could see them from her window, came toward Dick with their hands up, yelling that they wanted no part in this, and they wouldn't have been there at all if Mike hadn't made them.

Lennie put the Winchester down and leaned against the wall, her calico clinging to her body, and the thought occurred to her that now the people of San Fernando would say she was a devil, too. She'd just killed two men, hadn't she?

Mary asked: "Mike cash in?" Lennie nodded and gulped and felt like everything in her stomach was coming up. Mary was giving that ghastly grin of hers. She said: "Lennie, fetch me the will that shyster drew up the last time he was here. It's in my top drawer. I'm leaving everything to you. Mike was yellow, and Dick ain't very skookum, so I figured all the time you were the one. That's why my Winchester was there." She closed her eyes, and she said as if she was very tired: "I wanted the Starr name to go on, and I reckon it will. And I reckon you'll look out for Dick, too, like I always done for my men folks."

# The Ghost of Jean Lafitte

*Les Savage, Jr.*

✪

*Born in Alhambra, California, Les(lie) Savage, Jr., grew up in Los Angeles.
The first story he wrote was accepted by the publisher to whom it was sent—
"Bullets and Bullwhips" appeared in Street & Smith's* Western Story Magazine *(October 2, 1943). Almost ninety more magazine stories followed and
twenty-five novels. Due to Savage's preference for historical accuracy, he ran into
problems with book editors. As a result of the censorship imposed on many of his
works, only now can they be fully restored by returning to the author's original
manuscripts.* Table Rock *(Walker, 1993),* Fire Dance at Spider Rock *(Five
Star Westerns, 1995),* Medicine Wheel *(Five Star Westerns, 1996), and* Coffin Gap *(Nine Star Westerns, 1997) are among the first of these restorations.*
Six-Gun Bride of the Teton Bunch *(Barricade Books, 1995) is a notable
Savage short story collection now available in a trade paperback edition. Savage
died young, at thirty-five, from complications arising out of hereditary diabetes
and elevated cholesterol. However, his considerable legacy lives after him, there to
reach a new generation of readers. "The Ghost of Jean Lafitte" was the first story
Les Savage, Jr., set in the Gulf Coast region of East Texas in the bayou country.
It was purchased on February 6, 1945, and appeared in the Fall 1945 issue of*
Action Stories *under the title "Tonight the Phantoms Ride!" For its first book
appearance the author's title and text have been restored.*

## I

**T**hey wouldn't take him alive. Ernie Denvers had decided that even
before the bay horse had gone down beneath him. Whatever else happened, they wouldn't take him alive. He stood there beside the dying
animal, nauseated by the foul odor of rotten mud that rose from the
bayou to his left, surrounded by the hollow booming of frogs from the
pipestem canebrake at his back. So this was Texas. A helluva place.
Why hadn't he chosen Wyoming, or Kansas? No. He had to pick Texas.
East Texas at that.

His dust-grimed face became alert at the faint sound that rode the wind down his backtrail. Them? He turned with a curse, breaking through the first canes. Who else? They had been on his tail all last night and all today. They wouldn't give up now.

He might have stood five six, Ernie Denvers, fighting his way through the clattering brake, but there was something ineffably potent about his square, compact body that precluded any appearance of smallness. A three days' beard made a blue stubble-shadow over his adamant chin, and his eyes burned red rimmed and feverish beneath the straight black line of his heavy brow. He had no chaps, and the canes scraped his dust-grayed Levi's with an incessant, maddening clatter that knotted his nerves up inside him like snubbed dally ropes. Well, why not? A man that had been chased as long as he. Why not? They wouldn't get him alive, that's all. They wouldn't.

He whirled around to the sudden crash of pipestem canes at his side, and his reaction was automatic. The girl stood there, looking at him for a moment, and then a strange, wild smile caught at one corner of the fullest lips he had ever seen, and her eyes dropped to the big Artillery Colt in his hand. "You get it out pretty quick," she said.

Her hair was black and lustrous as the water in the bayous, hanging thick and tangled about the shoulders of a flannel shirt that was as old and tattered as the denim pants she wore. Her dirty Hyer boots were run over at the heels as if she did more walking than riding. She cocked her small head to the faint sound through the thicket behind them, and her black eyes flashed excitedly. "You're running from Giddings?"

"Giddings?" he said.

"Navarra was expecting you tonight," she said. "Uncle Caesar sent me out to meet you. He thought you might have trouble with Giddings, but he didn't expect you to come this way."

"I didn't choose the way," he said warily.

"I understand." Her laugh bubbled up from inside, like there was a lot of it down there, and then she caught his arm. "I'll show you the way. We can reach the house before Giddings does. Navarra will take care of the rest."

He pulled back for a moment, but her hand on his arm was insistent, and she was already turning to brush aside the pipestems. What was the difference? He didn't know why this was, but it looked better than what he'd been seeing. Nor could he guess how long they ran through the canes. It was all the same. Rattling pipestems beating against his face and salt grass whipping across his legs and the booming frogs never still. She stopped abruptly, and he couldn't help being brought up against her and was surprised at the clean sweet smell of her hair. It seemed out of place, somehow, in all the other odors of putrescent mud and decaying vegetation that rose humidly from the bayou they had reached. She took his hand again and led him across the shaky bank through a grove of gnarled cypress trees, festooned with streamers of Spanish moss that slapped wetly across his shoulders. Then the first of the breeze struck him, carrying the faint tang of salt air, and in a few more moments he was surprised to find the mud turning to sand beneath his feet. Had he been that near the coast?

"Dagger Point," said the girl, gesturing toward the row of breakers gleaming dully from the darkness ahead. "It's neap tide now, and we can wade across to Matagorda Island. Take off your boots."

Shrugging, he slipped off dirty Justins, rolled up his Levi's on lean, hairy calves. Again he had no measure of time or distance. The water was never more than knee high, except for the rollers that foamed up over his waist. But he jumped these, and farther out they ceased, and he was wading through quiet water. When the breakers began again, they were going the other way, and finally Denvers and the girl were standing on the wet sand of that shore. She led him over dunes bearded with thick sea grass and then through the higher bunch grass of the coastal prairie, and finally he saw the house, surrounded by a brooding cypress grove. It was old Colonial, with the tall columns along its front porch peeling white paint that must have been put on thirty years before. Its shuttered windows stared blankly from warped weather boarding, and the porch floor popped dismally to their boots and the huge, oaken front door swung in on creaking hinges to a dim, musty reception hall.

Denvers wiped sweating hands across his Levi's. All right. She took him into what he thought was the parlor, high ceilinged and heavily carpeted, filled with the same nameless sense of belonging to the past. There was a pair of Chippendale sofas facing each other in front of the fireplace, the harateen covering on their camel backs frayed and shiny, the *cabriolé* legs bearing scars that looked as if they might have come from spurs. The man stood beside a Pembroke table to one side of the hearth. The first thing Denvers saw was the thick streak of white through his jet black hair then his face, heavy boned and heavily fleshed with an indefinable dissolution. The thick lids of his eyes were turned a shadowed blue by the network of tiny veins patterning them and only added to the leashed violence slumbering in the eyes themselves. His shoulders filled out the tailored cut of his long black coat well enough, and Denvers couldn't see where he packed any gun. The spurs on his polished cavalry boots made a small tinkling sound as he shifted away from the table.

"He was way south of Dagger Point, Navarra," said the girl. "I heard him in the canes. Giddings was right behind him."

So this was Navarra, thought Denvers, and watched the man come forward, wondering how such a heavy *hombre* could move with such apparent ease. Navarra bent slightly to peer at Denvers, and for a moment Denvers saw the anger rise in his eyes, enlarging the black pupils, and then the heavy bluish lids narrowed like a veil and whatever the man felt was hidden.

"This isn't Prieto," Navarra told the girl, and his voice held the same slumberous violence as his eyes. "What's the idea, Esther?"

The girl's small hand rose in a confused gesture. "You said he'd be there and might have trouble with Giddings. What else . . . ?"

Navarra turned to Denvers impatiently. "You have a name, I suppose?"

"Denvers," said Ernie.

"You want me to keel him, Sinton?" Denvers hadn't heard the Mexican enter the room. He was barefooted, standing over by a serpentine chest of drawers. He had a pair of longhorn *mustachios* that flapped against a dirty white shirt, and his eyes glittered like a sidewinder's from beneath a huge straw sombrero. "I got my gets-the-guts all sharpened up." He grinned evilly, running his brown finger down the blade of a *saca de tripas* he held. "Nobody hears me keel 'im. Nobody knows."

"Shut up, Carnicero," said Sinton Navarra, and then his head rose to the sound of snorting horses outside, and Denvers's move toward the door was automatic because he knew who had come.

"No, *señor*," said Carnicero, moving in front of him with the knife. "I think you better stay, eh?"

"Out of my way," said Denvers.

"He can pull a gun pretty fast," said the girl.

"I can stick him before he gets it out," grinned Carnicero.

"Go and let them in, Esther," Navarra told the girl.

Denvers heard her move behind him and took a jump to one side, hauling at his big Artillery Colt. The Mexican threw himself at Denvers, heavy body hitting him before Denvers had his gun out.

"Carnicero!" shouted Navarra.

Denvers had to let go his gun, jerking up both hands to grab the Mexican's knife arm as it came down. With one hand on Carnicero's wrist and the other at his elbow, Denvers straightened the arm, using it as a lever to heave the Mexican backward against the wall.

"I have a gun pointed at your back, Mister Denvers." Navarra's heavy voice stopped Ernie Denvers. "If you will, forget whatever ideas you have about your own gun, and back carefully toward the chair on the right hand side of the fireplace, and sit down."

The girl slipped out to the reception hall, and Denvers could hear the front door creak open as he backed stiffly toward the wing chair, squatting dirty and tattered in the shadows beyond the pair of couches. He knew the surprise must have shown on his face when he saw the gun Navarra held.

"A singular weapon, is it not?" smiled Navarra sardonically. "French, Mister Denvers. A Le Page pin-fire, seven millimeters, twenty shots. A man is a veritable arsenal with one of these. Don't you think it's ingenious? The cylinder, as you see, has two rows of chambers, one set within the other, each row containing ten chambers. The inner set fires through the lower barrel, the outer set through the upper, and . . ."

He stopped talking with a sudden, enigmatic smile and slipped the gun beneath his coat up by the shoulder. Denvers stiffened in the chair, not knowing whether he meant to rise or what, and then let his weight back down because he saw the futility of that. Sheriff Giddings must have stood six four, and he came into the room with an arrogant swagger that pushed his heavy belly against his crossed gun belts and that caused the batwings on his *chaparejos* to flap with a soft, leathery sound every time he took a step. The red strings of a Bull Durham sack dangled across the dirty star pinned on his buckskin ducking jacket.

"Good evening, Sheriff," said Navarra easily.

"Not so good, Navarra," said Giddings, stopping in the middle of the rug and hooking hammy thumbs into his gun belts to stand there swaybacked and self-conscious as he swept the room with eyes that were meant to be hard. They settled on Denvers, and then met Denvers's glance. It was the sheriff's patent intent to force Denvers to drop his gaze, but Denvers stared wide eyed and waiting at Giddings's pale blue eyes, and finally Giddings's own gaze shifted uncertainly, and clearing his throat with a hoarse, blustering sound, he looked jerkily toward Navarra. "No. As I say, not a very good evening. Jale Hardwycke was murdered last night."

"Oh." Sinton Navarra's velvety tone rose at the end of the word, and he pursed sensuous lips. "Too bad. What brings you here?"

"We caught the killers red-handed last night on the old Karankawa Trail out of Refugio. Couple of saddlebums. Starting them back toward town when they put up a ruckus. We killed one. The other got away. Trailed him as far as Indian Bog. I'm not going back without him, Navarra."

"Very commendable," said Navarra. "I still don't see how we figure in it."

The sheriff's two deputies shifted uneasily in the doorway. One of them was short and squatty as a razorback hog, his cartridge belt shoved down by a beer keg belly, his wool shirt covered with mud and horse droppings and other filth. Denvers's hands tightened slowly on the chair arms. He even knew that deputy's name. Ollie Minster. He was the one who had killed Bud Richie. Remembering that moment brought back Denvers's rage so strongly that it blotted out the whole room like a roaring black curtain sweeping across his vision, and he could hear his own breathing grow heavy and harsh in the sudden, strained silence.

"You got a new man, haven't you?" said Giddings, looking at Denvers.

"So Hardwycke was killed," said Navarra, and his slumberous eyes passed across Denvers, and then he was watching Giddings. "Wart hogs go rooting around the outside of a bush, Sheriff, after their feed, when they could go straight in and save a lot of time."

Giddings flushed. "I ain't beating around any bushes. I'll have that man in the wing chair, Navarra."

"I'm glad you came to the point, Sheriff," said the other. "What makes you think this man is your murderer? You say you found them last night? It was singularly dark, as I remember, without a moon. Could you positively identify him?"

"I'd know the jaspers anywhere," growled Giddings. "Two of 'em. Acted all right at first. Even gave us names. Ernie Denvers and Bud Richie. Then, when we started figuring them in the murder, they got cagey."

"Names don't mean much," said Navarra. "Faces?"

Giddings jerked his head from side to side in a vague, evasive way, finally shrugging his arrogant shoulders. "Like you say, it was dark. Scuffling around and such, I didn't get much look at their faces. But this is him, I tell you. Denvers. Same height, same build."

Navarra's smile was sardonic. "Esther's about the same height as our friend in the chair."

"This *hombre* wasn't Texan," said Giddings. "He didn't talk Texas, and he didn't dress Texas. No leather leggin's, no ducking jacket. His hat was flat topped, and his pants was denim. . . ."

"Esther wears denims," said Navarra.

Giddings bent forward sharply. "You trying to say that Esther . . . ?"

"Don't be obtuse." The contempt gave Navarra's words a hissing intonation. "How could Esther have been there? I'm only trying to point out that you aren't really sure of anything concerning this man,

Denvers. It could have been Esther, from all the descriptions you give, or a hundred other men in the vicinity. I don't talk Texas. Everybody in this state doesn't wear a center-creased Stetson and leather leggin's. You could find a dozen men tonight that look like this man in the dark. In fact, Jale Hardwycke and I are about the same height and build. Could you have told us apart last night? How do you know it was Hardwycke who was killed?"

"Don't be a fool!" shouted Giddings apoplectically. "I know Jale Hardwycke when I see him. He'd been to Refugio and taken twelve hundred dollars cash out of the bank. We found his wallet with the money in it on this Bud Richie."

Denvers caught the sudden flicker of Navarra's eyes before his thick, bluish lids closed across whatever had been there. "Oh, the wallet. You have it now, then."

Giddings jerked his head from side to side that way then blustered: "No, dammit. I found Hardwycke's wallet on this Bud Richie and put it in my saddle bags as evidence. Then the ruckus started, and Richie got in the way of Ollie's bullet, and the Denvers jasper got away on my horse. Now, don't try to block me, Navarra. I'm taking this man."

"Did you see your horse outside?" said Navarra.

Giddings's voice was rising. "I said don't try to block me. I know you ain't fool enough to leave the animal showing. This is the only place he could have come."

"You're throwing your rope on the wrong steer, Giddings," said Navarra, moving in front of Denvers. "This man's been here since Tuesday."

"Has he?" said Giddings. "We'll find out soon enough. He'll have Hardwycke's wallet. I'm searching him."

"He's my guest, Sheriff," said Navarra, and his voice was velvety. "I wouldn't allow you to search him any more than I'd allow you to search me."

Blood flooded up Giddings's thick neck. "You and Caesar Sheridan think you're safe from the law, hiding out here on Matagorda Island, but you're under my jurisdiction just as much as any man in Refugio."

"Am I?" said Navarra sardonically. "I'm surprised you even came this far, Sheriff. The last lawman to reach Indian Bog was found dead. I'd be more careful if I were you."

"I'll get you for that one, too, Navarra."

"Do you think I perpetrate every crime that happens within a hundred miles of Matagorda?" asked Navarra. "These things were going on a long time before I came, Giddings, and will continue long after I'm gone. I think I'm the least worry you have when you're around Indian Bog, and I think you know that. Do you think you could get back across the channel with this man? Do you think you can get back alone?"

"Damn you, Navarra!" Giddings almost screamed it and took one lurching step toward Navarra with his hands held out. Then he stopped. A small vein had begun to pulse faintly across Navarra's temple, and Denvers could see his eyes. They were like the eyes of an enraged cat. The pupils were dilated until they showed black and feline between the heavy, blue-shadowed lids, flickering with an odd, ebullient light. Giddings stood there on his tiptoes, looking into those eyes, and his lower lip sagged slightly, and he began to pull his hands back toward himself in a strange, dazed way.

"I keel 'im, Sinton?" said Carnicero.

"I'm glad you didn't touch me, Giddings," said Navarra, running a pale, veined hand over that white streak through his hair. "Don't ever touch me. Don't ever lay your hands on me. It would be most unfortunate for you. Now, I'll ask you to go. You can't take this man from my house without a warrant. You can't even enter my house without a warrant, as a matter of fact."

Giddings's breathing had the driven, grating sound of a blown horse. He stood there for another instant, staring at Navarra. Finally he spoke, and his voice shook with his frustrated anger. "I'm coming back, Navarra. I'm coming back with enough warrants to send you and this whole household to hell! You've thrown your last dally on Matagorda!"

He whirled and stamped swaybacked out of the room, shaking the floor with each step, shoving his deputies ahead of him with a hoarse curse. His spurs clattered down the hall, the door slammed hard, and the squeak of saddle leather came faintly through the heavy red velvet curtaining the front windows. Denvers was on his feet by then.

"Why protect me like that?"

"Perhaps because of a singular dislike for our Sheriff Giddings," said Navarra, a soft ebullition in his smile. He held out his hand, a huge jade ring glinting on one finger. "And now, Denvers, the wallet. . . ."

The man coming through the door stopped him, voice filling the room like the roar of a rutting bull. "I saw Sheriff Giddings leaving, Navarra. Did he try to cause your man any trouble?"

"Prieto didn't come yet, Caesar," said Navarra.

The other glanced at Denvers. "Who's this, then?"

"I was waiting on the mainland for Prieto, like you told me, Uncle Caesar," said the girl. "I guess I brought the wrong one."

"Yes," said Navarra ironically. "Mister Denvers, would you meet Caesar Sheridan, Esther's uncle, the owner of this . . . ah . . . house, the ruler of Matagorda Island, the king of. . . ."

"Tie up your duffel, tie up your duffel," said Caesar Sheridan, waving one beefy hand disgustedly. He was a short man with enormously broad shoulders and a huge belly. His broad black belt pulled in tightly till a roll of fat slopped over it beneath his red wool shirt. He moved on into the room with short, quick steps, putting his boots down as if he wanted to poke their spiked heels through the floor. His face was puffy and discolored, purplish jowls patterned by a network of veins, eyes bloodshot and bleary above their dark bags. His lusty, violent approach to life was in every movement, and his thick lips curled back off broken teeth when he spoke, jerking his close-cropped head toward Navarra. "What was Giddings here for then?"

Navarra's slumberous eyes slid to Denvers. "Giddings was hunting the murderer of Jale Hardwycke."

Caesar Sheridan looked at Denvers. "You kill Hardwycke?"

Denvers moved a hand helplessly. "I. . . ."

"Giddings must have been pretty sure to come this far," insinuated Navarra.

Sheridan threw back his scarred head and let out a laugh that made the crystal chandeliers tinkle above their heads. "Good for you, Denvers, good for you. I always hated that Hardwycke's guts. He thought all the land in Texas belonged to him just because he dealt in real estate. Always claiming we had no legal title to Matagorda. You must be pretty good with a gun if you got him. Or did you do it drygulch style? Never mind, never mind. I don't care how you did it. Any man who finished Hardwycke's beans is good enough for me."

"It would be dangerous for him to go back to the mainland now," said Navarra softly.

"Dangerous?" roared Caesar Sheridan. "Hell, it would be suicide. Hardwycke was a big man on the coast. I'll bet they've got a dozen posses out combing the gulf. How about signing on here, Denvers? I need a man with a gun like that."

Denvers looked toward Navarra. "You were saying something about the wallet?"

"Wallet?" said Navarra. "What wallet?"

## II

The sand of Dagger Point shifted restlessly under a mournful wind sweeping in off the Gulf of Mexico, and somewhere above the hoary crest of a grassed-over dune a sea fowl squawked plaintively at the night. Denvers had a time getting his paint mare into the first foamy breakers piling up on the shore, but finally she was splashing knee deep after Caesar Sheridan's fat bay. Carnicero shoved up beside Denvers on a shaggy old mule, forking a ratty Mexican-tree saddle.

"Why did Navarra start to ask me about the wallet last night?" said Denvers.

"How do I know?" said Carnicero. "You better not ask too many questions. You better be glad Sheridan let you stay on Matagorda."

"Who is Sheridan?" said Denvers. "He owns that house on the island? It was when he came in that Navarra seemed to forget about the wallet. He passed it off like it didn't matter. Did it?"

"You keep prying and I keel you."

"That seems to be your only pastime," said Denvers. "Carnicero means butcher, doesn't it?"

"Why else should they name me that?" said the Mexican. "It is my life. I was born with a *saca de tripas* in my hand. They pinned my swaddling clothes together with stilettos. I ate my *frijoles* with a Bowie knife from the time I was strong enough to lift it. When they gave me my first machete, I was so happy I went right out and killed my grandmother. You should see what I can do with a blade, *señor*. I could cut your ear off so deftly you wouldn't know it was gone till your hat began to slip down on that side of your head. Colonel James Bowie himself could not slice a man into as many strips with one knife as I. . . ."

"Will you stop that gab," said Caesar Sheridan angrily. He halted his bay in the shallows breaking on the mainland shore, turning to Denvers. "Neap tide's in the channel now. About this time of year it lasts from midnight till dawn, and a man can wade across on foot at the shallow spots like Dagger Point. You saw how it was. Water didn't get above your stirrups. If you get separated from us on the mainland, just be sure you get back here before daylight. Miss neap tide and you're stuck on the mainland most of the day. Nobody can swim that channel when the water's in. There's a riptide that'll pull the strongest swimmer under. I've never seen a horse that could make it." He paused, looking ahead. "I guess this is Prieto."

The dim shadow emerged from the gloom shrouding the desolate beach, resolving itself into a horsebacker. As he drew closer, the faded denim ducking jacket became visible, hanging slack from the stooped shoulders of a tall man, and the *conchas* winked dully from the batwings of old bullhide chaps. Prieto had come in the night before, angry at not having been met on the mainland, and his voice was still acrimonious as he spoke. "Bunch of coasters grazing about two miles inland. Your man, Judah, made sure Sheriff Giddings was in Refugio."

Prieto fell in beside Sheridan, giving Denvers a close glance. Denvers caught a glimpse of the gaunt, acrid face with its bitter eyes and tight mouth. Denvers had gotten the impression last night that Prieto was new to Matagorda, and that he belonged to Navarra more than to Sheridan. Denvers wondered why Prieto should be over here tonight. Navarra wasn't.

They lined out of the water to cross the pale sand, and soon the salt grass was swishing at Denvers's *tapaderos*. Post oaks began to loom up out of the night, and they forded a bayou with the rotten mud sucking at the horses' fetlocks and the croaking of bullfrogs all around them. They were riding through a veritable swamp now, the rising moon casting a ghoulish light down through the moss-festooned trees. A bull 'gator bellowed somewhere out in the pipestem cane, and Denvers slapped continually at the mosquitoes that fogged the air around him. They finally reached a solid bit of ground where a giant mulatto was holding a train of Mexican rat mules.

"They still watering, Judah?" asked Prieto.

The mulatto nodded a bullet head set on a neck like a bull's, and the thick muscles across his bare chest caught the light wetly as he hitched at his white cotton pants. Sheridan slipped a Sharps carbine from his saddle boot, turning to Denvers.

"There's a bunch of coasters grazing and watering in that cypress grove farther on. We're downwind of them. We'll be able to get right close before they spot us. Drop as many as you can before they get out of the trees."

"*Drop* as many?" queried Denvers. "What kind of roundup is this?"

"It's the way we work," said Sheridan. "Any complaints?"

Denvers shrugged, loosing his big Artillery Colt in its worn holster. Sheridan booted his bay, leaning forward in the saddle, and worked through the cypresses. Following him with the others, Denvers finally made out the first coaster grazing in the tall salt grass, a big brindle steer with withers as sharp as a Barlow knife and horns that gleamed like scimitars. The others were farther on, wallowing in the bayou that ran through the cypresses, feeding in the knee-high grass. Suddenly the brindle raised its head, turning toward the men.

"Let's go!" whooped Caesar Sheridan and flopped his *tapaderos* out wide to bring them back in against the bay with a solid, fleshy thump. The horse shot out of the trees, and Sheridan's rifle was already bellowing. The brindle let out a scream of mortal pain, whirling to stumble a few steps away from Sheridan then sinking down into the muck. Denvers charged through the salt grass after Judah and Prieto, throwing down on the first beef he neared, a big, speckled heifer that got tangled up in the Spanish moss of a cypress when it tried to run.

Denvers put two .44 slugs into it before the beast went down and then pulled up his paint and charged after another cow, guns thundering all around him, men bellowing as loud as the cattle. Carnicero was on Denvers's flank, quartering into a big dun steer with a lobo stripe down its back. He got within ten feet of the animal, an ancient Navy pistol held above his head to throw down.

"Shoot dat steer," roared Judah, emptying a pair of six-shooters in wild volleys at the cattle, laughing uproariously every time a beef squalled and went down. "What's the matter with you, Butcher? Waiting foah him to come up and take the gun away from you? Shoot dat steer."

But Carnicero galloped on past the dun without firing, shouting something over his shoulder, and whirled to chase after a big black farther on. Denvers's paint stumbled in the muck, and the Spanish moss tore him backwards in the saddle. Struggling in the festoons of wet green growth, he whirled his paint out from among the cypresses, breaking into the open with streamers of moss flung out behind him like dripping pennons. Suddenly Carnicero's mule stumbled and went down, and the Mexican went over his head, landing sprawled in the muck farther on. Judah came charging from the cypresses at one side, splashing into the bayou after a huge steer with blood streaming down its black hide. The giant mulatto had emptied his guns at it, but the beast was still going headlong. It tried to gain the trees again, bellowing frenziedly, but Judah quartered it, once more forcing the steer out into the shallow bayou. Squealing in rage and pain, it floundered straight toward Carnicero.

The Mexican got to his knees, mud dripping off his white pants, and brought up his old Navy. He drew a bead on the charging steer. Denvers thought all sound had stopped as he waited for the explosion of the Navy. Then he saw the strange fear cross Carnicero's face.

"I can't," he shouted in a cracked voice. "I can't shoot. Judah, get that crazy *cimarron* before he runs me down."

"What's the matter?" roared Judah. "I can't get him. My guns are empty. Shoot him, you damn' fool!"

The beast had gained momentum now and was bearing down on Carnicero, mud and water showering up back of its churning legs.

Denvers spurred his paint into a floundering run through the bayou, slipping off solid land into the rotten muck with a loud popping sound, viscid mud shooting up into his face. He threw down on the steer, and the Colt jumped in his hand with a hollow click. Empty!

Carnicero was stumbling backward, knee deep in the muddy water, shouting in terror. Denvers dropped his empty Artillery into its holster and tore the lashing off his dally, turning his horse so he would run in between Carnicero and the steer. But there were only a few feet left, and Denvers was about as far away from the two of them as the steer was from Carnicero. He knew he would never be able to cut in front of the steer before it reached the Mexican. He was close enough to see the terror in Carnicero's face. The steer loomed above the man, huge and black. Denvers had his loop swinging, and he leaned forward as he tossed. While the rope was still in the air, he jerked viciously to one side on the reins, thrusting his weight that way as the paint whirled and, when the loop settled about those great horns, the horse was going full speed in the opposite direction from the steer. Denvers snubbed his rawhide dally on the slick horn, and the violent impact almost pulled his chunky paint off her feet, cinches cracking loudly with the strain, saddle jumping beneath Denvers.

He heard the steer let out a tremendous, raucous bawl, and then he was off the paint, leaving it to stand there with forefeet braced to keep the rope taut on the steer. At least they bred ropers in this godforsaken swampland. The beef was on its back in the bayou, feet flailing, great horns sending up spouts of foul mud as it tossed its head wildly from side to side. Denvers stumbled toward the huge beef through the muck, jacking empties from his Artillery and thumbing in fresh ones. He waited till the tossing head was turned his way and, as the steer lurched to get on its feet, he put a bullet between its bloodshot eyes. The beast suddenly stopped thrashing, and the rope went slack, and the tremendous black body sank back into the mud. Only then did Denvers see how close Carnicero was standing to the carcass. The Mexican hadn't moved from where he had been when the rope snubbed the steer, and he could have reached out and touched the animal's wicked, curving horn. Carnicero opened his mouth, letting out a shaky laugh, lips working around his words for a moment before he could make any sound. Finally he swallowed, stuttering.

"*Barba del diablo*, if that *ladino* had come one more foot, I would have been hanging on those horns instead of your rope. Where did you learn to swing a dally like that, Denvers?" The blood had come back into his dark face by now, and the grin faded, and he began to pout like a sullen child. "*Pues*, just because you save my life, don't think I won't keel you the first chance I get."

Denvers laughed. "Why didn't you shoot that steer when you had the chance? It was point-blank. You couldn't have missed."

Carnicero's eyes lowered uncomfortably, and he wiped his nose, sniffling. "*Dios. Sacramento.* I got my powder wet in the mud, that's all. What else? I got my powder wet. *Sí.*"

Denvers took the Navy from his lax hand, spun the cylinder, then looked up at Carnicero, frowning. "What do you mean you got your powder wet? It didn't even touch the bog. This whole gun's as dry as the top of my hat."


### III


They had hauled the carcasses up onto dry land, and Judah dismounted after the last beef had been dragged in. Taking a long skinning knife from his belt, he started to slice a beef's hide down to its leg.

"You going to jerk the meat right here?" said Denvers.

"Jerk the meat?" laughed Judah. "Jerk the meat, he says. Denvers, that meat ain't worth curing even. It's the hides. I guess you ain't been working this part of the country, eh? Two and a half cents a pound for beef in Kansas City. For what it costs to drive cows up there, you could make more profit on dirt. Cows ain't worth raising for their beef any more. Hides and tallow is all we take now. Where you come from, anyhow?"

"New Mexico," said Denvers.

"No wonder you don't know," said Judah. "You're right in the middle of the Skinning War, boy. Ain't you heard? A man in Refugio says that last year Texas shipped out three million dollars' worth of hides. How many hides is that, Butcher?"

"More than you'll ever be able to count," muttered Carnicero. "That ain't all. My cousin, he can read, and he saw in the *Galveston News* that a hundred million pounds of tallow was shipped out in Eighteen Seventy-Four. They don't have branding season any more in Texas. It's skinning season. Hides-and-tallow 'punchers we are now. Not cowpunchers."

"Quit blowing your air and get to work with that skinning blade, Butcher," said Caesar Sheridan.

"I tell you what," said Carnicero. "I'll haul them in, and you skin them."

"We've hauled them all in," growled Sheridan.

"There might be some we missed out there in the bayou."

"You get to work, dammit!" roared Sheridan.

"I hate to stain the blade of my knife with a cow's blood," pouted Carnicero.

"Maybe you never stained your blade with any blood," laughed Prieto.

"And maybe I keel you."

"Start skinning those hides," shouted Sheridan, rising up from a carcass with his beefy hands dripping blood and tripe. "Or do you want me to take your hide across the bay with the cows?"

Mumbling incoherently, Carnicero moved toward the black steer Denvers had thrown. He took out his gets-the-guts, regarding the long slim blade with a mournful expression then looked down at the steer. Denvers saw that his dark cheeks were wet.

"What's the matter with you?" yelled Sheridan.

"I can't," choked Carnicero and then began to cry like a baby. "*Madre de Dios*, I can't bear to think of cutting up this *pobrecito*. Such a pretty *bulto* he was, all black and young and strong. How would you like it if someone came along and shot you and took off your pretty *negro* hide? He never did anything to you. He never did anything to me. And now you want me to desecrate such a beautiful, wild creature by cutting him up."

Caesar Sheridan threw back his scarred, close-cropped head and sent the Spanish moss to fluttering with that thunderous laugh. Then he moved over to Carnicero in his quick, catty way, and shoved the Mexican toward the horse. "Go on, you old fool, haul them in if you like. I'll bet you never used that knife for anything more than eating *frijoles* with. 'Keel 'im'? You make me laugh. What happens when you come to using the knife on a man?"

"Oh, men are different," said Carnicero, his tears giving way to laughter with a sudden, child-like naïveté. "*Sí*, I slit their throats like this"—he drew his *saca de tripas* across his neck, chuckling—"I cut out their entrails with my gets-the-guts like this. I. . . ." He stopped with his *saca de tripas* pressed against his belly, and he was staring past Sheridan at something in the trees. Denvers followed the Mexican's glance. All he caught was a shadowy motion through the cypresses, but Carnicero's voice was shaking with terror. "*Madre de Dios. ¡Espíritu de Lafitte!*"

Sheridan whirled to look. "Lafitte's ghost? Where?"

Cringing, the Mexican raised a shaking hand to point toward the trees. "You saw him. Right there, Caesar. Cocked hat and satin knee pants and gold buttons and all. You saw him. Cross yourselves, *compadres*. You are cursed unless you do. You will die like Arno Sheridan."

Caesar Sheridan grabbed Carnicero by the arm, jerking him toward the trees. "No ghost killed my brother. You're showing me this thing, once and for all. I'm tired of hearing these stories. Whatever put that sword through my brother was human, and I'm proving it. Did you see, Judah?"

The mulatto was bent forward, whites of his eyes gleaming from his black face, lower lip slack and wet. "Lawd, Caesar, I saw somethin'. Don't go in there."

Still hauling Carnicero toward the trees, Caesar bent to scoop up his Sharps with a free hand. "There isn't any ghost, I tell you. If you saw something, it's human, and I'm getting it this time or my name isn't Caesar Sheridan. Come on, you puking dogie, show me."

"No. *Dios*, no!" Carnicero tried to pull back. "You can't catch a ghost, Caesar. I saw it. Cocked hat and satin knee pants and . . . !"

Caesar hauled him over the hummock of ground between the two cypresses, and they dropped into the lowland beyond, disappearing in the grove. Denvers started to follow, but Prieto caught his arm. "Never mind. It won't do any good."

"Yeah," muttered Judah, thickly. "How can you catch a ghost?"

"What are you talking about?" said Denvers. "This ghost."

"Lafitte's ghost," said Judah, looking over his shoulder. "You know, Jean Lafitte, the pirate? Who do you think built that house on Matagorda Island? It's where his mulatto mistress killed him. As long as there's a woman in that house, Lafitte's spirit is doomed to roam this coast. I've seen him before, over on the island. He'll kill us all, sooner or later, Denvers. You're crazy to stay on Matagorda. I'm crazy. I don't think I'll go back."

He whirled toward the cypresses, but it was only Carnicero, white pants dripping mud up to the knees as he came back through the trees. "Caesar caught sight of it again, and he was after it like a bull with a fly in his nose. I thought I'd come back."

"That was good work," said Prieto.

"But I really see the *espiritu*," said Carnicero huskily. "Right there between the trees. Lafitte's . . . !"

"I know, I know." Prieto waved a sinewy hand. "It was a good job. It got Sheridan away neat as a white Stetson."

"But I really saw the ghost!"

"Shut up," said Prieto. "We aren't talking about Lafitte's ghost. Sheridan's gone now, and we aren't talking about Lafitte's ghost."

A sudden grin flashed Judah's white teeth across his black face, and the thick muscles over his bare chest rippled as he flexed his arms, stepping toward Denvers. "That's right, Prieto. We better get it done before Caesar gets back."

Denvers noticed for the first time how the top of Prieto's holster was patterned with a myriad of faint scars that might have come from the man's fingernails raking the leather over and over again, and he suddenly understood that Prieto hadn't come with them tonight for the cows. For this? For what? With that same childish shift of emotion, the fear had left Carnicero now, and he was grinning at Denvers, caressing his *saca de tripas*. All of them, then. Denvers felt his throat close on his breath, and sweat broke out on his forehead. "Get what done?"

"Hardwycke's wallet," said Prieto. His holster made a soft, leathery sound against his bullhide chaps as he took a step toward Denvers, and the thin line of his mouth was as acrid and bitter as his voice. "We want it, Denvers."

"Seems a lot of folks want that wallet," said Denvers, trying to watch them all at once. "What's in it, Prieto? Twelve hundred dollars couldn't be so interesting. Something more?"

The salt grass swished eerily beneath Judah's advancing bare feet. "You don't need to worry what's in it, Denvers. You givin' it to us or we takin' it?"

Denvers understood fully now how it was, and he felt the spasmodic twitch of his hand curling above his gun. Three of them? He didn't think so. One, maybe, or even two, but not three. Not coming in from every side this way. Even if a man could pull his gun fast enough.

"I guess we're taking it," said Prieto.

The grass was wet beneath Denvers's feet, and a sudden shift of wind swept a streamer of Spanish moss between him and Prieto and then swept it out again. Their faces were turned ghastly by the moon, leering at him as each of them continued to move in, the lines of their bodies growing tense.

"Good," chuckled Judah. "Better this way anyhow."

From the corner of his eyes Denvers caught the ripple of Judah's heavy black chest. *All right, damn you.* Carnicero was easing his knife down, and Denvers had seen that kind of thrust before, used by all *saca de tripas*' men to rip a man's guts out. *All right.*

"I keel 'im?"

"You'll kill nobody," shouted Caesar Sheridan, plunging up out of the bayou on the other side, slapping the mud from his leggin's with the barrel of his Sharps. "What's going on here?"

Prieto turned with a palpable spasm, forcing a weak smile. "Nothing, Caesar, nothing. Get him?"

"What do you think?" said Caesar disgustedly. He looked narrowly from Prieto to Denvers and then the others. "Why didn't you come?"

"Nobody could catch a ghost," said Carnicero sullenly.

"Ghost?" Caesar Sheridan looked out into the somber depths of the cypress grove, shot through with pale, eerie moonlight. Somewhere a cat screamed, like a woman in mortal pain. Caesar moved his enormous shoulders, as if shrugging off something. "Let's get back to the skinning."

Denvers stood there a long moment, watching Prieto walk stiffly toward his horse, seeing Judah turn toward a carcass with a tight frustration in the twist of his lips. Finally Denvers moved over to a dead steer, surprised to find himself trembling. Reaction? He shrugged. He didn't know. He did know it hadn't been finished here tonight. At least he'd be expecting it next time. He had started to bend over the beef, but he stopped. "Pothook," he said.

Caesar was stripping off a hide. "Eh?"

"I said this steer carries a Pothook brand," said Denvers. "Esther told me what few steers you run on the island are marked with a Double S."

Caesar Sheridan's scarred, bullet head turned up. "So?"

"You got a bill of sale?"

Caesar straightened slowly, his long, thick arms hanging slightly forward from his squat, potbellied torso like a gorilla's. "And if I don't?"

"I might have known as much," said Denvers. "No wonder you made sure Sheriff Giddings was in Refugio tonight. I guess the bottom has really dropped out of the cattle business down here when a man rustles cows for their hides."

A slow grin spread Caesar's thick lips over his broken teeth. "You got your piggin' string on the right steer, Denvers. Now, get to work."

"I never took a cow that wasn't mine," said Denvers. "Even for the skin."

"You'd kill a man for a wallet that wasn't yours," said Caesar. "I think you'd better reconsider the cows."

"No," said Denvers. "I don't think I will."

Caesar Sheridan moved up to Denvers in that quick, catty way and stood there with his huge belly lopping over his tight belt. "You aren't in any position to be choosy, Denvers. The only reason you're safe, coming this far onto the mainland, is because we're with you and because we made sure Giddings and his posses weren't around this section of the coast. Try it alone and you'd run into those posses before your horse had time to dry the sea water off it. Or maybe you'd prefer a lynch rope."

"I'll take my chances," said Denvers and turned toward the paint.

He was yanked back around by Sheridan's bloody hand on his collar and pulled violently up against Sheridan's gross body, with the stink of blood and sweat and leather almost overpowering him. "Nobody's taking chances, Denvers, least of all me. If Giddings's posses caught you, you'd talk about tonight. I'm not having that. The only reason Giddings can't come on Matagorda with warrants for us is that he doesn't have anything to issue warrants for. The minute he gets positive proof of anything, that channel won't be any more protection to us than a mud fence after a big rain. And I'm not sending him that proof in the person of any witness tonight."

"Sheridan," said Denvers, "I'm leaving. Either you take your hand off me, or I'll take it off for you."

Denvers saw the slow flush creep into the man's sensual face, and for a moment the hand holding his collar trembled. Then Caesar Sheridan's lips drew back in that ugly grin. He threw back his close-cropped head and laughed. "You're not going anywhere," he roared. "And if you want to try it. . . ." His voice choked off in a gasp as Denvers's fist sank into his belly up to the wrist. Sheridan bent over spasmodically, and Denvers brought the same fist on up, smashing it into the hand holding his collar. With Sheridan's hand knocked away, Denvers swung his whole body into another blow at the man's gross belly. He felt his knuckles sink into the soft flesh until he thought they had gone through Sheridan. Caesar staggered backward, his face dead white, and twisted in a strange surprise, as if he hadn't believed a man Denvers's size could hit like that.

"I keel 'im," screamed Carnicero, and they were all in on him, shouting and yelling, Judah bringing his knee up against him and knocking him back into the salt grass. For a moment Denvers went to his knees beneath the weight of their bodies, fighting blindly, head rocking to someone's boot smashing his mouth. Then Caesar Sheridan came in from somewhere, roaring like a bull, tearing Judah off with an open hand and sending him backward in a spin that crashed him into a cypress, rolling Prieto aside with a backward swipe across the face. "This is mine!" roared Sheridan, grabbing Denvers by the collar again and yanking him onto his feet. "This is mine!"

Denvers ducked the man's first blow without having seen it coming, felt Sheridan's arm go past his head, and slugged for that belly. He heard Sheridan gasp and tried to tear free of the man, but this time Sheridan had him. He threw his ponderous weight to one side, blocking Denvers's next fist, and Denvers was taken off balance. They both rolled into the salt grass, boots spewing viscid, black mud. Sheridan got on top of Denvers's back and jammed his face in the mud, riding him like a bronc, slugging the back of his neck. Face driven deeper into the muck with each blow, Denvers tried to take a gasping breath and choked on the mud. He writhed over on his back, mud blinding him, reaching up to catch Sheridan's fist as it came down.

Gripping the fist in both hands, he rolled again, carrying Sheridan off him, and then he was on top. Sheridan grabbed him in a bear hug, and for the first time Denvers felt the incredible, driving strength of the man. He was pulled against Sheridan's gross body, unable to hit him, ribs cracking and popping under the inexorable pressure of Sheridan's massive arms. Somehow Denvers got his forearm in between Sheridan and himself, forcing it up until his hand was across Sheridan's face with the heel against the man's nose. Gasping weakly, he shoved upward, forcing Sheridan's head back. Sheridan made a desperate, strangled sound, rocking his scarred head from side to side in an effort to free himself, but Denvers kept his hand jammed against the man's nose and, finally, shouting in agony, Sheridan had to release his hug in order to tear himself away.

Denvers leaped up, the cypresses spinning around him, Prieto and Judah dim, unreal figures that seemed to sway toward him, bent forward with waiting leers on their warped faces. Then Sheridan was in front of him again, a massive wall moving in to crush him. Denvers spread his legs and once more sought the man's belly with his hard fists, trying to keep free of Sheridan's arms. He heard the man's gasps of pain every time he sank his knuckles into that roll of fat lopping over the broad black belt. Sheridan jumped back, sobbing for breath that wouldn't come, his crazy, roaring laugh echoing through the trees.

"By God, I haven't had a fight like this"—he broke off to grunt sickly as Denvers struck again and jumped on backward, bent almost double, shaking his bullet head—"damn you, Denvers, I'll kill you!"

He took a blow in the face to come in close with Denvers and caught Denvers's next blow with both hands, grasping his arm and swinging him around to slam against a tree. Denvers tried to get his shoulder in between himself and Sheridan, but Sheridan caught Denvers's lank, black hair and began beating his head against the furrowed bole of the tree. Denvers heard someone's desperate shout, realized it was his own, and felt himself writhing helplessly against the weight of Sheridan's gross torso holding him against the cypress, still beating his head against the trunk that way, and then he couldn't hear anything any more but the roaring in his head, or see anything, or feel anything, and finally even the roaring was gone.

## IV

Denvers's first conscious sensation, perhaps, was that of being suffocated. He reached out his hand with a sob, trying to shove away the heavy crimson damask all around him. A cool hand caught his, forcing it gently down again. Then, beyond his muddy boots, he saw the white and gold footboards of the bed, stuffed with the same color damask, and above his head the pulleys which drew the drapery of the four poster bed up, and finally the girl's face. She started to draw away, and he closed his hand on hers to keep her there. Then he felt the first real pain in his head, and it must have shown in his face, because her black eyes suddenly grew large with compassion.

"Nobody's ever whipped Uncle Caesar," she said. "You were a fool to try."

Denvers sat up, almost fell back, grabbed the fretted bedpost to keep himself erect. "Where's my gun?"

"I guess Uncle Caesar took it. He isn't mad at you, though. He's funny that way. He likes you all the better for standing up to him. He says you're the toughest"—she broke off to catch him as he tried to get up and almost fell on his face, stumbling against the marble-topped table by the window—"here, you can't do this . . . !"

"I'm getting out!"

She released him suddenly, allowing him to sink back onto the bed against the post, and her face was flushed. "The cattle?"

"I never ran wet cattle in my life, and I'm not starting now," he said. "Not even wet hides."

"I know, Denvers. I guess Uncle Caesar's been doing it ever since Dad died ten years ago. I've tried to make him quit, but what could I do? First it was cattle, rustling them from spreads on the mainland and running them across the channel at neap tide. They'd put them aboard a two-master Captain Garcia had waiting off Mocha Point and, by the time Sheriff Giddings got across with his posse, the only cattle on the island would be our own. Now, since the bottom dropped out of the beef market and this Skinning War started, it's been the same with hides." She stopped suddenly, anger pouting her full underlip. "I don't see what cause you have to be so finicky anyway."

It caused him pain to raise his head. "Hardwycke?"

"What's rustling compared to killing a man?" she said. "You're lucky Uncle Caesar let you stay. If you'd tried to get through the posses Giddings will have thrown along the coast, you'd be hanging from a cypress tree right now."

"You think I killed Hardwycke?" he said.

"You must have wanted that twelve hundred dollars pretty bad," she said bitterly, "to murder a man for it."

He shook his head dully. "Listen, I've kept my mouth shut because I didn't know where I stood here. The whole business is getting crazier all the time. I don't even know why I should tell you. How do I know you're not in this with your uncle, just as deep as the others?"

Her breath came heavily. "I'm not, I tell you. If I had any way to stop it, I would. But I can't turn in my own uncle to Giddings. I've tried. More than once, I've tried. But at the last moment I couldn't. It just isn't in me, that's all."

He waved a hand jerkily. "I'll take your word. Will you take mine?"

"For what?"

"That I didn't kill Jale Hardwycke," he said. "Bud Richie and me were driving a bunch of steers down from New Mexico to ship at Indianola. We were bedding down that night when we heard the shot. We came across somebody bending over Hardwycke's body there on the Karankawa Trail. The man jumped up and ran away into the brush. The wallet was still sticking out of Hardwycke's hip pocket. I guess we scared the other man away before he'd gotten it. Richie took the wallet out to see if we could identify the dead one. Giddings and his deputies showed up at that moment. I guess they'd been prowling the bayous for your uncle and heard the shot, same as us."

The girl was looking at him intently, and her voice sounded husky. "I want to believe you, Denvers . . . somehow."

He felt sick again and put his head into his hands. The back of his neck was wet, and he saw the china bowl of dirty warm water on the table. The rag beside it showed some blood. Sheridan had really done a job, beating his head against that cypress, then. Denvers became aware that the girl had moved closer, and he looked up. There was a strange, taut look in her face that drew him to his feet.

"I've got to believe you," she said. "You're the only one left."

"What do you mean?"

"Uncle Sheridan, Judah, Carnicero. I can't turn to them, can I? Uncle Sheridan's the one who's kept me on the island. When Sinton Navarra came, I thought, maybe, because he was an outsider"—she turned to one side, shrugging—"but he wasn't any help. He's mixed up in it, somehow. Denvers, please stay. . . ."

"Mixed up in what?" said Denvers.

Lamplight caught in her dark hair, with the vague, frustrated shake of her head, and she crossed her arms to rub her shoulders, as if she were cold. "I don't know, really. I can't name it. Something that's been going on here. Not the rustling. . . ."

"Lafitte's ghost?" She turned on him contemptuously. "Carnicero said he saw the ghost last night," said Denvers. "It's sort of a legend here? Your father. . . ."

"Arno Sheridan wasn't killed by a ghost," she said angrily. "Whatever killed him was human. My father was found stabbed to death farther up on the island when I was nine years old. I'm not talking about that anyway. The Lafitte legend was here long before I came. This is something different. Something recent. Maybe you saw it. Between Sinton and Uncle Caesar. Between all the men. They've changed. Watching for something. Waiting."

"You sure it doesn't have to do with this Lafitte business?" he asked. "What's the story?"

"About Lafitte?" She shrugged, turning to look out the window. "He was supposed to have built this house. Called it his Maison Rouge. French, for Red House. The real Maison Rouge was at Galveston Island. Lafitte settled on Galveston after the United States chased him out of Barataria. Then the Americans made him give up Galveston about Eighteen Twenty-One. Nobody really knows what happened to him after that. In fact, nobody really knows anything about the man. He's one of the greatest mysteries of the gulf, I guess. Most of the stories about him are just legends. This house is certainly old enough to have been built by him. We found some old-fashioned clothes in a chest out in the cypress grove. There's even a story about treasure he buried here on the island. But if you believed the legends, you'd be hunting buried treasure on every island off the Gulf Coast from Padre Island to Gran Terre."

"How about this one?"

She pulled aside the heavy crimson portière, and the open shutter rattled in the wind, and she stared absently outside. "Oh, on his last raid off Matagorda, Lafitte was supposed to have taken a Spanish ship, the *Consolada*, I think, down Cuba way. Half a million in doubloons and gold plate and all the other fixings you hear in one of those pirate stories. He brought it back here and buried it somewhere. You know his old custom of killing the two men he took out to help him dig the hole, so he'd be the only one left who knew its whereabouts? Then his mulatto mistress murdered him in a fit of jealousy, and Lafitte's men left Matagorda without having found the treasure. However, so the story goes, a letter had been written by Jean to his brother, Pierre, telling where this treasure was hidden on Matagorda. Such a letter, of course, would have to be carried by a man Lafitte could trust implicitly, so the tale chooses Dominique, his one-eyed gunner who had fought with Napoleon."

"You sound skeptical," said Denvers.

She shrugged. "I've lived here all my life, Denvers. It's no fairy tale pirate island spilling over with gold doubloons. It's just a bleak, lonely, empty sandspit, seventy miles long and five miles wide, full of squawking birds and crazy jackrabbits and crazy men."

She whirled away, dropping the portière, pacing restlessly toward the door, and he smiled. "You sound fed up."

She was facing him again, and the sudden intense bitterness in her voice was startling. "Fed up? I'm going crazy, Denvers. Don't you think I want to get off? I'd give my soul. The farthest inland I've ever been was Refugio and that was when I ran away. Uncle Sheridan found me there and brought me back. Even when I do manage to sneak away, about all I can do is wade across from Dagger Point and get my feet muddy in the swamps. What would I do if I went any farther? Ask someone to let me poke their cattle? I'm not a man. What chance has a girl got? Uncle knows that. He doesn't even bother keeping a very close watch on me. A girl can't run away from home like a boy. Nobody outside would give me a job. I've been in prison all my life. I've never seen the outside world. You don't know how I envy you." She had come toward him again, and he realized how near she was standing and how uncomfortable it made him. "And it isn't just that I'm fed up with the island, Denvers. I'm afraid. This last year, you don't know how I've been afraid. Something's happening here, Denvers. Something evil. . . ."

He stretched out an arm to express his concern. "Wait a minute, Esther. . . ."

"No." She stood rigidly now, looking down at him with a pale, strained face. "I'm not crazy, Denvers. You know it. You felt it when you first entered the house. I saw your face. I saw the way you looked around. It's something you feel and can't see. Tell me you didn't feel it?"

He frowned, mouth tightening. "Maybe I did. I thought it was because I was a stranger, maybe, coming in on this place, or because the house was so old."

She shook her head. "More than that. Something between Sinton and Uncle Sheridan. Something between all the men."

"Just who is Sinton Navarra?" he asked.

"The son of Esther's mother," said Sinton Navarra, "by her first husband," and closed the door as he came into the room. His black boots made no sound across the faded nap of the Empire Aubusson, and he moved with that light, swinging ease, so unfitting for such a large man, and his pouched eyes held that veiled inquisition, and a secretive smile played about his lips. "Yes," said Navarra. "Esther's mother had married before she came to Matagorda. Arno Sheridan was her second husband. Her first was Olivier Navarra, my father, who died of malaria at New Orleans in Eighteen Forty-Nine. I was sent to France to be reared and, while there, my mother married again. Thus, while I am really Esther's half-brother, I had not seen her until I came to Matagorda a few months ago. I take it my sister has been telling you of the horrible evil which hangs over this house. Ah. . . ." He held up a pale, long-fingered hand as the girl started to protest. "I understand, my dear, I understand. Matagorda has just gotten on your nerves, that's all. The incessant screaming of those beastly gulls. The never-ceasing pound of the surf." He cocked his dark head, moving to pull the portières aside. "You can hear it now, eh? You can always hear it. Beating, beating, beating, like some diabolical drum, calculated to drive a person insane. No, Esther, I don't blame you. I suppose she gave you the history of the house, too, Denvers." Navarra moved to the scarred Pembroke table at one side of the window, caressing a heavy, tarnished candelabra there. "She doesn't believe Lafitte built this house."

"I never said that," pouted Esther. "I just say you can hear legends about him almost anywhere along the gulf and very few of them own a shred of truth."

"Perhaps I am more of a romanticist," smiled Navarra softly. "The clothes you found in that old trunk in the garden, for instance, Esther. Or even the furnishings here. If a Colonial had furnished the house, everything would have been matched, don't you think? I mean Chippendale, or Georgian, or Late Empire. But look around you. The bed? French State, I'd say. And this candelabra? Undoubtedly of Spanish origin. And this Pembroke table. Hardly fitting together in one room.

My room's the same. A hodgepodge of Louis the Fourteenth and Spanish Colonial and Chippendale."

"You seem to know," said Denvers.

Navarra's shrug was deprecating. "I dealt in furniture in New Orleans for some years."

"I thought it was France?"

Navarra's heavy eyelids flickered with annoyance. "I have been many places, Mister Denvers. Many places."

"From New Orleans you should be an authority on Lafitte."

Navarra seemed to draw himself up. "An authority? I know every move Jean Lafitte made from the time he was born to the time he died, Denvers. I have been separating fact from fancy about Lafitte all my life. I know more about him than. . . ." He stopped abruptly, looking down strangely at Denvers, his brows raising as if in surprise. Then that soft, secretive smile caught at his lips, and he waved a hand. "But that is neither here nor there, is it? After all, Lafitte is long dead, and. . . ."

The scream came through the open shutter, above the sound of the surf, and Navarra was the one to jump for the door after the first stunned surprise had held them all there. "That wasn't any gull!" he said and took the stairs three at a time, stumbling across the dancing steps of the elliptical landing. Early dusk cast a dim luminescence through the circular fanlight above the door, limning a weird, shadowy form darting through the hallway. Denvers rose dizzly from the bed, and Esther rushed to help him keep his balance, while below Navarra tore open the front door and clattered across the pedimented porch. A few stunted cypresses surrounded the house, and Navarra thought he saw a form darting through them. He ran into the trees, taking a flagstoned walk, and stumbled across something, going to his knees. It was a man stretched out on the stones. He caught at Navarra's leg feebly. "I found where he stays," he gasped. "Just like Arno Sheridan I was up past Dagger Point and I found . . . where . . . he stays."

The man had stopped talking by the time Denvers and Esther reached him. Navarra shook him without response. Esther looked at Navarra. "Who is he?"

Navarra toed the dead body with an immaculate boot. "One of Sheridan's hands."

Carnicero came running through the trees, sobbing. "I saw it. *Madre de Dios*. I saw it. Lafitte!"

"Oh, now, Carnicero," said Navarra, raising his hand.

"You don't believe me?" blubbered Carnicero. He bent toward the dead man, pointing a shaking finger at the bloody wound in his side. "Look. Stabbed. The same as Esther's father was stabbed. Not by a knife, *señores y señorita*. Don't you think I've seen enough knife wounds to know? This man was stabbed by a sword!"

V

The stench of rotten meat was so strong it had begun to nauseate Ernie Denvers. The only sound for a long time had been the squealing birds and the dull pound of the surf. *No wonder the girl was fed up*, he thought. *Fed up? A man could go mad in a place like this*. He sat heavily on the paint mare they had given him, slitting his eyes against the biting sand blown up by the morning gulf wind. Ahead was Mocha Point, a long, rickety pier jutting out from the high spit of grass-topped land, and all along the shore were huge piles of decaying beef, covered black with scavenging birds.

"All legal," Caesar Sheridan was saying. "Nothing wrong with having our own packery on Matagorda, see? Shank Pierce has one across the bay. That's where most of the cows in Texas are going now. Private packing. Hides and tallow. And who can stop us from packing our own tallow and skinning our own beef here? Nobody. We run our herds on the island, don't we?"

"And if you wade across to the mainland every night after a few dozen of somebody else's hides, who's to know the difference?" said Denvers sarcastically.

Sheridan threw back his head to let out that roaring laugh. "That's right, boy, that's right. A fallen hide belongs to anyone who wants to skin it, no matter what the brand. Just like in the old days a maverick belonged to anybody who put his dally on it. That's the law. And that's the Skinning War. Texas is full of hide rustlers that help a hide to fall by filling it full of holes. That's why Giddings can't prove anything on us. All he's ever seen is the carcasses we leave. Could be any one of half a dozen gangs operating along the coast. Time Sheriff Giddings gets over here, our shipment of hides has left aboard the two-master Garcia docks here to load up, brands blotted out and everything."

Navarra had a silk handkerchief held across his nose. "That Mexican who was killed yesterday smelled almost as foul as this, Caesar. Was he one of the hands you have down here?"

Sheridan nodded. "This Lafitte thing is getting on my nerves. Any more trouble like that and my Mexicans are going to leave the island."

"Have you ever seen this ghost yourself?" asked Denvers.

Navarra waved his handkerchief disgustedly. "Of course he hasn't. These Mexicans are just a bunch of superstitious animals."

"Why would it necessarily have to be Lafitte's *ghost?*" asked Denvers. "You can laugh off Carnicero's stories, but not that dead Mexican a week ago. Killed with a sword? Who carries a sword nowadays?"

Sheridan frowned at him. "Don't be loco. Those Lafitte stories are so much tripe."

"Navarra doesn't really think so," said Denvers. "When was Lafitte supposed to have died, Navarra?"

"*Supposed?*" Navarra's voice was sharp. "He did die. You know the story."

"And a hundred others," said Sheridan. "I've hit just about every town along the gulf, from Port Isabel to New Orleans, and every one has Lafitte dying in their own town hall. I met an old sea captain at San Antone who claimed he saw Lafitte on his death bed there in Eighteen Thirty-One. I saw another one who swore he found Lafitte's grave near Indianola."

"He died in Eighteen Twenty-Six," said Navarra angrily. "He was in his middle thirties."

"And this is Eighteen Seventy-Five," mused Denvers. "Fifty years added to a man's middle thirties. Have you ever seen all of Matagorda Island, Sheridan?"

The older man shrugged. "No need to. Nothing up at the other end. We ran cattle down there. Island's too big to use all of it."

"This is fantastic," said Navarra. "Lafitte was a brilliant man, a vivid cosmopolitan, a gentleman of the world. Even supposing he didn't die, a man like that wouldn't isolate himself on a lonely. . . ."

"You said yourself this place could drive a man mad, Navarra," grinned Denvers.

"But fifty years . . . ?"

"I've seen a lot of spry old men past eighty."

Navarra turned away, swabbing angrily at his nose with the handkerchief. "I refuse to discuss it any longer."

Sheridan leaned back in his saddle, slapping his thigh with a raucous laugh. "He's gotcha, Sinton. That dead Mexican didn't meet up with no ghost and neither did my brother. How do you know Denvers ain't right? Maybe that story about Lafitte building this house is true. Maybe the old boy's been running around here with his sword like Carnicero claims."

"Don't be a stupid ass," said Navarra thinly.

Sheridan's laugh broke off abruptly, and he spurred his horse, jumping it around in front of Denvers's paint to bring the animal broadside across the head of Navarra's black. He grabbed the black's bridle, yanking it around till he held its head down by the rump of his horse and was facing Navarra. "Don't call me names, Sinton," he said.

All the indignant hauteur had slipped from Navarra, and his smooth, soft voice formed a sharp contrast against Sheridan's guttural roar. "Take your hands off my bridle. I don't like it."

"Maybe we better make it clear who bosses this island before I do that, Sinton," said Sheridan.

"Caesar," said Navarra deliberately, "don't threaten me. I'm not one of your Mexican hands. I'm not afraid of you."

Sheridan looked at Navarra a long moment. "No," he said finally. "No, I don't think you are, Sinton. But get this"—he yanked viciously upward on the bridle, causing the black to jump—"I'm running Matagorda and, nephew or no nephew, you'll do as I say when you're here.

You've been bucking me ever since you came, Sinton. I don't know what it is. I can't put my hands on it, but it's been there. Don't go any farther." He jerked the bridle again. "Don't let me get my hands on it. If you do, I'll tear it apart and you too."

He threw the horse's head away from him and necked his own fat bay around, flapping both feet out wide to bring them in with a solid, popping sound, and the bay jumped forward. Navarra sat his black there without moving, watching Sheridan go. There was an ineffable evil in the way his thick lids had closed almost shut over his eyes, the network of minute veins giving their pouched, dissolute flesh a sickly blue shadow. He seemed to become aware that Denvers was watching him and turned, glancing at him momentarily. Then, with an angry thrust of his head, he urged his horse forward.

There was a row of tallow vats along the shore near the pier and back of them was the slaughter shanty. Prieto and another Mexican were skinning carcasses by the shanty, and Carnicero was mounting a bloody-hoofed horse preparatory to hauling a skinned cow to the nearest pile of rotting meat.

"We tried salting the beef," Sheridan told Denvers. "But all we could get for a two-hundred-pound barrel was nine dollars. Even that tallow don't bring much more than what it costs to ship. The hides are the only things that really pay. You help Prieto with the skinning today."

Carnicero disappeared behind the piles of meat, hauling his carcass, and came back to dismount and climb up a ladder on the nearest tallow vat. Denvers was off his paint by then, rolling up his sleeves, when the Mexican *vaquero* came fogging through the piles of carcasses, his sombrero flapping against his back. "Another cut of steers disappeared from our north herd this morning," he called to Sheridan, hauling his lathered horse to a stop.

"Did you see anything?"

The man crossed himself. "*Madre de Dios*, does one see an *espiritu*!"

Sheridan turned to Navarra, face turning dark. "There's your ghost again. How do you explain that?"

"I don't purport to," said Navarra. "I just say Lafitte died in Eighteen Twenty-Six."

"Hell!" snarled Sheridan, turning to Prieto. "I'm going out to see what kind of tracks they found this time. You put Denvers to work."

The odor of rotting meat was oppressive, and Denvers reached for his bandanna to slip it over his nose. It was then he noticed how Prieto was watching him. The man's thin, bitter face was turned after Sheridan, riding away, but his glittering black eyes were looking sideways toward Denvers, and they held a sly, waiting light that stopped Denvers's hand with the bandanna just beneath his jaw. Then he heard the squeak of saddle leather behind him. Navarra?

"Did someone really cut out a bunch of steers this morning?" said Navarra.

"Strangely enough, yes," said Prieto, turning fully around toward Denvers, smiling mirthlessly. "I heard about it before sunup and sent word to have someone ride in with the news when Caesar came. If it hadn't happened that way, I would have found something else to pull him away."

Denvers caught his first sight of Judah coming down between the piles of beef, slapping at the swarm of flies buzzing around his great, black, sweating torso. He had a big meat cleaver in one hand.

"Good," said Navarra from behind Denvers. "Good."

Carnicero was now climbing down the ladder from the top of the tallow vat and moving with heavy feet toward Denvers from the opposite side of Judah. Denvers couldn't keep his eye on all of them at the same time.

"We've been wanting to get you alone like this," said Navarra.

"You mean you don't want Sheridan to know?" said Denvers, and his voice sounded like mesquite scratching saddle leather.

"You might put it that way," said Navarra, taking a small step around in front of Denvers. "I think you know what we want, Denvers."

Denvers had never wanted a gun so desperately. Four of them. Three on the mainland had been bad enough, and even there with his gun he had gone into it knowing how it would end. But now four. "This is why you didn't let Sheriff Giddings take me?" he said tensely. "What's in Hardwycke's wallet you all want so bad?"

"Surely you know," said Navarra.

"Not the twelve hundred dollars."

"Not the twelve hundred dollars," said Navarra.

"Maybe I don't have the wallet."

Navarra's blue-shadowed lids closed slowly across his black eyes. "I think you have. You can give it to us now. Or we can take it. Whichever way you prefer."

*Whichever way you prefer*. It almost made Denvers laugh. Whichever way you prefer. Sheridan wouldn't be coming back this time. All right. He still felt weak from the last fight but what the hell. He spread his feet a little in the sand.

"Am I to assume that you wish us to take it?" said Navarra.

"I can't give you what I don't have."

Carnicero had his *saca de tripas* out. That wasn't so much. Neither was Judah's cleaver. It was the gun. He wouldn't stand a chance after one of them pulled a gun. He couldn't let it get that far. All right. That would start it then. The first man to go for his gun would start it. He was still watching Navarra and remembering that French Le Page in the man's shoulder harness.

"If you don't have it on your person," said Navarra, "we'll find out where you put it."

"You won't lay a hand on me."

"We'll find out where you put it. If you don't have it on you. Either way. It doesn't matter. Once more, Denvers. Will you give us the wallet?"

The surf boomed dismally behind Denvers, and the gulls swarming over the rotten piles of meat made a horrible, raucous din, and the sweat had soaked through his shirt beneath the armpits. *The first man to go for his iron*. Judah's bare feet made a shuffling sound in the sand. Denvers ran his tongue across dry lips. The first man.

"Why waste time?" snarled Prieto.

"All right," said Navarra, and it was he.

There was no thought behind Denvers's move. He had been so keyed up to it that he felt nothing, actually, until he struck Navarra. He must have leaped, because he heard his own grunt, and then he was up against the big, dark man, grabbing for the hand Navarra had snaked behind his coat, and all of them were shouting around him.

Denvers's weight carried Navarra backward, and the two of them reeled across the sand, knocking Prieto aside as he sought to draw his gun. For that moment surprise robbed Navarra of any reaction. By the time he had recovered, Denvers had the man's hand twisted around, jerking the big French pin-fire from it. Still staggering backward to keep from falling, Navarra floundered into the surf and, with the first wet slap of brine against his legs, Denvers responded to the drive of a heavy body crashing onto his back.

"No, Judah, don't," screamed Navarra, tearing free of Denvers. "You'll kill him."

The blow that struck Denvers's head sent him to his knees with the Le Page still gripped desperately in his fist. Through the roaring pain in him he sensed that the giant mulatto was shifting to strike again and rolled sideways through the shallow water, trying to keep the gun held above it. Navarra tried to catch him and got one hand on his shoulder. In that moment Denvers felt the violence of the man's strength. Then he had torn free, with Judah's meat axe slapping the water where he had been a moment before. Still floundering away, he realized the mulatto must have been set to cleave him in two and had shifted the axe in the last moment to strike with the flat of the blade instead of the edge, when Navarra had first shouted.

Prieto's shot sounded sharply above the dull wash of the surf, and Denvers whirled toward him, struggling to his feet. Still stunned by the mulatto's blow, he was surprised to feel the French gun jump in his hand, and the explosion jarred him partly out of his dazed pain. He heard Prieto's shout, and Prieto's gun go off again, and the lead splashed water up at him, and then he had the Le Page going. It sounded like a whole crew of triggermen fanning their irons in front of his face, and he had never dreamed a gun could sling so much lead.

"Navarra," he heard Prieto yell, "stop him," and then Prieto stopped yelling and, knowing that was over, Denvers whirled to meet Judah as the mulatto floundered through the water toward him with the meat cleaver. Denvers's shot went into the foaming breaker at his feet, and he followed it, driven down by the man who had leaped on his back. He twisted around, firing blindly against the man's body, but the gun had been in the water now, and it made a soggy, clicking sound. Desperately he pistol-whipped the contorted face above him. Carnicero? It was gone, and he heard the man's pained cries, and he was trying to get to his feet again, gasping and choking, spitting out salt water, when he caught the flash of Judah's cleaver.

His plunge aside ducked his head beneath the sea again, and he threw himself at Judah, blinded by the stinging brine, feeling Judah's arm strike his shoulder with the blow that had missed. Inside the reach of that cleaver now, he struck at Judah's face with the gun. He heard the mulatto's hoarse scream and followed the falling body on back, straddling it to strike again, driving the man's bloody face beneath the water. The next breaker washed Denvers off Judah's limp frame, and he floundered backward, off balance, into Navarra, who had been stumbling toward him from the shallow water.

Waist deep they met, and Navarra's hands caught Denvers's wrist as Denvers tried to strike with the Le Page. They reeled back and forth with the breakers carrying them inshore and the backwash carrying them out again, Navarra trying to twist Denvers's arm around so he couldn't use the gun. Finally the heavy man twisted Denvers into position to apply pressure, and the pain brought a strangled shout from Denvers, and he felt the gun slip from his fingers, falling into the water. He tore his wrist free of Navarra's grasp, seeking the man's legs beneath the water. He found them and snaked one foot behind Navarra's knee, suddenly throwing his whole weight against the man.

Navarra stumbled backward, and at that moment a breaker struck them, carrying the larger man down with Denvers on top. It washed their struggling bodies inshore until Denvers was straddling Navarra in shallow water, his knees on the sandy bottom, his head above the sea. He found Navarra's neck with both hands and held the man's head down that way, feeling the thick muscles swell and writhe beneath his fingers as Navarra tried to rise above the water. Another roller foamed over, and Denvers's own head was submerged. When it had passed, he came out gasping and coughing, still holding the other man under with a desperate grip. Navarra jerked back and forth beneath Denvers in a spasmodic frenzy, hands clawing, legs kicking, but his struggles were growing weaker. A man was on Denvers's back then, tearing him off Navarra. He twisted from one side to the other under the blows, clinging with the last of his strength to the man beneath him.

"*¡Por Dios!*" shouted the one on his back, hooking an arm around his neck. "He's dead now. Get off him, will you? I keel you!"

Navarra's struggles ceased, and Denvers released his hold, turning to thrust feebly at Carnicero. The Mexican had one arm around Denvers's neck, the other drawn back with his knife. Denvers tugged weakly to one side, and they rolled off Navarra. A breaker swept them up on the wet sand at the water's edge. Carnicero rose above Denvers, straddling him. Denvers tried to catch the knife arm, but the whole desperate struggle had left no strength in him, and his grab missed, and his breath left him in a weary gust. Carnicero held the knife suspended above Denvers's chest for a long moment, a strange, indefinable expression crossing his face. Then the first lugubrious tear dropped from his eye.

"I can't," he said, and the tears began to stream down his face. "I was born with a *saca de tripas* in my hand. They pinned my swaddling clothes together with stilettos. I ate my *frijoles* with a Bowie knife from the time I was two. All my life they have called me Butcher for what I can do with a knife. And now, when I get the chance"—he began to whimper like a baby—"I can't keel you!"

## VI

Somewhere in an upstairs room a shutter slapped dismally in the wind. The chamber they had given Denvers was dark, and a rotten board creaked every time he paced past the Pembroke table. He halted at the window a moment, drawing aside the tawdry portières of crimson damask to look out at the somber clouds scudding across the slate-colored afternoon sky. He was hungry, and his boots were still soggy from the fight in the surf, and his head throbbed painfully from the blow Judah had given him with the flat of the meat cleaver. He turned back to start pacing restlessly again and then stopped abruptly, hearing the rattle of the door. Esther Sheridan pushed it open hesitantly and came in with a candle.

"It's getting dark," she said. "I thought you might like a lamp."

He watched her lift the glass reservoir on the Sandwich lamp, adjusting the wick spout until the candle flame caught. The camphine sent out a pungent odor, and the flickering light rose to glow against the curve of her cheek before she settled the glass again. Then she blew out the candle and stuck it in an empty socket of the candelabra on the Pembroke. It brought her close to him and, when she turned, there was a searching depth to her eyes. "What is it they have against you, Denvers?"

"Who?"

"Prieto's pretty badly wounded," she muttered, still studying his face. "They don't think he'll live. Navarra must have been pretty nearly drowned. He's still in his bed. Judah's face looks like a side of beef somebody's been chopping steaks off of. Or maybe it's not what they have against you. Maybe it's what they want from you."

He turned away from her, going shakily to the window again, wondering if he still feared that he couldn't trust her, or if it were himself he couldn't trust, now. It did something inside him to have her stand that close. Esther was only nineteen, and yet she did something inside him. He couldn't smell the camphine any more. He wondered what made her hair so sweet.

The girl began to laugh suddenly. "I guess they didn't know what kind of *cimarron* they were stringing their dallies on when they jumped you. Four at once and you haven't even got a scratch on you to show for it!"

"My head hurts, my body aches everywhere, and I have trouble standing up," he said and shifted uncomfortably as he sensed her beside him again.

"What is it?" she asked insistently.

He turned suddenly, driven somehow by her nearness, by the scent of her black hair, wanting to trust someone. "The wallet, the wallet. What else?"

She drew a sharp breath. "Hardwycke's wallet?"

"Navarra started to ask me for it when I first got here," said Denvers. "Changed his mind when your uncle came into the room. I didn't even realize Navarra had asked me for it. Then Prieto began putting on the screws when we went after those hides on the mainland night before last. Your uncle broke that up again. Yesterday afternoon they got Caesar away for good."

"They're afraid of him," she said.

"Navarra isn't," said Denvers.

"I don't think Sinton Navarra is afraid of anything," she muttered. "But the others are afraid of Uncle Caesar. You saw what he did to you. You can lick all four of them put together, but you can't lick Uncle Caesar. Do you blame them for fearing him? I'm afraid of him myself."

"Maybe they do fear him," he said, "but is that the reason they wanted him gone?"

"If Sinton's up to something, Uncle Caesar would kill him if he found out. What's in the wallet they want so badly?"

He shrugged. "How should I know? I don't have it."

Her voice was surprised. "Who does?"

"Sheriff Giddings," said Denvers. "He took it from Bud Richie."

"But you took his horse, he said."

Denvers jerked his dark head impatiently. "Giddings followed me here, didn't he?"

She caught at his arm. "But that doesn't mean he found where his horse had dropped beneath you, Denvers. I found you in that cane brake opening onto the sea. How far back had you left the dead horse?"

"At the head of the bayou," he said. "Beyond those canes."

Her voice was rising now. "That's Indian Bog. You must have come through the bog itself. Nobody takes that route. It's too dangerous. We've lost more cattle in there than any other bayou on this coast."

"I found a solid strip in the muck," he said. "They were right on my heels, and I had to take a chance."

"But Giddings wouldn't have followed you that way. It's the only reason you gave him the slip. He'd take the edge of the bog around to the coast before crossing at Dagger Point. And if he came that way, he'd never find his dead horse."

"If the wallet's still there. . . ."

"It might tell us what this is all about," she cried. "Listen. We can't leave the house together. Uncle Caesar thinks we're trapped here because the tide's in, and there aren't any boats on this side. He won't be watching so closely. When they all go back into the kitchen to eat, slip out the side door and meet me in the cypress grove."

## VII

Caesar Sheridan was sitting at the big oak table in the living room, playing solitaire, and he grunted as Denvers entered. "You seen Sinton?"

"Navarra? Not since yesterday."

"He ain't in his room," said Sheridan, slapping a queen down disgustedly. Then he turned in his chair, putting a beefy hand on his knee. "What happened yesterday, anyway? What's between you and Navarra?"

"Maybe he don't like the way I part my hair," said Denvers.

Sheridan snorted like a ringy bull. "Don't try to put that in my Stetson. Ever since Sinton hit this island, there's been something funny going on. You in it?" Denvers started to answer, but Sheridan went on, turning back to the cards, talking more to himself than to Denvers. "When Sinton first showed up, I let him stay because he was kinfolk. Now I'm afraid to let him go for fear the sheriff will tie onto him, and Sinton will talk. Same reason I'm afraid to let you go. You ain't planning a run-out, are you? I'll bet. Well, it won't do no good. Tide's in now, and you'll get pulled down by the rip if you try to swim. I've got a Mexican down at the barn with orders to shoot if you try to sneak a horse. I swear, Denvers, I don't know what to do with you. Messing up my men. Bringing the sheriff down on my head. Up to something, I swear. . . ."

"Beans on," said Judah from the kitchen door. He stood there looking at Denvers with murder in his eyes as black as the hide on his bruised, lacerated face. Sheridan shoved his chair back and rose with a grunt. "Coming?"

"I'm not hungry," said Denvers.

Sheridan threw back his head to laugh. "You mean you don't hanker to go in Judah's kitchen and let him hang over you with a butcher knife. Well, I can't say as I blame you. One time's enough for a while."

He stomped through the kitchen door, growling something at the mulatto. After a moment Denvers moved across the parlor to the side door. It was unlocked, and he slipped out. The cypresses acquiesced to the biting wind with a mournful sigh, heavy foliage beating into Denvers's face as he sought the girl. She startled him by stepping from behind a huge trunk. Without a word she led him over the short, rank prairie grass that covered the inland portion of the island, reaching the sandy shore finally. The moon had risen by then, and Denvers took off his high-heeled boots to walk the rest of the way. It took them an hour to reach the spot past Dagger Point where the tall sea grass flanked a bayou that cut back into the island. His feet sank ankle deep into the muck as he dropped down its bank toward the water. Finally the girl parted the growth from the prow of a skiff.

"Uncle doesn't know about this," said Esther. "I came across it last year, hidden up here. Somebody else must have been using it. I've found new pitch in the seams several times."

He helped her haul the leaky, battered skiff into the water. "Anybody else on the island?"

"Some Mexicans on the other end, but that's fifty-six miles. Maybe a few crazy hermits in between. Uncle says you always find them on a place like this. We had a couple helping us brand last fall. Maybe one of them."

He had never rowed a boat before, and they made heavy work of it across the choppy channel. About half way over they had shipped so much water that Esther had to bail with his hat while he worked the splintery oars. They reached the shore of the mainland and hunted along the coast until long after midnight before finding the mouth of the bayou leading toward Indian Bog. Finally the reeds and muck of the bayou became too thick for further rowing, and they hauled the boat ashore, hiding it in some salt grass. The air here was oppressive with the scent of hyacinth growing along the water, and the festoons of Spanish moss caught wetly at Denvers's shoulders as Esther led him inland. Stumbling wearily through the tangled marshes, tormented by the vicious mosquitoes, they at last found the pipestem

brake Denvers had broken through that night and hesitantly penetrated the rattling canes. The booming of the frogs rose all about
them, and somewhere a panther squalled. Esther's hand was suddenly
thrust into his, warm and moist, and her voice sounded strained.
"You'll have to lead the way from here on in. Think you can remember?"

The bellow of a 'gator startled him. He parted the canes with his
free hand, peering into the gloom ahead, hunting for that big spread
of water lilies he had stumbled through. Then his foot sank into rotten
mud up to his knee, and the girl caught at him with a sharp cry.
Indian Bog? Indian Bog. On the right he caught the sickly white gleam
of lilies. There was something revolting about the whole place. The
canes rattled like hollow bones, and the salt grass stank, and a foul
odor of decay rose from the mud, and the wild hyacinth waved feebly
in the breeze like dying hands. The first sign they had of the horse
was the buzz of flies. The moon was sinking with the coming morning,
and they barely made out the rotting carcass, covered with flies and
gnats, half eaten away by scavengers. Stomach knotting, Denvers
forced himself to approach the animal. The Mexican saddle bags Giddings had carried were called *alforjas* and, when Denvers bent to open
them, the flies swarmed up with a loud, angry buzzing, sending a
revulsion through him so sharp he almost jumped back. He ripped at
the pocket of the *alforjas* and put his hand inside.

"All right," said a soft voice from behind him. "Pull it out and
give it to me."

Denvers took his hand slowly from the saddle bags, turning to
face Navarra who stood in the cane brake. The man had recovered
his Le Page from the surf the day before, and it was in his hand now.
Behind him Carnicero's bucolic face showed dimly in the darkness.
The girl stood where Denvers had left her, a taut surprise on her face,
her hands to her mouth.

"We came across at low tide," smiled Navarra. "Been hunting up
and down the coast for that dead horse all evening. Thought maybe
you'd been telling the truth about not having the wallet. Then Carnicero spotted you coming down the shore in that skiff. We followed

you in through the bayou, going along the edge. Give the wallet to me, Denvers."

"The *alforjas* are empty," said Denvers.

He saw the little muscles bunch up beneath the thick flesh of Navarra's heavy jaw. With a muttered curse Navarra rushed at him, shoving him aside to stoop over the saddlebags.

"Never mind, Navarra. Denvers is right. The *alforjas* are empty."

Navarra stiffened perceptibly then straightened from the dead animal. Denvers saw him then, Sheriff Giddings, standing on past Esther, his big Colts gleaming dully in his hands. Navarra made a small, spastic gesture to raise his Le Page.

"Don't," said Giddings. "Ollie's behind you. Drop the gun or you'll be deader'n that hoss." The sheriff began moving forward. "Think we wouldn't figure on this? When I saw Denvers at your house on the island, I couldn't be sure he was my man. Like you say, it was dark that night of Hardwycke's murder and, even up close, I didn't get a good enough look at him to identify positive. But I knew that bullet I'd put in my hoss would drop him eventually. Took us a long time to find the animal. Think you'd reach it before we did, Denvers? When I found that wallet still in the saddle bags. . . ."

"You have the wallet?" Navarra asked.

Sheriff Giddings answered sharply. "That's right. You won't get the twelve hundred dollars, either. I been hunting thieves half my life, Navarra, and I know the way their minds work. Like I say, when I found that wallet still in the saddle bags, I knew Denvers would be back. I knew just how his mind would work. It was that twelve hundred dollars he killed Hardwycke for, and it would draw him back like a fly to molasses. Soon's he discovered he'd left it on the hoss, he'd be coming. So I just squatted with my posse. Looks like I got a bigger catch than I planned. That's all right, too. There's a little matter of some Pothook steers I'd like to discuss with you. It's getting near dawn now. Ollie, you get the horses, and we'll take these folks to Refugio."

Ollie Minster made a short, squat shadow back in the canes, moving to get the horses. Denvers saw the shift of other possemen. Two of them were closing in from behind a cypress, holding carbines. Denvers was half turned toward Carnicero when he saw the Mexican staring past the two men who had just appeared from behind the tree. He raised his hand to point, and his voice was hardly audible.

"*Madre de Dios*. There it is. Believe me now? See for yourself. *Madre de Dios*. Jean Lafitte himself!"

Denvers didn't actually see anything beyond the two men except that first shadowy movement in the trees, and then they turned with their guns. One of them shouted hoarsely, and the Spanish moss whipped around them with their scuffle. Then the man who had shouted staggered backward, gasping. The other began pumping his gun.

"Giddings," he shouted, and his voice was drowned by his racketing Winchester. "I saw him, Giddings. Damn my eyes if I didn't. I saw him!"

"John," shouted Giddings, whirling that way. "Stop, you fool. Carterwright! You'll get sucked down in that bog, John. Come back."

The posseman who had staggered backward was crouched down on his knees now, hugging his belly, and Denvers realized he must have been stabbed. The one Giddings had called Carterwright was running into the cypresses, still shouting. Giddings made a small, jerky move after him, shouting again. "John, don't," he called and for that moment was turned away from Denvers and Navarra. "Carterwright!"

Denvers jumped toward him, and Navarra bent to scoop up his Le Page. Giddings was whirling back as Denvers's body struck him. They went staggering into the canes, one of the sheriff's six-shooters deafening Denvers with its explosion. Denvers caught the gun between them, feeling it leap hotly beneath his hand as Giddings thumbed the hammer again. Giddings tried to beat at Denvers with the other gun. Denvers ducked the blow, tripping the man. They crashed down into the brake, and Denvers let his body fall dead weight onto Giddings. He heard the man grunt sickly, and for that instant the sheriff's body was limp beneath him. Denvers tore a Colt free from Giddings's hand, struggling to his feet. Navarra came in from behind him before he was fully erect, slugging at him with the Le Page. Denvers rolled aside, getting the blow across his neck instead of on the head. Dazed, he caught at the canes to keep from falling. Navarra bent over Giddings, striking him on the head with the barrel of his pin-fire. Giddings sank back, and Navarra pulled something from the sheriff's pocket. "Carnicero," he shouted. "I've got it. Come on. I've got it."

The Mexican stumbled through the brake from somewhere, panting. Then the sound of horses came to them, and Ollie Minster was shouting. "Giddings, Giddings? Where are you? Giddings?"

"Over in the brake," shouted the one named Carterwright, coming in out of the bog. "Navarra and that other ranny jumped Giddings."

The canes crashed as Minster drove his horse into them. Navarra dove to one side, disappearing in the pipestems, but the horse was on Denvers before he could follow. Then it went through his mind. Just in that instant while the horse was looming up above him big and black. Just the name. The name he had known so long before. All the way down from New Mexico. And the time even before that. Bud Richie. He didn't even try to get out of the way. He lunged for the animal, the shock of striking its chest knocking him aside. Then he had his hand on the stirrup leather, and the horse was dragging him off his feet. He had the Colt he had taken from Giddings, and he had that last moment before he had to let go. "Remember Bud Richie," he screamed up at Ollie Minster, the canes rattling and slamming all around him as he was dragged through them, his foot giving a last kick at solid ground. "Remember Bud Richie?"

Minster twisted on the horse, face ugly and contorted above Denvers, trying to bring his gun around in time. "Don't, Denvers. I didn't. Denvers . . . !"

Denvers's Colt cut him off, crashing just once, and Denvers saw Ollie slide off the opposite side of the horse with the pain stamped into his face. Then Denvers couldn't hang on any longer and let go of the stirrup leather to roll crashing through the pipestems. He came to a stop and lay there, hearing Carterwright call something from behind. He got to his knees finally, shaking his head, and crawled through the canes till he could no longer hear the man. He figured the girl would have made for the boat and tried to take a direction that would lead him to the bayou.

He had found the slippery, mucky bank of the bayou and was

stumbling down it toward the sea when the horses crashed through the canes behind him. He whirled, raising the Colt, hammer eared back under his thumb before he saw it wasn't Carterwright. "Ollie was leading the other possemen's horses," cried Esther, throwing him the reins of the animal she had been leading. "He let them go to follow you, and I got them."

He caught one pair of reins and threw them back over the head of a big buckskin. The heavy horse wheeled beneath him as he stepped aboard, and he slapped into the saddle with the animal already in its gallop. The other two horses followed Denvers and the girl for a while but soon trailed off and disappeared behind. Dawn was lighting the sky when he and the girl reached Dagger Point, and he saw the two horsemen ahead of them out in the channel.

"Neap tide came while we were on the mainland," called the girl. "It's about time for high tide to come in again. Looks like Navarra's already having trouble. It's suicide if the rip catches us before we're across. Want to chance it?"

Denvers pointed back of them along the coast. "We'll have to."

The girl took one look at the pair of horsebackers fogging across the shore from the direction of the bayou and turned her own animal into the rollers. Denvers could feel the riptide catch at his buckskin as he followed. He remembered the first time they had waded across here and realized how much deeper it was as the horse sank up to its belly in the first shallows. The animal threw up its head, nickering, and tried to turn back. Denvers bunched up his reins and drove it forward, water slopping in over the tops of his boots suddenly then reaching to his knees. The undertow swept the buckskin helplessly to one side, and Denvers felt the animal's feet go out from under for an instant.

Esther's horse was a little pinto, maybe two hands shorter than the buckskin, and its head was already under. Fighting it, she turned in her saddle to shout above the growing wind. "Don't let your horse start swimming. The rip will sweep you away from the shallow part as soon as its feet leave bottom, and you'll never be able to touch down again. Hurry up, Denvers, hurry up."

The solid feel was gone from beneath him, and he realized the horse was trying to swim. His reins made a wet, popping sound against its hide as he lashed it and yanked its head viciously from side to side. Long years of habitual reaction to that made the buckskin put its feet down and try to break into a gallop. Ahead the pinto was floundering helplessly, black tail and mane floating on the water. It began slipping to one side, and Denvers heard the girl's frantic cry. He raked his buckskin under water with his spurs, and the frenzied beast heaved forward, whinnying in pain, tossing its head. The pinto was already being swept away by the rip tide as it strove to swim, no longer able to touch bottom. Denvers unlashed his dally rope from the buckskin's horn, shaking out several loops and heaving the length to Esther. "You told me yourself," he shouted at her. "Don't try to fight that pinto. You're off the bar already. Grab my rope before you're out of reach. This buckskin's taller. Maybe he can make it."

Esther jumped from her pinto into the water, grasping desperately at the rope. Coughing, gasping, she pulled herself in. He hooked an arm about her wet, lithe waist, pulling her onto the buckskin behind him. Ahead he saw that Navarra and Carnicero had reached the surf and were climbing onto the island. Denvers raked the buckskin with the rowels again, hearing the horse's nicker above the wind, feeling it surge forward. The undertow kept sweeping at it malignantly, and every time the animal sought to lift its legs and swim, Denvers bunched his reins and yanked its head from side to side. His hands were raw from tugging on the leather, and the brine brought stinging pain to the abrasions. Soggy, dripping, they finally reached the surf, and the buckskin broke into a weary trot, urged on by the rollers at its rump. Navarra had dismounted on the sand dunes and, when he approached near enough, Denvers saw that the man had a wallet in his hands.

"It was on Giddings," said Navarra, throwing up his head to look at Denvers, voice suddenly ironic. "I suppose I owe you an apology, Denvers."

Still sitting his horse, Carnicero shouted and pointed toward the channel. Sheriff Giddings and Carterwright had driven their horses into the water and were coming across. Denvers didn't realize how strong the wind had grown until the girl screamed. "Go back," she called, and Denvers himself could hardly hear her voice above the whining blow. "Giddings, don't be a fool. High tide's coming in. We barely made it ourselves. You'll be swept off the bar."

She stopped shouting as Carterwright was abruptly turned aside, his horse floundering in the choppy sea a moment then shooting down the channel. Giddings tried to turn his horse back, but the rip caught it, and a high swell hit him. When the horse showed topping the swell, Giddings was out of the saddle. Esther put her face in her hands, and her shoulders began to shake. Denvers felt sick at his stomach, somehow, and turned away. He became aware that all this time Sinton Navarra had been pawing through the wallet. Money lay scattered all over the sand, and Navarra was tearing the last greenbacks heedlessly from the pocket of the leather case. "It isn't here, Carnicero. It isn't here!" He threw up his head that way suddenly, wind catching at the white streak in his long, black hair, and the wild light in his eyes was turned sly and secretive as his bluish lids drew almost shut over them. "You've got it, Denvers. You had it all along."

"What?"

"You know," almost screamed Navarra, and his suavity was swept away now. "You know what I've wanted all along. That's what you were after when you killed Hardwycke. Not the money. Are you from New Orleans? Give it to me, Denvers. I'll kill you this time, I swear I will."

"That's all, Navarra!"

Navarra had reached for his Le Page, but his whole motion stopped with his hand still beneath his coat. Denvers had stuck Giddings's Colt in his belt, and that was where he had drawn it from.

"I told you he could get it out pretty quick," said the girl, laughing shakily. Then she cast another look out to sea, and a sick horror crossed her face. She caught at Denvers's arm. "Whatever we do now had better be back at the house. This is a real blow coming up."

Denvers hardly heard her. "Navarra," he said. "What did you want in that wallet?"

# VIII

The ancient house trembled to the blasting malignancy of the wind, and somewhere on the second story a loose shutter clattered insanely against the warped weatherboards. The cypresses bowed their hoary heads and wept streamers of Spanish moss that were caught up by the storm and swept away like writhing snakes to tangle at Ernie Denvers's feet as he stumbled through the grove, one hand pulling Esther along after him. They hitched their horses to the rack in front of the long, columned porch. Denvers waved the Colt impatiently for Navarra to go ahead. He had taken the Le Page from the man, but had been unable to force Navarra to tell what he had wanted from the wallet. The front door creaked dismally, and Carnicero went in and stopped. Navarra went in and stopped. Denvers saw why as soon as he stepped through the portal. Revealed by the light of a single candle on the table, Judah was crouched over Caesar Sheridan, lying sprawled on the floor. The mulatto was looking at them, and the whites of his eyes gleamed from his black, sweating face.

"It killed Uncle Caesar," whispered Judah, and his voice got louder as he spoke. "It's here in this house. I saw it. My own eyes. I saw it."

Carnicero worked his lips a moment before he could get the words out. "Who?"

"You know who," said Judah. "All dressed up in his satin knee breeches and cocked hat, like he was going to a party. Rings on his fingers and gold buttons on his coat. You know who."

"*La fantasma!*" choked Carnicero and crossed himself. "Jean Lafitte. . . ."

The laugh stopped him. It came crazy and warped on the howling wind, partly drowned out by the clattering shutter. They all turned to look at the stairs, circling up the dancing steps to the top landing. It was a shadowy form, at first, moving down out of the darkness. The candlelight flickered across the gold buttons on the long, blue tailcoat then caught the gilt *fleur de lys* embroidered across cuffs and collar. Denvers had seen pictures of the dress worn in the early Eighteen hundreds. He recognized the high, Hessian boots, gleaming black against the skin-tight Wellington trousers, the short regimental skirts of a white marseilles waistcoat. There was something unearthly about the eyes, sunk deeply in their sockets, gaping blankly from the seamed parchment of the face. The hair was snow white, done in a queue at the back of a stiff, high collar. The apparition threw back its head to laugh again. "Yes!" he screamed. "Jean Lafitte! Did you think you could come and take my house like this? You'll all be spitted on my sword."

The wind outside changed direction, whipping in through the door, and the candle snuffed out, plunging the room into darkness. Denvers staggered back under the impact of a heavy body, felt the hard bite of a ring against his belly as a hand clawed the Le Page from where he had stuck it in his belt. He tried to tear it away but, when his own hand reached his belt, the Le Page was gone. Then the gun bellowed down by his belly, and he felt the bullet burn across his ribs. He fired blindly ahead of him and then stopped because the girl was calling, and he realized he might hit her.

"Denvers, Denvers, where are you . . . ?"

The mad laughter echoed through the high-ceilinged room, and Denvers stumbled across a heavy body. Sheridan? He brought up against the solid mahogany center table, trying to right himself, and another man charged into him. He slugged viciously with the Colt. Six-gun iron clanged off a steel blade, numbing his hand. He sensed the man's thrust, and the blade tore through his shirt as he leaped aside. The cackling laughter rose from in front of him. Ducking another thrust, he tripped over the stairway and stumbled violently backward, having to climb the stairs that way to keep from falling.

"Denvers, is that you on the stairs?"

Again he held his finger on the trigger for fear of hitting Esther and, cursing bitterly, backed on up the stairs.

"Strike your colors!" howled the madman, charging at him.

"Denvers?"

"Esther," he called. "Don't come up the stairs. I'll hit you if I shoot downwards."

A volley of shots came from down there, and the man in front of Denvers laughed crazily. "You can't kill me. I'm Jean Lafitte."

There was another thunder of shots, and Denvers shouted hoarsely: "Navarra, stop that. Esther's on the stairs."

"The devil with the girl," shouted Navarra from the lower blackness. "Get that madman, Denvers. Get him, I say." He stopped yelling, and there was a scuffle from down there, and Denvers heard the slam of the front door shutting. Then it creaked violently as if someone had torn it open again, and Navarra's voice sounded muffled by the wind. "Denvers? I thought you were on the stairs . . . ?"

The insane laughter drowned that out, and the man suddenly loomed up on the stairs in front of Denvers, leaping upward with his sword. Denvers lurched forward to meet him, trying to knock the rusty blade aside with his gun. The clang of iron on steel rang through the house again, and Denvers was thrown back, hand numbed as before, barely able to hang onto the Colt. Hot pain seared his shoulder, and he felt the slide of steel through the thick muscles there. With the blade caught in him, Denvers went to his knees on the dancing steps that led to the top landing above him. He hugged his shoulder in to keep the man from pulling the sword out again and turned as he rose, trying to stumble up those last few steps to the level hallway. Jerking desperately at the sword, the man threw himself against Denvers, and they both tripped on the final stair and stumbled across the hall to crash into the opposite wall. A blurred figure rose from behind the newel post and ran past them with a wild shout. Denvers got to his feet again, striking blindly with the gun, rolling down the wall in an effort to free himself from the screaming, clawing madman. He caught the line of light seeping from beneath a door. Then the door was thrust open and that second man who had crouched by the newel post was silhouetted in the lighted rectangle for that moment. "Carnicero?" called Denvers.

"Jean Lafitte," screamed the madman, grasping Denvers's gun wrist with the bestial strength of the demented, finally managing to pull the sword free. Denvers threw himself back from the man's thrust, bounced off the door frame, fell into the lighted room. He flopped over on the floor, tripping up Carnicero as the Mexican tried to jump over him and get out the door. He got one look at the Mexican's dead-white visage. *"Madre de Dios,"* screamed Carnicero frenziedly. *"¡La fantasma!"*

"Jean Lafitte," howled the demented creature and lunged at Carnicero.

Carnicero jerked aside, and the sword went through the leg of his flopping white pants, carrying him back against the table, the other man crashing up against him. Denvers shook his head, trying to rise. "See?" he panted. "Carnicero? It's no ghost. Get him, Butcher. He's real, and he's loco, and he'll kill you. Get him!"

Carnicero pulled his long *saca de tripas* out of his belt with a spasmodic jerk, catching the man's sword arm and whirling him around. Now it was the Mexican on the outside, bellied in on the other, holding him against the table. The man gibbered insanely, clawing with dirty, broken nails at Carnicero's face, trying to tear his sword free. Carnicero had the knife back above his head, holding the man by the throat.

"Get him!" shouted Denvers, stumbling to his feet and falling against the wall, pain blinding him. "He's crazy, Butcher. You've got to stop him."

"I can't," bawled the Mexican, still holding his gets-the-guts up in the air. "I never keel a man in my life, Denvers. That's why I couldn't stab you the other day. Not because you save my life on the mainland. I just never keel a man in my life."

"Jean Lafitte," roared the crazy man, tearing his arm loose finally and twisting from between Carnicero and the table. Leaning feebly against the wall, Denvers tried to line his Colt up on the man, but Carnicero's heavy body blocked him off. The Mexican was crying pathetically.

"I can't . . . I can't . . . !"

The man caught Carnicero's shirt front in one hand, slamming him around against the table, and shifted his feet to lunge. With a last desperate effort Denvers threw himself toward them, gun clubbed, left arm flopping useless from his bloody shoulder, but he saw the sword flash up and knew he would be too late. He didn't see exactly what happened then. He saw that Carnicero had dropped his knife arm down to try and ward off the thrust. The two bodies were up against each other for a moment, their feet scuffling on the floor. Carnicero was hidden almost entirely by the other man. There was a last spasmodic reflex; someone gasped. Denvers stopped himself from falling into them, and the crazy man slipped down against Carnicero, his face turned up in a strange, twisted pain. His arms were around the Mexican, and he slid all the way down, until he was crumpled on the floor with his arms still clasping Carnicero's legs.

"*Dios.*" Carnicero's voice was barely audible, and he glanced dully at the bloody knife in his hand. "It was so easy. I keel him. I didn't think it was like that. Just slipped in so easy. *Dios.* I keel him."

Denvers dropped beside the other man, pulling him off Carnicero's legs, shaking him. "Listen. Who are you? Really. What is all this?"

The man's eyelids fluttered open, and he cackled feebly. "Jean Lafitte. My island. They think Marsala killed me? They think many men killed me. There are a thousand legends. This is the only truth. My island. My Maison Rouge. . . ."

"You killed that Mexican the other night?"

"Aye, and Arno Sheridan," panted the man. "When Sheridan brought his family to this island, he drove me out of the house. Said I had no right to live there. I was just a crazy hermit. I'm not crazy. I'm Jean Lafitte. My house, understand? I caught Sheridan out on the range one day so long ago. He found where I was hiding. I put my sword through him. Just like I put my sword through that Mexican. He was riding herd on the cattle, and he found where I was hiding too, and I killed him. I'll kill all of you. I'll drive your cattle into the sea and take my house back. . . ."

"It was you cut those cows out the other day?" said Denvers.

Blood frothed the man's lips. "I've been cutting them out for years and driving them over the bluffs above Dagger Point. I had a skiff hidden up there. Somebody took it last night."

"What were you doing on the mainland last night?"

"I go there often. Often. You'd be surprised what I know. A man can hide in the canebrakes and hear many things. I heard Sheriff Giddings and his posse go by. They were talking about that dead horse everybody was hunting. I heard Sinton Navarra and Carnicero go by. They wanted the dead horse, too. I found it before anybody else." He giggled idiotically, coughed up blood. "I was very clever. I took the letter out of the wallet."

The sudden stiffening of Denvers's body caused pain to shoot through his wounded shoulder. "Letter?"

"Yes," laughed the man weakly. "I took it from the wallet, but I left the money in it, and put the wallet back into the *alforjas*, and nobody knew I had taken it, did they? You don't think I'm Lafitte? In my breast pocket. I wrote it. To my brother, Pierre, in Eighteen Twenty-Six. From this very house. How they got hold of it, I don't know, but I wrote it. My letter. You can't have it."

He tried to catch Denvers's hand, but Denvers already had the parchment half way out of the coat, bloody at one corner. It was then that Esther stumbled in, dropping to her knees beside Denvers. She made a small sound when she saw his wounded shoulder. Then she was looking at the man. "Denvers, who is he?"

"You said it yourself," Denvers told her. "Lot of crazy hermits on this island. Probably got hold of some of those clothes you found in that chest. Navarra?"

Her head rose at that. "Judah ran out the front door, and in the darkness Navarra thought it was you. He went out after Judah. He must have found out his mistake by now."

Her hands slipped off him as he got to his feet, moving toward the door, and his voice was unhurried and deliberate now, because that was the way it stood inside him. "Stay here. I don't want you in the way this time. Stay here till it's over."

## IX

"Denvers . . . ?"

The hall was dark lower down, but here a candle guttered, suspended in a cast iron holder, and he went down slowly into increasing shadows with his good shoulder against the wall to conserve his strength.

"That you?" asked Navarra.

Denvers decided he must be at the very foot of the stairs. "It's me. You wanted the letter out of Hardwycke's wallet."

Navarra's voice trembled slightly. "You had it all the time. I'm coming after it."

The creaking started, slowly, deliberately, with a small interval between each groan, as a man would make mounting the old stairway unhurriedly. Denvers felt the skin tighten across his sweating face. "You killed Hardwycke for the letter?" he said.

The noise stopped down there, and for a moment Denvers thought he could hear Navarra's breathing. "Not personally, Denvers. Prieto killed Hardwycke. Prieto and I left New Orleans together, but he stopped off at Refugio while I came on to Matagorda Island. If Prieto missed Hardwycke on the mainland, I'd get him when he arrived here."

"Why should he come here?"

There was a long pause, and Navarra might have been trying to place Denvers exactly during it. Then he spoke. "In New Orleans. Hardwycke had acquired some real estate which originally belonged to the Lafittes, and among the titles he found that the Sheridans had no legal claim on this end of Matagorda. Ostensibly Hardwycke was coming here to force the Sheridans off. However, one of the properties Hardwycke had acquired was the site of the old Lafitte blacksmith shop in New Orleans, and a Negro retainer of Hardwycke's let it leak out that in the floor of the blacksmith shop they had unearthed some old papers of the Lafittes, among them this letter. When I heard that, I knew why Hardwycke had really headed this way. I told you I was an authority on Lafitte. How do you think I became an authority? I've tracked down more of his legendary treasures than any man living and never found a doubloon. But this is the real thing. It's the most gold Lafitte ever had in one spot. I've been hunting that letter half of my life, Denvers."

"You aren't Esther's half-brother?"

"She had a half-brother under the circumstances I told you who died in France," said Navarra. "I was a friend of his, and he left me in charge of his personal effects. The Sheridans knew of him but had never seen him. When this came up, I took advantage of that. Prieto was my man. Judah hated Caesar Sheridan and feared him, and what man wouldn't have turned against his master for a share in half a million dollars? Carnicero is an old fool afraid of his own shadow. He was Sheridan's man, but he feared me as much as Sheridan and would do whatever I told him. And now I'm coming, Denvers. I'm coming. . . ."

Denvers saw the sudden shift down there, and Navarra made a shadowy figure behind the curving railing, charging up from the bottom tier of stairs and jumping for the protection of the newel post on that first elliptical landing. He covered his rush with a volley that seemed to shake the house. Denvers ducked down with the lead slapping into the wall behind him, snapping a shot at Navarra, and saw the man throw himself down behind the dancing steps.

"Hold it, Navarra," shouted Denvers. "Let me read you the letter."

"Don't try to stall me, Denvers," called Navarra. "I've come this far, and you won't stop me now. How many shots have you got left in that Colt? Is that what you're doing? You can't bluff me, Denvers."

Denvers spun his cylinder and was surprised to find in the flickering light only one fresh shell. Had he fired that many? He wiped a perspiring palm against his Levi's. "It doesn't matter how many shots a man has, Navarra," he said. "Only how he uses them. Listen to the letter. It's dated June eighteenth, Eighteen Twenty-Six. 'Dear Pierre.' That was Jean's brother?" There was just enough light so that he could make out the ancient script.

" 'Dear Pierre,' " he read, holding the letter in his left hand, trembling slightly from the injury to his shoulder, " 'I am writing you from Matagorda Island, where I have taken abode after I left Galveston. Do not believe any rumors that might reach you of what is happening here. Only what I write in this letter. The men are growing restless, and already one ship's crew has left in the *Pride*. The only one I can trust now is Dominique, and it is with him I shall send this letter. Even Marsala has turned on me. She left the house this morning in a fit of jealous rage and didn't come back until late into the night. Something about a Creole I have been seeing in New Orleans. Which one could that be? There will undoubtedly be talk of a treasure I took when I boarded the *Consolada* last month. It will be false. . . .' "

"Denvers!" Navarra's voice had a hoarse, driven sound. "You're lying. You're making that up to stall for time. There was a treasure, I tell you, and I'm coming. You can't bluff me, Denvers. You can't stop me. Twenty shots, Denvers."

Denvers eared back the hammer with his right thumb. *I'm coming, Denvers. One left against twenty shots.* He went on reading the letter, deliberately, barely able now to make out the old-fashioned script. " 'It will be false. Already there has come to my ears a rumor that I have buried treasure here on Matagorda. There is no treasure on the island. . . .' "

"Stop it, Denvers!"

Denvers caught the shift that must have been Navarra setting himself to rise from his crouching position behind the dancing steps. He grew rigid, the buzzing in his ears louder now, his feet feeling as if they were sinking into a soft, puffy cloud. *Twenty shots.* He remembered that fight on the shore, and what little chance Prieto had stood against that Le Page. *It doesn't matter how many shots a man has, Navarra. Only how he uses them.* Denvers read the last lines of the letter tensely, waiting for Navarra's rush. " 'There is no treasure on the island. The *Consolada* was the only prize I took during my stay here, and she was nothing but a blackbirder off the Gold Coast bound for New Orleans. The few Negroes I took off her didn't bring me enough to buy Marsala a new dress. . . .' "

"Stop it. Damn you!"

Screaming that, Navarra jumped erect on the landing, throwing himself up the last stairs with his gun bucking madly in his hand. Lead whining around him and hitting the back wall in a wild tattoo, Denvers dropped the letter from his left hand and with his right he curled his fingers fully around the Colt's butt. A bullet plucked at his shirt and another clipped his ear. He still couldn't see Navarra very well. The stairway seemed to spin before his eyes. One shot. Navarra shook the whole balcony, coming on up, his gun flaming in his hand. A veritable arsenal. Navarra rounded the turn completely and made a looming target over the Colt's front sight in the flickering light. *It doesn't matter how many shots.* Denvers flexed and winced as a bullet hit him somewhere in his left side. Then his finger pressed the trigger. He heard the boom of the Colt and saw it buck in his hand. Over the sights, Navarra's body stiffened, stumbled up one more step, hovered there, then crashed backward. Denvers swayed forward, dropping the Colt to catch himself before he fell. He was dimly aware of Esther's voice somewhere back of him. Her hands were on him, soft and supporting.

**X**

The wind made a faint whine now, fluttering the tails of the three horses as Denvers and Esther and Carnicero headed them up the last dune before the beach. Denvers was still weak from loss of blood, and his shoulder throbbed painfully, but as long as a hand could fork a horse he was all right. Esther looked across at him, hair blown over the curve of one flushed cheek. "I can't believe I'm leaving this place. What's it like on the outside, Denvers? Do women really wear satin dresses? My mother used to tell me. And that stuff they use on their hair to make it smell sweet."

"Perfume? You don't need perfume, Esther."

"You'll have to help me, Denvers," she said. "I guess I won't even know how to act."

"You'll know how to act," he said. "And as for helping you, I'll be there as long as you want."

Carnicero giggled. "It's funny, Denvers. All the time I've lived here, and she never looked at me like that."

The girl flushed and then, to hide her confusion, looked back toward the old house. "I guess it was best, that crazy man dying there. I don't see how an old man like that could be so strong. He must have been past eighty." She shivered suddenly, eyes darkening as she turned to Denvers. "Who do you think he was, Denvers, really?"

"Jean Lafitte," Denvers said, and there was only wonder in his eyes as he added, "or maybe just his ghost."

# Night Marshal

*Verne Athanas*

✪

*Born in Cleft, Idaho, Verne Athanas's father was a construction foreman and so his growing years were spent constantly on the move, wherever the present job happened to be. He began writing Western fiction for the magazine markets in the late 1940s. In his brief writing career, which spanned fourteen years, he wrote only three novels, but in them he sought to expand the conventions of the traditional Western story, and in* Rogue Valley *(Simon and Schuster, 1953) he produced his masterpiece. In* The Proud Ones *(Simon and Schuster, 1952), about a lawman and his limping deputy, he created a story which not only inspired a motion picture but also the long-running* Gunsmoke *series on radio and then television.* Maverick *(Dell First Edition, 1956) was his final novel, a cattle-drive story. If there is a predominant theme in his fiction, it is the specter of relentless determination required of a person in winning through on the American frontier in a life-struggle with the land and the hostile human environment. In his concern for psychological themes in his Western novels and stories he was clearly in the tradition of Les Savage, Jr., and T. T. Flynn, and in his care for accuracy in historical detail he emulated the work of another Oregon author, Ernest Haycox. "Night Marshal" first appeared in* The Saturday Evening Post *(July 2, 1960) and has not been previously collected.*

"**O**f course," said Lazar the Tailor, "I can give you a five-dollar suit right off the shelf, if it is what you want."

Bruce Harper fingered the bolt of material. "No," he said. "But my heavens, Lazar, sixteen dollars!"

Lazar the Tailor shrugged. "For the President United States," he said, "I couldn't cut it a nickel. Like iron, this material. Your son, someday he is going to wear this suit. You come to Lazar the Tailor ten years from now to cut it down for him, maybe twelve. This suit will make you tall, make you straight. You won't look like some mine mucker, you will look like the marshal."

Bruce Harper was already tall and straight, and he had no son, and he wasn't the marshal, but the night marshal, as Lazar the Tailor knew full well. He was a little sleepy now at ten in the morning after having gone on duty at midnight. He said: "I haven't got the money just now anyway, Lazar."

Said Lazar promptly: "I trust you. Turn around." Lazar measured. He hummed. He jotted figures. He said: "Day after tomorrow come back for the fitting."

"You mean it's going to take two days to make a suit?"

"I mean in two days vill be the fitting. In two days more maybe the suit is ready. So come in two days and do not be telling Lazar the Tailor how he should make the suit."

"In four days," said Bruce, "it will be pay day."

"Imagine!" marveled Lazar. "A coincidence!"

"Imagine," echoed Bruce. He left the shop.

Up the street John P. Ballard was approaching, escorting two women. One was obviously Mrs. Elsie Queen. The other obviously was not. Bruce spoke as they met.

John P. Ballard nodded. Mrs. Queen smiled. She said in her brash and cheerful way: "Good morning, Bruce. I don't think you've met Glory. Mister Bruce Harper . . . ? Miss Glory Fajen."

Miss Fajen raised eyes black as night and gave Bruce a look. Somewhere in his interior a small stallion neighed and cantered vigorously up his spine. He snatched off his hat and said: "I'm certainly glad to meet you, Miss Fajen!"

Her hair was black—crow's-wing black—and her brows and her eyes and the long lashes framing them. Her skin was white—oh, very white. And her lips were red—deep red, tongue-moistened red—and they parted in a definite murmur: "Mister Harper." A man could warm his hands at that voice as at a small, brisk fire.

John P. Ballard nodded again and escorted the women past. Bruce put on his hat. The small stallion nickered and pranced to and fro in his head. "Oh, hush now," said Bruce and went on his tour through the town.

Ophir was a straggle of shacks and slab houses and tents hanging precariously on the side of the mountain, menaced from above by the tailings dump of the Red Ophir Mine works and rapidly filling the gulch below with its own tailings dump of bottles and cans and castoff boots and sawdust sweepings and the general detritus of some three thousand hard-living souls. Ophir was rough and tough and rich, and proud of it.

Bruce returned to the office. John P. Ballard was not yet there. Bruce resignedly kicked the chair away from the desk and sat down and yawned. He thought about Miss Glory Fajen for a while, his eyes closed and his lips faintly smiling. A big fat horsefly came yammering through the open door and droned to a landing on the nose of one Juan Jesus Ortega who had killed several people, if the WANTED poster could be trusted.

Bruce drew his revolver and aimed carefully at the fly. Mr. Ortega was worth quite a bit of money, quick or dead. On the other hand Mr. Ortega was reputed to be some fast with a gun; so it was just as well that it was only his printed image which stared fixedly past the fly on his nose. Bruce reholstered his weapon, sighed, and yawned again.

In due time John P. Ballard made his appearance. Mr. John P. Ballard was, in a phrase of the day, a living legend. In younger days, before John P. himself wore the star, it was said that no less personage than Wild Bill Hickok had once left town for three days to avoid a meeting. One J. Wesley Hardin, it was said, came up the trail from Texas, witnessed a casual shooting match wherein John P. picked off four running rabbits twenty-five to fifty long paces distant, following which Mr. Hardin quietly rode on back to Texas. After he took up the peace officer's trade, John P. had served with distinction in many a town once famed and ferocious and now tamed or gone completely. Some said he had once been a United States marshal, though John P. never said yea or nay.

His mustache had gone gray, and his double-breasted vests showed a prosperous broadening, but when he laid a cold eye on an incipient causer of trouble, said trouble became downright conspicuous in its haste to be gone. Bruce Harper knew he walked in the shadow of the legendary John P., but there were times when it was a comforting shadow—say along about three o'clock in the morning with trouble a-brewing along Whiskey Row.

Bruce stood in the door and rocked on his boot heels. "A . . . ah . . . fine-looking young lady, Miss Fajen," he said.

John P. Ballard selected a cheroot from the box in his drawer and tucked it in under his gray mustache. "Hmm."

Bruce cut a surreptitious look at John P., who regarded the end of his cheroot.

"She is going to play piano in the Ophir Queen," said John P. quietly.

"Oh."

There was a short silence, and then John P. said: "Miss Cassiday will probably have your supper ready. Go along if you like."

"Sure," said Bruce.

He went upstreet, turned right to the house of Colin Cassiday, and came upon Colin himself just leaving, returning to his work as shift boss at the Red Ophir.

"Now," said Colin, "a man can wait till his dinner's cold and then eat it anyway because he can wait no longer, and then the sweet dallier comes in his own good time. Dammit, man, ye'll ruin me stomach yet!"

"Sorry," said Bruce. "Got held up."

"Now, Papa," said Jenny, coming out the door. She was a lovely creature, Jenny Cassiday, provided a man's taste ran to red-haired and blue-eyed colleens built as trim and solid as a little brick cottage.

Said Colin: "Dinner's done and over. I've got to get to me work. Let him eat at the Chinaman's."

"Oh, Papa, run along," said Jenny, kissing the tip of her forefinger and putting it on the tip of her father's nose.

"Well, mind you leave the door open. I won't have the neighbors talkin'. And when he's fed, he can go."

Colin departed, muttering about a man who'd not hold a decent man's job nor work a decent man's hours, and Jenny preceded Bruce into the kitchen. He made a small strategic maneuver of trapping her between the sink and the table, and got his knuckles rapped with a

wooden spoon. He sat at the table and nursed his knuckles and wondered aloud: "Now what's got our Jenny so uproarious?"

"Because I say not, and that's what."

"Why," he said soulfully, "it's not as if . . . I mean, we do sort of
have an understanding."

She turned a keen blue eye on him. "And an odd bit of a thing it
is, too, how much better the understanding is *between* Father Doolin's
visits."

He carefully rearranged knives and forks. "Why," he said, "I've
got . . . obligations around. And you know your father is always and
forever lecturing about how a man's got to be able to . . . support a . . .
well, you know. . . ."

"I know," said Jenny. "Here's your supper, or whatever it is in the
middle of the day."

He reached to catch her hand and got the spoon again. "Don't be
mad, Jenny. There's nothing to get mad about."

"Why, no," she said, vigorously pumping a pan of water at the
sink. "Me father fights off every man comes calling with a stick, for
fear he'll poison himself with his own cooking, and when one does get
past him, *he* has his obligations and his excuses, and mind you, now"—
wetting the pan to heat with such spirit the water sloshed and hissed
on the hot stove—"mind you, y'll feed one another one of these days,
and we'll see which poison's which!"

"Now, Jenny, what is it? What's the matter?"

"Why, no matter at all. If you think so much is the matter, why
don't you go and see if that black-eyed pussycat won't feed you!"

Bruce sat a moment, mouth agape. "Ah-ho!" he said finally.

"Ah-ho, indeed! I saw you watching her swinging that . . . that bottle full of . . . of . . . *hay!*"

"Why," said Bruce judiciously, "it didn't look like hay to me."

"And you looked close enough, too, didn't you? Well, why don't
you feed your gluttonous self, so you can run back down there and
have another look?"

Bruce, feeling somewhat put upon, said: "By George, I will!"
Which he did, not even looking around when Jenny banged the door,
and he was half way down the main drag before a heavy hunger pang

reminded him that he hadn't even sampled his supper, and here it was still four days before pay day.

The night deskman roused him at eleven, and he got up and washed and shaved by the light of the wall lamp and cut himself and swore softly. He went dourly up the street to the Chinaman's for breakfast—ham and boiled potatoes sliced and fried. The coffee was awful. He checked into the office at midnight precisely. John P. wasn't there. He debated hooking one of John P.'s cheroots from the desk drawer, decided against it, and stopped in at the Ore Bucket and ran half a dozen stogies on his bill, bit, and lighted one.

He got as far as the Ophir Queen before he saw John P. Ballard, standing at the bar, a thumb hooked in his vest, listening as Miss Glory Fajen played a grand piano at the far end of the room. Miss Fajen wore a gown as black and shiny as her hair, a great swirl of skirt supporting her slender waist, and none too far into the northern latitudes the black gown left off and the white skin began. As her dark-fringed eyes came on Bruce, they acknowledged his presence, and the red, red lips smiled, ever so fleetingly. He felt the quick rataplan of small cold-shod hoofs galloping up his spine.

*Hoo, boy*, he told himself. *Steady . . . steady!*

At his elbow John P. Ballard's dry voice said: "I think I will call it a night, Mister Harper."

"Fine," said Bruce absently. "I guess I can handle it all right now."

"You might check a couple of the other places . . . at your convenience, of course."

"Oh. Yes. Sure."

He checked the other places. It was nearly two o'clock before he got back to the Ophir Queen, and to his disappointment Miss Fajen was not in evidence, and the grand piano had been covered for the night. The professor was hacking away at his gutshot old upright. Bruce went on his rounds.

On Thursday he had his fitting, and on Saturday he collected his stipend, paid Lazar the Tailor, gave the bootmaker ten on account, paid his tab at the Ore Bucket and a couple of other accounts, and paid the Chinaman and then the Chinaman's cousin who did the laundry, and retrieved his shirts. He tunneled into the best one, with the pleated front, rubbed up the nugget cuff links and wished he had a gold chain to swing across the front of the waistcoat like John P., and whipped a high shine on his boots with dubbing and a soft cloth. He sallied forth, fragrant with bay rum.

Even John P. was impressed. "Fine suit," he said. "Excellent fit." He brought his gold watch out and popped it open. "Just a little early tonight? Only nine o'clock."

Bruce prinked his lapels into a faultless roll. "Oh," he said casually, "I just thought . . . Saturday night and all . . . might sort of look around a little before I went on."

"Certainly. Got your pay all right?"

"Ah . . . yes, yes, this morning." He rocked forward on his toes and back to his heels and clinked the coins in his pocket, a half dollar, his lucky silver dollar, and a quarter eagle, all the money he had in the world, excepting the half dime and three copper pennies in the stud box in his room.

John P. lighted up one of his cheroots, shoved the box across the desk. "Join me," he said.

Said Bruce, astounded: "Why . . . thank you, sir." He selected one, lighted it, and inhaled the implausibly fragrant smoke. He exhaled audibly. John P. said abruptly: "I haven't seen you going up the hill for your meals lately."

"No," said Bruce stiffly.

"Hmm. Cigar all right?"

"Fine . . . fine! Best I ever had."

"You never make a mistake on the best. No one but a fool buys shoddy." He puffed his cheroot, looked up keenly. "Well, run along. Have your fun. I'll see you at midnight."

Bruce went into the street, walked past the Ore Bucket and Bloody Bill's and the Oro Fino and the Square Deal. Here and there men spoke to him, and he nodded in reply. He stopped in at the Ophir Queen, but the cover was still on the grand piano, and Miss Fajen was nowhere in sight. He saw Mrs. Elsie Queen briefly as the door to the far room was opened and closed, Elsie, big and high colored and handsome in one of the rich gowns she always wore.

Bruce speculated a moment about her and John P. One seldom

saw them together during business hours, yet John P. was her escort, openly and without apology, on many a daylight excursion. He was the only one in the whole of Ophir who came and went through either the inner or outer door to the far room at his own apparent convenience. It was common gossip that John P. was a partner in the Ophir Queen, though he never publicly showed any more proprietary interest in the place than any other. Bruce tucked the thought away in his mind as he went out.

At the Mercantile Mart Mr. Pottinger was closing up. Out on his wide porch Jenny Cassiday was standing, two big tow sacks of groceries beside her, looking helplessly downstreet. Obviously her father had left her off to do her week's trading and had gone on for a glass or two with the boys, and time had slipped along on him.

"Hello, Jenny," said Bruce.

"Oh, Bruce." There was a short silence.

"Maybe I could . . . give you a hand . . . carrying these things?"

"Oh, I'm sure you have other things to do. Papa will be along soon."

"Why, I haven't else to do right now, Jenny."

"Oh? I understand you are being kept awfully busy, down at the . . . the . . . Ophir Queen, isn't it?"

"Ah," he said softly, bleakly. "You . . . understand this?"

"Oh," she said, "Papa tells me how busy you've been and all. And I knew you must be awfully busy . . . not ever coming around, and all."

"Well, now," he said with some heat, "I wasn't so sure I was welcome around any more."

"Nor am I so domned sure meself," said Colin, coming out of the dark. He looked Bruce up and down. "Trapped out like a trick horse," he said. "Spend yer days sleepin' an' yer nights prowlin' an' yer money on frippery. . . . Come along, girl."

Bruce kept his eyes on Jenny. Jenny looked almost wistfully back. Then at Colin's peremptory voice she followed, and Bruce stalked back toward the brightnesses and uproar of Saturday night and pay day on Whiskey Row. He turned in at the Ophir Queen deliberately, knowing Jenny and Colin could see him from the store, if they had by chance dallied this long.

Miss Glory Fajen sat at her grand piano playing something quiet and tinkly, the sound almost lost in the exuberance of Saturday night. Bruce stood a moment before deciding she wasn't going to look his way just now and went to the bar. Technically he wasn't on duty yet. He ordered a drink. He looked around. His eyes slid across one face, came back, and he idly thought of a big black horsefly, and then quite suddenly he saw the poster on the office wall. Here, in all-too-solid flesh, was the much-wanted Mr. Juan Jesus Ortega.

Bruce had three thoughts in flashing succession. He wished he was clean away from here. He wished that John P. Ballard stood at his elbow. He hoped he was going to get away with this. He moved clear of the bar and within jumping distance of Mr. Ortega.

The door to Mrs. Queen's far room opened, and John P. Ballard stepped through. Mr. Ortega, turning from the bar, casually reached down for the pistol at his thigh. Bruce made a lunging dive, embraced Mr. Ortega with wide-flung arms, drove him back against the bar and nearly got his foot shot off for his trouble. It did not seem possible that Mr. Ortega could have drawn so casually and still so rapidly, but he had and, though the bullet blasted into the floor a good half inch from Bruce's left foot, he found himself in roughly the same spot as the man who caught the bear by the tail. He needed help to let go.

Mr. Ortega kneed him swiftly in groin, belly, and chest, and simultaneously writhed, twisted, and wrenched. Bruce hung on desperately. Then came a thud from overhead, and Mr. Ortega collapsed atop him.

Bruce disentangled himself. John P. Ballard holstered his pistol. Mr. Ortega lay on the floor, with his hat caved in and a matted streak across his coarse black hair. "Well," said John P. meditatively, "I imagine we'd better take him over to the jail."

Mr. Ortega had a slender knife in the back of his pants, a jackknife in his right front pants pockets, a single-shot Colt .41 Derringer in his left front pants pocket, the usual assortment of matches and tobacco and papers, plus ninety-eight dollars in gold and one dollar seventy-five cents in silver.

"Nice round sum," said John P.

**Verne Athanas  559**

"He had a drink in front of him at the bar," said Bruce. "Prob'ly he had two. That'd be two bits."

"And he was cocked and primed and waiting for me," said John P. Ballard. He swiped his mustache right and left with a forefinger. "Might have saved a lot of trouble all around if you had just shot him."

"Wasn't time," said Bruce.

John P. regarded him steadily then reached out and touched him on the shoulder. "I'm grateful," he said quietly. "Thank you."

"Aw, hell," Bruce said, " 'twasn't nothin'."

"Possibly not," said John P. dryly, "but keep an eye on him for a while, will you? I want to check his backtrail a bit."

A few minutes after John P. Ballard left the office, Juan Jesus Ortega rolled his head to and fro, heaved a heavy sigh or two, then blinked his eyes and surveyed his surroundings. He sat up on the jail bunk and stared malevolently at Bruce through the bars. After a while he felt the small of his back gently, as if for a sudden pain.

"We got the knife," observed Bruce. "You can stop feeling for it."

Mr. Ortega spat on the floor. Bruce smiled. Mr. Ortega pulled an invisible Indian blanket about his shoulders and sat hunched on the bunk, looking glumly at the floor. Bruce looked up alertly, then stood up quickly in a pleasant confusion, as Miss Glory Fajen stepped in the door. She wore a trailing scarf of black net about her bare shoulders. Her face was almost anxious but, when she saw Bruce, she smiled with incredible brilliance. "Oh," she breathed, "you *are* all right."

"Why, sure," said Bruce, as pleasant confusion turned to blissful confusion. "Sure, I'm all right."

She placed a delicate hand on the expanse of white above the gown. "I was so frightened," she said. Then her face stiffened. Her heels clacked on the floor as she swept imperiously across the room to the barred door.

"Oh?" she said in outrage. "You! Of all the...." Mr. Ortega stared at her with deliberate insolence. "You," she said. "Stand up. Come over here. I want to see the face of a man who'd do such a thing."

Mr. Ortega got up. He slouched toward the front of the cell. Bruce said warningly: "Miss Fajen, I wouldn't stand so. . . ." But she stood, looking Mr. Ortega in the eye with the utmost contempt, and then she stepped aside as Bruce came up behind her, and Mr. Ortega said his first words.

He said: "Unlock this damn' door." He held a short, heavy-barreled revolver squarely on Bruce's body.

"Give me that gun," said Bruce without conviction.

"You bet! Now, I don' wanna shoot you, but I'm gonna if you don't move! You unlock this door right now, you dumb *cochino*, or I'm gonna blow your head right off!" There was enthusiastic conviction in his voice. Bruce unlocked the cell. "Turn around," said Mr. Ortega. Bruce turned around. Then the entire jail roof fell on him.

☉

He sneezed vigorously and was surprised to find himself flat on his face on the dusty floor. He pried himself up, and a good-size iron ball rolled from one side of his skull to the other and stopped just over his left ear with a terrible thump. Bracing a hand to keep the floor level, he looked blearily around. He sneezed again. His head was full of dust and that confounded iron ball kept rolling to and fro and banging up the inside of his head. His nice new sixteen-dollar suit was a mess. His revolver was gone. His prisoner was gone. Miss Fajen was gone. He closed his eyes and wished thickly the whole blasted thing would just go away. It didn't.

He got to his feet and went at a stumble and stomp to the gun rack and fetched down one of the heavy double guns, shoved a brass-cased load of double-aught in each chamber, and closed the breech. Then he went forth in search of Mr. Ortega.

He was perhaps half way up the street when the fireworks began in the alley behind Whiskey Row. There were two shots, one almost atop the other, a pause, and a third shot, by which time Bruce had ducked between two buildings and was running in that narrow passage with the ball in his head ricocheting off every inner cranny of his skull. He burst into the alleyway and saw John P. Ballard prone in the dirt and Juan Jesus Ortega prowling toward him, a hand clutching his bloodied side, his revolver thrust at a stark rigid angle toward

John P. At the sound of Bruce's running, Ortega wheeled and fired and missed, and in the next instant the battering ram of massed buckshot caught and lifted and dumped him messily against the side of the Ophir Queen.

Bruce knelt by John P.'s body, feeling an odd and poignant sense of loss. Gently he touched, feeling for a pulse, and incredibly John P. Ballard stirred and with great effort tried to lift himself. Bruce caught him and eased him over, and to the first of the cautious investigators approaching he shouted: "Get the doctor and get him now!"

John P. Ballard looked up at him palely and said: "Twice in one night is too damned many. I am going to quit this business." Then John P. grinned faintly and lapsed into unconsciousness.

The doctor came and looked, pursed his lips, and said: "Maybe," and they took John P. away. Bruce picked up his shotgun and walked to the alley door of the Ophir Queen. It was locked. He lifted a leg and kicked it open, hearing the clatter of the broken lock on the floor inside. He stepped through quickly and said quietly: "I never shot a woman, but I can if I have to. Put it on the table, honey, right where I can see it."

The two women froze. Mrs. Queen as always big and warm and handsome in a rich red gown, Miss Glory Fajen still in black, the scarf floating about her white shoulders, the wicked stub-barreled Derringer half raised in her hand. She looked into the muzzles of the shotgun and carefully put the vicious little gun on the table.

"Well, then," said Bruce, kicking the door closed. He looked at Mrs. Queen and felt sick. "Wasn't your share enough?" he asked.

She looked old suddenly—old and dumpy and sag jowled. She said thickly: "You don't know anything about it."

"Enough, maybe," he said. "You were partners, weren't you, you and John? And half of this wasn't enough. You had to have it all." He looked at Miss Fajen. "And you came in on it just because you owned Ortega." He shook his head wonderingly. "Now your fighting dog is dead. Where does that leave you?" The pale Miss Fajen went even paler with shock. "Why," said Bruce bitterly, "did you honestly think he was man enough to kill John Ballard . . . even from behind?" He looked again at Mrs. Queen. He said almost gently: "Elsie, you're a fool. How long do you think you'd have lasted if this pair had killed John?"

She said: "I can take care of myself."

"Like a rabbit between two wolves," he said unpityingly. He broke the shotgun, set the empty case alongside the Derringer, and closed the gun with one live round still chambered. "I don't want to tell John," he said. "And I don't want the pair of you fouling my jail. I'll be back at daylight. Don't let me find you." He pulled the trigger, and both women started at the snap of the pin in the empty chamber.

Mrs. Queen said thickly: "I'm just supposed to walk off and leave all this?"

"Why," said Bruce, frowning judiciously down at the shotgun, "that seems reasonable enough to me ... doesn't it to you?"

She sagged into a chair, looking sick. Miss Fajen began throatily: "Bruce...." He looked at her. She moved subtly inside the black dress. She looked at him through thick black lashes, and her red lips smiled, as enticing as Eve's apple. "Bruce," she said, "we can work out a better thing than that, you and I. You're smart enough, Bruce, to...."

"Smart enough to know better than that," he said. "Yesterday, maybe, but not today. What I said was daylight. What I meant was both of you." Then he scooped up the Derringer, left the empty shell standing on the table as he walked out of the room.

He came out onto the main drag, ablaze with flares and lanterns all along the noisy street. Through the street's dust, dodging the Saturday-night revelers, someone was running. He recognized her and went toward her, and Jenny ran straight into his arms, and she clung to him and wept a little and gasped: "Oh, Bruce, I heard the shooting, and I was afraid it was you, and I came down the hill, and somebody said it was the marshal, and I thought it was ...! Oh, Bruce!" She stopped to kiss him with great vigor, and he kissed her back, and what with one thing and another quite a little crowd began to gather before they broke apart. Jenny blushed bright red and clung to his arm and buried her face in his chest as he grinned and waved the shotgun and said to the gathering: "Go along, go along ... haven't you got any business of your own to tend to?"

He took Jenny under his arm and pushed through. As they came past a naphtha flare, she looked up, her face half weeping, half laughing with relief, and he kissed her gently, and she said: "Oh, your suit . . . your beautiful new suit. You come right along and let me sponge it before that blood dries and ruins it."

"It's all right," he said.

"It is not. I mean it is. It's a lovely suit . . . it's a beautiful new suit, and I wanted to tell you so before, but. . . ."

He grinned and tucked her arm a bit more securely under his own. "Why," he said happily, "it's like John P. Ballard always says . . . you never go wrong picking the best."

They walked up the hill together, leaving the Saturday-night uproar of Ophir behind them.

# Journey of No Return

## T. V. Olsen

✪

*Born in Rhinelander, Wisconsin, T(heodore) V(ictor) Olsen went on to become one of the most widely respected and widely read authors of Western fiction in the second half of the twentieth century. Such important novels as* The Stalking Moon *(Doubleday, 1965) and* Arrow in the Sun *(Doubleday, 1969) were made into classic Western films.* The Golden Chance *(Fawcett, 1992) won the Golden Spur Award from the Western Writers of America in 1993, and his historical novel,* There Was a Season *(Doubleday, 1972), has recently appeared in a mass merchandise paperback edition from Leisure Books. His most recent Western novel is* Deadly Pursuit *(Five Star Westerns, 1995). Olsen's novels have a visceral, wrenching involvement. Once past the first chapter, it is nearly impossible to put them down. They are stories that work on two levels—the gnawing question of what will happen next combined with a profound emotional involvement with characters about whom a reader comes to care deeply. He was equally adept at the short story. His first collection,* Westward They Rode, *has been reprinted by Leisure Books, and his second,* Lone Hand: Frontier Stories *(Five Star Westerns, 1997), has recently been published. "Journey of No Return" first appeared in* Ranch Romances *in the issue dated April 20, 1956, and is being reprinted here for the first time.*

**F**rank Kenton came back to Trail because he had nowhere else to go. And the first day back he knew it was a mistake. People never forgot.

He came in on the train in late afternoon and registered at the hotel then went for a walk. In this new-found freedom he could not get enough of the air and sunlight, of stretching his legs long and briskly just walking. The town talked behind their hands as he went up and down the streets. He had paid his score to the law; that should have ended it. He had not been especially bitter on his release nor up to the time he had begun this walk. Yet less than an hour later, when he returned to the hotel, there was room in his mind for only one thought: to kill a man.

When Frank Kenton left the hotel in the morning, he wore a large-caliber gun under the shoulder of his shabby black suit coat. After the meal at the cafe, served by the waitress in stony silence, he stood on the sidewalk outside and lighted his after-breakfast cigar. He was a tall, nearly gaunt man in the mid-thirties whose lined sensitive face was withdrawn and unfriendly. Standing, looking at the town he'd once called home, he was aware of the bitter knowledge that a man could pay forever for a moment's unforeseen violence.

He saw the man and girl leave a house down the street and proceed along the walk toward him, laughing at some joke. The girl's bright laughter reached Kenton, rippling a half-forgotten chord of memory in him. He watched her closely as they neared him. She was tall and slim in a plain bombazine dress, and the early sunlight struck white fire from her pale hair. *It's Carol,* he thought with a stir of emotion. Carol Langerfels had grown into womanhood. Sam Langerfels, her father, was walking at her side. She must not be married yet, Kenton thought in surprise, yet she would be about twenty-five now. He saw her start of recognition as she noticed him. A warm gladness began in her face. Then Sam Langerfels, also seeing Kenton, spoke sharply to her. She turned with slow obedience, but with trouble in her face, and started back toward the house.

Langerfels walked on toward Kenton, his black frock coat whipped by his long strides. Kenton dropped his suddenly tasteless cigar to the walk and ground a heel on it, thinking resignedly: *here it comes.* Kenton had a fleeting impulse to turn his back on the man but to what end? Inevitably he'd have to talk to Langerfels. And it might as well be now as later. Langerfels stopped before him. The man had not changed much in six years, Kenton decided, except that he was a little leaner, perhaps, a little grayer.

"How long has it been, Frank?"

*The hell with you,* Kenton thought, then caught Langerfels's gaze which was wholly neutral, without friendliness but without reserve. Kenton read the meaning of it accurately. This could be pleasant or stiff with antagonism: the choice was Kenton's. He shook the hand, saying quietly: "You know damned well how long it's been, Sam." His gaze mechanically fell to Langerfels's shirt pocket.

Langerfels chuckled softly, pulling his lapel back. The tarnished sheriff's badge caught penciled streaks of sunlight. "Yes, I'm still wearing it, Frank." Kenton said nothing. Langerfels studied him briefly. "How was it?"

"Like a beautiful dream. I enjoyed every minute."

"Yeah," Langerfels said dryly. "Now what did you really think, Frank?"

"All right, I'll tell you. I died every time I woke in prison and remembered where I was . . . every morning for six years. Is that what you wanted to know?"

Langerfels searched Kenton's dead eyes thoughtfully and Kenton's closed face. "That's part of it. Now, what about Costain? He's still around, you know."

"I didn't know," Kenton said, his voice curiously flat and emotionless, "but it doesn't matter. So I hate his guts. So do a lot of people. You can make anything of that you like, Sam."

The sheriff nodded pleasantly, but there was a perceptible tinge of ice to his voice. "All right, boy, I will. You keep away from Costain, hear?"

Kenton said: "You're a busy man, Mister Langerfels. Don't waste time with a man who's reached a point of no return."

"It could be worse."

"Could it?"

"A man can start over. You're educated, Frank. There are plenty of fresh opportunities for someone like you."

"That may be," Kenton said, but there was a note of bitter conviction in his voice that Langerfels did not miss.

"What's sticking in your craw, boy?"

Kenton mentioned the attitude of the town.

Langerfels said: "We're not all like that. I'll not give judgment on what a man's been, only what he is. And that's so with other people in Trail, Frank. You'll see."

"And Carol?"

A faint startlement touched Langerfels's face, and Kenton thought, *here's where he feels the pinch.*

"Keep away from her, Frank. She's not for you."

"I didn't think so."

"Wait a minute. I'm not looking down on you, but Carol could be hurt." Langerfels would not meet Frank's eyes squarely.

"I see," Kenton said, feeling a raw anger build in him. "I can start again, all new, with everything except your daughter."

Langerfels's eyes lifted, ice blue. "Make your start somewhere else, then. But keep away from Carol. Because if you don't, I'll run you out of Trail anyway." He turned on his heel and headed for his office.

Langerfels's harshness only hardened Kenton against any vestige of doubt still remaining about the job ahead. Kenton went to the livery, rented a nag, and headed out of town at a lingering gait. He was in no hurry. Now that he knew what he was going to do, there was a vast and fathomless reservoir of patience in him, even while his mood danced on the dark edge of violence. The sound of a horse coming up fast behind him turned him in the saddle. Then he checked his horse and hauled around as Carol Langerfels came up sidesaddle on a big-barreled appaloosa.

"Good day," Kenton said in a dry voice.

She asked: "Are you wondering why I'm here?"

"It's none of my business."

"I wanted to see you. Your coming back to Trail is no secret." Kenton considered that. If Costain knew of his return, there was trouble ahead. She added softly: "And it's no secret that I've waited for you, Frank."

He once courted this girl seriously long ago, it seemed now, and far away. He said: "I'm touched, very touched. Only why?"

A startled hurt began in her expression. "Frank, nothing's changed."

"Everything's changed."

"Oh." His indifference summoned an undercurrent of anger to her voice. "What could make a man so hard?"

"Ask your old man. He put me in jail."

"To pay up, yes."

"To pay up for nothing," Kenton said coldly. "There are two sides to a penny. Let's turn it over. Suppose I didn't rob Costain's safe. Want to hear about that?"

"Yes, please."

"All right. Charlie Duneen, the banker, went out to Costain's Single Bit that day to foreclose an impending mortgage. He took me with him because he thought having a lawyer along would settle a lot of details over legal points . . . in case Costain was of a mind to argue, which he always was. The three of us assembled in Costain's office. Charlie said there was no way Costain could hang on to his spread a day longer unless he had the money to pay in full now. An argument started, and Costain pulled a gun out of his desk and shot Duneen. I went after Costain, and he clouted me with the gun. I woke up in your old man's jail, charged with robbing Costain's safe. Then Herbelsheimer from the bank . . . who was next in line for the position vacated by Duneen . . . got on the stand at my trial and told two lies that invalidated my story of how Charlie died. First he said that Duneen had gone to Arizona for his health and was taking a new position there, which explained Duneen's disappearance. Two, he claimed that Duneen couldn't have gone to Single Bit to foreclose on it because there was no record at the bank that they'd ever held any such mortgage. Naturally that made my story of why I was at Costain's place look like an excuse to cover my real purpose there . . . to rob him. When a respected banking man and a big rancher say one thing, and an out-at-the-pants shyster says another, who is any right-thinking jury going to believe? Three he asked who would have better reason to commit robbery than a struggling lawyer who hadn't eaten a square meal in a month?"

"I remember. You told your story at the trial."

"You didn't believe it either, did you?"

Carol bit her lip. "But why, Frank? Why should Herbelsheimer lie?"

"He and Costain were always close friends. Also, Herbelsheimer stood to profit by Charlie's death. Why shouldn't he be grateful to the man who brought about his promotion to a better job? He did get Duneen's position, didn't he?"

"Yes, he still has it. But why was Duneen's body never found?"

"¿Quien sabe? There are any number of gorges and wash-outs you can tumble a body in, and nature will do the rest."

"I believe you Frank," Carol said quickly. "But where were you going now? Not to see Costain?"

"Why not? I had time to think of things . . . six years of it."

"Oh no, Frank! It isn't as though you had spent your life in prison."

"It isn't his fault I didn't."

"Strange," she said softly, "but I had thought you would be too big for hate."

"It's funny," he said almost musingly. "I thought so too. Only it isn't really Costain. It's a lot of things he kind of symbolizes."

"What things?"

He shrugged evasively. "Just a lot of things . . . that began when I got back to Trail."

"Did Dad say something to hurt you?"

He shrugged. "What's the difference?"

Her mouth tightened. "I think you enjoy playing the martyr."

This struck too near the mark, and strangely it had the power to irritate Kenton. "Don't do that, Carol. Don't do that to me."

"You're doing it to yourself."

He looked at her, erect and lovely, and a terrible and mocking bitterness was suddenly on him. "I'm not young any more, Carol. I can't go back and start starving all over again. There's no life for you now with an ex-con."

She looked at him for a long five seconds. She said: "I remember when we were children. Life was so simple then. I was ten and you were fifteen, but all I thought of, even then, was that someday . . . it couldn't be any other way . . . that someday we'd. . . ." She bowed her head and could not go on.

"And live unhappily ever after. Is that it, Carol?"

"Frank, don't. This doesn't get us anywhere."

"Neither does talking."

"And you'll still try to get Costain?"

He said nothing. She looked at this tall, cold-eyed man who was a stranger to her, and there was a small sob in her throat. "You'll have your pound of flesh, then, won't you?" A sudden passionate anger caught in her voice, "You fool, Frank!"

Carol wheeled her horse and plunged it full tilt back for town. For a moment Kenton wanted to call after her, to tell her he had not meant to take this bitterness out on her, that he was not responsible for what he said because he was no longer a man but a husk, living now only to even scores with Will Costain.

Continuing on the road to Costain's Single Bit, the portly figure of the rancher bulked hatefully through the darkness in Frank's mind. He meant to make Will Costain sweat blood, to telescope into minutes the mental torture that had filled not minutes but six wasted years in the life of Frank Kenton. He spurred the livery horse, setting a brisk pace. Time would crowd him now, for Carol would tell her father of his intent, and Langerfels would hurry to prevent it.

On the wagon road, still a mile from Single Bit headquarters, Kenton sighted a light spring wagon. Nearing it, a strange smile shaped his straight mouth as he recognized the driver. As the rig reached him, Kenton sidled his horse off the road as though to let the other pass then reached out and caught the headstall of one of the team and stopped the wagon. He reined in close to the driver, a hugely obese man whose massive legs almost split the trousers of his conservative brown suit. His eyes were blue-irised slits nearly hidden in the rolls of fat pouching his cheeks, his bristling yellow hair, close-clipped so that his head sat his shoulders like a fat burr. "A fine morning for a drive, Banker Herbelsheimer."

The big man watched Kenton stolidly, incuriously, with no surprise.

"You don't know me?"

"Nor care to, *mein* friend."

"Look harder, Hans."

Herbelsheimer did then nodded his massive head. "You've been away a long time, *Herr* Kenton."

"Why, you ought to know that," Kenton said. "You've come from seeing Costain, I'd say. You and he were always thicker than thieves, as I should know better than anyone."

Herbelsheimer gave him a look of pure, sustained hatred and fingered the reins uneasily. "What are you after, Kenton?"

"There's hell to pay, Hans, and I'm here to collect from Brother Costain."

The wariness in the banker's shrewd eyes heightened in sudden knowledge. "*Teufel!* You mean to give him a chance!"

Kenton nodded. "As much as he gave me."

Herbelsheimer's pink face puckered, and he looked as though he were about to cry. The blood rushed to his heavy features. "But, damn you, Costain is my friend!" He flung an arm behind the wagon seat, coming up with a shotgun. Kenton hadn't seen it and was caught off guard. He ripped open his coat, his hand diving to the shoulder holster and hauling out his gun just as Herbelsheimer let go with the shotgun.

The shot sprayed Kenton's left shoulder, and he rolled back in the saddle, bringing his six-gun up. It roared deafeningly, and Herbelsheimer dropped the shotgun and slid heavily down in his seat, holding his torn arm. Kenton, still holding his gun, grabbed the reins of his spooked horse and quieted him. He felt the hotter pain, running from his shoulder and down his own stiffening left arm. He said hollowly: "It's a draw, Hans."

Tears squeezed from Herbelsheimer's pain-squinted eyes and rolled down his round cheeks. "Damn you, Kenton," he said. He almost wept. "Damn you, Kenton. I'll see you in hell for this."

Kenton said savagely: "I'll be waiting for you on a bed of coals with a pitchfork."

He kicked out with a boot, slashing with it at the nearest wagon horse's rump. The team, already nervous, moved forward now, carrying the slumped Herbelsheimer toward Trail and a doctor's care.

Kenton ripped his shirt open and tied his pocket bandanna on his shoulder. The bleeding and pain did not lessen. He headed on toward Single Bit and Will Costain. Half a mile from the ranch Kenton left the wagon road, where it crossed the slender meandering thread of Hackberry Creek, then followed the willow-choked creek bank to a grove of giant cottonwoods at the rear of the big Single Bit wagon shed. He sat his horse at the fringe of the grove, screened by a meager stand of brush, giving cold attention to the expanse of rolling, park-like lawn surrounding the low stone ranch house. He saw it was deserted and heard nothing but the clean measured tap of the blacksmith's hammer on the anvil, ringing distantly through the clear morning. His shoulder was filled with a tortuous sickening pain, but it could not stop him now.

Kenton half hitched his horse to a tree and started across the open lawn toward the house. He was tense with the fear of being sighted and ridden with the vicious, angry urgency of knowing that Langerfels would be here soon, if Carol had told him. Edging to an open window of the front room, he crouched in some low shrubbery. He drew his gun out slowly with the hand of his good arm, listening warily. He heard footsteps entering the room.

"I'll have my coffee in the office, Martin." That was Costain's voice. "I have market reports to study. You stay here."

"Sure you'll be all right, Mister Costain?" Martin's voice was a musical Texan drawl.

Costain laughed indulgently. "There is only one window opening on my office. I have a gun, and I can watch one window, don't you think? I'll call you if anything happens."

Costain was scared enough to hire a bodyguard, Kenton thought, feeling a cold drawing of his muscles. He waited till he heard the door to the office close then, with painstaking caution, he holstered his gun, took off his hat and raised his eyes just above the level of the window sill. Martin, he saw, was sprawled in a comfortable leather chair, smoking, one booted foot propped on the arm while he leafed through a magazine. He was lean and unshaven, wearing often-patched range clothes, typical of the ragged earthy riffraff of rawhiders that drifted up from Texas. He wore a belted .45 and an old .40-.40 Henry leaned against the chair.

Kenton sank down in a quandary. He had to take Costain by surprise to keep him alive. But how could he do it with Costain watching his office window and Martin guarding the front room onto which the office door opened? The sick blood pounded through Kenton's temples as he restlessly quested out what he knew of the layout of this house.

There was a kitchen and a pantry to the rear, for Costain liked to do his own cooking, a large bedroom and, up front, the living room and Costain's office. Thoughtlessly Kenton reached up to rub his stiff arm. His had brushed his trousers pocket and the handful of pistol shells there. The suggestion of a crystallizing idea, a scheme in embryo, touched his mind. It would be a tall chance, but there was no time to consider alternatives.

He moved at a low-crouching run to the rear of the house, eased the back door open, and stepped inside. He stumbled on the door sill and almost fell. A living flame wracked his shoulder, paralyzing thought and muscle. He leaned against the wall for a moment. *Take it slow*, he thought numbly, *take it easy. Get him first, then it won't matter.* Fighting down the nausea that gripped him, he moved to the iron stove in the corner and lifted the stove lid with infinite care. He set the lid down silently to one side, seeing, as he had hoped, a banked layer of glowing coals. He worked quickly to stir up the coals with the poker. Then, selecting a thin, narrow strip of kindling wood from the wood box by the stove, he emptied out his small handful of shells and laid them down in a row on the wooden strip. He lowered them delicately onto the surface of red coals.

He returned silently and swiftly to the front room window and crouched there, listening tensely over the heavy strike of his heart, feeling a rising excitement mount to his tight nerves. When the crash of fire-touched gunpowder came from the kitchen, he heard Costain speak over it loudly. "What's that?"

Martin left the front room to investigate. *Now*, Kenton thought. Gun ready, he slung a leg over the windowsill and stepped into the room. Nine fast steps took him to the office door. It was unlocked, and he stepped quickly inside and closed it noiselessly behind him. Only then did Costain, behind a desk of expensive walnut, look up. His hands, on the desk, moved.

Kenton said in a voice of steel: "Don't."

Costain became motionless, watching as Kenton walked toward the desk. The man had not changed at all in six years. Costain was a gentleman rancher. A heavy, portly man in the black business suit of a well-to-do cattleman he could at fifty-five have passed for forty. His black banjo eyes revealed nothing at all. Kenton hooked a leg over the desk corner and sat there, his gun trained loosely on Costain.

"You know," the rancher said presently, "you won't leave this house alive, Frank."

"You won't, either," Kenton said idly. "That's more important."

Costain said with a soft, contemptuous smile: "You haven't the shadow of a chance, Frank. Give me the gun."

Kenton could see the small lance of fear playing behind the opaque eyes, and a wicked pleasure filled him. He thought: *Costain's head is on the block now. He's cracking. Let him crack some more.*

"You'll not go through with this."

"Ask Herbelsheimer."

Costain stiffened. "What about Herbelsheimer?"

Kenton didn't answer. He only watched the man's growing fear and felt the strength draining from himself. Weary with pain, he thought: *the hell with the pain. The hell with the blood. The thing now is to make Costain sweat.*

There was a tap at the office door. Kenton half swiveled his gun toward it with a curt nod at Costain.

"Yes?"

"Some bullets in the stove, I reckon, sir." That was Martin's drawl. "Some of your crew playing games?"

"Yes. It's all right, Martin."

Kenton listened to Martin leaving the door then smiled gently. "You did fine, Will. Fine."

"Frank, listen. I'll pay . . . pay any damn' thing."

"You'll pay my way. That's how it'll be."

Kenton saw Costain's face receding then in a giddy blur, and he silently called on a hidden reservoir of strength. He fought back the sickness and blackness, and the room swam back into focus. He lifted his left hand from the desk without taking his gaze from Costain. The blood pooled quickly under his palm.

Costain began to babble. "Frank, I'll confess. I'll tell Langer-fels. . . ."

"About how you killed Duneen, eh?"

"About that, about anything!" Costain spoke in a frightened voice.

"Fine, Will. All right, Frank, drop it." The voice from the window at Kenton's back brought him half around. It was Sam Langerfels.

Weak from blood loss, trying futilely to steady the gun, Kenton felt himself slipping down on the desk and knew belatedly that he had waited too long. His last conscious thought was of Costain clawing open a drawer of his desk and bringing up a pistol. Then it was as though a bright light were turned off, and Kenton thought he heard a gunshot before a roaring void of blackness filled his eyes and ears.

He lay in the big bed of the front corner of the room of the Langerfels house and listened to the sheriff talk.

"I was right behind you most of the way, Frank. I watched from the grove while you got inside the house. And I listened to you and Costain outside his office . . . every word."

"You could have picked me up at any time, then. Why didn't you?"

Langerfels smiled and scratched his graying head. "Why, when Carol told me about what you had in mind, I figured a jasper wouldn't get that het up against a man who put him in jail, even for six years, unless he had a good reason for thinking he didn't deserve it. So I waited. And it was a good thing I did."

"Yeah." Kenton stirred his bandage-stiff shoulder. "So what about Costain now?"

"I just winged him when he pulled that gun. Both he and Herbelsheimer will get a taste of what you got for six years. Only they'll both get life sentences for Duneen's killing. I doubt if they'll appreciate the diet." He paused with a trace of embarrassment then added: "Apologies for those six years would sound cheap, Frank."

Kenton had already sensed the man's hurt, his regret; and he had been making a fact-facing, self-searching appraisal of himself and not liking what he saw. He wondered now whether he would really have cold-bloodedly pulled that trigger on Costain. And Carol? Hesitantly he put the question to Langerfels, who cleared his throat. "She waited for you for six years with the town making a lot of rotten talk about a girl who'd wait for a con. And I gave her as much hell about it as any, I'm ashamed to say." The sheriff looked at Kenton with intent bright eyes. "She helped Doc Bishop fix your shoulder but, when you started coming to, she left the room. She said she didn't think you'd want to see her after what you'd said before." He laid a hand on Kenton's arm, saying gently: "Be good to her, Frank. I'll ask no more than that."

"Sam?"

"What is it, son?"

"Please ask her to come in now."

# Virginia City Winter

*Dorothy M. Johnson*

✪

*Born in McGregor, Iowa, Dorothy M. Johnson grew up in Whitefish, Montana. She began to write for magazines while working as a editor in New York, where she lived between 1935 and 1950. In 1950 she returned to Whitefish, where she was news editor for the local weekly paper. Her first book,* Beulah Bunny Tells All *(Morrow, 1942), is a collection of short stories about a fictional schoolteacher whose adventures had previously appeared in* The Saturday Evening Post. *Her reputation as one of the finest Western short story writers has come to rest on two collections of short stories—*Indian Country *(Ballantine, 1953) and* The Hanging Tree *(Ballantine, 1957)—both consisting of stories previously published in* Collier's, Argosy, Cosmopolitan, and The Saturday Evening Post, *her primary magazine markets. "Lost Sister," included in* The Hanging Tree, *won a Golden Spur Award from the Western Writers of America. Johnson was a masterful storyteller, equally at home writing about men or women, whites or Indians. It is the simple, stark beauty and truthfulness of her stories that make them so memorable. "Virginia City Winter" first appeared in Johnson's later story collection,* Flame on the Frontier: Short Stories of Pioneer Women *(Dodd, Mead, 1967), and has not been otherwise reprinted.*

The Flanagans reached Alder Gulch in August 1863, after a long, difficult journey from the States. There were five of them: Pat and his wife, Norah, Timmy, thirteen but looking younger, Katie, eight years old, and Baby, who was just getting the idea that it would be a fine thing to walk instead of crawl. They had almost no money left when they reached the gold gulches, but there was work a-plenty in the raw new settlements along Alder Gulch. They stopped in the biggest one, roaring Virginia City.

Before they had the horses unhitched, a bearded man rode up on horseback, tipped his hat to Norah, and said to Pat: "I got a mine up that way half a mile. You ever done any placering?"

"No, sir," answered honest Pat, "but, if it's a matter of digging, I've sure done that."

So he had a job right off, and two more offers before he got his camp staked out. He went to work next morning, and the wages were high. So were the prices of everything there was to buy, but Norah was used to stretching a dollar, even if it was in unfamiliar gold dust. They had no house to live in; most people didn't, in spite of the constant racket of building. Nights are cold in that high country, and there wasn't much Norah could do about heating a covered wagon or keeping an active baby clean when the baby was on the ground most of the time. Timmy, curious and excited, investigated along the gulches, found that many miners lived in dugouts, and started to dig one before his father got home from work the first day.

That night there was a shooting up the street—a miner killed his partner in a drunken quarrel, jumped on his horse, and left town. So the Flanagans moved into the vacant cabin twenty minutes before someone else tried to. It had two small rooms and even an expensive little iron stove, which had been freighted up the Missouri by steamboat and then down from Fort Benton by wagon.

"Aren't we the lucky ones!" caroled Norah. "Will they catch the murderer and bring him back for trial?"

"Around here, one more shooting is just one more shooting," Pat said gravely. "They won't even try."

"It's a fine cabin," said Norah, "or will be with a bit of chinking between the logs."

"I'll do the chinking," Timmy promised, and he did, and then they were well set for the winter. Pat worked till all hours on his job, because after freeze-up there would be little washing of gravel to get the gold out.

Every night when Pat came home, his wife had a kettle of water hot for him. She cleared the children out of the front room—that is, the one that was not the kitchen—so he could scrub off his dirt and warm his feet and, if he wanted his shoulder muscles kneaded, all he had to do was ask. In his own home Pat Flanagan was a king, and nobody questioned that it was his right and his family's duty. He wore a kind of glory, which they provided, and it shone upon them, and none of them gave the matter a thought because that was the way it had always been.

"I am learning something about gold and how to find it, from listening to the talk," Pat reported. "Partly it's luck, but there's something in knowing the signs of what to look for."

"You've always been the lucky one," Norah assured him proudly.

He smiled at her and answered: "I have indeed. So maybe in the spring I will go prospecting a little, and we'll have our own gold mine."

"Why, maybe we'll be rich!" Norah suggested with the voice of faith.

In a lull in the conversation Timmy spoke: "I got work today. At the barbershop." His parents stopped eating and looked at him with pride and concern. "It's to carry water and wood for the barber and his bathhouse and run errands, like to the Chinese laundry, and if a customer wants his boots cleaned or his back washed, there I am, handy."

Then he held his breath, because if either of them said no, then no it was. Pat looked at Norah, and they nodded together. "It's honest work that needs doing," said Pat, and Norah agreed, "It is indeed. And how will they pay you?"

"From the barber two dollars a week to carry water and cut wood and keep the boiler hot, and from the customers whatever they want to give for the boots and the errands and to get their backs scrubbed. A pinch of gold dust or a small nugget. But I think," he said, frowning, "it should be more for cleaning boots if they're on a man instead of off."

"I think so too," agreed the father, but Norah asked, "Why?"

"He ought to get more for going down on his knees before a man, that's why," Pat explained.

Norah showed her dimples. "And if he tells them that, I don't doubt there'll be many will prefer it that way."

So the Flanagans were pleased with life and ate their bread and beans with thankfulness. Baby even had a cup of milk, although it was terribly expensive, cows being scarce.

"I saw a pretty lady today," said Timmy one evening. "Riding down the street with her husband, and her laughing and proud. The barber said her name was Missus Slade, from the toll house out in the hills." Encouraged to describe her, he stammered, because he was half in love from his respectful distance. "She rode a fine black horse, and her hair was black and glossy, hanging down in curls. A handsome lady, acting like she would not be afraid of the devil himself."

"No more she would," his father agreed. "The one she's married to has a reputation of a devil, with no fear in him and considerable cruelty. Captain Joseph Slade . . . we heard of him coming across the Plains, you'll remember."

"Oh, that one!" cried Norah. "Him that carries a dead man's ears around in his vest pocket, and he killed the man that wore them."

"Before they came here, that was," Pat emphasized. "Captain Slade hasn't killed anybody here."

"Another man he tried to burn up, the way they were talking," Timmy added, "but I didn't hear all the story."

Pat had heard it; he picked up plenty of talk at his work. "When Slade was superintendent of the stage line, dishonest men tried to cheat him, selling him hay that was weighed with rocks in it. So he chained one of them to a log and set the hay on fire against it."

"I declare, I think that's terrible!" Norah objected.

"He only let the man singe a little and promise not to do it again," Pat explained. "After that, nobody cheated the stage line."

"And to think," Timmy said sadly, "I didn't look at him twice for admiring his lady!"

"A few more years on you, and you'll be a great one with the ladies, I don't doubt," his mother said fondly, making him feel gallant so that he blushed.

"The lady is perhaps not quite a lady that you'd stand around and chat with after Mass, if there was Mass and if she went," Pat said cautiously. "But she is a loyal wife to Captain Slade . . . ah, loyal she certainly is. They were saying that she saved his life once. Three men captured him in a cabin, going to kill him, and he begged to say a last good bye to his wife. So they sent for her, and she came weeping and pleading, and into the cabin she went and, when she came out, she had a pistol in her hand and Slade, behind her, had another that she'd carried under her skirt, and the two of them rode away triumphant."

"Ah, the loyal lady!" breathed Norah.

Life and hard work went hand in hand with the Flanagans, and they had nothing to complain about until—Timmy, in between cleaning boots, was looking out the shop window while the bearded customers talked about hold-ups when he saw four men tramp across the street, carrying a man on an improvised stretcher, and his heart leaped with pity. Half an hour later his sister came running and blurted out: "Pa's hurt."

Timmy was appalled to find Norah crying. No matter what happened, she had never cried in the presence of her children. "Your father's alive, and the doctor is with him," she sobbed. Then she drove the children out of the house, saying: "It's not right that his children should hear him groan with his pain, and him a king among men!"

For the next week Timmy's tips were very good at the shop, because the customers were sympathetic. Then they forgot. He began to worry, for the firewood at home was getting low, and Pat would not be going out to buy more. Timmy wrestled with his conscience and left it bruised and cringing. On the way home Saturday night—very late, and no supper in him—he picked up a stick of wood back of the barbershop. But he came back and returned it. He couldn't steal from the barber. He went softly through the alleys in the darkness, hiding when he heard a sound or saw a light, and took one piece of firewood from each back door where there was any. At home he arranged it carefully, scattering it so his mother wouldn't notice it was new. It was better to bear the shame of thievery than to let the family freeze. And he vowed he'd return it, some day.

The children slept on the kitchen floor, as they had from the beginning. Norah sat up nights in a rough chair, ready to help Pat if she could. She did not sleep very much at any time, and that little in the daytime on the floor, with Katie sitting big-eyed beside her father's bed.

Timmy learned so many exciting things at the shop and couldn't tell them at home that he felt bottled up and about to burst. There had been hold-ups on the road to Bannack and beyond; a man named Nick had disappeared with a team of mules he did not own and was blamed for stealing them; then his body was found, shot and frozen, several miles out of town. Angry storekeepers and miners formed a posse, rounded up several men who seemed guilty, and held a great trial out of doors at Nevada City. Four days before Christmas they hanged a handsome young man named George Ives for the murder. Then a dozen angry men rode out looking for more murderers and on the way back strung up two more men. The riders were the new Vigilantes, and the men they pursued were the infamous bandits known as road agents. They were making history. But Timmy Flanagan told none of this at home for fear of disturbing his mother, who had enough on her mind.

Just after New Year's Norah shut the door of the front room and held Baby on her lap and told her two older children: "Now we play a game for the rest of the winter. The king is in yonder bed and will be till he gets his health and strength again. Katie, you are the big princess. You will look after the king when I'm away, and also tend the little princess. Timmy is the crown prince, and he will go on doing what he has been doing. And the queen will go out and find work somewhere because we need the money." She added sadly: "Your father, the king, does not hold with this plan of mine, and I never thought I'd cross his will, but this is what we have to do. The crown prince will go with me till I find my job that the good Lord has waiting somewhere."

With her warm shawl around her and Timmy by her side, she went into Dance and Stuart's store. Mr. Stuart was shocked. "But ma'am," he explained, "you couldn't lift a keg of nails or measure a miner for a pair of pants." He filled Timmy's pockets with dried apples before they left, and Timmy kept thinking of the dried ears Captain Slade carried in his vest pocket.

Norah tried the bakery, and the baker smiled. "This is man's work," he said. "I bake for my family," she argued. "Can you lift a hundred-pound sack of flour?" he challenged. She admitted that she probably couldn't do it any more than once. He grinned. "Do it once and you can have it."

Norah looked with calculation at the costly sack of flour that had been freighted by wagon over the mountains from Salt Lake, almost five hundred miles away. "How high do I lift it to please you?' she asked coolly.

"Clear of the floor," he said, looking ashamed of himself.

So she drew a deep breath and lifted it and let it drop again, and the baker said: "I don't think you weigh that much yourself, ma'am, my apologies. I'll deliver it to your cabin myself, and good luck to you." "Don't disturb my husband," she warned. She added: "Thank you" but distantly, like a kind queen accepting a vassal's back taxes.

"Now we will go to the boarding house," she told Timmy.

The proprietor there argued: "But the men are rough and dirty, and the work is hard, and you wouldn't want to hear the talk that goes on sometimes."

"As for the talk I am hard of hearing," said Norah. "I'll wait tables and wash dishes . . . and it's time somebody did." She took off her shawl and neatly folded it and kissed Timmy and rolled up her sleeves.

When he got home late that night and quietly spread his stolen firewood around by the chopping block, his mother was not waiting in the house. Katie woke up under her quilt on the floor and reported sleepily: "Ma came in dancing, just about, all gay and happy. She's asleep now in the other room, so I guess she was tired."

"I guess she was," said Timmy.

On days when he came home earlier, he noticed that Norah always acted the same way. She came in smiling, light footed, full of talk and gaiety. She kissed the children and could hardly wait to run in and tell Pat all the things she had heard—or the things she didn't mind having him know she had heard.

The way she acted puzzled Timmy. She jumped around so, once she was in the cabin, and laughed so much that a person would think she had just found a hundred dollars. But he saw her once or twice before she reached the cabin, trudging up the path as if her feet were too heavy to lift, with her head down and her eyes half closed, shivering in her worn and faded shawl. She's tired, Timmy thought, and Pa must know it, so why does she try to fool him?

The tenth of January was a date Tim remembered clearly, because it was his birthday, and startling news came from Bannack, and that was the day he had a memorable experience with Captain Joseph Slade. Years later he could boast about it, but the day it happened he did not tell his own folks. Slade came in for a haircut and shave— unlike most of the men, he was clean shaven. When he came, he was drunk and good natured. While he waited his turn in the chair, he said: "Boy, kneel down and clean my boots."

He talked big, Captain Slade did, with the other customers listening politely, and pretty soon he demanded: "Boy, what do you think you're doing?"

"Cleaning your boots, sir, like you told me."

"And if I tell you to go to Hades, will you do that too?"

Timmy answered stoutly: "No, sir. You ain't going to pay enough for that."

Slade burst out laughing, and so did the others, because it was wise to laugh at what Slade thought was funny. Then he snarled: "Think you're smart, eh?" and kicked.

Tim Flanagan tumbled tail over teakettle across the floor. When he could see again, past his rage and pain, he observed that the barber was standing in front of Captain Slade with the open razor in his hand. "The boy charges extra for that, sir," the barber said softly. "Get out your gold, sir, and give him a good big pinch of dust."

Slade grinned at the razor. "I'll give him half an ounce if he'll hold out his poke for it. Boy, are you scared of me?"

"I sure am," gasped Timmy as he pulled his leather poke out of his pocket.

They weighed the yellow dust on the gold scales, and Slade went out, laughing, unshorn, and with one boot still muddy. The barber fanned himself with a towel. There was such a sigh of relief in the shop that one man said later it blew the door off the hinges. But it was really an excited miner who threw the door open and announced: "The Vigilance Committee over to Bannack strung up Sheriff Plummer and two deputies!"

Nobody answered. It was dangerous to say: "They had it coming because they were really road agents pretending to be lawmen," and a lie to say: "Too bad." In embarrassed silence the customers filed

**Dorothy M. Johnson   585**

out, each to look for someone he dared talk to frankly. The barber closed the shop for the day. Timmy went home with eight dollars' worth of dust he had earned in a hurry but could not say anything about it for fear of worrying his folks. But Norah heard about it next day and whispered: "Did he hurt you badly, son?" and kissed him and managed not to cry.

On the fourteenth of January she came back white as a sheet, before she had gone a hundred yards from home. "Look!" she whispered. "Look!" All around the town, on the ridges of the hills, there was something new and grim: men armed with rifles, almost shoulder to shoulder, tense and watchful, black against the early morning sky. "They wouldn't let me through the street," she said. "They're going to hang some men. Timmy, my work, my job! I'm needed at the boardinghouse with so many men in Virginia from the gulches!"

Timmy stared out at the armed pickets. They were moving a little, stamping their cold feet, never relaxing their watchfulness. "They'll pay no attention to a boy," he said. "I think the shop will be closed, the barber being a Vigilante. Everybody will go to the hanging."

Norah stared at him solemnly. "Very well, you go. But promise me you won't watch the hanging."

"Oh, Ma!" he mourned.

"Promise!" she insisted, so he did and kept the promise, but it seemed like a terrible thing to miss the free show.

He worked hard and awkwardly at the boardinghouse all day. He saw armed men tramping by, and he heard shouts and catcalls and the mob's roaring. He did not go down the street for the hangings, although the cook did and said he could. When he went home that night, he looked at the unfinished building where five men had died, swinging from ropes tied to a rafter: Clubfoot George Lane, Frank Parish, Haze Lyons, Jack Gallagher, Boone Helm. He regretted that he could not take home any firewood—there were still too many men on the street too excited to settle down.

He was tired enough to fall into bed, but Norah said his father was restless, wanting to know what had happened. "They strung up five road agents and another got away," Timmy said briefly. "The

Vigilantes did it. All of a sudden pridnear every man in town claims he's a Vigilante."

"They're good men," Pat said. "Brave men."

Norah sassed back: "With all their virtue they're killers just the same!"

Pat sighed. "They've took a bill of sale on a herd of nightmares," he agreed. "But it was something that had to be done."

The rest of the winter was relatively quiet—a few fights, an occasional gunshot, plenty of talk. But there were no more hold-ups anywhere near, because the road agents had either been executed or scared out. Pat Flanagan's leg healed enough so he could sit up in bed. Baby learned to walk, and her father crowed with delight when she tottered into his room and sat down with a thump on the floor but didn't cry.

"I'll be learning to walk myself one of these days," promised Pat. "But I ain't going to thump down on my bottom like that." He sighed. "I ain't going to dig gravel for a while, either," he admitted. "Have to get an easier job . . . and what is there?"

"You said once you learned the shoemaking trade," Timmy remembered.

"That I did, in my youth." Pat suddenly got so excited he couldn't lie still. "The shoemaker's gone . . . Clubfoot George . . . one of the five they hung! Run quick to Dance and Stuart's . . . is his bench and tools still there? Meanwhile . . ."—he looked around the room, calculating—"I can mend boots here, along about next week. Son, help me up." He stood for a moment, white and shaking, leaning on Timmy. "Now run!" he commanded.

Clubfoot George's tools and leather were still at the store, unused except by an occasional unskilled man trying to patch his own worn-out boots. Tim made a deal to get the lot delivered to the cabin next time a wagon went that way.

Early in March Norah came home out of breath, not dancing but pale and frightened. "Mister Slade's drunk and troublesome," she reported. "I heard he slapped the judge or spit in his face! They've warned him out of town, but he won't go. I came home through Daylight Gulch to miss the crowds gathering."

"Before you set foot out tomorrow," Pat ordered, "Tim will walk along the street and make sure it's safe."

It was safe enough; there were rumbles of anger in groups of miners arguing, but they were sound men, not road agents. Some of them were Slade's friends, and none was his enemy, but there were those who felt strongly that this time the man had gone too far with his bullying and had to be stopped. Tim escorted his mother to her work then went on to his own, but the shop was locked. A loafer said pompously: "Barber's not coming. He's at a meeting."

"Meeting" had taken on a new meaning that winter. "Meeting" meant Vigilantes secretly assembled, with something dreadful happening soon thereafter. Tim walked moodily home. Slade was drunk most of the time lately and always a man to be avoided, a dangerous man. But he had not robbed anybody, and he had not shot anybody since coming to Alder Gulch, and what a man had done before he got there didn't count. Everybody arrived with a clean slate.

Exactly the same arguments were being discussed in a secret meeting at that very moment. Every man there was angry, but they were not in agreement. It took them a while to make a decision.

Tim was glad to get home. Later, standing tiptoe at the high widow in the front room, he described to his father what he saw. "Big crowd down in Daylight Gulch," he reported. "Say, a rider just cut out for the hills in a hurry."

"The tollhouse is that way," Pat said. "Can you see the scaffold? If so, stop looking, for I will not have you see Slade die, if he does die."

"There's a building in the way," Timmy reported. "I think the scaffold is the gate of the corral that used to belong to George Ives."

For a long time nothing happened except that the crowd down there moved and squirmed, and he could see arms wave angrily. Then there came an angry roar of the voices of a thousand men; even in the cabin they heard it. Pat crossed himself and murmured: "May the Lord have mercy on his soul. Come away now, boy."

"A rider is coming down the toll road," Timmy said, unable to obey. "It's a woman, I do believe, and her riding like a maniac . . . yes, a woman, with her long black hair streaming out behind her!" Then he turned away because he could not bear the sight of the Widow Slade riding down into the crowd in hopeless fury with her mouth open in a scream he could not hear and a pistol in her right hand and the black horse spraying lather.

"Ah, the poor lady," Pat groaned. "The lady so loyal to a man like that! Go to your mother now, son, and stay with her and escort her home, for it's not fit she should walk alone among murderers, no matter if they call themselves Vigilantes. A badman he was, but he had not killed anyone here, and it was for pure anger they hung him, and I think they will regret it."

A day or two later both Norah and Timmy heard news they reported to Pat as he painfully patched a pair of boots. The Widow Slade, like a black angel in her fury, had vowed she would not have her man's body rest beneath the earth where such wicked men as his executioners lived. She was having a coffin made, lined with metal. She would fill it with whiskey to preserve the body she had loved and, when the snow was gone from the passes so a wagon could get through, she would take her man to Salt Lake City for burial in a decent cemetery. She is keeping him in the same house with her, the whisper went. Pickled in whiskey in a coffin lined with metal. Over and over men described her wild, useless ride down the hill. "With a pistol in each hand and the reins in her teeth!" That did not match the fact of what Tim Flanagan had seen, but he heard it so many times from men who hadn't actually seen her at all that he learned to accept it. So that was how he remembered her: with a pistol in each hand and the reins in her teeth.

Pat Flanagan could stand alone. He could walk four steps and back with help. Then four steps alone. Among the Flanagans there was one triumph after another.

There came a day of sunshine, of spring that could not be denied, and on that day Tim Flanagan saw a sight that sent a cloud over the sun. He saw a wagon moving through the street, a wagon well loaded, with a canvas over the load, and a man named Kiscadden driving the team. Beside him on the seat, wrapped in a black shawl, sat the Widow Slade with a face of stone, looking neither to one side nor the other. Tim Flanagan took off his cap and held it so until the wagon passed, carrying Captain Joseph Slade to his last rest. He trudged home, wanting to weep for the tragic lady, but what he saw in his own yard was so splendid that he forgot his pity. His father was out of doors, walking slowly, without crutch or cane. Norah's hand was on his arm as if he were supporting her frailty as a man should. Tim heard the sound of their breathless, triumphant laughter. Like a flash of light he understood something that had puzzled him all winter. He knew at last why his mother, tired out, always came home to the cabin dancing and gay and lively. Why, every time, he thought, she was galloping in to save her man, with a gun in each hand and the reins in her teeth.

Tim was hungry, and his feet were cold. He rubbed his chapped hands, where drops of blood had oozed through the cracks and dried. He shivered in his patched jacket. He was accustomed to these things and did not think about them. With his teeth chattering, he smiled, because the winter was over.

# Deep in This Land

*Ernest Haycox*

◉

*During his lifetime Ernest Haycox was considered the dean among authors of Western fiction. He was born in Portland, Oregon. In the 1920s his name became established in all the leading Western pulp magazines of the day. His first novel was* Free Grass *(Doubleday, Doran, 1929). In 1931 he broke into the pages of* Collier's, *and from that time on was regularly featured in this magazine, either with a short story or a serial that was later published as a novel. In the 1940s his serials began appearing in* The Saturday Evening Post, *and it was there that modern classics such as* Bugles in the Afternoon *(Little, Brown, 1944) and* Canyon Passage *(Little, Brown, 1945) were first published. Both of these novels were also made into major motion pictures although, perhaps, the film most loved and remembered is* Stagecoach *(United Artists, 1939), directed by John Ford and starring John Wayne, based on Haycox's short story "Stage to Lords-burg." No history of the Western story in the twentieth century would be possible without reference to Haycox's fiction. He almost always has an involving story to tell and one in which there is something not so readily definable that raises it above its time, an image possibly, a turn of phrase, or even a sensation, the smell of dust after rain or the solitude of an Arizona night. "Deep in This Land" was among the stories he wrote but held in reserve. It was first published posthumously in* Playboy *(January 1990) and has not previously been collected.*

**H**e dismounted and went ahead to break trail through hip-deep drifts and so came out of the pines to the rim of the valley and paused there to rest himself and his hard-pressed horse. The great wind had quit; the flakes fell in thick, wavering laziness; and the trees were brittle-still. The weather pall hung low, and he had only a shadowy view of the rough bare land that ran away toward the plains of central Oregon, but directly below him in the valley a figure stirred against the painful whiteness, walking away from a wagon half buried in snow.

He went rapidly down the slope, even then knowing he had come upon a bad thing.

The figure stopped and waited for him and, when he got near, he saw it was a girl bundled inside a heavy overcoat, a shawl wrapped around her head and an axe in her hand. Her mouth was tight with misery, and her eyes held a dead-beat look.

"You're walking straight toward nothing," Hill Beachey said.

She pulled the shawl from her ears. "I mean to get some wood for a fire."

"How long have you been here?"

She did some counting, some remembering. "This is the third morning."

"Where's your man?"

"The sheep drifted. The first night . . . first night of the storm. They went out to head off the sheep."

"Who did?"

"My father . . . my brother."

He took the axe and turned her about and walked on to the wagon. She had searched for the men, for her tracks made widening rings around the wagon and struck off to the west and came back to the wagon. He knew this country, and now he knew this story. He said: "Wait," and followed her trail until, about 400 feet from the wagon, it ended at the rim of a cañon whose floor lay fifty feet below. That was the trap into which the sheep, pushed by the violent wind, had fallen; he couldn't see the sheep, but he saw the hummocks of snow scattered along the cañon, and he knew the sheep were below the hummocks. Her men had tried to head off the band in the crazy, whooping blackness, and they'd gone over the rim with the sheep. He looked along the cañon; he surveyed the cañon's farther rim. *No*, he thought. *Two nights of it. They are dead.*

He turned back. She was at the head of the wagon, waiting for him, her eyes watching him. He stopped at the tail gate and pushed aside the canvas to look at the gear and sacked stuff and household goods into which she had burrowed during the storm. He thought of her crouched there in a night as black as the bottom of a well, the storm screaming around her and her men dead or dying somewhere near at hand. Maybe she'd even heard them calling.

He said: "It's five miles to my cabin. We'd better start before this weather fires up again."

She looked beyond him to the cañon. For a moment there was the softness of hope on her face, but that left and the punished expression appeared once more.

"Want anything from the wagon?"

"Not now."

He led off with the horse to tramp the trail ahead of her. At the top of the ridge he stopped, and she rested herself against the horse and watched the valley. "You're sure?" she said.

"Well, they might have made it to timber and dug in." But he knew that was impossible, and he knew she knew it, too. "I'll come back tomorrow."

She continued to watch the valley, and he knew there was nothing in her mind but those three days, the scream of wind, the blackness, the cold creeping deeper into her flesh and death and aloneness, and the fear that turned to terror and the terror that finally numbed her. It was in her eyes—frozen there. He went on through the trees, his front muscles aching as he pressed against the snow. From time to time he looked back at the girl and, when they came into a meadow and crossed it to the next ridge, he put her sideways on the saddle, knowing she wouldn't tell him of her exhaustion.

A light wind arose to whip the snow; a steel-cast twilight closed them in a narrow world. Beyond the second ridge a valley opened with cattle clustered about fenced-in stacks of hay, and a creek made a ragged streak through the snow. An Indian lodge and a cabin with tacked-on sheds sat near the creek and, as they passed the lodge, two old people—Indian man and woman—came from the lodge to stare at them. Beachey helped the girl from the saddle and stepped into the cabin with her. It was a windowless, dirt-floored bachelor's place with sacked supplies piled about and clothes and gear and bacon sides hanging from the pole rafters, but a flame on the fire hearth lighted and warmed it, and an Indian girl turned from the fire to look at the white girl with surprise wiping her face smooth. Beachey spoke to the Indian girl and left the cabin to catch up a pitchfork in the lean-to; and, riding down the slope through the fast-falling darkness, he moved from stack to stack to throw down hay for the waiting stock.

Black, blind night squeezed the land when he came back. The Indian girl had gone. The other girl had settled against a wall, still wearing the overcoat. She faced the fire, and her hands lay idle before her, palms turned up. She was a big girl, firm body and wide hips, but there was no motion or interest in her, and her eyes—the color of thick, faded, blue velvet cloth—seemed to see nothing in the fire. He bent down and untied the scarf; he unbuttoned her overcoat and went at the business of making supper with the air of a man to whom such a chore was a necessity but a nuisance.

"How many cattle?" she said.

"Three hundred . . . if the wolves didn't drag some down last night."

"We had eight hundred sheep. We were driving over from the Willamette Valley, looking for new range. The storm caught us. My father's name is John Templeton. It's my brother's name, too. I'm Maria." She ate a little food, drank a good deal of coffee, and returned to her place by the fire. "Are they dead?"

He lighted his pipe and clenched it between his teeth. "Yes," he said.

"Can we go back in the morning?"

"First thing." He washed the dishes and stepped into the night to stand at the break of the valley, facing the flurry of heavier snow flung on by a quickening wind. There was no sky, no valley, no silhouette of hills, no shadows—only the uniform dead, sea-bottom blackness, only this and the bitter emptiness of the land moving like a threat against him. From the valley's upper end came the wind-carried sound of wolves and, although he couldn't see his cattle, he knew they were drifting from the sound, for the sound meant the same thing to them that it did to him. He stepped into the cabin and found the Indian girl again at the fire.

She was pure Umatilla strayed a long way from home, for her

tribe lived a hundred miles from this lonely part of Oregon, and she had no parents, only the old people—her grandparents in the lodge. Her face was light brown and smooth and round, and her eyes had a liquid darkness that was the perfect breeding place for mystery. She wore a white woman's dress over doeskin leggings and her hair, parted in the center, moved back to a done-up braid unusual for an Indian girl. She was neat and quiet and pretty, and an accumulative curiosity had brought her back to study the white one. Presently she turned her attention to Beachey, her glance dropped, and she left the place.

He closed the door, found a wagon cover in a corner, and hung it from the rafters to split the room into two separate cells. "You take the bunk," he said. After she had gone to her side of the canvas, he made himself a bed on the floor, piled wood on the fire, and turned in. She made no sound beyond the partition; and, because he had risen at four in the morning and had been on the move for sixteen hours, he soon fell asleep.

✪

She wore an old shirt and a pair of trousers inside the big coat, the shawl wrapped around her head, and she rode his horse while he went ahead with his two big team horses through a steady-falling snow and through the sullen grayness that was an omen of more weather to come. It was a two-hour trip to the snowed-in wagon. He found the harness of the strayed horses inside the wagon, threw it onto his team, hitched them, and left her with them while he went on with the saddle horse to the cañon's rim and skirted it until he found a break that led to the bottom. The hummocks lay about him, one large mound showing where the main body had cascaded down and smaller mounds made by those that had straggled and had fallen separately. He stepped to the large mound and scooped away the snow until he got down to the carcasses; and he straightened and looked about him, thinking of the hopelessness of this search, and then his eyes touched the darkness of what seemed to be a coat sleeve on the far side of the cañon, and he went over there and found both men locked face to face together, one man bearded, one man young. They had survived

**Ernest Haycox 595**

the fall, and they had tried to climb from the trap before exhaustion had caught them. When he pulled the two apart, he knew why—the younger man's leg had been broken.

He stood a moment to consider the weight and awkwardness of those bodies and of the hard climb to the rim's surface, and it occurred to him that it would be easiest to use horse and rope to tow them out of this place, but he thought of the girl and changed his mind and set to work. The girl came over from the wagon when he brought her father's body to the top of the incline and settled on her knees and bent to brush the snow from her father's face. After he got the second man from the cañon, he drove the team and wagon around and lifted the bodies inside. "You drive the wagon," he said, got on his horse, and started ahead.

They had used up the morning. By the time they reached the ridge behind his cabin, middle afternoon was on them, and the grayness came in again. On the out trip he had noticed a windfall shaken down by the blizzard and, when they passed it again, he stopped the wagon and pointed into a pit created by the wrenched-out roots of the tree. It was a better grave than he could dig in the frozen earth. "It will have to be here," he said and waited for her approval.

She stared at the pit, and her glance went around the bleak and dark and cold forest, and the desolation of it stiffened her face and blackened the color of her eyes. She nodded without speaking.

He found axe and shovel in the wagon. He used the shovel to clear the snow from the pit and from the ground near the pit, and he took two blankets from the wagon and laid them at the pit's bottom and placed the bodies on these. She dropped into the pit to bring the blankets around and over the two men, but she thought of something and drew the blanket from her father and took his watch and wallet from his pockets and covered him again. Beachey gave her a hand out of the pit. "My mother's picture is on the back of the watch," she said. "And that's my mother's ring on the chain."

He stood by with the shovel, not anxious to fill in the grave before her eyes. He said: "You want to pray?"

She dropped to the bottom of the pit again and drew back the blankets to give her father a long study and to touch her brother's head. Then she covered them and came out. "No," she said and walked around the wagon beyond the sight of this.

He chipped away at the half-solid rim, breaking the earth into the pit. When he had it half filled, he took the axe and dropped a pair of stunted pines and chopped them into ten-foot lengths and laid these as a solid covering over the grave and went on with his digging until the logs were buried three feet beneath the dirt. He dropped another pine and cut it into sections to blanket the graves; he had to fell two more trees to make the job complete. The girl came from the wagon and stood by him. "I feel better about it," she said. "They're safe," and she looked directly at him and raised her hand to brush the sweat from his cheeks.

"When the snow's gone," he said, "I'll make a fence and put up a mark."

She looked at the scarred earth below her, and her voice was soft. "They're safe," she repeated and turned back to the wagon seat. He threw the tools into the wagon and led the way down the ridge into the cabin clearing. He set the wagon against the cabin's back side, took the gear from the horses, and walked into the valley with his pitchfork. It was dark again when he returned to the cabin. She had cooked supper.

After they had eaten, he hauled in a log for the fire and filled his pipe and squatted straight before the flame, feeling her presence behind him. The food's nourishment was a quick thing in his blood, dissolving the dog-weariness of the day. He said: "What stock you have besides the sheep?"

"Six horses and two milk cows."

"The horses will be all right. They'll turn up. The cows might."

She finished the dishes and sank in the corner beside him, and firelight danced in her eyes and her hands fell idle, palms up before her. Her body loosened to the heat. Her will lost its grip on her thoughts, and she dropped her head and was silent. He put his hands together, softly scrubbing his knuckles; he bit the pipe between his teeth and stared at the fire's heart, eyes half shut. There was nothing but lean meat on him, and his bones showed—knuckles and wrists and hip corners and jaws. Sun and wind had stained his skin as walnut juice would stain it, and he had that air of sharp listening that comes to a man long living alone. Health moved out of him as a current; restlessness played back and forth along his nerve tracks. He said: "The nearest house is Burnt Ranch, sixty miles. The Dalles is a hundred and eighty miles. We'd not make more than ten miles a day, and I'd be gone from the cattle too long. I'm tied to the beasts. It'll be early spring before this snow melts from the passes. That's the soonest I can take you out."

Her head lifted to study him, and in a moment he turned to meet her glance and saw the light ripple of interest cover her face, like water slowly working up through the frozen crusts of a creek. He said gently: "No doubt you'd like to leave sooner, and I wish I could do it for you, but it can't be."

"It will do," she said. She drew back against the wall, doubling her knees, and he watched her long fingers interlace and lie quietly together. Her mouth softened; she rested her head against the wall logs and rolled it and drew her lids down until they shuttered the blueness and the pointed brilliance of the firelight's shining. Behind him he heard the door open and the Indian girl's light feet move over the packed earth of the floor. He sat still and waited for her to come about him and stand motionless in the corner, looking down at him. She drew her arms across her breasts with a gesture that was like a stubborn decision. The white girl opened her eyes and watched.

Beachey said in jargon: "It is not good for you to be here," and made a straight line across the air with one finger. He lowered his glance and waited for her to leave and heard her feet make a soft treading behind him. A tin pan dropped from the table, and he swung to see that she had made this commotion deliberately, for she had her eyes on him. The door slammed behind her.

The white girl said: "You want me to sleep in the wagon?"

"No."

"Then I'll sleep by the fire, and you keep your bunk. It will be handier for me mornings when I cook breakfast."

He knocked out his pipe and rose to draw the canvas down across the room, splitting it into its two halves. He removed his boots and rolled into bed and lay quiet, watching the firelight's leap on the raw roof shakes above him, hearing her leave the cabin and rummage in the wagon, and return; and silence came, and the long day struck him a blow across the forehead, and he fell asleep as he listened to the wolves far down the valley.

An unfamiliar sound wakened him and rolled him from the bunk. She was crying but trying to cover it, and wind struggled in and out of her, rasping the quietness. He pushed the canvas aside and found her lying flat and tense, facing the ceiling with both hands pressed over her mouth. Light flashed on her tears, and through that brightness he saw the blue bottomless depth of her sadness. He got down beside her and drew her head in and felt her arm cross him and touch his shoulder, felt the great wave of misery rise and wash everything before it, and shake her body with its crowding. Her breath thickened, and then she was crying without restraint, her fingers digging into his shirt, the warm tears rolling along his arm. Her eyes were closed, her face stern, her mouth vibrating with actual pain. She closed her fingers on him until she hurt him unknowingly. She rolled her head onto his chest and poured out the formless thing, the everything and the nothing, death and blizzard and being lost and bravery that could no longer be brave, and pieces of strength and chunks of hope, and endurance that had borne too much—it all came out faster and faster, in greater volume and harsher physical punishment; and, when there was nothing left within her, she lay silent, every muscle loose. He waited until he was sure she was asleep and got his arms away from her, covered her with the blankets, and returned to his bunk. He put a hand on the solid wetness of his sleeve and lay for an hour awake.

☒

She had risen before him to light the fire and make breakfast— oatmeal in the pot, the coffee steaming, bacon spitting in the pan. She had changed into her dress and had done her hair. Her eyes were a light blue, the strain gone from them, and she moved about her work with the first show of certainty he'd seen in her. Coldness struck him when he stepped out to the yard—it was like walking straight into a board wall. The snow had stopped, but the first stain of daylight showed him the low-hanging pall in which more weather hung suspended, and all around him silence lay not soft but hard and unpeaceful. She had, he saw, knocked the ice from basin and bucket, and she had gone to the creek to fill the bucket, her tracks breaking the deep carpet of snow.

He came into the room half angered. "I don't expect you to do any rough work." Then he saw the strike of the remark in her, the moment's blurring of her brightness, and he was sorry.

"I've done it all my life. If I'm to be here till spring, I can't be helpless."

"Well," he said, "do as you wish. I'll be gone most of the day. There's a rifle in the corner . . . Spencer. Know how to use it?"

"Yes. But what for?"

"Nothing, I expect." He sat across the table from her and fell to his meal. "Now that you ask, it occurs to me maybe I have got the habit of bracing myself against things that won't happen. That's from livin' alone. There's nothing around here but space. When you look at space a long time, you get the idea that something's ready to break out of the timber . . . and you're not sure it'll be anything good." He finished the meal and stood a short time at the fire with his pipe to soak in heat against the long day he would be abroad. "You look better."

"I slept. Have you got any meat besides bacon?"

"Piece of venison hanging in the shed."

He got into his coat, made sure he had matches and tobacco, took his Winchester, and went out to saddle his horse. Riding back, he found her waiting at the doorway with a package wrapped in cloth, a pint whiskey bottle filled with coffee and a small tin bucket. "Bacon and bread. Light a fire and heat the coffee. You always ride without something to eat?"

"Never bother."

"Well, bother. It's twenty below this morning."

He rode the incline into the valley and turned to see her raise her hand to him from the doorway. He lifted his hat and gave out a quick call that shot through the stillness and set the morning-salted horse into a fit of bucking. He stiffened his back and jammed his legs full length in the saddle. Breakfast fed its lustiness into him; he felt good;

he felt restless. Riding toward the valley's foot, he counted the cattle standing dumbly around the haystacks, and he read the ground for animal prints and meanwhile tried to guess the weather. There was no motion anywhere; a steel-colored ceiling hung low; a dirty-wool twilight lay packed in the trees of the roundabout ridges. The earth had quit breathing but, when it let out that accumulated wind, it would come with a rush. At the foot of the valley he turned and followed the far ridge back toward the pass where the valley began. From this distance he had no view of the cabin.

He found an old cow standing half stalled near the timber and spent half an hour driving it into the flats, and he went on with the weather in his mind, and the cattle in his mind—and the girl in his mind. He remembered the way he had seen her at the wagon after three days of being alone, her eyes like two holes bored deeply in wood; and he remembered this morning, the lighter blue come back, the woman's look come back. He thought, *I'll leave out Salt Meadow today and get home a couple hours earlier. What the hell I been going over there for, anyhow?* He rose into the deeper snows of the pass and looked into the narrow corridor of another valley running east, only the foreground visible; and on this high spot he got the shock of being alone, as sometimes he did. From this place the land ran away in every direction to hidden valleys and pine-black ridges and clay-yellow cañons and sagebrush flats mixed in with lava-flow reefs, mile after mile of it, so empty that sometimes he felt his own queerness for having pushed this deeply into it. Strange things were out yonder that nobody'd set eyes on, deep places in the earth, high places, places so old with timber that it couldn't be ridden through, thousands of years of emptiness pushing against him to make him feel he didn't belong here.

He scraped away a patch of snow at noon, lighted a fire to boil his coffee, and went over a ridge into afternoon's grayness. He crossed a meadow and drifted west; he got down to buck through a breast-high patch of snow caught in the timber and came upon a small clearing in the middle of the trees—an old burn, round as a saucer and not much more than fifty feet across. In the center of the clearing a cow lay down, dying, bleeding at her back quarters, torn at the throat; and a gray shadow scurried across the corner of his vision at the same time he plucked his rifle from its boot and pumped a cartridge into the chamber. In the trees, at the very margin of the trees, he saw the shadow stop and harden into the shape of a wolf—a big one, sitting on its haunches to watch with its sharp shoulders sticking up from the shaggy winter coat, stiff ears erect, lean face set in its solemn intelligence, eyes burning green even in this new light.

He threw the gun to his shoulder for a snapshot but held fire, for the wolf was at once gone; and he lowered the weapon and caught the evasive blue of other bodies moving in the timber around him, half a dozen shadows, a dozen shadows—a pack driven by hunger from the higher hills. He put a bullet into the dying cow and heard the shift and scutter of feet on the crusty snow in the trees. He got down, leading his nervous horse forward with a good grip on the reins, feeling the watchfulness of hidden eyes upon him. They had their meat, and they'd not go away. He got his knife and slashed the cow in a dozen places and, still hanging on to the reins—for he was careful in a situation like this—he got an envelope from his pocket and doused the knife slashes with strychnine. Deeper in the trees he saw a wolf broadside, one foot lifted and head turned, clever mind thinking about him and not much afraid of him. He eased the rifle across his saddle, let it be idle a moment before the wolf's watchful eyes, then he drew it rapidly before him and fired. The wolf leaped high and fell and threshed briefly on the ground before it died, and other gray bodies, stirred by the shot, went flickering in and out of the trees, lightly running and stopping, and waiting, cautious but not afraid. He turned over the small clearing to retrace his way through the trees and found a big gray shape halted before him. He looked about, his thoughts running close and careful and quick, for now he knew he was in narrow quarters. If hunger and bravery hit them at the same moment, they'd rush in to hamstring his horse, and they might make a try at him. The big one still stood before him, head stretched forward, the crease of its mouth lean against the long snout. There was no wind, but its muzzle trembled as though it caught the blood smell, and it made a brief motion forward and froze, the greed-shining eyes round with thought. Beachey tipped the gun's muzzle for a snapshot and caught the beast in the hind quarters as it leaped aside. When he ran forward, he lost sight of the wolf in the darkness of the trees, but he saw the drip of blood and scurried snow lead away into the quickening gloom.

He moved back along the tracks he had previously made through the timber, sharply watching to either side and to the rear. The horse pulled back and surged forward and tossed its head against the reins. Behind he heard a swift snarling among the animals and a quick fading of the quarrel, then he noticed shadows flickering in and out of the trees to his right, ducking near, retreating—but flanking him with a calculated intention almost human in its insolence. He bucked through the drifts and was knocked down by the surge of the anxious horse against him; he sprang to his feet and saw the swift retreat of a gray body that, in that single moment, had rushed forward for attack. He threw a shot into the trees and went on over the ridge and came upon the valley. He walked a hundred feet into the valley before he stopped to rest, knowing the pack wouldn't follow him into the open. His mouth was dry, sweat dampened his hands, and his legs shook; then he got onto the saddle and turned home.

It was late afternoon, the sooty shadows moving in, and as he rode along the valley, he discovered that the stock was feeding on hay pitched out from the stacks. Light trembled through the pall and towed him home. The girl waited at the doorway.

"I heard shots."

"Big pack of wolves. They had a cow down."

"Hungry beasts."

He said: "Who pitched the hay? That Indian won't work."

"I had time on my hands," she said.

Short anger stirred him again, and the shadow of it came to his face.

She said: "I can't be idle . . . I have to keep busy."

He shook his head and put away the horse and brought his gear into the cabin and found his washed clothes hanging on lines across the rafters. The fragrance of fresh-baked bread was sweet in the room; the big kettle bubbled with supper. She had spread a canvas wagon cover over the dirt floor. He washed, sat up to a venison roast, browned onions and potatoes, dumplings, a dried-apple pie, and he rose from the table with a wonderful contentment and stood at the fire with his pipe. He watched her move about the dishes; he watched the quick turns of her body as she worked, the flash of light in her eyes, the broad white hands lightly moving.

"Long time," he said. "Long time alone."

"How long?"

"Came in here summer before last. In a year and a half I have seen four white faces . . . till you came." He found a dish towel to wipe the dishes, but she shook her head, almost sharp with him.

"This is my business. Where was your home?"

"At The Dalles. My people had a farm and twelve children. The country was filled up and no room to spread, but I had to spread. Had to make my try. So I worked till I got a herd together and drifted south across central Oregon, just kept going. What I wanted was grass that wouldn't die and water that wouldn't stop . . . and no neighbors close enough to keep me from spreading. I have got ten lean years waiting for the beef to multiply and cover the range. But when that's over, I'll look down from Bald Peak and see my range run out yonder till she drops off."

She put away the dishes; she swept the floor and moved about the narrow space to take down the dried clothes; she stacked them and said half to herself: "I will iron tomorrow." She was through with her work, and she stood idle at the doorway and looked through it into the darkness with a closed-down expression, so that he knew she was thinking of her men buried on the hill. She came to the fire and spread her hands together before it; she was idle, but even in idleness energy moved out of her and whirled around him until it was as though he stood braced against water running fast. Firelight made gloss-bright tracks across her hair. Her lips lay softly rolled together, motionless but impatient for motion. She looked at him, and the violet blue was a sudden opening of a bottomless place. Then she looked away, and her lips stirred and came to their broad, soft rest.

Beyond the cabin, toward the lodge, feet broke the snow's surface with squealing sounds and the old Indian's voice lifted, and a woman's voice—the girl's voice—answered, and the footsteps ceased.

The white girl said: "How do Indians get married?"

"Man makes a present to the old man. Indian girl moves in. That's all."

She nodded. Presently he knocked out his pipe, lowered the canvas from the rafter, and went to bed.

○

There was no snowfall; into the gloom of first daylight a yellow cast appeared, and the silence around them had a strained and trembling quality to it. From the saddle Beachey listened into it and swung his glance from valley to hills. She handed him his sandwich and flask of coffee and little tin bucket. "Take care, this will get worse." The old man and old woman were at the flap of the lodge; a moment later the old man appeared again and walked toward the ridge, soon disappearing in the trees.

Maria crossed the yard and stepped into the lodge. The girl and the old woman were squatted at a little fire, half talking and half whispering. They quit. They raised their eyes to her, and she saw that they hated her; the old woman's eyes gleamed with it; the girl's eyes were flatly colored by it. She looked about her for some white man's object that would tell her that Beachey had bought the girl for his wife, but she saw nothing that wasn't Indian except a long butcher knife in the old woman's lap. *No,* she thought, *that's not a thing a white man would trade for a woman* and turned back to the cabin. The man didn't value this girl enough to buy her; the girl wasn't in his heart.

She stood a short time in the center of the cabin room, hands folded, slowly turning to look at everything about her, and restlessness disturbed her hands, and a determined expression came over her face, and she set to work. She dragged everything to one end of the cabin and swept it, ceiling and walls and floor; she transferred the things to the clean end and swept the other end. In the lean-to she found some pine poles and chopped them to proper length and made a kind of half attic over part of the room and stored part of Beachey's possessions there; she got a big canvas tarpaulin from her wagon and spread it on the floor and arranged the food stores and the gear and the clothes around the room to please her sense of order. At noon she drank coffee, ironed the clothes, and filled the fireplace; then she stood by it to listen into the strangled stillness of the day, and she thought of her people, and she thought of Beachey, and of the Indian girl, and of herself. Fire's light danced against the indigo shade of her eyes, and she turned to Beachey's bunk and watched it with her firm mouth rounded into its calm; her shoulders rose and settled. It was a gesture, but it was the outward ripple of her mind's decision. She turned out to the lean-to, and brought in a wooden tub, and set forth with the bucket to fetch water from the creek.

The old Indian, returning from the ridge, watched her. He called into the lodge, bringing out both women. The three stood with bent heads, glances slanted on her, thinking about her and angered by her; and the old woman stepped into the lodge and came back with the butcher knife and, issuing a shrill cry, rushed forward.

Half way to the cabin with a filled bucket Maria turned in time to dash the water into the old woman's face. The woman checked herself; the old man growled at her; the Indian girl stood back, intent with her watching. The old woman made a gouging motion toward Maria with the knife, pointed at the cabin, and pointed into the valley, her fingers making a signal of walking away. She waited until she saw that the threat was no good and crouched and crept forward, old knuckles white against the knife's handle. Maria stepped sideways, circling as the squaw came on, and she raised the bucket and swung it toward the squaw. The old woman jumped and ran straight in, slashing the knife downward. Maria brought the bucket across the woman's arm and knocked the knife to the ground; and, as the old one dropped in the snow to recover her weapon, Maria ran into the cabin, seized the rifle, and came out. In the day's strained silence the bolt made a hungry sound when it drove a shell into the gun's breech. Squaw and man and girl were all at once shouting at her with their rage, and the shouting went on until the squaw rose to her feet; then the three stopped their crying and stared.

Maria aimed her finger at the lodge. She made a turning, dropping motion with her hand; she pointed to the ridge. Old man and old woman shouted at her again, but the Indian girl spoke to the old people and went into the lodge. Maria retreated to the cabin's doorway and watched the old man go into the valley to catch up his ponies; there was furious motion inside the lodge, both women talking, the skin walls trembling, and as soon as the old man got back, the women knocked down the lodge in a dozen quick motions, lashed it to its poles, and hitched the poles to one of the ponies. They didn't look at her. The old man and travois moved away toward the ridge, the two women riding behind, and in a little while they were gone, and there was nothing in the yard to mark them save the round circle where the lodge had been. Maria drew back the gun's bolt, lifted out the shell in the chamber, and laid the gun aside. She watched the valley a moment, and took her bath, and combed her hair. Twilight came in, and somewhere not far off there was the rumor of great motion in the sky, and the motion reached forward, and the trees began to tremble, and first wind sighed on the cabin. She had supper half done when Beachey called through the quickening fall of snow. From the doorway she saw him break through the dense gray wall of weather, bent forward on the horse, eyes black as coal against the beaten redness of his face. He noticed the lodge's absence, and his glance went along the churned tracks in the snow.

"They gone?"

"Yes."

"Trouble?"

"I had the gun."

"I'll feed the stock," he said and faded into the blind night.

Wind shook the cabin, and its beginning cry was at the eaves. She put on the supper when she heard him drive the horse back to the lean-to. She waited at the fire, listening to the door of the cabin open and close. She waited for him to speak of the change in the room. "Looks good," he said and sat down to his supper, ate it, and dropped before the fireplace with his pipe. "Floor wouldn't hurt this place," he observed.

"Be cleaner," she said and went at the dishes.

"I'll make it soon as the storm lifts."

She did her chores and came to the fire, standing beside him and above him. Her hands lay quietly together. Wind struck its steady hammer blows on the cabin; the night was a void—and the void was a cold and bitter and unbearable thing; and there was no world save this lone bright cell. He sat up and raised his glance.

"There's no way of getting out of here until spring. You understand? No way until the passes clear."

She kept her eyes on the fire. "People have to live," she said.

He bent to catch some thin torn echo wavering in the flood of other sounds rushing by. She listened with him, thinking she heard the sound of wolves. She looked down upon the top of his head, and her mouth stirred and made a new line. He saw that; he had been watching for it; and his eyes drove his thought into her. Her hands began to stir with their restlessness, and she sank slowly to her knees, and her body began to turn inward as he rose to meet her.

# The Business of Dying

## Richard S. Wheeler

◙

*Born in Milwaukee, Wisconsin, Richard S. Wheeler emerged as an author of the Western story at the age of forty-three with* Bushwhack *(Doubleday, 1978), followed by* Beneath the Blue Mountain *(Doubleday, 1979). Even this early his work was characterized by off-trail storylines, avoidance of any appeal to myth or legendry, and a rejection of upbeat resolutions. Following a hiatus of a few years in which he published nothing, Wheeler brought out what remains his masterpiece,* Winter Grass *(Walker, 1983). It was finalist that year for the Golden Spur Award from the Western Writers of America. It was, however, his later novel,* Fool's Coach *(Evans, 1989), that earned him his first Spur Award. His more recent work,* Cashbox *(Forge, 1994) and in particular* Goldfield *(Forge, 1995), has been more ambitious, taking a wider spectrum of history into account in narrating the complex lives of his characters set against distinctive historical backgrounds. The period between 1989 and 1993 was an extraordinarily productive one for Wheeler, during which he published no less than eighteen novels and averaged 250,000 words a year. He also deserves recognition for his special talent as an editor—for eight years he worked for Walker and Company and brought a number of notable writers to the fore by recommending their first novels for publication. After much prodding from the editors, he finally agreed to provide this collection with what is his first published short story.*

$H$omer Winslow knew that they were going to plant him at the age of twenty-four. He lay in his tent thinking about that, mournful, desolated by the unfairness of it. But he couldn't escape it, short of a miracle. The weakness oppressed him. They called it the stomach complaint, and a lot of the men grubbing gold out of the gulches of the Sierras had succumbed to it. No one had a cure for him nor were there doctors or hospitals in California, though he'd heard that plenty of physicians had come West with the rest of the forty-niners. The doctors would call it dysentery, but that was too fancy a name for the polyglot gold grubbers clawing nuggets and dust out of all the bars and branches of the American River. All Homer knew was that the complaint was a mortifying, demeaning, cruel, and undignified way to shuck his mortal coil. Every time he crawled for the bushes, a breathtaking hurt and weakness and dizziness overwhelmed him.

He had tried every cure his rough colleagues had recommended. Even though vegetables were nigh impossible to get, he had bought some, following the advice of those sages who said he'd do better once he varied the salt pork and beans. Others had condemned coffee or tea, while others insisted that he take not the slightest drop of ardent spirits. Still others insisted that he eat fish only and never a slice of red meat. One fellow, a Wisconsin farmer before he came West in the rush, told Homer to try salt. What was needed, he explained, was something with an affinity to water, that would lock water in Winslow's desperately dehydrated and weakened body.

Nothing worked. He would have liked to go on down to the great tent city of Sacramento for help, thinking maybe the rough conditions of the mountains or the thinner air was at fault. He even dreamed of continuing to that other tent city, San Francisco, where surely he could find a competent surgeon, but he was too far gone. He would never survive the trip, strapped to the top of some freight wagon or handed onto the deck of one of the great steamers plying the river trade.

Each day his strength ebbed, and he knew the end would come soon. He had lost hope. His mind was clear, even though his body suffered waves of cold and nausea that gripped him and twisted his guts. The men of Mad Mule Gulch had actually been tender, and he could ask nothing more. Homer had a good gravel claim, a foot to bedrock, ten feet wide and stretching from bank to bank, according to the miners' law for that locale. He had left his tools there, the inviolable mark of a claim, and no one had jumped it. Even better, should any stranger try to jump it, every gold-grubbing man in the gulch would deal swiftly with the interloper.

Even kinder was Homer's tent mate, Phineas Parsons. They had met here, formed a partnership as was the custom, and helped each other. Phineas never abandoned Homer. He prepared the daily broth that Homer managed to swallow and even washed Homer's soiled clothing. But Phineas's kindest act was to devote an hour a day to Homer's fine claim, usually panning out an ounce of gold for Homer, which bought necessaries. Before the complaint took him, Homer had grubbed almost nine hundred dollars of flaky gold with an occasional nugget as a bonus. This he kept in a lidded butter crock beside his head. No one would steal it. No sensible miner ever stole. It was live and let live on the western slope of the Sierras and swift, merciless justice for those who violated that code. But things were changing. Whole shiploads of Australians, mostly convicts shipped out from England, were arriving in the camps, bent on looting and pillaging. And Homer had heard there were even pigtailed Chinamen and Chileans flooding in, galvanized by the awesome news from Sutter's Mill, though he had never seen any of them.

Dusk came, and Homer sensed the cessation of toil around Mad Mule Bar. Twilight fell earlier and earlier these autumnal days, and soon winter would chase the miners out of the mountains. Most would flee to San Francisco or Sacramento and try the fandango with the *señoritas* or drink some of the whiskey shipped in plentiful amounts around the Horn. But not Homer. He would not be leaving the mountains this time.

He heard Phineas rustling about outside the tent, smelled smoke, and knew his partner was starting the cook fire. Presently Phineas poked his bearded face into the darkened interior. "You all right, Homer?" he asked.

"No."

"Getting worse?"

"I'm done for."

"You figuring on heading for the other shore?"

"Day or two."

"Wish I could help. Don't know how in tarnation to help."

"There's no way."

Phineas crawled in and settled beside Homer. Skinny, bleached, sunburned, scraggle-bearded, and worn down from the brutal mucking and digging, Phineas had been a cooper in Ohio once. The perfection that he once brought to his trade, making water-tight, flawless kegs, he brought to his mining. No man on the bar got as much color out of a panful of gravel. That was one of many reasons Homer considered himself lucky in his choice of a partner.

"It ain't fair," Phineas said. "Just ain't the way things are supposed to be."

Homer appreciated the sympathy but didn't feel like talking.

"Partner, if you're thinking the time's come, you've got to make some decisions," Phineas said then.

"Leave me be now, Phin."

"I won't. This is the time. It's come up now, and you've got to wrestle with it. You're clear-headed, and you can give me some answers." Resignedly Homer listened. He didn't want to deal with death. "You've got a jar full of gold there. What do you want done with it?"

"I don't know."

"Well, should we send it to your family? We can get it cashed out in San Francisco and send a draft."

Homer had two married sisters and a mother scattered through western Indiana. They could all use the money, though none was hurting, and he didn't want them to know he was dying. They'd all opposed him. He'd come anyway, getting up a small outfit consisting of a mule and packsaddle, off his mother's farm. It had turned out to be the best way to come. He had walked to California, leading the mule, arriving with the vanguard, well ahead of most of the overland forty-niners, with the mule in good shape. He had sold the valuable beast for a tent and gear and grub. "I'll think about it," he said, wishing he didn't have to.

"No, I'm wanting an answer now."

That irritated Homer and he slid into a melancholia that closed out the world. What earthly difference did anything make?

Phineas stared a while, his lips forming and rejecting words. "You're not acting like the old Homer Winslow I partnered up with," he said softly. "It's important how a man checks out. You can quit, or you can go in style. You haven't much choice, I'll confess that. But a fellow can put up a good show of it."

Homer wished the man would back out of the tent and fix his supper, but Phin had some sort of itch and was going to babble on. "I'm thirsty," Homer said.

Phin slipped away and returned with a tin cup full of icy water. He helped Homer to sip, not that it did any good. Homer was always thirsty but not a drop stayed in him. "Well, Homer, are you glad you came . . . to the gold fields, I mean?" Phin asked.

"Yes," he said.

It had been the great adventure of his young life. He hadn't considered himself reckless, though others thought that anyone crazy enough to cross a continent on foot was reckless. He'd defied his family—hurt his ma, who had had to hire a man to plow her fields. And he was going to die here, but he didn't regret coming. He'd seen things he hardly knew existed. He'd seen wild Indians, Sioux and Pawnees. He'd seen vast herds of black buffalo. He'd seen mountains with a load of snow on top, right in summer. He'd seen mountain men wearing fringed leather, carrying big percussion-lock rifles with octagonal barrels and talking a peculiar tongue. He'd been scared by a grizzly with two cubs, had a prairie rattler crawl right over his bedroll, chased off a red varmint trying to steal his good mule, and almost got clubbed doing it. He reckoned he'd stuffed most of a regular lifetime into the past ten months, and that made dying a little easier. And he'd done it all on his own, against the entreaties of his ma and Sara and Josephine, too, and that made him right proud, as if he'd cut loose and come up a man.

But, if it made dying easier, it didn't make it any better. He'd sparked Melissa a few times back on the farm. Melissa lived two farms over and across the creek, which he negotiated by walking over a fallen tree. She was Abe Stowell's youngest, but it hadn't come to anything, and now he was dying without ever knowing a woman, or having a wife, or having a child, and that knocked his spirits into the dirt whenever he thought of it. Nothing about dying was more of a cheat than that.

"Yes, I'm glad I came," he said. "No regrets about coming here. I did a lot of living."

"It took something to come, I'll say that," Phineas agreed. "Lots of people didn't. Some didn't even believe the news, even after the government in Washington announced it. Some came. I came. A mess are sailing around the Horn or crawling across Panama right now.

They'll be here. Seems to me, a fellow who's done all that, grubbed out well over two thousand and still has nine hundred in good dust after paying the freight, well, it seems to me a fellow like that should do some mighty good dying."

It irked Homer. "I'm the one not going to see anything anymore, not you, so button your lips."

Phin retreated but wouldn't let go of it. "I'm sorry, Homer. You have any thoughts about the hereafter? You want us to fetch a preacher? There's a dozen on the bars, to hear tell of it. We'll ask around."

"Oh, I don't know. I never did figure it all out, Phin. I've tried to live up to what was expected of me and be a decent fellow. I guess it's like trust. I'll just trust that, if there's something good waiting for my soul, it'll be there for me."

"You want me to fetch a preacher to say some words when the time comes?"

Phin wasn't going to let go of it, Homer could see that. Well, maybe there was some good in it. Even this talk had wearied him so much, he felt pure cold death crawling up his limbs. "Don't look special for one, but if one's handy, it's all right. It's mostly for you, not for me. What a preacher does is give heart to the living, and that's fine with me. I won't be hearing it."

"All right," said Phin. "Now, tell me who to write in Indiana. You've got folks there. I'll send word. I promise I will, with the next man leaving the bar for Sacramento."

Something stirred in Homer. Memories flooded back on him. "Phin, when I croak, don't you say one word. Don't you write them. Just bury me proper."

"Homer, they're your kin."

"You listen to me. This is what I want, and a dying man ought to get what he wants!"

Phin was plainly puzzled, but Homer was remembering some bad moments back there in Greene County, moments that had irked him then and enraged him now. "Listen," he said urgently, "when I let 'em know back there that I was going to head West and make my fortune, I never heard the like. It wasn't just Ma and my sisters, though they were bad enough. Everyone in the county! Like Abe Stowell. He had eighty acres and some dairy cows, and I was sweet on his girl. I told old Abe what I was fixing to do, and he got sort of stern and thundercloudy, and I could feel the wind coming up and the rain start landing on me. He said, 'Don't go.' It would all come to nothing. There was too much risk. I was chasing moonbeams. A fellow running across a continent full of wild Injuns wasn't the type to make a good husband.

"And that was just the start. The grocer, he told me it was folly. Said I'd come to nothing and take sick and go broke. Said it wouldn't profit me. And Missus Hope, she was the minister's wife. She said it was all wrong. I'd fall into evil and all that. The truth of it, Phin, was that I stood alone, and left alone. There wasn't a man or woman or girl or fellow that ever gave me a blessing or said that I was doing something pretty fine, pretty special, pretty daring, pretty smart, pretty courageous! They all saw what was wrong with it and not a one saw what was right. By the time I'd heard the whole lot, I felt like telling them they didn't know what this big new land was for. It's for making dreams come true. It's for risking and trying and making it. But they'd gotten all narrowed down, trying to make a good life out of avoiding trouble or challenge. So I just took off. I said to myself, they don't know how to live! You following me?"

"You're making mighty good sense. Half the men on this bar had to wrestle with skeptics and naysayers. Most won't get rich here, but not a one regrets coming and trying, and even if they take only memories out of here, they'll make better lives out of what they've been given just because they came, Homer."

Homer liked that. His partner had it right. "Phin, don't let all those folks back there know. Don't let 'em think they were right. After I go, you just tell people I was a big success, and no one's seen me for a while."

"I'll do that, Homer. You're a success. You made a good claim, took thousands out, and everyone admired you."

"That's right, and you tell every fellow on Mad Mule Bar that's how I want it. My folks, they'll find out I croaked eventually, even if we have lost contact, but don't you tell 'em. If my ghost has to hear all those I-told-you-sos, I'll come and haunt you!" Homer laughed. He hadn't laughed in weeks. It hurt his body.

Phineas laughed, too, with a strange tenderness. "It's a promise. And I'll make every man here swear to it. Now, Homer, what about that dust?"

Something almost feverish seemed to grip Homer. "I want a little celebration, a little hurrah. There's over five pounds of dust. It'll buy me a big hurrah. I want a good box, and I don't care about the cost. There's mahogany and teak coming into the Bay and everything else. Find a cabinetmaker and make me a good box. I want a fancy one, and I want a parade somewhere. Maybe after winter closes in. I want all my friends on this bar to make a parade right through Sacramento City, carrying that mighty fine box, and I want you to tell 'em I grubbed a lot of gold, and I wanted to check out in style, and there I am. After that, you pick out a good saloon and set up drinks with that dust until it's gone. When they ask who I am, you tell 'em I came West and I found gold and I did what I set out to do, and no one can argue it."

"Ah, Homer, that's a good plan," said Phin softly. "Count on me. I won't let you down."

Excitement coursed through Homer. All this seemed impossibly important. "Now, Phin, there's something else. You remember that week we took off because it was so hot a man couldn't pan gold except for a couple hours after dawn? We took off. We put our tools on the claims to hold them a bit, and we got a ride to Stockton with that freight outfit. And we went to that fandango."

"I remember, Homer."

"Phin, I'd hardly set eyes on a woman for months, and there were those *señoritas*, nice girls, daughters of all those *hacendados* around there, and they let us in and let us do some fandangoing. Well, Phin, I danced with the prettiest lady I've ever laid eyes on, golden and laughing with shining eyes and her feet patting around so fast I couldn't keep up. Do you remember her?"

"Sort of."

"Well, her name was Margarita." Homer hesitated, collecting his thoughts. "This'll be awful hard on you, Phin, and say no, if you don't want to. I'd like a lock of her hair going into the box with me. Maybe she won't remember me. Maybe you'll need another lock. Just some shiny black hair, but don't tell my ghost about the switch."

"What was her surname, Homer?"

"Blamed if I know. Just Margarita."

"I'll try, Homer."

Homer sighed. "It's important. Dying's hard when you haven't sampled all of life. I've never gotten hitched up, and I never had me a child, and I never woke up in the morning to find some sweet Margarita beside me, sleepy, trusting, smiling, awaiting a hug and a smile from me. On that account I don't like this dying at all, but, Phineas, just put a lock of a lady's hair in with me. Wherever I'm going, I'll take it up there and tell the boss I got shortchanged a little, and I want to take this in there." Phin turned aside and hid his face in deep shadow. The light out there was fading fast. "You go fix your supper, Phin," Homer said. "Now you've got the whole plan."

"I have the whole plan, Homer," Phin said, sliding out.

"I don't want anything," Homer said.

"But you've got to eat. And the broth helps a little."

"Not anymore," Homer said. He lay back, sensing that life was fleeing him, and he wouldn't see the dawn. But it was all right. Thanks to Phineas he had done his accounting and found he'd made a profit. He might have hung on for a day or two or three, but he didn't need to anymore. "It's been mighty fine," he said, feeling the night come.

# Moving On

## Jane Candia Coleman

☒

*Born and raised near Pittsburgh, Pennsylvania, Jane Candia Coleman majored in creative writing at the University of Pittsburgh, but stopped writing after graduation in 1960 because she knew she "hadn't lived enough, thought enough, to write anything of interest." Her life changed dramatically when she abandoned the East for the West in 1986, and her creativity came truly into its own.* The Voices of Doves *(Ocotillo Press, 1988) was written soon after she moved to Tucson. It was followed by a book of poetry,* No Roof But Sky *(High Plains Press, 1990), and by a truly remarkable short story collection that amply repays reading and rereading,* Stories from Mesa Country *(Ohio University Press, 1991). Her short story "Lou" in* Louis L'Amour Western Magazine *(March 1994) won the Golden Spur Award from the Western Writers of America, and she has also won three Western Heritage Awards from the National Cowboy Hall of Fame.* Doc Holliday's Woman *(Warner Books, 1995) is her first novel and one of vivid and extraordinary power. Her new story collection is* Moving On: Stories of the West *(Five Star Westerns, 1997). It can be said that a story by Jane Candia Coleman embodies the essence of what is finest in the Western story—intimations of hope, vulnerability, and courage—while she plummets to the depths of her characters, conjuring moods and imagery with the consummate artistry of an accomplished poet. "Moving On" is published here for the first time.*

**N**ell Pomerene stopped on the edge of the stubble field and looked down at the house in the valley. It seemed lonesome in the middle of the bare yard where a few chickens scratched the hard dirt, and the sunflowers she'd planted in an effort to pretty the place drooped for lack of water. Their heads hung sadly, like hopeless faces, like the faces of her parents, who had come here filled with dreams and seen them dashed, one by one, by the winds, the drought, the blizzards, the grasshoppers that cleaned off crops like a mowing machine and left bare ground behind them.

She stood on the sandy track for a minute, listening to the silence. Where *was* everybody? Where was her mother? It was wash day, but the big iron washtub stood empty over the ashes of last week's fire, and the clothes—work shirts, diapers, shirtwaists that should have been drying in the breeze—weren't there. Where were her baby brothers, Luke and John, toddlers but active, so that the yard always resounded with the sound of little feet and infant squabbling? Where were the mules, Roy and Sally, their long ears cocked, their big mule heads hanging over the wire fence, waiting for supper?

She stood still and watched and listened, and when nothing familiar reached her but the sound of the wind in her ears, she began to run toward the house, her feet kicking up small spurts of dust.

"Mama!" she called. "Mama!"

No answer came. She stopped and stared at the blank face of the house, and then she was running again, terror at her heels.

"Mama! Mama!"

And the rustle of the prairie was around her—wind, crickets in the weeds, in the bending red grass. In the house there was nothing. The pots and pans were gone, the bedding, the quilts, the trunks where clothes were kept. In the house was only the sweep of wind through the sagging door and the echoes of voices she could almost, but not quite, hear. In the house was a note scrawled in her mama's hand on a torn piece of brown paper.

*We moved on.*

That was all. That and the empty feeling in her stomach, the mockery of the silence that wasn't silence at all but a thousand small sounds that added to her terror. She was alone. She, Nell Pomerene, was all that was left, all that there was to prove that once a family had lived here, had laughed, and loved, and worked the fields, hoping for prosperity. She didn't cry. Couldn't. Tears never solved anything, and besides, only babies cried—her two brothers, their faces red and crinkled, roaring like healthy young animals. Luke and John, gone, with her parents, leaving her, Nell, fourteen years old, on her own.

She sat down on the edge of her bed and thought her way clear to her bones, and what she found was herself—alone, abandoned, but with a gut feeling that she wasn't meant to die for a long while. What lay ahead was struggle, and strife, and years. She knew that. Took it on her small shoulders, tried it, and found herself able.

After a long time she got up and went to the kitchen, where she found an overlooked pot with dented sides, two shriveled potatoes, and a small onion in the back of the bin. Food first. Then sleep if it came. Trouble would keep until morning.

✪

The sun rolled like a wheel on the edge of the plain, and the house creaked around her the way it always did except that, empty now, the sound was threatening. She lay still, wondering if she had dreamed it all, thinking that any minute now her mother would come in saying: "You going to sleep your life away?"

But no one came, and after a while she got up and went outside and drew some water from the well. She looked at her reflection in the bucket and saw blue eyes, brown hair in long braids—an ordinary face, nothing to be ashamed of or to gloat over, either.

"Why me?" she asked the girl in the mirror. "Why'd they go off and leave *me*?"

Of course, there was no answer. She hadn't expected one, simply had wanted the companionship of a voice, had felt the need to ask the question though she knew she'd never know the truth of it. She thought of going to school, then realized she never had to go again if she didn't want to. She could do as she pleased, now and forever. She, Nell, was boss, but somehow the idea was frightening, and she shied away from it like a new colt that sees the open field for the first time and sticks beside its mother. But she had no mother.

"We moved on." She said the words aloud, finding in their brevity a coldness that implied she didn't count, was as easily erased as a figure drawn in the dust, as quickly forgotten as a leaf blown from a tree. What to do? She sat on the splintered log that served as a step, chin in her hands, and thought, looking out over the rise and fall of the prairie. There were families who needed a hired girl and who would take her in. And they'd likely work her to death because she had no one to speak for her. She supposed she could go to the Reverend Mason. He'd see she was treated right, would probably ship her off to the orphanage, an uncertain fate at best. She wasn't clever with her hands, except around animals, so work as a dressmaker was out, too. So many choices, yet so few. She shook her head. Her hair had come loose from its braid and blew across her face gently as cobwebs. Without thinking, she rebraided it, splashed water on herself, and shivered because the October air was cold. Soon it would be winter. Too soon. And she with no place to go, alone, hungry for a family as well as for food.

She heard the wagon before it crested the hill and came slowly down the track, and she squinted against the morning light, hope like a sweetness in her mouth. Maybe they'd come back! Missed her! She stood up and trotted across the yard, stopped and leaned on the fence, a woman waiting for life to happen.

☼

Levi Solomon had been on the road since he was fourteen. At first he had gone on foot, carrying his peddler's pack until it seemed he'd been born with it, like a hunchback, felt naked without its bulk. And then one day he'd gotten lucky. In the far corner of Kansas, where the plain stood drought-seared and wind blasted, a homesteader was packing up, turning his back on dream turned nightmare.

"Take the damned mule!" he shouted at Levi. "Take the damned wagon! There's a curse on all of it!"

He stood by the grave of his wife and child, his beard blowing around his face, his eyes wild so that he looked like a prophet shouting doom except to Levi, who didn't wait to be told twice. He hitched up the mule and drove away toward the West, the poor farmer's keening growing fainter and fainter until at last it was no more than the wail of a coyote, the scream of a hunting hawk. After that he prospered, bought another mule, and replaced the wagon with one designed as a home as well as a place to store his goods.

The whole West was his for the taking: the sand hills, the prairie, the mountain passes and meadows of the Rockies, and he went where he chose with his pots and pans, his needles and thread and bolts of cloth, his seeds and saplings, tablets, tools, and patent medicines, and the stories that flowed out of his mouth like honey. He was welcome at all the farms, the ranches. He brought news, gossip, messages, a touch of the theatrical for wives starved for the sound of a voice, for husbands bored with the sameness of it all.

The night before he had camped out and lay watching the stars and sniffing the frosty air like an old hound that feels the approach of winter. He was feeling old for the first time in twenty years of traveling, and he allowed himself the odd pleasure of imagining a home in a town, a store that wasn't ambulatory, a fire in his own hearth during long winter nights. "Ach, Levi," he had said out loud because he often talked to himself or to his mules that listened stolidly. "And what would you do in a house without the land for company?" He had shaken his head. The road was what he knew, the road and the land beckoning, he and his mules and wagon bobbing along like a small ship on waves of grass in a prairie sea.

He had climbed into the back of the wagon and slept, and in the morning had had a cold breakfast of bread and cheese. Then he had hitched his team and driven on until he had reached the stubble field and saw the sad house, the figure that leaned on the fence.

"No money there," he said, assessing the barren yard, the sagging roof. But the woman—at least he thought it was a woman—seemed to beckon him, standing alone in the center of it all. He clucked to his team and headed down the hill. "Good morning."

He tipped his old straw hat as he spoke, realizing that the person he had thought was a woman was a young girl and a frightened one, if he was any judge. In his years on the road he'd seen many such, women and girls, some with bloodied faces, some whose men had gone away, burying their dead. But none had aroused the compassion that this girl did, with her blue eyes the color of sky and her shoulders squared as if she would take on the world in spite of her fear.

"Hello." Her voice was low, but there was music in it, back in her throat like a songbird.

"Are you the lady of the house?" He spoke jokingly, hoping to put her at ease.

She shook her head. "No," she said. "No."

"Well, then, your mama. Is she home? I have needles and good thread. And some fine wool for winter." He stepped down and came to stand beside her.

"She isn't here." He had to tilt his head to catch her whisper. "They left. Moved on."

*Mein Gott!* he thought. *To leave a child, a girl-child, out here alone. What kind of people were these?* "This is true?"

She nodded. "It's just me now." Her voice broke, and there was a glint of tears in her blue eyes, but she lifted her chin proudly.

"You have friends? Relatives?"

"Nobody who'd want me."

It got worse and worse. If he had sense, he'd get back in the wagon and leave, but he knew in his heart that he'd remember how she looked, standing in the yard with the empty house behind her, knew that she would haunt him no matter how far away he went. He said: "This is very bad."

She scuffed the toe of her worn boot in the sand then looked at him, at his mules, at the wagon with its water barrel, pots and herbs and harness bells strung on the outside like a Christmas tree. "Take me with you," she said.

"I can't. It isn't possible. People would talk. Say bad things."

"What people?"

She was being deliberately hard-headed. What people, indeed! "My customers." He raised his voice. "Good women. What will they say when Levi Solomon comes to trade with a little *shiksa* sitting in his wagon? What?"

"Why should they say anything?" she wanted to know. "What you do isn't their business."

"My business is everybody's business. I have to be careful. People trust me. But they won't if they think they have to look out for their daughters in case I kidnap little girls."

Her head shot up. "I'm fourteen."

"And that makes you a grown-up?"

"My mother was married at fifteen."

" 'Marry in haste, repent at leisure,' " he quoted. "Look what happened. She left you." Then, seeing the hurt in her eyes, he wanted to cut off his tongue.

Strangely she came to her mother's defense. "She probably had reasons!"

He put a hand on her shoulder. "Listen to me," he said. "There is no good reason to leave a child, a daughter, out here alone. It was a bad thing. Wrong. But I won't make it worse. Get your clothes. You can come with me. At least," he added, "until we get to a town. Someplace where maybe you can find work. Maybe even find your mama, who can tell?"

The look she gave startled him. He had thought her a plain little thing, but her eyes suddenly blazed with blue fire, and she smiled, it seemed with her whole body. "You won't be sorry," she said, breathless. "I can cook, and drive a team. And I'm good with animals. They like me. And you can say I'm your daughter. We'll be a family. I don't want to find mine. I don't want to see them again. Not ever!"

He thought how he would give anything to see his mother once more, but then she had never abandoned him, not until her death. Bitterness was a disease. It ate at a person from inside, and this child with her stubborn chin and fiery eyes was too young for such knowledge. "What's your name?" he asked her.

"Nell," she said. "Nell Pomerene. Not that I'm proud of it."

"So, then, Nell," he said. "Get your things. Me, I'll catch some of these chickens to take with us. It would be a shame to leave them for the coyotes."

She stopped on her way back to the house. "Do you have anything to eat?"

"I have enough," he said. "And tonight we'll have chicken. Hurry now. We have places to go."

They headed southwest. Levi wanted to put distance between them and the coming winter, but she was too relieved to care where they were going—and a little doubtful, too. Maybe it was a foolish thing, what she'd done. Maybe she should have stayed at the house, waiting and hoping instead of going off with a stranger, this black-bearded man sitting beside her on the wagon seat. "You think I did right?" she asked finally. "Coming with you?"

He was annoyed. She could tell by the way his mouth tightened. "What would you have done?" he asked. "Tell me. With winter coming, no food, nobody? Anyway, it's too late now. I don't go backwards."

"Why not?"

"A waste of time." He flipped the reins. "Rocinante! Sancho!" he called to the mules. "Walk faster! Don't be lazy."

"What did you call them?"

He told her.

"Those sure are funny names," she said.

His annoyance vanished, and he smiled. "Not so funny. They are out of a book. About a man and his servant who wandered around Spain and had adventures."

"A book?" she said. "You have a book?"

His smile broadened. "Ach, child, I have many. A life without knowledge is no life at all, and knowledge is written in books."

"Can I see them? I'll be careful. Honest. All I ever had was the reader in school, and it wasn't mine."

"Not only can you see them, you may read them," he said. "And we'll talk about them afterwards, if you want." Which, he reflected, would be quite different from talking to himself. Life on the road was often a lonely thing, knowledge or no.

She gave a little bounce on the seat and turned toward him, her eyes once again filled with that strange fire. "I want to start now, please," she said, and her voice, polite but determined, told him she intended to do just that.

He pulled up and got down. She didn't wait for him but hopped out and followed him to the back of the wagon. Slowly he opened the trunk, where he kept the things that were precious to him—a tintype of his parents, the certificate of his birth in a city he had forgotten, and the books that had been his friends since his youth.

She peered inside, then carefully lifted out the books, one by one, caressing them as if they were jewels. "So many!" she whispered.

"There are libraries with thousands of books," he said. "More than you can count." She set her chin. "Then I better get started."

Her excitement was infectious. Back on the seat he found himself singing, and the mules whose names had started it all laid back one long ear each to listen.

☉

He felt the storm long before it was visible, felt the darting tongue of wind against his cheek and smelled the dampness of snow. It was a day of such brilliance, of a flood of sunlight from a sky so empty of clouds that a newcomer to the prairie would have laughed at the notion of an approaching blizzard, made fun of his sudden attention. He drove down into a small dell that was protected by the coming together of two hills. Wild plum trees, bare of leaves but with thickly laced branches, formed a screen there, and a pond reflected them as they moved to the music of the wind. Levi was no stranger to weather. He knew.

"What's happening?" Nell stuck her head out of the wagon. "Why are we stopped?"

In answer Levi gestured to the north, where a cloud, purple and black, had appeared suddenly on the horizon. "We'll stop here," he said. "There's good shelter. Maybe we have a couple hours before it hits."

He unhitched the mules, watered them, and fed them corn before picketing them on the lee side of the wagon. Nell, with the instinct of one born on the prairie, made a fire. "Dinner," she said. "Probably we won't have another hot meal for a while."

He gulped his coffee and eyed the storm that was closing in on them now, the edges of the clouds curling and misshapen. "I'll need to sleep in the wagon tonight," he said carefully, wondering how to bring up the subject.

"Where else? Only a fool'd sleep under it in this weather."

"Thank you," he said.

"What for?"

"For trusting me. I didn't want you to think . . ." Embarrassed, his voice trailed off.

She didn't understand his hesitation. People froze to death in blizzards, or got lost in the blowing whiteness only a few feet from their doorsteps. Storms such as this one was going to be were no time for fancy manners. "Levi," she said, "it's *cold,* that's what I think. And we'd better clean up these dishes and get inside before it gets colder."

They made their beds at opposite ends of the wagon with the lantern flickering in between. She put on mittens and a knitted cap and pulled a shawl close around her shoulders, all the while listening to the roar of the wind driving the first particles of snow against the board and canvas sides of the wagon. If she were home now, she'd be doing the same thing, trying to stay warm, the snow coming through cracks in the walls and no voice but her own to drown out her fear.

" 'Blow, blow thou winter wind. Thou art not so unkind as man's ingratitude,' " she quoted across the space that separated them.

"You've found the Shakespeare," he said, his eyes gleaming.

"Yes. And I just now thought I'd never really thanked you. That maybe I seemed ungrateful. But I'm not. If it wasn't for you, I'd be back there alone and likely freezing to death."

"That can happen here," he reminded her.

"Yes, but at least there's two of us. That makes a difference."

It did, indeed. Two people could keep the world at bay, could bring a faint warmth to the inside of the fragile little shell that was all that stood between them and death. Two people could laugh and drown out the wolf howl of a storm.

"It's a good thing I came along that day," he said gruffly. "Your being here is a good thing."

She fought down a happiness so intense it nearly choked her. "I think so, too," was all she said. She lay down in her nest of blankets and curled in upon herself to keep the warmth of it all. And she never noticed when he placed another blanket over her and blew out the lamp.

She awoke to gray light and the soundlessness of snow falling on snow. "Levi!" she called.

No answer came. To her it seemed that she had always been calling for someone who wasn't there, who would never be there again. She sat up and threw off the blankets.

"Levi!" she called again and heard the death of her own voice in the deepness of snow.

"Out here."

She stumbled down the narrow aisle toward the rear of the wagon. Outside was a white curtain, blank and thick as cotton, but she thought if she put out her hand, she would touch the hardness of stone. "Where?"

"Feeding the mules. Don't come out. It's drifted."

Levi's head appeared in the opening, then the rest of him, his breath making clouds in the air. Icicles hung from his beard, and his eyebrows were white.

Unexpectedly, she laughed. "You look like Father Christmas!"

He laughed with her. "But I have no gifts."

"Yourself," she answered. "You've brought yourself."

"Such as I am." He wiped his beard and looked down at his boots and trousers that were coated with ice.

She followed his glance. "Take them off," she ordered. "Get dry. If you don't, you'll get frostbite. You'll get sick." She tugged at his arm and forced him to sit. "Do what I tell you."

It was pleasant to be fussed over, to have her chafe his frozen hands and feet, to be handed dry socks, and all the while her voice swooping like a flock of sparrows. Do this! Do that! Take care of yourself! When will it stop? Will we ever be warm and on our way again? At that thought her tears came, too many to be turned to ice, and he held her, patted her, said words of consolation and hope.

"Yes, yes. Soon the sun will shine, and we'll be moving. Don't worry. Levi Solomon has weathered many storms."

But she felt their isolation, knew her own. Always, in the past, there had been four walls and a roof, parents, her little brothers beside her in the bed giving and taking warmth. There had been the old stove casting its inadequate heat through the curtain that separated the rooms. There had been many bodies, not just her own and this man's—still a stranger. Yet she stayed in his arms, needing the closeness of another, the beating of a second heart in a world empty of all but the falling snow.

It seemed a miracle when the blizzard passed and the sun poured out of a sky as blue as turquoise. The white world seemed to absorb its light and give it back, sparkling and radiant. She looked out, held her breath for a moment, and put out her hands as if she could preserve the beauty, could capture the blue shadows of the plum trees, the erratic tracks of a rabbit, the blackness of a raven overhead, his wings defining the sky.

Beside the wagon, Rocinante and Sancho stomped and blew, and looked toward her, hopeful, their ears and whiskers still coated with ice. Behind her Levi coughed, and the sound filled her with sudden dread. She turned, blinking in the dark, trying to see him where he lay in his blankets.

"You're sick," she said.

"Just clearing my throat." His voice was hoarse.

She stumbled toward him, knelt down, put her hand to his forehead. "You've got fever."

"A cold. Nothing more." He tried to smile but a violent shiver wracked his body.

And she had thought she was safe! She had rejoiced in the sunlight, the coming of day! Perhaps never again would she trust life or believe in its innate goodness. For all purposes she was alone again, marooned in a sea of snow that was too deep to travel over. Once again everything rested on her shoulders—her life and this man's to whom she was beholden. "Lie still," she commanded. "I'll see to the mules. And then I'm going to start a fire and get you some tea."

"You can't. . . ."

"Try me." She stood up, looking tall and determined.

"Child, child," he said.

And she answered, "I'm not a child. I already told you. Not anymore. Not since *they* left me. Now lie there and keep warm."

Even when she was an old woman with much of a happy life behind her, she never liked to remember the time that followed. How she dug down through the drifts and struggled to build a feeble fire, scarcely hot enough to warm water, how she searched her mind for remedies her mother had used and pulled patent medicines from Levi's stock, how she piled blankets on him, washed him, and finally, in desperation, slept beside him during the long, cold nights, warming him with her own warmth, willing him to stay alive so hard that it hurt. And when the snow melted enough to travel, she hitched the team and drove on in search of a farm, a town, the winter camp of Indians, she didn't care as long as whoever was there had the ability to cure.

She shot rabbits for food, she who hated the killing of animals. She skinned them, gutted them, wiped the blood on her skirts and cooked them, forcing the meat and gruel through Levi's dry lips and trying not to hear the rattle in his lungs. Sometimes she read to him, straining her eyes in the lamplight, the words of the Bible resonant and somehow comforting, though she never really felt their meaning. It was the sound of her voice that was important, a link between her and the man who lay in rumpled blankets burning with fever.

And then one day, far in the distance, she saw mountains rising up out of the plain, and she stared at them in wonder and wished that Levi was beside her to share her excitement, to tell her their names. As it was, she had only herself to talk to, only her own questions that she could not answer. Was the whole country empty? Where were the people? She had seen only the rabbits she shot, and antelope, and once a herd of buffaloes like a dark river passing over the land. And there were always a few small birds buffeted by the wind that never stopped, that sang in her ears like the deepest notes of a fiddle, dark and mournful.

How long a time she spent on the road she was never able to determine later, but it was long enough to turn her into the woman she knew that she was, supple and tough as a sapling, and as determined to live. When she saw the little settlement tucked against the side of the mountain, she didn't change her pace, just moved toward it, not blinking, watching for fear that, like the mirages of the Plains, it would suddenly lift and disappear, a trick of light and distance.

People came out to meet her, and she said without thinking and before the world went dark, "Please. My husband is very ill. Please help us."

⚙

She awoke to warmth and the rich scent of roasting meat, and for a moment she struggled to remember where she was. A tall woman crossed the room and stood looking down at her.

"You're awake," she said.

"Where's Levi?" Nell held her breath, waiting for the answer.

"In the other room."

"Is he . . . is he all right?" She hated how she sounded, weak and babyish.

"He'll make it. But it was close."

She forced back tears of relief. "Can I see him?"

The woman smiled. "Sure. He's been asking for you, but I told him you were asleep."

"How long?"

"A day and a night. You were worn out. Must've been quite a trip."

Nell closed her eyes. She felt a thousand years old. "We were caught in a blizzard. That's when he took sick."

"You were lucky," the woman said. "That storm wiped most of the cattle off the range. Killed some people, too." She shook her head as if she was casting off memories. Then, abruptly, she changed the subject. "I'm Lucy Wickers. I run the post office, such as it is. My husband's a freighter."

"Oh." Nell was quiet a minute, picking at the quilt, her own words echoing in her head. *My husband is sick*. Had she really said that? And if she had, how could she explain such a lie? "I'm Nell," she said finally. "And he's Levi . . . Levi Solomon," she added.

"Well, Nell, have some breakfast. Then you can take some to him. You both look half starved. How long've you been on the road?"

It seemed like forever since that day when she climbed into the wagon and left her past behind. She shrugged. "A long time. I kind of lost track."

"You poor kid. You ought to settle down someplace. Open a store. You could do it here. There's enough in that wagon of yours to get you started."

"I guess," Nell said.

What happened next really wasn't up to her. All that she owned were the clothes she had with her. She was shocked when she saw Levi. He was pale, and his eyes were sunken in their sockets, and someone, probably Lucy, had trimmed his beard so that it clung to his thin cheeks like a shadow.

"How do you feel?" she asked, suddenly shy, remembering how she had slept beside him in the wagon, held him close night after night, keeping death and the cold away.

"I'm alive," he said, his dark eyes glowing. "And I thank you."

"I didn't do much."

"Yes," he said. "Yes, you did. You saved my life."

"Then we're even," she said.

He thought he didn't want the slate wiped clean. With a clear conscience she could leave, go out into the world where he would never see her again, never hear her voice reading his precious books aloud.

She said, so low he wasn't sure he understood: "I told a lie. I didn't mean to. It just came out. But you'd better know."

He cocked his head at her. "Was it very bad?"

"Bad enough." She twisted her hands in her lap. "I said . . . I told them . . . you were my husband."

"So? So, what's wrong with that?"

"Because you're not. I'm not your wife."

*But she could be. If only. . . .* He sighed. "Would it shame you if you were?" he asked.

That startled her. "Why should it? Why should I be ashamed?"

"I'm a peddler. A Jew. I have no home, no place. Some people laugh at me. Call me names and throw stones. Maybe even you once."

"I never," she said, indignant, although part of what he said was true enough. She'd seen it happen, so long ago she'd almost forgotten. She'd been sitting beside her papa on the wagon seat. They had driven to town, and she saw the boys, three of them armed with sticks and stones, and they were shouting at a peddler, an old man with a pack. What they said she couldn't recall, but their faces were clear in her mind, ugly and twisted, unlike the old man's with his white beard, blood on his forehead, his face filled with sorrow. "I never," she repeated, fiercely this time. "And if it happened . . . to us I mean . . . why, I'd stop them. I'd throw stones right back. What does anybody know about you? How good you are. How kind."

He watched her face, and the quick flame in her eyes, and knew she was telling the truth. She would fight, for herself as much as for him. Had she not brought them through illness and storm to safety? Suddenly he couldn't imagine going on without her, just him and the mules and his own somber thoughts. "What shall we do, then?" he asked, and thought his heart would stop while waiting for her answer.

When it came, it wasn't what he'd hoped. "Lucy says we could stay here and open a store."

"And? Would you like that?"

She folded her hands in her lap and sat quite still, looking at him, at his hollow cheeks, his eyes that seemed to be pleading with her. Running a store would mean staying in one place, building a home, having neighbors like Lucy to help when help was needed. It would mean the comfort of four walls, a fire on the hearth when the storms drove out of the north. But then she thought of the miles they had covered together, the land rolling away in front of them calling, always calling. She thought of the cold nights, of days filled with the dazzle of sun, and how, without him, she was empty, a water jug holding only the sad music of the wind. And she found she didn't want the life without him, didn't want life the way it had been before in that lonely house on the silent prairie.

She spoke slowly, awed by her knowledge. "I think," she said, "I think you and I should move on. Together. If you wouldn't mind."

He held out his arms, and she went into them, carefully but surely, for it was where she knew she belonged.

"Ach, Nell," he whispered. "I wouldn't mind at all."

# Guipago's Vow

## Cynthia Haseloff

☉

*Born in Vernon, Texas, and named after Cynthia Ann Parker, perhaps the best known of nineteenth-century white female Indian captives, the history and legends of the West were part of Cynthia Haseloff's upbringing in Arkansas, where her family settled shortly after she was born. Her first novel was* Ride South! *(Bantam, 1980), an unusual book featuring a mother as the protagonist searching for her children out of love and a sense of responsibility. Another unusual female protagonist is to be found in* Marauder *(Bantam, 1982). Both of these novels have subsequently been reprinted by Chivers Press in hardcover reprint editions. Haseloff's characters embody the fundamental values—honor, duty, courage, and family—that prevailed on the American frontier and were instilled in the young Haseloff by her own "heroes," her mother and her grandmother. Her stories, in a sense, dramatize how these values endure when challenged by the adversities and cruelties of frontier existence. Her talent, as that of Dorothy M. Johnson, rests in her ability to tell a story with an economy of words and in the seemingly effortless way she uses language. Haseloff's most recent novels are* The Chains of Sarai Stone *(Five Star Westerns, 1995) and* Man Without Medicine *(Five Star Westerns, 1996). The story that follows was especially written for inclusion here.*

Guipago stuck the blade of his knife into the earth and dug his hands into the blood-red sand. He clawed it into his fists. Raising his slashed arms, he let the sand trickle slowly back to the earth as the piercing lamentation flowed from his throat.

"Aheeeeeee! Tanankia, my son," he said over the scattered bones and remnants of clothing before him. "My son, I will bring you a white man and kill him for you here where your bones now lie. Great Spirit, hear my vow."

Guipago rose to his feet and turned to the men around him. The young men, his son's friends, stood awkwardly with heads down. Red

Horse, Guipago's brother, was still bent over the bones of his son, weeping. Their boys, cousins, had ridden off in the first adventure of young manhood, full of hope, full of pride, hungry for war honor that would give them a place of honor among the Kiowa people. Now both were dead, their bodies left by their companions as the Mexican lancers had forced them and the Comanches, with whom they rode back across the border.

Guipago closed his eyes against the glare of the spring sun and the burning tears that seared his eyes. "You have heard my vow, all of you. I will kill a white man where my son's bones now lie."

Guipago stood now in the trees, watching the schoolhouse, waiting for the man he knew was inside. Five years had passed. Five hard years for the Kiowas and for Guipago. He had refused the peace road after Tanankia's death. He had led his people away from the agencies. He had hit the Texas Rangers at Lost Valley, turned north, and fought General Miles's soldiers, holding up Lyman's supply train for four days, pinning the dispatch riders in the buffalo wallow for two. And then he and the People had fled across the Staked Plains and into the depths of Palo Duro Cañon with their Comanche friends. Ranald Mackenzie and the Fourth Cavalry found them there and drove them farther onto the plains, where the winter winds blew unimpeded by land or structure, where there was no food, and the children died.

Only a Kiowa could have found them then. Zepkoeete came. "Come in," the warrior who hated white men said. "Come in and live in peace. They are too many to fight. You have been to Washington. You have seen their ways. To white men we are as wolves, running on the prairie."

Zepkoeete's words were true. When Guipago brought his people in, the white men put him with the other chiefs and warriors in the unfinished ice house at Fort Sill and threw chunks of meat over the high walls to feed them as if they were wolves. Zepkoeete was given immunity for bringing them in. Guipago, and the others, Woman's Heart, Bird Chief, White Horse, Buffalo Bull's Entrails, Double Vision, Mamanti, all of them, together with the Cheyenne, Comanche, and Arapaho chiefs, were sent in May to prison at Fort Marion, Florida.

Gray Beard, a Cheyenne chief, had died fleeing from the train as it drew ever closer to the prison. Mamanti died in the prison. Some said it was because he had used his spirit powers to curse and kill Kicking Bird, the peace chief who had named the war chiefs and their warriors, *named* them for the whites to imprison. Some said simply that Kicking Bird was poisoned with strychnine, and medicine had nothing to do with it. But Mamanti had died. And others had died too, not really victims of the heat of Florida but of their own hearts. A Kiowa cannot stand prison. Satanta had said that even on a reservation they grow pale and die, but he knew nothing anymore of the life of a free man who had spent his whole life on a horse moving over endless prairies once he was in a thick-walled cell with a small window covered with bars. Now Satanta was dead, too. Guipago had not been with them in Florida where, at least, they were all Indians together. He was put alone in the prison at Huntsville, Texas. Enfeebled, life draining from him with each day, he had run off the second floor of the hospital and found again his freedom.

To live in prison a man must have patience, and he must have a purpose. Some men found ways to be patient, passing the time with drawing or working or gambling or sleeping. Some men found purpose in the hunger again to see their children and wives and mothers and fathers. Guipago had found patience and purpose in his vow to Tanankia.

The white man came out of the schoolhouse. Guipago watched him closely. John Goforth Ditsworth climbed the ladder propped against the building and returned to his work on the shingles. The teacher had not changed. He was still thin and tall. His cropped hair still stuck out where he had run his hands through it as he read. Rimless spectacles still aided his gray myopic eyes.

*So, Johngi,* Guipago thought as his fingers touched the cuffs and chain that hung from his saddle. *You have not gone home. You are still meddling with the poor Kiowas. Will your gentle God protect you from me? This time I do not think so.* Then, as he trotted his pony into the school yard, he called out: "Johngi! Johngi, come down and talk to one who has been away a long time."

Friend John, called Johngi by the Kiowas from his first introduction as John G. Ditsworth, looked down on the Kiowa chief who sat looking up at him. Unlike many Kiowas, Guipago was lean and sinewy. His face was tight copper skin stretched over hard angles. A few deep seams allowed it to move. Prison had not changed him much outwardly. His hair was dark as ever, worn in the old way, with the left braid cut off below the ear and the right wrapped in red flannel. Earrings of shells and watch chains ornamented the margins of his ears. He wore a white shirt under a white man's vest and a pair of frayed gabardine trousers, but on his feet were moccasins, beaded and trailing long fringes. Guipago was dressed up.

John did not see but felt there was something about the chief that was not there before, a sadness. Perhaps he grieved for Tanankia, the lost People, the lost years. The Quaker laid down the shingling hatchet carefully on the new split wood. "Guipago, the children said thou was home. Why hast thou taken so long to come to the school? There are many things I want to show thee." After ten years among the Kiowas the schoolteacher could speak their language without thought, but he spoke now in a Quaker's English.

As John backed down the ladder, Guipago spoke softly to himself. "And I you, Johngi."

"Get down Guipago," John said, reaching up to shake the Kiowa's hand. "I have my lunch inside, and we will eat something." John had never entered a Kiowa lodge without being offered food. Many times he had eaten while his hosts had nothing. Guipago stepped down from the pony, tossing the rope reins high on the horse's neck. The horse followed him like a puppy. "I see your horse has not forgotten you."

"No." Guipago stroked the broad jaw. "He has not forgotten the old ways."

"Best buffalo pony I ever saw," the Quaker said, remembering the pony's quick swerve as he heard the twang of the bow string and took himself and the rider away from the dying buffalo's fury.

"Where is your woman, Johngi?" asked Guipago as they walked together toward the shade of the porch.

"She has taken the children back to Ohio during the summer recess," the schoolteacher said. "Their grandparents are hungry to see them."

"Yes," said Guipago. "One can grow hungry to see a child."

Ditsworth looked down at the dust he kicked as they walked. On the porch he found his lunch and offered a sandwich to the Indian. They ate together in silence on the steps, watching the sky and land around them.

"Come, Johngi," Guipago said as he stood. John looked up. "It is time to go from here."

The teacher left his sandwich and stood beside the chief. He wiped his hand on his trousers, ready for the final handshake that always formally ended a visit. "I had hoped thou would stay and talk with me as we once talked," he said.

"There is something I want to show you," the chief said as they walked to his horse. He removed the chain and cuff from the saddle. "Look, Johngi. This is what the white men put on me when I surrendered."

Ditsworth looked at the shackles, his gentle jaw set. All his life the man had hated chains and the power of one man over another that they stood for. He had seen their marks on the fleeing slaves he and others of his faith had smuggled north. He had felt his own shame and the disgrace of his people when they fitted shackles over the Indians' wrists and ankles.

"Hold out your hands, Johngi," Guipago said softly. "I will show you how iron feels on flesh."

The Quaker offered his wrists and watched as the Kiowa placed the cuffs over them and clamped the iron together. "There," the Indian said. "We can go now."

John Ditsworth looked up into the Kiowa's black eyes. "Go?" he said.

"Yes," said the Kiowa. "You are my prisoner."

The Quaker straightened. A frown compressed his open face. "Thou art my friend," he said.

"You are my white man," Guipago said.

"This will cause trouble, Guipago."

"No, Johngi. This will not cause trouble. I have thought about this. You are the perfect white man. Your woman is away and will not miss you. The other white men and the Indians know that you travel about among the bands. They will think you have gone somewhere with someone else. They will not miss you. And your God will not let you fight me."

"And what dost thou intend to do with me?" asked John Ditsworth.

"I will kill you."

The teacher looked about him. He did not doubt that Guipago had the will and the power to kill him. He was a Quaker, not a fool. He had never been blind to the depredations of the Kiowas even as he had loved them. He had put his life in their bloody hands many times in the belief that a man, red or white, can change when he is led gently to a better way.

Guipago dropped the rope noose over John Ditsworth's head. "Come, Johngi. We will find your horse. Our road is long."

The two men rode away from the empty schoolhouse. Tied in the saddle with Guipago leading his horse, John looked for someone to whom to call out. The only living thing he saw was a sandhill crane at the edge of a withered cornfield before all civilization disappeared behind them. Guipago led Johngi through the broken land and sand hills into the twilight and across the moon-made shadows. He did not stop to rest, to eat, to sleep. He let the horses drink at the streams they crossed. He did not let John drink or eat. They rode on into the coming day, into the heat of noon, and into the blessed benediction of twilight before Guipago pulled Johngi from the saddle and tossed him a slice of dried meat and a gourd of water.

"Sleep now," Guipago said.

"This is about thy vow, isn't it?" asked Johngi after the water quenched his thirst and cooled his parched lips.

Guipago checked the knotted rope around Johngi's neck and tied the end around his own arm. "Johngi, if you run, I will only find you. Sleep now," Guipago said and rolled into his blanket.

John shivered. The night was as cold as the day was hot. He looked at the shackles on his wrists. The flesh was red and worn away. "Friend

John," he said aloud to himself, "thou *art* a fool." *Friend John,* a thought skittered across his brain, *get up and smite this loathsome, heathen Indian to death and make thy escape.* Then the small voice inside said: *Friend John, will thy faith stand though sorely tried?*

On the third day Guipago arose from his blankets refreshed and ready for the day's journey. After he untied himself from John, he removed the noose casually and coiled the rope and dropped it over his saddle. He bathed his face and sang his morning song to the Great Spirit. Hollow-eyed John Ditsworth sat against the rocks with his shackled hands draped over his outspread knees.

"You should sleep, Johngi," Guipago said.

"This is about thy vow to Tanankia, isn't it?" asked the Quaker.

"Yes," said Guipago, eating a strip of jerky and washing it down with a long drink of water. He rinsed his mouth and his hands and stood up.

"Thou propose to take me to Mexico and kill me on the spot where Tanankia was killed?"

"Yes. That is the vow. How do you know this vow?" Guipago asked.

"It is a famous vow," said John. "Once Kicking Bird warned me, but that was so many years ago. It was washed away."

"You should have listened. A famous vow must be kept. It is never washed away. A man would lose his face. Then he would have to die." Guipago rose and went to the grazing horse. "Come, Johngi. Saddle your horse."

John picked up his saddle, blanket, and bridle and started toward the horse. When he forced the bit gently between its teeth, he lifted the headstall and pulled the thick ears through. With his thumb he worked the coarse forelock from beneath the brow band and smoothed it. He put his arm to the elbow through the reins and picked up the blanket.

"You are good with the horse," Guipago observed. "Not like an Indian, but good. A quirt would move that one better," he added, lifting his own highly ornate whip.

"We do not strike other creatures . . . beast or man," said Johngi.

Guipago laughed. As John lifted the saddle to throw it onto the horse, he considered it. It was a Western saddle, heavy with horn and cantle and wide leather skirt. He had removed the showy *tapaderos,* although he found them functional for safety in rough country. Now the thick wooden stirrups were exposed. The metal rings of the double cinches clanked together as he started to swing up the saddle. Compared to the Eastern saddle, he thought, it was monumental.

John glanced at Guipago, busy with his own horse. The lead rope hung from his saddle. The Indian had not yet placed it over John's or the horse's head. The two men stood together between the animals, the Indian working and preparing to mount from the right, the white man from the left. John turned back to his horse, smoothed the saddle blanket, and pulled it to the ground. "Guipago," said John. The Indian turned to see what he would say. With a grunt Ditsworth swung the saddle up and into Guipago's face, catching him hard with one of the heavy stirrups. Guipago fell back. John threw himself onto his horse and kicked it away into a full gallop. He lay low over the horse's neck and held tightly to the mane as the animal streaked across the prairie. "Come on, come on," he said, listening to the horse's labored breathing.

The best buffalo pony that John had ever seen soon closed the distance to the big American horse without any effort. When Guipago came alongside, he struck the Quaker full force with the backward swing of his fist and forearm, sending him tumbling off. The buffalo pony cut away. Guipago circled it into a stop in front of the fallen man. John saw the blood on the Indian's cheek where the stirrup had hit him. He lay back, letting air return to his empty lungs.

Guipago turned his horse and rode after the other animal that had stopped to graze. He led it back to John. The teacher stood up, dusting his clothes, rubbing an elbow hurt in the fall. "Johngi," the warrior commanded. The fallen Quaker straightened. Guipago looked straight into his eyes as he stuck a rifle behind the ear of John's horse and pulled the trigger. The horse crumpled after the concussion of the gun. John looked down at the dead horse then up into Guipago's face. Guipago tossed his rope over John's head and tightened it. "You will walk now, Johngi." Guipago turned his horse away and led the teacher behind him. John barely heard Guipago's words. "You are a child in these matters."

The next days were agony even for a man who was accustomed to walking. John suffered. Grilled by day and frozen by night with feet that swelled and ached, he followed Guipago deeper and deeper into the empty land and away from any salvation. Most of the hours and days passed in silence. Both men were used to silence and did not fight it with idle words. Guipago, though once thoughtful and sometimes eloquent in council, now found words tiresome, even useless. He had spoken his vow. Action was all that was necessary. Each step was one closer to the fulfillment of the only important words that remained. John G. Ditsworth had learned as a child to wait in silence for the still small voice within him. These past days he had missed it in the tumbling thoughts of his mind. His fear had ruled him, leading him to the foolish escape attempt. As he walked behind Guipago, he worked to quiet the tumult. He was not surprised when, at last, it began to speak.

*Thou hath lost thy faith back there.* John heard the words clearly in his mind, but if asked he would have said they impressed themselves on him. *Thou ran without being sent . . . taking matters into thine own frail hands. Friend John, thou are not a warrior and not suited to contend with men of war on their own terms. Remember thyself.*

That night John retrieved the worn journal from his jacket pocket and began to write. Guipago watched as the sunburned man bent over the pages beside the fire. John wrote:

*July 19, 1879. Guipago and I are traveling now toward the site of his son's death in Mexico. Kicking Bird told me that, when Guipago found his son's body lying on the ground, he kneeled down over it and vowed to the Great Spirit that on that ground where his son was killed he would take the life of some white man. Now, to kill a white man on that ground, he would have to catch one and take him there. Guipago says that I am the perfect white man for his purpose.*

*I have been among this people with much sorrow and many tears; under discouragements and heavy burdens; in heat and in cold; in hunger, in thirst, and in weariness; in sickness, in weakness of the flesh and weakness of the spirit; in perils, in privations, and in cruel besetments of the enemy; alone as to the outward, and a stranger among a strange people. Yet hath the Lord supported, and by the right arm of His power, notwithstanding my many slips by the way, sustained and upheld me in all and through all.*

*Even at times when His presence has been, or seemed to be, withdrawn, His hand has been underneath to bear up and keep me from falling, to make a way where man could make no way, and to overrule the counsels of the most hostile men. It may be, though Guipago does not mean it for good, that I am the perfect man for his purpose.*

"What do you scratch upon the papers?" asked Guipago.

"I am writing a record for my family," the Quaker said as he closed the book. "I do not want them, when they learn what becomes of me, to worry that I suffered from great anguish or fear."

"You should be afraid," said the Kiowa.

"I was about to write about that truly hard and dangerous time," said John, "when Satanta and Adoltay were in prison and I was held hostage by the whole Kiowa tribe."

"Oh, that was not dangerous, Johngi. They were only holding you, *maybe* kill you if things go wrong. I am going to kill you for sure. Do not think I will not. You are nothing to me one way or the other. Perhaps I even like you a little, but I will keep my vow."

"Yes," said the Quaker as he kicked a brand back into the fire, "I also made a vow long before I knew thee or these circumstances. I had nearly forgotten it in the cares of life. I broke that vow. I repent me of it." John cleared his throat. "Guipago, I ask thy forgiveness for hitting thee with the saddle and causing thee pain."

Guipago laughed and slapped his hands down on his knees. "I forgive you, Johngi." The Kiowa continued to laugh as he made his bed and crawled into it. "Pain? A mosquito bite!"

☼

When Guipago awoke, John G. Ditsworth stood over him with arms raised and a large rock between his shackled hands. "Lie still," the Quaker said.

"So you can kill me easier?" asked the Kiowa. "You have fooled me again, Johngi." Guipago started to lift the covers.

**Cynthia Haseloff 643**

John hurled the rock down with all his force. The Indian lunged for him, shoving him back until they both lay on the ground.

"I will kill you," the Indian said through clinched teeth.

"Thou cannot," John whispered. "To kill me here would break thy vow. Thou must take me to Mexico *alive.*"

"Then perhaps I will gouge your eyes out or burst your eardrums." Guipago spoke the words, pushing his thumbs into Johngi's eyes beneath the sparkling spectacles.

"Then who will see and hear thy rattlesnakes?" whispered John, holding the wrists of his captor.

Guipago jerked his hand free, looked at the teacher, grasped his hair beside his ears, and banged his head down hard against the ground. Releasing his grip, he rose to his feet. "There had better be a rattlesnake under that big stone," Guipago stated as he moved toward the rock hurled by the Quaker. The Indian stooped and raised the slab, revealing a very flat snake.

"I got him," exulted John.

Guipago's mouth twisted wryly. He taunted. "Smashed the poor thing to bits, gentle John. Took pride in your cunning, too." More seriously he added: "Killed your deliverer, Johngi."

As the days of long marches continued, a pattern began to evolve. They rose early. Guipago bathed his face and sang his morning prayers. John sat in silence, listening to his inner voice. During the day the men rarely spoke at all. Guipago was not generous with food or water but merely sustained his prisoner. He kept the rope on his neck and rode triumphantly before him. In the evening they made a small fire. Guipago had coffee and sugar, which he did not share. John wrote in his journal. The Indian played cards.

"Johngi, play cards with me," he said.

The Quaker looked up. "I do not play cards, Guipago."

The Indian tossed a card toward John's hat. "You don't play cards. You don't drink whiskey. You don't smoke cigarettes. And you have only one woman. Johngi, you lead a pitiful life, and soon you are going to die." Another card sailed into the black hat. "I should take you to the Comancheros and show you a good time before I kill you."

John closed the book. "I am not discontent with my life. I have chosen it, knowing its joys and disciplines, just as thou hast chosen to be a warrior and know the heathenish joys and disciplines of that life. As a result, I do not gamble away my family's food or house. I do not make a fool of myself with whiskey and wake up with a bursting head and heaving stomach. I do not regard the lack of any of these things to be a sacrifice or even a loss."

"You are not a man, Johngi."

"Thou defines a man by his vices, Guipago, not by his spirit." It was the teacher speaking.

"A man would fight me." Guipago sailed another card. "Why do you not fight me, Johngi?"

"Thou art not my enemy," the Quaker said simply.

Guipago smiled. "But I am your enemy." The Kiowa pulled the long gleaming knife from his belt, turned it, observed it in his hand. "I will kill you with this knife, Tanankia's knife. I *am* your enemy."

The next day Guipago pulled up his horse at the top of a jagged escarpment. John walked to his side. A shimmering desert lay before them. "There is no water from here or even on the other side that a white man can find." The Indian spoke softly. He looked down at John, clad in his dust-covered black hat and dirty black coat and trousers. "That is the no-water country. Today, Johngi, the land will test you."

As far as John Ditsworth could see, the emptiness stretched out. There was not color in it or the sky. The unimpeded sun rose over it, crossed it at leisure, and pulled away the color as well as the moisture. The great orb was the cruel prince, the self-consumed monarch of the heavens who would tolerate no glory but his own as he strutted over the land. At John's feet the earth split and fissured, unable to grasp and hold itself together under the pressure of the sun's relentless power. He stood looking at the scene until the rope tightened against his neck, then he stepped off behind Guipago.

At noon they had not reached the center of the plain. John saw lakes with tree-lined banks and tree-covered islands. They floated before him then disappeared just as their shade and water seemed but a few more steps away. He closed his eyes at last, denying the mirages the chance to tantalize him further. The faces of his wife and children moved against the backs of his eyelids. His tongue swelled, filling the cavity of his mouth. He pressed back against the rope around his neck, letting it draw him on, pulling him, towing him through the waterless sea.

Many times John fell. The rope never went slack. Sometimes he grasped it with his blistered, bleeding hands and let Guipago pull him across the sand. But the heat burned through his hat and shirt, and he called out. The Kiowa let him get to his feet, then moved on.

Guipago rode under a shade made from his blanket, propped by his bow and quiver. When John fought with thick fingers to loosen and throw off the shirt and jacket, the Indian jerked hard on the rope. "No, Johngi," he said and moved them ever on.

The strong boots the Quaker wore became leaden weights, anchoring him to the searing ocean bottom. The thought flickered across his mind that, if he kicked them off, he might rise and break the surface and breathe again. But there was not time to reach down and pull them off. They became wet and clung to his feet until the blisters broke and the leather chewed the raw flesh. He walked on until the boots became brittle with salt and fell away in pieces.

"Johngi," the voice came through the humming in his ears. "Johngi, drink." Guipago poured a thin stream of water onto his burned lips. John grabbed his hands and held them as the measured drops ran into his mouth. "Roll the water around on your tongue. Hold it in your mouth a long time before you swallow." John looked up into the face above him and, as a child, held the water obediently until he had to swallow.

"How much farther?" The words cracked as they struck the dry air. "We are across," Guipago said.

☒

The warrior scraped the sand away with his hands. He let the water fill the depression before pushing the empty gourd beneath the surface. When it was full, he walked back to the place in the shaded cañon where John lay. The Quaker was little more than a skeleton dressed in scraps of clothing. Guipago wet the rag that now covered his eyes. John twisted away. Guipago held him and ran the rag over his stubbled face and throat, then replaced it over his eyes. He sat back on his heels.

For three days he had watched over John, stripping off his coat, soaking it and the blankets in the scraped pools, covering him with the wet, cool cloths until the bursting heat of his body came down. "Do not die, Johngi. You must be alive when I kill you or the vow will be broken."

"The vow," murmured John. "I must keep my vow."

"I am tired of you," Guipago said. "If we were on a raid together, I would leave you. It is customary. I have done it before without a thought. A man expects to be left if he cannot keep up, if he holds the others back and endangers them. That is the way of warriors." Guipago became thoughtful. "It is not a good way, but it is the way of warriors. Once some raiders had a man wounded very bad. He was no use to them. Waiting for him to die would take too much time. So that night they decided to leave him. They left him at a water hole, near enough so that he could get water if he lived. They left him a little meat. And they piled rocks over him so, if he died, he would be buried and, if he lived, the animals would not eat him. They left him very well off.

"After they had gone, a wolf came and ate the meat. He was grateful to the man, so he dug away a few stones and lay down beside him. He kept him warm when it became very cold. When other animals came to see if he was dead and could be eaten, the wolf ran them away. He stayed by the man. And the man knew he was there. And he thought his medicine had sent him the wolf as a protector. So he began to live. He got water. He got some game. The wolf hunted with him. They became brothers. When he came home, the wolf came with him, but he would not stay in the camp. The People did not hurt that wolf ever because he had saved a Kiowa. But finally that man moved away to live with the wolf. He lived with him many years. And when he came back, he was a quiet man." Guipago concluded: "I have often thought of that man and that wolf. How could this be . . . two enemies?"

Trapped by the sickness of this white man as he had been trapped by the prison bars, Guipago grew restless. The smooth cañon walls suddenly reminded him of the interior of his cell. He wanted to breathe. He picked up his rifle and went to look for something to fill his empty belly, something for Johngi to eat.

✹

When he opened his eyes, John Ditsworth saw the sliver of moonlit sky between the cañon walls. His head thumped, and he was thirsty. He sat up on one elbow and looked about. The fire smoldered, sending threads of gray into the air. Down the cañon he saw the white markings of Guipago's paint pony. John reached out and took the water gourd and drank. He wiped his mouth and sat up. "Guipago?" he called weakly, then, mustering strength, called hoarsely but more loudly: "Guipago." There was a faint echo from the cañon, but nothing more.

John stood. His legs gave way. He sat back on the sand. Sweat popped onto his forehead, and his head swam. "Guipago," he said and lay back.

As he lay, John began to shiver. He pulled his coat and the blanket to him, but his feet were still cold. He raised himself to pull the short blanket over them. He noticed they were no longer swollen. He ran his hand over the raw redness and knew that they had been oiled and tended.

"Guipago," he said softly to himself.

When the Indian had not returned and the moon had come full over the cañon, John made himself stand. He walked feebly to Guipago's saddle and gear and dropped to his knees. The coffee and sugar, the playing cards, the heavily beaded moccasins, all lay where their owner had left them. This, along with the grazing pony, convinced him that the Indian had not simply abandoned him to die. He looked again at the gear. Only the carbine was missing. Most likely that meant that Guipago had gone to hunt. John rested, thinking. He looked at the sky. The cañon made it difficult to tell the time, but the teacher was sure the moon had passed the zenith and was descending slowly into the morning. If Guipago had gone hunting, he would have gone in daylight. He would not have gone so far that he could not have gotten back before night. Perhaps the game was heavy. John considered that. If he'd expected to take big game, he would have taken the horse. Would he have taken big game by chance? If he had, surely he would have come back for the horse. John sat up. Something was wrong with Guipago. He could not get back.

*Take the horse. Leave,* a voice said inside him. *There will never be a better chance.*

John pulled on Guipago's beaded moccasins. The Indian's women had made them for him, anticipating his return, honoring him, making it special—new road, new moccasins. The Quaker limped and staggered toward the pony, then led him back to the saddle and gear. After slipping on the simple, bitless bridle, he placed the blanket, but it took several tries to lift the saddle atop. He rested before tightening the cinch. John put a moccasin in the stirrup and climbed aboard. The little pony's head came up, and he eyed the new rider.

Holding the reins, John suddenly realized he had no real power over the horse—no bit, no white man's training. Guipago moved the animal with his legs, even his thoughts. John squeezed the belly. The horse moved forward. He released his legs, drew the reins to him, and sat back. The pony stopped. John smiled. "Friend horse, I want to leave here, and thou must carry me," John said. "Where I do not yet know, but away will do for now."

He squeezed the sides and released his hands. The paint moved off down the cañon, away from the fire and Guipago. John rode for some time. All and all he was well pleased to be moving away from his own death.

*Wilt thou run again without being sent, John?* the still small voice asked.

"What didst thou say?" John asked aloud.

*Wilt thou run again without being sent, John?*

"But everything was there," the Quaker said. "Everything for my escape."

*Wilt thy faith stand though sorely tried?* asked the voice. John blinked. *In thy vow thou put thy trust in God, not in men or circumstances. Thou knowest Guipago is in trouble, or he would have returned. Thou knowest that there is no other help for him but thee. There is no love in what thou plan to do, John. Thou art only taking up thine own life again.*

John turned the horse around. By the time he returned to the camp, first light was coming into the well of the cañon. He rode down the winding way to the cañon floor, following Guipago's faint footsteps in the red sand. At last he found where Guipago had begun to climb. The teacher dismounted weakly and hobbled the pony. He crawled after Guipago. Coming into the open, he looked around him. A clear path led off toward the east. He followed until it twisted out of sight and back into the rocks and crevices.

"I will love, but I will not live forever. Mysterious Moon, you only remain. Powerful sun, you only remain. Wonderful earth, you remain forever."

John recognized the voice and the words of the Kiowa death song. He followed slowly, tentatively, feeling his way toward it. It grew louder, but he saw nothing.

"Guipago," he called, leaning his trembling weakness against the rocks. "Guipago, where are you?"

"Here, Johngi," the voice called out. "The rocks collapsed with me, and I am now in this crevice."

" 'And the Lord will hide thee in a crevice in the rocks,' " John said to himself and ventured to the edge of the path. Below him Guipago stood looking up from a chamber. Smooth as polished marble, its walls offered nothing to grab hold of and nothing to stand on. It was too deep for him to leap up and catch the lip. It was too large for him to put his arms and legs and back against the walls and climb out. It was a perfect prison.

*He cannot follow you from there,* a voice inside said.

John turned and started away. He walked hastily back the way he had come. He leaped a small gap, fell, and cut his hands but got up and walked quickly on. He slid the last thirty feet and fell at the horse's feet. The pony shied. John caught the reins as he rose. Taking the ropes from Guipago's saddle, John made the return trip as quickly as his weakness could carry him. At the pit he stopped. He looked around for a spot to secure the rope. There was nothing except an outcropping above his head. He would have to toss a loop over it. He made three tries before it caught.

John dropped the end of the rope to Guipago. The Indian leaped for it. He tried again, then again. The rope dangled inches out of his reach.

The trembling Quaker leaned out and caught the rope. He loosened the line and tried to shake it off the outcropping. It stuck. Below him Guipago was cursing. John tried again, and the rope came off.

"Canst thou climb, Guipago?" John asked. Guipago nodded. "I will try to hold thee."

"Speak louder, Johngi," the Indian shouted.

"I said," the Quaker returned, "I will brace myself to hold thee, but thou must use thy strength to climb out. I do not think I can pull thee up by myself, and the horse is too far away. I will call out when I am set."

John tied the rope around his waist. He moved back into the rocks where he could wedge his long body and secure a hold.

"Climb, Guipago."

The rope jerked tight on his waist. John winced and pushed harder against the rocks. Guipago caught another hold. The rope jerked again. John slipped but grabbed and held. "Hurry," he said. "Oh, hurry. Dear God in heaven, I know we can do this together. Amen."

The jerks continued on John's skeletal body. Each time he thought he would come loose, but he held. John was still pushing the rocks when Guipago released the constricted rope and pulled it roughly over his shoulders. The Quaker relaxed and smiled into the Kiowa's face.

"This changes nothing," Guipago said, tightening the noose around John's neck and starting away. "I am still going to kill you, Johngi."

The Quaker followed. "Did you get anything to eat?"

"I lost my gun," Guipago said.

"Good," the Quaker said under his breath. "Now thou will have to slit my throat."

"I have done it before," said Guipago.

As they walked along the winding cañon, the two men shared the last of the jerked meat and some ground mesquite beans. Guipago led John as before with the noose around his neck. At nightfall they made their last camp.

"I do not understand you, Johngi," Guipago grunted. "I would have left you."

"But thou didst not leave me," John said. "Thou nursed me after the desert. Cooled me, fed me, dressed my feet with oil."

"I must have you alive for tomorrow." Guipago spoke to the small fire where his coffee boiled.

The Quaker sat quietly for a time. "Guipago, I did leave thee."

"But you came back." The Indian poured coffee into a cup and dropped in a handful of sugar. He handed to it John. "What made you come back, Johngi?"

He thought. "All my life," he said, "I have gone haltingly. If I had left thee, I would never walk sure. I would have left my faith for good."

"You kept your vow," said Guipago.

"Guipago," the Quaker asked, "doth thou remember the time I came to thy camp with the telegram from Washington that demanded the People turn over the five young raiders or Satanta and Adoltay would not be released?"

Guipago nodded.

"When thou heard the message, thou went away to think, and the next morning thou gave me thy answer. Doth thou remember what thou had me write?"

Guipago looked at the fire as John drank the burning coffee. "I said I wished Washington would let it pass. If those foolish young men have killed any of the people of Texas, they are dead. If some of these young men have been killed, they are dead. Let it all pass . . . do not let it make trouble among the living."

"Then thou learned that Tanankia had been killed. And thou took the war road. Thou did not let it pass, Guipago," said John.

Guipago took a deep breath and released it. "Tanankia was my son. The wolves had eaten his body. A father cannot look on the scattered bones of his child without remembering his vow to give that child a good life. I failed that vow. I will not fail the one I made to his bones."

John Ditsworth handed the cup back to Guipago. "We drink from the same cup, Guipago. Good night." The Quaker lay down and closed his eyes.

Guipago pulled up his blanket and rolled onto his side. Before he closed his eyes, he thought he saw in the darkness beyond the fire the shining eyes of a wolf. He sat up and chunked a stone at the spot then lay back.

In his dreams that night Guipago saw the wolf digging up the buried Kiowa and lying down beside him to warm him. He saw the bared teeth as the wolf fought its own kind to protect the Indian. *Why? Why?* he thought when he awoke. *A wolf and a man are enemies. And yet that wolf had one spirit with that man.* Guipago went back to sleep.

At sunrise Guipago went off, washed his face, and sang his morning song to the Great Spirit. When he returned, he woke John. "Come, Johngi," he said, dropping the noose again over the teacher's head.

Guipago wore only his moccasins and a breechcloth. In his hand he carried his son's knife. The sun caught the blade as he led the Quaker away from the dead fire. Reflections danced into John's eyes.

Guipago stopped at last and turned to John. His eyes never left the Quaker's face. Quickly, with a rough sure hand, he thrust the knife toward John's throat. The rope fell away. Guipago grabbed the man's arm, jerked it forward, and cut a gash across the palm of his hand. John winced as the blood spurted. Guipago slashed his own hand and grasped John's, letting their blood flow together. They stood. Each held the other's hand as tightly as he could, forcing his blood, his spirit, into the other. Blood ran down their forearms and dropped into the sand where Tanankia had died, now red with blood again.

Guipago released John's hand and walked away. John stood watching the Indian. Guipago stopped on a small rise and turned back, looking at John and the bloody place where his son had died.

"Come, Tangui, let's go home." John stood, without moving, questioning the Indian with his whole being. "Have I not killed the white man?" the Indian asked. "Your old man is dead. You are my brother, Guipago's brother, Lone Wolf's brother. I give you a new name, Johngi. You are now Little Wolf, Tangui. You never left the dying Kiowa, and you made him hope to live again. Come, we are men to make a new road together. I have kept Guipago's vow."

# About the Editors

Jon Tuska and Vicki Piekarski are authors or editors of numerous works about the American West, including Piekarski's *Westward the Women* (Doubleday, 1983) and Tuska's *Billy the Kid: His Life and Legend* (Greenwood, 1994). Together they are coeditors in chief of the *Encyclopedia of Frontier and Western Fiction* (McGraw-Hill, 1983), which is now being prepared in its second edition. Together they were the cofounders of the Golden West Literary Agency and the first Westerners in the history of the Western story to coedit and copublish twenty-six new hardcover Western fiction books a year in two prestigious series, the Five Star Westerns and the Circle (v) Westerns.